Gerrit and His Dog

~ and ~

The Royal Law

Grace & Truth Books
Sand Springs, Oklahoma

ISBN # 978-1-58339-138-9

Current printing, Grace & Truth Books, 2004

Cover design by Ben Gundersen

Grace & Truth Books
3406 Summit Boulevard
Sand Springs, Oklahoma   74063
Phone: 918 245 1500

www.graceandtruthbooks.com
email: gtbooksorders@cs.com

TABLE OF CONTENTS

Page

Gerrit and His Dog

The Royal Law

Chapter 1

THE GAME WARDEN

Gerrit uttered faint cries as he followed the narrow path, which freakishly wound its way through the motionless, silent moor. He had wandered far from the village. Between the fir trees behind him the slender church steeple pointed upwards in the darkness of the approaching night. The houses were already hidden from view in the twilight darkness. But Gerrit took no notice of this. Time and again he stood still, bent over, and listened.

"Brownie! Brownie!"

His words were muffled. The sound of his voice reached no further than the dense growth of junipers, which rose from the ground a few feet from each side of the path in this wild moorland. The boy's eyes stared vacantly in the dusk.

"Brownie! Brownie!"

He squatted down on the path, took off his cap, and with it wiped his damp forehead. Looking for Brownie, his lost dog, his eyes stared into the heath. He left the path and walked straight toward the dark wood through which the September wind was whistling the song of harvest.

It had become completely dark by the time Gerrit, tired and hungry, sat down against the trunk of a beech tree and fell asleep. In the branches above him wild pigeons busily fluttered their wings before they came to rest. Deeper in the forest a fox was slinking out of its den to seek its prey. It would roam to the farms a few miles distant to fall upon its prey. Far away echoed the call of a deer, and a black grouse fluttered amid the brushwood.

Gerrit Datema, feeble-minded Gerrit, was asleep, far from the home of the foster father who took very little interest in him. The clock in the village tower struck eleven; the sound echoed through the wood.

The game warden took his gun from the rack and walked outside into the dark night.

"Come, Sasta!"

The hunting dog followed and soon the two of them disappeared into the dark fir trees of the large hunting reservation. At times they followed the trails; then again they suddenly wandered from the paths and struggled through the thick under-brush, for poachers do not keep themselves on the beaten paths.

Suddenly Sasta shot away like an arrow. The experienced hunter did not call the dog back but followed as quickly as he could. He listened to hear whether the dog was attacking something – it remained quiet. Seeking safety, a frightened rabbit started up from its hole.

Then, yes, Sasta was barking loudly without letup – he was attacking something. The hunter hastened his pace and hurried in the direction of the noise. As he approached he shone his bright searchlight straight ahead and saw a dark form.

"Sasta, come away, I say!"

The dog immediately obeyed, placing himself in front of his victim. Cautiously the game warden kept his eyes on the trembling figure before him. The figure was resting his back against the trunk of the beech tree under which he had been sleeping.

"Hey there, young man, what are you doing here?" The voice of the hunter was harsh and the light beamed mercilessly in the boy's face.

"Feeble-minded Gerrit," the hunter mumbled to himself. "What is he doing here in the middle of the night?"

Stiff and shivering from the cold, the boy rose to his feet. His eyes pierced through the darkness toward the game warden, who had turned off the searchlight.

"Gerrit, what are you looking for here, boy?" the hunter asked with friendliness in his voice.

"Brownie, Brownie, have you seen Brownie?" was the boy's faint response.

"Is Brownie lost, Gerrit?" asked the game warden, realizing what the trouble was.

Sasta growled.

"Quiet, Sasta," commanded the dog's master.

The boy was afraid to move one step forward because of the dog. The warden affectionately laid his hand on the lad's shoulder.

"Come, Gerrit, together we will look for Brownie," said the hunter reassuringly. Then he took Gerrit by the hand as if he were a small child. The lad willingly followed along. Sasta came on behind.

"Brownie, Brownie," the voice of the feeble-minded boy continually echoed through the quiet of the night.

Van Vliet, the game warden, knew Gerrit well. Like everyone else in the village he was very fond of the boy. The love which this simple lad bestowed on his dog demonstrated a far better attitude toward the animal world than did the cruel poachers who without compassion ensnared defenseless rabbits.

Little by little Van Vliet began to realize what was troubling the poor boy. "Hm, hm," he mumbled inwardly, "his dog is gone, and now, it is only natural, he is without comfort. Poor boy!"

"Are you hungry, Gerrit?" the warden asked aloud.

"Hungry, yes." The boy was so hungry his body shook.

The warden opened his game bag and gave the lad a slice of bread. Eagerly he bit into it — but then he suddenly lingered behind.

"Come, Gerrit," said Van Vliet, "walk with me or I will lose you in the dark."

At that moment the hunter heard Sasta chewing and immediately knew what had taken place. Gerrit had shared his bread with the dog. "How touching," the hunter thought. He patted the boy on the shoulder and said, "That's good, Gerrit. Take good care of the animals."

The boy pressed close to the warden. He was thrilled by this word of praise. He continued to cry out constantly, "Brownie, Brownie, why don't you come?"

Van Vliet was moved with compassion for the poor, parentless, feeble-minded child. They approached the edge of the forest. A speck of light shone right in front of them. There near a large oak could be seen the roof of a small farmhouse. Everything was still.

This was the house of Peter Datema, Gerrit's uncle and foster father. Van Vliet knew that Datema was a rough customer, a cruel poacher. The game warden was incensed when he realized that Datema was asleep. Apparently Gerrit's foster father was unconcerned that the poor boy who was entrusted to his care was not at home.

With a dull thud Van Vliet hit the rickety door. No answer. Perhaps the fellow was out poaching. Or might it just be possible that the warden was mistaken in his opinion of Datema and that he was out looking for the boy?

With his heavy fist Van Vliet gave the door a harder thump. This time he could hear someone stumbling around in the house. Soon the door opened with a grating noise.

"What is going on so late at night?"

The warden's searchlight shone right into the bristly face of the rough, untidy man. "Datema, here is Gerrit! I brought him home; I found him asleep in the forest. I'm surprised to find you at home." The warden's words shook with suppressed anger.

"Oh, is that so! And is the game warden drawing his wages for bringing runaway boys home?" A scornful laugh broke the silence.

Without giving an answer to this sarcastic remark, the warden said, "The boy lost his dog; do you know where the dog is?"

"What do I care about the dog? He is gone, and good riddance!" A mocking laugh followed.

"Am I to understand that you have taken from this poor, parentless boy what little he does have? Man, don't you have a heart?"

"It is my business, and my business alone, whether I have a dog around here. You can kindly concern yourself with your own affairs. Come inside, boy, and quick … go to bed. Now is there anything else you want, Mr. Warden?" These last words were uttered in a tone of great impudence.

"Datema, I warn you, don't you lay a finger on that boy. If you do, you will have me to answer to. Do you understand?"

The door slammed shut.

For a while the hunter remained, listening for any sign that the boy was being harmed. But all was quiet.

After a while Van Vliet's voice broke the silence, "Come, Sasta, time to go."

The game warden walked home with many thoughts preying on his mind. Was the dog dead? Had Datema taken the dog far away? How happy the warden would have been could he have had the privilege of returning the dog to his poor master! As it was, Van Vliet's heart was filled with discouragement and indignation.

Chapter 2

GERRIT

Whether it was Verdont the mailman, Geertsen the basketmaker, Tuenis the shoemaker, or Van Lenging the butcher, everyone thought a great deal of Gerrit Datema. Even Katie, the wife of farmer Verwijen, liked him and she wouldn't even let anyone pick up a rotten apple from her orchard. As far as she was concerned, Gerrit Datema could do no wrong. Even miserly Art Duiker, who, as people said, wouldn't lay aside a few pennies each Saturday night to give to the church collection, made a habit of buying several rolls of peppermints at the candy counter from Gijsje Bertelds so that he might give one to Gerrit every time he saw the lad.

If anyone ever teased Gerrit, it was so much the worse for the villain. Job Rijpma made this mistake once. The boys at school gave Job such a working over that he was laid up at home for three weeks. Of course those boys were punished, and severely at that. However, behind the glasses of bespectacled Principal Van Buren they saw his eyes twinkling so mischievously that the punishment was far from being a punishment. It was impossible to think of the village without thinking of Gerrit as a part of it.

As for Gerrit himself, his story is a sad one. A month after he was born his father died and he was left with his mother and Uncle Peter, who lived with them. Uncle Peter, a brother to Gerrit's father, was a lazy man. But what choice did the poor woman have but to try to run the farm with Uncle Peter's help? Approximately a half year after Gerrit's father's death his mother was faced with a new trouble. One morning the doctor told her that Gerrit would never be able to learn well at school.

Gerrit's mind did not function properly. The older he grew, the more evident this became. Yet Principal Van Buren had said, "When Gerrit is old enough, he should come to school anyway." The kindly man wanted to do whatever he could for the lad. And so it was that when Gerrit was of age he went to school.

"Look, boys and girls," the teacher would say, "if you get seven or eight answers right and Gerrit gets two, just remember that he had to work harder for his two than you had to for your seven or eight." This the children understood very well.

At another time the teacher would remark, "Why do you have a healthy mind? Only because God gave it to you and you should use it to good purpose. And whereas your healthy mind is not of your own doing, you should not tease those who have not been so blessed."

With this type of encouragement the children learned to associate with Gerrit and they took him under their protection. As a matter of fact, protecting Gerrit became what might be termed an unwritten law of the village.

One day Gerrit's mother gave him a puppy. His teacher, who was very fond of dogs, came to see the new pet. How happy Gerrit was!

"Have you given your puppy a name, Gerrit?" asked the teacher.

Gerrit couldn't quite grasp the meaning of the question. Because the puppy had a nice reddish-brown color the teacher suggested, "Why not call him Brownie?"

Gerrit decided that Brownie was a fine name for his pet. And as the years passed, boy and dog were virtually inseparable.

Then one afternoon as he came home from school Gerrit saw a large automobile parked in front of the farmhouse door. Strange men were carrying a long chest and they put it into the car. They rode away just as Gerrit arrived home. Uncle Peter stood there crying. Gerrit understood nothing of what had taken place.

"Come inside, Gerrit," said his uncle, and he set a dish on the table and filled it with soup. After Gerrit had finished the soup his uncle took him by the hand and together they walked to the center of the village. They went to the house of Gerrit's teacher. After Uncle Peter had exchanged a few words with the teacher, he left. Gerrit had noted that the two of them looked sad but he did not understand why.

Then the teacher showed Gerrit some pictures and told him stories as only he could tell them. They looked at a picture of fishermen caught in the middle of a storm. The teacher explained that all Jesus had to say was, "Be still!" and the storm would subside. Gerrit looked at the picture and saw the high waves and the small ship. He extended his arms high in the air and then threw them down. The teacher knew Gerrit understood the storm was very severe.

When it was dark Uncle Peter came and together they returned to the farm. The teacher and his wife had wept long, very long, but Gerrit still did not understand why.

Gerrit never saw his mother again. She never came back. At times Gerrit asked about her but she remained away so long that eventually he stopped asking. He didn't really understand. The people in the village became even friendlier than before but Gerrit never quite understood why.

Wherever Gerrit was, there Brownie was too. Woe to anyone who attempted to lay hands on Brownie's master. The big dog would spring up and growl angrily. But who in the village would ever harm poor Gerrit? Surely, no one!

Parents gave strict instructions to the small boys and girls, "Remember, never tease Gerrit! Do you hear?"

At catechism the minister told the children about sick and palsied people who had been brought to Jesus. With serious expression he would add, "Boys and girls, just think of Gerrit Datema." Then it was quiet — very quiet. The minister knew very well what the children were thinking. He said, "If only the Lord were still on earth to heal the sick." He could see from the faces of the children that he had spoken what was on their minds.

"If the Lord were to walk one day through our village, I am sure all of you would bring Gerrit to Jesus and say, 'Lord, wilt thou make Gerrit whole?'" Shyly the children nodded. If this could only be!

Then the minister continued: "That cannot take place now because the Lord Jesus is no longer on earth but in heaven. He performed miracles on earth so that men would believe in Him as God's Son. But the Lord is still the same Almighty God today! He is omnipresent. That means He is present everywhere, even in our remote village near the forest. You should ask God for a new heart for yourselves and for Gerrit Datema also. He cannot ask for himself. He doesn't really understand."

With these words the room became even quieter. The minister continued: "You can see, boys and girls, the great difference between yourselves and Gerrit. You know the way from God's Word; Gerrit does not know it for his mind does not function properly."

Because of the minister's explanation the ties between Gerrit and the other children grew even stronger. They made a point of protecting him. And many boys and girls prayed in the evenings, "Lord, give me a new heart and give Gerrit a new heart too."

Gerrit was enrolled in Mr. Van Buren's class. He always sat in the front row. He was never promoted; from the very beginning he sat in the same seat and his greatest delight was to play with the youngest children.

Gerrit never missed a day of school. On a sheet of white paper he would draw long lines with a large pencil or he would try to read from a book with large letters and lovely pictures. It was only with great difficulty that Gerrit learned to spell his name, but when he finally succeeded he burst out in loud laughter.

Whenever Gerrit learned something new, the teacher would say, "That is good, Gerrit. You did that very well." And Gerrit would shake his uncombed hair back and forth from sheer joy. Whenever he wasn't in school, he was out playing with Brownie.

Things did not go well for Gerrit's Uncle Peter. As a result, he took very poor care of the boy. He often teased the boy, and everyone in the village knew it. Alas, he began to think of the boy as a heavy burden.

At night Uncle Peter went out to poach on the game reservation. He left the boy to his own fate. The farm deteriorated; the fields were overgrown with brush and weeds. During the day Uncle Peter did not till the fields, but went to the city to sell his illegal spoils. Often he came home drunk and cursed the boy when he saw him asleep at the table with his head in his arms.

Now to explain why Uncle Peter got rid of the dog. One night he came home drunk again and on seeing Gerrit asleep he flew into a rage. The boy simply did not understand that he should have gone to bed.

"Go to bed, you dummy! What have I done to deserve you? Take that, you simpleton!" And he struck violent blows at the head of the frightened boy.

Uncle Peter was yelling at the top of his lungs. Sensing that his master was in great danger, Brownie sprang at the man and bit into his chest. The dog let go, ready to attack a second time. Not knowing what the result would be, Gerrit called the dog off, and Brownie obediently lay down. Had not Gerrit done so, the dog might have torn Uncle Peter to pieces.

As a result Uncle Peter was terribly afraid. He realized that if he did not get rid of the dog, his life would be in danger. So the next morning Uncle Peter decided that Brownie would have to be taken to a farm far away.

Gerrit was now without comfort. A storm had arisen in his life. But the Lord whose eyes see over the whole earth also took notice of Gerrit Datema. He who maintains all things and blesses man and beast also said to this storm, "Be still!" He will maintain the cause of orphans. He is the helper of the fatherless.

Chapter 3

THE POACHERS

About fifty yards from the main trail, which ran along the eastern edge of the forest toward the village, stood a small, dilapidated, whitewashed house. The forest trail was bordered on each side by low-growing heather. Colorful phlox and dahlias bloomed around the house. From the windows of the house one could see the village in the distance through the tall trunks of the fir trees. No stranger passing by would guess that in this house lived the most notorious poacher of the neighborhood.

Everyone knew the poacher as Wild Harry. When he shot, he seldom missed. While poaching, he ran daring risks. Many times his cunning had brought the game warden into a state of desperation. On several occasions when he had come close to being caught, Wild Harry had even threatened the warden's life.

There was a feeling of great hostility between the two men. Finally the game warden had only one aim in life — to stop Wild Harry. Several times he succeeded in catching the poacher and giving him a summons. And every time, though the culprit had to pay a higher fine, he escaped a jail sentence. This continued until the warden caught him trapping a young red deer. Then the judge sentenced the poacher to a year's imprisonment. Wild Harry never forgave the warden for this. When he was released, he poached more than ever before, but the warden was seldom able to catch him. At the tavern in the village the poacher made a practice of boasting that he would someday avenge himself on the warden. "I shall reckon with him," he threatened. "He will know the vengeance of a man who has served time in prison."

Van Vliet was not the sort of man to be intimidated by such threats. Nonetheless, he did keep on his guard. Duty called him and, as the keeper of the forest, he could not neglect his work. After all, the people who paid his salary had a right to expect that he would keep the poaching within reasonable limits.

The poacher was aware of Van Vliet's devotion to duty and swore he would not rest until he had made matters impossible for the warden. The hunting season was approaching. As the nights lengthened, the wild boar became more careless. At this season of the year poaching was widely practiced in the forest. At this time the struggle between warden and poachers became most intense.

In the quiet of the night the deer could be heard again. The poacher whistled a tune and sharpened his knife on a stone, so he could do his work quickly when the time came.

The night after the game warden had found Gerrit Datema in the woods, Wild Harry and Peter Datema were playing cards in the small white house. In the poorly furnished room were only a rickety old table and two chairs. Above the chimney place hung the antlers of a deer, and on the wall Wild Harry's gun. In the corner lay a dark brown heap. It was Brownie, held fast by a heavy chain.

There was blood clinging to the dog's fur, a sign that he had been beaten. The dog groaned softly. Datema had brought the dog to his friend with the intention of planning what was to be done with him.

Wild Harry half-closed his eyes. "Well, Peter, what do you intend to do with that monster?"

"Do you know of a place far away from here?"

"Why not give him a stab in the ribs? Then you would be rid of him once and for all."

Datema twisted uneasily in his chair. "No, Harry, I would rather not do that. It was my sister-in-law's dog, you know."

"You act as if you were a little girl, so gentle and mild," said the poacher scornfully.

The dog looked at the two men as if he understood every word they were saying. Datema shuddered visibly.

"Well, yes, Harry, but don't you know of a place I could bring him?"

"Certainly. Tomorrow morning I'll take him away and you'll never see him again. Is that all right?"

"Don't kill him. Do you hear?"

"No, I'll take him so far away he'll never return."

"All right, we'll keep it at that," agreed Datema. "Let's drink to it, Peter," said Wild Harry, and he fetched a bottle and two glasses from the cupboard.

Both men drank one glass after another. They kept playing cards for hours.

"I have another plan, Peter," said the poacher.

"What is that?" asked Datema.

"The day after tomorrow I'm going to set traps at the feeding grounds of the wild pigs. The game warden will sure be shocked when he sees the swine being trapped before his very eyes." Harry laughed hoarsely. "You will help me, won't you?"

Of course Peter Datema would. What a great trick they would play on the warden and what a lot of money they would make!

Late that night Datema went home. He had difficulty finding the way even though the moon shone brightly. He was satisfied. The dog was gone.

Early the following morning Wild Harry took hold of the heavy chain, which was securely fastened to Brownie's collar. "Come!" Brownie began to walk. But then he came to a halt, looking in the direction of his home.

"Come on!" bellowed Harry impatiently. Outside he was readying a wagon with a brown horse harnessed to it. The dog jumped into the wagon and was fastened to a wooden peg. The poacher took the reins, clicked his tongue, and the horse moved forward.

They rode far. First they followed the main trail. Then they traveled down a few country roads between luxuriant cultivated fields. Then they disappeared into the forest. Brownie pulled uneasily at his chain. He remained in an alert position — head raised, ears pointed straight up, nostrils wide open. Now and then he uttered a short dull bark. He took no notice of the poacher; his instinct told him he was going far away from the house and boy he was so fond of. He felt helpless as he was carried away beneath the high shady trees from which the first golden leaves were falling on the moss-covered ground. Indignantly he pulled at the chain. Wild Harry grumbled a few curses at Brownie and threatened him with the stick he brandished in his hand. The dog cringed.

Thus they rode for several hours. Finally the horse came to a standstill and Harry let himself slide limply from the wagon. He loosened the chain from the peg and pulled Brownie behind him. They walked up a narrow twisting path where children were playing in the sand. The poacher brought the dog to a small farmhouse from which a man in stocking feet emerged. The two men spoke with each other for a while. Then the poacher turned about and went away.

Brownie watched him for a moment without moving. Then he nervously tried to follow but he was roughly restrained. He was brought to a large doghouse where his chain was securely fastened to an iron bolt in the wooden wall. A tray of food and some water were placed before him. Then he was left alone … alone. And Brownie sensed that he was alone.

Clouds floated in the heavens. The moon kept itself hidden behind the clouds but a silver border suggested that the light of the moon would soon be visible. The forest was so black that the blackness could almost be felt. On this dark night two men prowled through the forest, each with a sack slung over his back, which contained the strong steel wire with which they were going to set the traps. Stealthily they approached the open range in the forest.

The ears of corn, which the game warden had set out for the wild boars, glistened in the moonlight. The idea was to keep the boars in the woods where they belonged. The potatoes were yet unharvested in the fields, and the farmers' property had to be protected. The poachers decided to take advantage of this situation.

A large dark cloud floated over the face of the moon. Motionless, the poachers lay face down upon the ground. Overhead in the leaves a rustling was heard like falling drops of rain. The fir trees swayed. An inquisitive weasel scurried past on its limber paws.

Wild Harry put his ear to the ground to listen. It was quiet. His trained ear could always detect the approach of wild boar.

With the wind blowing toward them, the two poachers waited. Wild Harry kept putting his ear to the ground. At last he gave Peter a nudge. They were coming. He heard the dull thumping of approaching hoofs. Without a doubt, the boars were coming. But their approach was delayed because they stopped to burrow in the ground; they were looking for acorns among the dead leaves, which the trees shed every autumn. Finally the poachers could hear the corn being munched. Fiery eyes glowed between tree trunks. A couple of the pigs snorted.

Suddenly one of the boars came close to the spot where the poachers were lying. It shook its bristly head and the men could see its grinders shine. The animal began to grind its teeth together wildly and from under the hairy eyebrows its eyes looked around searchingly. Then the pig spied the men. With a jump it turned around and ran with haste into the thick woods. The other pigs all fled in frantic fear behind the leader. They dashed straight across the broad fire lane into the dark woods.

The poachers got up. Wild Harry spit a stream of tobacco juice into the darkness.

"That one pig betrayed us," whispered Peter nervously.

"That isn't so bad, man. Mark my word, tomorrow night they will return at the very same time!"

"Then we'll have a good haul," said Peter.

Wild Harry agreed. Both men walked stealthily back along the well-known secret path to Wild Harry's white house. The poachers well knew that the wild boar would return to that spot and that, when they set the traps, they would be well rewarded for their trouble.

The game warden stepped out from behind the tall tree trunks. His sharp eyes detected the figures of the men moving away. He understood why the herd had fled and just what the two poachers had been planning.

Chapter 4

UPROAR IN THE VILLAGE

The butcher was singing his favorite tune. The door of his market stood wide open. The sun shot its rays over the village and between the branches of the old trees. In the distance the hills took on a golden glow.

"Hi, Van Lenging, how's the bologna today?" A few smiling boys peeked their noses in the door.

"Well, boys, you are wide awake, aren't you? Are you on your way to your lessons?" Then Van Lenging and the boys teased each other in a spirit of good fun. Laughter rang through the market. The butcher always had a good time exchanging jokes with the children.

"Here, would all of you like to have a thick slice of bologna? But don't go broadcasting that Van Lenging gives out free samples."

"Thank you so much, Van Lenging."

There were no customers in the market, so the butcher came out from behind the counter. "Listen, boys, I'll tell you a story about a mischievous prank I played when I was just about your age.

"It happened when I was still a schoolboy. Mr. Stuik was my teacher. Of course you boys don't know him. I was very mischievous and was often punished for it, believe me, just like Philip Duvans today. But let's get on with the story. Mr. Stuik had given us a great deal of homework and this made us very rebellious. Another lad — his name was Philip too — and I decided to get even with him. When it was dark we each took a piece of glass under our arm and went to his house. He lived in the very house where Mr. Van Buren lives today. But unbeknownst to us another teacher, Mr. Stuwe, had seen us take the glass and he kept us in his sight. He stood right behind the big elm tree by Van Buren's house. Do you know what we did? We banged hard against the windows and then let the pieces of glass fall. There was an awful racket of shattering glass. We started to run away as fast as we could. Imagine our terror when in the dark we were grabbed by the collar. We were panic-stricken. Philip stammered, 'Oh, Mr. Stuwe.'

"'Quiet,' I heard the teacher say. And we kept quiet out of fear. Just then the door of the house flew open. Out stepped Mr. Stuik. He was wearing slippers and had no coat on.

"'They are all broken,' we heard him say.

"'Where are they?' yelled his wife. The neighbors came running out of their houses. It was a ridiculous affair. Fragments of glass everywhere and not one window broken! The lights went on upstairs and even the windows in the attic were inspected. But every window was untouched. Mr. Stuik couldn't figure out what had caused the shattering noise and the broken glass.

"When the excitement was over, Mr. Stuwe said to us, 'Now what must I do with you bad boys?'

"'Teacher, we will never do it again.'

"'Will you promise me that?' he asked and at once he put out his hand. We grasped it, thankful that everything had turned out as well as it had. 'Go home at once!' he said and off we went. Mr. Stuik never did understand why the two of us did so well in school after that day.

"There goes the bell. Off to school with you." Full of laughter the boys continued on their way to school.

Tanis, the village policeman, came in to see Van Lenging. "Van Lenging," he said, "I need you."

"What is the trouble, Tanis?"

"You know that Peter Datema and Wild Harry are busy poaching again. Last night the game warden discovered that very likely they are going to set their traps tonight to catch the wild boar. They made a first attempt last night but suddenly the pigs ran away. The warden had been spying on them all the while, hoping to catch them in the act. I'm asking you to help us tonight. We must catch those fellows. That scoundrel Peter Datema totally neglects poor Gerrit. It seems the boy has lost his dog and now he wanders with a blank look on his face through the woods and fields. We suspect his uncle put the dog away. A few nights back the warden found Gerrit sleeping in the forest. There isn't one good word that can be spoken about Peter Datema. We must see if we can catch him poaching tonight. Then perhaps at the same time we can put an end to the lad's misery. Can you help tonight?"

"Indeed I can. Count me in. So the boy lost his dog. That's why I don't see him anymore. What time, Tanis?"

"Ten o'clock at Van Vliet's house."

"Agreed."

"Not one word to anyone about this."

"I understand."

The report of the dog spread through the village like wildfire. Everyone was indignant. A meeting was held on the village square to decide how best to deal with Peter Datema. Even the minister came in his shirtsleeves from the porch of the parsonage. He wanted to hear what was going on. His face was red with anger but he admonished the people not to take the law into their own hands. He advised, "Let's leave it to God and meanwhile we will get Gerrit another dog." His advice was accepted by all.

But the whole village also shared Geertsen's sentiment: "The boy should be taken away from that man." The minister and Gerrit's teacher promised to make work of it. Everyone then went his way but the mood of the village was far from calm. When Gerrit came to the village in the afternoon, the minister took him into his house. The villagers waited. Woe to Peter Datema if he dared to show his face. The village was in an uproar.

Brownie was tied to a doghouse among strange people. He was alone. He took no notice of the children who were playing a short distance away and who occasionally came to look at him. He had no interest in the woman who was chopping wood in the farmyard nor the man who had tied him up and was now working in the fields under the warm September sun.

Brownie became more and more fearful. He even forgot to bark. He stretched his head out flat on the ground and peered off into the distance. He didn't touch the food placed before him. The children patted him on the back and pushed the trays of food and water under his nose. But Brownie turned his head away, breathing heavily.

One of the children forcefully pulled Brownie's head down while the other encouraged him, but Brownie growled viciously until they let him go.

"He's a mean dog, leave him alone," they said discouraged. They ran away to play again. Brownie was alone. With angry short sniffs he strode around his coop and then lay down with his back toward it. He wouldn't even look at it.

He searched around in the distance for something familiar. He constantly tugged at his chain, but to no avail. It remained fastened to the iron bolt. At a safe distance the children kept their eyes on him.

"He is wild," they thought, "a trapped wolf!" They laughed at his angry growls and behavior. They didn't go near him again.

Night came; the family went into the house and put on the lights. Now and then the moon was visible from behind the clouds. The dog lay before the coop – solitary, huddled up, motionless.

Now and then Brownie groaned in his sleep. It became quieter. The people had gone to bed. Brownie trembled and stood upright. A desperate instinct for freedom set his muscles in motion. He pulled stubbornly on the chain; he began to bite and chew it. A wild rage took possession of him, like a storm roaring over the sea. He strained with all his might as if he were tugging a heavily laden cart. He pulled and bit, twisted and fought until the collar rubbed painfully on the battered skin of his neck. With a howl he sank down for a moment.

But untiringly he tried anew. This time his body jumped up and down like a lever. White bubbles of foam formed around his mouth. He kept jumping until the iron bolt, which held the chain into the wall, swung loose.

Brownie was free ... and bewildered. He shook himself and licked his sore neck. The chain jingled softly. For a moment he stood still and motionless. The hairs on his back shuddered frightfully. Then he set his paws in motion and fled as if he were mad. With long strides he ran over the farmyard, down the pathway, and disappeared into the forest.

Chapter 5

CAPTURED

The two poachers sat together in the scantily furnished room of the small white house. They were waiting for the time when they could execute their plans. "The darkness serves to our advantage," observed Wild Harry.

A dark September heaven hung over the forest and moorland. The sun had gone down. In the waning light the beech trees looked like fire-red torches amid the soft golden foliage of the poplars. It looked as if the white of a few birch trees was trying to ward off the darkness, and high in the air the wind was blowing.

Wild Harry looked toward the forest. His thoughts went back to his youth. "Don't become sentimental," he chided himself. "Don't give way to your feelings."

"How can a person get to be so tough?" he asked Peter.

"What are you talking about, Harry?"

"Well, I was thinking back to the days of my childhood when I was afraid to look at blood. I remember the first time I was allowed to go hunting with my father. How ironic that he was a game warden! I was fifteen years old and had been instructed to remain close to him. Toward the end of the chase one of the other hunters came toward us. Suddenly I noticed a small roe coming out of the bushes. I couldn't take my eyes off the graceful little animal. The roe didn't suspect a thing. It stood there calmly in the sunlight. Then my father also saw it, but he didn't shoot. Finally the animal became aware of us. Then right next to me I heard the report of a gun. I ran over to the felled animal and softly stroked its soft brown hide. Tears flowed from my eyes. Yes, these very eyes [and Harry pointed to his eyes with his finger] have wept over a slain animal. My father was furious. He scolded me severely, 'Are you an old woman?' I couldn't bear his reproach so I promised myself that in the future I would be hard … always." The poacher fell silent.

"And at that you have succeeded very well, Harry," said Peter.

"I can't change what I am now, but you don't have to be like me, Peter." Wild Harry's eyes looked penetratingly at Peter Datema.

"Come, Harry, you're beginning to irritate me; we must be going. It's half past eight," said Peter. To himself Peter thought, "Something is very strange tonight; Harry is never like this. Could it be that Harry is human too?"

The men went on their way, their thoughts again completely centered on their purpose. Yet for some reason Wild Harry was not able to shake a strange misgiving. It kept coming back.

At ten o'clock they reached the feeding area. Cautiously they prowled forward. Near the tree trunks they scattered some corn. Then they took a steel wire from their sacks and carefully intertwined it with some moss. At the least sound they stretched out flat on the ground. With his arm Harry measured the length of the loop — he was judging the size of the pigs. Then he drew the wire tight around the trunk and pulled with all his might. Thus the trap awaited its prey.

After the snares had been laid, the poachers went off a short distance with the wind blowing toward them. It was whistling over their heads. They heard the deer in the distance. The forest life was awakening.

The poachers waited.

The game warden scanned the darkness with his intent, sharp eyes. The policeman and Van Lenging kept a little behind him, ready at the first signal. Here and there a rustling was heard in the woods, branches cracked. The head of a deer peered between the tree trunks; cautiously it walked forward. A second deer approached. The night hung threateningly over the black forest. The warden was sure that the poachers were in the immediate vicinity, but he wanted to catch them in the act. Carefully he laid himself flat on the ground. With his ear to the ground he could hear the boars hoofs. They were approaching quickly.

The leader appeared and very cautiously looked about for signs of anything suspicious. The men could hear the animal sniff the air. It suspected man. The men lay motionless. Perhaps the animal would not come into the open. With a clatter of its teeth it suddenly disappeared into the brushwood.

Once again the animal stepped cautiously forward; it inspected the open feeding place. For a brief moment its enormous head with white shining teeth, its short neck, and its high hack could be seen in the dim light of the moon. Then it came forward toward the food, which had been purposely laid there. Branches cracked and more wild pigs appeared. The way seemed to be safe. The men could hear corn cracking between the strong jaws. Further in the woods pigs' eyes glowed in the dark like flaming fire.

Then a scream pierced the night. At the same moment the moon reappeared from behind a cloud. In the brightness Wild Harry saw the white teeth of a wild boar. The animal pulled and tugged at the wire, which was cutting its sides. The trapped creature gasped wildly. A dark human form rose quickly from the other side and cautiously approached the infuriated swine. A knife gleamed in the poacher's right hand and with a quick leap he jumped upon the broad neck of the raging creature. The man's legs wrapped themselves around the hairy body while his knees dug into the back. The animal ground its teeth like a scissors; foam was flying into its face. In one hand the poacher held his razor-sharp knife while with the other he tried to expose the boar's throat in order to give it a deadly thrust. Peter stood behind Wild Harry ready to help. The other animals fled at a wild gallop. But just as Wild Harry was about to give the fatal blow a voice was heard through the night.

"Hold it right there, Harry, and you too, Peter Datema."

Peter tried to run away but Van Lenging's strong arms encircled him like tongs. The game warden leaped forward. He barked out the command, "Put out your wrists!" The handcuffs were locked and the poacher stood there powerless.

As soon as Wild Harry saw the game warden, a wild rage took possession of him. He would fight. He jumped up, but before he could inflict one blow he lay sprawled on the ground. The warden's fist had hit him squarely in the jaw. In a short time Wild Harry was also handcuffed. The warden then put the wild pig out of its misery by shooting it in the head.

"So," said the warden, "your time is up, Harry." The poacher was silent and tight-lipped. The whites of his eyes flashed in the darkness. He was filled with powerless rage.

Both scoundrels had been taken – caught in the act.

Meanwhile Brownie continued his journey. His nose sniffed along the ground. In the distance a stream quietly rippled over the rocks. His throat was parched. Panting, he sought the cool brook and eagerly lapped the refreshing water. Now and then he looked behind him.

The following day he roamed for miles, passing along fields, woods, and small villages. Sometimes he seemed to recognize something. Then again a strange hostility oppressed him because the unknown landscape offered no trace of his faraway home. At one time a group of screaming people tried to catch him. Fatigued and soaking wet he was able to hide himself in the thick brush. Near a small hamlet a pack of dogs tore after him. They were ready to fight to drive away the stranger. He withstood their attack, fighting desperately because the loose-hanging chain impeded his body movements. Finally the pack retreated and he ran away, covered with bleeding wounds and more dead than alive.

But he continued to search. Suddenly he recognized something lying on a narrow path between the imprint of horse-hoofs in the loose sand. He made a dash for it; he rolled over it; he rubbed his front paws over it; he laid his head upon it. It was his master's cap. While looking for Brownie, Gerrit had lost it there unawares.

Brownie was on the right track. His strength was renewed because instinct told him that the home of his master could not be far away. The morning light dawned in the east. The golden light spread itself all over the forest.

Chapter 5

A MIRACLE

Rev. Van Merwe and Principal Van Buren agreed that Gerrit could not continue to live with his uncle. Since Uncle Peter was the boy's foster father, however, it was necessary for them to bring a complaint before the judge. Before doing this, they decided they should speak to Datema.

It was early in the morning when Mr. Van Buren and the minister set out to Datema's farm. Gerrit walked between them. The big fifteen-year-old boy held his teacher's hand much as a small child would. He kept shaking his head and calling for his dog, "Brownie, Brownie!"

"The big question," said the minister, "is whether another dog will satisfy the boy."

"I doubt it very much, pastor," replied the teacher.

"I find it heartwarming to see the people sympathizing with the lad," continued the minister. "Last night a little girl brought a bunch of common dandelions to my home and asked me to put them in Gerrit's room. Isn't that touching?"

"It certainly is," the teacher responded. The two men walked on in deep silence.

The farmhouse was hidden behind an old oak at a curve in the trail. "He is home," observed the minister. "Look, smoke from a newly kindled fire is rising from the chimney."

"Good morning, pastor, good morning, Van Buren," the cheerful voice of Van Lenging echoed through the heavy foliage of the forest.

"Van Lenging, what are you doing out so early?" inquired the minister.

The butcher took the minister aside. "We caught both of the scoundrels last night," he reported with obvious delight. The minister looked at him in bewilderment.

"Wild Harry was just about to cut the throat of a wild pig when we apprehended him; everything went very smoothly, pastor."

"What about Datema?" asked the minister.

"Yes, he was caught too. Both of them have been released temporarily, but, mark my words, both can depend on long sentences in jail." The butcher laughed aloud and slapped himself on both knees from sheer joy.

Rev. Van Merwe laid his hand on Van Lenging's shoulder and looked straight into his eyes. "Van Lenging, don't ever forget that it is solely by grace that we are not in their position."

The face of the butcher suddenly became very serious. He fumbled with his cap and said in shame, "I won't forget that, pastor. Good-bye." He walked hastily back to the village. After that reminder all the enjoyment he had felt vanished.

Under his breath the minister informed the teacher, "Last night the two of them were caught. This will change the situation drastically." The teacher nodded his agreement.

Both men walked toward the house. Peter Datema, looking worn out, was just coming outside. The sight of the three approaching frightened him. "Pastor ... Van Buren?" His greeting was bewildered.

"Yes, and Gerrit too!" the minister exclaimed loudly.

The face of the farmer turned pale and a rising rage could be read in his eyes. "What now?" he thought to himself, "as if last night weren't bad enough."

"We have come to talk with you, Datema. Where will it be — here or inside?" The minister's voice was stern.

"It is all the same to me," answered Datema, trying to appear nonchalant.

The minister sat down on a bench, the arm of which creaked. With a courteous gesture, which the farmer could have interpreted as mockery, he invited Datema to sit beside him. Gerrit leaned heavily against the side of the house and kept calling for his dog, "Brownie, Brownie."

At first the minister spoke softly. Then he raised his voice and anger rang through his words. The farmer was silent. More and more Datema lost his self-confidence and arrogance in the presence of this servant of the Lord, who reminded him of

God's law and the fact that God will punish those who transgress His commands. Then the minister spoke about the practice of loving our neighbor. Datema's heart was self-accusing — he had no defense to offer in his own behalf.

Suddenly there was a strange noise in the distance — the sound of a chain being dragged over stones. It grew louder and louder. Then could also be heard the sound of paws running on the hard ground. The men turned around in fright.

There, in the early dawn of the morning light, while the dew was still sparkling on the grass, came the dog. He was fatigued and shabby-looking. Blood had congealed and clung to his wounds. He was dirty, thin, and trembling. He stopped for a moment before them and looked at them squarely with his deep brown eyes.

Then the dog gave a loud bark, ran to his master, and stood up on his hind legs. With his front legs he embraced the boy. He licked him, wagged his tail as if beside himself with joy, then barked and licked his master again. But he was exhausted, hungry, and wounded. He laid himself down on the ground. With his dark, tender eyes he looked at his master as if to say he would lay all his devotion at the boy's feet.

Gerrit bent over Brownie, then stood erect and a lustre sparkled in his eyes. He brought the dog food and water. He spoke to him encouragingly with a few short and simple words, but what feeling there was packed into those words: "Brownie, Brownie ...

nice ... good dog." Suddenly the boy was off into the house like a shot. He returned with a rag clumsily crumpled up in his fingers. He intended to use the rag as a bandage.

After the minister had recovered from his astonishment, he took the rag from the boy's hands. "Get water, Datema, and a bandage, an old shirt or something like it; I'll bandage up this faithful dog myself."

The teacher was wiping his handkerchief over his eyes. "It is impossible to have dry eyes after seeing something like this."

Peter Datema returned meekly with water and a cloth. Gerrit kept right on talking, his arms swinging back and forth from sheer excitement. His joy was so unbounded it shone from his eyes.

The minister bound up the wounds skillfully. The dog kept wagging his tail and begging to be caressed. Peter Datema stood there ashamed, his arms hanging limply. Even to him this was a miracle!

"Pastor," said Datema shyly and confusedly, "if you think it better for Gerrit to live with you in your home until I return from prison, it is all right with me. Afterward I will be different, pastor, I promise you. Can you ever forgive me for what I did to the boy?"

Rev. Van Merwe gladly extended his hand. "Datema," he said, "will you consider what we have just been talking about? And above all seek forgiveness from God!" He looked fixedly and earnestly at the poacher.

Then without saying a word Van Buren also extended his hand. The Lord Himself had spoken! The minister took Gerrit's hand and placed it in the coarse hand of his weeping foster father.

Then, followed by the dog, the trio returned to the village. Their silent thoughts were on the miracle.

* * *

Rev. Van Merwe approached Wild Harry's small white house. Harry was sitting downcast on a rickety chair and had an empty glass before him on the table. The minister stopped at the open door.

The poacher started up with a fright. The only word he could blurt out was an astonished, "Reverend."

The minister ordered, "Come here, Harry." The poacher got up and stood at the door next to his visitor. The minister pointed to the phlox and dahlias ablaze in the midday sun. "Under the fir trees bouquets are standing here praising God, making a poacher's cottage into a palace."

The poacher looked at the minister in bewilderment, not understanding his meaning. But then a hand was placed on the rough man's shoulder. "But now, how do matters stand with the master of the palace? What is going on inside him?" The voice was penetrating and yet kind. The minister had touched the tenderest cord of this worldly man. At once Wild Harry began to sob loudly.

The two men talked for a long time — until the long shadows of evening fell over the moss-covered pathway. When the minister walked this path toward the main road, a despondent voice was heard: "Pastor, will you still pray for me?"

The echo rang loud and clear through the trees, "I'll do that, Harry. Good-bye now."

Goldfinches fluttered away before his feet.

* * *

That night Brownie slept in the room with his young master. Every once in a while the dog seemed to awaken, although he lay motionless, his head down. But there was an alertness in his open eyes, which indicated that he was listening to the breathing of the sleeping boy.

* * *

It was Sunday and the church bells had echoed over the distant moor. The church was full to overflowing. Rev. Van Merwe was standing behind the pulpit. His text consisted of only a few words: "And the fame thereof went abroad into all that land."

"This fame, the fame of God's wonder-working hand also goes out through our village near the forest. God is a God of wonders in nature and in grace. Who is it that causes to grow the grass, which we trample with our feet? Who causes it to rise up after rainstorms have flattened it? Who unfurls the flower so that honey may be produced? Who cares for all things? Who? It is God, the Lord, who performed miracles from of old!"

The people understood what the minister was driving at. They had seen the miracle.

"God performs miracles each and every day. We walk amidst the wonders of His hands. But He can also humble the hardest hearts, no matter whether they reside in a poacher's hut or a king's palace.

"Listen to His voice as His report goes through our village streets and along the paths of our forest and moor. It is the voice of Him who permits His sun to shine on the wicked and the good. Listen to His law which shines with a perfect lustre even in the hearts of sinners."

Gerrit was sitting in the pew reserved for the minister's family. He was staring at the minister. To the side sat Van Lenging. He was also looking straight ahead. The game warden was sitting a little in front of them and wiping his hand over his eyes. Yes, it is a miracle that God is willing to live in the hearts of broken sinners, even in the hearts of poachers who have come to repentance. The warden now understood this glad tiding in a way that he never had before.

With gladness in his heart the minister's last words vibrated along the church arch, "God also remembers the feeble-minded!"

The Royal Law

Adelpha

Chapter 1

A NEW FRIEND

One Sunday morning Hans Wiggers stood leaning against a lamppost and watching eagerly as the people left the church. He had not been in church because his shirt and pants were torn and ragged. It was bad enough that he had to walk the streets in his ragged clothes on Sunday. At first he had not dared to do it but he became used to it. He had almost forgotten that he had ever had a shiny black cap and a nice suit that mother always laid out for him. He never thought of it anymore except when he saw other boys wearing their Sunday clothes. He remembered how happy he, and his mother and Hester had been. The house in which they had lived was always so neat, quite different from their covered wagon, in which they had no room to keep things. The eyes of Hans filled with tears as he thought of the kite Miss Anna had given him. His father made him put it away because he didn't want so much "stuff" lying around.

How happy all those people looked. Hans used to go to church sometimes, and every Sunday he went to Sunday school. But now he couldn't, because he was hardly ever in the same city for two

Sundays in succession. Besides that, who would want to have such a shabby-looking boy in his class?

The street was almost empty, for the worshipers were hurrying to their homes. But Hans had no reason to hurry home. Why should he? Only Hester would want to see him. Maybe he wouldn't even be let in! Hadn't his father said that he must not try to come back today? Father might even hit him if he disobeyed.

"Well, my boy, what is the matter?" a voice spoke to him. Hans looked up to see who was speaking. The friendly young man repeated his question and laid his hand on Hans' shoulder. He too had come from the church, but he gave more than a passing glance at the little boy standing by the lamppost. The man's name was Otto Dalhaven and his heart was full of love for his Master and also for children. Whenever he saw a child in trouble, he tried to help.

"Are you hungry, my boy?" he went on.

"No Sir, I mean, I am," Hans stammered, "but not very. I wasn't thinking about that."

"Oh, no? Then what were you thinking about? What makes you sad? Can't you tell me about it? Perhaps I can help you."

Hans was surprised to have a stranger speak to him that way. That had never happened before. He was not usually bashful and after a moment he replied, "I don't know, Sir. There is so much that isn't right, but I don't believe you can help me."

"If I cannot help you, I have a friend who will surely help you if you ask Him."

"I don't believe he can help us," Hans said with a sigh. "Is he rich?"

"Yes, very rich."

"As rich as a king? Mother says it wouldn't help if we were as rich as a king, for father would spend it all."

"My friend is a king," said the stranger with a smile. He was going to continue, but Hans interrupted him.

"Oh," he said, disappointed, "I know who you mean. God."

"That's right, I mean the King of all kings. Do you know Him, too? Is He your friend?"

"I don't know," said Hans slowly. "I have asked God to help us because Miss Anna said He would, but He never did."

"Every king has laws for his people. Perhaps you have never tried to live according to God's laws. If you haven't, He is not your King. Do you know His laws?"

"I don't know, Sir," Hans said again with a tired voice, "I never think about it anymore."

"Will you come to my Sunday school class this afternoon? Then I shall tell you about the laws of my King," said the friendly young man. "But first tell me your name and where you live."

Hans gave his name and said, "We don't really live anywhere. We have a covered wagon just outside the city near Low Gate. Do you know where that is?"

"Yes, I know. Have you been there long?"

"No, Sir, just three days, and we won't stay much longer," said Hans, looking about him. "You see, we sell things, and only in the larger cities do we stay longer than three days. Perhaps you need something. We have all kinds of things. May I come to your house?"

"Yes, you may come tomorrow," said the stranger, smiling at the little salesman. "But now you must come with me. I'll show you where I live."

Hans happily followed his new friend through a few side streets to a square white house standing apart from the others. "Can you remember the way?" asked Mr. Dalhaven, as he opened a gate for the boy to enter. "Come here again this afternoon. The Sunday school begins at 1:30 sharp. Wait a moment, and I'll give you something, because you told me that you were hungry."

As Hans returned home he was in a much happier mood than he had been when his father had sent him out that morning. The loaf of bread the kind stranger had given him made him sure that he would be welcome at home. So he hurried through the streets as fast as he could to tell his sister all about it.

Hans soon reached the large covered wagon, which had once been painted yellow, but now had almost no color. The horse was unharnessed and was nibbling near by at the dry hard grass. The poor horse looked as if he had had very little food. On hearing his master approach, the horse lifted his head to look at him with big sad eyes, as if asking for food.

"Yes, Brownie," the boy called happily, as if he had heard the question, "I brought you something." He ran to Brownie, and breaking off a piece of the loaf he had received, fed it to the horse.

Hans and Brownie were good friends. The horse knew that if his master had something special, he would share it with him. The boy petted the long silky mane. The wagon door opened and a little girl looked out. Her blond hair and light blue eyes made her look quite different from Hans, but the shapes of their faces were just alike.

"Oh, Hans, are you there?" she called when she saw him. "Come here quickly. Father and mother are gone, but I stayed home to wait for you."

Hans did not have to be called twice. After giving the horse another pat, he took the bread and hurried toward the wagon. The little girl opened the door wide, letting out the dog, which jumped up at his young master happily.

"Look, Hes," said Hans, "I have something to tell you." And while cutting slices of bread, he told her the whole story. "You may come, too, Hester," he said as he finished. "So put your hat on. Hurry! Let's go before mother comes home. She probably wouldn't let you go."

Hester quickly got her hat and old, worn-out shawl from a chest that also served as a seat. She took the rest of the bread Hans had given her and followed him out of the wagon.

"No, Tommy, you may not go with us," said the lad. And although the dog begged, Hans tied him to a rope. "There, now you can take care of the house."

"Hes, we'll first wash ourselves, because at a Sunday school everyone looks clean. Come here, I'll help you." He took a wooden pail from under the wagon and ran to a nearby creek.

In a moment he came back and took off his sister's hat and shawl. With much splashing they washed and wiped themselves dry on an old towel. They tried to pin together the biggest rips in their clothes. Ignoring Tommy's begging, they went on their way.

The cold March winds made them shiver, and so they started to run to keep warm. When they had reached the edge of the city, they heard the town clock strike one.

Hans came to a halt. "It's only one o'clock," he said, "and the class starts at half past one. Where shall we go to wait?"

"Into the city," replied Hester. "The wind doesn't blow as hard there."

And so they hurried on until they felt the protection of the buildings. After they had walked around for fifteen minutes, they went to the big white house. A few boys and girls were standing in front. Although most of them wore ragged clothes, they did not seem to be quite as poor as Hans and Hester. As more and more children came, they began to play together. Three or four boys near Hans played marbles. Hans watched them, moving ever closer until he stood in the circle of players.

"Say, what are you doing here?" a big boy suddenly snapped. He was one of the few who were wearing nice warm clothes. "Get out of the way. You're bothering us."

"I have just as much right to stand here as you," said Hans, angrily. He wasn't about to let anyone send him away.

"No, you don't, you beggar," called the other boy. "Get out of the way or I'll ..."

"Come on, if you dare," said Hans, standing ready to fight.

"I wouldn't want to fight with you," retorted the big boy. "Do you think I didn't see you begging at my mother's door yesterday?"

"I did not!" shouted Hans, boiling mad. Without giving it a second thought, he jumped on the big boy. It might have become a serious fight, but just at that moment Mr. Dalhaven opened the door and stepped out.

"Come, boys, what does this mean?" he called sternly. "No fighting here. Marinus, are you at it again? When will you learn to stop bothering other people?"

At Mr. Dalhaven's first words the two boys let each other go. When he called them to come in, they followed slowly. Marinus found time to whisper to Hans, "Just wait, I'll pay you back, I promise!"

There was no time to answer, for they had reached the door where Mr. Dalhaven stood. Hester, who had watched the fight with frightened eyes, took Hans' hand and held it very tightly in her own. They were the last ones to enter. Hans was ashamed of himself when he saw Mr. Dalhaven's eyes on him. However, Mr. Dalhaven said nothing. He closed the door and led them all to a large square room arranged like a schoolroom with bright colored texts on the walls.

When all were seated, Mr. Dalhaven opened with prayer. Although Hans closed his eyes and folded his hands, he didn't hear a word of the prayer, nor of the first part of the talk that followed. His mind was filled with what had happened outside. What a mean kid! Why did he have to call Hans a beggar? Hans worked for his living, and had never asked anything of anyone! Besides that, Marinus wanted to chase him away as though he had no right to watch that game of marbles! Who did Marinus think he was? Hans would show him. He planned how he would wait for his enemy after class. Then they would see who was the stronger. Nobody could insult Hans Wiggers and get away with it!

Just then a word of Mr. Dalhaven caught Hans' attention and he started to listen carefully.

"We have been speaking about the greatness and the power of King Jesus. Let us now see what laws He has made. For without knowing what His laws are, we cannot obey them. If we do not know His laws, we do not belong to His kingdom, and we cannot expect Him to help us when we are in trouble. One of God's laws is: 'And as ye would that men should do to you, do ye also to them likewise.'

"This is a law that all of us disobey often, for it is not easy to keep it. And yet this is what the King wants: He wants you to think about this law in everything you do. If you do, your life will be different from the life you have led. If you treat others as you want them to treat you, you will not live for yourself but for others. Then you will not grumble when your father or mother asks you to do something you don't want to do. Those of you still in school will not try to make it hard for your teachers or to make them angry.

Hans thought these words were meant for him alone, and his face became very red. But Mr. Dalhaven was looking toward the other side of the room.

"If you obey this law, it will not be hard for you to forgive someone who has wronged you because — and this is the wonderful part of the laws of our King — if we really try by grace to keep just one of His laws, we will keep the others as well. If we do unto others as we would have others do unto us, we will be loving our neighbors as ourselves. And if you do that, you will also love your enemies. You will also do good to those who hate you and pray for those who despitefully use you. This seems to be impossible; and, in fact, if you try to do it in your own strength, it is impossible. But the King will help you. He goes about through the cities and towns of the whole world. Although you cannot see Him, He is wherever you are and sees all you do. He is even in this room and is looking into your heart. He knows what you are thinking about at this very moment. He knows what you are going to do. If it is something against His laws, you grieve Him just as much as if you were to say, 'I don't want you for my King.' Instead, while you are still here, you should say in your heart, 'Lord Jesus, forgive me for disobeying. Be my King and give me strength to fight against sin.'"

The Sunday school was over, and Hans and Hester walked slowly to their wagon home. Mr. Dalhaven had given each of the children a little card on which was printed in big letters:

THE ROYAL LAW

**As ye would that men should do to you,
Do ye also to them likewise.
— Luke 6:31**

Hans held his card carefully. Mr. Dalhaven's words had gone deep into his heart. He knew very well that he had never served King Jesus, but he was resolved to from that day forward. He asked Jesus to help him, knowing that Jesus surely would. Hans was so busy thinking about these things that both children hardly said a word on the way home. Hester's thoughts were not on what she had heard, for she could not understand all of it. Yet she knew her brother was deep in thought and did not wish to disturb him.

Hans was exactly twice as old as Hester. As a matter of fact, she had been born on his sixth birthday. Perhaps that was why he thought she belonged to him alone. When she was very young, he had carried her everywhere; once she was able to walk, she had followed him everywhere. If you saw one, you could be sure the other was near by. Yet Hans and Hester were not at all alike. Hans was unafraid and talkative; Hester was bashful and quiet. Only when the two were alone together would she talk freely. But when, as now, Hans didn't feel like talking, Hester didn't say anything either.

All at once they heard a loud, rough voice saying, "Well, well, there is that beggar again. I wonder how much the teacher gave him for listening so attentively."

Hans became so angry his whole face turned red. He was about to say a bad word, but suddenly he remembered what Mr. Dalhaven had said.

"The King would not want me to fight," he thought. Then he whispered, "Oh, King Jesus, keep me from getting angry." He took Hester's hand and hurried away.

"That horrid boy!" cried Hester, turning to look at Marinus, who was now calling them bad names.

Hans made no answer but kept his mouth closed tight. Marinus stopped his teasing as soon as he realized that his name-calling wasn't making

Hans angry. So the two children were able to walk home in peace.

How happy Hans was that he had fought against getting angry. Had not Mr. Dalhaven said that the Lord would be pleased with him now? Now Hans knew that he wanted to belong to the Lord, and it was in his mind never to grieve Him again. He would always obey Him, always!

Filled with such thoughts he arrived home at the wagon. "Hester," he said, "aren't you glad the King sees us everywhere? He always knows when we do something for Him. I never want to make Him sad again, do you?"

"No, I don't either," said Hester, as though it were the easiest thing in the world. What Hans wanted was good, of course, and so she wanted it, too.

Hans hurried up the steps of the wagon and quickly stepped inside. He had thought of something. He knew that in the bottom of the chest that held the family's clothes was a little Bible that Miss Anna had given him. When he had attended her Sunday school, he read it occasionally, but lately he had never thought about it. Now he wanted to read again what Mr. Dalhaven had said. He could easily find the verse, for the reference was written on the card.

Hans was disappointed to find that his mother had come home while they were gone. She was sitting as usual — head in arms — on a low stool by the rusty stove. When the children came in she raised her head, but said nothing. So Hans was hopeful that he could still do what he had intended. He pulled the chest out into the light of the only window. Hester looked, too, to see all the things of long ago that were in the chest.

"What are you doing there?" asked his mother in a cross voice.

"I'm looking for something, Mother," replied Hans, as he uncovered some books and letters.

"You don't have to look for anything in there," said his mother. "Close the chest and keep your hands off."

"Right away," said Hans without looking up.

The woman got up, and without saying a word pulled Hester away from the chest and let the cover fall down. Hans cried out with pain. He had just found the Bible, and as he was taking it out the heavy cover fell on his hand.

"If you won't listen, you'll have to feel," said his mother. Hans was so angry he swore and kicked the chest against the wall.

Poor Hans! He had forgotten the Royal Law. "I shall have it!" he cried, and again he raised the cover to retrieve the book he had dropped.

"You will not, you naughty boy," said his mother. She pulled him away by the shoulder, shook him, and with a flood of words pushed him out of the door and locked it.

Poor, poor Hans! He tried to open the door but could not, so he went down the steps and threw himself down on the cold, hard ground. Sobs shook his body. He kicked the grass, as if it had been the grass that had been cruel to him.

The cold air soon calmed his anger, and gradually he became more and more ashamed of himself. Only a few minutes ago he had said he would never grieve the King again, and now he had just grieved Him with his anger. How small he felt now, just when he thought he was beginning a new life.

Hans failed to realize that he had fallen into sin precisely because he was so sure of himself. He had decided in his own strength to serve the great King. He did not know that he needed to feel small and humble, to expect nothing from himself, but everything from the King who gives help to those who ask for it. Hans needed knowledge of himself.

Hans did not know how long he had been lying there, but all at once he decided to find a place that was not so cold. He got up slowly and walked to the other side of the wagon where the cold wind did not blow in his face. He sat down against a wheel. Feeling ashamed and sad, he covered his face with his hands. Would the King believe him if he again promised to serve and belong to Him? Would the King still help him if he asked for help? How sorry he was that he had become angry. It hadn't helped any either. Perhaps if he had asked his mother quietly and politely, she would have given him the little Bible, but now he was sitting all alone, cold and tired.

Suddenly Hans felt something warm on his hands. He wiped his eyes and saw the black, hairy head of his dog. The dog looked at Hans sadly, as if he understood the boy's sorrow. Hans took him on his lap and petted him.

"Well, Tommy," he said with a sad smile, "did you come to comfort me? Poor dog, you don't like it out here in the cold either, do you? Come on, let's run to warm up."

So he untied the dog's rope. Tommy was so glad to be free that he jumped up at his master happily. Hans didn't pay much attention to him, but stroked his head and followed him quietly.

A few hours later, as it was beginning to get dark, Hans returned to the wagon and saw that the door was slightly ajar. Thinking this meant that he could go in, he softly opened the door and walked in.

It was very dark inside. At first he could see nothing but soon the dim light through the only window revealed his mother sitting by the dying fire. She had fallen asleep and so had Hester, sitting against the chest, with one arm under her head and the other carefully hidden under her apron. When Hans touched her, she woke with a start.

"Oh, Hans, are you here?" she whispered. "Shh — mother is sleeping, but I got it for you." With these words she took out a package hidden under her apron and gave it to him.

"What is it, Hester? The Bible? Oh, no," said the lad sadly but firmly. "I'm sorry but I may not have it until I ask mother for it. The King would not think it is right." Without making any noise he lifted the cover of the chest and put back the book, which he had wanted so badly.

A few moments later everything was quiet. Both children were sleeping in a corner on some straw, which served as their bed.

Chapter 2

A NEW LIFE

Although the city near which the covered wagon was parked was quite small, the Wiggers family sold so many goods that they remained there day after day. Whether this was because Mr. Dalhaven had recommended them to his friends, or whether the people liked the polite little salesman and his sister, they did not know, but during the week following that Sunday they did more business than they had done for several weeks.

Still, Hans had a harder time than ever. That the family had more money did not make conditions much better, for the more money Hans brought home, the more money his father spent at the tavern. Yet Hans gave no thought to taking some of the nickels he had received and buying some food for his sister and himself. Or, rather, he did think about it, and in times past he had occasionally done so; but now he knew better. He knew that by keeping some of the money he would grieve the King who had said, "Thou shalt not steal." That thought was enough to make him bring all the money home, that is, if his father had not already taken it from him on the road.

Hans began to love the King more and more, for now he not only remembered the stories that Miss Anna had told him two years before, but he was able to read them over for himself. Because he had not read for such a long time, his reading was very slow, but perhaps because he read so slowly, the words sank deeper into his heart.

Hans had been given his Bible. After that unhappy Sunday he had asked his mother whether she would give him the little book given to him by Miss Anna. His mother had given it to him without saying a word. Perhaps she was pleased that he had asked for it when he could so easily have taken it for himself while she was gone. Perhaps she was sorry for the way she had behaved. But at any rate Hans had his treasure and always kept it near him.

Although the wind was still cold, the sun was getting warmer, and often on his long trips about the city and to the neighboring towns Hans found a sheltered corner behind a woodpile or haystack where he and Hester could sit while he read slowly to her the words of his King. They both liked best the stories of the wonders Jesus had done while He was on earth, but invariably they turned back to the chapter in which was found the text which Mr. Dalhaven had explained. Hans needed to hear those words very often: "Love your enemies, do good to them which hate you." The reason was that more than once he had almost forgotten this commandment and wanted to pay back evil for evil. Every day Marinus Helm teased Hans and his sister.

Whenever Marinus saw them coming, he thought up some new way to be mean to them. They always gave a sigh of relief whenever they passed the Helm meat market without being bothered. They would have liked to go another way, but the market stood on a corner, which they had to pass on their way in and out of the city. Marinus especially enjoyed teasing their dog, so that Tommy always growled whenever he saw Marinus and would have jumped on him had Hans not held the chain very tightly.

It was the second Tuesday after the beginning of our story. The Sunday before, Hans and Hester had been to Sunday school again, and Mr. Dalhaven had promised that he would come to visit their parents. But he must have been busy on Monday, for he had not yet visited the covered wagon. Anxious to hear whether the expected visitor had come, the children hurried home.

All at once Hester asked, "Where is Tommy? Oh, Hans, he must have run ahead of us. I hope he didn't go into the meat market. Marinus said that if he did it again, he would hang him."

"Marinus knows better than that," said Hans. Hans seemed calm, but he was looking anxiously about for Tommy. "He wouldn't dare do that; he says that only to make us afraid. Tommy must have run home."

At that very moment the children heard loud barking, and with a wild yelp their dog darted out of the meat market. He was hobbling on three legs.

"There, ugly mutt, is another one for you," shouted an angry voice, and a large stone just missed Hans' legs as the dog tried to hide behind him. That was really too much! Hans would not allow anyone to mistreat his dog. He would punish Marinus for that!

"Poor Tommy," said Hester, petting the dog that was still yelping behind her. These words made Hans forget his anger long enough to pay attention to his wounded pet. While bending over the dog, Hans thought of the words he had read to Hester that very day. So, though there were tears of sorrow and anger in his eyes, he picked up his dear Tommy and walked on without a word.

Poor Tommy! He lifted up the paw that had been badly hurt and tried to show his thankfulness by licking his master's face.

It was a good thing that they were not far from the wagon, for Hans had to carry both his basket of wares and the dog. As soon as they reached the wagon, Hans as best he could bound up the sore paw with an old handkerchief his mother gave him. Then he took the dog inside the wagon.

"Mother, may Tommy sleep with me tonight?" he asked as he entered the wagon with the dog in his arms.

"Sure," said his mother, "but dear me, Hans, what a fuss you are making over that dog. You act as though it were a sick baby."

Hans laughed, and with Hester's help fixed the straw in the corner to make a soft bed for the wounded dog.

"What is the matter with him?" asked Mrs. Wiggers, who for the past few days had not been as listless as before. "Was he run over?"

Hans' anger rose again. Should he tell his mother? She would surely go to Marinus' parents and Marinus would be severely punished. And he certainly deserved it. Suffering would be good for him. It might teach him a lesson. But all at once his eye fell on the Royal Law which he had fastened on the wall: "As ye would that men should do to you, do ye also to them likewise."

"He ran away from us and went into a meat market," he answered simply. "Then the boy in the store kicked him out."

"Then it was Tommy's own fault," said mother. Tears came into Hans' eyes. He didn't want his mother to think that. "Poor Tom," he said in an effort to make an excuse for the dog, "he must have been hungry."

After a few minutes Hans asked, "Has anyone been here today, mother?"

Mrs. Wiggers was sitting on the only chair in the room and trying, by the dim light of the lamp, to mend the biggest holes in an old sweater. She used to enjoy keeping things clean and neat. But now, why should she work so hard for a husband who spent almost all his money for drink, leaving her hardly enough to keep the family from starving?

Her efforts did no good. Everything, she reasoned, was his fault.

"Has no one been here, mother?" Hans asked again after receiving no answer.

"Been here? Why, no, child. Who would think of coming here? I can't imagine. Besides, I was out with a basket this afternoon, or do you think we can live on what you earn?"

Hans sighed. He knew that the eight or ten nickels he made were not enough for the family to live on. So of course his mother had to go out selling too. Perhaps, then, Mr. Dalhaven had come to a locked door. That was too bad! It would have been a good thing for Mr. Dalhaven to talk with Mrs. Wiggers about the King. It would make her much happier if she knew about the King who could prepare her to live in His kingdom after she died.

Mrs. Wiggers was far from happy. She thought herself to be the most unhappy and most neglected person in the world. She did not see that most of her unhappiness was her own fault.

She had been a lovely young girl, but while still in her youth had married a man who enjoyed drinking a glass of beer now and then, but never became drunk. Although the woman she worked for had warned and begged her not to marry him, she did not see the danger and did as she pleased. The first year of the marriage everything went well. Mr. Wiggers was a good worker and always brought his pay home. But when Hans was about a year old, everything changed. His mother was not feeling well, and his father began to go to the tavern regularly. When she recovered, instead of making her home a happy and pleasant place, she became angry and scolded her husband so much that their happy home life seemed lost forever.

Hoping to earn more money in the city, Mr. Wiggers quit his job at Woodlawn. And for a time he did earn more money. But soon he couldn't find any work at all and the family moved from one place to another until Mrs. Wiggers had to work so they could earn a living. Then, within a short space of each other, Mrs. Wiggers' parents both died. They left her a covered wagon with which they had traveled through the country for many years. At first she thought she would sell it, but then decided to move into it with her family.

That was two years ago. Since that time Mrs. Wiggers had been without food in the house several times. She didn't understand that God's hand was bringing her through those difficulties in order to draw her to Himself. She blamed her unhappy life on everyone and everything but herself. She failed to realize that she had disobeyed the King's command, "Seek ye first the kingdom of God," and that as a result she had no right to the promise that "all these things shall be added unto you." She had not sought the Lord in her happy days, so He had to send her hard times in order that she might see the faithfulness and love with which he had watched over her all those years, even when she did not bother to think of Him at all.

After sharing his supper, a slice of bread, with Tommy, he sat with Hester on the chest, which they had pulled nearer to the table. A few evenings before, Hans had started to teach his sister to read. Sometimes the pupil did not understand immediately, but the teacher was usually quite satisfied. Hester already knew some letters and was anxious to learn more.

All at once the quiet in the little family was disturbed. Hester and Hans were still happily bending over their book, the little Bible, when they heard someone stumbling on the steps. They looked up.

"There is father already," said Hans, looking fearfully toward the door, and, sure enough, the door opened and a large man walked in.

Hans quickly closed his Bible and slipped it into his pocket, for he knew that was the best way to stay out of trouble. Mr. Wiggers flopped down on the chest next to his boy and looked about darkly. "Well, rascal," he stuttered finally, "where is the money? Come on, hand it over; how long must I wait?" And with that he pulled on the boy's ear.

"I've given it to mother already," Hans cried, trying to free himself from his father's hand. Tommy had kept quiet, but when he saw his master attacked he growled and came limping toward Hans.

"What is that mutt doing here?" scolded Mr. Wiggers, turning around and letting go of his son.

"It's only Tommy; be still, Tom," said Hans, picking up the dog and laying him on the straw.

"Throw the animal out," commanded Mr. Wiggers in an angry voice.

"But, Father!" begged Hans.

"Throw him out or I'll do it myself," repeated the drunkard, rising.

Fearing further punishment, Hans bent down to pick up the dog and do as his father had ordered. Either he was not fast enough about it, or another notion came into the drunkard's head. All at once he grabbed his son by the arm, shook him angrily, and then cast him aside.

The boy fell hard against a corner of the chest. He gave out a scream and then lay quietly, a stream of dark red blood oozing from his head.

"Hans," shouted Mrs. Wiggers as she jumped up and bent over her boy. "Look what you are doing. You might kill someone in your drunken frenzy."

Mr. Wiggers stood by in a daze. The sight of his boy lying there so pale and motionless shocked him out of his drunkenness. He watched uncertainly as his wife lifted the lad and tried to put him on the chair.

"Quick! Get some water!" she shouted sharply at Hester, who was clasping her skirt in fear. The dog had scurried to the straw in the corner.

Silently Hester obeyed. Mrs. Wiggers grabbed a cloth and started to wash the boy's head. Hans opened his eyes for a moment, but closed them again with a groan. He seemed seriously injured. The sharp corner of the chest had cut a deep gash, and he was unconscious for some time. After his mother had stopped the flow of blood as best she could, she laid him down carefully on the straw and then sat down beside him.

She could not think. Without words, without tears she gazed on the pale face of her boy, her poor, patient boy, who lay there perhaps on his deathbed. She remembered how sweet and willing and obedient he had been, especially the last few weeks, and she remembered how often she had said unkind words to him. She thought back to the time when he was little and the family had been so happy. All her love for him seemed to revive. It was as though her heart were pulled out of her breast at the thought of losing him.

It was late. Hester had cried herself to sleep some time before. Mrs. Wiggers continued to sit by the still body of her boy, watching his pale face. She did not look up; had she done so, she would have been surprised at the change in her husband.

He had slumped down on the chest on which his little boy had been sitting. His little boy. Was he … what had he done? Had he become a murderer? Had he killed his own child … his child whom he had loved so much and whom lately he had made so unhappy? He had not meant to do it. Oh, what had drinking done to him! If his boy recovered, he would never taste another drop of that awful stuff. It had brought nothing but misery to him and his family. And now this! Oh, it was not possible. No, not this, not this! Large drops of sweat stood out on his forehead. With his head in his hands he cried like a child.

That sound caused the boy to come to. Slowly, as one waking from a dream, he opened his eyes and looked around. Then he seemed to remember what had happened. His lips moved, but his mother bending over him could hear only a single word, the meaning of which she did not understand.

"He is out of his mind," she whispered to her husband. "I think he said something about a king."

It was an awful night, which Hans' parents spent watching over him, but it was a night which began a new day for all of them. Toward morning the boy was running a high fever and still seemed delirious. The poor father could stand it no longer and walked out. He didn't know where he was going; he only wanted to go far, far away, away from the sight of the boy on the straw.

But later on in the morning he returned to the wagon. He found that the fever had run its course. Hans was lying quietly on his bed of straw with his eyes shut. Hester was sitting beside him and looked up with fear in her eyes when her father came in and spoke to her. How it pained him that his child had learned to fear him! How much wouldn't he give if

it were different! But now it would become different
— surely it would!

Mr. Wiggers sat on the old chest and took
Hester on his knee. Not used to such kindness, the
little girl was afraid. But she soon lost her fear when
he softly asked where her mother was.

"Mother went out to buy something for
Hans," she said shyly, "and I stayed here to give
him a drink when he wants one."

The sound of voices woke Hans up. "Father,"
he said softly. Immediately the poor man knelt
down and tearfully begged his son to forgive him.

"Forgive you? Oh, Father," said Hans with a
happy smile that brightened his face, "you didn't do
it on purpose."

"No, not on purpose," answered Mr. Wiggers,
"but it certainly was my fault. If God had not
graciously prevented it, I might have been a
murderer. This has taught me something, and I
promise you, my boy, never again shall I touch a
drop of that awful stuff, so help me God!"

A few weeks can sometimes bring about a big change in the life-style of a family. So it was with the Wiggers family. Five weeks after the events we have recorded the covered wagon couldn't be found near Low Gate. Even the marks of the wheels had been hidden by a growth of young grass.

Yet our friends were not as far away as might be supposed. They were living on the other side of the city in a neat little home quite different from the covered wagon. The only familiar object was the Royal Law hanging in a frame above the mantle.

Now the family was living in accord with that law, for great changes had taken place in their hearts. Whenever Hans looked back upon the hard times, he was thankful because, although they were very difficult, they had borne wonderful fruit.

On the day after Hans had been injured, Mr. Dalhaven came to visit as he had promised. He was shocked to find his pupil lying on the straw, with Tommy in his arms. Hans tried to tell Mr. Dalhaven what had happened, but the boy was very weak and as a result his story seemed somewhat confused. Fortunately just then Mr. Wiggers came in. After hearing who the visitor was, he told Mr. Dalhaven the whole story, much ashamed of what he had done.

And it was a good thing that he did so. Although Mr. Wiggers had made his promise to Hans in all sincerity, he was relying on his own strength to keep that promise. Mr. Dalhaven prayed earnestly to God, who alone can give strength to fight against a sin which has so much power over its victims.

Mr. Dalhaven would gladly have carried his little friend to a more comfortable place, but since there was no hospital in the town he made Hans as comfortable in the wagon as he could, and sent him little treats very often. But Hans enjoyed Mr. Dalhaven's almost daily visits even more than the treats.

Those visits were a blessing to the entire family. Both Mr. and Mrs. Wiggers listened gladly as Mr. Dalhaven told them of the love with which the great King looks down upon sinners. He told them that the Lord was willing to forgive all their sins if they would confess them with true sorrow and ask for His help in beginning a new life. They listened gladly, for they felt a deep need of that love.

Hans slowly recovered. When he was well enough to go outdoors again, the family moved to their new home. On Mr. Dalhaven's advice they decided to sell the horse and wagon. To their great surprise Mr. Wiggers found work quite soon. Spring had come late, so the farmers needed extra laborers to help them with their work. Mrs. Wiggers was able to stay home to take care of her family, and she kept her house clean and shining.

When father came home from work, he usually took Hester, who had started going to school, upon his knee and read to his family the wonderful words of the King. How happy the family was that the Lord had made all things well.

As soon as Hans was well and strong again, there was another happy surprise. Mr. Dalhaven offered him a job as office boy. He didn't have to be a salesman anymore.

Hans was very happy, almost too happy. There was only one thing that still bothered him — Marinus Helm's teasing. But Hans was sure that some day, with his King's help, he would win Marinus by being kind, never returning evil for evil, but living according to the Royal Law:

**As ye would that men should do to you,
Do ye also to them likewise.**
— Luke 6:31

Praise for
We Are Not Ourselves

Shortlisted for the Flaherty-Dunnan First Novel Prize

Longlisted for the Guardian First Book Award

Nominated for the Folio Prize

New York Times "100 Notable Books of 2014"

Washington Post "Top 50 Fiction List for 2014"

Entertainment Weekly "Ten Best Fiction Books of 2014"

Esquire "5 Most Important Books of 2014"

Publishers Weekly "Best Books of 2014"

One of Janet Maslin's "Ten Favorite Books of the Year" in the *New York Times*

Cleveland Plain Dealer "Best Books of 2014"

Fort Worth Star-Telegram "Books We Loved in 2014"

Glamour "Best Books of 2014"

Popsugar.com "2014 Must-Reads"

Bustle.com "Best Books of 2014"

Indie Next List book pick for September 2014

One of Amazon's "Best Books of 2014"

One of Barnes & Noble's "Best Books of 2014"

One of Apple's "Best Books of 2014"

"[A] devastating debut novel . . . an honest, intimate family story with the power to rock you to your core . , rich, sprawling . . . Mr. Thomas's narrow scope (despite a highly eventful story) and bull's-eye instincts into his Irish characters' fear, courage and bluster bring to mind the much more compressed style of Alice McDermott. . . . This is a book in which a hundred fast-moving pages feel like a lifetime and everything looks different in retrospect. . . . This is one of the frankest novels ever written about love between a caregiver and a person with a degenerative disease."

—Janet Maslin, *The New York Times*

"A long, gorgeous, epic, full of love and caring . . . one of the best novels you'll read this year."

—*The New York Times Book Review*

"*The Corrections. The Art of Fielding.* Most years, there's a mega-hyped American epic that's heralded as a literary breakout. This year's, a saga about an Irish-American family in Queens, is refreshingly unpretentious but packed with soul—and profoundly moving characters."

—*Entertainment Weekly*, The Must List

"A great novel about hope, heartbreak, family, and failure in America . . . written with the tensile strength of a thriller. . . . *We Are Not Ourselves* doesn't pile on, doesn't hector; rather, with profound compassion and understanding and at times majesty it painstakingly lays out the three seemingly unexceptional lives as they're lived, in the end summoning the only truly universal verity governing life in America: You can be anything you want, but in the end you'll always be yourself."

—*Esquire*

"Stunning . . . The novel is a formidable tribute to the resilience of the human spirit, to the restorative and ultimately triumphant supremacy of love over life's adversities. . . . The joys of this book are the joys of any classic work of literature—for that is what this is destined to become—superbly rendered small moments that capture both an individual life and the universality of that person's experience."

—*The Washington Post*

"Astonishing and powerful . . . Thomas's finely observed tale is riveting. As a reflection of American society in the late twentieth century, it's altogether epic, sweeping the reader along on a journey that's both inexorable and poignant."

—*People*, Pick of the Week

"The fallible, everyday nobility of the woman at the center of Matthew Thomas's auspicious debut, *We Are Not Ourselves*, lingers in the memory: a daughter of the twentieth century whose dashed dreams find their realization in this tale of hard-won compassion and dignity."

—*Vogue*

"Masterly debut."

—*Vanity Fair*

"An ambitious, beautifully written novel about ambition and what it can do and not do [that] deals with the classic American Dream in all its messy complications."

—USA Today

"Engrossing . . . [Eileen's] unflagging fight against an invincible opponent is carefully and compassionately portrayed."

—The Wall Street Journal

"A vividly open-ended reflection of how life works (or doesn't), with its unexpected turns, its false promises and betrayals and divides . . . We Are Not Ourselves is a solid first novel, unsentimental, multilayered, evocative of a lost world."

—Los Angeles Times

"A sweeping novel about striving, disappointment, and resilience featuring nurse Eileen Leary, a tough-as-nails daughter of Irish immigrants in dogged pursuit of the elusive American dream."

—O, The Oprah Magazine

"In his powerful and significant debut novel, Thomas masterfully evokes one woman's life in the context of a brilliantly observed Irish working-class milieu. . . . A definitive portrait of American social dynamics in the twentieth century. Thomas's emotional truthfulness combines with the novel's texture and scope to create an unforgettable narrative."

—Publishers Weekly, starred review

"Mr. Thomas's prodigious observational and storytelling skills could at first make the reader believe that the Learys are exceptional people, living eventful lives. But they experience no more than almost any family does or will. It offers up achingly beautiful words about lives which may seem ordinary, but aren't. We Are Not Ourselves ennobles us all."

—Pittsburgh Post-Gazette

"We Are Not Ourselves is a meticulous and moving debut that eschews the sweep of the big picture for the emotional truth of the extreme close-up."

—San Francisco Chronicle

"*We Are Not Ourselves* stands with the giants of Irish American literature, from McDermott and William Kennedy to the family dramas of Eugene O'Neill."

—*Irish America Magazine*

"It's so achingly sad you want to put the book down; it's so elegantly etched that you can't. There's a calm beauty to Thomas's prose, and a warm but unsentimental understanding of human nature. By the book's end, when we're given just a little hope to grasp, you feel as if you've been through a real family's tragedy."

—*Seattle Times*

"As anybody who has cared for a loved one in decline knows, the most devastating changes are often the smallest: the hand that doesn't grip as tightly as it did last week, the memory that is slightly but noticeably slower. Thomas does a brilliant job of dramatizing these small moments, which, in the aggregate, create an emotionally powerful reading experience."

—*Los Angeles Review of Books*

"Alluring prose, often depicting the simplest and most heartbreaking moments . . . Through one family, Thomas shows us the American journey—daily life with all its complexities, the gritty stories people live and the unseen heroes who endure them."

—*Paste Magazine*

"These are rich draughts of memory drawn from the well of American life, and we do well to savor them."

—*Buffalo News*

"Ambitious and beautifully written . . . Thomas spurs readers to reflect on and re-consider the constituent elements of love and a life well-lived."

—*Psychology Today*

"Impressive . . . delicately written and extraordinarily moving."

—*Grantland.com*

"An elegy for the middle class in urban America, and for the social mobility we insist on believing in. . . . [*We Are Not Ourselves*] spotlights a dark place that most of us can count on visiting at some point—and shining that light on our collective fear is what a novelist, often, does better than anyone."

—TheMillions.com

"A magnificent piece of work, not only the best first novel in memory but the best American novel in a very long time."

—John Podhoretz, *New York Post*

"Without bells, whistles or flourishes, this is so fluid, so straight to the point and so wrenching in its denouement that closing it, I felt I had lived the lives myself. . . . I eagerly await Mr. Thomas's second, third, etc. He is a master writer for the twenty-first century."

—Liz Smith,
NewYorkSocialDiary.com

"A gripping family saga, maybe the best I've read since *The Corrections*."

— Melissa Maerz, *Entertainment Weekly*

"The greatest Alzheimer's novel yet . . . visionary and challenging . . . Matthew Thomas's realist epic, *We Are Not Ourselves*, exceeds the usual boundaries of fiction on the subject."

—Stefan Merrill Block, "A Place Beyond Words,"
NewYorker.com

"Matthew Thomas's *We Are Not Ourselves* is just a stunning, stunning book. A huge, ambitious story that spans three generations. . . . Possibly the most emotionally engaged I've been with any book this year."

—Phil Klay, "Year in Reading,"
TheMillions.com

"*We Are Not Ourselves* is a powerfully moving book, and the figure of Eileen Leary—mother, wife, daughter, lover, nurse, caretaker, whiskey drinker, upwardly mobile dreamer, retrenched protector of values—is a real addition to our literature."

—Chad Harbach, author of *The Art of Fielding*

"The mind is a mystery no less than the heart. In *We Are Not Ourselves*, Matthew Thomas has written a masterwork on both, as well as an anatomy of the American middle class in the twentieth century. It's all here: how we live, how we love, how we die, how we carry on. And Thomas does it with the epic sweep and small pleasures of the very best fiction. It's humbling and heartening to read a book this good."

—Joshua Ferris, author of *Then We Came to the End*

"*We Are Not Ourselves* delivers the deepest, most involving and best pleasures of reading. A true epic in the best sense of the word, encompassing the big great gorgeous heartbreak that was our American Century. Each page is suffused with a relentless and probing genius, as well as a generous and humane heart, and the result not only explodes across the darkening sky, but remains with you long after you've finished the last page and handed it to someone you love. So long as there are novels like *We Are Not Ourselves*, so long as there are writers like Matthew Thomas, the form of the novel is more than alive, it is thriving, palpitant."

—Charles Bock, author of *Beautiful Children*

"*We Are Not Ourselves* is wonderful on the position of the striving classes and our longings on behalf of our families, and on how we deal with unexpected disaster. It's as fiercely passionate and big-hearted and memorable as Eileen, its *I'm-holding-this-family-together-with-my-two-hands* protagonist."

—Jim Shepard, author of *Project X* and *You Think That's Bad*

We Are Not Ourselves

Matthew Thomas

Simon & Schuster Paperbacks

New York   London   Toronto   Sydney   New Delhi

Simon & Schuster Paperbacks
An Imprint of Simon & Schuster, Inc.
1230 Avenue of the Americas
New York, NY 10020

First Simon & Schuster trade paperback edition June 2015

SIMON & SCHUSTER PAPERBACKS and colophon are registered trademarks of Simon & Schuster, Inc.

For information about special discounts for bulk purchases, please contact Simon & Schuster Special Sales at 1-866-506-1949 or business@simonandschuster.com.

The Simon & Schuster Speakers Bureau can bring authors to your live event. For more information or to book an event, contact the Simon & Schuster Speakers Bureau at 1-866-248-3049 or visit our website at www.simonspeakers.com.

Interior design by Nancy Singer

Manufactured in the United States of America

10 9 8 7 6 5 4

The Library of Congress has cataloged the hardcover edition as follows:
Thomas, Matthew.
  We are not ourselves : a novel / Matthew Thomas..
    page cm.
  1. Irish Americans—Queens (New York, N.Y.)—History—20th century—Fiction. 2. Ireland—Emigration and immigration—History—Fiction. 3. Queens (New York, N.Y.)—History—20th century—Fiction. 4. Domestic fiction. I. Title.
  PS3620.H63513W4 2014
  813'.6—dc23
                                                        2013044414

ISBN 978-1-4767-5666-0
ISBN 978-1-4767-5667-7 (pbk)
ISBN 978-1-4767-5668-4 (ebook)

To Joy

Darling, do you remember
the man you married? Touch me,
remind me who I am.
                    —Stanley Kunitz

We are not ourselves
When nature, being oppressed, commands the mind
To suffer with the body.
                    —*King Lear*

We Are Not Ourselves

His father was watching the line in the water. The boy caught a frog and stuck a hook in its stomach to see what it would look like going through. Slick guts clung to the hook, and a queasy guilt grabbed him. He tried to sound innocent when he asked if you could fish with frogs. His father glanced over, flared his nostrils, and shook the teeming coffee can at him. Worms spilled out and wriggled away. He told him he'd done an evil thing and that his youth was no excuse for his cruelty. He made him remove the hook and hold the twitching creature until it died. Then he passed him the bait knife and had him dig a little grave. He spoke with a terrifying lack of familiarity, as if they were simply two people on earth now and an invisible tether between them had been severed.

When he was done burying the frog, the boy took his time patting down the dirt, to avoid looking up. His father told him to think awhile about what he'd done and walked off. The boy crouched listening to the receding footsteps as tears came on and the loamy smell of rotting leaves invaded his nose. He stood and looked at the river. Dusk stole quickly through the valley. After a while, he understood he'd been there longer than his father had intended, but he couldn't bring himself to head to the car, because he feared that when he got there he'd see that his father no longer recognized him as his own. He couldn't imagine anything worse than that, so he tossed rocks into the river and waited for his father to come get him. When one of his throws gave none of the splashing sound he'd gotten used to hearing, and a loud croak rose up suddenly behind him, he ran, spooked, to find his father leaning against the hood with a foot up on the fender, looking as if he would've waited all night for him, now adjusting his cap and opening the door to drive them home. He wasn't lost to him yet.

Part I

Days

under Sun

and Rain

1951–1982

nstead of going to the priest, the men who gathered at Doherty's Bar after work went to Eileen Tumulty's father. Eileen was there to see it for herself, even though she was only in the fourth grade. When her father finished his delivery route, around four thirty, he picked her up at step dancing and walked her over to the bar. Practice went until six, but Eileen never minded leaving the rectory basement early. Mr. Hurley was always yelling at her to get the timing right or to keep her arms flush at her sides. Eileen was too lanky for the compact movements of a dance that evolved, according to Mr. Hurley, to disguise itself as standing still when the police passed by. She wanted to learn the jitterbug or Lindy Hop, anything she could throw her restless limbs into with abandon, but her mother signed her up for Irish dancing instead.

Her mother hadn't let go of Ireland entirely. She wasn't a citizen yet. Her father liked to tout that he'd applied for his citizenship on the first day he was eligible to. The framed Certificate of Citizenship, dated May 3, 1938, hung in the living room across from a watercolor painting of St. Patrick banishing the snakes, the only artwork in the apartment unless you counted the carved-wood Celtic cross in the kitchen. The little photo in the certificate bore an embossed seal, a tidy signature, and a face with an implacably fierce expression. Eileen looked into it for answers, but the tight-lipped younger version of her father never gave anything up.

When Eileen's father filled the doorway with his body, holding his Stetson hat in front of him like a shield against small talk, Mr. Hurley stopped barking, and not just at Eileen. Men were always quieting down around her father. The recording played on and the girls finished the slip jig they were running. The fiddle music was lovely when Eileen didn't have to worry about keeping her unruly body in line. At the end of the tune, Mr. Hurley didn't waste time giving Eileen permission to leave. He just looked at the floor while she gathered her things. She was in such a hurry to get out of there and begin the wordless walk that she waited until she got to the street to change her shoes.

When they reached the block the bar was on, Eileen ran ahead to see if she could catch one of the men sitting on her father's stool, which she'd never seen anyone else occupy, but all she found was them gathered in a half circle around it, as if anticipation of his presence had drawn them near.

The place was smoky and she was the only kid there, but she got to watch her father hold court. Before five, the patrons were laborers like him who drank their beers deliberately, contented in their exhaustion, well-being hanging about them like a mist. After five, the office workers drifted in, clicking their coins on the crowded bar as they waited to be served. They gulped their beers and signaled for another immediately, gripping the railing with two hands and leaning in to hurry the drink along. They watched her father as much as they did the bartender.

She sat at one of the creaky tables up front, in her pleated skirt and collared blouse, doing her homework but also training an ear on her father's conversations. She didn't have to strain to hear what they told him, because they felt no need to whisper, even when she was only a few feet away. There was something clarifying in her father's authority; it absolved other men of embarrassment.

"It's driving me nuts," his friend Tom said, fumbling to speak. "I can't sleep."

"Out with it."

"I stepped out on Sheila."

Her father leaned in closer, his eyes pinning Tom to the barstool.

"How many times?"

"Just the once."

"Don't lie to me."

"The second time I was too nervous to bring it off."

"That's twice, then."

"It is."

The bartender swept past to check the level of their drinks, slapped the bar towel over his shoulder, and moved along. Her father glanced at her and she pushed her pencil harder into her workbook, breaking off the point.

"Who's the floozy?"

"A girl at the bank."

"You'll tell her the idiocy is over."

"I will, Mike."

"Are you going to be a goddamned idiot again? Tell me now."

"No."

A man came through the door, and her father and Tom nodded at him. A draft followed him in, chilling her bare legs and carrying the smell of spilled beer and floor cleaner to her.

"Reach into your pocket," her father said. "Every penny you have stashed. Buy Sheila something nice."

"Yes, that's the thing. That's the thing."

"Every last penny."

"I won't hold out."

"Swear before God that that's the end of it."

"I swear, Mike. I solemnly swear."

"Don't let me hear about you gallivanting around."

"Those days are over."

"And don't go and do some fool thing like tell that poor woman what you've done. It's enough for her to put up with you without knowing this."

"Yes," Tom said. "Yes."

"You're a damned fool."

"I am."

"That's the last we'll speak of it. Get us a couple of drinks."

They laughed at everything he said, unless he was being serious, and then they put on grave faces. They held forth on the topic of his virtues as though he weren't standing right there. Half of them he'd gotten jobs for off the boat—at Schaefer, at Macy's, behind the bar, as supers or handymen.

Everybody called him Big Mike. He was reputed to be immune to pain. He had shoulders so broad that even in shirtsleeves he looked like he was wearing a suit jacket. His fists were the size of babies' heads, and in the trunk he resembled one of the kegs of beer he carried in the crook of each elbow. He put no effort into his physique apart from his labor, and he wasn't muscle-bound, just country strong. If you caught him in a moment of repose, he seemed to shrink to normal proportions. If you had something to hide, he grew before your eyes.

She wasn't too young to understand that the ones who pleased him were the rare ones who didn't drain the frothy brew of his myth in a quick quaff, but nosed around the brine of his humanity awhile, giving it skeptical sniffs.

She was only nine, but she'd figured a few things out. She knew why her father didn't just swing by step dancing on the way home for dinner. To do so would have meant depriving the men in suits who arrived back from Manhattan toward the end of the hour of the little time he gave them every day. They loosened their ties around him, took their jackets off, huddled close, and started talking. He would've had to leave the bar by five thirty instead of a quarter to six, and the extra minutes made all the difference. She understood that it wasn't only enjoyment for him, that part of what he was doing was making himself available to his men, and that his duty to her mother was just as important.

The three of them ate dinner together every night. Her mother served the meal promptly at six after spending the day cleaning bathrooms and offices at the Bulova plant. She was never in the mood for excuses. Eileen's father checked his watch the whole way home and picked up the pace as they neared the building. Sometimes Eileen couldn't keep up and he carried her in the final stretch. Sometimes she walked slowly on purpose in order to be borne in his arms.

• • •

One balmy evening in June, a week before her fourth-grade year ended, Eileen and her father came home to find the plates set out and the door to the bedroom closed. Her father tapped at his watch with a betrayed look, wound it, and set it to the clock above the sink, which said six twenty. Eileen had never seen him so upset. She could tell it was about something more than being late, something between her parents that she had no insight into. She was angry at her mother for adhering so rigidly to her rule, but her father didn't seem to share that anger. He ate slowly, silently, refilling her glass when he rose to fill his own and ladling out more carrots for her from the pot on the stovetop. Then he put his coat on and went back out. Eileen went to the door of the bedroom but didn't open it. She listened and heard nothing. She went to Mr. Kehoe's door, but there was silence there too. She felt a sudden terror at the thought of having been abandoned. She wanted to bang on both doors and bring them out, but she knew enough not to go near her mother just then. To calm herself, she cleaned the stovetop and counters, leaving no crumbs or smudges, no evidence that her mother had cooked in the first place. She tried to imagine what it would feel like to have always been alone. She decided that being alone to begin with would be easier than being left alone. Everything would be easier than that.

She eavesdropped on her father at the bar because he didn't talk much at home. When he did, it was to lay out basic principles as he speared a piece of meat. "A man should never go without something he wants just because he doesn't want to work for it." "Everyone should have a second job." "Money is made to be spent." (On this last point he was firm; he had no patience for American-born people with no cash in their pocket to spring for a round.)

As for his second job, it was tending bar, at Doherty's, at Hartnett's, at Leitrim Castle—a night a week at each. Whenever Big Mike Tumulty was the one pulling the taps and filling the tumblers, the bar filled up to the point of hazard and made tons of money, as though he were a touring thespian giving limited-run performances. Schaefer didn't suffer either; everyone knew he was a Schaefer man. He worked at keeping the brogue her mother worked to lose; it was professionally useful.

If Eileen scrubbed up the courage to ask about her roots, he silenced her with a wave of the hand. "I'm an American," he said, as if it settled the question, and in a sense it did.

By the time Eileen was born, in November of 1941, some traces remained of the sylvan scenes suggested in her neighborhood's name, but the balance of Woodside's verdancy belonged to the cemeteries that bordered it. The natural order was inverted there, the asphalt, clapboard, and brick breathing with life and the dead holding sway over the grass.

Her father came from twelve and her mother from thirteen, but Eileen had no brothers or sisters. In a four-story building set among houses planted in close rows by the river of the elevated 7 train, the three of them slept in twin beds in a room that resembled an army barracks. The other bedroom housed a lodger, Henry Kehoe, who slept like a king in exchange for offsetting some of the monthly expenses. Mr. Kehoe ate his meals elsewhere, and when he was home he sat in his room with the door closed, playing the clarinet quietly enough that Eileen had to press an ear to the door to hear it. She only saw him when he came and went or used the bathroom. It might have been strange to suffer his spectral presence if she'd ever known anything else, but as it was, it comforted her to know he was behind that door, especially on nights her father came home after drinking whiskey.

Her father didn't always drink. Nights he tended bar, he didn't touch a drop, and every Lent he gave it up, to prove he could—except, of course, for St. Patrick's Day and the days bookending it.

Nights her father tended bar, Eileen and her mother turned in early and slept soundly. Nights he didn't, though, her mother kept her up later, the two of them giving a going-over to all the little extras—the good silver, the figurines, the chandelier crystals, the picture frames. Whatever chaos might ensue upon her father's arrival, there prevailed beforehand a palpable excitement, as if they were throwing a party for a single guest. When there was nothing left to clean or polish, her mother sent her to bed and waited on the couch. Eileen kept the bedroom door cracked.

Her father was fine when he drank beer. He hung his hat and slid his coat down deliberately onto the hook in the wall. Then he slumped on the couch like a big bear on a leash, soft and grumbling, his pipe firmly in the grip of his teeth. She could hear her mother speaking quietly to him about household matters; he would nod and press the splayed fingers of his hands together, making a steeple and collapsing it.

Some nights he even walked in dancing and made her mother laugh despite her intention to ignore him. He lifted her up from the couch and led her around the room in a slow box step. He had a terrible charisma; she wasn't immune to it.

When he drank whiskey, though, which was mostly on paydays, the leash came off. He slammed his coat on the vestibule table and stalked the place looking for things to throw, as if the accumulated pressure of expectations at the bar could only be driven off by physical acts. It was well known what a great quantity of whiskey her father could drink without losing his composure—she'd heard the men brag about it at Doherty's— and one night, in response to her mother's frank and defeated question, he explained that when he was set up with a challenge, a string of rounds, he refused to disappoint the men's faith in him, even if he had to exhaust himself concentrating on keeping his back stiff and his words sharp and clear. Everyone needed something to believe in.

He didn't throw anything at her mother, and he only threw what didn't break: couch pillows, books. Her mother went silent and still until he was done. If he saw Eileen peeking at him through the sliver in the bedroom door, he stopped abruptly, like an actor who'd forgotten his line, and went into the bathroom. Her mother slid into bed. In the morning, he glowered over a cup of tea, blinking his eyes slowly like a lizard.

Sometimes Eileen could hear the Gradys or the Longs fighting. She found succor in the sound of that anger; it meant her family wasn't the only troubled one in the building. Her parents shared moments of dark communion over it too, raising brows at each other across the kitchen table or exchanging wan smiles when the voices started up.

Once, over dinner, her father gestured toward Mr. Kehoe's room. "We won't have him here forever," he said to her mother. As Eileen was struck by sadness at the thought of life without Mr. Kehoe, her father added, "Lord willing."

No matter how often she strained to hear Mr. Kehoe through the walls, the only sounds were the squeaks of bedsprings, the low scratching of a pen when he sat at the little desk, or the quiet rasp of the clarinet.

They were at the dinner table when her mother stood and left the room in a hurry. Her father followed, pulling the bedroom door closed behind him. Their voices were hushed, but Eileen could hear the straining energy in them. She inched closer.

"I'll get it back."

"You're a damned idiot."

"I'll make it right."

"How? '*Big Mike doesn't borrow a penny from any man*,'" she sneered.

"There'll be a way."

"How could you let it get so out of hand?"

"You think I want my wife and daughter living in this place?"

"Oh, that's just grand. It's *our* fault now, is it?"

"I'm not saying that."

In the living room, the wind shifted the bedroom door against Eileen's hands, making her heart beat faster.

"You love the horses and numbers," her mother said. "Don't make it into something it wasn't."

"It was in the back of my mind," her father said. "I know you don't want to be here."

"I once believed you could wind up being mayor of New York," her mother said. "But you're satisfied being mayor of Doherty's. Not even owner of Doherty's. *Mayor* of Doherty's." She paused. "I should never have taken that damn thing off my finger."

"I'll get it back. I promise."

"You won't, and you know it." Her mother had been stifling her shouts, practically hissing, but now she sounded merely sad. "You chip away and chip away. One day there won't be anything left."

"That's enough now," her father said, and in the silence that followed Eileen pictured them standing in the mysterious knowledge that passed between them, like two stone figures whose hearts she would never fathom.

The next time she was alone in the house, she went to the bureau drawer where her mother had stashed her engagement ring for safekeeping ever since the time she'd almost lost it down the drain while doing dishes. From time to time, Eileen had observed her opening the box. She'd thought her mother had been letting its facets catch the light for a spell, but now that she saw the empty space where the box had been, she realized her mother had been making sure it was still there.

A week before her tenth birthday, Eileen walked in with her father and saw that her mother wasn't in the kitchen. She wasn't in the bedroom either, or the bathroom, and she hadn't left a note.

Her father heated up a can of beans, fried some bacon, and put out a few slices of bread.

Her mother came home while they were eating. "Congratulate me," she said as she hung up her coat.

Her father waited until he finished chewing. "For what?"

Her mother slapped some papers on the table and looked at him intently in that way she sometimes did when she was trying to get a rise out of him. He bit another piece of bacon and picked the papers up as he worked the meat in his jaw. His brow furrowed as he read. Then he put them down.

"How could you do this?" he asked quietly. "How could you let it not be me?"

If Eileen didn't know better, she would have said he sounded hurt, but nothing on earth was capable of hurting her father.

Her mother looked almost disappointed not to be yelled at. She gathered the papers and went into the bedroom. A few minutes later, her father took his hat off the hook and left.

Eileen went in and sat on her own bed. Her mother was at the window, smoking.

"What happened? I don't understand."

"Those are naturalization papers." Her mother pointed to the dresser. "Go ahead, take a look." Eileen walked over and picked them up. "As of today, I'm a citizen of the United States. Congratulate me."

"Congratulations," Eileen said.

Her mother produced a sad little grin between drags. "I started this months ago," she said. "I didn't tell your father. I was going to surprise him, bring him along. It would have meant something to him to be my sponsor at the swearing in. Then I decided to hurt him. I brought my cousin Danny Glasheen instead."

Eileen nodded; there was Danny's name. The papers looked like the kind that would be kept in a file for hundreds of years, for as long as civilization lasted.

"Now I wish I could take it back." Her mother gave a rueful laugh. "Your father is a creature of great ceremony."

Eileen wasn't sure what her mother meant, but she thought it had to do with the way it mattered to her father to carry even little things out the right way. She'd seen it herself: the way he took the elbow of a man who'd had too much to drink and leaned him into the bar to keep him on his feet without his noticing he was being aided; the way he never knocked a beer glass over or spilled a drop of whiskey; the way he kept his hair combed neat, no strand out of place. She'd watched him carry the casket at a few funerals. He made it seem as if keeping one's eyes forward, one's posture straight, and one's pace steady while bearing a dead man down the steps of a church as a bagpiper played was the most crucial task in the world. It was part of why men felt so strongly about him. It must have been part of why her mother did too.

"Don't ever love anyone," her mother said, picking the papers up and sliding them into the bureau drawer she'd kept her ring in. "All you'll do is break your own heart."

2

In the spring of 1952, Eileen's mother made the amazing announcement that she was pregnant. Eileen had never even seen her parents hold hands. If her aunt Kitty hadn't told her that they'd met at one of the Irish dance halls and found some renown there as a dancing pair, Eileen might have believed her parents had never touched. Here her mother was, though, pregnant as anyone. The world was full of mysteries.

Her mother quit her job at Bulova and sat on the couch knitting a blanket for the baby. When she tied off the last corner, she moved on to making a hat. A sweater followed, then a pair of bootees. Everything was stark white. She kept the miniature clothes in a drawer in the breakfront. The crafting was expert, with tight stitches and neat rows. Eileen never even knew her mother could knit. She wondered if her mother had made clothes for her family in Ireland, or to sell in a store, but she knew enough not to ask. She couldn't even bring herself to seek permission to rub the bump on her mother's belly. The closest she got to the baby was when she went to the drawer to examine the articles her mother had knitted, running her hands over their smoothness and putting them up to her face. One night, after her mother had gone to bed, she picked up the knitting needles, which were still warm from use. Between them swayed the bootee to complete the pair. Eileen tried to picture this baby who would help her populate the apartment and whose cheeks she would cover in kisses, but all she saw was her mother's face in miniature, wearing that dubious expression she wore when Eileen went looking for affection. She concentrated hard until she stopped seeing her mother's face and saw instead the smiling face of a baby beaming with light and joy. She was determined to have a relationship with this sibling that would have nothing to do with their parents.

Eileen was so excited to get a baby brother or sister that she physically *felt* her heart breaking when her father told her that her mother had miscarried. When a dilation and curettage didn't stop the bleeding, the doctors gave her a hysterectomy.

After the hysterectomy, her mother developed a bladder infection that nearly killed her. She stayed in the hospital on sulfa drugs while it drained. Children weren't encouraged to visit the sick, so Eileen saw her mother less than once a month. Her father rarely spoke of her mother during this period that stretched into a handful of months, then half a year and beyond. When he intended to bring Eileen to see her, he would say something vague like, "We're going, get yourself ready." Otherwise, it was as if she'd been erased from their lives.

It didn't take long for Eileen to figure out that she wasn't supposed to mention her mother, but one night, a couple of weeks into the new order, she brought her up a few times in quick succession anyway, just to see how her father would react. "That's enough now," he snapped, rising from the table, evidence of suppressed emotion on his face. "Clean up these dishes." He left the room, as though it were too painful for him to remain where his absent wife had been invoked. And yet they spent so much time fighting. Eileen decided she would never understand the relations between men and women.

She was left to handle the cooking and cleaning. Her father set aside money for her to shop and go to the Laundromat. She rode her bike to one of the last remaining farms in the neighborhood to buy fresh vegetables, and she developed her own little repertory of dishes by replicating what she'd seen her mother make: beef stew with carrots and green beans; London broil; soda bread; lamb chops and baked potatoes. She took a cookbook out of the library and started ranging afield. She made lasagna just once, beating her fist on the countertop when it turned out soupy after all that work.

After doing her homework by the muted light of the end table lamp, she sat on the floor, building towers of playing cards, or went upstairs to the Schmidts' to watch television and marvel over the mothers who never stopped smiling and the fathers who folded the newspaper down to talk to their children.

At school she usually had the answer worked out before the other girls put up their hands, but the last thing she wanted was to draw any kind of attention to herself. She would have chosen, of all powers, the power to be invisible.

One day, her father took her to Jackson Heights, stopping at a huge cooperative apartment complex that spanned the width of a block and most of its length. They descended into the basement apartment of the super, one of her father's friends. From the kitchen she looked up at the ground level through a set of steel bars. There was grass out there, blindingly green grass. She asked to go outside. "Only as long as you don't step foot on that grass," her father's friend said. "Not even the people who live here are allowed on it. They pay me good money to make sure it stays useless." He and her father shared a laugh she didn't understand.

A frame of connected buildings enclosed a massive lawn girdled by a short wrought-iron railing. Nothing would have been easier than clearing that little fence. Around the lawn and through its middle ran a handsome brick path. She walked the routes of the two smaller rectangles and the outer, larger one, wending her way through all the permutations, listening to the chirping of the birds in the trees and the rustling of the leaves in the wind. Gas lamps stood like guardians of the prosperity they would light when evening came. She felt an amazing peace. There were no cars rushing around, no people pushing shopping carts home. One old lady waved to her before disappearing inside. Eileen would have been content to live out there, looking up into the curtain-fringed windows. She didn't need to set foot on that grass. Maybe someone would bring her upstairs and she could look down on the whole lawn at once. The lights were on in the dining room of one apartment on the second floor, and she stopped to stare into it. A grandfather clock and a beautiful wall unit gazed down benignly at a bowl on the table. She couldn't see what was in the bowl, but she knew it was her favorite fruit.

The people who lived in this building had figured out something important about life, and she'd stumbled upon their secret. There were places, she now saw, that contained more happiness than ordinary places did. Unless you knew that such places existed, you might be content to stay where you were. She imagined more places like this, hidden behind walls or stands of trees, places where people kept their secrets to themselves.

When the soles of her shoes wore through, her father, in his infinite ignorance of all things feminine, brought home a new, manure-brown pair Eileen was sure were meant for boys. When she refused to wear them, her father confiscated her old pair so she had no choice, and when she complained the next night that the other girls had laughed at her, he said, "They cover your feet and keep you warm." At her age, he told her, he had been grateful to get secondhand shoes, let alone new ones.

"If my mother were well," she said bitterly, "she wouldn't make me wear them."

"Yes, but she's not well. And she's not here."

The quaver in his throat frightened her enough that she didn't argue. The following night, he brought home a perfectly dainty, gleaming, pearlescent pair.

"Let that be an end to it," he said.

Mr. Kehoe came home late, but he never seemed drunk. He was unfailingly polite. Despite the fact that he'd been there since she was two years old, it always felt to Eileen as if he'd just moved in.

She took to cooking extra for him and bringing a plate to his room. He answered her knock with a smile and received the offering gratefully. Her father grumbled about charging a board fee.

Mr. Kehoe had a smear of black in a full head of otherwise gray hair. It looked as if he'd been streaked by a tar brush. When he wasn't wearing his tweed jacket with the worn cuffs, he rolled his shirt sleeves and kept his tie a little loose.

He started battling through fitful bouts of coughing. One night, she went to his door with some tea; another, she brought him cough syrup.

"It's just that I don't get enough air," Mr. Kehoe said. "I'll take some long walks."

Even through severe coughing fits he managed to play the clarinet. She'd stopped trying to hide her efforts to listen to it. She sat on the floor beside his door, with her back to the wall, reading her schoolbooks. In the lonely evenings she felt no need to apologize for her interest. Sometimes she even whistled along.

One night, her father sat quietly on the couch after dinner with a troubled look on his face. Eileen avoided him, occupying her usual spot by Mr. Kehoe's door. Heat rattling through the pipes joined the clarinet in a kind of musical harmony. She looked up and was unnerved to find her father looking back at her, which he never did. She concentrated on her beautifully illustrated copy of *Grimm's Fairy Tales*. The day before, when she'd told him that Mr. Kehoe had given it to her, her father had grown upset. She'd seen him knock on Mr. Kehoe's door a little while later and hand him some money.

She was absorbed in "The Story of the Youth Who Went Forth to Learn What Fear Was" when her father startled her away from the door. She barely had time to step aside before he had thrown Mr. Kehoe's door open and told him to quit making that racket. Mr. Kehoe apologized for causing a disturbance, but Eileen knew there had been none; you could barely hear him playing from where her father had been sitting.

Her father tried to snatch the clarinet from Mr. Kehoe's hands. Mr. Kehoe stood up, clutching it, until its pieces started coming apart and he staggered backward, coughing wildly. Her father went out to the kitchen and turned up the radio loud enough that the neighbors started banging on the ceiling.

When she came home the next day, Mr. Kehoe was gone.

For almost a week, she didn't speak to her father. They passed each other without a word, like an old married couple. Then her father stopped her in the hall.

"He was going to have to leave," he said. "I just made it happen sooner."

"He didn't have to go anywhere," she said.

"Your mother is coming home."

She was excited and terrified all at once. She'd started thinking her mother might never come back. She was going to have to give up control of the house. She wouldn't have her father to herself anymore.

"What does that have to do with Mr. Kehoe?"

"You can move your things over there tonight."

"You're not getting another lodger?"

He shook his head. A thrilling feeling of possibility took her over.

"I'm getting my own room?"

Her father looked away. "Your mother has decided that she's moving over there with you."

3

On the Wednesday after Easter of 1953, eight months after she'd left, her mother came home from the hospital. The separate rooms were as close as her parents could ever come to divorce.

Her mother got a job behind the counter at Loft's, a fancy confectioner's on Forty-Second Street, and started coming home late, often drunk. In protest, Eileen let dirty dishes stack up in the sink and piles of clothes amass in the bedroom corners. When she got teased in the schoolyard for the wrinkles in her blouse, she saw she had no choice but to continue the homemaking alone.

Her mother began drinking at home, settling her lanky body into the depression in the couch, in one hand a glass of Scotch, in the other a cigarette whose elongated ash worm would cling to the end as if working up the nerve to leap. Eileen watched helplessly as the malevolent thing accumulated mass. Her mother held an ashtray in her lap, but sometimes the embers fell into the cushions instead and Eileen rushed to pluck them out. Her mother fell asleep on the couch many nights, but she went to work no matter her condition.

That summer, her mother bought a window air-conditioning unit from Stevens on Queens Boulevard. She had the delivery man install it in the bedroom she shared with Eileen. No one else on their floor had an air conditioner. She invited Mrs. Grady and Mrs. Long over and into the bedroom, where they stood before the unit's indefatigable wind, staring as though at a savior child possessed of healing powers.

When both her parents were home, an uneasy truce prevailed. Her mother closed the bedroom door and sat by the window, watching night encroach on the street. Eileen brought her tea after dinner. Her father stationed himself at the kitchen table, puffing at his pipe and listening to Irish football. At least they were under the same roof.

She hated thinking of her mother riding the trains. She saw her mother's body sprawled in dark subway tunnels as she sat at the kitchen table for hours watching the door. As soon as she heard the key shunting the dead bolt aside, she rose to put the kettle on or wash dishes. She wouldn't give her mother the satisfaction of knowing she was worried about her.

One night, after she had cooked the dinner and washed the pots and pans, she nestled exhausted into the couch, where her mother sat smoking a cigarette and staring ahead. Tentatively, she laid her head in her mother's lap and kept still. She watched the smoke pour through her mother's pale lips and the ash get longer. Other than a few new wrinkles around the mouth and some blossoms of burst blood vessels on her cheeks, her mother's skin was still smooth and full and porcelain white. She still had those dramatic lips. Only her stained teeth showed evidence of wear.

"Why don't you give me hugs and kisses like the mothers on television?"

Eileen waited for her to say something sharp in response, but her mother just stubbed out the butt and picked up the pack to smoke another. There was a long silence.

"Don't you think you're a little old for this?" her mother finally asked. Eventually she moved Eileen aside and rose to pour herself a tall drink. She sat back down with it.

"I wasn't like your father," she said. "I couldn't wait to escape the farm. I remember I was packing my bag, I heard my father say to my mother, 'Deirdre, let her go. This is no place for a young person.' I was eighteen. I came looking for Arcadia, but instead I found domestic work on Long Island. I rode the train out and back in the crepuscular hours. *Cre-pus-cu-lar.* You probably don't know what that word means."

She could tell her mother had begun one of those sodden monologues she delivered from time to time, full of edgy eloquence. Eileen just sat and listened.

"I used to daydream about living in the mansions I cleaned. I liked to do windows, everyone else's least-favorite job. I could look out on rolling lawns. They didn't have a single rock, those lawns. I liked to look at the tennis courts. Perfectly level, and not a twig out of place. They suggested . . . what!—the taming of chaos. I liked the windswept dunes, the spray of crashing waves, the sailboats tied to docks. And when I went out to run the rag over the other side, I looked in on women reclining on divans like cats that had supped from bowls of milk. I didn't begrudge them their ease. In their place, I would have planted myself on an elbow from the moment I rose in the morning until the time came for me"—her mother made a languorous gesture with her finger that reminded Eileen of the way bony Death pointed—"to be prodded back to the silken sheets."

"It sounds nice," Eileen said.

"It wasn't *nice*," her mother said sharply after the few beats it took her thoughts to cohere. "It was—*marvelous*, is what it was."

A few days before Christmas, her mother told her to take the train in to Loft's a little before the end of her shift. When Eileen arrived, her mother looked so effortlessly composed that one would never know she'd become a serious drinker. Eileen walked around the store in stupefaction, gaping at the handcrafted, glazed, and filigreed confections.

When her mother was done, she gave Eileen a box of truffles to take home and walked her over to Fifth Avenue and down to Thirty-Ninth Street, to the windows of Lord & Taylor, which Eileen had seen only in pictures in the newspaper. The scenes behind the windows, with their warmly lit fireplaces and silky-looking upholstered miniature furniture, gave her the same feeling she'd had when she'd stood before that great lawn and peered up into the perfect world of the garden apartments. Gorgeous drapery framed a picture she wanted to climb into and live in. Brisk winds blew, but the air was not too cold, and the refreshing smell of winter tickled her nose. In the remnant daylight, the avenue began to take on some of the enchanted quality visible behind the windows. It thrilled her to imagine that passersby saw an ordinary mother-daughter pair enjoying a routine evening of shopping together. She checked people's faces for evidence of what they were thinking: *What a nice little family.*

"Christmas gets the full treatment," her mother said in the train on the way home. "Mind that you remember that. It doesn't matter what else is going on. You could be at death's door, I don't care."

That night, her mother tucked her in for the first time since she'd gone into the hospital. When Eileen awoke in the middle of the night and saw the other bed empty, she stumbled out to find her mother sitting on the couch. For a terrible instant, Eileen thought her mother was dead. Her head hung back, mouth open. Her hand clutched the empty tumbler. Eileen drew close and watched her chest rise and fall, then took the ashtray from her lap and the tumbler from her hand, careful not to wake her, and brought both to the kitchen sink. She took the blanket from her mother's bed and spread it over her. She slept with the door open in order to see her from where she lay.

The package she received in the mail contained a book on how to play the clarinet and, beneath it, Mr. Kehoe's own clarinet. A note on legal stationery said that he'd died of lung cancer and left it to her in his will. She slept beside it for several days until her mother found it one morning and told her to stop, calling it ghoulish. She tried to play it a few times but grew frustrated at the halting noises it produced. With an undiminished memory for its muffled, sensuous sound through the walls, she thought of Mr. Kehoe. She could hear whole songs when she shut her eyes and concentrated, as if the music were waiting to be extracted from her by a trained hand. She could never even string together a couple of familiar-sounding notes. Eventually she took to laying out its pieces and looking at them awhile before fitting them back into the soft pink felt that lined the case. She didn't need to play Mr. Kehoe's clarinet to appreciate it. Its parts were sleek and expertly wrought, their burnished metal protuberances shining with a lustrous gleam. They filled her hand with a pleasant weight. She liked to press the buttons down; they moved with ease and settled back up with a lovely firmness. The mouthpiece where Mr. Kehoe had pressed his lips came to a tapered end. She liked the feel of it against her own lips, the pressure against her teeth when she bit down.

The clarinet was the nicest thing she owned, the nicest thing anyone in her family owned. It didn't belong in that apartment, she decided. When she was older she would live in a beautiful enough home that you wouldn't even notice the clarinet. That was what Mr. Kehoe would have wanted. She would have to marry a man who would make it possible.

When she was thirteen, she started working at the Laundromat. The first time she got paid, after kneading the bills awhile between her thumb and forefinger, she spread them on the table before her and did some math. If she kept working and saved every dollar she could, she wouldn't need anything at all from her parents once she was done with high school— maybe even before. The prospect excited her, though excitement gave way to sadness. She didn't want to think of not needing anything from them. She would save her money for them.

Her mother drank harder than her father ever had, as though she were trying to make up for lost time. Eileen started tending to her needs in a prophylactic rather than merely reactive way. She made coffee, kept a constant supply of aspirin waiting for her, and laid a blanket over her when she fell asleep on the couch.

One night, Eileen came into the living room and saw that her mother's head was bobbing in that way it did when she fought sleep to hold on to a last few moments of conscious drunkenness. Sitting with her was easiest then. She was too far gone to say something tart and withering but could still register Eileen's presence with a tiny fluttering of the eyelid.

Eileen took a seat next to her and felt wetness under her hand. At first she thought her mother had spilled her drink.

She was terrified to change her mother's clothes, because there was a chance her mother might realize what was going on, but she couldn't just let her sit there in that sopping spot all night. She managed to remove her wet clothes and wrap her in a robe. Then she lay her back down on the dry part of the couch. Getting her to bed would be much harder.

Eileen sat on her haunches next to the couch and guided her mother's head and shoulders from her lap to the floor, then dragged the rest of her down. Once she had her there, she slid her along by hooking her arms up under her mother's armpits. Her mother was making murmuring noises.

When Eileen got her to the bed, though, she couldn't lift her up into it. Her mother had stirred to more wakefulness and was trying to stay on the floor.

"Let me get you up, Ma," she said.

"I'll sleep right here."

"You can't sleep on the floor."

"I will," she said, the end of the word trilling off. Her brogue came back when she was drunk or angry.

"It's cold on the floor. Let me lift you up."

"Leave me be."

"I won't do that."

Eileen tried for a while and then gave up and lay on her mother's bed to rest. When she awoke it was to the sound of her father coming home from tending bar. She went to the kitchen and saw him sitting at the table with a glass of water.

"Can you pick Ma up? She's on the floor."

He stood without a word and followed her. It occurred to her that, except on Mr. Kehoe's last night, she'd never seen her father enter that bedroom. In the light streaming in from the kitchen, her mother looked like a pile of dirty sheets on the floor.

Eileen watched him pick her mother up with astounding ease, as if he could have done it with one hand instead of two. One of his arms was cradling her head. Her long limbs hung down; she was fast asleep. He took his time laying her in the bed. He looked at her lying there. Eileen heard him say "Bridgie" once quietly, more to himself than her mother, before he pulled the blanket over her and smoothed it across her shoulders.

"Go to bed now yourself," he said, and shut the door behind him.

"Imagine all of Woodside filled with trees," Sister Mary Alice was telling her eighth-grade class. "Imagine a gorgeous, sprawling, untouched estate of well over a hundred acres. That is what was here, boys and girls. What is now your neighborhood, all of it, every inch, once belonged to a *single family* that traces its roots back to the very beginnings of this country."

A garbage truck in front of the school emitted a few loud coughs, and Sister paused to let it pass. The rolled-up map above the blackboard swayed slightly, and Eileen imagined it unfurling and hitting Sister in the head.

"The grandson of one of the early Puritan founders of Cambridge, Massachusetts, built a farmhouse near this spot, on a massive plot of land he'd bought," Sister started walking around the room with a book held open to a page that contained pictures of the house. "His heirs converted that farmhouse into a manor house. This *manor house*"—Sister practically spat the words—"had a wide hall leading to a large front parlor. It had a back parlor with a huge fireplace, a grand kitchen, a brass knocker on the door. It had an orchard to one side." The insistent way Sister counted off the house's virtues made it sound as if she was building a case against it in court. "After a few generations, they sold the estate to a Manhattan-based merchant from South Carolina to use as a weekend retreat. Then, in the latter half of the last century, when the train lines expanded, a real estate developer saw an opportunity. He cleared the estate's trees, drained its swamps, laid out the streets you walk on today, and carved it into nearly a thousand lots that he distributed by random drawing. He opened the door to the middle class, letting them pay in installments of ten dollars a month. Houses were built. The last vestige of the estate, the manor house, was razed in 1895 to make room for the church, and, eventually, the school you're sitting in right now."

Eileen was watching the frowning white face of the clock at the front of the room when Sister came up to her with the book. Her gaze drifted lazily to the pictures, but once she saw them she couldn't take her eyes off them, and when Sister moved down the row, Eileen asked her to come back for a second.

"The Queensboro Bridge was completed in 1909, and then the LIRR East River tunnel the following year, and they began laying out the IRT Flushing line—the seven train to you—station by station, starting in 1915. The Irish—your grandparents, maybe your parents—began coming across the river in droves, seeking relief from the tenement slums of Manhattan. They wound up in Woodside. Imagine ten people to an apartment, twenty. Then, in 1924—providence. The City Housing Corporation began building houses and apartments to alleviate the density problem." Sister had made it back to the front of the room. The faint outline of a smile of triumph crept onto her lips as she addressed her final arguments to the jury. "This is the way the Lord works. To those who have little, he gives. Isn't it nice to think of all of you here instead of just one privileged family in a mansion in the woods? Wouldn't you agree, Miss Tumulty?"

Eileen had been daydreaming about the demolished mansion she'd just seen the picture of. Sister's question snapped her to attention. "Yes," she said. "Yes."

But all she could think was what a shame it was they'd knocked that house down. A big, beautiful house in the country with land around it— that wasn't a bad thing at all.

"And think of this," Sister Mary Alice said in closing. "Not a single one of you would be here if that estate were still around. None of us would. We simply wouldn't exist."

Eileen looked around at her classmates and tried to conceive of a reality in which none of them had come into being. She thought of the little apartment she lived in with her parents. Would it be a loss if it had never been built?

She pictured herself on a couch in that mansion, looking out a window at a stand of trees. She saw herself sitting with her legs crossed as she flipped through the pages of a big book. Someone had to be born in a house like that; why couldn't it have been her?

Maybe she wouldn't have been born there, but she'd have been born somewhere, and she'd have found a way to get there, even if the others didn't.

Some nights she went up the block to see her aunt Kitty and her cousin Pat, who was four and a half years younger than her. Her uncle Paddy, her father's older brother, had died when Pat was two, and Pat looked up to her father like he was his own father.

Eileen had grown up reading to Pat. She'd delivered him to school an early reader, and he could write when the other kids were still learning the alphabet. He was whip-smart, but his grades didn't show it because he never did his homework. He read constantly, as long as it wasn't for school.

She sat him at the kitchen table and made him open his schoolbooks.

She told him he had to get As, that anything less was unacceptable. She said there was no end to what he could do with her help. She told him she wanted him to be successful, and rich enough to buy a mansion. She would live in a wing of it. He just rushed through his work and read adventure stories. All he wanted to do when he grew up was drive a Schaefer truck.

Her mother's morning powers of self-mastery, so impressive in the early days, began to dry up, until, when Eileen was a freshman in high school—she'd earned a full scholarship to St. Helena's in the Bronx—they evaporated overnight. Her mother went in late to Loft's one day, and then she did so again a couple of days later, and then she simply stopped going in at all. One day she passed out in the lobby and the police carried her upstairs. After the officers left—her father being who he was meant nothing would get written up—Eileen didn't say a word or try to change her mother into clean clothes, because her mother would be embarrassed, and Eileen still feared her wrath, even when her mother was slack as a sack of wheat, because the memory of her mother taking the hanger to her when she misbehaved as a child was never far from her mind.

The next day, when they were both at the kitchen table, her mother smoking in silent languor, Eileen told her she was going to call Alcoholics Anonymous. She didn't mention that she'd gotten the number from her aunt Kitty, that she'd been talking to others in the family about her mother's problem.

"Do what you want," her mother said, and then watched with surprising interest as Eileen dialed. A woman answered; Eileen told her that her mother needed help. The woman said they wanted to help her, but her mother had to ask for help herself.

Eileen's heart sank. "She's not going to ask for help," she said, and she felt tears welling up. She saw her mother's darting eyes notice the tears, and she wiped them quickly away.

"We need her to ask for assistance before we can take action," the woman said. "I'm very sorry. Don't give up. There are people you can talk to."

"What are they saying?" her mother asked, pulling the belt on her robe into a tight knot.

Eileen put her hand over the receiver and explained the situation.

"Give me that goddamned phone," her mother said, stubbing out her cigarette and rising. "I need help," she said into it. "Did you hear the girl? Goddammit, I need help."

A pair of men came to the apartment the following evening to meet her mother. Eileen had never been more grateful not to find her father home. She sat with them as they explained that they were going to arrange for her mother to be admitted to Knickerbocker Hospital. They would return the next evening to take her in.

That night, as soon as the men had left, her mother took the bottle of whiskey down off the shelf and sat on the couch pouring a little of it at a time into a tumbler. She drank it deliberately, as if she were taking medicine. They'd told her mother to pack enough clothing for two weeks, so Eileen filled a small duffel bag for her and slipped it under the bed. She would explain things to her father once her mother was in the hospital.

Eileen spent the school day worrying that, with so many hours left before the men returned, something would go awry. Her mother seemed okay, though, when Eileen got home. All in the apartment was still. The kettle sat shining on the small four-burner stove, the floor was swept, the blinds were pulled evenly across the windows. Eileen cooked some sausage and eggs for them to eat together. Her mother ate slowly. When the men arrived, shortly before six o'clock, both wearing suits, her mother acquiesced without denying she'd agreed to go. The strangely tender, sorrowful look she wore as she shuffled around the apartment gathering the last of the things she needed—toothbrush, wallet, a book—made Eileen's chest ache.

Eileen rode with them to the hospital. At the end, the two men drove her back. When they reached the apartment building, the driver put the car in park and sat motionless while the man in the passenger seat came around to open her door. She stood outside the car, thinking she might like to say something to express her gratitude, but there wasn't a way to do it. The man took his hat off. A strange, knowing silence filtered into the air around them. She was glad these men weren't the kind that said much. He handed her a piece of paper with a phone number on it.

"Call if you need anything," he said. "Any hour." Then they drove off.

Her mother stayed in for nine days. When she reemerged, she attended meetings and took a job cleaning grammar schools in Bayside. She complained about being beholden to the Long Island Rail Road schedule, but Eileen figured what actually bothered her was all the time she had to herself on the train to consider how she hadn't gotten very far in the years since she'd made similar trips.

Eileen dreamed of taking a dramatic journey of her own. When she learned about Death Valley in geography class, how it was the hottest and driest spot in North America, she decided to visit it sometime, even though she wouldn't be able to leave her alabaster skin exposed there for long without suffering a terrible burn. A vast, desert expanse like that was the only place she could imagine not minding the absence of company.

4

I n the fall of 1956, when Eileen was a sophomore, another round of relatives started coming over from Ireland. How she loved it! Sure, at times the apartment was like a sick ward, teeming with newly landed, sniffling relations who commandeered a bit of the floor or even her own bed, but still: with all those people crowded around, her father came alive, charming them like a circus animal keeping a ball aloft on the tip of its nose, and her mother worked alongside her to keep the peace in cramped quarters.

Over a dozen people passed through their little space: her mother's youngest sister Margie, who was only a few years older than Eileen and whom her mother had never met; her aunts Ronnie and Lily; her uncles Desi, Eddie, and Davy; her cousins Nora, Brendan, Mickey, Eamonn, Declan, Margaret, Trish, and Sean. Two or three or even four would stay with them at a time, until that group found an apartment in Rockaway or Woodlawn or Inwood and the next moved in. Nothing came close to the feeling Eileen got when they gathered at the table for meals, and when she awoke in the night and heard the gentle snoring and the shuffling sound of their rolling sleep, she was sure she'd never felt happier.

Uncle Desi, her father's youngest brother, was the first to arrive. He moved into the room with her father. The first time her father wasn't around, Eileen peppered Desi with questions. It wasn't hard to get him to talk. It was as if he'd turned a faucet on and the words came pouring out.

"Your father loved Kinvara," Uncle Desi said. "He was the happiest fellow you could imagine. A smile from ear to ear all day long. Then we were made to move to Loughrea when the Land Reform laws came. We went to better farmland, but I believe he never got over the sting of leaving those fields and that house he'd helped to build as a lad."

The apartment and neighbors and outside noises seemed to succumb to Desi's charms. All went hush as he rubbed his bristled chin.

"I was much younger than him, seven or so when we moved, so I had a grand time building the new house. We pulled it up out of the land. We boys and our father dug clay, dragged timbers from the bog, and harvested the thatch for the roof. I tell you, it was plumb and solid, still is. Everyone was satisfied but your father. He said that if they could take one house from you against your will, they could take another. He never settled into it. The sky was his ceiling, I suppose. One thing: he never had to be asked twice to work. Jesus, he never had to be asked once. He was always working. The stone walls he built—you would have thought they were a mile around.

"All he ever wanted was a little money to play cards. There'd be poker games that would last five days. That, and a chance to work in the fields. When I tell you he had strength enough to bend a hammer, I don't know if you'll believe me. The only thing he wanted it for was to pull up stubborn vegetables. Then, in 1931—your father must have been twenty-four—my eldest brother Willie, he was a beat cop in Dublin, well, he developed a cataract. He went blind in that eye and had to come back to the farm. The plot wasn't big enough to support two men and my father, and there wasn't a job to be found on the entire godforsaken island, not even for a man like your father."

He raised one brow and clicked his tongue dramatically, as if to suggest that the failure to find room for his older brother spelled doom for the country he had left behind.

"The best our father could do for him was buy him a ticket over. It was Willie who'd wanted to emigrate, not your father, but that was out of the question. This country didn't admit the infirm.

"Our father gave him three months. Your father spent the time plowing, harrowing, and sowing, barely stopping to eat or sleep. A man could be forgiven for wondering if he were trying to die in the fields. His friends threw the biggest good-bye party in memory; it lasted three days and nights. What a time! At the end, your father went directly from the revelry to the crops. People tried to get him to go in and sleep, but he wouldn't listen. He worked through the night. Our father went out in the morning, the ticket in his hand; I followed behind. He found him ripping out weeds. I'll never forget what he said."

Desi paused. He stood up to act out the scene.

"'Michael John,' he said, handing it over." He stretched an imaginary ticket toward her. "'You have to go. And that's that.' Then he turned back to the house." Desi faced away, took a couple of steps and looped back. "I stood there for a while with your father in perfect silence. Our mother took him to the boat."

He sat back down and eyed his empty teacup. She got up to refill it for him.

"I remember the first letter from your father," Desi said as he chewed some shortbread. "He said the hardest part about leaving was knowing that Willie had no idea what to do with the crops he'd planted, that he'd let them linger in the earth too long. And that's exactly what happened. He wrote that the whole way over, he saw, in his mind, the crops moldering there, sugaring over, their rich nutrition going to waste. He said he was never planting another seed. My brother Paddy—your cousin Pat's father, God rest his soul—was here already a couple of years. Paddy referred your father to Schaefer Beer. As soon as they got one look at him, they put him to work hauling barrels."

She knew how much pride her father took in being able to write, since not everyone he grew up with could, and she watched with interest whenever he slipped on his reading glasses to sign his name to checks and delivery slips, but the idea of him sitting down to write a letter—especially one that revealed his thoughts and feelings—simply baffled her. The closest he got to expressing a feeling was when the foolishness, idleness, or venality of certain men moved him to indignation.

She'd always understood that her father had been young once, but she'd never really considered what that meant. Now she saw him as a young man crossing a sea to start life anew, a courageous man carrying a kernel of regret and heartache that he would feed with his silence. There was more in him than she'd grasped. She wanted to find a man who was like him, but who hadn't formed as hard an exterior: someone fate had tested, but who had retained a little more innocence. Someone who could rise above the grievances life had put before him. If her father had a weakness, that was it. There were other ways to be strong. She wasn't blind to them.

She wanted a man whose trunk was thick but whose bark was thin, who flowered beautifully, even if only for her.

Maybe having all those relatives around had given her father a reason to settle in, or maybe it was the power of a management salary to keep a person in line. Whatever it was, when her father was promoted from driver to manager of drivers, something extraordinary happened: he stopped going out and began to do his drinking at home, where she'd never seen him put a glass of alcohol to his lips. There was such a self-possession about the way he drank at home, such an air of leisure and forbearance, that rather than signal chaos as it had in her mother's case, it suggested urbanity, balance, a kind of evolution.

He bought nice glasses and stacked them with ice cubes and sipped a finger of expensive whiskey once or twice a night with whichever relative was there, as if it were no more than a salubrious activity to pass the time, an efficient way to filter the sludgy residues out of the engine of his planning. He bought new furniture, a dishwasher, a handmade Oriental rug. He bought a television; in the evenings they all watched it together. The only time the spell of Eileen's happiness was broken was when she sneaked a look at her mother's face at a moment of great drama in the program, expecting to see her squeezed along with the rest of them in the tightening grip of a tense plot, and saw her intently focused on the drink in her husband's hand, like a dog watching for a scrap to fall from a table.

She went to Anchors Aweigh in Sunnyside with Billy Malague. Billy was a year older. After he'd graduated from McClancy, he'd approached her father for help getting a job at Schaefer. Apparently he'd been in love with Eileen for years, or so her friends said. She wasn't interested in him; she only went out with him to be able to say she'd given him a chance. A lot of girls would have thrown themselves at Billy. He had thick locks of blond hair that looked strong enough for a person to suspend from. He was rugged and charismatic, and well liked by other men. She could see the appeal in him, but she couldn't be with a man who didn't have his sights on anything higher than driving a truck for thirty years.

Anchors Aweigh was dark and a little musty. A band was playing when she and Billy first arrived, but they soon packed up their fiddles and the jukebox came on. A lively energy emanated from the crowd, which was a healthy mix of generations.

She'd never taken a drink before. She scanned the menu and ordered a zombie, figuring she might as well dive in headfirst. Billy raised the ends of his mouth in an appreciative grin.

"I remember my first day. Your father called me a narrowback. He calls anyone born in America a narrowback. I tell you, it feels like an honor coming from him." She couldn't avoid noticing the way Billy rattled the ice around in his tumbler, the way he wiped his mouth with the hairy back of his hand after he took a sip. "He gave me a route that went into Staten Island. That means extra zone pay. My first day, an upstart kid like me, and he's making sure I get some money in my pocket. He said, 'You have twelve stops. You'll be done in six hours. You should stay out ten.' I didn't under-stand. I didn't want him to think I was a shirker. I said, 'If it takes six hours, sir, I'll try to get it done in five.' He looked at me like I was a stone-cold idiot. 'If you get back here in less than ten hours,' he said, 'don't come back.'"

He was so excited talking about her father that she wasn't sure which of them it was he was supposed to be in love with. She surprised herself by how quickly she drained the tall glass, sucking the sugary drink up through the straw. It made her nervous to look at the empty glass and feel herself begin to lose control, her brain tingling slightly, her lips taking their time to come together when she spoke, her head a little heavier on her neck. She wondered if she'd taken the first step on the road away from her dreams. What scared her was how easy it had been to do it. All she had to do was get the contents of the glass into her stomach. To chase her agitated thoughts, she ordered another drink immediately. The chatter in her head quieted down as she sat drinking and trying to return Billy's insistent gaze. All she could focus on were his strangely doughy cheeks and protruding ears. She imagined him a couple of feet shorter, in a T-shirt with horizontal stripes, and a bowl haircut. In the middle of a little story he was telling, she laughed to think that what was evidently a boy before her somehow struck the rest of the world as a full-grown man. The bartender, whose age wasn't in question—he must have been a year or two shy of her father—gave her a look that Billy didn't see, in which there seemed to be pity for the boy. The first drink had been too syrupy sweet, but she liked the second one so much that she ordered three more after it.

It was after midnight when Billy carried her in, begging her father, she later learned, to spare his life, explaining that she'd been possessed, that she'd smacked his face whenever he'd tried to get her to leave, that he hadn't wanted to give anyone the wrong idea and get escorted out and have to leave her there with those animals.

Her father woke her early in the morning. She spent a couple of hours on the tiled floor of the bathroom, leaning her head on the rim of the bowl and sitting up straight when the urge to throw up possessed her. When she'd emptied her guts completely, her father told her to take a shower. Then he walked her to Mass at St. Sebastian's.

"You're no different from the rest of us," he said. "You don't get a special dispensation."

The air conditioning in the new church cooled her sweat and set her to shivering. Once, she had to get up to go to the sacristy bathroom. When she fell asleep, her father elbowed her awake. When communion came, she had to choke down the host. For a terrible moment up by the altar, she feared she'd have a retching spell. She took deliberate steps and deep breaths all the way back to the pew, and she ended up missing a day of school.

That Friday night, after dinner was over and the kitchen was clean and her mother had retired to her room, her father sat her down on the couch.

"If you're going to be fool enough to do this," he said, "you can't go about it half-cocked."

He went to the liquor cabinet and brought over a couple of tumblers and set them down on the coffee table. Then he went back and returned with a number of small bottles of different types of whiskey.

"What's this?"

"You'll be getting a lesson."

"I can't," she said.

"You will," he said.

"I've learned my lesson already."

"This is a different lesson," he said. "We'll start with the good stuff."

He told her he would take her methodically through everything there was to drink and everything there was to avoid. Then he poured a couple of fingers of whiskey into her glass. What struck her more even than her revulsion at the idea of taking a drink was that her father had come up with a plan, that he'd thought ahead about all this. He seemed to have bought the bottles for the occasion, as if he'd plotted the lesson out like an actual teacher.

She took a small sip; it burned her throat. He told her to take a bigger one. It smelled like charred wood and tasted like ashes. He poured a drink from each bottle and made her drink it in turn. She could tell there was a difference in quality, but only barely. When he got to the fourth, he poured some for himself and told her to drink with him slowly. It went down easily and left no trace except a warmth in her belly that spread out and seemed to heat her body a part at a time.

He put the whiskey bottles away and brought out several small bottles of vodka. She hated every one. He didn't drink any. He was wearing his reading glasses. There was something scholarly in it. She couldn't tell if it was supposed to be a master class or a form of house arrest. Then he brought out several varieties of gin. He took the wrapping off each and poured a small amount in her tumbler for her. He had stopped drinking after the whiskey. She wondered if by boring her with a scientific approach he was trying to take away whatever fascination attached itself to alcohol in her mind.

He went to the refrigerator and brought back a bottle of Schaefer.

"Drink this," he said.

"I don't like the taste of beer."

"Drink it down and get it over with."

He took the cap off and handed it to her. She took a few small sips and tried to push it back toward him.

"Finish it," he said.

When she'd finished, he told her she wasn't to be seen drinking any other beer. Then he brought out bottles containing drinks that were fruitier and more colorful than anything she'd imagined him permitting in his house. Cointreau. Crème de menthe. Crème de cassis. Grand Marnier. He made her taste each in turn. She liked the taste of the crème de menthe and he shook his head and poured a full glass.

"Enjoy it, then," he said.

"I don't want to drink that much."

"If you want to stay under this roof, you'll finish that glass." He took out another tumbler and filled it. "And this one when you're finished with that."

He came in when she was done and poured out another glass.

"What's going on?" she asked, feeling woozy.

"Drink this."

She woke in the morning with a headache, grateful it was Saturday.

"You will never again drink anything you can't see through," her father said when he saw her in the kitchen, leaning on the counter after taking an aspirin. "You will never pick up a drink again after putting it down and taking your eye off it."

"Okay," she said.

"Drink whiskey," he said. "Good whiskey. Not too much. That's the long and short of it."

"I don't think I'm ever drinking again."

She thought she saw a trace of a smile cross his lips.

When New Year's Eve came around, he raised a glass to her, and everyone else gathered did too.

"Here's to my Eileen for making the honor roll again," he said to a loud cheer. "God bless her, we'll all be working for her one day." He paused. "And let me tell you, there must be something right with her if she can stand after half a dozen zombies. She's definitely my daughter."

She's definitely my daughter. She heard a lifetime of unexpressed affection in the words. She imagined she could go for years on it, like a cactus kept alive by a sprinkling of rain. Still, she was so embarrassed that she decided never to drink anything but whatever the most boring girl in any group she was in was drinking.

5

From the moment students entered the doors of St. Catherine's Nursing School, on Bushwick Street in Brooklyn, until the day they graduated, the one bit of knowledge instructors seemed most concerned to impart was that they'd be thrown out for poor performance, but Eileen was used to those tactics after thirteen years of Catholic education, and she knew that even if nursing wasn't the field she'd have chosen, she'd been training for it without meaning to from an early age. There was nothing these veterans could throw at her that life hadn't thrown already, and they somehow knew this themselves. There were times she could feel them treating her with something like professional courtesy. She couldn't help thinking this was what it felt like to be her father, to be praised for something you'd never had any choice about, to wonder if there was a way out of the trap of other people's regard.

Martyrdom was never her aim, the way it was for some of the halo polishers she went to school with. They might as well have joined the nunnery for all the secret satisfaction she heard in their voices when they complained about the exhaustion and thanklessness of it all. But they wouldn't have lasted five minutes at a nunnery. They lacked the mental fortitude.

She'd never dreamed of being a nurse. It was just what girls from her neighborhood did when they were bright enough to avoid the secretarial pool. She would've preferred to be a lawyer or doctor, but she saw these professions as the purview of the privileged. She didn't know how she'd ever have gotten the money to pursue them. She thought she might have had the brains for them, but she was afraid she lacked the imagination.

• • •

After St. Catherine's she went on scholarship to St. John's for her bachelor's, enrolling in the fall of 1962. Her plan was to take summer classes, finish in three years instead of four, get through grad school, and begin the path to administrator pay. She earned spending money—and savings for the nursing administration degree tuition to come—as a dress model at Bonwit Teller. Women came to look at dresses and she showed them how they could look if they lost a few inches from their waist, or were taller, or had neat divots by their clavicle, or a galvanizing shock of black hair, or smooth skin, or arrestingly heavy-lidded, owlish emerald eyes. What they had on her was money and the insolent ease that came with it. Despite herself she became the preferred girl in the showroom. She didn't try to push dresses on potential buyers by slinging a hand at the waist and jutting an elbow out. She simply put a dress on and stood there. She didn't smile or not smile; make eye contact or avoid it; speak to customers or remain silent; she did whatever came naturally to her. If her nose itched, she scratched it. She turned to show them the dress at all angles when they asked her to, and when they were done looking at it, she went back to the dressing room and took it off. The other girls seemed to linger more, attempting to convince themselves of what they hadn't convinced the customers of.

She daydreamed that the next person who walked in would be a rich man looking for a dress for his girlfriend, who would see her and change his mind about the drift his life was taking. He would let her forget about nursing, fly her around the world, care for her parents' needs. She could sleepwalk through life, never changing a dirty bedpan, never batting away an exploratory hand when she leaned over a man in his senescence, never pressing through a fog of halitosis to take an old lady's temperature, never working another day, never thinking another thought. She would come back to this store and sit in the chair and put the girl through her paces. She'd make it seem as if she was going to leave without buying anything, that she'd wasted everyone's time, and then she would order one of everything to remind them that they had no idea how women like her really lived. But the only people who showed up were women a little older than her, or teenaged girls with their mothers. They said how radiant she looked, but she could hear them thinking of themselves.

One afternoon in April of 1963, a girl about Eileen's age came in looking for dresses for her bridesmaids. The girl made apparently random
selections, projecting a nervous aura. She looked familiar—alarmingly
so; only after Eileen had modeled a handful of dresses did she realize
the girl was Virginia Towers, who'd left St. Sebastian's in seventh grade to
move to Manhasset. Eileen prayed she wouldn't recognize her, but while
Virginia was examining the seams she started patting excitedly on Eileen's
shoulder.

"Eileen?"

"Yes?"

"Eileen! Eileen Tumulty!"

Virginia's voice was all heedless abandon. Eileen raised her brows in
silent acknowledgment, perturbed to be addressed so familiarly in a place
where she'd worked to keep her distance from the other girls.

"It's me, Ginny. Ginny Towers."

"Virginia, my goodness," she said mutedly.

Kind, sincere Virginia had been the only kid in her class with an investment bank executive for a father. Her father was also a Protestant,
though her mother was a Catholic who'd grown up in the neighborhood.
No one teased Virginia, even though she'd been shy and fairly awkward;
it was as though her family's means draped a protective cloak across her
shoulders.

"What are you doing here?" Virginia asked.

There was no answer that wasn't awkward, so Eileen gave the dress a
demonstrative little tug in the chest and raised her hands in amused resignation.

"Right!" Virginia said. "Dresses." She had two in her hands and three
more draped across the armoire, none promising. "Well, hell. Do you like
any of these?"

If Eileen had the money to buy bridesmaids' dresses this expensive,
she would buy different ones entirely—sleeker ones, less vulgar, more ver-
satile. She was convinced she had nicer dresses hanging in her closet than
Virginia did. She owned only half a dozen, but each was perfect. She would
never buy five dresses for twenty dollars each when she could snag one

truly gorgeous one for a hundred. She went out infrequently enough that she never worried about being seen too often in any of them.

"I think the one I tried on a couple of dresses ago is quite nice," Eileen said.

"The lavender one? I knew it! I liked that one too. I'll just have them order that one then."

Standing in the billowing dress, Eileen felt like one of those men in sandwich boards advertising lunch specials.

"Eileen *Tumulty*," Virginia said, as though it were the answer to a quiz-show question. "I'm guessing this is just your day job."

"I'm doing my bachelor's," she said. "I went to nursing school."

"I figured you'd be on your way to being a doctor or something. You were always the smartest one of us."

She felt her face redden.

"I'm finishing at Sarah Lawrence this year. And I'm getting married! But you knew that already. He's a Penn man. Very square—he makes me giggle he's so square. My father has set him up with interviews at Lehman Brothers. We're going to live in Bronxville. I'm going to walk to school my last month!"

She knew of the town; it was a wealthy bedroom community in lower Westchester County. "That sounds just lovely."

"And I know you won't guess what I'm doing next year."

"What's that?"

"I'm going to law school. At Columbia."

"You were always intelligent," Eileen said, stifling her surprise.

"Not like you. You were a whip."

"You're very kind."

"You were more of an adult than the rest of us," Virginia said. "I often think about that day in sixth grade when you took me to Woolworth's and made me buy a notebook for every class. Do you remember?"

She remembered, but she didn't relish recalling what an excess of energy she'd had then for grand improving projects, as though she'd thought the moral balance of the world could be restored by a regimen of directed efforts.

"I remember you weren't the most organized girl, but I don't remember going to Woolworth's, no."

"I think you'd had enough of watching me never be able to find anything when I needed it. You made me separate my notes. That was one of the most helpful things anyone's ever done for me."

"I'm glad," Eileen said, feeling a churning in her gut.

"You should come to law school with me. We could be study partners. I'd get the better end of that deal."

It was as if Virginia was speaking to her from the outside of a circus cage, clutching a bar in one hand as she absently held a lamb chop in the other. Eileen had to get away before she said something she'd regret.

"Maybe in my next life," she said, and the awkwardness she'd kept at bay came rushing back at once. The dress's low cut left her feeling exposed. A new customer had arrived, and the other girl was busy with someone else, so Eileen asked Virginia if she was sure about the lavender dress and left her with the woman who arranged the accounts.

"Please look us up," Virginia said on her way out. "Give us a couple of months to settle in. Bronxville, don't forget. We'll be in the phone book. Mr. and Mrs. Leland Callow. We'd absolutely love to have you over. There's nothing so valuable in life as old friends."

Her mother told her to save her money, to buy used if she had to have a car, but her father was the one to go with her to the showroom.

The new Pontiac Tempest was on the floor, the 1964 model.

"It's most of what I have saved," Eileen said.

"You'll make more. You'll save again."

"It's a bad investment."

"It's an investment in life," her father said. "If this is what you want, this is what you're getting. It beats the piss out of a beer truck, I'll say that. Maybe I'll get one myself. Or I could get one of those convertible types over there. What did he call that one? The GTO? I could drive your mother around in it. Do you think she'd take to it?"

For a moment, he sounded serious, and Eileen wanted to say, *Daddy*,

I think she would, but instead she just said, "Now *that* is a *terrible* investment," and asked him whether cherry red or navy suited her better.

She could buy used and save for the future, or she could make a statement about where she thought her life was heading, and shape the perceptions of others about that trajectory, and maybe sway the future by courting it.

"What the hell do you think I'm going to tell you?" her father said.

She went with cherry red.

She was at the table when her mother got in from work.

"Studying again?"

Eileen barely grunted in reply. In shedding herself of her effects, her mother had dropped her keys on Eileen's splayed notebook. There were so many keys packed onto the interlocking rings; each represented a room, or several, that her mother had to clean. Eileen slid them off the notebook as if they were coated in pathogens.

"Why don't you put those books aside for five minutes," her mother said. "You can drive me and my friends."

"Drive where? Which friends?"

"My meeting friends."

Meeting friends, Eileen thought crankily. *She almost makes it sound pleasant.*

"Take my car," she said, not looking up from her book.

"I'm nervous to drive it."

Her mother had only had her license for a year, and she was shaky on the road. The Tempest was still brand-new.

"I've got a test."

"We started a car pool," her mother said. "I said I'd pick everyone up this week."

"And how had you planned on doing this, exactly?"

"Come on," her mother said. "It's getting late."

The first stop was in Jackson Heights. She was surprised to pull up outside one of the co-ops; she'd always imagined that people of means were spared some of the sadder aspects of man's nature. As soon as her mother left the car, Eileen took out her textbook. She was planning to study at every stop, even with others in the car. There wasn't time for the squeamish propriety of small talk; the fact that she had submitted to this depressing task was enough.

When her mother returned, there was a brightness in her voice.

"Hiram," she said to the man getting in the backseat, "this is my daughter, Eileen."

"So I guess you're Charon tonight."

"*Eileen*," she said.

"Charon. The ferryman. On the river Styx."

"Oh," she said. "Right."

"Shuttling the dead."

He had bumped his hairpiece on the doorframe in getting in; instead of adjusting it with a furtive hand, he had taken it off completely and was resetting it with such nonchalance that it seemed he wore it not to disguise his baldness but to bring it out in the open.

"You're very much alive, Hiram," her mother said, beginning to titter. "Though I can't say the same for that rug you're wearing."

"I'm supposed to give you a tip," he said. "How about this: avoid men in borrowed hair."

"Sound advice," Eileen said.

"Tell it to my wife. Not that I had this when she met me. You should have seen the locks. I was Samson."

In the rearview mirror she watched him look contemplatively out the window. He returned her gaze alertly, as if he was used to being watched.

"Beware of women bearing scissors," he said, chuckling. He was in on some private joke that made even the heaviest things weightless. "Beware of three-drink lunches."

"One-drink lunches," her mother said.

"Well, if we're going to hell, at least we're doing it in style. This is a beaut."

"Thank you," Eileen said.

"You've got it backwards," her mother said. "We're leaving hell."

"Yes, yes," he said agreeably. "We're in purgatory, but we're hopeful. Or if we're not hopeful, at least we're not succumbing to despair. Or if we're succumbing to despair, at least we're in this beautiful car."

Her mother was buoyant as she rang bells and led her meeting friends to the car, where she peppered them with chatter to put them at ease. Eileen couldn't bring herself to open the book even when it was only Hiram in the car. She ended up having a marvelous time. In even a few minutes with some of them she could see they radiated hard-won perspective. She made three trips; then she parked up the block and watched in the mirror as her mother and the final quartet, a spectrum of widths and heights, disappeared down into the church basement.

On the way home, after they'd dropped everyone off, her mother blew smoke through the cracked window and talked with a quick and ceaseless fluency. Upbeat as her mother seemed, Eileen saw that the corners of her mouth were being pulled down, as though by a baited hook. She could tell that her mother didn't entirely believe in her own forgiveness. Eileen wasn't sure she believed in it herself, even though she'd been the one to grant it, through tears, after her mother had sat her down at the kitchen table and unearthed mistakes Eileen had successfully buried and said how sorry she was for them. Her mother had worked hard to kill the past, but it clung to life in Eileen's mind, in the thought that this apparently solid form might dissolve back into the liquid that had seeped into every corner of her childhood, bringing disorder and rot. The smell of the past, that irrepressible smoke, was spoiling the air between them, where, in the absence of others to filter it, an acrid cloud now hung.

"Roll that down further, please."

Without a word, her mother did as asked. She stared straight ahead, smoking and avoiding Eileen's gaze as she used to at the height of her drinking days. Eileen pulled over and got out to roll down the rear windows. She stood briefly outside the car gazing at the back of her mother's head, which for a strangely exhilarating moment looked as if it belonged to someone else. Whatever her mother was going through, Eileen would allow herself to care only so much about it. She had her own life to worry about. Life was what you made of it. Some of the houses she'd dropped these people off at would have been enough for her, so why couldn't they be enough for them? If she lived in one of these houses, she wouldn't need to get into another woman's car and head to a damp lower church for a meeting. She could look at her fireplace, her leather sofa, her book-lined drawing room; she could listen to silence above her head; she could peer in on empty bedrooms lying in wait for fresh-faced visitors, pleasantly useless otherwise. It would all be enough for her to put a drink down for. And yet there these people were. The fact that they were there, that everything they owned wasn't enough somehow, disturbed her, suggesting a bottomlessness to certain kinds of unhappiness. She shook the thought from her head like dust from an Oriental rug and decided that a house would have to be enough.

6

She spent the entire fall of 1963 trying to convince her cousin Pat to apply to college. Then December rolled in and the application deadlines were around the corner, and many of them had already come and gone. She went to him to make one final appeal.

"I'm not college material," Pat said, his big feet up on the coffee table in her aunt Kitty's apartment, where Eileen sat with her knees together under the pressed pleats of her cotton skirt.

"Bull."

"I've never been big on school." He leaned over and tapped ashes into a coffee cup, stretched back again.

"You could have been a great student. You're smarter than all those boys."

"You need to give up on this idea of me as a Future Leader of America."

The truth was, she already had. He was smart enough to make it to his senior year without doing a lick of homework, and he possessed an intuitive ability to make men champion his causes that reminded her of her father's own. He was pissing away his apparently unbearable promise at underage bars, but she didn't care about that anymore. All she wanted was to keep him safe.

"You could get As in your sleep," she said, "if you gave it a tiny bit of effort." She crossed her legs and played with the pack of cigarettes. She resisted blowing away the smoke that was traveling in her direction.

"I can't sit and study. I just get restless."

"I'll do the applications for you."

"I need to *move*. I can't be cooped up." He snubbed out his cigarette and folded his hands behind his head.

"You'll have plenty of chances to move in Vietnam," she said bitterly. "Until you're in the ground, that is."

He turned eighteen that February, 1964, and she tried to get him to marry the girl he was dating, but he wouldn't do it. When he graduated in June and received the notice to report for his physical, she was terrified, because he was a perfect specimen, big and strong and almost impossibly hale, with 20/10 vision, practically, and great knees despite the family curse, so there was zero chance of his getting declared 4F. She tried to get him to enlist in the National Guard to avoid a dangerous posting, and then after the Gulf of Tonkin resolution in August she was *sure* he'd find some college to enroll in, but instead a couple of weeks later he went to the recruiter for the Marines.

He'd been on the winning side of every fistfight he'd ever been in, so he might've thought he could simply stare down whatever trouble was to come. He went to Parris Island for basic, got further training as an antitank assaultman, and was assigned to Camp Lejeune, where he stayed until June of 1965, when he volunteered to go over after the first waves of the ground war had landed in South Vietnam.

He called before he left. She couldn't picture him in a crew cut at the other end of the phone, wearing that one outfit they all seemed to wear, a polo shirt and chinos, as if they all shopped in the same store. All she could see in her mind's eye was him standing in his St. Sebastian's blazer, five grades behind her, shifting impatiently from foot to foot while she fixed his tie. He was the closest she'd ever had to a brother.

"You'd better stay alive," she said.

"There are some scared-looking fellas I could hand the phone to if you want to give them a little pep talk. This is Pat you're talking to. Pat *Tumulty*. I'll see you in a while."

"Fine."

"Tell your father I'll make him proud," he said.

Her father had filled her cousin's head with so much patriotic rhetoric that he thought he was embarking on a noble adventure.

"Don't you even *think* about trying to impress him," she said. "He'd never say so, but he's scared to death that something's going to happen to you."

"He told you that?"

"He doesn't have to say it for it to be obvious. He just wants you home in one piece. The bullshit around that man is piled so high you can't even see him past it."

"He'd take my place if they'd let him."

"Even if that's true, it doesn't mean a goddamned thing. The only thing he's ever been afraid of is regular life. Come home and live a regular life and impress *me*. Forget about my father."

She could almost hear him straighten up.

"Tell him I'll make him proud," he said.

She sighed. "Tell him yourself. He'll be where you left him, in that damned recliner. He doesn't go anywhere. Everybody comes to him."

"I will."

"Good-bye, Pat," she said, and then she thought, *Good-bye, Pat*, in case she was really saying it. She waited to hear him hang up.

7

She began to look forward to the day when she would take another man's name. It was the thoroughgoing Irishness of Tumulty that bothered her, the redolence of peat bogs and sloppy rebel songs and an uproar in the blood, of a defeat that ran so deep it reemerged as a treacherous conviviality.

She'd grown up around so many Irish people that she'd never had to think much about the fact that she was Irish. On St. Patrick's Day, when the city buzzed like a family reunion, she felt a tribal pride, and whenever she heard the plaintive whine of bagpipes, she was summoned to an ancient loyalty.

When she got to college, though, and saw that there was a world in which her father didn't hold much currency, she began to grasp the crucial role the opinions of others played in the settling of one's own prospects. "Eileen" she couldn't get rid of, but if she could join it to something altogether different, she might be able to enjoy her Irishness again, even feel safe enough to take a defensive pride in it, the way she did now only on those rare occasions when her soul was stirred to its origins, like the day just before her nineteenth birthday when President Kennedy was elected and she wept for joy.

She wanted a name that sounded like no name at all, one of those decorous placeholders that suggested an unbroken line of WASP restraint. If the name came with a pedigree to match it, she wasn't going to complain.

It was mid-December 1965. She was in a master's program in nursing administration at NYU after getting college done in three years, as she'd planned. Between classes, she met her friend Ruth, who worked nearby, under the arch in Washington Square, to head to lunch together. It was an unusually mild day for December; some young men had on only a sweater and no jacket.

"Well, it's not that he *needs* a date, necessarily," Ruth was saying as they walked toward the luncheonette on Broadway. "He just doesn't have one."

Eileen sighed; it was happening again. Everyone always believed they'd found her man for her, but more often than not he was a blarneying, blustering playboy who'd charmed her friends and the rest of the bar and whom she couldn't ditch fast enough.

"I'm sure one will turn up," she said. "Tell him good things come to those who wait."

The men that stirred her—reliable ones, predictable ones—were boring by other girls' standards. She didn't meet enough of these men. Maybe they couldn't get past the guys who crowded around her at bars. If they couldn't at least *get* to her, though, they weren't for her. She'd rather be alone than end up with a man who was afraid.

"You are *impossible!*" Ruth said. "I am trying to look out for you here. No—you know what? Fine. That's just fine." Ruth fastened the buttons on her coat.

Eileen could feel Ruth burning. In front of the luncheonette, Ruth stopped her. "Here's the thing," she said. "Frank asked me to do this favor, and we just started, so I want to come through for him. I don't care what you do on New Year's. You want to miss the fun, that's fine by me. You want to be alone the rest of your life, that's fine too. I've tried. I even set you up with Tommy Delaney, and look what you did with that."

"You think you're safe with a West Point man," Eileen said, as though to herself. "You think he'll have a bit of class." She watched a cab stop at the corner and a man with a newspaper tucked under his arm pay his fare.

"Tommy's a *fine* man," Ruth said.

"Oh, I'm sure he's swell," Eileen said. "I have no way of knowing. He couldn't sit still long enough to say two words to me. He spent the whole time making sure every back in the place got slapped."

"Tommy has a lot of friends."

"He bought everyone a round and said I didn't know it yet, but he was my future husband. There was a big cheer. The *nerve!*"

The man with the newspaper got out of the cab. He was tall and handsome, with dark cropped hair and striking eyeglasses. She imagined he was a visiting professor, Italian or Greek. She took her eyes from him before he turned in her direction.

"He liked you. He wanted to make an impression."

"An impression!"

"Look, this one is different," Ruth said lamely. "He won't be trying to win you over. He doesn't want to be there any more than you do."

"What's the problem with him? Is he queer?"

Eileen didn't know why she was still resisting. She would normally have done her friend Ruth this small favor, but she wasn't in the mood for disappointment, not on New Year's Eve. She watched the taxi launch off from the curb, only to stop again up the block to let a young couple pile in. The sun came back out from behind a cloud. Ruth unbuttoned her coat.

"He's a grad student at NYU. A scientist. Frank's in an anatomy class with him. He's obsessed with his research. He never leaves the library. Frank is worried about him. He wants to get him out."

Eileen didn't say anything. She was trying not to believe in the promising picture she was forming in her mind, for fear of disappointment.

"So what Frank told him is that I was nagging him to find a date for my friend for New Year's."

"Absolutely not!" Eileen said. "I will not pretend to be somebody's charity case."

"He's a gentleman. He couldn't resist a woman in need. It's the only thing that would have worked."

"Ruth!"

A pair of girls pushed past them into the luncheonette. Eileen could see the counter seats filling up and could make out only one empty booth.

"Would it help if I told you he's handsome? Frank even said it himself. He said all the girls they know think he's very handsome."

"Let them have him," she said, not meaning it. She couldn't believe she was feeling defensive about this man.

"Just do this for me and I'll never bother you again," Ruth said, putting her hand on the door to open it. "You can go become an old maid after this."

"Fine. But I'm not going to pretend to be grateful he went out with me."

In the interval between the setup and the date, she'd convinced herself that this was nothing more than a good deed she was doing. When the bell rang at Ruth's, though, she was seized by nerves. She ran to the bedroom and locked the door.

"Come on! I have to answer the door."

"I'm not going. Tell him I got sick or something."

"Come *out* and say *hello*!" Ruth whispered forcefully as the bell rang again.

She heard Ruth invite them in. She liked his voice: it was soft, but there was strength in it. She decided to open the door, but not before resolving to give him the hardest time she could. She wasn't going to have any man thinking she needed him there, certainly not some spastic recluse she'd have to lead around the room by the sleeve.

Before she had a chance to say anything sarcastic, Ed rose to his feet. He was indeed handsome, but not too pretty; neat and lean, with clean lines everywhere, including those in his face that gave him an appealing gravity when he smiled.

He leaned in and whispered in her ear. "I realize you didn't have to do this, and I promise to try to make it worth your time."

Her heart kicked once like an engine turning over on a wintry afternoon.

He could dance like a dream. When he pressed her close, his substantiality surprised her. The glasses, the neatly combed hair, the chivalry on the sidewalk and at doors made an impression, but the back and shoulders let her relax. The girls at their table thought him the most polite man they'd ever met. When she first heard him speak in his articulate way that was oddly devoid of accent, she thought he was like the movie version of a professor, but without the zaniness that emasculated those characters. Still, he was refined in a way that might have raised eyebrows among the men of her set. He could discuss things they didn't understand. He didn't so much drink a beer as warm it in his hand as an offering to the gods of conversation. She fretted over how he'd get along with her father, and so she brought him around earlier than she would have otherwise, in case she had to cut him loose, but something in Ed's carriage disarmed the big man. Eventually she had to feign annoyance at how well they got along. She shouldn't have been entirely surprised. He'd been a neighborhood kid, the kind who knew how to throw a punch when a friend was in trouble and could talk everybody's way out of it before it started—the kind men listened to because the way he spoke suggested he wasn't telling them anything he thought they didn't know already.

He was a natural athlete. They went to the driving range with her old friend Cindy and her husband Jack, who was into golf. Ed teed up and smacked the ball so soundly that when she saw it next it was a tiny pea at the end of its parabolic journey.

They headed out to Forest Hills one weekend to see her friends Marie and Tom Cudahy. There was a tennis court near the Cudahys' townhouse. They borrowed tennis whites from their hosts and the four of them hit the ball around in doubles, no keeping score or serving, just volleying. Ed returned shots he shouldn't have been able to get to in time. At the end, Tom asked him to play him solo, and Eileen turned and saw the embarrassed look on Marie's face. They both knew what was coming. Tom had been a letterman at Fordham and had a powerful serve, and though he mostly kept his competitiveness in check during mixed doubles, he liked to throttle his counterpart for a while afterward.

The two men took their positions and Tom fired a blistering smash. The ball raced up Ed's body off the bounce, as if it was trying to hit him more than once. The second serve came in on Ed's hands. He flicked his wrist at the last second and deposited the ball just over the net. Tom hustled but the ball died, bouncing again before he got to it. They traded points and games. Ed's serve was careful and reliable, his returns determined and vigorous. She liked the way he whipped his racket across his chest, dismissing offerings with sudden ferocity. He tucked the ball into corners and moved it around the court. Tom won the set, but Ed made the contest closer than anyone in their circle had.

They walked back to the Cudahys' to shower and change. She had one hand in Ed's, while the other held down the hem of Marie's mod minidress. On the court she'd felt protected by all the activity, but off the court she felt almost naked in it. Ed looked terrific in Tom's spare whites, as if he was born to wear them.

"When did you get so good at tennis?"

"I'm not that good."

"You looked pretty good to me."

He bounced a ball as he walked. "I cleaned up trash one summer in Prospect Park. I stuck around after work a few times and played at the Tennis House. I was always running after shots, trying to catch up to them. There was a pro who gave me some free advice. 'Go where you think the ball's going,' he said. 'Beat it there.'"

"I have a good strategy too," she said. "I don't move at all. I let it go past me to you."

He laughed. "I noticed."

"I'm flat-footed."

The smell of honeysuckle wafted up at them from a garden. Ed put the ball in his pocket. "Well, we can't exactly have you sweating through this white dress." He pulled her to him and gave her hip a squeeze. "This *little* white dress." They took a few stumbling steps together. "It just wouldn't be decent."

"The term is *tennis whites*, Tarzan," she said, shoving him playfully. "And they're very proper. So behave yourself."

Tom was walking ahead with Marie, his racket slung at his shoulder like a foxhunter's spent rifle. His clothes were casually disheveled, his shirttail hanging out in a way that suggested he'd never had to worry about money, but Eileen knew he was wearing a costume, trying to blend in. He worked for J. P. Morgan, but he was from Sunnyside, his father was a laborer like hers, and Fordham was Fordham, but it wasn't Harvard, Princeton, or Yale.

When the waiter came over, Tom wrinkled his nose up and pointed at something on the wine list, and she knew it was because he didn't want to mispronounce the name. He ordered for the table without asking what anyone wanted to eat. Ed gave her hand a little squeeze, and it felt as if a pulse passed between them. For a moment she knew exactly what he was thinking, not just about Tom, but about her, and himself, and all of life, and she liked the way he saw things. She could spend her life tuning into the calming frequency of his thoughts.

He wasn't a stiff, and he wasn't a weakling either. What was the word for it? *Sensitive* was the only one that came to mind, amazing as that was to consider; he was a sensitive man. He soaked up whatever you gave him.

His name was Leary, as Irish as anything, but she decided she could marry him anyway.

8

Ed's family had been in New York since just before the Civil War, but their sole claim to distinction was that his great-great-grandfather had had a hand in building the USS *Monitor*. Ed said his father liked to suggest by a looseness in his wording that his ancestor had been some sort of naval architect, but the truth was he'd punched the clock with the grunts at the Continental Iron Works in Greenpoint, where they fashioned the hull.

Ed's mother, Cora, had a soothing voice and a velvety laugh. Friday nights, Eileen sat with her and Ed, drinking tea and eating oatmeal cookies in the kitchen Ed grew up in, in a railroad flat on Luquer Street in Carroll Gardens, near the elevated F tracks. Cora kept the window open on even the coldest days, to drive off the steam heat. Eileen liked to watch the lacy curtains kick up in the breeze. Cats stalked the adjacent lot, curling into old tires. When they hopped onto the windowsill, Cora swished them away with a dish towel. Trains rumbled by at intervals, marking the passage of time. Whenever she rose to leave, Eileen found herself pulled into Cora's bosom for a hug. She never got over her surprise at receiving maternal affection, and she returned the hugs awkwardly, with an abstracted curiosity, though she welcomed them all the same.

Ed's father, Hugh, had been dead for a few years. Eileen knew little about him; Ed released that information in a trickle, and Cora never brought him up. The only evidence of him in the apartment was a framed picture, on one of the end tables, of him wearing a hat, an overcoat, and a slightly furtive half smile. Eileen knew he'd played the piano to accompany silent movies; that he'd scaled up paint cans in the Sapolin factory, once earning a small bonus when he suggested they paint a giant can on the water tank on the roof; that he'd worked as a liability evaluator at Chubb; and that World War II had given him his only real feeling of purpose.

Ed seemed to feel safest talking about his father's experience during the war years, though he had no memory of that time. It was all just stories he'd heard.

"You could get him going for hours if you asked about the war," Ed said.

The government had urged civilians to pursue activities essential to the war effort, and Hugh landed on the docks, in Todd Shipyard, sticking bolts in steel plates in the bulkheads and hulls of damaged ships. The work itself wasn't stimulating, save for the mild danger of hanging out over the water, but he liked toiling under the sun alongside other men, breathing in the salt air and thinking of what his labor led to—never mind the irony that after three generations in America, the Leary line was still working on ships.

Ed said his father and the other men modified ships from regular freighters into tankers, adding a second layer to the hull. They converted luxury liners to barracks for troop transport. The peak of their activity, in terms of both industry and importance, was working on the *Queen Mary*. They stripped her of her furniture and wood paneling, replaced her bars and restaurants with hospitals, painted her a dull gray to confuse rising submarines, and gave her smoke suppression. She could go as fast as a destroyer, reaching speeds of thirty knots where an average submarine could only go ten. At the height of the conflict, in 1943, she carried sixteen thousand men from London to Sydney without a gunboat escort.

One night, Eileen stayed late at Ed's house. Cora had gone to sleep. They were sitting on the couch, which was worn along the seam by its skirt, some of the filling rupturing through. Eileen picked the picture of Hugh up off the end table.

"What was he like?"

"I suppose he was like a lot of fathers," Ed said. "He went to work and stayed out late. He wasn't around a lot."

"What about as a man? All I see when I try to picture him is this coat and hat."

A pair of end table lamps provided the only illumination in the room, which was like a parlor in a shabby club. Cora had installed cute statuettes in every corner, but personality only went so far in making an apartment feel like a home. Eileen had a new appreciation for how her mother had kept things neat and in working order, how her father had paid to replace the furniture whenever it got run down. Ed had grown up with less.

"He liked to laugh," Ed said. "He told raunchy jokes. He always had a cigar dangling from his mouth. It made him look like a dog hanging its tongue out on a hot day. He was always hustling, working angles."

"What else?" she asked, putting the photo down. She sensed he was on the verge of candor. "Tell me more."

"He liked to drink," Ed said. "It wasn't pretty when he did."

"I know a little about that," she said, and they shared a moment of quiet understanding.

"I'm sorry," he said. "You deserved better."

She felt her emotions catching in her throat. "You can tell me anything, you know."

"I wouldn't know how to say it if there were anything to say."

"Just say what comes to mind."

He was silent, and she worried she'd pushed him too hard. In her nervous state she had picked off the material that covered the sofa's arm, and now she tried to fit it back into place with one hand while keeping her eyes on Ed. She should have left him alone, rather than risk angering him and making him shut down, but she didn't want to revert to the surface-level interactions she'd had with other men. She had never wanted to talk to anyone more than she wanted to talk to Ed. She wanted to tell him things she'd never told anyone, and to learn more about him than she'd learned about anyone else. She used to think a bit of mystery was a prerequisite to her feeling attracted to a man. For the first time, her attraction didn't diminish the more she knew, but actually grew.

"You remember Charlie McCarthy?" Ed said after a while. "Edgar Bergen's dummy? My father used to say I looked like him."

Eileen folded her hands in her lap and held her breath, trying not to look too eager to hear what he had to say.

"I figured out early on I could make him laugh if I did a Charlie McCarthy impression. So I practiced. I got to the point where I could do the voice pretty well. When my father got in from the bar, I'd hop up on the couch and twist up my mug for him." Ed showed her, forming a rictus and opening his eyes wide, looking from side to side with an eerie, doll-like blankness. "Sometimes he laughed. Sometimes he told me to cut it out and said I looked nothing like that doll. I never knew which it was going to be. I remember the last time I did it. He laughed and laughed. Then he smacked me in the mouth, *whack!*"—Ed brought his hand down on the coffee table—"and told me to stop embarrassing myself."

Their hands migrated toward each other on the couch. After their fingers sat intertwined for a bit, she clasped his hand in both of hers, pulled it to her, and gave it a little kiss, then shifted closer to him.

Ed said he and his mother had never discussed his father's drinking, but it was his understanding that his father hadn't been a drinker before the war. "If the war had gone on forever, or if he'd been a park ranger or done something outdoors, maybe things would have been different."

When peacetime returned, Hugh went back to Chubb and sat at a desk all day. He didn't have any hobbies. "I think the only way he knew how to drive off the anxiety in him was to go to Molloy's," Ed said. "Everybody raised a glass when he walked in. They laughed at his jokes. They let him buy rounds."

By the time Ed was nine, he said, his mother was sending him by train on pay Fridays to pick up his father's check. If he didn't get there in time, they were stuck for the week. If he did, his father wasn't necessarily stuck. With his beautiful singing voice, he could make twenty-five dollars, or two-thirds of his weekly salary, as the cantor at a single funeral Mass at St. Mary's Star of the Sea. Ed only knew his father did this because he served funerals during the school day as an altar boy.

"The first time he sang," Ed said, "I walked out of the sacristy with the cross to start the funeral and there he was, standing off to the side with this sheepish grin on. When the time came, he walked up to the lectern. He gave me a nervous look, like I'd caught him in something. Maybe one of his friends knew what kind of voice he had and set him up with the gig. I remember *knowing* he'd been drinking beforehand. It's just something you can tell."

She nodded.

"Then the organ started up, and he started singing, and it was like he was surprised by the sound of his own voice. Like he was hearing it for the first time. I couldn't believe how good he was. He sang his heart out. There were tears on some faces in the pews."

"My father can't sing," she said. "But he thinks he can."

Ed gave her a warm smile. "He came to collect the cash afterward. I was in the rectory changing out of my alb. He put his finger to his lips. 'Don't tell your mother.'" Ed's face took on an intense expression. "I already knew enough not to say anything, you know?"

She nodded again. Sometimes, she thought, life makes you grow up early. And some people never grow up at all.

"He started showing up often. I don't know how he did it without getting fired at Chubb. It was a pretty decent round-trip on the train. He must have been gone two, three hours at a time. He did it for years. I doubt a penny of that money made it home to my mother. To think that he was a block away from her all that time. She would have loved to have lunch with him."

Once Ed started talking, the dam broke. They went out once a week to eat in Manhattan, and the conversation turned often to their early years. She found out that in grammar school Ed was a model student, but by the time he reached high school he'd turned his back on his studies. After he was kicked out of his second school, Cora used her influence in the parish to get him admitted on probation to Power Memorial in Manhattan. The long train rides settled him down enough to get him graduated. He took a job mixing paints and dyes at the Kohnstamm factory on Columbia Street, a short walk from home. He brought his paychecks home to his mother.

At Kohnstamm's, Ed said, he found someone to look up to—the scientist who directed the mixers. The chemical processes awoke a scholarly impulse in him that had lain dormant. He got to know the chemicals so well that soon other men began coming to him instead of checking the manuals. He moved over to Domino for a better paycheck, turning slag into sugar, paying attention to the reactions, the reagents, the products. He

began taking night classes at a community college, then quit Domino to
enroll full-time at St. Francis College, where his younger brother Phil was
a student. Cora paid both their tuitions with the money she'd saved from
what Ed brought home.

Their flat had no hallway. To get from the kitchen to the living room,
you had to brush against the foot of every bed, one of which Ed shared
with Phil until he was twenty-one, when his sister Fiona got married and
moved to Staten Island. Until the day Hugh brought a desk home from
his office, Ed and Phil studied together at the kitchen table, the only good
surface to spread out on. Cora never had to call them to dinner; she only
had to tell them to put their books away.

Friday nights, when his friends were out, Ed waited for the bartender's call. He would pull up in front and honk, and Hugh would keep him
waiting while he had another. Ed wouldn't go in, because he didn't want to
watch his father drink. Once, he waited so long that he woke up slamming
the brakes, thinking he'd nodded off while driving and was about to plow
into the car in front of him. He started beating on the horn; a few guys
came out to see what was the matter. Hugh joined them and stared as if it
were somebody else's crazy kid. Ed kept slamming on the horn. When he
finally stopped, his father screamed at him. After that, Ed said, when he
drove up he gave a quick toot and shut the car off.

Ed was named to the Duns Scotus Honor Society, like Phil the year
before. They were the first pair of brothers in St. Francis's history to receive
the honor.

They were at Lüchow's on Fourteenth Street, eating Wiener schnitzel and
sauerkraut, when Ed told her about the day his father died.

"A few days before I graduated," he said, "my father had a heart attack
on the couch. I drove him to the hospital. I must have flown through every
light. I had my arm on him to keep him from slumping forward"—Ed
pressed it against her to show her—"like I did when I picked him up at the
bar. I was burning through intersections. When I got there, I saw that he'd
died. I slapped his face a few times. Then I threw him over my shoulder
and ran him in."

Only after Ed had heard definitively that his father was gone, while he sat weeping in the waiting room area, did he realize he'd wrenched his back. As he alternated in spasms of grief and pain, he understood that he loved all the things he'd always thought he'd hated about carrying his father's body home all those nights: the weight of him hanging on him, pulling at the sockets of his arms; the drunken heat that came off him; the roughness of his beard against Ed's neck; the soft sound of his voice as he mumbled; the sickly sweet smell of whiskey.

"There are things you feel that you can't explain," Ed said. "You know other people won't understand them."

"I know just what you mean." She was thinking she was referring to how she'd felt at times about her own parents. Then she realized she was feeling something like it just then for Ed. You had to hope the love you felt would get recorded in the book of time. "You don't have to say another word," she said.

9

S he wanted to buy her husband-to-be a luxurious wedding gift. It happened that her father's best friend, in addition to regularly occupying the stool next to him at Hartnett's—where her father had shifted from Doherty's when he'd started going back to pubs—was a vice president at Longines, which distributed LeCoultre in North America. For six hundred dollars, Eileen purchased a prototype of the next line of LeCoultre watches. It was slung with a beautiful eighteen-karat gold band and would have retailed for two thousand dollars. She paid in three installments.

She tried to think of a creative inscription that would encapsulate her feelings for him, some intimate notion to commit to posterity, but everything she came up with sounded too fanciful by half. In the end she settled on his full name, middle included, and hoped he'd hear a rough sort of poetry in the lack of embellishment and a tenderness in the identification of him as her man.

They went to Tavern on the Green a week before the wedding. They emerged from the subway and took a horse and carriage up to the entrance. She had never been to the Tavern before. She loved the banquet tables, the big picture windows, the austerity of the trees in winter.

She presented the watch to Ed after the salad course. He undid the bow, neatly removed the green foil wrapping, opened the box, and held the watch.

"It's beautiful," he said. Without trying it on, he put it back in the box. "I can't take it, though. I'm not the kind of man who's ever thought of wearing a gold watch. You should return it to the store."

In an astonished instant she'd gone beyond words, beyond anger, to a disappointment so deep it made her stomach ache.

"It's a prototype, Ed. I can't." She refolded the napkin in her lap, smoothed down the silk of her dress.

"Why not?"

"It's unique."

"I'm sure they'd listen—"

"It's *engraved*, goddammit."

Ed was still talking, but she didn't hear him. Quickly, dispassionately, she ran through the mechanics of how she would exit the restaurant. She wouldn't say a word. She would of course leave the watch on the table. She would go home and tell her parents that the wedding was off. She was disappointed that she wouldn't get to see her father in a top hat and tails. A busboy stacked and removed the salad plates, and now another stopped to replenish their water glasses, taking his time to keep too many ice cubes from tumbling out of the pitcher. His conscientious presence was the only reason she hadn't risen yet.

"Maybe you could have them take off this gold band and put a leather one on it for me instead, if you don't want to take it back," this man to whom she'd sworn her devotion was saying in lordly ignorance of how far from him she'd flown in her mind, how almost absurdly vulnerable he was to her at that moment. "I'm a regular guy. I don't know how to wear a watch like this."

She saw how unfathomably easy it could be for her to walk out on her own life. She was awash in sudden sympathy for Ed. Then the cloudburst passed, and she sat in a little puddle of resentment over how benighted and pinched her future husband was.

They endured a tense dinner, even managed to make it through dessert. After they'd risen to leave, a surge of spite compelled her to fish the watch out of her pocketbook and make him read the engraving on its back.

He looked at it quietly. For a moment, it occurred to her that he might be moved enough to change his mind, and she grew unaccountably nervous. Then he handed it back.

"I'll give you love and devotion and work hard all my life," he said.

"And I appreciate your getting this for me, more than I could say. It's the nicest thing I've ever gotten. But I know I'm not going to wear it. If you take it back, we can put that money in an account to send our kids to college. I'm sorry. I can't help the way I am. I wish I could. It'd be easier sometimes to be someone else. Right now, for instance. You look so beautiful tonight. I hate that I've disappointed you."

A couple of days later, her father saw Ed and asked where the watch was. When Ed told the truth—it was home in the box, he didn't feel comfortable putting it on—her father didn't react with the fury she'd anticipated. Ed's answer put him in a contemplative mood.

Later that night, her father called her into his room. "There's a reason he can't accept nice things," he said. "His family's been in this country a hundred years, but they never owned a house. That's a sin. If you're not in a house by the time I'm dead, I'll haunt you from my grave."

They got married a little over a year after they met. They spent a honeymoon weekend in Niagara Falls. It wasn't what she'd dreamed of—France, Italy, Greece—but Ed was researching a paper that would synthesize part of his dissertation work, and they couldn't afford to go away for long.

The *Maid of the Mist* didn't run in the off-season, so they had to experience the falls from the viewing areas. Large blocks of ice had gathered in sections of the falls, and the cold spray made it hard to stay long. They went to restaurants and took scenic walks.

On their final day, as she stood in the Prospect Point Park observation tower wrestling with the thought that all bodies of water were part of one larger body, Ed announced that when they returned home, there would be no time to go out while he did his research, which would take the better part of a year. She didn't take this threat too seriously. She figured he *believed* he needed that kind of sequestration, but more likely he was just trying on the role of head of household—making a show of arranging his affairs with an exaggerated masculine correctness. He'd been doing the same research in the run-up to the wedding, and pretty much the whole time they were courting, and he'd managed to make himself available to her. True, they'd only seen each other on the weekends, but she'd been busy with work herself.

They got back in late March 1967 and moved from their parents' apartments into the second floor of a three-family house on Eighty-Third Street
in Jackson Heights. She was elated that part of the dream she'd conceived
for her existence had been fulfilled. For years, the neighborhood had exerted a powerful pull on her imagination, and now it was the one she came
home to and slept in at the end of every day. The details were familiar, but
they burned with a new intensity. Flowerpots at intersections announced
the birth of new life, and the smell of spring through the windows lingered
in the pillowcases.

She was happy to put the turmoil of life in her parents' apartment behind her. She wanted to be conservative, if not in politics—her father would
disown her if she made that shift—then in comportment, in demeanor.
She'd always behaved a little older than her age, but now she found herself
making extremely prudent choices, like dumping expired milk down the
drain, even when it didn't smell, and driving more slowly on curves or in
the rain. She bought Ed a beautiful new tweed jacket and made him get rid
of all his old shoes, replacing them with wing tips and oxfords.

There was still a little lingering restlessness in her spirit, though. It
hadn't been her dream to live in an apartment like the one she and Ed had
ended up in, sandwiched between two ends of a family. The Orlandos, the
owners, lived on the first floor, and Angelo Orlando's older sister Consolata took up the third by herself. Angelo worked for the Department of
Sanitation, and Lena was a housewife. They had three children—Gary, ten;
Donny, nine; and Brenda, seven. The Orlando home was full of the sort of
ambient noise she associated more with apartment buildings than houses.
She had convinced herself that moving into a house, even a multifamily
one, meant diving into a pool of blessed silence. The Orlando boys played
tirelessly in the driveway with a small army of neighborhood kids. When
it rained, they roughhoused indoors for hours, crashing into walls, and Lena's voice rang out in shrill rebukes. The insistent murmur of a radio rose
at night from Brenda's room, which was below Ed's office. Ed wore ear-
plugs and possessed advanced powers of concentration, so the radio didn't
faze him, but it incensed Eileen. And Angelo and Lena's fights, though in-
frequent, were of the screaming, door-slamming variety. The noise came at

her from both sides. Most nights, Consolata made a restless circuit of her apartment, pounding between rooms with oddly heavy steps for a woman so thin, turning the television off in one room and on in another, leaving it on until programming ended and sometimes beyond, so that the rasp of a lost signal harassed Eileen to sleep.

Three months into the marriage, Eileen was astonished to realize that she hadn't entered a bar, restaurant, or party with her husband. She'd grown tired of making excuses to her friends; when they called and she had to say she couldn't go, she wanted to hand the phone to Ed to have him explain. She showed up alone if she went at all when they got together at each other's houses, and after she'd faced enough inquisitions about where Ed was, she decided it wasn't worth it to go. She'd envisioned playing euchre with him at the Coakleys', or watching him save Frank McGuire from grilling disasters, or seeing his entertainer side come out at the piano after everyone downed a couple of banana daiquiris at Tom Cudahy's place. She'd envisioned her own dining room, which was finally appointed hospitably after Ed had agreed to let her spend the money on furniture, thronged with friends around the table, Jack Coakley clapping his hands and dramatically sniffing the roast chicken's lemon-pepper aroma as she carried it proudly past him, but instead what she had for company were the dog-eared pages of novels as she sulked in the armchair. The only reason she even had that damned chair was that her mother had shamed Ed into buying it so she'd have somewhere civilized to sit when she came over. Her mother flatly refused to sit on their ratty couch, which they'd inherited when Phil left for Toronto. As long as Ed had a place to rest his head—and it could have been the floor for all he cared—he was content to go about his work as though the body's needs were nuisances and the soul's demands, illusions. The only thing he seemed to consider authentic was his work—not work in the abstract, because he hardly listened when she spoke about her day, but *his* work, his precious, important work that was going to make a contribution to science. She would pause in the doorway for a moment before she headed out for solitary walks around the neighborhood, looking at his back hunched over his infernal notebooks, his hand not even rising to give her a perfunctory wave good-bye.

She walked the path her youthful self used to tread on dates, when Jackson Heights was the neighborhood to be seen in. She'd pass Jahn's, where she used to have a burger and a shake after the movie, and remember how whatever hopeful young man she was with would escort her up and down both sides of Thirty-Seventh Avenue before returning her home on the train. Sometimes she'd take them on detours onto side streets, not to find an alley to make out in—though she did that too—but because she liked to look at the co-ops and houses and imagine a future in which she lived in that privileged setting.

Sometimes, she would feel that sense of possibility reenter her chest, and then she'd keep walking until it had worn off and the blocks looked strangely unfamiliar. She would stop at Arturo's and gaze in at the couples dining in neat pairs, or the families passing plates around, and wonder when things would settle down long enough for her to enjoy some of that hot bread with him, buttered to perfection, a glass of red wine warming the stomach, the two of them in no hurry to get anywhere, choosing from an inviting menu. There needed to be time for that kind of leisure, or she didn't see the point in living.

One day, the heat was unusual for early spring, and Ed was at his desk in his underwear and T-shirt. She'd begun to resent that desk, beaten up around the legs and stained a dull brown. She knew she'd never be free of it, that it would follow her wherever she went.

Getting that desk, Ed had told her, had been one of the few happy times he'd shared with his father as an adult. His father walked in from work one day and told him to get up and come with him. They drove into the city; his father wouldn't say what it was about. They went to the Chubb offices. "The place looked like it had been cleaned out," Ed said. "He led me to a storage closet. There was a desk and chair in it—his desk and chair. He'd had a handyman buddy hold them for him. They were getting new furniture for the whole office the next day. 'Sit down,' he said. 'Pull out the drawers. Pretend to work.' It was strange to have him watching me. My mother was the one who peeked over my shoulder when I worked. 'Can you get your work done at it, or what?' he asked. I said, 'Who couldn't get work done at this desk? It's beautiful.' My father, being my father, said,

'Good. Now I can read the paper at the table.' But I knew he was glad to do something nice for me."

The story had touched her when she'd first heard it, but now the ugly desk seemed a symbol of how little her husband would ever be equipped to see beyond the limits his biography had imposed on his imagination.

She watched him work, his pasty legs sticking out absurdly from his briefs, and waited for him to swivel in his chair to face her, to be a normal man for a moment. Angry, disappointed, she walked over and turned the air conditioner on. Ed rose without a word and turned it off again, then went back to work. He didn't even look in her direction. They went back and forth like this several times. She couldn't believe she'd signed on to live with a man so committed to his own pointless suffering. They weren't poverty-stricken by any means; they were even able to put aside a bit of money from every check for a down payment on their future house. But Ed thought even minimal indulgences were best lived without.

When they were courting she'd seen his eccentricities as a welcome change. There was a bit of continental flair about him. Certainly he was more charming than the doctors at work. He was as smart as any of them; he only hadn't gone to medical school because he was too interested in research to stop doing it. There was something romantic about that, but living with him made his eccentricities curdle into pathologies. What had been charmingly independent became fussy and self-defeating.

The heat broke her. She told him she'd had enough and started walking to her parents' apartment in Woodside. She sweated through her blouse, her resentment spurring her forward. Ed could have all the heat he wanted in that apartment by himself. She wouldn't be cooped up for another minute with him.

When her father came to the door and saw her fuming and drenched, he knew what was up. "That's your home now," he said. "Work it out with him."

In her rush to leave Ed, she had neglected to bring her purse. She asked for change for the bus.

"You walked here," her father said. "You can walk back."

By the time she got home, she had grown so angry at her father that

she'd forgotten all about being angry at her husband. Ed didn't say anything when he saw her, but after she showered she emerged to an apartment bathed in the cool of a churning air conditioner.

They made love for what felt like forever that night. She didn't mind
the sweat at all.

She was in Woodside visiting her parents when she saw a sign taped to the
window of Doherty's: "Big Mike Tumulty vs. Pete McNeese in a footrace.
Friday, July 21, 7:00."

She knew Pete, and she'd never much liked him. He was tall and skinny,
and he always seemed to speak a little louder than came naturally, as if he
were imitating another man's voice.

"What's this about a race?" she asked her father as she walked into the
kitchen. He was sitting sideways at the table with a cup of tea, looking out
the window. He wore a new white undershirt and slippers.

"He was running his mouth off about how fleet of foot he was."

"You're almost sixty years old."

"So what?"

"Pete is barely thirty." Her father put the kettle back on.

"So he's half my age," her father said. "He's also half the man."

She thought the whole thing ridiculous, but on the race's appointed
day, she couldn't help dropping by Doherty's on the way home from work.
The bar was fuller than usual, almost visibly crackling with static energy, as
if a prizefight was about to take place instead of an absurd pissing contest.
Happy shouts rose over the din, and everywhere she looked, men huddled
and clapped their palms to the backs of each other's necks. Someone asked
her father how he planned to beat Pete. "I'll blind him with the tobacco
juice," he said through a cheekful of chaw, to a round of hearty laughter.
Guys were taking final book. "Two dollars on Big Mike," she heard one say
proudly, and she imagined that if all the money her father's adherents were
willing to lose to support him were piled on the bar, it would be enough
to buy the establishment from the owners, or do something worthwhile.

The course was set: they would start in the bar, at the back, run out
to the sidewalk, circle the block once, and return to the bar. It wouldn't be

easy to watch. Pete and his horse-long legs would come around the corner upright and easy, and her father would follow with his cheeks puffed, his face carmine red, his legs churning. Everyone gathered would watch an era end.

"Give me a glass of Irish whiskey," her father said, gently rapping his knuckles on the bar. "I'm warming up." He took his shirt off, then his undershirt. He resembled a bare-knuckled fighter. Pete tried to smirk, but he looked unnerved. Her father put his foot up on a stool. There were packs of muscle shifting under his skin, and when he leaned over to tie his shoe, his back looked broad enough to play cards on.

"Jimmy," he called out with mock sharpness. "Get those kids out of the street. I don't want to run any of them down."

Guys laughed, exchanged looks. Her father and Pete toed a line in the back of the bar. The bartender counted down from three and they headed through a crowded gauntlet on either side, reaching the door at the same time. Her father shifted his massive body laterally like a darting bull and crushed Pete in the doorframe. They never made it outside. Pete staggered, out of breath before he'd even begun.

"They broke at the gate," her father said as he returned to his stool, heat radiating visibly off his naked skin, a slight glower to him, a hint of violence in his eyes, the pride of a clan chieftain in his heavy step. She watched his friends retrieve their money and felt their eyes on her long, lean body, which her work suit clung to in the summer evening heat. They regarded her appreciatively, with a slightly wistful longing. She was the chieftain's daughter, and she'd married outside the clan.

They hadn't won anything, but they hadn't lost anything either— neither money nor their idea of Big Mike. Her father had played Pete's game, but by his own rules. It was a Solomonic solution, and she thought sadly of the difference he would have made with his gift for inspiring men if he'd been born into another life.

10

E d was an expert on the brain. His subspecialty within the field of neuroscience was psychopharmacology, specifically the effects of psychotropic drugs on neural functioning. While doing his dissertation research, he ran an experiment in the aquaria of the Department of Animal Behavior at the American Museum of Natural History, studying the relationship between the neurotransmitter norepinephrine and learning in the black-chinned West African mouthbrooder fish, whose female laid eggs and whose male spat sperm at them and gathered them, then heated them under its tongue. Ed housed them individually in small aquaria in a greenhouse whose temperature was maintained at 26°C, and performed experimental tests in a separate room at the same temperature, injecting them with drugs that either enhanced or depressed action. The fish saw a red light, and if they didn't jump over a barrier in five seconds, they received a shock. He was testing the effects of drugs on an organism's ability to augment its decision-making abilities—in short, to learn.

The subject of learning fascinated him. He told Eileen it was because it had happened almost by accident in his own life. "If I hadn't run into that chemist at Kohnstamm's," he said, "I don't know what would have become of me. I think about that narrow escape."

He experimented on the fish faithfully six days a week for almost a year, going in even when it was supremely inconvenient to do so, missing family functions and dinners with friends, leaning on colleagues for favors when she put her foot down and demanded a sliver of his time. He never slept enough, he seldom ate enough, and his back always hurt because he sat too long at his desk, but the way the work was coming together gave him so much energy that he glowed as he neared the end, so much so that she went shopping without him and put a coffee table, two couches, a pair of end tables, and some lamps on the American Express, thinking he'd be too happy to complain. Still, she was so nervous about the cost that a few weeks later, on the Saturday when the furniture was supposed to be delivered, she still hadn't told him it was coming. She was relieved when he left early for his lab to gather data, and after the men delivered the pieces and hauled the old couch to the backyard until the Monday pickup, she sat on one of the couches, fretting over what she'd say. When the front door finally opened, she leapt to her feet, ready to spar, but Ed stepped in from the vestibule wearing that tranquil expression he wore when he was deep in his work, that made it look as if he'd just come from meditating. As he took in the room, she waited to see his face fall and readied to say she'd send it all back, but all he did was sit on the couch and say how nice and firm the pillows were compared to the lumpy ones they'd been living with. She'd never even thought he'd registered the lumps.

He was about two weeks shy of having gathered all the data he needed when the heating plant broke down and the aquaria froze, killing his specimens.

He didn't smash equipment or hurl insults at the plant manager. He didn't come home and make life miserable for her. He ate a quiet dinner and lay on the floor in the living room, between the glass-topped coffee table and one of the couches. She lay on the other couch reading to keep him company. She understood he didn't want a pep talk. When it was time to turn in, she leaned over him and saw in his eyes not sadness but extreme fatigue. She knew enough not to tell him everything would be fine. She gave him a kiss on the lips, told him to come in soon, and shut the light off. He remained behind in the silent dark. He came to bed very late, and the next day he began again from the beginning, with new fish, because he needed a full set of data.

When he finished a year later, he had worked on the fish for so long that the species' scientific name had changed twice, from *Tilapia heudel-otii macrocephala* to *Tilapia melanotheron* to *Sarotherodon melanotheron melanotheron*.

"You never get anywhere worthwhile taking shortcuts," he said when she asked how he'd gotten through that difficult time. She couldn't have agreed more. Not taking shortcuts—not settling for someone inferior—was the only reason she'd been free to marry him.

They started going out again. Ed got them a membership at the Metropolitan Symphony Orchestra. Once, when they were heading to the symphony, he picked a wounded fledgling off the sidewalk and carried it in his handkerchief for a few blocks, until he bowed to her protestations and deposited it in a planter. He gave her the silent treatment until they got home. When she was shutting off the light she said, "Good night, St. Francis of Assisi," and he laughed despite himself and they made love and fell asleep.

In December of 1970 she headed to the city with Ed to see the window displays on Fifth Avenue. She was excited to see them, despite how corrosively ironic Ed had been about them the year before, when at one point in his jeremiad he'd called them "altars to consumer excess." She wasn't about to let his grousing spoil her enjoyment of a tradition she'd observed whenever she could since she'd first gone with her mother as an eleven-year-old.

Ed refused to pay for a parking garage. It took them half an hour to find a spot, and they ended up on Twenty-Fifth and Seventh, almost a mile from Lord & Taylor. He refused to let them take a cab, even though she was wearing heels and it was twenty degrees out, with a wind that whipped up the avenue. The sun was setting, and store gates were being pulled down as if in protest of the cold. The sidewalks of Seventh Avenue were unusually empty. She noticed that most of the cabs that passed were occupied.

As they neared the store, the sidewalks grew more crowded, the bells of the Salvation Army collectors jingling on each corner. They saw a pack gathered in front, which quickened her step and made Ed sigh and slow down.

She had been delighting in the scene of a golden retriever pulling at the corner of a wrapped gift when Ed—who had been munching his way toward the bottom of a little bag of roasted nuts— broke the spell.

"These things seem here for the purpose of entertainment," he said, "but really they're here to get you to come in and part with your money."

He spoke in a breezy, careless way that suggested he believed a new understanding had sprung up between them. "They're like organisms that have evolved elaborate decorative mechanisms to lure you in. People fall for it. It's fascinating, actually."

"Listen to yourself."

"The bee orchid, for instance, has flowers that look like female wasps. Males try to mate with it, and in the process they get pollen on their feet and spread it around. It's not about the window. It's about pulling you into the store. It's about getting you to leave with something."

She was attempting to concentrate on the little animatronic girl whose hand was traveling slowly to cover her mouth, which had fallen open at the sight of Santa Claus's ebony boots disappearing up the chimney.

"It's a stupefying, hypnotic loop. It puts you in a suggestible state."

"Do you have to be so heady about everything? Do you have to analyze everything to death?"

"What's amazing is that they're exactly the same every year."

"That's an *ignorant* remark," she spat. "They're not the same at all. They put a lot of work into these. Months of planning."

She wouldn't have minded his objections so much if he hadn't insisted on drawing her into a dialogue about them. Was it too much to ask to share a moment of joy?

She looked around at the other husbands. They didn't look any happier to be there, but they stood back dully, hands folded behind them or scratching their noses. They couldn't have been as cleverly cruel about it as Ed if they'd tried.

"And the battling of tourists," he said. "Every year it gets worse. The jostling, the jockeying for position. They're descending on the imperial city for their bread and circuses. I wish we didn't have to do this."

She started walking to the train. A couple passing in the other direction gave her curious looks, as though they could see the intensity of her disgust in her expression. She found herself unaccountably smiling at one man, giving him a manic sort of grin full of the slightly breathless ecstasy of being unmoored, and he returned it with a delighted blush. By the time she felt a tug on her elbow, she was at the next corner.

"Don't be hysterical," Ed said. "I was just making a few observations."

"The world isn't a lab."

"Come on," he said. "Let's go back and look."

In his worn jacket with the frayed sleeve ends, he looked like a war veteran about to ask for change for the subway.

"You've ruined it."

"Don't say that. Listen, I can't help myself sometimes. I don't know what's wrong with me."

"I do," she said. "You didn't have enough fun as a kid."

He pulled her arm, but she wouldn't budge. She watched steam rise from a manhole cover and felt in her chest the rumbling of a passing bus. She was keenly aware of the limits of the physical world. She wanted to be in one of those scenes in the windows, frozen in time, in the faultless harmony of parts working in concert, fulfilling the plan of a guiding, designing hand. It would be lovely not to have to make every decision in life, to be part of a spectacle brought out once a year, for the safest of seasons, and put to work amusing people who stared back in mute appreciation. The real world was so messy, the light imperfect, the paint chipped, the happiness only partial.

"One of these years," she said, "we will come here and you will enjoy it and not make me feel miserable about it. I dream of that."

"Let's let that be this year," he said. "Let's go back and look at those windows. Please, honey. Let me make it up to you."

"It's too late," she said.

"It's never too late," he said. "Don't say that."

She hadn't been looking at him; now she stopped to. Streams of people flowed past in either direction, rushing toward obscure destinations. This was her life right here, petty as it seemed at the moment, and this was the man she'd chosen to spend it with. He was holding his hat in his hand as if he'd taken it off for the purpose of beseeching her, and she saw that he would always have flaws, that he would always be a little too intense in his objections, a little too unbending when it came to the decadence of the world. She thought, *We can't all wear a hair shirt all the time.* But there he was, trying to pull her back to the scene he despised, and she saw that he couldn't live in a way other than the one he thought was right, and when he saw what the right thing was, like now, he cared about it as if it were the only thing that mattered. Everyone else around seemed as insubstantial as the air they moved through, the shopping bags they carried the only things anchoring them to the ground.

"Did I tell you I love what you did with your hair?" he said, and she let herself be mollified, because she'd thought he hadn't noticed. She took his hand. They retraced their steps, the street around them thrumming with life. She saw that there was something perfect about the imperfection of her husband—her mortal, living husband with his excessive vigilance about the effects of capitalism and his unmistakable pair of bowed legs that she watched carry him forward. She kept her eyes on his shoes hitting the pavement and let him guide her wherever he was going.

11

Shortly after getting his PhD, Ed came home with the news that he'd been sought out by an executive at Merck, who'd read an article of his in a journal. Eileen was in the kitchen cutting vegetables for stew.

"He said I could have my own lab, with state-of-the-art equipment, everything top of the line. I'd have a team of assistants."

"Did he say how much you'd be paid?" She pushed the peppers into the stewpot and rinsed the knife in the sink. She could smell something fried and sickly sweet coming up from the Orlandos' apartment below.

"He didn't have to. More than I'm making now. Let's just say that."

"How *much* more?" She began to cut the beef into cubes. It was a thick cut with veins of fat. Ed would not have approved of how much she had spent on it.

"We'd be very comfortable."

He didn't appear terribly enthused to be able to make such a statement.

"Honey!" she said, hearing herself squeal as she put the knife down. "This is amazing!" She threw her arms around him.

"We'd have to move to New Jersey."

"We could live anywhere we wanted," she said, letting him go to take a few steps and get the motor started on her thoughts. She was already envisioning a house in Bronxville. "If not New Jersey, then Westchester County, for instance."

"That's too far to commute."

"Then we'll move to New Jersey."

"Not me," he said.

"How do you want to do this, then? What would make you comfortable?"

"Staying where I am," he said.

She looked at him. He was seriously considering not taking the job. If she had to say, he had already made up his mind. She picked up the knife and cut the last slab.

"You love research. Think of the lab you'd have. I'd have to drag you home."

"It's not research. It's making drugs." Ed paced toward the living room and back.

"Drugs that *help people*," she said, pushing the meat into the pot.

"Drugs that make a lot of money," he said.

This opportunity looked like their destiny. There had to be a way to get him to listen to reason. She added salt and pepper and two cups of water and turned the burner on. "You research drugs already. What's the difference?"

Ed stood in the arched doorway between the kitchen and living room. He stretched his hands up and flexed his muscles against the doorway. "Researching drugs and making them are not the same," he said. "On my own I can be a watchdog. For them I'd be a lapdog. Or an attack dog."

"What about when we have kids?" She put the caps back on the oil and the spices. "Don't you want to be able to provide for them?"

"Of course I do. I guess it depends what you mean by *providing*." He gave her a meaningful look, let down his hands, and peered through the glass lid of the stewpot. He switched the radio on and played with the antenna to relieve the static. The kitchen filled with the violins and flutes of a classical orchestra.

"I could make you do it," she said. "But I won't."

"You could not."

"I could. Women do it all the time. I could find a way. But I won't."

He straightened up. "You're not like that."

"Lucky for you, that's true," she said, though what she was thinking was that she was more like that than Ed understood. If her husband wasn't going to fight to secure their future, someone had to. "I just want *you* to know that *I* know what I'm not doing here. What I'm not *making you* do."

"Don't forget I'm on the fast track to tenure," he said, and she could tell it was a done deal in his mind.

Ed was an assistant professor at Bronx Community College, where he'd started teaching while in graduate school at NYU. One day soon he would be an associate professor, and then, probably soon after that, a full professor.

"There's nothing fast about the track you're on," she said bitterly, looking at him in the window's reflection in order not to have to look right into his face. "I don't care how quickly you get there."

Five years into their marriage, when Eileen was thirty-one, they decided to stop using birth control and try to conceive a child. At Einstein Hospital, where she worked, she had established a reputation as a head nurse and was confident she'd be able to return to the field after a short absence. She would have to go back to work eventually, something she wouldn't have had to do if Ed had said yes to Merck.

Seven months passed with no results and she started to worry. She wasn't too old yet by any means, but she also knew the time for rational calculations had arrived. They'd been going about it haphazardly, having sex when they felt like it and leaving it to chance. She decided to make getting pregnant a conscious project, turning her attention to managing it as she'd managed so many others. She drew up ovulation charts and held Ed to a schedule. They both went in for tests. Ed's sperm count was normal, his motility strong. Nothing was wrong with her ovaries. Every month, she cried when her period came. Every month, Ed reassured her.

Then, finally, after another six months had passed, she got pregnant. A new lightness entered her spirit. Things that had once annoyed her hardly registered with her anymore. She laughed more easily, gave Ed more rope, and was practically a pushover with the nurses she supervised. She surprised herself with how serene she felt. She never thought she'd be one of those egregious earth mothers, but there she was, tired all the time and yet still making meals and keeping the place in order and smiling through it—laughing, even, at the comedy of being alive. She didn't get angry at the evening news. When she got cut off on the highway, she shrugged her shoulders and shifted over a lane and hoped everybody arrived safely where they were going.

Her mother was over at her apartment, reading the newspaper. She grunted in appreciation and handed it to Eileen.

"Here," she said. "Read this. You might learn something."

It was an article about Rose Kennedy; one paragraph discussed how the Kennedy children used to hide the coat hangers so their mother couldn't deploy them on their backs. Eileen seldom thought anymore about her mother using the hanger on her, both because the memory was so unpleasant and because it was woven so thoroughly into the fabric of her childhood that it barely merited conscious thought, but even this many years later, as she pictured her mother cracking her with that little metal whip, she could almost physically feel it on her body.

"See?" her mother said proudly when Eileen handed it back. "I'm not the only one. If Rose Kennedy can do it, I can too. You should do it yourself, but you won't. You're too soft."

If Eileen hadn't been pregnant, she might have said something about how all that money doesn't necessarily buy you class, you can still act the same as a cleaning lady from Queens, because it would have cut to the quick, but she just said, "I guess it takes all styles," and decided then and there that she would never lift a hand in anger at her child.

A few months into the pregnancy, she suffered a miscarriage. The sadness she felt was ruinous, unspeakable. Almost worse was the awakening in her of a dormant foreboding that went back, perhaps, to her mother's own miscarriage and the effect it had had on both their lives. She'd never acknowledged it consciously, but in the blind alleys of her mind she'd feared that if she ever did manage to get pregnant, she'd have difficulty bringing the child to term.

She tried not to let Ed see how distraught she was. She needed to keep him on task trying to get her pregnant again, and she didn't want him thinking it would be gallant to take the pressure off her for a while. Another year passed with no results. She started having an extra glass of wine at restaurants. She took to suggesting wine with nearly every home-cooked meal. She began buying cases of wines she liked and storing them in the basement to have something on hand when company came over, and because buying in bulk was cheaper. She felt she was acquiring a little more insight into the way her mother's life had played out. She was still in control, though; she kept going to work every day, kept depositing money into her savings account.

Ed no longer made efforts to reassure her. He seemed to have resigned himself to not having children. At times she wondered if he weren't relieved. Despite his protests to the contrary she imagined he wouldn't terribly mind preserving for himself some of the time that fatherhood would claim. Once, when he said he was too tired on a night they were scheduled to try, she accused him of sabotaging their plans. She knew she was being hysterical, but she couldn't help herself.

Her friends ran into no trouble having babies. Cindy Coakley had three girls in five years until she finally delivered Shane to Jack. Marie Cudahy followed up Baby Steven with the twins, Carly and Savannah. Kelly Flanagan's Eveline was born with a cleft lip, but then Henry came out a couple of years later looking like the Gerber baby. One after another, the calls came in with the cheerful news, and the cards arrived celebrating fecundity. The only holdout among her close friends was Ruth McGuire, who had raised the last two of her seven younger siblings herself. When Ruth told her she was done raising kids, Eileen felt herself drawing even closer to her. They would greet the childlessness together.

Whenever they gathered around to watch whichever of her friends' kids was celebrating a birthday open presents, Eileen bit her nails down to the quick. She was sure everyone could read her thoughts in her mortified grin. She always spent too much money and bought too many gifts. She felt a nervous expectancy whenever the kid began to tear the paper open. She needed to have gotten the essential gift, the inevitable gift.

Having no kids freed Ed to pursue his professional interests without the burden of nighttime feedings or diaper changes or pediatric visits. He did important work on neurotransmitters, gave talks at conferences, and was named full professor faster than his peers.

She stopped thinking of each menstruation as a referendum on her femininity. She threw herself into her work with a compensatory vigor and was promoted several times. She sensed that her bosses and coworkers saw her as one of a new breed of women—it was 1975—willing to sacrifice motherhood on the altar of career. The men deferred to her and the mothers hated her, and there was an opportunity here if she was willing to pursue it fully.

Still, the miscarriage haunted her. She had dreams of sitting on the toilet bowl and hearing an unusual plop and finding in there a tiny baby who'd open its eyes at her—she couldn't tell its sex—and look at her angrily, blinking slowly, and she would wake with a start and shake Ed awake. She avoided looking into the bowl when she went to the bathroom. Eventually, she and Ed settled into the rhythms of a childless life, which offered undeniable compensations: they could go out with other couples without having to arrange for child care; they could indulge in the leniency reserved for aunts and uncles; and they were free to nurture their careers in the way they might have nurtured offspring. Maybe this was why she was so upset when Ed was offered the chairmanship of the department and turned it down to devote more time to teaching and research. It was as if he was telling her he didn't love their child.

To make up for the money he'd left on the table in passing up the chairmanship, Ed started teaching night anatomy classes at NYU. He'd pop home for dinner and head into the city by train. On dissection nights, he came home smelling like a pickled corpse himself. She couldn't stand to have him touch her after he'd been handling dead bodies, and when he teasingly ran his hands over her anyway, she squealed and squirmed out of reach.

A tenure-track position opened in NYU's biology department. One of Ed's advisors was on the search committee. He said Ed would be given serious consideration if he applied.

She urged him to do it. NYU would be an obvious bump up in prestige.

"They need me at BCC," he said. "Anyone can teach at NYU. What's important to me is having my students leave knowing they got a real education. I want to help them get into NYU. I want them prepared to meet the demands that will be placed on them when they do." There were other reasons to stay: the city had an airtight pension plan and great health benefits; there was no guarantee of tenure at NYU; he had a pretty good lab at BCC and could do the same research there that he'd do at NYU; there were grants out there to be procured. "It's all about having the right ambition," he said.

In the end, he never applied. To all the people she'd excitedly told about the NYU possibility, Eileen defended Ed's choice by saying that when the opportunity arose, which was bound to be sooner rather than later, he would be a natural choice for dean of the college. That prospect, she said, wasn't something you just flushed. That was the sort of career experience that could be parlayed into a parallel administrative position in a more prestigious institution.

He kept teaching the night classes. Now when he came home stinking of embalming fluids, not only wouldn't she let him near her in bed, she made him shower before she'd even hug or kiss him hello. Dinner and dishes would intercede after that, and often she could get to bed without having to touch him at all. She didn't feel bad withholding herself from him. He had made his choice. He shouldn't have expected to have everything he wanted, not if she had to give so much up to keep him happy.

The tall tree in the backyard, whose crown eclipsed the apex of the Orlandos' gabled roof, blocked much of the light in their bedroom. They were into their midthirties, and hints of seniority crept into their thoughts; they held them off by making love. Sometimes the activity was tinged by anger. Neither of them was going anywhere, even if in the middle of fights that lasted for days she entertained thoughts of divorce and suspected he did, though neither raised its specter aloud. They knew they would never sever their union, and this knowledge opened a door to the basement of their psyches. They became familiar enough to each other to begin to feel like strangers in bed, which infused their love life with a new potency. She wondered whether her friends had wandered down similar alleys, but she never had the courage to ask.

When she was thirty-five, after she'd long since given up worrying about it, she conceived a child and carried the pregnancy to term, delivering at dawn a couple of days before the ides of March, 1977. She and Ed had been struggling for weeks to come up with something to call the baby if it happened to be a boy, and by morning of the second day they were no closer to an answer, to the consternation of the girl with the birth certificate paperwork. Ruth took the train in to visit and accidentally left her book behind on the hospital nightstand. When the girl came around again on the morning of the third day and said Eileen could always take a trip down to City Hall to file the documents herself, Eileen's gaze landed on the name of the author of Ruth's book, *Mrs. Bridge*, which she had never heard of. She had a distant relative named Connell, but the real reason she chose it was that it sounded more like a last name than a first name, like one of those patrician monikers the doctors she worked for often bore, and she wanted to give the boy a head start on the concerns of life.

When Connell was a couple of months old, she realized, as though she'd awoken from an extended slumber, that his coming into the world had been a matter of grave importance. She had escaped a trap without knowing she'd been in it. For a while, she pushed Ed to conceive another child, until she stopped for fear of what misbegotten creature might result if she succeeded at her age. She would build the future on the boy.

It surprised her how much she enjoyed bathing her baby. She suspected it would have surprised anyone who knew her. As soon as she put the stopper in and opened the tap to fill the sink, a remarkable calm settled over her. She held his neck and head with one hand, her inner forearm cradling his body, and cleaned him with the other, pressing the cloth into the little creases in his skin. He smiled mutely at her and she felt a terrible unburdening of pent-up emotion. A little water splashed up in his face and he coughed and resumed his uncanny placidity. When he grew bigger and could sit up in the sink, she handed him a sopping washcloth to grip and suck on while she washed him with another, and she delighted in the sound of his draining it, the sheer vital pleasure he took in pulling it in his little teeth.

When he was old enough to be bathed in the tub, she loved the sight of him leaning over its lip, standing on tiptoe as he reached for the water with his swinging hand, his little back muscles shifting in the effort. In his enthusiasm he nearly fell in headfirst. He splashed waves out of the tub with a succession of quick slaps at the water's surface. He giggled and gurgled and pulled at his penis with exploratory joy as she rubbed shampoo into his black hair. He grabbed the rinse cup and took a long draft of the soapy water before she could seize it from him. She loved to wrap the towel around him when she was done, powder his little body, secure the diaper, and work his limbs into pajamas, sensing the calm and ease he felt when snug in the garment's gentle pressure. Snapping the buttons gave her an unreasonable pleasure. She would breathe his baby smell and wonder how she could ever have lived without it. Her heart swelled when she bathed him, when she dressed him for bed, when she combed the last wetness out of his washed hair, when she gave him the breast, when she gave him the bottle, when she laid him down, when she went to check on him at night and felt his chest rise and fall under her hand and his heart beat through her fingertips. She thought of him as she lay awake, and though she was always exhausted, and though there were nights she imagined she'd rise in the morning and the enchantment would have worn off, the well of her affection filled up in her sleep and she plucked him from the crib and pressed him to her, kissing his soft neck. There were some things that couldn't be communicated, and this was one—how much pleasure a woman like her could take in the fact and presence of her beautiful baby boy. She knew it wouldn't be like this forever; soon she'd make demands on him, expect the world of him. She was going to enjoy this part. She was going to fill up her heart with it enough for years.

12

After Eileen's mother got sober, sitting idly took more out of her than working long hours, so she continued to haul herself out to Bayside to clean up after grammar school kids even into her midsixties, long after Eileen's father had taken the watch and pension and tossed the truck keys to the younger bucks. When her employer lost its contract with the schools, though, her mother didn't look for another job. She had talked for years of putting money down on a beach home in Breezy Point, but Eileen suspected she'd realized she couldn't make a vaulting leap forward in the time she had remaining. She started reading the *Irish Echo* instead of the *Daily News* and making trips to Ireland using the savings she'd accumulated. The line of her allegiances began to blur, as if her time in her adopted homeland had been an experiment whose hypothesis had proved unsound.

Eileen had long been able to tell her mother about the fights over Ed's career and know that she would click her tongue and shake her head in censure of his lack of drive. Some change was occurring in her mother, though, to make her less pragmatic. She seemed less bothered by her station in life. She stopped complaining about politics, or the idiots on the subway, or the ugliness and stench of city life. She read novels and met with a group to discuss them. Eileen couldn't help feeling a little betrayed. She figured part of this transformation was her mother trying anything to avoid taking a drink. "Negative thoughts back you into a corner," her mother said to her, smiling, one afternoon after returning from a picnic with the baby in Flushing Meadow Park. "They multiply and surround you. Don't think of what you don't have. Try to focus on the simple pleasures." It was rich, this spouting of shibboleths, this late-stage wisdom-mongering. It was the tactic of a woman who'd played her hand and lost, or worse, never played it to begin with. But her mother had picked the wrong audience for her speech. It may have gone over well with down and-outers at AA who'd wrecked their lives and slipped into a spiral of regret, but Eileen's problem wasn't negative thinking, it was too little positive thinking on the part of everyone around her. She had a vision, and she wasn't turning away from it for a second, even if her husband, and now her mother, saw some ugliness in it. At least she had her father on her side though God bless him, he supported anything you threw your heart into. She was going to do that, no question about it. What waited ahead, if only Ed would walk the path she'd laid out for him, was a beautiful life, an American life.

"One day at a time," her mother said, and Eileen thought, *And everything all at once.*

Christmas of 1980 Eileen bought Ed a VCR. They'd looked at them together, but when he'd seen what they cost—about a thousand dollars—he had decided they could live without one. Eileen hadn't worked hard all her life to sit on her hands when she could afford to buy something. She was making decent money now that she was the nursing director at Lawrence Hospital in Bronxville. It was the perfect gift for him, considering how much he loved old movies. Starting in August, she paid for it on layaway.

When he unwrapped it, he looked horrified, as if it were a relic unearthed from a sacred burial ground that would bring a curse down upon their heads.

"How could you do this?" he asked, seething in front of the three-year-old boy. "How could you think of buying this?"

A few days later, she came in from the shower and saw him on his haunches putting a tape in the machine. She gave him a sardonic look.

"All right," he said. "I was wrong. It's a great gift."

"Save it."

"I mean it. It was thoughtful of you." He was clutching the empty sleeve of the VHS tape to his chest. "I appreciate it."

"I can't believe this."

"Look, I know I get set in my ways."

"You're telling me."

"Doesn't mean I can't learn a thing or two."

He wheeled the TV cart over, so that it was right next to the bed. PBS was on, the fund-raising appeal between programs. Ed patted the bed. "Get in," he said.

"I've got to brush my hair out."

"Come on," he said. "I want to make sure I get this whole thing on tape."

"Anyway, I'm happy you're using it."

"What can I say?" He threw his arms out in amused resignation. "You're good for me. I don't know what I'd do without you."

"Really?"

"Really and truly. I'd be lost without you."

Sometimes it felt like all the difficulty he put her through was worth it. It was a rare man who'd admit so thoroughly that he'd been wrong.

"Honey," she said, and she dropped her towel and stood naked before him the way he was always trying to get her to do. At first she hunched a bit, and then she stood tall, her hands at her hips, feasting on his gaze and letting him drink in her body. The movie was starting, but Ed didn't take his eyes off her. She felt herself blush. "You'd better hit record," she said. Ed didn't stop looking at her. She climbed on him and hit the button.

"We can watch it later," he said, kissing her neck. "That's the genius of this thing." He moved his hand down her back, squeezed her butt, touched her sex.

"Anytime we want," she said breathlessly.

She rolled off him and ripped the sheet away. He lowered the volume and yanked his underwear off. She reached across him to switch off the bedside lamp and he thrust up into her, flipped her onto her back. The tape whirred rhythmically. The television pulsed, filling the room with light and plunging it into darkness, outlining their bodies in the lovely deep of night.

• • •

In January of 1981, her mother was diagnosed with cancer of the esophagus.

A nurse came to the apartment, but her father did his share of nursing too. Eileen would go over after work and find that he'd given her medicine, bathed her, changed her clothes, made her a liquid meal—she could no longer eat solid foods—and tucked her in. He'd moved into her room, and slept in the other twin bed.

The day her mother entered the hospital for good—November 23, 1981—her father mentioned some pains in his chest. They admitted him and found that he had been concealing his own cancer, which had spread throughout his chest cavity, colonizing the organs. They gave him his own room, down the hall from her mother. They rolled them out to see each other once a day.

Her parents had slept in separate rooms for thirty years, but a few days before Christmas, when the doctors rolled her mother away from her father for what would turn out to be the last time, she called to him from down the hall.

"Don't let them take me away from you, Mike, my Mike!" she said, for all on the floor to hear.

What they didn't hear was what she asked Eileen later that night, with the tubes in her.

The curtain was drawn. The lights were off except for the one above her bed. Eileen had filled two cups with ice water, but both were left full and the ice had long ago melted.

"Was it worth it?"

Eileen leaned in to hear her better. "Was what worth it, Ma?"

"I didn't touch a drop for twenty-five years. Did it make a difference?"

She felt an uncomfortable grin forming on her face. She wasn't at all happy, but she couldn't keep this ghoulish smile away. She didn't want to show her mother how much she was hurting. Through the open door, she heard the distant beeps of call buttons and voices in intercoms. She had worked in a hospital for twenty years, but somehow she felt she was in a place she'd never been before. Under the green glow of the fluorescent lamp, her mother looked like a wraith, her skin so thin you could count the veins.

"How can you ask that?"

"I'm asking you." Her mother shifted her head on her pillow with great effort. Her cheeks were two smooth hollows beneath large, alert eyes. "Was it worth it?"

Eileen had thought of the time since her mother had gotten sober as the happiest of both of their lives. There had been a quiet thawing of the glacier in her mother's heart, with occasional louder crackings-off of icebergs of emotions, until, after Connell was born, it had melted so thoroughly that all that remained in an ocean of equanimity were little islands of occasional despond. Her mother appeared almost joyful at times. But perhaps it had been a performance.

"Of course," Eileen said, taking her hand.

"I wish I hadn't stopped." Her mother didn't look at her but gazed at the folds of the curtain, her other hand palm down on the blanket.

"Think of all the things you wouldn't have had. Think of all the lives you touched. We had some great years."

Her mother pulled her hand back, folded it into her other one. "I would have given it all away for a drink."

"Well, you didn't."

"I still would."

Eileen took her hand again and held it with force. "It's too late. You did all that. You can't take it back. You had a great life."

"Fair enough," her mother said, and in a little while she was dead.

Her father died two weeks later. In going through the papers, Eileen learned that he had cashed in the bonds and sold the life insurance policies decades before. Maybe that was how he'd gotten her mother's ring back from the pawnbroker. Or maybe he'd incurred bigger debts than she'd ever suspected. She knew he'd always played the horses, but it had never occurred to her that he'd had an actual gambling problem. If so, he'd been good at keeping the consequences from her. She remembered something she'd witnessed when she was ten, at her friend Nora's apartment after school. Nora opened the door to a man in a dark suit and hat who told her to give her father the message that he should pay what he owed. Eileen was standing behind her. "You kids will pay if he doesn't," the man said, pointing at Nora and herself. "Tell him." Eileen went home frightened, and when she told her father what had happened, he said, "He didn't mean you. He thought you belonged to that girl's father. But you don't. You belong to me." It was impossible to imagine any man having the courage to show up at her father's apartment that way, not when her father counted every Irish policeman in the city as an ally, and many of the non-Irish too. But that didn't mean he wasn't in someone's debt. Maybe that explained why they'd never lived in a house. And maybe it explained why he'd been so adamant that she own one herself. In any case, she had to dip into her savings to pay for her parents' funerals.

The wakes were so close together that she worried few relatives would be able to return for her father's, but those who'd flown in for her mother flew back, and if they hadn't there would still have been standing room only at the parlor.

She was staring at his coffin trying to understand how he could fit into that little box when a black man about her age came over and introduced himself as Nathaniel, the son of Carl Washington, her father's longtime driving partner. Nathaniel asked if she knew how their fathers had come to drive together. With all the stories told about her father over the last couple of days, she was amazed there was one she hadn't heard.

"My father was the first black driver Schaefer ever hired," Nathaniel said. "The first morning my father showed up for work, none of the other drivers were willing to be paired with him. There were rumblings of a walkout. My father wondered if he was going to have to go find another job. Your father walked into the warehouse after the others and took one look at everyone back on their heels with their arms across their chests and said, 'Get in this truck with me, you black son of a bitch.' Then he hopped up in the truck without another word."

She cringed, but Nathaniel was smiling.

"His language could be rough," she said.

"My father heard worse," he said. "Your father wouldn't drive with anyone but my father after that. For twenty years. I don't know if you remember, but he used to hold a Bronx route."

She nodded.

"Once he had my father with him, he insisted on being switched to the Upper East Side."

"I remember when he switched."

" 'There's enough blacks in the Bronx,' he told my father. 'Let them see a black face in that neighborhood for a change.' "

She put a tissue to her eyes and handed him one as well.

"Big Mike this, Big Mike that," Nathaniel said. "Growing up I heard your father's name around the house more than the names of people in my own family."

He waved his wife and children over and she greeted all of them in turn.

She was embarrassed to learn that Mr. Washington had died a few years before. She was even more embarrassed to see in Nathaniel's face, when she said, "I wish I'd known," that he never would have dreamed she'd show up at his father's funeral.

13

n February of 1982, Bronx Community College announced that the dean would be stepping down at the end of the semester. They offered Ed the job and even mentioned the possibility of his becoming president someday. She felt like a chess master who had seen several moves ahead. Taking the deanship would mean the end of Ed's teaching career, but there was no question of his refusing: he would strap the boy and herself to his back and carry them further up the ladder of respectability.

Working at Lawrence had opened her eyes to how people lived on a higher rung of that ladder. She found herself walking or driving around Bronxville after work, to marvel at the manicured shrubbery, the gorgeous houses set back from the street, the shining plate glass windows behind which every table looked set for Christmas dinner. From time to time her car was in the shop and she had to take the Metro-North, but it was almost a pleasure to do so, because the Bronxville station was quaintly beautiful, with no graffiti in sight and the lambent glow of the station house and cars idling amiably as they dropped people off. She waited in the strange serenity of the platform's airy expanse, and when the train came around the bend, it bore the dignity of another era. Drowsing riders slipped past sleepy towns on the way to Grand Central Terminal. She began to dwell on the idea that she could finally begin to really live her life if she came home to an enchanted place like that, but they would need more money to live there. Ed's job offer had come just in time.

She thought she'd made her feelings clear to Ed, and that he'd understood and agreed, but one day he came home and told her he'd turned the deanship down. "The classroom is too important," he said. "I want them getting the education they'd get at elite schools, and I know that, at least in my classroom, that's what they're getting. I can control that much."

This about-face infuriated her—the caprice in it, the self-indulgence. This wasn't the sober man she'd thought she'd married. Sure, he had his arguments: his ambition had never been for fancier titles and fatter paychecks; he was after something unquantifiable, philosophical, the kind of aim never properly rewarded in earthly terms. She grew increasingly impatient with his disquisitions, but she found herself parroting them to her friends, wrapping herself in the chastening rhetoric of sacrifice and duty.

She wanted Ed's idealism to trump her pragmatism, and for a couple of weeks it did, until one night at dinner she said that she was tired of living in their apartment, and that after fifteen years it was time for a change, time, even, to own a house. Ed made his case for the low rent the Orlandos charged and the fact that they were socking away money for Connell's education and avoiding the expenses and headaches of ownership. Another day Eileen would have let herself be appeased, turned the temperature down on the conversation, but now she allowed her anger to boil up at Ed and his unbecoming lack of courage. She felt herself on the verge of screaming one of those unforgettable phrases that could alter the dynamic of a relationship forever, and so she told him to put the boy to bed and slammed the door on her way out the room.

After work the next day, when that regular crowd that were never in a rush to get home to their families went to a bar in the vicinity of the hospital, Eileen for once accepted the invitation to join them. She was determined to stay out until God knew what hour, even with the young boy at home, and do whatever these people did as they watched their numbers dwindle to a determined few, but she was only halfway into her first glass of wine when a memory rose up of one particularly lugubrious episode during the period when her mother went out after work. She reached for her wallet to settle up, but the others wouldn't let her pay. As she drove home, she decided that she couldn't just pretend to Ed that nothing had changed. She felt a timer ticking on the way they were currently arranging their lives. She was getting restless. She had thought they were walking a mutual path toward greater stakes in a shared dream, but the more he insisted on staying in their apartment, the harder it was for her to see him as a fully vested partner in her future. She needed him to be her partner, because she loved him terribly, despite the difficulty of living with him sometimes, and so she was going to save him from himself, and save their marriage if that was what it was coming to, by insisting that they leave. He had always been good at listening to her. As he got older and more fixed in his fears and habits, she had to shout a little louder to be heard, but once he heard her, if he could stomach what she was asking for, he did what she asked. She did what she could do for him as well. He needed a real home no less than she did. His mind had grown smaller as he'd bunkered himself in his ideals. He needed space for his thoughts to breathe. He needed to regroup, to see new possibilities, to think bigger than ever. If there was anything she could help him with, it was thinking big.

She'd almost reached her landing with the basket of folded clothes when she heard the doorbell ring. Ed was teaching his night class. She groaned in frustration and elbowed the door open, hustling to the front stairs to get down there before the bell rang again. The boy had always been a light sleeper, but in the months since he turned five he'd seemed to awaken at the mere suggestion of activity. This constant up and down—two flights to the laundry room, a long flight to answer the door—was driving her crazy.

When she saw Angelo standing there, she wondered if she'd forgotten to slip the rent payment under the door. She found the whole exercise so humiliating every month—stooping in subservience, struggling to slide the envelope past the stubborn insulating lip—that she might unconsciously have followed her desire to forget about it and see how long it would be until they said something.

"Is this a good time to talk?"

"Sure, come in."

She was in a form-fitting sweat suit, which made her a little self-conscious walking up the stairs in front of him. When they got upstairs, she asked him to have a seat at the dining room table, but he chose to stand in the doorway, leaning against the doorjamb, holding the knit cap he'd taken off his head.

"Can I get you some coffee? Water?"

"No, thank you."

She sat.

"I've run into a little financial trouble," Angelo said.

"I'm so sorry," she said, and because she didn't want to hear the details, she began to worry the upholstering on the chairs.

He inhaled deeply, cracked his swollen knuckles. "I don't want to burden you with the whole story. Long story short, I'll have to sell the house."

"All right," she said.

"I wanted to see if you had any interest in it."

Recently, she and Ed had begun to seriously discuss the possibility of buying a house. She'd campaigned to sway him to the virtues of home ownership by appealing to his practical side. Owning would mean an added financial burden, but they'd be building equity instead of flushing rent money, and they had already put enough aside for a down payment. The only things holding them back were his conservatism about expenses and general fear of change. She hadn't been thinking multifamily, but the rental income would offset part of the mortgage, and it struck her that it wasn't going to get any easier to convince Ed to buy a house than telling him she wanted to buy the one they were already in. They wouldn't even have to get a moving truck. This was her best chance to capitalize on his recent softened stance; the longer they waited, the more time he'd have to convince himself that they shouldn't tie their money up in a home. And when he heard that Angelo was in trouble, he would want to help him out.

It didn't hurt that her father, who had promised to haunt her until she and Ed owned a house, would be appeased. She'd been thinking of her father's curse more and more lately. She could make the case that she'd been in a house long before he was dead, and that it was just a matter of signing a few papers to make it officially hers. He would appreciate the neatness of such a solution.

"This is all very sudden," she said.

"I'd sell it to you at a discount," he said. "I'd only ask that you keep my family on at an affordable rent."

"I'll talk to my husband about it."

"Please do," he said. "I'm going to have to move quickly, one way or the other."

Her mind was churning. She didn't like being on an upper floor, especially after Ed's cousin's kid in Broad Channel, playing Superman, had climbed out onto a second-story roof, jumped, and broken an arm and a leg. And she was tired of not having a driveway of her own. She used to consider herself lucky that Angelo allowed her and Ed to park in the driveway at all, but that gratitude had worn off, and now it nettled her to have to walk around the house to get to her door, or to have to ring Angelo's bell when she was blocked in.

"There's one thing I would want," she said.

"You name it."

"I would want to switch apartments. I would want to be on the ground floor."

"It's your house," he said.

"And one other thing."

"What's that?"

"I would ask you to park your car on the street," she said. "I would want the driveway clear for our use."

He seemed to chew on what she'd said. His mouth rose at the corners in a forlorn smile at the concessions his situation—she realized that she didn't care to know the first thing about it, not the first thing—had forced upon him.

"No problem," he said, regaining the momentum he'd briefly lost. "There's plenty of parking around here. Worst case, I walk a block or two."

"And we'd need the garage cleaned out."

"Everything will come out of there."

"And the cedar closets in the basement. You can have the ones we use now."

She thought she heard him whistle. She couldn't tell if he was taken aback or impressed by the bargain she was driving. "All of these details can be arranged," he said. "We can work together on this."

"I just needed to get these things out in the open."

He picked up her keys from the bowl on the mule chest and let them twirl in his fingers. "I got you."

"I'll talk to Ed."

"And you'd keep us on?"

"Yes."

He dropped the keys and straightened up. "At affordable rents?"

"I wouldn't charge an arm and a leg," she said. "You folks are like family now."

"Even if I die?"

"Angelo! My God."

He gave her a look that suggested he saw her not as a woman but as another man. "I'm asking: even if I die?"

"Even if you die. Of course."

"I just want to know my family is taken care of," he said. "I'm not looking to break the bank. I just want to take care of my people." He backed toward the stairs.

"I understand," she said, stepping toward him.

"Why don't we find out how much houses like this are going for, and then you can give me less than that."

"I need to talk to my husband," she said again. "We'd have to qualify for a mortgage."

"Don't worry." He had taken a step downstairs and he turned, smiling fully now, so that he almost appeared mirthful. "People like you, with all your affairs in order—you can have anything you want in this country."

Part II

The

Salad Days

Thursday, October 23, 1986

14

Eileen was understaffed again, so she had to stay late filling out charts and writing notes, and when she went around to dispense a final round of meds in little paper cups, one patient crashed his fist into his mouth in that way stupid people did when trying to look cool taking pills or eating peanuts, and he missed and sent the pill skittering across the linoleum floor. Pharmacy wasn't picking up the phone, and she was out of that medication, so she got down on all fours and searched for it. A quarter of an hour later she found it covered in dust under the far bed. She reached her arm up with it from under the bed in a gesture of mutual victory, but as she crawled out backwards on her hands and knees, she saw that he was staring idiotically at her rear end, which she'd left hovering as she focused on the task at hand. She wanted to cram the pill in his mouth and slam his jaw shut, cracking his teeth, but she wasn't about to let a useless fool like this defeat her poise, so she just placed it back in the little cup. In her chosen profession (in fact she felt it had chosen her, in a kind of malevolent possession) even administrators weren't spared feeling like pieces of meat.

It was almost six thirty when she hit Eastchester Road. The Hutch was moving, thank God, and the Mets were in Boston, so maybe it wouldn't be so bad on the other side of the bridge. The traffic during the playoffs had been a nightmare: mindless, endless, pointless; very nearly proof of the randomness of the universe. Her sciatic nerve was throbbing and her feet were going numb, and she didn't have it in her to sit there inching along.

As she approached the Whitestone and the road sloped up toward the start of the cables, she felt her mood lift. Her time on the bridge was the only part of her commute she didn't mind. She loved the way the cables shot up in a triumphant curve as the first arch neared and then plunged down immediately afterward. Sometimes—it was happening now—the music on the radio matched the rhythm of the bridge. The cables climbed toward the second arch, and she felt herself in the uncanny presence of beauty. Nothing else in her day stirred her to the contemplation of abstract ideas. The bridge was making an argument for its own soundness as she drove over it. High above the East River, the sharp focus of ordinary life gave way to hazy impressions as the eye worked to contain the vastness it beheld. Then the cables rolled into anchor, the landscape resumed a human scale, and that hopeful notion she'd conceived for the evening at the peak of the span began to recede.

At least the traffic was flowing. She'd be home by seven at this rate. She had called at five to say she expected to be quite late and to ask Lena to feed Connell, and then she'd called again before she left and said not to feed him. Lena had assured her it was no trouble, and Eileen had heard the touch of sharpness in her own voice when she'd said she wanted to have dinner with the boy herself. She had put chicken in the fridge to defrost it, and if she didn't cook it, it was going to go bad.

That morning, she'd decided that they were going to have a family meal, even though Ed wouldn't be there with them. If he was forcing her to compromise on her ideal of family time by continuing to teach these night classes, then a compromise was all she could stand anymore, not the complete capitulation she'd made lately on nights he taught, when she let Lena feed the boy and took a restless bubble bath before she went up to get him. She and Connell were enough to make up a family; in fact, they were plenty. In some families, mother and child was all there was. She didn't need Ed to be happy.

She was angry at Ed for the class that met two nights a week, and she was angry at him for staying late another night to attend to his research. If he was going to be away this much, at least he could be making good money doing it. His turning down the job at Merck still bothered her, and the fact that he'd spent these years taking on extra instruction only served to make him seem more irresponsible somehow.

At the exit for Northern off the Whitestone Expressway, she took pleasure in seeing Shea Stadium empty. Soon enough—it couldn't come soon enough—this endless season would be over. At 114th Street, she headed over to Thirty-Fourth Avenue, because she didn't like driving through Corona on Northern. It depressed her to live next to a neighborhood that run-down, though things closer to her end of town weren't all that great lately either. Some of the reliable old stores were becoming junk shops, and the number of signs with Spanish in them was on the rise.

She wasn't looking forward to fetching Connell from the Orlandos. It used to be, when he was in kindergarten or first grade, he'd come running when she appeared at the back door, but lately she'd had to fight to get him out of there. They always had the television going, that was part of it, and the place was comfortable in a way that appealed to a kid, with knick-knacks everywhere and interesting clutter. Brenda's four-year old daughter, Sharon, was usually there. The number of Orlandos present never seemed to dip below three. It reminded her of her apartment during the happy period in her teens when a new wave of relatives came over from Ireland. There were differences, of course: the Orlandos were louder, more physical, certainly more affectionate. She'd dealt with smoke as a kid, but there were more smokers in the Orlando house; everyone but Sharon seemed to have lit up at some point in Eileen's presence. She suspected that whatever fun Connell had up there paled in comparison to the afternoons she'd enjoyed with all her cousins around, but he didn't know the difference. Or maybe it was like when she went up to the Schmidts' apartment to watch television as a girl. She always felt she was escaping the reality of her life. Was that how Connell felt? If so, he had no reason to. She and Ed provided a calmer home than she'd ever had. Still, these days he never wanted to come down. She had to admit that for the first few minutes after they got downstairs, until she put the kitchen radio on and started cooking, her house felt empty by comparison.

She parked and went inside, took her shoes off, and changed quickly out of her stockings. She put her slippers on and went up the back stairs. Lena answered the door in a smock and said, "Come in, come in," with the carefree informality of a woman perfectly comfortable in her own home. Behind her, Angelo sat at the table in the dining room that had once been Eileen's own, smoking a cigarette and flipping through the *Post*. He still had his Sanitation Department shirt on, unbuttoned and untucked, with an undershirt beneath it. His hands were thick, and his fingers were stained from cigarettes, but there was an elegance in the way his hair was cropped and the longer strands on top were slicked back. He gave her a warm smile and welcomed her with a small gesture of the hand. The only books in the house were a few dusty volumes in the glass case behind him, and he hadn't finished high school, but still he gave the impression he could summon up reliable answers to almost any question put to him. She watched him luxuriously turn the pages of the newspaper, licking his finger and sliding his hand behind the page to flip it as though it were a leaf in an illuminated manuscript. Since Consolata's death a few months back, he was less quick to yell, and he sat at the table and talked to Connell more, which the boy delighted in. The family was still paying the rent for Consolata's apartment, presumably out of whatever small inheritance she'd left them. Lena and Angelo were planning on moving upstairs with Gary, to give Donny, Brenda, and Sharon room to breathe. The kids were grown, but it was evident they wouldn't be striking off on their own anytime soon.

Gary and Brenda were on the couch, Sharon between them, resting her head on her mother's lap while her uncle held her feet. Donny was in the easy chair. Connell had the smaller couch to himself. They were watching *Jeopardy*. Connell barely looked up when Eileen walked in. Donny waved; Gary looked embarrassed to be noticed. He was wearing corduroy pants and a T-shirt that was too tight in the gut. He wasn't fat so much as the shirt was a shrunken relic of his youth.

The question at hand was about which president served the shortest term in office, thirty-two days. Eileen couldn't remember the name.

"Harrison," Gary called out, just before the contestant buzzed in with "William Henry Harrison." Connell said "Yes!" with gusto and Donny grinned proudly at his older brother. The next question in the category asked for the name of the man who shot James Garfield at the Baltimore and Potomac Railroad Station.

"Charles Guiteau," Gary said quietly, and a moment later the contestant did too.

It was easier for her when Gary stayed in his room. She didn't like to think about him. He was the oldest of the siblings, but he'd never held down a job. He had an air of resignation about him, as if he'd already given up on life. At the same time, he had a good deal of intellectual ability. She didn't like to acknowledge that people with real ability might not arrive at comfortable stations in life. Her cousin Pat had been a bad enough disappointment; she didn't want to consider the possibility that Connell might fall through the cracks like Gary. She certainly didn't like to think that something similar had happened to her too, on a smaller scale. She had achieved professional status, but her existence wasn't ideal, and hard as she tried to hack her way through the thicket of middle-class living, she couldn't find a way out to the clearing. It would have been easier to see Gary as a savant with an overdeveloped capacity to absorb trivia, but the truth was he was a complex, intelligent individual. She'd heard him discussing issues of the day and couldn't help agreeing with him, even being enlightened by observations she couldn't have made herself. And yet there he was, living in the margins, talking to a television, dying half an hour at a time. A claustrophobic sensation swept over her. She needed to forget that people like Gary existed, to forget even the possibility of failure. She needed to spirit her son away or Gary would suck him into the black hole of his life.

Connell rose and slapped Donny five across the coffee table. Then he looked up at her.

"It's time to go," she said. "I'm making dinner."

"Can I come down when it's ready?"

"*No,*" she said sharply, then collected herself. "You're coming down now. They've had enough of you up here. Let the Orlandos have their evening in peace."

"He's no bother," Angelo said over his newspaper. "He can stay as long as he wants."

"Thank you, but he's going to help me get dinner ready." She hadn't had any intention to ask Connell for help, but she needed a good excuse.

"We were discussing politics before," Angelo said. "He said you wanted him to be a politician. I asked him if he knew what a politician was."

Eileen offered up a little embarrassed laugh. "What I mostly want is for him to get downstairs right now," she said, loud enough for Connell to hear.

She said her good-byes and walked to the door. Connell lagged behind, standing and watching the show. Gary got another question right, and Donny and Connell broke into hysterics.

"*Connell*," she said. "Come *on*."

He took his time getting his schoolbag and followed her down the stairs. She got him set up chopping lettuce while she grilled the chicken. She was going to make salad for dinner, with the chicken spread over it. She'd given in to pizza too often recently, and the nights Ed cooked it was grilled cheese in a lagoon of butter, or cheeseburgers, anything with cheese. The boy was too chubby for her liking. It was true that he hadn't hit a big growth spurt yet, but it was also true that the tendency toward physical largeness on her family's side could edge into overweight if it wasn't watched scrupulously. In the absence of worldly cares, Connell stuffed his face with candy and ice cream. She hadn't had time to get fat as a kid. When she was only a few months older than he was now, she was planning meals, shopping, keeping the house—things she couldn't imagine him doing. When she sent him to the store, she had to write a list, and he still inevitably forgot something on it.

She was going to start mapping some order onto his life. Ed wasn't a big help in that area. He loved the boy so much, was so permissive, seemed delighted by everything he did. Connell brought home a ninety-five and Ed beamed; she was always the one forced to ask where the other five points went. She resented the way Connell walked around oblivious of how carefree his existence was, how little responsibility he had.

She put some cherry tomatoes in the salad and cooked the chicken quickly in the pan. She grabbed some dressing, tossed it all together, and told him to sit down. She served him salad and put the chicken over it.

"This is dinner?" he said.

"You need to eat more leafy greens. *Some* leafy greens."

It was seven thirty. Ed was just half an hour into his class, with an hour to go. She spent a few moments of pique in wondering if she and Connell were crossing his mind at all. Connell was eating too fast, as usual. He

didn't even like salad, and yet he was rushing to eat it. There was something irrepressible in the way he ate. Maybe he was trying to speed through
dinner so he could get to dessert. He knew the rules: no dessert until his
plate was clean. It had been a couple of years since she'd had to stage one
of those nightlong sit-ins to get him to eat his meal. She'd figured out what
to avoid, and he'd stopped trying to slip it in the garbage when she wasn't
looking and just ate what he was served. Dessert held that power over him.
She always kept something in the house, for herself as much as for him, but
she took only a little portion, nothing like the heaps he wolfed down. He
was going to have to learn restraint if he ever wanted to make a success of
himself among serious people. It was unseemly to behave with that kind
of abandon. She told him to slow down and he nodded at her and kept on
eating at his pace. "Slow *down*," she said, annoyed. "You're going to choke."
She got up to refill her water glass. She stood at the sink drinking it and
filled it again. When she turned around she saw him waving his arms, his
fork on his plate, and then she saw him leap to his feet, his hands on his
throat. She told him it wasn't funny, and then she saw his face and began
screaming, "Are you choking?" but she already knew he was. It had happened a few times when he was a toddler, but it had always been a mere
scare, some dense foodstuff, tuna fish or peanut butter, compacted in his
esophagus, and he'd been able to breathe through it, but now he wasn't
making a sound. It was time to grab him coolly and dislodge the food with
one fist to his abdomen and the other shoving up, but she couldn't do it.

She'd dealt with choking a number of times in her career. You got your
hands in the midsection and gave the diaphragm a healthy shove and out
the food popped. A couple of seconds and it was over. You had more time
than people thought, a lot more, four full minutes until brain damage set
in. But this was her son and she had no room for error.

She had him by the shoulders. She began to panic. She knew she
shouldn't panic, but she couldn't help herself; she loved the boy so much.
She was thinking *Please don't die, please don't die* and she started screaming
for help, and then she was shoving him out the door and pulling him toward the back stairs. She got to the stairwell and screamed, "Angelo! Angelo!
Angelo!" and ran upstairs and banged on the door and screamed, "Come

down!" and then she ran back down, because she had left the boy alone. Her hands were shaking. "He's choking!" she screamed. Connell was turning blue. She heard someone flying down the stairs, and then Donny was shoving her aside, and then he was standing behind Connell, giving him a muscular approximation of the Heimlich, and then something flew out of Connell's mouth onto the carpet. He started coughing and wailing a terrified wail that sounded more like a cat's than a child's. It was a cherry tomato. He must have swallowed it whole. She picked it up and crushed it angrily in her hand. She sat him at the dining room table. Angelo, Gary, and Brenda came in. Connell kept coughing, though the wailing subsided. She went to get him a glass of water. In the kitchen she saw the plates and slammed them into the trash with their contents. She could feel the feelings rising up, getting ready to wash over her, take her over. He took the water down quickly. She would never get angry at him for eating fast again. It was Ed she was angry at, for not being there, for exposing Connell to this danger by his absence. She was grateful the Orlandos were reliably present in the evenings, and mortified that she, a nurse, hadn't been able to save him herself.

"Are you going to slow down now?" was all she could think to say when she went back to the dining room. Then she burst into tears. Connell seemed too dazed to cry.

"If you'd been Gary," Donny said, "I would have let you choke. What do they call that, Gary? Euthanasia?"

Connell gave a little chuckle through his coughs.

"Don't you do that again," Angelo said. "I don't need another heart attack. Two is plenty."

"You good?" Brenda asked, putting her hand on Connell's shoulder. He nodded. "Slow down. Your food's not going anywhere."

"Well, my work here is done," Donny said. "I better go find a phone booth to change in."

"Why don't you go pick up your dirty drawers from the bathroom floor instead," Brenda said. "I don't think the hamper's made of kryptonite."

The laughs were welcome, but she could see that Donny had been affected by the brush with disaster. He was wide-eyed and shaking his head. The whole Orlando family seemed unnerved. Connell spent the afternoons up there, but it had never occurred to Eileen that they might in some way have thought of him as being part of their family too.

"*Wheel of Fortune* is on," Gary said. They made their way up the stairs. She sat at the table with Connell.

"Are you okay?"

He nodded.

"Shaken up?"

He nodded again. "I couldn't breathe," he said.

"I know."

"I couldn't talk."

He couldn't know how hard on her he was making this.

"Horrible," she said. "I froze up."

"Donny saved me."

"I don't know what happened. I've done it before. I guess it never meant as much to me."

"Thank God they were here," he said.

"I would have done it eventually," she said. "My training would have kicked in. I think because I knew they were here, I didn't have to go into lifesaving mode."

"He saved my life," the boy said thoughtfully.

"Let's not go overboard," she said. "You were going to be fine. We had time."

He looked like he was in shock. She went to the freezer and scooped some ice cream into a bowl for him.

"Here, have this," she said. "I don't think you can choke on this. Maybe you'll find a way."

Ordinarily at this time of night she would have made him sit down with his homework, but she didn't say anything about it. At the moment she didn't care if he never did his homework again. Maybe this was how Ed felt all the time.

She told him he could take the ice cream to the couch—another first— and she went to get the television for him. The only set in the house was the little black-and-white one in their bedroom. They had been wheeling it out to the living room during the playoffs and the World Series. She cleaned up the pan from the chicken while he watched *Entertainment Tonight,* and joined him when she was done. The games usually started at eight, or before eight, but when he got up to change the channel to NBC, *The Cosby Show* was on. It took only a moment to understand that preempting *The Cosby Show* would have cost the network ad revenue. They lay on separate couches. It wasn't easy to see the set from that far away. The girl, Vanessa, was trying to wear makeup to school, against her mother's wishes. The boy, Theo, was attempting to organize his family to do a fire drill. It could have been *Leave It to Beaver,* except that everyone was black. The world was changing fast. It was hard to fit her son's America into her memory of how the world had been ordered when she was a child. She felt like a member of an in-between generation, straddling sides in a clash of history. Her life was as remote and ancient to Connell as the stories of the pilgrim settlers had been to her when she was his age.

The Cosby Show ended and the game was about to come on. She told him she was going to the bedroom to lie down, and he gave her a stricken look.

"You're not watching the game?"

She could tell he was disturbed by what had happened to him, that he didn't want to be alone. "I'll watch for a little while," she said, relenting.

She didn't blame him. Over and over she had been reliving in her mind the moment when she'd watched Donny pop the tomato out. She wanted to sit next to Connell, to hold him close to her, but she had no idea how to do it. She had no interest in watching another of these games she'd had to sit through so many of in the run-up to the playoffs, so after a few minutes she rose to get *Lonesome Dove.* She flipped through it distractedly, reading and rereading the same page several times. The Mets fell behind early, and by the end of the fifth inning they were down 4–0.

She knew she wasn't the softest mother in the world. She worked a lot. She worked, period. Other mothers stayed home, baked cookies, talked to their kids all the time, knew everything their kids were thinking. It had never occurred to her to try to be Connell's friend. She did her best to encourage meaningful conversations at dinner, the three of them talking as a family, and not only because it would be constructive in lubricating Connell's future advancement among people who judged a person by how he spoke, but also because she liked to hear what he was thinking. She had worked hard to give him a comfortable life. That was as valuable as providing emotional sustenance. Life wasn't only about expressing feelings and giving hugs. Still, she couldn't figure out how to break through the defenses her son had put up, and it bothered her, an intellectual problem as much as an emotional one.

She placed her bookmark in the page and held the book in her hands. "I'm thinking of turning in," she said.

"Can you stay here and read?"

So, he needed her there. He couldn't say it in so many words, but he had more or less admitted it. She opened her book again and started in on the first page of the chapter she'd been reading.

Ed walked in before ten. They heard the door, and then they heard him hanging his coat in the vestibule, and then they heard him dropping his briefcase on his desk in the study before he came into the living room.

"Still four–nothing?" he asked when he walked in.

Connell nodded. "Gooden got smacked around."

"They were saying on the radio his velocity is down."

"El Sid has been great in relief. But the bats are ice cold."

"Something happened," she said, interjecting. "Connell choked."

"What?" Ed turned to her, then back to him. "What happened, buddy?"

"I was trying to concentrate on not choking, and then the next thing I knew I was choking."

He looked at her. "*Really* choking?"

"It was in his windpipe."

"What was?"

"A cherry tomato."

"You got it out?"

"Donny did."

He pointed upstairs. "You ate with the Orlandos?"

"Donny came down," Connell said.

"To eat with us?"

Her blood ran cold at the thought of discussing the particulars around the boy, who would see on her face how unsettled she still was.

"I'll explain later," she said.

"Come here," Ed said, and he sat on the couch and put his arm around Connell, who leaned into the lapel of his father's tweed jacket. It was so easy for Ed to connect to him. She always had to be the scold. Maybe Connell had hardened his heart to her. He leaned in further, so that his chubby belly pressed against the waistband of his sweatpants. He had his face in Ed's flannel shirt and started sobbing. Ed kissed the top of his head and rubbed his back. Connell kept his face buried there for some minutes. Ed was looking to her for a mimed narrative of what had happened, but she kept waving him off. After a while, Connell lifted his head.

"Will you do what your mother has asked you to do a few times now, if I'm not mistaken," Ed said in a firm but gentle voice, "and try to slow down when you eat? Can you do that for me?"

Connell nodded.

"Good."

And then, without another word, they had transitioned out of that conversation and were watching the game. She stopped reading *Lonesome Dove* and directed her attention to them. It was something to behold, Ed's physical comfort with the boy, who had his leg draped over his father's. She'd been affectionate with Connell when he was very young, up until he was about three, but then something had interceded to make it subtly harder for her to connect to him. She knew Ed could do it, so she'd never spent much time worrying about the boy being deprived, but now she had the sensation that she was on the other side of something important. She wasn't angry so much as hurt and darkly fascinated.

The Mets scored a run in the top of the eighth inning, and then, in the ninth, after Ray Knight grounded out and Kevin Mitchell popped out—she'd sat through so many playoff games of late that she knew the players' names by now—Mookie Wilson doubled, and then Rafael Santana singled him in. Ed said this team had a knack for getting two-out hits. Lenny Dykstra came to the plate as the tying run, but a few pitches later he struck out swinging and the game was over. The Mets were down three games to two in the World Series. Another loss and their season, which seemed to have united New York for a while and which even someone like her, who paid little attention, knew had been an extraordinary success, would be over.

"Complete game for Hurst," Ed said. "Impressive."

"They couldn't get to him," Connell said.

Ed rose and shut the volume off but left the screen on, and they watched the Red Sox players celebrate as the credits rolled and the news came on. Then he shut the television off and pulled the plug on it to prepare to roll it back into the bedroom.

"Clemens is up next," Connell said, foreboding in his voice.

"Yes, but they're in New York."

"They have to win two."

"They'll do it."

"It's Roger Clemens."

"What did Tug McGraw say?" Ed asked Socratically.

" 'Ya gotta believe,' " Connell answered.

"Well, then."

It was after eleven thirty, much later than Connell's bedtime. They said quick good nights and the boy headed off. Ed wheeled the television in front of him as if he was piloting a projector cart. She got into bed, and Ed came in a few minutes later, after he'd tucked Connell in. She told him the story of how the boy had choked and how she'd responded to it, or failed to respond, and Ed nodded and said it was over now and everything was fine, and it calmed her to hear it; Ed was good at putting her at ease. He gave her a kiss and she rolled over and lay thinking about what had transpired, with a clarity of thought the clamorous broadcast hadn't allowed. Why had she frozen? As Connell had stood there not even gasping for air, but silently motioning toward his throat, a feeling for him more intense than love and more mysterious had risen up from the depths of her mind. She felt that he was part of her own flesh again, as he'd been once, and that she was on the brink of dying along with him. Nothing would be the same if he died. She would go on, but her life would lose its meaning and purpose. This kid who annoyed and infuriated her so often was walking around with her fate in his hands. She didn't trust him with it. She felt fragile, exposed. She was going to make him be more careful going forward.

At one thirty in the morning, she was awakened by Connell nudging her, asking if he could come into the bed. She was too sleepy to object. She moved aside and let him slide into the space between them. She couldn't remember the last time he was in bed with them. She had policed that boundary well when he was younger, not wanting to become one of those couples whose marriages were held hostage by a child in the bed every night. Forget about sex: she just wanted to get a good night's sleep. Eventually Connell had stopped trying to join them.

She began to groggily recall the events of earlier, and it made sense that he was there. She could hear him nudging Ed awake, the two of them talking.

"I almost died," Connell said.

"You're fine," Ed said.

"I was scared. I'm still scared."

Ed rolled over. "You are completely fine. You're safe. You have a long life ahead of you. A long life."

"I didn't want to die," Connell said.

"Well, now you have to remember that feeling. Go out there and make the most of life."

"You really think they're going to win?"

"The Mets? Yes."

"Both games?"

"Both. You'll see."

"You're sure?"

"Have faith," Ed said. "They'll pull it out. Now go to sleep."

As she listened to them talk, she was taken back to the row of beds she slept in when Mr. Kehoe was still living in the other room. She had no memory of any conversations taking place among the three of them once the lights were out. Both her parents faced away from her. She remembered wondering what it would have been like for the two of them to sleep in the same bed. Now she wondered whether she'd have had the nerve to crawl between them and feel their heat radiating on either side of her. Maybe if they'd slept in the same bed, she would have grown up as the kind of girl who had that nerve. Maybe your imagination stopped at the boundaries that contained it. She had taken comfort in the placement of her bed between theirs. Maybe you took what you could get. She could have reached out and touched their backs. That had been enough for her. It wouldn't be enough for her son. She was glad, on this night when she hadn't been able to save him herself, to have one bed they slept in and to be able to give him this opportunity. She hadn't had it as a girl, but that didn't mean he shouldn't have it. She wondered if he'd lost some of his trust in her tonight. So much of life was the peeling away of illusions. Maybe she'd only hurried that along. Maybe that wasn't the worst thing. He was going to have to fend for himself at some point.

She felt Connell roll away from Ed and nuzzle up to her in a way that she hadn't anticipated him doing. His forehead was pressed against the top of her back. Within a minute, he was asleep. She couldn't move without waking him, but she also couldn't sleep without moving him. She decided to wait. She felt oddly touched having him there. Still, it was going to be a long night, and she'd be exhausted in the morning, so she'd eventually have to move him off her.

She lay there thinking, *I almost lost him. I'm never serving goddamned cherry tomatoes again. Ed better be right about the Mets, or this kid is going to be more disappointed in his father than he is in the Mets. Then again, he has to learn that things don't always work out the way you want them to.*

She went back and forth between thinking it would be nice if Connell got the outcome he wanted and thinking it would be character-building for him not to get it. Fatigue from a long day at work and the effects of adrenaline withdrawal must have been enough to overcome her need for space, because she felt herself drifting off, even though he was still attached to her.

The kid would be thrilled, she thought. *Let them win.*

The next thing she knew she was waking up. Somehow in the night she had gotten herself to face the boy, who was still sleeping, and Ed behind him on his back, out cold. Connell breathed in and out softly. His lashes were long like his father's, and in the muted sunlight peeking through the blinds his cheeks looked sweet and full. As if he could sense her looking at him, he opened his eyes and blinked a few times in that half-conscious, slightly perturbed way he used to as a toddler when he hadn't yet fully come to. He gave her a slumber-drunk smile; then he was back asleep. She didn't know what to do with everything she was feeling for him, even for her husband, so she got up to take a shower and left the two of them to wake up and find each other there.

Part III

Breathe

the Rich Air

1991

15

After Connell turned in, Ed surprised her by not moving to the study to grade lab reports or read journal articles. He lay on the couch with the newspaper listening to Wagner. She didn't have to know music to recognize that it was Wagner, because the swelling crescendos and singer's deep voice gave it away. Ed often listened to Wagner when he was in a contemplative mood.

She sat on the other couch with her book, happy to share with him the beaten-back chill of a February night, which made itself known in the frost on the windows. She switched the light on in the artificial fireplace, pausing briefly to rattle the glass coals and hear them clack against each other. It pleased her that the man she'd married, in addition to possessing an erudition that impressed even worldly friends, read the sports section in its entirety. At one point he rose and went to the study, and she thought she'd lost him for the night, but he returned with a pen to do the crossword. She loved the carefree way he called on her for help when flummoxed by a clue. It suggested an abiding faith in the soundness of his intellect that he could meet head-on those swells of ignorance that might capsize another man's confidence; they were wavelets lapping against his hull.

"I've done everything I can do," he said, as he lay the quarter-folded newspaper on the coffee table. "I want to be realistic. Maybe it's time for me to relax."

She glanced up from her book to catch his eye, but he was looking at the ceiling.

"I'm not sure what you mean," she said.

"I'm turning fifty soon. I'm slowing down. I've earned a rest."

"Nonsense," she said.

"I'm going to become one of those guys who come home and call it a night. Maybe I'll watch some TV."

"I'll believe that when I see it."

"I can start right now."

Her heart leapt a little. It was pleasant to imagine him spending more time in their bed. He had finally given up the night classes, thank God, but he still worked so hard, often coming in from the study long after she was asleep.

"I don't know how long you could keep that up," she said. "You'd get bored."

"I'll be fine."

"Well, if it makes you happy," she said.

He'd already moved to the stereo to change the record. He plugged his headphones in and had them on before she could hear what he was listening to. He lay back down and closed his eyes.

She waited for him to acknowledge her gaze. He liked to lie like that and slip into a reverie, but he usually opened his eyes between movements to give her a little review with his raised brows. She wondered if he were sleeping, he was lying so still, but then he began tapping his foot rhythmically. When the side ended, he lay there, arms crossed across his chest, impassive. She shut off her light and stood to head into the bedroom. She called his name, but he didn't reply. She watched for some kind of acknowledgment of her departure, but he only shifted his glasses. She went to him and stood over him. He must have imagined he could outlast her in this game, but she was starting to grow disturbed by it. She leaned in to kiss his cheek good night; before she reached it he had opened his eyes and was staring back at her in a kind of horror, as if she'd interrupted him in a reflection on something monstrous.

"I'm heading to bed," she said.

"I'll be right in."

After a few bouts of fitful sleep—she never slept well without him beside her—she headed to the living room. She found the end table lamp on and Ed still wearing the headphones. A record was spinning, and he'd set up a stack to be played by the autochanger. She shut the stereo off and called his name. He put a hand up to silence her.

"I'm just going to lie here a minute," he said.

"It's four in the morning." She switched off the lamp, but ambient light still filtered into the room from the coming sun. "You need good, quality sleep. You're always saying that. Don't lights interrupt sleep? You need REM sleep. *Restful* sleep. Come on inside. You have to teach in a few hours."

"I think I'm going to cancel class," he said. "I'm not feeling it."

"Huh?"

He hadn't missed a class in twenty years. They'd had fights about it. *You can miss a single class*, she would say when something came up. *They can't fire you for it. They can't fire you, period.*

"I think I've earned a day off," he said.

"Well, either way, just come to bed. It's late."

She stood over him until he got up. They shuffled down the hall together. In the morning when she woke he was sitting at the foot of the bed.

"Maybe you'd better call for me," he said.

After she'd made the call, she showered and dressed. When she headed to the kitchen, she saw him lying on the couch again, as if he hadn't moved from the night before, the only difference being the cup of tea on the table.

"You're taking this whole 'taking it easy' thing pretty seriously," she said.

"I'm just gathering my energy," he said. "I'll be all right tomorrow. I'll go in tomorrow."

He let himself be kissed good-bye. She went to work. When she returned she was surprised to find him in the same spot, wearing the same clothes. She hadn't really believed he'd stay home all day; it was unlike him. His record of never missing work was a matter of somber pride. Connell's bag and jacket were slung over a chair in the dining room.

Ed's eyes were closed. His feet beat the time. She stood over him, tapped him on the shoulder. As she spoke, he motioned to the headphones to indicate he couldn't hear her. She mimed pulling them off her ears.

"I'm listening to music," he said.

"Plainly."

"How was work?"

"Work was fine," she said. "Did you stay there all day?"

"I got up to eat."

"So this is the new thing?"

"I'm trying it out. I'm feeling enormously refreshed."

"I'm glad to hear that," she said.

"I've been meaning to spend more time attending to my needs," he said. "This is step one. I've had a cloudy head for a while. I'm trying to get back to basics."

"What about work?"

"I'm going to need you to call in again for me tomorrow."

In the big mirror in the other room she saw herself in the coat she'd been meaning to replace. She had once thought of thirty as a terribly old age, but now she was turning fifty at the end of the year, and thirty seemed impossibly young.

"How long do you plan to do this?"

"I hadn't formulated a plan."

"Shall I expect you to eat with us tonight?"

"Of course," he said, waving her off and putting the headphones back on.

As she began to prepare dinner, she reflected on what this thing could be. It was clearly some kind of midlife crisis. Something was spooking him: getting old, probably. She was confident it wasn't another woman. They were coconspirators in a mission of normalcy. A stronger deterrent to infidelity even than love was the desire to maintain a stable household, a stress-free life. She knew he was reliable, and not only because he wasn't going to miss work to sleep off a drunk, or gamble his paycheck at the track, or forget their anniversary. He was, in a subtler way, reliably knowable. Some women yearned for a hint of mystery about their men; she loved Ed's lack of mystery. It had shade, depth, texture; it was just complex enough. His heart contained too little passion for him to attempt a grand affair, and too much for him to endure a scurrilous one. He was too preoccupied with his work to love two women at once; he lacked that tolerance for superficial interaction every successful adulterer wielded.

A few days later he returned to work, but the headphones ritual persisted in the evenings. One night he returned to his study, and she felt relieved. She assumed he was grading lab reports, but when she went in to bring him a plate of cookies she found him writing in a notebook, which he took pains to block from her view. When she went back later that night to look for it, it was gone.

Their dinners began to feel strange to her. Ed looked away when she tried to meet his gaze, and he never wanted to talk about his work—or about anything, really, but Connell's day and the happenings at school.

"And then," Connell said, "they lifted him up to grab the rim, but they didn't give him the ball to dunk. Somebody pulled his shorts down. And then they pulled his underwear down! He just hung up there until Mr. Cotswald ran over and got him."

"Ha!"

Ed laughed with just a bit too much gusto. She'd expected him to condemn the boys' behavior. It was as if he hadn't really absorbed what Connell had said. Something in the warmth in his voice, the distraction that flickered in his eyes, made her wonder if she'd been too hasty in ruling out an affair. A listlessness had come over him lately that seemed at times like a species of dreaminess.

"Well." Ed pushed back his chair. He gave Connell a perfunctory pat on the head and retired to the couch and the privacy of his headphones. Connell looked embarrassed, as if he'd extended a hand for a shake and been rebuffed. She knew enough not to compound it by speaking to him.

She went to bed feeling frowsy. She squeezed the deposits of fat at her hips and wondered how they had managed to sneak up on her. She knew the doctors at work still turned to look at her in the halls, but if Ed didn't see her that way, then the interest of other men felt less a vote of confidence than a shabby habit that in its mindless lack of differentiation—she saw the way they looked at so many of the girls—called into question whether she had ever been beautiful at all.

Ed came in after midnight. He stood over her, gazing oddly. She could feel herself stiffen.

"Anything you want to tell me?"

"Not really," he said.

"What are you listening to, anyway?"

"Wagner's *Ring Cycle*. I have so many records I haven't even cracked the plastic on. It makes me anxious to see them all sitting there. I'm working my way through them."

She was surprised by how relieved she felt to hear this. It was sufficiently particular to actually be plausible. It was the kind of thing she imagined people did when they came to a point where the roads to the past and the future were equally muddy—retreat to the high ground of a major project.

She had long measured a meal's success by the range of colors arrayed on the plate, but it felt hopelessly middle-class now to conceive of food in this fashion, and she looked askance at orange carrots, bright green beans, white mashed potatoes, the dark pile of meat and onions, picking at it with her fork in the way she resented in her child.

She used to love to sit at her kitchen table and watch the drapes kick up in the wind, to look through the window across the little divide and see the Palumbos gathered in their dining room, but now the house next door felt far too close. She hated its plain brick face and the shabby décor visible within. She had long tolerated this vulgarity because she felt privileged to have a house at all, but now she found it too disappointing to bear.

Lately she couldn't stop thinking about Bronxville. When she'd left Lawrence in 1983 for the nursing director job at St. John's Episcopal in Far Rockaway, she'd missed going to Bronxville every day. When she returned to Einstein a couple of years later to be head of nursing, she'd begun to think the timing might finally be right to move to Bronxville. The commute would be shorter for both of them, she was making good money now, Ed had gotten into a decent pay class himself, and they'd made a few good investments. They had put eight thousand dollars into oil shale stock on the advice of one of Ed's colleagues, a geologist at NYU, and it had climbed to forty-four thousand. But then in '85 the shale oil company went bankrupt. That year, they also lost twenty grand on a penny stock scam with First Jersey Securities. The final nail came in 1987, when her boss left for a government appointment, and the new head of the hospital fired those he could and appointed his own leadership team. Though she landed on her feet at North Central Bronx, she had to take a pay cut to do so.

She couldn't look across at the Palumbos' just then, with their dreadful chandelier glowing like margarine and the two of them looking all their years as they sat down to a cheerless meal, so she got up to close the drapes. Ed took her rising as a cue that the meal was over and headed for the couch.

When she and Ed moved in, the neighborhood was Irish, Italian, Greek, and Jewish, and they knew everyone on the block. Then families started to trickle out, and in their place came Colombians, Bolivians, Nicaraguans, Filipinos, Koreans, Chinese, Indians, Pakistanis. Connell played with the new kids, but she never met the parents. When an Iranian family—they called themselves Persian, but she couldn't bring herself to refer to them as anything but Iranian—bought her friend Irene's place up the block after she moved to Garden City, the son, Farshid, became a classmate of Connell's at St. Joan of Arc and started hanging around the house.

It wasn't hard to feel the pull of the suburbs, because the neighborhood was half suburb already, arranged around mass transit but also around car travel. There were driveways next to every house, and gas stations and car dealerships at regular intervals along Northern Boulevard. LaGuardia Airport was a short drive away, and Robert Moses's highways, and the massive parking lots at Shea, and the husk of the World's Fair, which had left detritus like a glacier.

Most of the stores she loved were gone, replaced by trinket shops, T-shirt shops, fireworks black marketeers, exotic hair salons hidden behind heavy curtains, over-the-counter purveyors of deadly martial arts paraphernalia, comic book stores, karate schools, check-cashing places, Korean-run Optimo-branded cigar and candy stores that sold cheap knockoffs of popular Japanese toys, taxi depots, sketchy bars, fast food, wholesalers of obscure cuisines, restaurants suggestive of opium dens, bodegas stocked with products she would never consider eating. The Boulevard Theatre on the corner was now a Latin dance hall with neon lights flickering late into the night and an insistent beat that hectored the remaining old guard to leave. Cars piled up outside it and the cops were always breaking up fights. The gloomy little Irish bar was the last stand against the invasion, but she couldn't take some specious pride in it now after avoiding it all these years.

The memory of wealth haunted the nearby garden apartment buildings. She imagined gaunt bachelors presiding over dwindling fortunes, long lines coming to a silent end. There were remnants of the way it had been, like Barricini's Chocolates and Jahn's, but stepping into them only reminded her how few of the old places were left.

She knew it was possible to see the changes as part of what made the city great, an image of what was to come, the necessary cycle of immigration, but only if you weren't the one being displaced. Maybe even then you could, if you were a saint. She had no desire to be a saint, not if it meant she'd have to blunt the edge of her anger at these people. It certainly wasn't saintliness that led her to attempt to get past her resentment at the break-in that occurred a couple of years back, while they were on a cruise in the Bahamas. Rather, it was a desire to continue living in the neighborhood without boiling over into outright vitriol whenever she stepped into the grocery store, where anyone she laid eyes on, worker or customer, unless they looked respectable, could have been one of the offenders. She had returned from that cruise to find her jewelry box rifled through and her drawers turned inside out. Luckily, she'd long ago overridden Ed and spent the money to rent a safe deposit box at Manufacturers Hanover, where she stored Ed's LeCoultre watch and her mother's embattled engagement ring. All the bonds were in the box as well. She took a certain satisfaction in thinking of how little the thieves had made off with; for once it seemed an advantage that Ed had never been the sort to buy necklaces and bracelets for her birthday or their anniversary. The degenerates had pinched Ed's stereo, that was true, but he'd needed a new one for years, and this was an excuse for her to buy one for him. She was angry too at the Orlandos, who'd been home at the time. She couldn't imagine how they hadn't heard anything, or done anything if they'd heard. What kept her awake some nights, though, fantasizing about revenge, was the fact that they'd taken Mr. Kehoe's clarinet from the bedroom closet. What could they possibly have wanted with a clarinet? How valuable could such a thing have been on the secondhand market? There was no way they were keeping it for themselves, because the swine wouldn't know what to do with such a delicate instrument. She pictured them back in their sty of an apartment, surveying their loot, sniffing it, looking at the clarinet's pieces in stupefaction and dropping them into a garbage can.

She couldn't blame everything on the latest waves of immigration. Her immediate neighbors had been there longer than she had and both had fallen on tough times. Both houses used to look respectable, if a little dull, with dingy lace curtains in the windows and bleached paint on the trim, but now a rusted-out car sat on blocks in the Palumbos' backyard, next to a rain-filled drum, and Gene Cooney's house was under permanent construction, with ugly scaffolding marring the facade and a garden box full of crabgrass and construction debris. Gene stalked the perimeter all day with an edgy intensity, wearing a tool belt around his waist. Wild rumors had sprung up about him and his family, spread by newer residents. He was said to be an IRA arms smuggler lying low. There were whispers about his daughter, who wore short skirts and fishnet stockings and kept nocturnal hours. Eileen knew the truth: he'd gone off the rails after his wife had been killed on Northern Boulevard by a hit-and-run driver, and his daughter wasn't a prostitute but a girl who had fallen victim to the fashions of the Hispanics she'd grown up around— though one could be forgiven for confusing some of them with hookers.

When she'd first moved onto the block, the garden boxes in front of the houses were lush with flowers in bloom and respectable attempts at horticulture, but many had since returned to the wild, with giant weeds poking up over their walls. She was committed to making hers an oasis against decay, although she hadn't inherited her father's sympathy with all manner of vegetable life. Angelo had helped her keep things alive, and she'd picked up a bit of knowledge working alongside him, but ever since his third heart attack had killed him a few years back, she was constantly buying new plants to replace the ones that wilted in the middle of the night.

She overspent on furniture. She had the rugs cleaned and the walls painted every two years. She'd found a beautiful crystal chandelier on sale on the Bowery. The house wasn't fancy, but it had a certain luster. The one thing she couldn't escape was the sound of the Orlandos' footsteps above her. The fact that she owned the whole building didn't make it any more pleasant to hear them.

Ed was seated at the table as she fixed the tea. His back was to her, possessed of that solidity that so delighted her the first time she put her arms around him. Now she wanted to pound on it. He was hunched over and rubbing his temples. She put a hand on his shoulder and he flinched at her touch. She thought, *Who the hell does he think I am?*

She considered flinging herself on him before he could get the headphones plugged in. She thought of ripping the plug out once he'd settled into his pillow and filling the room with sound, screaming over the music the invectives she'd held in. But she didn't do that. She sat in the armchair and read a book until she headed to bed.

She wondered whether she was being hard on her husband. He had, after all, more than earned a rest after teaching for so many years. She hadn't heard anything from Connell yet about it, and she expected that the boy, who was becoming a more sullen presence in the house as he slunk into adolescence, would be oblivious enough to his father's new routines to allow her to conclude that it was all in her head.

Connell noticed, though. "So what's with all the record listening?" he asked one night, snapping his gum in that insouciant way that usually annoyed her. Now she saw that the attitude gave him the courage to speak.

Ed looked up but didn't respond.

"What's up with the headphones?" he asked again, stepping closer to his father.

Given the strange way Ed had been behaving lately, she thought he might fly into a rage, but he simply took the headphones off.

"I'm listening to opera."

"You listen to it all the time now."

"I decided I didn't want to die not having heard all these masterpieces. Verdi. Rossini. Puccini."

"Who's dying? You've got plenty of time."

"There's no time like the present," Ed said.

"You don't have to use those," Connell said, pointing to the headphones.

"I don't want to disturb anyone."

"You don't think you're disturbing anyone this way?"

Another night, when she picked him up from track practice, Connell asked her in the car if his father was unhappy.

"I wouldn't say that," she said. "I think he's quite happy."

"He always says, 'You have to decide in life. You deliberate awhile, you think of all the possibilities on both sides, and then you make a decision and stick to it.'"

She'd never heard this particular line of reasoning from Ed. This must've been one of those things he and the boy talked about when she wasn't around. She could almost feel her ears pricking up.

"Like with girls. He says, 'When you're getting married, you make a decision and that's it. Things aren't always perfect, but you work at them. The important thing is that you decided.'"

Her stomach tightened.

"But what I don't get is, if it's such a chore, if you're talking about having to stick to it because you decided it, why do people do it in the first place?"

"They do it because they're in love," she said defensively. "Your father and I were in love. *Are* in love."

"I know," he said.

It occurred to her that perhaps he didn't know. Overt affection had always been uncomfortable for her, but in front of the boy it felt impossible. Ed used to squeeze and kiss her when Connell was a baby, but she would wriggle out of it. Certainly she didn't reach for him herself, but he knew when they married that he'd have to take the lead. She wasn't like the women a few years younger who wore miniskirts. What she offered instead was the negotiated submission of her fierce independence. She was different in bed with him than she was anywhere else, but this wasn't something her son could have any idea about.

"Your father is happy," she said. "He's just getting older, is all. You'll understand someday. The same exact thing will happen to you."

It didn't feel like the best explanation, but it must've been good enough, because the boy was silent for the rest of the ride.

16

His father was always on the couch now, but that morning he came to Connell's room and told him he wanted to take him to the batting cages. They drove to the usual place, off the Grand Central Parkway, in back of a mini-mall.

Connell picked out the least dinged-up bat from the rack and tried to find a helmet that fit. His father came back from the concession stand with a handful of coins for the machines. Connell headed for the machine labeled Very Fast. He put the sweaty, smelly helmet on and pulled his batting glove onto his right hand. He took his position in the left-handed batter's box and dropped the coin in. The light came on on the machine, and then nothing happened for a while, until a ball shot out and thumped against the rubber backstop. Connell watched another one pass and wondered if he was going to be able to hit any of them. They were easily over eighty miles an hour, though they weren't the ninety miles an hour they were presented as.

The next pitch came and Connell timed his swing a little too late and the ball smacked behind him with a fearsome *thwack*. The next pitch he foul-tipped, and the one after that he hit a tiny grounder on, and then the next one he sent on a line drive right back at the machine. It would have been a sure out, but it was nice to hit it with authority. His father let out a cheer behind him, and Connell promptly overswung on the next pitch, caught the handle on the ball and felt a stinging, ringing sensation in his hands and hopped in place, then swung through the next pitch entirely.

"Settle down, son," his father said. "You can hit these. Find the rhythm."

The next pitch, which he foul-tipped, was the last, and he stopped and put the bat between his legs and adjusted his batting glove. There wasn't a line forming behind him, so he could take his time. Balls pinged off bats in nearby cages and banged off piping or died in the nets. His father had his hands on the netting and was leaning against it.

"You ready?"

"Yeah."

"Go get 'em."

He put a coin in and took his stance. The first pitch buzzed past him and slammed into the backstop.

"Eye on the ball," his father said. "Watch it into the catcher's mitt. Watch this one. Don't swing."

He watched it zoom by.

"Now time it. It's coming again just like that. Same spot. This is all timing."

He took a big hack and fouled it off. He was getting tired quickly.

"Shorten your swing," his father said. "Just try to make contact."

He took another cut, a less vicious one, more controlled, and drilled it into what would have been the outfield. He did it again with the next pitch, and the one after that. The ball coming off the bat sounded like a melon getting crushed. The whole place smelled like burning rubber.

When the coins ran out, he held the bat out to his father. "You want to get in here?"

"No," his father said. "You have fun."

"I don't mind."

"I don't think I could hit a single pitch."

"Sure you could. You're selling yourself short."

"My best days are behind me," his father said.

"Why don't you take a few hacks? Come on, Dad. Just one coin."

"Fine," his father said. "But you can't laugh at me when I look like a scarecrow in there."

His father came into the cage and took the helmet from him. He took the bat, refused the batting glove. He was in a plaid, button-down shirt and jeans that fit him snugly, and Connell thought that he actually did look a little like a scarecrow. His glasses stuck out from the helmet like laboratory goggles. Connell stepped out of the cage and positioned himself where his father had been standing. His father dropped the coin in and took his place in the batter's box, the lefty side, Connell's side.

The first pitch slammed into the backstop. The next one did as well. His father had the bat on his shoulder. The next pitch came crashing in too.

"Aren't you going to swing?"

"I'm getting the timing," his father said.

The next pitch landed with a thud, and the following one went a little high and came at Connell. His father didn't offer at any of them.

"You have to swing sometime," Connell said. "Only three left."

"I'm watching the ball into the glove," he said. "I'm waiting for my pitch."

"Two left."

"Okay," his father said.

"*Dad*. You can't just stand there."

The last pitch came and his father took a vicious cut at it. The ball shot off like cannon fire and the bat came around to rest on his father's back in text-book form, Splendid Splinter form. The ball would have kept rising if it hadn't been arrested by the distant net, which it sank into at an impressive depth.

"Wow!"

"Not bad," his father said. "I think I'm going to quit while I'm ahead."

Connell went in and took the helmet and bat from his father, who looked tired, as if he'd been swinging for half an hour. He dropped the coin in and found the spot in the batter's box. His father's hit must have freed his confidence up, because he made solid contact on all but one of his swings, and then he put another coin in and started attacking the ball, crushing line drives.

"Attaboy," his father said.

He hit until he was tired, and they drove to the diner they liked to go to after the cages. Connell ordered a cheeseburger and his father ordered a tuna melt. They shared a chocolate shake. Connell drained his half and his father handed him his own to drink.

"That's okay, Dad."

"You drink it," his father said.

The food came and his father didn't really eat. Instead he seemed to be looking interestedly at Connell.

"What's up?" Connell asked.

"I used to love to watch you eat. I still do, I guess."

"Why?"

"When you were a baby, maybe two years old, you used to put a handful of food in your mouth and push it in with your palm. Like this." His father put his hand up to his mouth to show him. 'More meatballs!' you used to say. Your face would be covered in sauce. 'More meatballs.' You had this determined expression, like nothing was more important in the world." He was chuckling. "And you ate fast! And a lot. You used to ask for more. 'All gone!' you said. I used to love to watch you eat. I guess it was instinct. I knew you would survive if you ate. But part of it was just the pleasure you took in it. A grilled cheese sandwich cut into little squares. That was the whole world for you then. You getting it into your mouth was the only thing that mattered. You couldn't eat it fast enough."

His father was making him nervous watching him. He hadn't eaten any of his sandwich.

"You going to sit there and watch me the whole time?"

"No, I'm eating."

His father took a couple of bites. Connell called for more water and ketchup.

"I wish I could explain it to you," his father said after a while.

"What?"

"What it's like to have you. What it's like to have a son."

"You going to eat those fries?"

"They're all yours," his father said. Connell took some. "Eat as many as you like." His father slid the plate toward him. "Eat up."

17

She decided to scrap the intimate dinner they'd agreed upon for his fiftieth birthday and throw a full-scale surprise party instead. One thing it couldn't fail to do was get him off the couch for a night, but she wanted more than that: she wanted to wake him up, set him on the course to recovering his lost enthusiasm. He'd spent so much time alone lately that it would be good for him to be forced to mix with others.

Until she was drawing up the list for the party, she'd never noticed how weighted toward her side their social group was. So many of the friends they'd lost touch with were Ed's. When she considered her friends' husbands, she saw the same thing—a withdrawal, a ceding of the social calendar to the wife. It was her responsibility to ensure that her husband didn't get domesticated entirely. She would go beyond the usual crowd. She decided to track down some of the guys who were his regular buddies when they first got married and reach out to the cousins he never saw. She would remind him how much there was to look forward to.

She gave her garden box a full makeover, even though she knew the early-March chill would kill everything right after the party.

As she finished patting the soil down around a rosebush, a car zoomed past at a murderous clip bound for Northern Boulevard, salsa music pounding from its four-corner speakers. If she were a man she would have spat in disgust. She hated the driver; she hated the drug cartel he likely worked for; she hated worrying that people taking the train to the party might run into some kind of trouble. God forbid any of them got propositioned by the prostitutes that had begun to walk Roosevelt Avenue. One of them had approached Ed while Eileen and he were coming off the stairs holding hands.

She hoped that the NCB executives she'd invited wouldn't judge her for her current situation. Her career depended on their seeing her as the kind of person who belonged in their midst. How could she ever explain to them the way Jackson Heights used to be?

She didn't think of herself as racist. She was proud of her record of coming to the aid of black nurses who'd been unjustly targeted by superiors. She enjoyed an easy rapport with the security guards at NCB, most of whom were black.

She loved to tell the story of her father's stepping forward to drive with Mr. Washington when no one else would. She also enjoyed recounting the tale of how, when none of the old Irish guard would shop at the Chinese grocer up the block, and the new store was on the verge of failure, her father had paid the man a visit to take his measure. Satisfied that the man, Mr. Liu, was a hard worker and an honest proprietor, her father had stood for a few evenings on the corner near the grocer with the suspect vegetables and stopped people and said, "Go spend some money at the chink son of a bitch's place," and they'd listened. Now the whole of Woodside was Chinese grocers. She wondered if the newer generation would do for an Irish immigrant looking to make an honest living the same thing her father had done for one of their own years before. She wondered if some of the black nurses she'd helped along the way would lift a finger for a white woman in need. She'd watched the Bronx spiral downward over the years, and she hadn't flinched. The security guards marveled at her driving into the neighborhood alone every day. They never let her walk to her car unescorted at night.

No, she couldn't be called racist. That didn't mean she had to like what they were doing to her neighborhood. They were making it into a war zone.

The day of the party, her house had never seemed so small. An hour before Ed was supposed to arrive, there was barely room to pass in the halls; she had to ask her cousin Pat to carry a side table down to the basement. Still, as soon as people began assembling in the kitchen, she felt their presence as a kind of armor around her. She tended to the ham and the broccoli casserole in the stove and the separate duty of each pot on the stovetop. She had made nothing to offend anyone's palate, and so she presented it without anxiety. When the caterer arrived with trays containing more food than could possibly get eaten, she told herself it was safe to begin to relax.

When Connell called from a pay phone and said they were ten minutes away, she was surprised to find herself seized by terror. She passed the news to the living room, which filled with that clamor particular to a crowd silencing itself. A quiet grew louder than the din that had preceded it; she could almost hear her pulse in its murky depths. She moved through the wall of people to be near enough for him to see her when he entered.

As Ed stepped into the room, Eileen closed her eyes, obeying a strange compulsion not to look at his face. A frenzied chorus rang out around her. When she opened her eyes, she saw him beaming and being passed from person to person, shouting as he encountered every new face—shouts like war whoops that could have been either exultant or lunatic. He was red with excitement, and sweat was gathering on him. As she moved close to hug him, she heard him whoop the way he had for the others, as though he hadn't seen her in years. His whoops went on; they wouldn't die down. He greeted each successive person with the same ecstatic disbelief.

She was afraid to leave him, afraid to stay. She saw him engulfed in friends' arms and ducked into the kitchen to get him a drink. When she returned he was miming his own shock for them over and over. She didn't want anyone else to notice the unconvincing mirth in his performance. She shouted to Connell to cue the stereo. Ed was ushered into the dining room. In the mirror she tried to look at other people's reactions but was inexorably drawn back to her husband's expressions. When he saw his brother Phil in from Toronto, he let out a howl that sounded like that of a dying animal. She reached for a tray of hors d'oeuvres to pass. The food smells were mingling successfully; no trace of dust came off any surface she touched; nothing was out of place. The only messes were the ones guests were making themselves—someone bumped into the punch bowl and sent a couple of crystal mugs crashing to the floor—and for those she had great patience.

She poured herself a glass of wine and drifted into the living room, where she gave herself over to conversation. Behind the timbre of any individual voice lay the lovely murmur of the group, but she couldn't distract herself from the thought of her husband's frenzied surprise, and she went in search of him.

She went out on the stoop with Pat and the smokers and the kids, but no one had seen him come outside. The bathroom was locked, but after a little while her aunt Margie came out. She went down to the basement and searched its recesses, where she found no sign of him.

When she got back up to the landing at her back door, instead of heading inside she called up the stairs. There was no response, but she had an instinct to proceed upstairs anyway, and she found him sitting on the flight between the second and third floors, just sitting there, looking directly at her as she approached, in a way that unnerved her, as though he'd been waiting for her to find him. The music and talking muffled through the intervening flight rose and fell in waves, following the rhythm of its own respiration. There had been no dip in the revelry yet.

"Frank wants to take your picture," she said. "Fiona just got here. I don't know if you saw her."

He sat in silence, though he didn't look away.

"Pat's only here to see you. He doesn't go to parties anymore. You should have heard him when I finally got him on the phone. 'For Ed?' he said. 'Sure. Anything.'"

"Keep him away from the bar," Ed said.

"He won't even come inside," she said, chuckling. "He's on the stoop."

She could feel her eyes watering, though she wasn't consciously sad. "We're having a real party downstairs," she said. "It'd be even better if you were there."

He patted the spot beside him. The gentleness of the gesture touched her, and being moved when she was also angry confused her, so that she wanted to go back down alone, but she gave in, gathered her skirt under her and sat.

"I'm getting old," he said. "I can feel my body breaking down."

"You just feel that way because it's your birthday," she said. "Everyone gets old."

"I didn't expect to see all these people. I thought we'd have a quiet night."

She looked at him wryly. "Haven't we had enough quiet nights lately?"

"I don't even know half these people."

"You know almost every single one of them," she said. "There are maybe four people that you've never met."

"Then I don't remember them."

"Of course you do. I'll go around with you and start conversations and you can hear who they are that way."

He looked away.

"You love parties," she said. "You grumble and complain that I entertain too often, but once the party's going, no one enjoys it more than you. Those people are here to see you. I don't know what to tell them when they ask where you are."

"Tell them you saw me a second ago in the other room."

"What's wrong with you?"

"I'm tired. I can't tell you how tired I am. I'm tired of standing in front of a bunch of people and being the center of attention. Do you have any idea how much energy that takes? You're never off. *Never.* You can never have a bad day. I feel like I've been trying to keep all these juggling balls in the air, and I can't let them hit the ground or something bad will happen. I'd love to just lie down right now."

"Well, you can't. Everyone's here. We have to make the best of it. I'm sorry I did this."

"You don't need to be sorry."

"I am. This was a stupid idea. Stupid, stupid."

"I just need the school year to end," he said. "That's it. I can't tell you how much I'm looking forward to vacation. No summer classes for me this year, that's for sure. I'm just going to stay put."

Another day, she might have hissed at him to get off his ass and get down there, but something prevented her. She was about to say she'd come back and get him in five minutes when he slapped his knees and stood.

"Okay," he said. "Let's go."

Before they reentered the party, she ran down to the basement to grab a bottle from the rack.

"Wave this around when we get in there," she said. "In case anyone noticed you were gone."

Frank McGuire had the camera around his neck and called Ed over, as relieved as a retriever reassembling the pack. She watched him arrange the guys in a row in the dining room, the group waiting for him to focus, and then a moment of stillness that seemed to expand and breathe. She tried to memorize the scene—not the visual details, which she could recall later by looking at the photograph, but the mood, the nimble camaraderie, the way they clutched each other, the hint of annoyance at having to pose, the way afterward they laughed off the brush with intimacy. Every picture of men in a row, she thought, ended as this one did, with them expelled as if by force, dispersing into separate corners to get a drink, a plate of food, to smoke a cigarette. Ed looked vulnerable standing there in the lee tide. She decided not to leave his side for the rest of the party, and ushered him around with a subtle steering of her arm. He was a perfect sailboat, responding to the slightest tug on the line, tacking when she wanted him to tack, coming about when she wanted him to come about. She could feel him relax with her there, and soon she was having fun again. She had to resist her impulse to leave him and head to where the good conversations were taking place. She'd always considered it a luxury that she could count on her husband to entertain himself at parties. From across the room they would check in with each other with a wave, a nod, a wink, and a charge of desire would run through her as she watched the way women's eyes danced when they were near him. It was hard to see him as well up close; something was lost in the foreshortening.

Cindy Coakley brought the cake in. They sang "Happy Birthday" and Eileen put her hand on his back as he blew out the candles with a remarkable lack of wind, so that a few stray flames survived his second and even third attempts. The lights came on and Cindy passed him the knife. He stood for a moment brandishing it before him, and Eileen couldn't help finding something menacing in the image. She put her hand over his in what she hoped would look like an evocation of the gesture of unity with which they'd cut their wedding cake, and she pressed his hand down into the thin layer of frosting and the forbidding brick of ice cream beneath it. When she released her hand he struggled to free the knife from that frozen denseness and, failing, threw up his palms in defeat and took a step back from the cake. She laughed with an expression she hoped said something universal and vague about the uselessness of men and took his face in her hands and gave him a big, unrestrained kiss. To do so in front of all those people went against every ounce of culture she'd ever absorbed. He stiffened at first, but then he relaxed and let her kiss him. People began hooting and cheering. She let him go and pulled the knife from the cake and started serving little slices.

She hated to wake up to a messy house; it felt like paying a bill for something consumed without being savored. Still, when the last guest left, she went straight to bed. Ed slept on his back, inexorably flat. It was nearly her favorite thing about him. She'd read that it took confidence to sleep on one's back, because it exposed the internal organs. He'd always been confident in bed. She loved how small he made her feel, how she could nestle up to him and be enveloped in his reach. She thought of the first time they'd danced, her surprise at his size, which he had hidden in his overlarge jacket. He had a rangy athleticism that put him at ease in the company of men who made their living with their hands. He allowed her to bridge two worlds, the earthbound one she'd come from and the rarefied one she aspired to. And he was the only man in whose arms she'd ever been able to fall asleep.

In the morning, she fixed herself tea and got to work dispatching the pots and pans. When she'd cleaned the countertops and cabinet doors, she ran the mop over the kitchen floor, but her usual feeling of pride at the glossy shine and the piney scent didn't come. How had she tolerated the floor's permanently dingy linoleum this long? The wallpaper had bubbled up in places, and the joints in the window frames were so slack that the glass shifted like a loose tooth when the window was lifted. In the dining room she felt better for a while as she ran the rag over those stately pieces and breathed in the easy astringency of Murphy's Oil Soap, but soon the tarnish along the bottom edge of the wall-length mirror was all she could see. In the bathroom, she noticed places where the enamel had worn away in the tub, exposing the black beneath it.

She began to obsess over the details of her guests' attentions. Had they seen the stains on the rug under the ottoman? The evidence of rot on the vanity? She imagined them picking up objects and finding a layer of dust beneath.

She moved to the basement to clean the laundry room. She would have to have a talk with Brenda about the dryer sheets she always found in the machine and the empty detergent boxes she ended up throwing out herself. These little quality-of-life infractions added up to a diminishment of her happiness on the planet. When she was done, she moved to the storage shelves to organize those and decided she'd have to talk to Donny about keeping his tools better organized. Then came the cedar closets. This time she chided her own inattention, because a few of her favorite sweaters had been eaten through by moths. Then she went upstairs and started to give the grout between the bathroom tiles a proper scouring. When she looked up, Ed was standing in the doorway, Connell behind him. They were wearing their Sunday best.

"What are you doing?" she asked.

"We're going to Mass," Ed said. "Isn't that what we do on Sundays?"

"What time is it?"

"Four forty-five," Connell said.

She had missed every Mass except the five o'clock service. She felt them regarding her strangely and looked down at rubber gloves on hands that seemed to belong to someone else, one of which held a crumbling green sponge.

"Wait for me," she said, as she peeled them off and closed the door to freshen up.

18

Connell dreaded when the teacher left the room, because in that vacuum of authority he was subject to a tribunal of his peers. And so when Mrs. Ehrlich went to the bathroom during geography class and brought Laura Hollis up to the board to take names, Connell knew the general contours of what was coming. That day, Pete McCauley ran up to the blackboard and grabbed an eraser, missing badly when he threw it at him. Somebody in the rear made up for this errant toss by throwing a pencil, then another, the latter of which hit him in the back of his impassive head. The laughter in the room clattered like shutters in a howling wind. Even his nerd friends chuckled a little. Laura wrote nothing down, as Juan Castro stood by the door keeping the real watch. Pete retrieved the eraser and ran over and stamped it on his back. He couldn't get the chalk splotch off his blazer, though he rubbed at it the rest of the day.

He used to hang out with these kids. Most of them lived in apartments, so his backyard made him useful. They'd meet there, drop their bikes off. He'd go with them to Woolworth's to steal Binaca. He never stole it himself, but he went on the expeditions and spent the whole time fretting that he'd be grabbed by a guard. When they were just outside the front door, they'd pull it out conspicuously and spray it into their mouths like it was some kind of drug. They said they needed it for their girls. Shane Dunn and Pete McCauley claimed to have already had sex, and Connell had no reason to doubt them. Every summer at CYO camp there was at least one pregnant seventh- or eighth-grade girl riding the bus.

Then, in the spring of fourth grade, something happened that changed his life. One day they rode over to Seventy-Eighth Street Park because of some dispute Juan's older brother had gotten into. Connell found himself walking with his classmates and a bunch of older kids in a line, toward another group coming at them. He saw one of the kids on his side take out a knife, but he kept walking forward as though powerless to do anything else, and he was sure he was going to get stabbed in the melee to come. Then he heard sirens and everything slowed down and he could see it would end with him in the back of the squad car, his future ruined. The lines atomized in all directions. He ran with his friends to the bikes. They rode down Thirty-Fourth Avenue to his house. He pedaled furiously, his heart pounding in his chest, feeling like a crocodile was snapping at his heels.

After that, he hung out with the nerds in his special math group. Starting in fifth grade, he never got less than ninety-five on anything. He won the math bee twice, the spelling bee, the science fair. He didn't show people up when they were wrong the way John Ng did; he didn't crow about his accomplishments the way Elbert Lim did; but still he was everybody's favorite target, probably because he acted like a wooden soldier, sitting stiffly upright and barely ever turning his head. He wouldn't respond when kids tried to get his attention, because he didn't want to get in trouble with the teachers. He didn't let kids copy off his tests anymore. It didn't help that he was chubby. Starting when he was in third grade, the fat came on stealthily, as though in his sleep. Now, in eighth grade, he'd grown several inches, and the fat was hardening into muscle, but that didn't matter: he was the fat kid. Being the only one in his class to get into the best Catholic high school in the city made matters even worse. It felt like it'd be years before he ever got to kiss a girl. It was like the other kids smelled something on him. He used to talk to his father when he'd had a bad day. Now he just went to the basement and started lifting weights.

At lunchtime, he served a funeral Mass. He'd started serving funerals whenever he could, to avoid the cafeteria. He wasn't eating lunch anyway. When he did, sometimes he threw it up afterward. He wanted his muscles as tight as the skin on action figures.

The church was tall and long, and dark everywhere except the altar, which had spotlights and floodlights on it, especially the tabernacle. He liked to look at the faces in the pews. He was the best altar boy they had. He arrived early and knew the ceremony as well as the priests. He didn't sway the way other kids did when they stood holding the big book. He was a human podium. He offered the cramps in his legs and arms up to God.

Gym was his least favorite class, despite the fact that his athleticism made him a temporary asset to whoever his teammates were on a given day. Changing for gym was a nightmare. Someone sadistic had decided that they should wear their gym clothes under their uniforms and shed their outer layers in a proto-striptease. They peeled their uniforms off in front of each other, girls on one side of the auditorium, boys on the other. He made sure not to look across at the girls, because the fallout of being caught doing so by one of the other boys would be unspeakable. He couldn't look down or to the side either, because then someone might call him a fag. So he looked at the high ceiling, almost as tall as the one in church, and the high windows up at the ground level, which were always open and which made the outer world seem tantalizingly near.

There were a couple of minutes of milling around before Mr. Cotswald blew the whistle to start class. He kept to himself the way he had ever since the day he'd allowed himself to be hoisted up to the basketball hoop by Pete and Juan, who'd interlocked their fingers to make a step for each of his feet. Other kids had been getting lifted up there and getting the ball passed to them, and then dunking and dropping off, and since it looked like fun he'd let his guard down when Pete and Juan waved him over. Instead of passing him the ball, Shane had pulled his shorts and underwear down. He still felt weird about telling his parents it had happened to someone else. He still had no idea why he hadn't just dropped off the rim when they'd done it.

At the end of the day he sat in homeroom waiting for the bell. He wanted to spring to his feet when it rang, but he knew better than to let that happen again. Last week he jumped the gun on the okay-to-rise sign and the class erupted in laughter.

Mrs. Balarezo gave the signal for everyone to stand. Then she gave a second go sign to John Ng to lead the ordered procession out. Connell was at the head of the second row. He slid in behind Christina Hernandez and waded out into the sea of kids heading down the stairs. Thank God Ms. Balarezo sat him up front. It gave him a fighting chance to escape. It was the one good thing that had come of being singled out. A while ago she'd switched his and Kevin's desks. She didn't have to say why she was doing it; everybody knew he was getting murdered back there.

He got down the stairs and out to the street, no lingering, no talking to anyone. Passing through the gate he exhaled deeply. He loosened his tie, undid the button. He couldn't relax entirely. It was a long couple of blocks, each house feeling slightly safer than the last. The route was a fist slowly releasing its clench.

The first block was the avenue that ran along the school. It was a short stretch before he turned at Eighty-Third, and it should have been the safest one, with all the cars and adults around, and the church on the corner, but it wasn't; it was the worst. He walked past the rectory. Somehow they had all gotten there first, as if by teleportation, and were sitting on the steps. He felt them deciding his fate: Tommy, Gustavo, Kevin, Danny, Carlos, Shane, Pete. Danny lived on his block; that meant something—after school, any-way. At school, Danny was like everybody else. When they cracked jokes, he laughed louder than the others. He never hit Connell, though. He'd push him, but he wouldn't fight.

As Connell passed the church, his mind was afire. Did he do anything today to get their notice? Did he talk to a girl? Did he talk to anyone at all? Did he offend anybody by *not* talking? Anything was possible. He wanted to be invisible. If he could get to the corner unnoticed, and across the street, the chances of their following him home dropped, but then it was one and a half long side-street blocks, narrow ones, less busy, and he had to hurry. If they wanted to get him in that stretch, he was a man in the desert without a horse.

He crossed the avenue. Out of the corner of his eye he could see them following him. When he reached the other side, they were upon him. They surrounded him quickly, a phalanx closing its gaps. There was a moment of indecision, in which the fact of their outnumbering him seemed to hang in the air like a question. He thought they looked vulnerable in this in-between moment, as though they saw something absurd in the ritual of his submission. He imagined them calling the whole thing off, Danny saying, "Hey guys, let's forget about it," and then the group breaking up and walking home.

Sometimes lately he looked at them, even at times like this, and saw not bullies but lost children and, down the road, lost adults. He didn't know why he thought all this stuff, why he did laps around the block after dinner, saying hello to strangers and waving at old ladies perched on their stoops.

The hiccup of indecision passed. As though propelled by an electric wind, one kid shot out of the circle. Today it was Carlos Torres, quiet Carlos, disappearing Carlos, and the role was bigger than him, so he puffed himself up to fit it. He approached Connell awkwardly, jabbing at the air. Connell did his best to avoid the blows. He felt his shirt riding up on him, the buttons straining as he darted around. It was only a matter of time. The circle grew smaller and smaller. A stinging slap landed on his ear and he heard a deafening pop. The one thing he needed to do was hold on to his bookbag; God forbid they should get that from his grasp. Another smack landed hard on his face. The kids gaped in a kind of amazed half respect as they watched him take the blows. Then it turned to anger: why wouldn't he defend himself? He wondered too. He was bigger than them, stronger too. Maybe it was the fact that some of them carried knives to school. He saw them show them off. One recent graduate, whose older brother was in the Latin Kings, had become a legend for bringing in a gun. It would be nice to have an older brother, Connell thought sometimes: to be in a band of brothers that took on the world, instead of getting his solitary ass beaten to a pulp. It wasn't always fear that he felt, though, when he didn't fight back. It was something else, something mysterious.

His hands went up to cover his face and he felt a thud in his side. He was winded, and he focused on keeping his feet. If he fell he would have to cover his body with his arms, leave himself to their mercy and hope they didn't kick him in the head. Something about his keeping his feet kept them civil. He staggered around, Carlos screaming at him, growing in confidence with every blow he landed.

"Fight back!"

He looked to the blurry group for help. It was the same way he always looked at them, and he sensed something like sympathy in the way some of them looked back, but they were also revolted, and they joined Carlos in hectoring him.

"Fight, *maricón!*"

They pushed him into Carlos.

"Oh, snap, Carlos, you gonna take that?"

He kept his hands up.

"You wanna fight, huh? You wanna fight?"

"No," Connell said. "No."

He felt a fist explode in his gut and he doubled over. His stomach was burning, but the tears didn't come. He wasn't afraid for them to come. He had wanted to cry for a while, but he just couldn't.

Carlos was grinning maniacally. For a second he looked like he was sharing something with Connell, letting him in on a joke. "Fight back!" he screamed. "Faggot!" Connell saw the hatred in his eyes, tried to watch his hands. Carlos smacked him so hard that Connell could actually hear it resound, as though it had happened to someone else. The kids were startled. Connell staggered, and an adult, a stranger, came to break up the fight. Everyone scattered.

Connell let himself in with his key. He collapsed on the couch and awoke to the sound of his father coming home. He could hear him in the study, where he always stopped to drop his briefcase. Soon he would move to the living room. Connell didn't want to be on the couch when he walked in. He didn't want him to see any marks or bruises and start asking questions, but more importantly, he didn't want to deal with the weird negotiations that could ensue if he were there, his father hovering over him, waiting for Connell to move so that he could resume his headphoned isolation.

He thought of how he used to tell his father anything. His father knew how to make him feel better about things. He would hang on his father and cover his face and neck in kisses. It embarrassed him to think of it. He knew it wasn't as long ago as he liked to pretend.

He stood up. "I'm going out," he said to his father's back, which was bent over the desk. His father nodded wordlessly. He started walking up the block. He turned up Northern, heading toward Corona. He had started taking longer trips into areas he didn't feel safe in, but it didn't matter. He would walk until it was time go home and eat. He could feel the fat on him burning up with every step.

They sat through another dinnertime silence, every clinking fork magnified as though by a set of speakers. His parents' former banter had given way to remorseless, efficient eating, like that of lions after a hunt. A vague unease hung in the air, localized for Connell in the spot above the doorway where a pair of plaster doves sat perched on a heart, locked in a kiss. The doves were a wedding present from friends his parents had since lost touch with. They hung loosely on the nail and were dislodged by the slightest bump or bang. A year ago, one of those falls broke off a chunk of the heart. His father had Krazy-Glued it back together, and there were white cracks in the broken places. Connell wanted to take it off the wall, thrust it up under their noses, and say, "You see this! This is supposed to be you two! Lovebirds!"

The silvery clinks grew more frequent as the meal progressed, as though his parents were hurrying to dispatch the business of eating so they could return to the more complete nourishment provided by their private thoughts. His mother hadn't noticed that he'd slipped most of his fatty steak into the napkin in his lap. He would deposit it into the garbage when she wasn't looking.

His mother slapped her hands on the table. "Since when does this family have nothing to say to each other?" His father kept chewing, so Connell did too. They had a nice little solidarity going. His father was looking down at his plate. Connell tried to do the same, but he could feel his mother's eyes on him.

"Fine," she said. "I'll start. What about school? Any interesting assignments?"

Lately he'd felt called upon to drive the silences away. Never before had his comings and goings generated so much fodder. He felt perpetually on the verge of blurting out something embarrassing.

He shook his head.

"Okay," his mother said. "I've had enough of the both of you." She stood up to clear her plate.

"I'm writing an essay about Uncle Pat," he said. He hadn't wanted to mention it, because he resented the responsibility of keeping conversation alive in their family, but the assignment was real, and if it could bring his mother back to the table, it would take some pressure from his father.

"Why Uncle Pat?" his mother asked, resuming her seat.

Uncle Pat wasn't really his uncle. He was his mother's first cousin. He put Connell on stools in dark saloons and introduced him as "the Dude." He had a scar on his face from the time he stopped the mugging of an old lady. Wherever they went, Uncle Pat knew everyone.

"I have to find someone in my family with an interesting job," Connell said. "Go where this person works if possible, and write five hundred words about it."

"I'll tell you who has an interesting job. Your father does. You can watch him teach."

His father put down his knife and fork and looked up. "He doesn't want to watch me teach," he said firmly. "Let him follow Pat around the cages. He can learn some valuable lessons."

"Ed," she said.

"He can ask him why he's cleaning up canary poop after owning one of the most successful bars on the North Fork. He can ask him why we had to write a check to pay his state taxes last year."

"I'd rather you watched your father," his mother said.

"I can't watch Dad," he said. "It's due tomorrow."

"*Tomorrow*," she said, snorting. "That's just great. And when exactly were you planning on getting out to the Island?"

"I've seen the farm," he said. "I can just make it up."

"No, you can't. I won't let you avoid the research."

"Jeez."

"I'll call the school in the morning and say you're sick. You'll turn it in a day late."

"Cool! I'll take the train out to Uncle Pat."

"You're dreaming," his mother said. "You're going to the college with your father." She threw her napkin on her plate. "I'm going for a walk. I cooked, you two can clean."

He and his father exchanged glances as the front door slammed. His father didn't notice him emptying the napkin into the garbage.

Normally he needed a raging fever to stay home. People died on his mother's gurneys; a guy once died in her arms.

"Tomorrow's your lucky day," his father said flatly. "I don't teach until eleven."

Connell did a victory dance. He expected his father to laugh, but his father kept his head down and his hands plunged in the filmy water.

Connell awoke to the odd sensation of a motherless house and stumbled out to the study to find his father leaning over his desk writing something. He started to speak, but his father put up a hand to cut him off.

"Get in the shower."

He hadn't finished his cereal when his father told him to start the car. Connell loved to sit in the driver's seat when the engine was running. The rumbling under him spoke of power and freedom, as well as great potential for danger. If he shifted the gears incorrectly, he could go crashing through the new garage door, or back into a pedestrian on the sidewalk.

"Move over," his father said. "This isn't the time. And keep that thing off." He snapped at the radio knob before Connell could.

"Let me tell you about my students," he said after some silence. "They're tough." He had that look in his eye that he got when he was moved by something. "They're proud. They can spot a faker a mile away. They don't tolerate being treated like children. There's too much at stake for them."

Connell had no idea what his father was getting at.

"When we get to the lecture room, I'm going to introduce you, and I want you to sit in the back and listen. I don't want you to distract anyone.

I won't be able to talk to you, so you can't ask any questions. Please don't interrupt me, because I have to concentrate."

They arrived at the campus and parked in the garage. His father shut the engine off and sat still. He had his eyes closed and was taking deep breaths. Connell waited for something to happen. His father started rubbing his temples. After a while he opened his eyes and looked at him.

"You ready?"

"Yeah," Connell said.

His father reached to the back seat for his briefcase. "I was just doing a little relaxation ritual I have before I go in to teach."

It was hard to believe his father needed such a thing. He'd always projected such easy command, and there were plaques on the wall attesting to his excellence as a teacher.

He was looking for something in his briefcase, not finding it, and growing agitated. He pulled a pile of papers out in a panicked frenzy and rifled through them. In the close quarters of the front seat, Connell could almost hear his father's heart pounding. When he found what he was looking for, a legal pad, the heaving in his chest and the kinetic fury of his hands settled into an eerie stillness that overtook his whole body. Connell had no idea what to say. His father was staring straight ahead.

"It's nothing," his father said. "It's that you're here. I want everything to be perfect."

They walked through the campus, passing people his father knew. His father introduced him quickly, barely stopping to do so, even though the people sported those deliberate expressions of instant delight that all people, however curmudgeonly, were required to produce upon meeting the progeny of their colleagues. He was walking so fast that Connell had a hard time keeping up with him, and eventually he broke into a little trot, which prevented Connell from taking in the sights as he would have liked. It looked like one of those fancy campuses in movies, with buildings with august columns and stonework, not like a place for people hanging on by a hair.

"This is nice," Connell said.

"This campus was designed by a famous architect named Stanford

White," his father said automatically. "At one time, it was the Bronx satellite
of New York University." His voice sounded distant, as though he were delivering a lecture. "When NYU built this campus, their chancellor said he
wanted it to look like the American ideal of a college. In the early seventies,
after it had gotten too expensive to maintain, NYU sold it to the State of New
York, and we moved over here from the old Bronx High School of Science."

"Dad," he said.

"Yes?"

"Are we late?"

"No."

"Then why are we running?"

Something in his voice must have given his father pause, because his
father stopped and put a hand on his shoulder.

"This isn't how I would have wanted this to go," he said. "Believe me.
There's a lot here I wanted to show you. There's a beautiful overlook point
called . . ." He rubbed his nose. "The Hall of Fame for Great Americans,"
he said after a few seconds. "You can see for miles up there. It has a lot of
statues arranged in a circle around you. Maybe if everything goes well I
can take you there after class."

They arrived at the building, but instead of marching directly into the
lecture hall to a throng of expectant students, as his father's pace suggested
they might have to do, they headed to his lab, where he closed the door
behind him. His father told him to absorb himself in whatever he might
find interesting, so long as he didn't break anything. He waved at a human
skeleton suspended in the corner, a row of rat cages along the far wall, and
a lonely assemblage of beakers and petri dishes. Then he took out his legal
pad and paced back and forth, quietly reading aloud.

Connell left the beakers huddled in their fragile little gathering. He
avoided the accusing eyes of the rats and hurried past the hollow ones of
the skeleton. Finding nothing more promising, he circled back to tap on
the glass of the rat cages and listen to what his father was reading.

"You can feed them if you want," his father said, gesturing to the rats,
which almost seemed to listen along over his shoulder. "There's a bag of
pellets in the drawer behind you."

"I'm okay," Connell said.

"I'm trying to focus," his father said, "and it would help if I didn't have to worry about you listening to every word."

His father searched around. "Here, take this," he said, tossing him an issue of *Scientific American.* Connell didn't like that magazine; they had a lot of them at home. His father was always drawing his attention to articles on black holes or glaciers or acid rain, but Connell stuck to *Sports Illustrated* and the "People" page in the back of *Time.*

"Why don't you sit outside and I'll come get you when I'm done?"

Connell wanted to tell him he didn't have to come to his stupid class at all if he wanted him gone that badly, but he held back. He did have to write the report. But something else told him not to make a big deal of it. "I'll just go to the class and wait for you," he said.

"Great," his father said, visibly relieved. "Two flights up. Room four forty-three. Introduce yourself."

As Connell left, his father was splashing water on his face in one of the sinks at the end of the long tables.

He took the stairs three at a time. The classroom door was open; he walked past it as casually as he could. The room was more full than he'd expected. How was he supposed to introduce himself to a room full of college students? He could barely get up in front of kids his own age without worrying about his voice betraying him with squeaks and squawks.

He mimed absorption in a bulletin board, then doubled back, passing the room again. The floor sloped upward from the front, so that the people at the back stared down from a lofty perch. A box on the wall taunted him: In Case of Emergency, Break Glass. The words took on a sudden poignancy; he would've been helpless even with an axe in his hand. He was beginning to see the wisdom in his father's having prepared a speech.

He stepped into the room and hustled to one of the empty seats in the back. He waited for the thumping in his chest to subside. They could figure out who he was for themselves if they cared so much.

When his father walked in, he didn't look up but headed for the podium and started reading from his pad.

"Today we are going to begin our discussion of the central nervous system," he said. "I have quite a bit of material to cover, and it is crucial that you assimilate this material for the final exam, so I would ask you to take careful notes, because I will not be able to repeat myself or interrupt the lecture to answer questions. Should you happen to find yourself confused at any point, please write your questions on a sheet of paper to hand to me at the end of class, and I will provide you with a written response when we meet on Thursday. Additionally, I am sorry to report that, due to the demands of a long-term research project, I will be forced to cancel office hours for the remainder of the semester."

The room erupted in incredulous groans. His father didn't look up but only held his finger on the page and waited for the furor to die down.

"At the end of each remaining class session, I will collect your questions. After I do so, I will pass out the detailed responses I have written to your earlier questions. Writing these responses will come at the expense of a considerable amount of my time, so I hope you will rest assured that any lost office hours will be more than adequately compensated for in this fashion. If on occasion I appear sluggish or distracted, or seem to need a second to compose myself, be aware that I am likely exhausted from the busy schedule I am keeping.

"One other point of note. Beginning today, I will be reading exclusively from prepared lectures and leave off answering or posing questions. In recent class sessions, we have covered comparatively less material than we did in the earlier part of the course, as you are all no doubt aware."

There were murmurs of acknowledgment, though his father didn't stop to notice them.

"I ask your forgiveness for the relatively inert nature of my presentation of the material from now on, but I assure you that a certain briskness is vital to your being adequately prepared for the final examination. And so, without further ado, I would like to begin."

When his father walked in, an indignant chatter had percolated throughout the room. At the beginning of his speech, a few students scanned the room for the reactions of others, but now several who didn't have notebooks out before took them out, and many pens were poised over pages.

He began.

"The central nervous system," he said, "represents the largest part of the nervous system. It consists of the brain and the spinal cord. Along with the peripheral nervous system, which we will learn about later, the central nervous system plays an essential role in the control of behavior."

All around Connell, people were writing down everything he said.

"The central nervous system is contained within an area known as the dorsal cavity, which can be broken down into two subcavities, the cranial and the spinal. The cranial cavity contains the brain, while the spinal cavity contains the spinal cord."

A few hands went up; it was evidently a hard habit to break immediately. If his father saw them out of the corner of his eye, he didn't give any indication. He flipped pages in his pad as he read.

"The central nervous system is protected by an elegant, two-tiered system. First, both the brain and the spinal cord are enveloped in a sheath of membranes known as the meninges. The meninges are three continuous sheets of connective tissue. From the outside in, these sheets are known as the dura mater, the arachnoid mater, and the pia mater."

The students seemed confused. Most had stopped writing. They were looking at each other and adding their hands to the gathering chorus in the air.

"The second tier of protection of the central nervous system is provided by bone. The brain is protected by the skull, while the spinal cord is protected by the vertebrae."

Now most of the class had its hands raised. His father had said he didn't want questions, but Connell was sure that if he knew how many hands were up, he would want to clear up the point so everyone could move along.

"The brain receives sensory input from the spinal cord as well as from its own nerves—which we will name and discuss later. It dedicates most of its capacity to processing sensory inputs and instigating motor outputs."

He had to think of something. His father obviously couldn't hear the grumbling that had overtaken the class. He was in some kind of zone. No one was taking notes anymore. Connell didn't want to anger him, but he knew his father would thank him later if he helped him solve this problem now.

His fingers tingled as he stood and felt everyone turn to face him. All he wanted to do was get his father to look up from the page. He cleared his throat.

"Dad!" he said sharply.

His father must not have heard him, or if he did, he must not have understood the seriousness of the situation. Connell wanted to sit back down, but now he couldn't. He felt short of breath.

"The spinal cord serves three main functions," his father went on. "It conducts sensory information from the peripheral nervous system to the brain. It conducts motor information from the brain to various effectors. And it serves as a minor reflex center."

"Dad!" he said again, this time more emphatically. "Dad!"

His father looked right at him. It felt as if they were the only two people in the room. All the hands in the air fell at once. His father looked around at the faces staring back at him. Everyone seemed to wait to see what would happen next. His father bent over the pad again. As he did so, hands shot up all over the room. Voices called out.

"Professor Leary!"

"Professor!"

But he didn't hear them. "The second tier of protection of the central nervous system," he said, to a round of groans, "is provided by bone." One man hopped in his seat, as if he were about to run up and tackle him away from the lectern.

"The brain is protected by the skull . . ."

Connell knew he had heard this already.

"What is this shit?" the hopping man asked.

"Hello!" shouted a lady a few rows up. "You can't just *ignore* us here."

Connell had seen his father determined before. When he wanted to do something, when he really wanted to do it, he put his head down and got it done.

A growing outcry was filling the room, so that you could barely hear him reading.

"Dad!" Connell shouted. "*Dad!*"

His father stopped again. This time he backed away from the pad and the lectern. Connell saw the pages he'd folded under the bottom flip back onto the pad. His father looked at him again in that uncanny way, as if Connell was the only other person there. He backed up to his briefcase and squeezed the handle as though to keep it away from someone trying to snatch it from him. Then he seemed to recover a bit and approached the podium again. Connell sat down.

"Today we are going to begin our discussion of the central nervous system," he said. He stopped talking and looked around at the room. They were eerily quiet. Connell was desperate for someone to say something. He knew he couldn't do it himself.

After a few seconds, his father gestured to a woman in the front who had been taking notes through the chaos.

"Karen," he said. "Karen? Is that right?"

"Yes, Professor Leary."

"Karen, if you don't mind, would you tell me where I left off?"

"You had just finished telling us that the spinal cord serves as a minor reflex center."

"Okay," he said. "That's good. That's good. Thank you. That's exactly what I needed. The spinal cord as a reflex center."

He flipped through the pad furiously. When he had gone through all the pages, he flipped back through them again so hard that it looked like he might rip them off.

"You see," he said. "I'm tired. I've been working hard. And there's a lot on my mind. In fact, there's something specific on my mind that's distracting me, and I hope you'll forgive me for letting it get in the way today. If you'll all turn and look, you'll see my son at the back of the room."

Connell could feel the blood rush to his cheeks.

"My son came along with me, as you can see," his father said. "Today is an important day for him." His father was looking directly at him. "Isn't it, son?"

He was going to make him talk about the project.

"Yes," Connell said.

"Today's his birthday," his father said.

Everyone was staring at him. It had been almost a month since his birthday. He could see it all: the metal bat, the batting gloves, the high-end tee, the netting, the boxes of balls, the bucket to keep them in; heading out into the cold and the whipping wind after dinner and setting up at the back of the driveway; under the moon, in the quiet of the evening, slamming balls into the net and delighting in the *ping* produced by a ball squarely struck.

The faces smiled. He heard a volley of clucking. One lady near him asked him how old he was.

"I'm fourteen," he said.

"Fourteen today," his father said. "And he's been such a good kid, waiting for me. You see, we're going to the Mets game right after this class. Opening Day. And I've had that in the back of my mind. I've been worried about the traffic. We're going to be cutting it a little close. So I apologize for not being all here today. Really, if I'm being honest with myself, I should ask you all if you wouldn't mind if we just ended class early and made up for it next week. I realize some of you have come from far away. Would you forgive me if we canceled today's class and made it up next time?"

The students looked around at each other. Some grumbled; one man slapped his desk in frustration, yelled "Bullshit!" and walked out. Others shrugged.

"Good. Good. That's great," his father said. "Then we'll end class now."

They started packing up their stuff. "I'll draw up a handout explaining in depth what I was going to go through today, and I'll spend a little time at the beginning of next class taking you through it point by point." He picked up the briefcase from the floor and began gathering his things. "Thank you all," he said, over the rustle of bags and jackets. "This is kind of you. I apologize for imposing on your time like this."

Some of them wished Connell a happy birthday as they left. His father waved them out the door. Connell remained seated until everyone had gone. He walked up to the front of the room. His father stood facing the blackboard, his hands on the chalkwell. Connell could see his shoulders rising and falling.

"I have to pee," Connell said, though he didn't really have to.

In the bathroom, he looked in the mirror. He lifted his shirt up, then took it off and flexed with both arms. There was more mass and definition. He brought his fists to his ears and squeezed his muscles like Hulk Hogan. He smiled a big, crazy smile with lots of teeth. He drew close to the mirror, leaned his forehead against it. His breath collected on it and evaporated. He slapped at the little bit of baby fat still on his stomach, hard enough to leave a red mark.

"Go away," he said. "Go away!" Then he started to worry that someone would walk in on him.

He put his shirt on and went back out. They walked to the car in silence.

"I don't have tickets to the game," his father said after they'd been driving awhile. "We can still go. We can try to get in."

"We don't have to."

"It might be hard to get tickets."

"Yeah."

"I was thinking we could go watch some planes."

Connell turned the radio on and the volume up a few clicks. He watched his father's face for flickers of anger, but his father didn't seem to notice the change in volume. Connell turned it up even more. His father's hand shot to the knob.

"That's too loud," he said. "Not too loud."

It was lower now than it had been before he raised it the first time, but he didn't want to chance it. He looked out the window.

"Hey, Dad?"

"What?"

"What was all that about?"

"I just didn't feel like teaching today."

"Why did you say it was my birthday?"

He could see his father's face reddening, his hands gripping the wheel tighter.

"Don't you think I know my own son's birthday? It's March thirteenth!" His father took a deep breath. "I just wanted everything to go perfectly. I wanted you to have good material for your project."

"You seemed confused."

"I was fine!" he shouted. "That's the end of it! I wanted things to go well while you were there. I've never had you in the classroom with me before. End of discussion!"

The pitch in his voice rose along with the volume, and his words became a kind of shrieking. Then he stopped and his breathing settled down.

"I didn't want to be cooped up inside today," he said.

They drove in silence.

"I'm sorry about your project," he said. "Maybe you can come back and watch me sometime."

"It's all right," Connell said. "I can make it up. I already know what kind of teacher you are. You teach me every day."

They drove back to Queens, heading to the strip of grass they'd come to call their own, along a road that led to LaGuardia Airport. When they parked, his father turned to him.

"Can you do me a favor? Can you not tell your mother about this?"

"Coming here?"

"No. The other thing."

"Sure. Sure."

"She won't understand it the way you do."

They walked to the fence near one of the landing strips. In the distance, Connell could see planes coming in in a line, separated by long intervals. Planes took off around them; engines roared. They stood there dwarfed by arrivals and departures. His father's arm was around him, and his own fingers clung to the chain-link fence.

They listened to the game on the way back. When they got home, instead of putting a record on and breaking out the headphones, his father put the game on the radio and they sat on the couch listening to it. The Mets beat the Phillies by a run, Gooden throwing eight solid innings and Franco nailing down the save.

He thought about telling his mother how weird it had been, but so much about his father was weird that it was hard to say where the weirdness began and ended. It wasn't a generation gap so much as a chasm that had opened up and swallowed a whole lifetime. Instead of hanging out with the flower children, his father had haunted laboratories and listened to

Bing Crosby. He loved foreign languages and corny puns. How often, when Connell reached for another helping at breakfast, did his father stop his hand and ask him in mock earnest if one egg wasn't *un oeuf*?

Who could forget the events of that past Thanksgiving? They went to the Coakleys. The Coakleys used to live a few blocks away in a three-family house like their own; now they lived on Long Island, in a house with plush carpets and a low-lit den that had a couch on all sides and a large television perfect for watching the game. Cindy Coakley had been his mother's friend since first grade at St. Sebastian's.

His parents were getting ready in their bedroom. Connell was lying on his bed reading. The radio was on in the living room; his parents must have thought he was out there listening to it, because his mother started laughing in a girlish way that made him feel as if he was hearing something he wasn't supposed to be hearing. He crept to his door.

"Oh, Ed," he heard her say. "Don't do it!"

"Why not? I think it's a great idea."

"It's a *terrible* idea," she said, but the delight in her voice said otherwise. "I insist—no, I *demand*—that you not do this."

"I'm doing it," he said. "Here I go."

"Ed!" she squealed. "That's brand new!"

It wasn't strange to hear them laughing, but this was different; this was playful. Around him they laughed like parents, with a certain restraint. He had never heard his mother sound so young.

"How does that look?" his father asked.

"You are not going to show that to anybody. Do you hear me?"

"You're afraid the women won't be able to handle it," he said. "You think they'll swoon."

A few seconds passed in silence. He went right up to their closed door, his heart pounding in his chest. He heard some muffled sounds.

"We don't have time," his mother said, but she sounded as if she was saying they had all the time in the world.

She made little moaning noises. Connell's blood ran cold. He had never seen them kiss on the lips, and yet there they were, kissing and doing God knew what else. He thought of all the times he'd watched Jack Coakley pull Cindy to him in brute affection, the times he'd silently urged his father to sweep his mother up in his arms in front of everyone.

"We'd better get going," his mother said. He heard the sound of the zipper on her dress.

"Maybe I'll give Jack a laugh. He needs a laugh."

Connell dashed back to his room. When his parents emerged, he watched for some sign of the mischief he had heard them discussing, but there was nothing.

They drove in a pleasant silence to the Northern State Parkway and the Coakleys. The men watched football in the den while the women talked and transferred food from pots to serving dishes. The dining room table was set with good silver and wineglasses, salt and pepper in sterling silver shakers, and two layers of tablecloths. As everyone trickled in, Connell was already at the table, looking forward to the painful bloat about to overtake him. After the meal, he would sit on the couch with the rest of the men and pat his swollen belly, burping quietly.

Jack carved the turkey. Everyone began passing dishes.

"Ed," Jack said. "Why don't you take your jacket off? Join us awhile."

Everybody knew what was coming.

"I can't," Connell's father said. "There's no back to this shirt."

A little wave of laughter passed over the table. Connell felt his face redden. They played this routine out every year. Connell didn't care if everyone else was amused by the line; why did his father have to be so weird? He was the only one in a suit; everyone else wore sweaters and khakis. Even on the hottest days of summer he wore long-sleeved shirts and pants. Connell didn't care about his warnings about skin cancer and the shrinking ozone layer. All he knew was his father looked like a dork.

"You know, Ed," Jack said. "You always say that. What does that mean? What are you trying to tell me?"

Jack was six-four, two-fifty, an ex-Marine. When they watched the game in Jack's den, it wasn't hard to imagine Jack on the field protecting the quarterback. In a booming voice, he told stories that ended in uproarious laughter; Connell's father spoke gently and people leaned in to hear him. Jack's face lit up whenever Connell's father talked, but Connell always wanted his father to finish quickly; he was nervous that Jack would see how strange his father really was.

"Just that the shirt I'm wearing happens not to have a back, and so I can't take my jacket off."

"Now why would a shirt not come with a back?"

"It's cheaper this way," his father said. "Less material."

"I don't think anyone here would have a problem with seeing your back," Jack said with an odd edge in his voice. He turned to Frank Mc-Guire. "Do you have a problem with seeing Ed's back?"

Frank looked back and forth between Connell's father and Jack, like he didn't know what the right answer was. He broke into nervous laughter. "Come on, guys," he said. "He wants to wear his jacket, he wants to wear his jacket. It's Thanksgiving."

"I realize he wants to wear his jacket, Frank. But I'm asking him to take it off. He's making me nervous."

"Is that what you want? You want me to take my jacket off?"

Jack was giving Connell's father a hard look. Cindy, who had only belatedly caught on to the tension in the scene, as though it were occurring on a frequency only dogs could hear, put a hand on Jack's arm in a silent plea.

"Yes," Jack said. "That's what I want."

"Well, it is your house."

"Last time I checked it still was."

"Jack!" Cindy said.

Even Connell's mother, who had been smiling at the outset, looked concerned. Connell wasn't supposed to know what his parents both knew, which was that Jack's airline was planning major cuts and Jack was worried about getting laid off. At night Connell stood in the darkened door of his room, listening down the hall to his mother on the phone in the kitchen.

"It's okay, Cindy," Connell's father said. "This jacket is really bothering you, huh?"

"Nobody else has a jacket on."

"Okay," his father said, rising. "I understand. I'm sorry to have caused a disturbance." He took one arm out of his jacket slowly, then the other. He had cut the entire rear panel from what looked like an expensive shirt. The sleeves clung to the shirt's outline like windsocks in a strong gust. His skin was a blank, ridiculous canvas flecked by freckles and scraggly hairs. For a moment, the room seemed suspended in time.

"Is this what you wanted?" he asked. "To see this? Does this make you happy? Behold, then!"

Then Jack let out a bark of laughter so loud and sudden it could have been a death rattle; another followed to punctuate it; then his laughs came quick and plentiful, like the little skips a stone makes on the water's surface after the first big few. The laughter was passed around the room like a contagion.

"Sit down at this goddamned table and eat some of my turkey, you goofy son of a bitch," Jack said after he'd composed himself. The look on Jack's face said he'd charge into battle for Connell's father if he had to. Connell had seen people give his father that look before. Maybe you had to be an adult to really appreciate him.

That fall, he had made Connell do a project on habituation for the science fair. They tapped a bunch of roly-poly bugs a number of times with a pen. Some stopped rolling up quickly; the rest just kept getting annoyed. Eventually they all quit responding. This was supposed to be extremely significant, the fact that they could learn to ignore millions of years of inherited instincts after five minutes of pointless irritation. Connell gathered the data; his father helped him draw up the findings on a couple of poster boards—charts, graphs, everything low-tech. When he arrived at the auditorium, Connell knew he didn't stand a chance. Other kids were setting up huge working volcanoes, radio-controlled cars, and full ecosystems with convoluted loops that ran the length of two tables. He didn't even have a box full of bugs. When the teachers came around for the presentation, he started sweating. He explained the way they—*he*—had gone about it, as best as he understood it, which was less than he should have.

In awarding him first prize, they cited the project's elegant simplicity and its careful application of the scientific method. Other parents hooted and hollered when their children's names were announced. His father kept his seat and gave him a cool little nod and pumped his fist. Connell was never more impressed by him in his life. It was as if his father had known all along that they were playing a winning hand.

When his mother got home, she pulled him aside. "What was it like at Daddy's school?" she asked. "How was he?" Her expression was strangely intense, and she was practically whispering. Connell was so unnerved that he almost said something. Then he remembered his promise.

"Dad was Dad," he said. "I didn't understand a word he was saying."

19

An article in a nursing journal said that a fixed routine had a deleterious effect on the mind of a person prone to depression and that shaking up elements of a depressive's environment could be a productive way to introduce treatment. She didn't know for sure that Ed was technically depressed, but she knew she'd never be able to get him to a psychiatrist to find out.

What Ed needed—what they all needed—was to climb out of a rut. She started to wonder whether a move to another house might not be just the thing to jolt him out of his torpor. The timing was right: Connell was starting high school next year and could commute into the city from almost anywhere; the value of their home, given the encroaching neighborhood decay, would only go down. In a few years, they'd be trapped.

A house could make all the difference. Things improved for the Coakleys after Jack got promoted to director of cargo for SAS and they moved out to East Meadow. Jack had shown some signs of depression himself when they were still in Jackson Heights, but in East Meadow he started making furniture in his big garage and got into gardening and landscaping. He established an idyll in their backyard for all to enjoy: the echoing pool, the radio raised to drown out the rattle of distant mowers, wet footprints drying on hot concrete, the ubiquitous smell of sunblock.

It had been five years since she'd raised the rate on the already far-below-market rent she charged the Orlandos, and even then she'd raised it only a pittance. The knowledge that her son was safe had always offset in her mind the revenue she'd lost by floating the Orlando clan. Connell went up to one or the other of their apartments after school and stayed until she and Ed came home. Now that he was getting old enough to take care of himself, though, the protection they offered meant less than it once had.

"I've been thinking about this house," she said. Connell was having dinner at Farshid's, and they were alone at the dinner table. Ed didn't respond. She'd gotten used to these one-sided exchanges. She'd learned to read different meanings into his silences. That night's silence was auspicious; it lacked the heaviness of other varieties. It was like a sheet she could project her thoughts onto.

"I've been thinking that it might be nice to have a place of our own, where we don't have renters. I'm tired of being a landlord. Aren't you?" She filled a plate with chicken, potatoes, and steamed green beans and handed it back to him. It looked bland, but it was just the two of them, and Ed never seemed to care either way.

"This is our home," he said.

"I know," she said. "I was just thinking we could look for a place that would be . . . *more* ours."

"We've done a lot of work on this house." Ed cut into his chicken. Rather than cut a small bite, he sawed it in the middle until it was in two halves.

"You're happy here?"

"I am." He began cutting the halves in half, his head into his work.

"You're not happy," she said. "You're miserable. You won't get off the couch."

"I'm happy."

"We could move to the suburbs. Get a nice house."

"We have a nice house right here." He looked up at her for the first time. His chicken was arranged in a neat mosaic of bite-sized pieces, but he hadn't begun to eat.

"This neighborhood is going to hell."

"I'm a city boy," he said. "All those empty streets. All the space between houses." He gestured dismissively with his fork.

Space between houses was all she wanted in the world.

"Wouldn't it be nice to get out of here? Start somewhere else? The timing is perfect. Connell's starting a new school next year. We've saved so well."

"This place is a lot better than what I had growing up," Ed said.

"Yes," she said. "You're right about that."

She hated being made to feel churlish. She wasn't looking for a palace, just a step up from where they were. It was for him that she was thinking of all this, but how could she talk to him about it without alerting him to her line of reasoning?

"I don't want to have anyone walking over my head anymore," she said.

"We'll switch apartments with Lena. She'd jump at it. Those stairs probably kill her."

She gave him a withering look. His green beans were all cut in half now too.

"Our life is here," he said.

"Wouldn't you like to get to know another neighborhood?"

"I don't want to be isolated," he said. "I don't want to have to get used to a whole new way of life."

She bit her tongue, then said it anyway. "You already have a whole new way of life."

She watched him finally begin to move some food into his mouth and chew it slowly, as if considering the mechanics of chewing anew. It was driving her crazy. She put her knife and fork down and waited.

"We can't afford to move where you want to move," he said, but it was as if he wasn't in the conversation anymore, so caught up was he in bringing small bites to his mouth, gnashing them between his teeth, and swallowing.

"You don't know the first thing about where I want to move," she said bitterly.

She had long ago stopped concerning herself with the details of their money management. They had a common bank account that he balanced fastidiously. He also handled their investments. Since he was conservative in his portfolio choices (the First Jersey Securities investment had been her idea, based on a tip she'd gotten from a doctor at work; Ed had reluctantly agreed to it), they'd seldom suffered the effects of overexposure, and they were in a strong position relative to peers of similar or even greater income. This was one decision, however, that she couldn't afford to let him control. If she couldn't get him excited about this project, she would have to generate enough excitement for both of them.

She began searching through the listings in Bronxville.

"This place looks perfect," she said, as she showed Ed an open house notice in the newspaper.

"You know how I feel about this."

"Humor me. It's on Saturday. We'll make a day of it."

"I've got something lined up for us for then."

He almost never made plans. She couldn't help but smile at the obvious ploy.

"Do tell," she said.

"Mets tickets," he said.

"You've *bought* these tickets? It *has* to be this Saturday?"

"Somebody at work is holding them for me. I said I had to check with my wife's schedule."

Such a hopeful look came over his face, as if he really thought she hadn't seen through his ruse, that she couldn't bring herself to argue. The next night he showed off the tickets, undoubtedly purchased at the stadium on the way home from work. He'd even bought four, the unnecessary fourth there to lend verisimilitude to the bit of theater.

Saturday came. It was a sunny, mild day in early May, and, she had to admit, a perfect day for a game. With the other ticket, Connell brought Farshid. On the 7 train, adults in the infantilizing garments of fandom buzzed with an adolescent excess of energy. When the doors opened at Willets Point, she felt carried along by the buoyancy of the crowd. Instead of following the switchback ramp to the top as they usually did, though, they stopped after a single flight. When they emerged from the corridor and were flooded with light, they saw that the players looked unusually life-sized.

The boys took their seats with palpable pride at being envied from above. Batting practice was still going on, and they got their gloves out. Connell never failed to bring his glove to games and wear it for hours in an uncomfortable vigil, despite having never come close to snagging a ball; they were always in the wrong seats. On the lower level, though, having a glove was good planning.

Ed took their orders and went for refreshments. In the absence of his moderating influence, the boys fired fusillades of obscure terms at each other: *hot smash, can of corn, high and tight, round the horn, hot corner, filthy stuff, the hook.* As she listened to them speak, a meditative calm came over her. She did some of her best thinking at ball games, or while Ed was listening to them on the radio. She'd always understood the basic mechanics of baseball, and Ed had successfully explained a good deal of the more complex aspects to her, but she'd never cracked the code of the priestly solemnity her husband and son greeted the game with, in which old bats and split-leather gloves were revered like relics, as saints' fingers and spleens had been in earlier centuries. In truth, she was impressed by the range of her son's knowledge. It was an arrested form of scholarship he was practicing when he allowed his brain to soak up these facts. It was really history men craved when they fixated on the statistics of retired athletes—men who hadn't been to war, in a nation still young enough to feel dwarfed by the epochal moments of its onetime rivals. The rhetoric of baseball was redolent of antiquity, the hushed tones, the gravitas, the elevation of the pedestrian into the sublime. Connell and Ed would read write-ups of games they'd watched or listened to on the radio, even ones they'd attended. The narrative that surrounded the game seemed as important as the game itself. Ed raved about the descriptive power of some sportswriters, but she never saw what he was talking about; it seemed like boilerplate stuff, dressed up as the chronicle of an epic clash. She focused on the visceral particulars of the stadium experience instead: the smell of boiled meat, nestled under sauerkraut; the thunder of the scoreboard exhorting them to clap; the feel of her son's hand as he slapped her five.

Ed had been gone a long time. She panned around for his Members Only jacket. After some restless searching she spotted him a section over, leaning into the railing, staring around with his hand over his eyes like a lookout in a crow's nest. She had his ticket stub in her pocket, so he couldn't show it to the ushers, one of whom was trying to move him along. She could see Ed growing agitated as he swatted a second usher's hand from his shoulder. She hated making a spectacle of herself, but any second now the guards would be called, and that would create an even bigger scene. She stood and shouted his name, waving her arms. He finally saw her and broke free of the ushers, who gave no chase, seeing order restored. He made his way down the aisle encumbered by trays; she distributed the quarry to the boys.

He stood in front of his seat. "Where the hell were you?"

She stole a glance around to see who was listening. "I was right here," she said, trying to urge him toward calm. No one had cocked an ear yet, but she and Ed were on the border of a full-on commotion.

"I couldn't find you," he said sharply.

"I realize that, honey. But you're here now."

"I was looking all over for you."

"Ed," she said. "I'm here. You're here. Enjoy the game."

The boys were too caught up in the food to notice Ed. He still hadn't taken his seat but was standing looking into the crowd as if the answer to what confounded him were projected on the backs of their heads. Farshid listlessly fingered a waxy-looking pretzel. Connell wolfed down a hot dog in two bites and started in on his own pretzel. When she picked up on annoyance behind her, she tugged on Ed's sleeve and he fell into the seat and began to smooth out his pants with an insistent repetitiveness, as though trying to warm himself or clear crumbs from his lap. He had bought nothing for the two of them to eat.

"Where's the food for us?"

"I didn't get us anything."

She shook her head in disbelief. "What are we going to eat?"

"You didn't ask for anything."

"I have to *ask* to eat now?" She took a piece of Connell's pretzel.

"Hang on," he said. A hot dog salesman had entered their section, and Ed flagged him down.

"I feel like you don't *think* anymore," she said when they were settled in with their dogs. "I need you to get with it, Ed."

"Let's just enjoy the game," he said.

A couple of innings later, a Met lifted a high foul ball toward their section. She could feel it gaining on them. As it approached, time seemed to slow; an awful expectancy built. It shifted in the wind, so that it appeared to be headed elsewhere; then it was upon them. People all around reached for it, but it was headed right for Ed. He stabbed at it clumsily and it bounded out of his hand, snagged by a man behind them in the ensuing scrum.

For a moment, Connell appeared stunned. He had been brushed on the neck by the hand of destiny. His body seemed to shiver with contained nervous energy, and he hopped like a bead of oil in a saucepan.

"Wow!" he said, to her, to his father, to Farshid, to anyone who would listen. "Can you believe it?"

The victorious fan stared into empty space with a determined expression as he received the forceful backslaps of his friends. His studied lack of fanfare had the effect of holding the note of his triumph longer.

Ed was miserable. "I'm sorry, buddy," he said. "I tried to get it for you."

"No problem, Dad."

"I'm really sorry." He looked bereft. "I feel terrible."

"Maybe if you'd had a glove," Connell said sweetly, extending his own. Ed turned and asked if the boy could see the ball, which the man handed over more warily than Eileen thought appropriate. Connell held it covetously. She worried that he might ask to keep it, but after a few moments in which he seemed to communicate wordlessly with it, he gave it back, and the man secreted it into his jacket pocket. Something about these talismanic objects, spoils of an ersatz war, reduced men to primal feelings. Connell pounded his glove every time a foul ball was hit in their general direction, no matter how far away it was, and she could think of nothing to say to stop him.

20

She sat beside Connell on the top step, wondering about all the fuss people made over the constellations. The webs of light poorly described the forms they were meant to evoke, and even if she'd known what those forms were, she doubted she could have suspended her disbelief enough to see them characterized there.

On an average night the stars glimmered weakly, if they were visible at all, but that night they were unusually prominent. This was another reason to move—maybe in the suburbs he could see the stars well all the time.

"What do you see?" she asked.

"A lot of stars," he said. "What about you?"

"There's the Big Dipper," she said.

"And the Little Dipper."

"Yes."

"And the North Star."

"Yup."

They had come to the limit of their knowledge. She was relieved to have a son who didn't spew forth a stream of facts about the sky when he looked up at it. One fear in marrying a scientist had been that her children would be ill-equipped to live in the world of ordinary men.

"I like to imagine people thousands of years ago looking at the same stars," he said.

She smiled at his philosophical tone.

"And people in the future long after we're dead," he said.

A shudder came over her. She was the one who was supposed to put it into perspective for him, not the other way around. She had lived through the loss of two parents and witnessed death nearly every day at work, and yet she was spooked to hear him invoke their inevitable finality.

"Come inside," she said. "It's late."

"I want to see if the stars get brighter the later it gets."

"It's a school night." She felt her grip on her temper begin to slip. The males in her life refused to cooperate with her. "You can investigate this in the summer."

She stood in the hallway watching him trudge to his room. Then she found herself stepping back onto the stoop and looking again to the night sky, trying to divine what ancient people might have seen in it—animals, hunters, maybe kings. Nothing came into focus, except when she thought she saw a dog with a long leash around its neck. When she looked up again it was gone.

That night, when she couldn't sleep, she concentrated on the steadiness of the stars, their transcendence of human sorrow and confusion, the reassurance offered by the unfathomable scale of geologic time.

21

On Sundays, they went to one o'clock Mass. Ed was never the driving force in their church attendance. When Connell was a baby, Ed had loved to usher him out the back of the church at the first hint of a meltdown.

For someone whose responsibility it was to get everyone to Mass, she didn't feel confident of her own belief in God anymore. It had been years since she'd thought of the world as the product of a divine plan. Maybe working as a nurse was too much for belief to fight against. She'd seen people expire on the table in every way—noisily, quietly, thrashingly, completely still. Death had come to seem no more than the breaking down of an organism: the last exhalations of the lungs, the final pumpings of the heart, the brain deprived of blood.

That didn't mean she was going to stop going to Mass. She liked the moral lessons for the boy, and the good works the Church did were the most important reason to attend—God or no God. When alone with her thoughts she couldn't help detecting some frequency she was tuning into, and she prayed to that frequency after communion when she knelt alongside her pew mates, though most of the time she felt like she was talking to herself.

The previous Sunday, Pentecost Sunday, at the end of the last Mass he would celebrate at the parish, Father Finnegan, who had been there thirty years, had introduced his replacement, Father Choudhary. Everyone registered the new, dark figure up there preparing the gifts as a harbinger of the future. Over the last decade, the priests had gone from being mostly Irish to mostly Hispanic; now, apparently, they were coming from India too.

Every year, there were more Indians around her at church. A few months ago, an Indian family had bought the Wohls' house up the block, and because she'd assumed they were Hindu, she'd been surprised to see them at Mass the following week. She'd lingered a bit so she wouldn't have to walk down the block with them, something she hadn't been proud of when she lay in bed thinking of it that night. The next Sunday, she made sure to catch them on the way out and walk with them. It had felt good to make amends for a slight no one knew she'd committed, and thereafter she felt comfortable letting them walk home alone.

Ed was more open-minded about other cultures. When they walked through Greenwich Village, he marveled appreciatively at the stratospheric Mohawk haircuts of the punk rockers, while she felt only disgust. So when they found themselves at Father Choudhary's first Mass, she wasn't surprised that Ed seemed extra attentive. To her, Father Choudhary looked spooky under his stark-white vestments, with the effigy of Jesus behind him on the altar. He spoke in a trilling accent. Even the Hispanics looked around as if to say, *This guy isn't one of us.* Ed just sat with his arms folded in amusement, or tapping the church bulletin against his thigh.

During the reading, Ed was usually good for a flip to another section of the liturgy—he was more into the literature of the Bible than the sacred text aspect—but with Father Choudhary at the pulpit, he held the book open to the reading. At least she could understand Father Choudhary better than Father Ortiz, who she wished would give in and speak Spanish with an interpreter beside him.

It was a reading from the book of Proverbs, on how the wisdom of God was born before the earth was made:

When he established the heavens I was there,
when he marked out the vault over the face of the deep;
When he made firm the skies above,
when he fixed fast the foundations of the earth;
When he set for the sea its limit;
so that the waters should not transgress his command;
Then I was beside him as his craftsman,

and I was his delight day by day,
Playing before him all the while,
playing on the surface of his earth;
and I found delight in the sons of men.

When Father Choudhary closed the book to begin his homily, Ed settled in to listen. Father Choudhary began preaching about matters wholly unrelated to the reading: the idea that if we are all made of dust, then the same dust, cosmic dust, he called it, could be found throughout the universe; that this cosmic dust might have been created by the Big Bang; that somehow our sharing in this dust called us to responsibility to each other. Ed looked positively enthralled. Father Choudhary spoke of the smallness of man in relation to the vastness of the universe, and how that smallness was instructive, how it reminded us that part of our humanity was a sense of humility. He exhorted everyone gathered to allow themselves to feel wonder and awe in the face of all creation, big and small. Then he quoted from a French Jesuit named Teilhard de Chardin: "He recognized with absolute certainty the empty fragility of even the noblest theorizings as compared with the definitive plenitude of the smallest fact grasped in its total, concrete reality." She had never seen Ed more enthused at church. He slapped his hand on the back of the pew in front of him, and for a moment, as she watched him shift in his seat in restless indecision, she thought she would have to reach over and keep him from standing and applauding.

After Mass, a crowd gathered outside the church. Eileen worked her way to the curb, but when she turned, only Connell was behind her. Ed was on the steps, waiting in the receiving line to greet the priest like a well-wisher at a wedding. This was too much.

She reached him just as he was extending his hand for a shake.

"Great speech," he said absurdly, as though congratulating a politician. "Where are you from?" She was mortified, but Father Choudhary seemed delighted as he pumped Ed's hand. They talked at length, the receiving line at a standstill.

She waited until they had gotten far enough away.

"What was all that about?"

"All what?"

Connell had produced a tennis ball from his pocket and was bouncing it to himself.

"Since when are you so interested in the lives of priests?"

"He did a good job," Ed said.

Connell lost the ball and Ed fetched it from the street, flipping it in his hand as he walked, infuriating her. In her anger she twisted the bulletin into a baton that she smacked into her open palm like a nightstick.

"You really needed to ask where he's from? He's from India."

"He's from Bangladesh."

"You needed to know that?"

"I like to learn new things. If we don't learn, we die." Ed threw the ball to Connell. "Isn't that right, buddy?"

When they arrived home, Ed stood rooted to a spot on the sidewalk in front of the house. She waved Connell inside, and the boy hesitated, then went in. Ed didn't budge. She began to climb the stairs, hoping Ed would follow.

Ed bounced Connell's ball on the ground and caught it. "I saw the paper," he said. "The houses you circled."

She tucked up her skirt and sat on the top step. She felt as if she'd been caught canoodling with a boyfriend. The ball went *thwunk* as it hit the sidewalk; Ed cradled it back into his cupped palm.

"I don't want to leave," he said. "We have a perfectly nice house. We know the neighborhood. Doesn't that count for anything? Plus, we have this new priest."

"He's *Indian*," she blurted out incredulously before she could catch herself. "Look around you. Look at what's happening to this neighborhood. What's already happened."

"It's home," he said.

"How about that?" she asked, pointing to some graffiti at the base of the big apartment building across the street.

"That too," he said.

"How about when you walked in covered in eggs on Halloween?"

"Kids horse around everywhere."

"How about when Lena got mugged?"

"You can't live in a bubble," he said.

"How about what happened to Mrs. Cooney? You want that to happen to me?"

"Of course not. But that was an accident."

"I'd say it was closer to murder."

She paused, feeling herself shift from anger to resolution. She didn't need to argue with him. She could do this without him if she had to.

"I want us to look," she said. "Just to know what's out there."

He shook his head. A tiny patch of bald was forming, but she could only see it from this angle. He stopped bouncing the ball and put his hand on her foot and gave it a squeeze. The touch electrified her, as if he had channeled all his energy into his hands.

"I can't explain why I can't give you more in this," he said. "I just really don't want to go anywhere. Have you ever felt like life was getting away from you, and people were lapping you and you couldn't catch up? And if you could just stop the world and take it all in, and nobody would go anywhere for a little while, you'd have enough time to understand it? I wish I could do that. I don't want anybody or anything to move an inch."

"People move," she said. "That's life."

"I'm lodging my protest," he said, and he put the ball in his pocket and rose to go inside, leaving her alone on the stoop.

22

The first house she saw cost nine hundred thousand, at least twice what they could afford. She had to see it, though, to have a basis for comparison.

She wore a nice gray suit, a ruffled blouse, and heels. She drove up a long driveway that turned into a circle in front of the house, along whose perimeter a few cars were parked: a BMW, a VW, an Audi. She was embarrassed to be driving a Chevy Corsica. She was glad that Ed's torpor hadn't led to an attenuation of his car-washing habit; at least she had neatness on her side.

The door was open. She entered a capacious vestibule with marble floors, oil paintings on the walls, and an enormous chandelier hanging from the vaulted ceiling. She took in the sweep of the place for only a few moments before an effervescent real estate agent descended the stairs, trailing behind her a young couple who were dressed more casually than Eileen and looked more comfortable there. She had made a mistake. She removed her jacket—it was too warm for one—as they took the final steps of what seemed an endless staircase.

"Welcome," the agent said, extending both arms as if drawing her in for a hug. The couple had to be ten or fifteen years younger than Eileen. She felt she was intruding. She wanted to turn around and head to the car.

"I saw the door open," she said.

"Of course! Of course! We were just about to look at the back patio. Join us, or take a look around yourself if you like."

"Thank you," she said. "I think I'll walk around."

She stood there while they made their way outside. She thought again about leaving but couldn't bear the idea of their talking about her after she was gone. The inevitable simmering potpourri wafted in from the kitchen. She didn't want to fall for it, but she couldn't resist the mood it put her in. She headed upstairs. In the bedroom at the top she was surprised by another couple who looked closer to her age and had two girls in tow, the younger of whom was bouncing lightly on the bed. When the mother saw Eileen standing there, she told the girl to stop. The husband was admiring the craftsmanship of the window. He took Eileen in with an appraising glance from top to toe, as though she were part of the house, and smiled. The wife ushered the girls out, but the husband lingered behind, making pronouncements about the bones of the house as though he imagined being trailed by an audience of onlookers.

After they left, she drifted to the window the man had been admiring. Her car looked like a miniature version of itself. Birds and acorns had taken a toll on its roof; it needed a paint job.

She fluffed up the pillows the little girl had leaned against. She tried to resist the impulse to sit but felt suddenly tired and didn't know what else to do in the room, which she now felt trapped in, as she didn't want to face the young couple and the agent downstairs. She heard the low murmur of voices and labored to slow her breathing. She hadn't noticed until this moment that her heart was racing. She tried to calm herself by gazing at the beautiful sunlight coming through the window and feeling the lace of the duvet, but what put her at ease eventually was the quiet of the house. There were no horns honking outside. She breathed deeply and remembered that these people did not know she was an impostor; for all she knew they were impostors themselves. Maybe no one visiting the house really belonged there—including the agent, who had to project an air of aristocracy to blend in with her surroundings, but when it came down to it was working a job like anybody else.

She had almost willed herself into equanimity when she noticed three photos, each nicely framed, standing sentry around a bedside table lamp. Nothing in the photos could have explained the twisting in the gut she felt.

She saw a tableau of a family, possibly from the holidays; a wedding portrait in black and white; and a picture of an elderly couple on horseback, the husband wearing a grin of effortless control. The house was probably being sold so they could move to an inviting snowbird locale or else as an inheritance after the death of one or both of them. It seemed they had lived a full life. The husband possessed a heartiness that belied his years. She felt a surge of nerves that verged on nausea.

What Ed didn't understand was that in a house like this she would finally be able to breathe enough to put things in order for both of them. Here, she could make herself into the kind of wife who wasn't always rushing to get lunch made before he walked out the door in the morning. She didn't even mind thinking that the next place she lived could be where she died.

She gathered the courage to head downstairs. She found the agent and the young couple outside on the patio, the husband taking in the sweep of the yard, the wife inspecting the grill. She straightened her blouse before she slid the glass door open.

"I've got to run. I don't have much time to stay and chat."

"Of course!" the agent said. "Did you pick up a brochure?"

"It's a lovely house, but it may not be exactly what we're looking for."

"Everyone has a checklist, right? Otherwise it'd all be one big house!"

"My husband and I would like to look at other properties in the area."

"Please! Take my card. Where are you now?"

"The city," Eileen said. Queens was technically the city, but she knew that wasn't what she was conveying.

"I'll be happy to show you other properties."

"Thank you." She turned to the couple. "I wish you the best of luck in your search."

"And you in yours, wherever it leads," the young man said in a grand way that struck her as ungracious.

When she got home Ed was on the couch with his eyes closed and the headphones on. She stood there waving both arms, trying to draw the gaze of his inner eye. Then she went into Connell's room.

He was lying on the floor in his baseball uniform. It touched her to see how cute he looked in it. It was small on him; he had grown a lot over the past year, and his arms were wiry and long. He had begun to fill out in the upper body. She wondered how concerned she should be about how much time he spent in the basement lifting weights. She'd heard it could stunt his growth, but there was so much else to worry about lately, and she was just glad he wasn't getting into anything really destructive.

He'd had the sense to take off his mud-caked cleats, but the rest of his uniform sported a layer of that clayey dirt that never came off in the wash.

"How did it go?"

"We lost. I stink. I walked nine guys."

He was flipping a ball to himself and catching it; it was coming close to hitting his face. One toss would have crushed his nose if he hadn't turned away at the last second.

"You'll get better."

"I threw pretty hard, though," he said, a proud smile spreading across his face.

"Just don't dent the garage door," she said. "I don't want to have to spend money on yet another one right now."

He nodded. "Dad came to the game," he said.

"Really?"

"He did something weird."

She felt herself begin to panic. "What happened?"

"He wigged out on me after the game. I had to stay and help with the ball bag and bases and stuff. Dad went to get the car. When I got in, he started screaming at me. I've never seen him like that before. He kept yelling, '*You kept me waiting! You kept me waiting!*'"

"Well, it's not good to keep people waiting," she said halfheartedly, wondering if he could hear how tenuous her solidarity with his father was at the moment.

"I couldn't leave all the bats and stuff. My coach asked me to help. And I wasn't that long, I really wasn't. He screamed all the way home."

"Your father's going through a hard time right now," she said. "You can't take it personally."

"I didn't ask him to wait for me. I didn't ask him to come."

"He loves going to your games."

"Whatever."

"Don't say that."

"Mom, you weren't there. He was crazy."

A careless toss caused the ball to roll out of reach and he sat with his hands on his knees looking like a little man, already beleaguered by experience. He was a smart kid; he knew some kids had fathers who beat them or simply weren't there. Still, it was hard to see him disillusioned. Normally she was jealous of the bond between the two of them, but now she wanted to defend it.

"Daddy has a thing about being made to wait in the car," she said. "You can't take it personally. I'm sure he's sorry."

"He made us sit in the driveway for half an hour so he could apologize."

"See," she said. "There you go."

In bed that night, though, she confronted Ed.

"Connell said you flipped out on him."

"I lost my temper."

"He's just a kid, Ed."

"That's not going to happen again."

"It had better not. I don't give a damn what your father did to you. That boy's not him."

She parked a few blocks away and walked to the realty office on the chance that the agent hadn't seen her car the first time. The ruse would be exposed eventually, but she liked being taken seriously as a contender for these places. It was like when she was younger and would ask that a certain item be placed on hold at a store. The cashier would write her name on a slip of paper, and she would be granted time for consideration. The mere idea of possessing it in that allotted limbo was sufficient to quench the desire for it and she would almost never come back to complete the purchase. Perhaps it could be like that with the expensive houses; a few minutes in them could inoculate her against the need to live in them.

The office was in the center of Bronxville, and though it was sandwiched between two boutique shops, it had the feel of an old dentist's office. There was paneling on the walls, a thin blue carpet, and a few worn desks on either side of an aisle that ran through the center. The desk chairs didn't have wheels. The office made Eileen feel she was not completely out of her realm. One other agent talked quietly in the corner.

Gloria wore her brown hair cut short, like a politician's. There were ghostly remains of blond in it. She wore a navy business suit with what looked like a silk blouse. Her teeth were bright white, and level and straight enough that they could have been caps. She was around Eileen's height.

Once again, Gloria extended both hands in greeting. Eileen wondered whether this was something she had learned in a real estate textbook. And yet, she found herself succumbing to it as she had to the potpourri. They sat at the desk.

"Why don't we start by talking about what kind of house you're looking to see? Is there a style you're particularly interested in?"

Eileen had no real grasp on the terms of art that governed houses. Colonial? Edwardian? Tudor? These were terms she'd heard. As much as she'd always wanted a house in the suburbs, it was an abstract desire. It was about what the house represented: polish, grandeur, seclusion, permanency.

"I liked the house I saw last week quite a lot," she said.

Gloria looked surprised. "I thought it hadn't appealed to you."

"Well, yes, that's true. In some ways it didn't. But in many ways it was a perfect house."

Gloria looked like she was weighing whether to let her off the hook or not. Then she smiled. "It has to be a perfect house in every way," she said. "That's what I want for you."

"Thank you."

"If you don't mind my asking, was it a matter of price?"

"Not at all," Eileen said. "Money wasn't the issue."

Gloria raised her brows. "Okay," she said, clicking her pen into action. "Well, if I'm going to find your future home, I'm going to need certain guidelines."

"Of course," Eileen said.

"Why don't we just start from the top, Eileen. It's Leary, right?"

"Yes."

"And you live in the city, you said?"

"We do."

"Which part?"

"Queens."

"Parts of Queens are so lovely, aren't they? I actually have a brother in Douglaston."

Douglaston was another world entirely. Eileen paused. "We're in Jackson Heights," she said.

"One of the garden co-ops?" Gloria asked, raising her brows again in what looked like a hopeful manner. "I hear they're quite beautiful."

"We own a house," she said. "A three-family house."

"Okay." She was writing things down. "And you're looking to move to Bronxville specifically? Or is it this general vicinity you're interested in?"

"Bronxville."

She looked up from the pad, beaming. "Isn't Bronxville just beautiful? When my husband moved us here I thought I'd died and gone to heaven."

"I used to work at Lawrence Hospital," she said. "Years ago. I remembered loving it."

"So you liked the house you saw. What did you like most about it?"

"The size."

"How many bedrooms do you want? Three? Four? Five?"

"At least four," Eileen said, feeling like a drunk picking the figure in the middle.

"Okay! That's a start. Now, what's your price range?"

Eileen thought for a minute. "It depends," she said, "on whether you're asking me or my husband."

Gloria laughed. "But that's why we love them, isn't it? Men will lay their heads anywhere. I'm always trying to get my husband to consider moving to a bigger house, to tell you the truth. There's nothing wrong with living up to your means. Does your husband work on Wall Street? The train ride down is so easy."

"He's a college professor."

Another silence ensued, another appraisal from Gloria.

"So, four bedroom. Close to the train, or no? Does he teach in the city? NYU? Columbia?"

"We'll both be driving," she said flatly. "He teaches at Bronx Community College."

"Do you want to be in the school district?"

"It's not necessary. My son Connell will be going to school in the city." She paused for effect, then added, "To Regis," expecting the revelation to inflate a protective balloon of prestige around her, and indeed the agent raised her brows.

"Well!" Gloria said. "He must be a bright young man!" Then she punctured the balloon. "My husband went there. It's all he ever talks about. I get tired of hearing about it. I have all girls, but if I'd had a son, I would have sent him there myself."

Eileen had to fight to suppress her urge to correct the woman. You didn't "send" your son to Regis: your son took the scholarship exam in November and you prayed for a letter inviting him to the interview round; then, after the interview, you prayed again that he'd aced it—actually prayed, no figure of speech, even if you never prayed otherwise. Then you gathered around your son as he sat at the dining room table and opened the letter that informed him he'd been admitted, and when he said he didn't want to go to an all-boys' school that was full of nerds, you told him he was going and that he'd thank you later, and you saw a little grin flash across his face, though he was trying to pretend to be annoyed. And when you said, "Your grandparents would have been so proud," you felt something in your spirit lift, because you had a responsibility to them that you'd carried for years, and now you could hand off part of it to him. And you saw that he understood somehow what it meant for this to have happened, that he wasn't the only person involved. You imagined your father looking over your shoulder, nodding silently, and your mother, that enigma, was there too, and you could almost see her smile at the thought of what might become of the boy, of all of them, the living and the dead.

"So what's a comfortable range? Over a million? Under a million?"

She had been thinking she could afford as much as four hundred thousand. Once they sold the Jackson Heights house and paid down the taxes and commissions, they'd have enough for a good down payment, but four hundred thousand was the upper limit. It was a long way off from "under a million," but that was her reply.

"Anything else I can work with?"

"I want a house that makes an impression from the street," Eileen said. "A house that almost pulls you up into it. A big, impressive house."

Sunday after Mass, instead of taking to the couch, Ed packed a picnic lunch for the three of them and drove them to their spot near LaGuardia. She spread the blanket and they ate the strangely spartan sandwiches he'd prepared: turkey on bread, no mayo, no mustard, no lettuce or tomato; they weren't even cut in half.

It was the first hint of repose they'd had in who knew how long. She wanted to enjoy it as a family, but Connell took out the gloves, bounding around like a buck, and Ed rose to gratify him.

The sun was out after a sojourn behind some clouds. Planes glinted in the sunlight and gradually diminished in the distance, leaving a trail of noise. A light breeze took the edge off the heat. The moment struck her as perfect, in the way that quotidian moments sometimes did. She tried to freeze it in her mind: the acid sweetness of her apple, the crunch of it against her teeth, the smell of the grass. It was cheating, in a sense, to circumvent the natural sifting process of memory, but she found that those moments when she stopped and thought *I'm awake!* as though in the midst of a dream, were ones she remembered with an uncommon clarity.

Ed stood sturdily, a bit stodgily, as he waited for throws to arrive, though a surprising spring entered his step when he had to move laterally. His button-down shirt and dress slacks weren't conducive to the activity, but he adjusted gamely. Connell's accuracy suffered in his enthusiasm to return the ball almost as quickly as it landed in his glove. They started out close together. Connell seemed to want to spread out and drifted steadily back. Ed arced his throws in broad parabolas, and Connell threw on a line, though in his zeal he would sometimes overshoot and send Ed scurrying to retrieve the ball before it reached the street. A row of parked cars flanked them on either side. The last thing she wanted was for the pastoral quality of the moment to be shattered along with a window. Ed began to call Connell closer. The boy resisted at first but crept forward when Ed held the ball in his mitt and waved him toward him. They were back to a distance not much farther apart than they'd been when they first started throwing. Ed signaled to him to slow it down.

"Not so fast," he said. "We're just having fun."

"I'm not throwing that hard, Dad," Connell said.

But she could tell he was. He seemed to be reaching back and giving the throws all his strength. Ed was catching them, but he looked almost frightened at their speed.

"Slow it down," Ed said, his voice skirting anger.

"Why? Can't catch it?"

Connell unleashed a throw that came at Ed like a fist. Ed stepped aside and let it sail past. He gave the boy a look and went to retrieve it.

"That's enough," she said when Ed was out of earshot. "Your father asked you to stop throwing so hard."

"I'm not! I'm not throwing my hardest."

"Just listen to him."

"Okay," he said. "Relax, Mom."

Ed looked more defeated than angry. He was at the mercy of the Darwinian logic of an adolescent, and he stood for a minute, seeming to consider his options, then threw the ball to Connell, who snatched it out of the air midhop.

She could see it before the ball left his hand, the coiled fury in Connell's body. There was something majestic about the physical changes that turned a boy into a man, the inexorability of the need to advance, to clear away the previous generation and make room for the current one. There was also something terrifying about the impending clash between the males in her life. Neither would come out unscathed.

Maybe he was angry with his father for yelling at him in the car. Maybe he was upset that his father was having a hard time corralling his throws. Maybe it was that his father had always been a step behind some other fathers. Ed wasn't just older, he was also old-fashioned, but he and Connell had always had baseball in common. Maybe it was too much for Connell to withstand aging's incursion into his father's ability to carry out this ritual. Whatever it was, he put everything he had into the throw, so that as it left his hand she let out a little involuntary gasp.

It came so fast at Ed that he seemed to freeze in anticipation of it. He didn't even try to get out of its way. She could see, as time slowed for her observation, that sometime since she'd married him there'd been an attrition in his motor functions. His hand was no longer as fast as his mind. Even from that far away, she could see his eyes widen. The ball struck him square in the chest. He staggered and fell backward, first on his rear, then on his back.

She shouted and leapt to her feet and started running. Connell did the same. He was on his knees talking to Ed when she got there, and she pushed him aside. Ed was clutching his chest as though he'd had a heart attack. Connell was stammering apologies. He kept trying to get at Ed as she shoved him away. Then Ed was stiff-arming her as he rose to his elbows and looked at both of them.

"I'm fine, goddammit," he said. "Let me stand up."

As Ed stood, Eileen raised her hand at Connell and held it there, poised to smack him. She could feel the way the three of them were suspended in the moment as though in the relief of a sculpture. Her hand throbbed with the need to connect. Her son almost quivered in anticipation of the blow. She smacked him once, hard, on the face.

"The boy doesn't know his own strength," Ed said, taking hold of her ringing hand. He picked up the ball from the ground. "Get back out there."

"Let's go back to the blanket," she said quietly.

"We've got a few more throws left."

"We don't have to play anymore," Connell said to Ed. He wouldn't look at her.

"We're not done," Ed said.

"Ed," she pleaded, uncomfortable with every possibility she could imagine.

"Have a seat," he said, pounding his glove. "Get going," he said to Connell.

Connell walked out halfheartedly. Ed threw it to him and he lobbed it back.

"Harder!" Ed said.

Connell threw again with less force than he could have.

"Harder!" Ed yelled. "Air it out!"

That night, as they lay in bed, Eileen could see, at the V of his undershirt, the mark the baseball had made on his chest. She ran her hand over the spot; he picked her hand up in an oddly vertical way, as though lifting the cover to a butter dish, and moved it away in one swift motion.

They lay in silence, both flat on their backs, not an inch of their bodies touching, their arms flush against their sides, as though they were mummified. Her hand against her own thigh still registered a ghostly vibration of the smack she'd given Connell.

No matter how much they'd fought, the bedroom had always been an inviolate space. She could express things there that she couldn't express elsewhere. She could cuddle up to him in a way that would have surprised the nurses she supervised. There was something old-fashioned, she knew, in the way she waited for him to take the lead. He'd never had a problem doing so. Touch was their high ground when the slick cliffs of words proved treacherous.

"I have a confession to make," she said. "Yesterday, when I said I was with Cindy, I was really looking at houses."

He gave her an irritated look and then shut his eyes as if he were sleeping. "I don't know why you're obsessed with leaving," he said. "I like it here."

"How can you say that? You're not even *here*. You spend all your time on the couch. You could be in a sensory-deprivation chamber. You put those headphones on and don't hear the horns honking or the car stereos pumping. I do all the grocery shopping, so you don't get jostled in the aisles of Key Food and you don't have to deal with the checkout girls not speaking English. You're not a woman, so you don't have to fear for your safety after dark."

"Now's not a good time," he said.

"It is *too* a good time. Connell's done at St. Joan's. Haven't we been in this hellhole long enough?"

"Jesus," he said, finally opening his eyes. "Who are you all of a sudden?"

"I was fine with it until recently. But now it feels like some pressure is going to cave my head in."

"I've been engaged in a project of recuperation, of rejuvenation," he said, as if he'd been having a different conversation entirely. "I've become preoccupied lately with things I haven't done. I didn't want that pile of records staring at me. So I decided to take action, even if it wasn't popular with you, or Connell, or the chattering classes of your friends."

She burned to hear him talk of her friends. She hadn't said a word to them about how he was behaving, afraid as she was to hear what they might have to say.

"It's time I did some things for myself," he said.

She should have been furious. *Do things for himself?* What about all the sacrifices she'd made to get him through graduate school? But his speech sounded vaguely rehearsed. Something rattled around in it, like a dead tooth that hadn't fallen out. Was it that he didn't believe it himself?

"I can't live like this forever," she said.

"It's almost summer. I'm going to have more time to fix this place up. I've got projects in mind. I can revamp the garage. I can paint the house."

"Can you bring back our old neighbors? Can you drown out the noise?" She smirked. "For the rest of us, I mean. You're doing a fine job of doing it for yourself. Can you give us a lawn in front?"

"You need to relax."

"Don't tell me what I need. And don't patronize me. Not when you've been half-crazy yourself. This all started when you started going crazy, come to think of it."

"Things are going to get better now." He reached to stroke her hair. Now it was her turn to recoil from his touch.

"I want you to go with me. Just come to look at them with me. I hate going alone."

"What's the point of looking if we're staying put? I'm going to fix this place up."

It was like talking to a child. She felt something in her snap. "You may be staying here," she said slowly. "But I can't."

"And I can't leave. I told you."

"You can't go back in the womb, Ed."

"Don't be a bitch."

He'd never called her that in all their years together. She looked at him savagely.

"I'm sorry," he said. "I didn't mean that."

She ground her teeth. "Don't talk filth to me," she said, practically hissing. "You want to talk that way to a woman, get a girlfriend. Is that what this is about? This mooning, this philosophical mumbo jumbo? Is there a girl in the neighborhood you can't bear to leave? A *chiquita*?"

Ed rolled over. "Good night," he said.

She wasn't going to be the one to break the silence. She lay there turning her ring on her swollen finger, chafing at the discomfort of its digging into her skin. The salty corned beef she'd cooked for dinner had made her fingers expand as if they'd been inflated. She wanted the ring off, not so much because of the discomfort but just to have it off, just so that Ed wouldn't have any claim on her at the moment, even if he didn't know he didn't, but she couldn't get it past her knuckle.

"You're all wrong," Ed said after a while. She felt his hand between her shoulder blades. "There's no girl. You're my only girl. You know I adore you."

She didn't turn over. She stared at the handles on the chest of drawers. "Then why won't you do this for me?"

He slapped at the bed in frustration. She felt it shake. "I can't right now," he said. "I just want to stay in place."

"That's what the suburbs are *for*—staying in place." He didn't respond. "Honey, listen. Is everything all right with you? Really? You don't seem yourself lately."

"I'm fine. It's just been a long year."

They lay in silence again. Finally she turned to him. "We wouldn't be moving right away," she said. "It takes months to move. Maybe even more than a year."

"I just can't!" he said, pounding the pillow. "Don't you hear me?"

She fooled with the little raised flower at the front of her camisole, to disperse the humiliation she felt at being spoken to that way.

"I'm not going to stop looking, and I'm not going to sell the house out from under you, Ed. I need your consent."

"I'm going to work on the house this summer," he said. "Maybe you'll want to stay after that."

"Do it if it makes you happy," she said. "But don't go thinking it'll make a difference. You can't put out a fire with a thimbleful of water."

23

Eileen went in Gloria's car. One house had six bedrooms, more space than she'd ever imagined in even her most lavish dreams of dinner parties and extended visits, and she wanted Gloria to leave her there to sleep on the floor in the master bedroom and wake in the night to roam the dark spaces like a watchman in an empty office building. She registered her approval of touches Gloria pointed out, the beauty of which she needed no vocabulary to understand. It was impossible not to be enchanted by the exquisite good taste of the wood running everywhere, the quiet granite of the countertops.

"I want to see as many houses as I can," she said giddily as they left. "I want to take them all in."

Gloria was a willing enough conspirator that Eileen allowed herself to relax. She'd been afraid of wasting the agent's time, but Gloria did such a good job of projecting professional aplomb that Eileen decided to believe in the durability of her patience. Gloria would tell her the price on the way and what she thought they could get them down to. Eileen could see Gloria watching her for some reaction that would establish benchmarks to strive for, and she gave her none; she merely marveled indiscriminately at the gorgeous interiors, the manicured lawns, the impeccable patios, the huge kitchen windows that might look out, in the future, on grandchildren at play. Every time, Eileen said the same thing: "Wow!" or "Gee!" or "Beautiful!" or some other blandishment that kept Gloria off the trail of what she really felt, which was terror. She dispatched that terror with manic exuberance and affirmation. They would sit in the car for a few minutes talking, then head up to begin another simulation. The afternoon passed in a haze.

After perhaps the fifth house, Gloria paused before turning the key in the ignition.

"This is fun, isn't it?"

"Enormous fun," Eileen said. "I could do this all day."

"Yes. Well, at some point we have to settle on some parameters."

"It's so hard to say. They're all so beautiful. Who could ever leave some of these houses, except to move to the others?"

"I'm pretty sure you're going to love this next one," Gloria said determinedly. "I'm not even going to give you the fact sheet. I just want you to react. I want to see what tickles you."

They drove to the house, which turned out to be the most impressive yet. It was a gray brick center hall colonial—she knew that term now—set high off the road, with a front lawn that sloped gently downward. It had long black shutters, a gorgeous front porch, and a room off to the side with floor-to-ceiling glass windows. It must have had three times the space of the floor they inhabited in their house. After they'd walked through it, Eileen studiously wide-eyed the whole time, Gloria led her to the porch.

"Do you mind sitting for a minute?"

"Not at all," Eileen said, and took a seat in one of the tall white rockers. Gloria sat on the top step and faced her. It felt as luxurious to sit on the porch as it had seemed it might from the curb.

Gloria took out a pack of cigarettes. "Care if I smoke?"

Eileen shook her head.

"I don't normally smoke around clients. Believe me, it's not easy not to."

"Please feel free."

"I feel comfortable around you," Gloria said.

Eileen looked down. Gloria was a working girl, like her. Her shoes were slightly scuffed, and Eileen could tell she painted her nails herself. She wondered what her father would have thought of this performance of hers. Her lip began to tremble.

"When I said under a million, I think I wasn't being entirely realistic."

"What's a better number?"

"You're not going to like it," Eileen said.

"I can work with any number. I just need to know where to start."

"I don't even know if I can convince my husband to move."

"Look at you. You're a beauty. He'll go wherever you want."

"You're sweet," she said. She could feel sadness gathering in her chest, as though scattered shards of it were being pulled from her extremities by a powerful magnet.

"What are we talking about? Eight hundred? Seven?"

Eileen felt anxious talking about money this explicitly; she felt as if the agent had held a bright light up to her face and could see the imperfections on her skin.

"More like four," she said. "Five at the most."

"Hoo-wee!" Gloria exhaled a deep puff and stabbed the butt out on the step. "Do you have any idea how much this house is listed at? Take a guess."

"Eight hundred thousand."

"Nine *fifty*," she said with a flourish, like she was calling out someone's weight at a carnival. Gloria laughed. "We're going to have to change our strategy."

"I'm sorry I've wasted your time," Eileen said miserably.

"Look, I'll be straight with you. We've wasted some time. But I don't really mind. I like looking at houses. I'll find you a good one. One your husband won't be able to resist."

They agreed to go looking again the following week. As she returned Gloria's hug good-bye, it occurred to her how grateful she was that this woman who weighed her fate in her hands hadn't humiliated her.

She had an electrolysis appointment scheduled at her regular place in midtown. She didn't feel like going, but it was impossible to get an appointment, and she had begun to obsess over the little hairs that poked through her top lip and dotted her jawline. She wondered if they were harbingers of greater changes to come. Lately her skin tingled and itched a little more than usual. She felt warm at odd times; she wasn't ready to call them hot flashes. Her breasts seemed slightly less full. She'd always had irregular periods, so there wasn't anything to read into those, but she did have more headaches lately, though it was hard to imagine anyone *not* having headaches under her circumstances. She wasn't going to bury her head in the sand when the change began, but she also wasn't ready to conclude that it had begun before she had firmer proof. In the meantime, she was going to fight to hold on to her beauty as long as she could.

To avoid the traffic snarl, she took the train. On the way back, the crowd on the 7 platform pressed close, and the train offered no relief. At every stop the car got more crowded instead of less, until at Seventy-Fourth Street the train bled riders making connections to other lines. The walk home from Eighty-Second Street thrust in her face the horrors of the change. The street had once been the jewel in the neighborhood's crown. The white stucco storefronts were crisscrossed with wooden planks to give it a Tudor charm—Tudor was another style she recognized now when she saw it—and the streetlamps were made of ornate iron, but now gangs clotted its great arterial expanse, and the mom-and-pop stores had given way to bodegas, check-cashing places, and dollar stores with cheap signs that obscured the old facades. The globes that used to adorn Eighty-Second Street's lamps were gone. Similar ones could still be found on Pondfield Road in Bronxville, which might have been part of why she was so drawn to the town: it was like a time capsule of Jackson Heights before the collapse.

As she made her way down the street, a group of young men in sweatshirts and baseball caps—they looked Hispanic to her, but she couldn't always tell—were heading in her direction, taking up the width of the sidewalk. One of them walked backwards in front of the others, gesturing wildly with his arms outspread as the others clapped and hooted. A collision would ensue unless she went into the street, and she wasn't about to do that; they should all be able to share the sidewalk. The one with his back to her wasn't turning around. She decided to stop and hope they would filter around her, like water around a branch lodged between rocks. She held her hands in front of her protectively. The young man reacted too slowly to the wide-eyed looks of his friends and bumped into her.

"Excuse me!" she said, more shrilly than she'd intended. He spun around in a defensive posture, as though in preparation for a karate chop. When he saw her he dropped his hands.

"Sorry, lady," he said. The others snickered. She knew she should just keep moving and not say anything. She had an instinctual fear of groups of young men like this. She'd heard stories of ugly incidents. Still, she felt a wave of righteous indignation pass over her.

"This sidewalk's for everyone, you know."

"Sorry," the young man said. "It was an accident."

She had wrung a second apology from him; she knew this was probably the time to stop. They could run off and have a laugh at the crazy white lady. Maybe they'd shout curses at her as they receded from view. The perfunctory way he'd apologized irked her, though. She was going to teach this young man how to comport himself, even if no one else was bothering to take the time to do so.

"You should watch where you're going," she said. "It's hard enough to get down this sidewalk. There was no room to get past any of you."

"Whatever you say." There was a restrained quality to him, as though he were a tiger waiting to pounce.

"It's my neighborhood too," she said. "Just because you're taking over doesn't mean I'm leaving."

One of the boys standing behind the one who had bumped her moved forward. She knew what was coming: *Fuck you, white bitch!* But the other put up his hand to restrain him. "Hold up," he said. "I'm sorry for running into you. I didn't mean to crowd the sidewalk. Nobody's taking over your neighborhood. I was born here. There's room for all of us."

His articulateness shocked her. He parted the group to make room for her and indicated with a pacific gesture that she should pass. As she hastened to leave she replayed the incident in her mind, trying to make sense of the inscrutable turn it had taken. She had expected hate to be directed at her and had almost been disappointed not to face it. The kid had been raised well, there was no denying it. She wanted to forget the encounter. It unsettled her more than a brush with violence would have. A vision of the future loitered in it, an intimation of her obsolescence.

That night, when she told the story, she substituted for the young man's oddly delicate apology a bowdlerized version of the slurs she'd anticipated hearing—which was, in any case, closer to the truth of her lived experience than this inexplicable aberration. "I wouldn't repeat some of the vile things

I heard," she said, "even if Connell weren't here." It was a venial sin, she knew, but she didn't have to labor to justify it to herself, because it was in everyone's interest that they move to the suburbs. Ed, though, offered up only a muted version of the chivalric indignation she'd expected to hear, which stoked the fire of her anger at the gang members. Within a few days, she'd begun to consider the possibility that they'd actually said some of the things she'd put in their mouths, and there was a decent chance they had, memory being such a slippery thing.

When she went back to the realty office, she parked in front this time, and Gloria greeted her in a more familiar and less overtly warm way. A bridge had been crossed, a confidence shared. There was perhaps a greater investment on Gloria's part in finding a house for her.

They began their rounds. On the way to each house, Gloria enumerated the positives in what Eileen was about to see but also addressed certain ineluctable realities, a little confidentially, as if to allow her to encounter these realities in a mood of mutual trust. Then they went inside. If the memory of the previous visits hadn't been fresh, Eileen might have found the houses appealing; they were, after all, in a neighborhood more desirable than her own. But what a falling off! Where there had been five bedrooms, there were now three; where marble, now linoleum; where wood, some sort of composite, or else actual wood in a state of such severe neglect as to necessitate its wholesale removal and replacement. Expansive atriums became foyers not much larger than the claustral vestibule in her current house. And the magisterial light that pervaded the earlier houses, born of high ceilings and plentiful windows, gave way to a darkness that was all too familiar. Eileen's expectations sank with the price of the houses.

Gloria saw the shift in mood and tried to bolster her with recitations of hidden advantages, but Eileen would have none of it. She could live down the road from the houses she coveted, she could make friends with their inhabitants, but she could not live in them, not in this life she had with Ed. She had enjoyed years of intellectual partnership, and she'd raised a happy, healthy child, and this was far more than some women ever came close to having. She felt churlish even beginning to wonder what life would've been like if she'd married someone else. And yet as she sat outside the latest disappointing house, she couldn't help thinking that these were the wages of self-respect, sitting in a car outside a house she couldn't afford anyway, turning her nose up at it.

A baleful air hung in the car. She wanted to reassure Gloria, to express her gratitude for the kindness and patience she'd been shown. "I had unrealistic expectations," she said. "I can't get what I want with the money I'm capable of spending."

"Some of these houses are pretty nice, actually," Gloria said.

"Some of them remind me of where I live now," Eileen said. "The neighborhoods are on the border. They could go either way. I'm looking for this next house to be the one I settle down in. I don't want to have to look over my shoulder. I might as well stay in Jackson Heights if I'm going to do that."

The houses Gloria had shown her were in areas like Yonkers and Mount Vernon, where poor and comparatively wealthy populations—they happened to be drawn along black and white lines—abutted each other. It wasn't that she wanted to avoid black faces. She wanted to avoid black anger, black retribution, black vigilante justice. She wanted a buffer from the encroachment of crime. She didn't want to have to watch a neighborhood go to ruin again and preside over the memory of it like a monk guarding the scrolls of a dwindling people.

"Don't give up yet," Gloria said. "Give it some more time."

"Of course," Eileen said.

24

On days Connell didn't have games or practice at Elmjack Little League, he went to Seventy-Eighth Street Park, even though it scared him to go there sometimes. They played softball there—no league, just pickup—and during the games he felt protected. The older white crew came around, guys in their twenties who wore bandanas and sweatpants, blasted classic rock on boom boxes, and played roller hockey when they weren't playing softball. They drank beer out of bottles in paper bags. Somehow they didn't have to be at work in the late afternoons. The girls his age swooned over them.

He liked to throw with the high school kids who sometimes came around, because they didn't complain if he gassed it up. He was playing catch with one of them when Benny Erazo sauntered up in a way that looked like he was carrying bricks in his pockets. Benny had gotten kicked out of St. Joan's the year before. He went to IS 145 now. Connell had helped Benny through fifth-grade math by letting him copy his homework and look at his tests. Benny's little brother José was still at St. Joan's and was sometimes in the group that jumped Connell after school.

"You need to worry about your rep," Benny said.

"My rep?"

"Your reputation on the street is that you're soft." Benny was wearing a Bulls jersey. He had a light mustache and smelled of cologne under several layers of clothes.

"I didn't even know I had a rep on the street."

"I'm just saying."

"I'm not soft," he said.

"People say shit. You need to take care of your rep."

"Thanks for telling me." Connell slapped the ball into his glove.

"Come with me and tag up later. You need to have a handle."

"I already do." He didn't know why he was saying this.

Benny looked at him dubiously. "Yeah? Really?"

"Yeah."

"What is it?"

He thought quickly. "PAV," he said, because they were the first letters that came to mind.

"I've seen that shit," Benny said.

He hadn't thought he'd stumble on a tag that easily. "Don't tell anyone it's me," he said nervously.

"What does it mean?"

He thought again. "People Are Vulnerable," he said.

Benny considered it for a second. "Deep."

"Thanks."

"Somebody hears you claiming his tag, that's it for you."

"It's mine."

"Draw it for me later," Benny said. "When I come back from my moms."

"I don't do that anymore," he said, trying to sound cool.

"Why?"

"I almost got caught once."

"You really are a pussy-ass white boy."

"No, I just have to worry about my reputation." He paused. "With my parents." He was trying to make a joke of it. Benny pushed him and he staggered back a step. The guy he'd been playing catch with walked away.

"I'm not fooling with you," Benny said. "Your rep is that you're soft. I was telling you to tell you."

Connell knew what he was about to do might look crazy, but he did it anyway. He rolled up the sleeves of his T-shirt. "You think this is soft?" he asked, flexing. Benny reached into his pocket and took out a switchblade.

"Tell me again you're not soft," Benny said quietly. "Tell me again."

Connell stood there in silence.

"Tell me you tagged up." There was menace in his voice. "Tell me, Connie." Benny switched the blade out for a second and showed it to him, then popped it back in with the heel of his palm. He kept it in his hand.

"What do you want me to say?" Connell asked, his terror confusing his thoughts.

"Say, 'I'm a pussy-ass pussy motherfucker.'"

"I'm a pussy-ass pussy," he said, and paused. He wasn't comfortable saying that word. Benny laughed like he'd read his mind.

"Motherfucker!" Benny corrected. "Pussy-ass pussy *motherfucker*."

"Pussy-ass pussy."

Benny showed him the knife again. "*Say it!*"

"Motherfucker," Connell said, his stomach tightening.

"Say the whole thing. 'I'm a pussy-ass pussy motherfucker.'"

"I'm a pussy-ass pussy motherfucker."

Benny howled with laughter. "You want to take care of your rep, you better not go around telling people that!" He put the knife in his pocket. "Man—I wasn't going to use this shit on you." He motioned to push him, and Connell flinched. Benny laughed again. "You want to stay alive, you better not go around claiming someone else's tag. They'll end you. That's it for today's lesson."

The whole way home, Connell replayed in his head what he'd said. *I'm a pussy-ass. I'm a pussy-ass pussy.* When he got there, his father was on the couch with the headphones on. Connell stood over him and watched him. He watched his hand going back and forth, the index finger raised. His father's eyes were squeezed shut, as if he was trying to see something he needed absolute dark to see. When the dull murmur coming from the headphones rose to a crescendo, the upward thrusts of his arm lifted his body off the couch. When the symphony lulled, he lay there, eyes still squeezed shut, and his chest rose and fell with his breathing.

Connell dropped his bookbag on the dining room table and headed to the basement. He added a ten-pound plate to either side of the bar and then lay on the bench. *Lift it, pussy-ass*, he thought, but he couldn't make it budge. He took the plates off and did a couple of sets of ten.

While he was lifting, he thought of something he could have said to Benny to make him laugh. When Benny asked, "What does it mean?" he could have said, "Pussy-Ass Virgin." But he only ever thought of that kind of stuff after the fact. He even knew a French expression to describe coming up with witty things too late; *that* was the kind of pussy he was. His father had taught it to him: *Esprit d'escalier*, the spirit of the stairs; the thing you think of when you're already gone. The kids who thought of snappy things on the spot never had to worry about being fat or smart or pussies. You had to have a little meanness in you to do it. You had to be willing to embarrass other people sometimes. He didn't want to have to embarrass other people. Deep down, or not even that deep, he knew he was a pussy-ass, maybe that was why it hadn't been that hard for him to say what he'd said to Benny.

Maybe it was partly his father's fault that he was such a pussy-ass. His father was a nice guy. Not that he told Connell not to fight back. The last time Connell had come home with a swollen eye, his father had said, "You have my permission to fight back. You're not going to get in trouble with me." But Connell hadn't wanted to risk it. He hadn't wanted to get a JD card or suspended or worse. He'd been thinking of his permanent record. He hadn't wanted to ruin his chances of getting into a good high school or having a good life. He'd needed the teachers on his side, the principal. He'd wanted to get out of the neighborhood. Well, now he was going to a fancy school in Manhattan on scholarship. You couldn't get more out of the neighborhood than that. Maybe he was a total pussy-ass, but at least he wasn't an asshole like Benny.

He put the plates back on. He thought, *Lift it, motherfucker*, and then he said it aloud, like he was uttering the password to a new club. He got the bar up once; it came crashing down with a loud bang. His father didn't come running down to see whether he'd hurt himself, because his father couldn't hear anything with those headphones on.

Pussy-ass pussy, he thought. *Motherfucker*.

25

Ed had been working in the garage since she woke up. He had emptied much of its contents into the backyard, which now bore an uncomfortable resemblance to those of their immediate neighbors. It was a hot May morning, and sweat was pouring off him.

"I'm taking Connell," she said.

"Okay."

"You sure you don't want to come?"

"I'm a little busy." He gestured to the clutter. She felt bad taking the boy, who probably should have been helping him with whatever this project was, but she couldn't face those houses alone again.

In the car, Connell found Z100 and turned the volume up.

"How come you're not telling me to turn it down?"

"It's not that loud," she said.

"Dad doesn't let me turn it up when he's driving. He says he needs to concentrate."

"I don't mind." She started tapping the fingers of her free hand on the door. It was a song she'd heard while driving to work. Connell smiled at her, and she felt like the favored parent for a change. He'd always gravitated toward his father—a consequence, she suspected, of her having returned to work so soon after he was born. It probably wasn't just that she was out of the house so much; it was also the way she got on the phone with her friends after dinner as though punching the clock at a second job. But some of that, she saw now, had been the need for escape. There would be less of that when they moved. She could begin to be more of the mother he wanted.

"Your father's got a lot on his mind," she said generously.

"He's the most uptight person in the world. He grips the wheel with both hands the whole time. You can't say *anything* to him."

When they first met, he would pick her up with one elbow hanging out the window, like a cool guy in a movie.

"You don't know what it's like to be an adult," she said. "There's a lot to think about all the time."

"He wants me to have the change ready for the tollbooth about a mile in advance. He gets all weird about it. He freaks out if I don't have it in my hand, counted out. And then he throws it in that bin with all this force, like he's throwing a baseball. It's so awkward. What's up with him? Why is he so weird?"

She had been a passenger of Ed's herself. It was as if he was doing brain surgery instead of driving a car. "Fathers are just weird sometimes," she said. "Don't think too much about it."

"It's so embarrassing."

A song came on that he liked and he bobbed his head up and down and tapped his hands on the dashboard.

"I want your input," she said. "I've been looking at all these houses and I can't tell what I think anymore."

"What about Dad? What does he say?"

"Your father and I have a difference of opinion right now about whether we should move," she said. "I'm going to have to ask you to be a man about this. I might need you to keep quiet about it for a while if we find a place we really like."

"Sure."

She felt her foot falling heavier on the gas pedal as they hit the Grand Central Parkway. A new spirit entered the car. She had a conspirator. She could feel it making a difference already. She felt freer than Ed as she drove. She was cool enough to appreciate her son's music, to pick up a little speed on the highway, to let the coins wait until they got right up to the booth. She had enough energy to make important changes in her life, to pull her husband out of a pit, to yank her whole family out of the maw of a neighborhood that threatened to swallow them whole.

• • •

Gloria gave Connell the full open-armed treatment. She seemed inordinately glad to meet him. At first Eileen thought it was a salesperson's come-on, but then it occurred to her that by existing, Connell might have been confirming that his mother wasn't a fantasist.

"I've found the perfect place for you," Gloria said. "It's gorgeous. It's slightly out of your price range, but only slightly. I want you to consider it. It's as close as you can get to your perfection with the money you can spend."

They drove up Palmer Road toward Yonkers, past the stately complexes of condos and leafy gardens, but turned off it before they'd gone too far. She had studied the area enough to know that this was an outpost of Bronxville with Bronxville post office boxes and Yonkers schools. But the schools wouldn't matter with Connell heading into the city in the fall. A sign announced—either proudly or defensively, it was hard to tell which—"Lawrence Park West."

The area was promising. It was a mixture of old and new homes, but the road was curvy and lined with enormous oaks, and between the wooded plots, she caught glimpses of stucco Tudors with carriage houses, and even what may have been a tennis court. They turned onto a wider street and the road flattened and the houses were all easy to spot but majestically elevated above the road. They stopped in front of a gray colonial with overgrown hedges and columns that linked the porch on the first level to one on top. Stone pillars flanked the driveway, and next to the front walk was a jockey holding a lantern. His red coat had been chipped and bleached to pink in the sun. The house looked as if it had been built sometime in the first half of the century, but built well, and it was twice as large as the houses she'd seen the week before. She was hopeful.

Gloria led them up the driveway to a staircase at the back entrance. A patio of moss-covered brick, framed by a stone wall and a terrific amount of growth, resembled an English garden gone to seed. It opened up onto the craggy slope, which contained an enormous stone blanketed by ivy. Atop the hill were houses accessed by another street.

The kitchen looked like it had been despoiled by squatters. Cabinet doors didn't close right, the wallpaper bubbled, and the brick floor was coated in a thick, dingy skin of polyurethane. Everything on the rear side

of the house—the kitchen, the den, the dining room—was dark as a cat-
acomb, but she could tell that light would penetrate its depths on a good
day, particularly if she trimmed some of the bushes, and while the dining
room had a matted rug and a rickety-looking chandelier, she could envision the grand meals she'd serve there, and the living room was practically
bleached by light. Next to it was the brick-floored foyer and the entrance
proper, and a flight of banistered stairs leading to the second floor. Off the
landing at the bottom of the stairs was a little flight down into what could
be a reading room, next to what would be Ed's study, with a bay window
and built-in bookshelves.

Gloria went to the two front doors and threw them open with a flourish. Light flooded in. Looking left from the front porch, which was fringed
by a rotting wooden fence, Eileen could see where the road curved and
headed down to Palmer Road, the main artery into the town that lent this
house its respectable mailing address.

Eileen stood on the porch, imagining people opening the big metal
gate at the bottom and making their way up the gently winding path. The
thought of their approach thrilled her, the moments of anticipation, the
embraces, the handing off of wine bottles, cakes, presents. And then she
turned and saw Connell looking out the window in the living room, an
ethereal light flooding against him, so that he resembled a figure in one
of those portrait paintings of the children of nobility from centuries past.
These days and years would act as a crucible in which his fate was distilled.
The closing down of possibilities had begun, almost imperceptibly. She
had to act quickly to preserve her image of the life she imagined, in which
Ed toiled happily in his study, turning over ideas until they yielded fresh
hypotheses, and she was a grand hostess and the matriarch of a respected
clan. This house would be the backdrop to the second act of their lives
together. It was Connell's contemplative gaze that gave her that assurance.

"What do you think?" Gloria asked rhetorically as she drifted into the
room. She was a maestro of timing: there was no need to respond. She led
them up the stairs like a groom guiding his bride to the bower.

"I'll show you the other bedrooms first," she said, "and then the master
suite."

She led them to a room so massive it could have swallowed Connell's current bedroom whole, along with the spare, with room left over.

"This could be your bedroom," Eileen said.

"Sweet!" He darted into the room and walked its perimeter like a cat marking its territory. He opened and closed the closet doors and then lay in the center of the room and stretched his arms and legs as far as he could. She laughed out loud at his exuberance.

"Come on," she said. "Get up now."

"It's okay," Gloria said. "He can be excited."

"You could land a plane in here," he said.

"Maybe a helicopter," Gloria allowed.

"There's no doubt it's a big enough house," Eileen said cautiously. How "slightly" out of her price range was this house? This might be another tease, only this time she wouldn't have done it to herself.

"You haven't even seen the master bedroom."

"I'm a little worried about the price."

"You're prepared to spend four hundred thousand," Gloria said. "Five at the most."

"The uppermost," Eileen said.

They were in the hallway now, their voices low.

"This house is five sixty."

"That's a big difference." Eileen tried to hide the panic and disappointment that had already set in.

"Not when you think about the fact that when it's fixed up, it's a three-quarter-of-a-million-dollar house. Minimum. *Minimum*." Gloria spoke coolly, a little impatiently, as if they were discussing an artwork she didn't want to sully with considerations of money. "There are some catches, though."

"Catches," Eileen said.

"Not necessarily deal breakers. How handy is your husband?"

She thought of Ed at home in the garage, tools strewn around him in a blast-radius circle, trying to make the house presentable enough to entice her to stay in it. Everything he knew about home improvement he'd learned from how-to books. Whenever he made a study of something, though, he could do it at least passably well. "If I can earn a PhD," he'd said when they'd had a short in the hallway light, "I can figure out how to fix some faulty wiring." And he had. The handiness came at the expense of great effort. Doing a big project around the house always left him exhausted.

"He's pretty handy," she said. "Why?"

"This house was on the market for over a year, then taken off and relisted. They just dropped the price."

"What's wrong with it?"

"It's suffered some water damage. It's a twofold problem. It's at the bottom of a hill, so there's always runoff. And it's built on a rock, with a rock behind it, so everything just flows into it. On top of that, the pipes burst this winter. There's a lot of damage in the basement. A lot of it needs to be ripped out and rebuilt. Plus there's no guarantee the water won't come back. You're going to need a new roof in a couple of years. It's an expensive proposition to fix this place, but it's a steal if you can do any of the work yourself."

"My husband can do it," she said.

It would be good for him. He could sweat this thing out through manual labor. She could see him drinking a beer in jeans and a T-shirt, wiping his brow and holding a baseball cap at his hip.

"Let's make our way to your room," Gloria said. They left Connell and stopped briefly at each of two average-sized bedrooms and a bathroom with matching sinks below bulb-lighted mirrors like those in dressing rooms. A toilet hid demurely behind French doors.

The master bedroom suite contained a closet as large as her current guest bedroom. She pictured a sitting area in the corner of the bedroom proper. The same light poured in as below but unencumbered by tree cover. It would be impossible to dwell on sad things in that light.

In recent years, a tentative mood had obtained in their bedroom. They fumbled over each other's bodies. It was as if they'd entered a new phase of life and had to get reacquainted. She needed light for play, discovery. Something could be gained if they saw each other naked in the bright light of day.

The wallpaper was all seams and bubbles, and something would have to be done about the stain on the ceiling in the corner of the room. There would be time and money to worry about such particulars in the proper order.

She made her way to the window. She'd heard all about suburban ennui, but she couldn't imagine feeling it in a house like this. If the abundant space and light failed for a moment to confirm for her how far she'd gotten from what she'd left behind, and a shadow of uncertainty drifted over her, she needed only to throw open the curtains on this window, gaze out onto the empty street, and wait for a car to drive down the block, and then another. In the substantial interval between them, she would feel a calm settling in: there was no reason to be there unless you had someone to see; there was no way to stay there long unless you had a reason to stay.

"I think you like it," Gloria said.

"I do," she said quietly. "I like it a lot. I'm trying to figure out how I can afford it."

She was in the middle of the sort of reverie that invented the future by imagining it. The spell would be broken in a moment, but she lingered in it, telling herself to remember the details.

They wouldn't be able to put as big a percentage down. They'd have a much higher monthly payment. They might not be able to immediately do all the renovations she had in mind. They'd have to work in stages. They'd have to live lean, not go to restaurants or shows.

"What about you?" Gloria asked Connell.

"Can we put a hoop in the driveway?"

What a simple thing, Eileen thought. *What a different set of concerns he has.*

"I don't see why not."

"Yes!" He pumped his fist.

"Someone's excited," Gloria said.

"I'm excited too," she said, "but the person we need to convince is his father. Provided the structure is sound and the repairs are possible and the finances are in order, I think this might just be the perfect house for us."

Gloria clapped her hands. "That's the spirit," she said. "You wouldn't get this house at this price except under some very specific circumstances. Now, having said that, why don't we go take a look at those circumstances."

They headed downstairs. Gloria pointed out some flood marks that

Eileen hadn't seen earlier, and then she took them into the house's bowels. Eileen passed her eyes over everything Gloria pointed to, but she did her best not to register it. Connell poked at a section of rot. When he pulled a piece off, she barely mustered enough indignation to scold him. She heard, as though from underwater, the litany of troubles the house had endured. She nodded when she needed to nod and pulled long faces to demonstrate concern. She even heard herself sigh when Gloria showed her a section of foundational wall in the garage that had been soaked through and was threatening to collapse. She was determined to let these subterranean details remain subterranean. They could be handled in due time. The issue now was preserving her vision. The base of the house might be rotting, but the visible portion was commanding enough to chase any qualms away.

"It's not an inconsiderable amount of work," Gloria said.

"We could make it work." Eileen turned to Connell. "You and Daddy could take this on, don't you think?"

"No way."

"He just doesn't want to have to do anything around the house," she said to Gloria. "But they could handle it. I'm confident."

"If you say so, Mom."

"Maybe we'll pay you like a contractor. Maybe it's time you earned your allowance."

"There are things he can't do. There's the roof, as I said. You've got a little time on that. The electrical wiring is old. You might not have enough amp service. You might blow some fuses. Some of the outlets don't work. Am I scaring you yet?"

"I'm just listening."

"There's asbestos around the plumbing and ductwork. That could make it hard to resell. So could the underground oil tank."

"I'm not worried about selling it. I'm worried about buying it."

"Water gathers in the fireplace. Some of these are expensive jobs. Thankfully there's no mold from the flooding. That we know of."

"It sounds like we need a plumber. And a roofer."

"And a general contractor," Gloria said. "And an electrician. And a willing husband."

"I can live without a few outlets for a while. I don't know if I can live without this house."

They stopped for gas on the way home. When she went in to pay, she bought a couple of scratch-off tickets, something she'd thought she'd never do, and scarfed a pair of Twinkies while she rubbed a quarter on the tickets. She didn't win, and she bought five more. Then she got two more with the free tickets she'd won, and those were losers too. She bought five to take home with her and another package of Twinkies to split with Connell and headed out to the car, where the boy sat oblivious of the turmoil she was in.

She drove with an anxious feeling in the pit of her stomach, fidgeting with the button for the electric window. When they pulled in, she saw one of her good sheets strewn like a makeshift tarp over whatever tools Ed had left in the driveway. Cinderblocks held the sheet down at the corners, and the garage door was closed. The stark whiteness of the sheet put a chill in her.

Ed was sitting at his desk. The vestibule abutted his office, a glass-paneled door between them. He had a pleasant habit of wheeling around in his chair whenever he heard her come home, but he didn't turn this time. "We're home," she said. When he didn't respond, she went over and stood behind him. He was calculating his semester grades. His desk was cluttered with tests and lab reports; little piles of them abounded. He jotted notes on a legal pad as he did his calculations. She'd never seen him do his grades with such elaborate exactitude. He had written the last name of each student, along with the roman numerals from the test sections, in a long row. She watched him meticulously check each number against those he'd written on the exams. It was double work, and moreover it was the kind of task he usually dispatched in his head.

When she placed a hand on his shoulder, he almost leaped out of his seat. He didn't turn around to her.

"What's the matter with you?" he exclaimed.

"I didn't mean to frighten you."

"Don't bother me when I'm doing my grades."

"Since when?"

"I want to get these right. It's a big class, and I've graded a lot of assignments in the last few days, so I feel a little fuzzy, as you can imagine. I don't want to make any mistakes in my calculations. When I look at this stuff long enough, I feel like I'm seeing double."

"What's up with the sheet?"

He took off his glasses, the way he sometimes did when he was going to give thoughtful consideration to a question, but then he just dropped his shoulders.

"Sheet?"

"Outside," she said. "The bed sheet."

"I wanted to leave things there."

"Why did you use a good sheet?"

"Good sheet?"

"There were other sheets you could have used."

He slammed his pencil down. "What's the difference?"

"You used one of the sheets I put on the bed. There are about ten old sets in that linen closet that you could have used."

He spun around in his chair. She backed away from him instinctively. His face was red and his mouth contorted. "I took the first sheet I could find!" He was on his feet now. "I didn't have time to work out which sheet was which. I just grabbed a sheet!" He had begun to shout. "I took the first sheet!" He had his hand in front of his face, as if to strike her or bite it. "People walk by the house all day long, peeking back there. I needed to cover everything up!"

She had intended to let it go, but now she had to ask. "Why did you leave it out in the first place?"

"I didn't want to have to set it up again," he said. "Is that okay with you? God damn it! God damn it!"

She was quiet. She wondered whether Connell could hear.

"I'm sorry," he said. "There's a lot of pressure on me to get these grades right. Dealing with these kids has upset me. This younger generation has no respect. It's disgraceful."

"What do you mean? What's happened?"

"What's happened," Ed said, "is that with everything going on lately, I've been distracted."

She wanted to know what he meant, because it seemed at times as if nothing was going on, hence the big pile of ungraded papers, but she held back.

"In my distraction, I've made a few calculation errors. And they've raised a stink about it. That's all. These kids today feel entitled to everything instantly. You say you'll review the grade, and they say they can't wait until the next class. They go berserk! I like to take my time with things, give them an honest going-over. That's impossible with a crowd of people at your desk. Especially when they speak in such a fresh and disrespectful way."

So much of what he was saying was odd. He was one of the most popular professors in the department, a status made all the more remarkable by the fact that he was no pushover in the grading arena. They wanted to work for him, to impress him. His belief in them made them want to believe in themselves. It also made her want to kill him sometimes, because she didn't believe they deserved it.

After taking an old sheet from the linen closet, she went out to the driveway and picked up one of the cinderblocks holding down the good sheet. Beneath the sheet lay two-by-fours that had been sawn in an irregular fashion. Ed had been attempting to construct something. She couldn't tell if it was supposed to be ornamental or structural. What it resembled more than anything was a pile for a bonfire. There were none of the heavy tools she'd imagined Ed hadn't wanted to move several times, only this inert, enigmatic heap. She folded the good sheet up and replaced it with the old one in a way that would discourage his noticing she had done so. When she had finished, she hurried away as she sometimes did when she got spooked in the basement and felt something closing in on her.

She considered saying something to Ed on the way back in. Then she decided the time for checking things with him had passed. If he noticed it was a different sheet tomorrow—by no means a certainty—he would just have to deal with the fact that she had messed with his arrangement.

• • •

She awoke to find herself alone in bed. She stumbled out to the living room and saw Ed's light on in the study. He was hunched over, as if so many hours of sitting at the desk had sapped the energy in his back. His hair was wild. The desk lamp radiated tremendous heat. The smell of sweat mingled with the mushroom odor of old books to give the room a greenhouse quality.

"Come to bed," she said.

"I'm working."

"It's three in the morning. Come to bed."

"I have to finish this." His voice sounded weak, as if he'd fallen asleep in the chair, but his expression was oddly alert. His eyes were sunken and dark, like he'd reached the end of a long fast.

"Can you finish it tomorrow?"

"I can't."

"Let me see," she said.

She leaned over him. He shifted his body to block her view, but she could see the piles on either side of him on the desk, the calculator between them. She picked up the pile of tests and flipped through them. They all had grades on their first page, which surprised her, because what was Ed doing if not grading these things? She put the tests down and picked up the lab reports, over his protestations. The same was true of those: grades had been assigned, red numerals in distended circles emblazoning their upper right corners.

"These are all graded," she said. "Why don't you come to bed?"

"I'm still working."

"You have more to grade?"

"I do."

He covered a pad on the desk with his hands. She could see it was the set of names and numbers he had been working with earlier. Yet another pad lay next to it.

"What's that?" She pointed to the second pad.

"Will you leave me alone? Will you go back to sleep? I'll be in when I'm done."

She picked up the second pad, fending off Ed's hands. On it were written all the same names and numbers as on the first pad. They appeared to be identical.

"What is all this?"

She answered her own question by looking at the first test. Each number listed on the pad corresponded to the student's performance on a section of the exam. His grade book lay splayed open at the back of his desk. She picked it up to check her hunch; indeed, the grades weren't there. Was he that nervous about making a mistake? Just how fresh had the kids become that a teacher of his stature could be moved to such excessive scrutiny of his no-doubt flawless math well into the night? He should have been resting and quelling the psychic demons that were draining his confidence in the first place. All of this had become far bigger in his sleep-addled mind than it ever should have been allowed to be.

"Let me help you with this," she said, careful not to describe what "this" was. He surprised her by capitulating quickly. She gathered his things and led him to the kitchen table. "You keep the grade book," she said. "I'll tell you the number to enter."

He held his pen poised over the book. She took the first test off the pile. Edwin Alvarez had earned an 84. She flipped through the test, making sure the subsection grades added up to the indicated total. Eighty-four it was. This was probably the kind of kid Ed was proudest to see achieve, a kid from the neighborhood.

"All right," she said. "Edwin Alvarez."

"Wait!" Ed said, suddenly panicked. "Wait! Wait!"

He stood up and bolted out of the room. Before she could follow he reappeared holding a long ruler. He squared himself in the chair and lined the ruler up under Edwin Alvarez's row of boxes. She had to laugh at his intensity. He didn't share the laugh, though; he didn't look up at all, as though he had to stare unblinkingly at the name in front of him in order to prevent it from disappearing.

"Okay," he said. "Go."

"Edwin Alvarez."

"Edwin Alvarez," he said hesitantly, as if cross-referencing it with the names in the list, an odd thing considering it was the first.

"Eighty-four on the test. We're only dealing with the test right now."

"Yes," he said. "The test only."

"Okay? Can we move along?"

"Eighty-four?"

"That's correct," she said, biting her tongue. As disturbing as this drill was, now wasn't the time to discuss it. She had to get them both back to bed.

"Okay," she said. "Lucy Amato. Give me one second."

She flipped through the test, adding the numbers in her head. She saw how this could get to a person; late at night, numbers ran together. Ed had added them correctly again. She could see it would play out as an exercise in redundancy. It was the kind of thing you signed up for when you got married, idiosyncrasies that bordered on obsessions at times, quirks that became handicaps if allowed to thrive. It could have been worse: he could have had a wandering eye, a gambling habit.

He had located Ms. Amato's name; his ruler was brought to a sharp congruency with the line underscoring her performance for the semester.

"Seventy-three," she said.

"Seventy-three." The desperate edge had left his voice. Despite her tiredness, she was touched by the feeling of working together with her husband on a project; it beat being adversaries. Maybe she'd even be able to tell him about the house.

They went through the stack, she calling out the name, he orienting himself in the ledger, she checking his addition, which grew quicker the more she saw he'd been accurate in his math, she calling out the number like a bingo caller, he repeating the number before committing it to paper, he confirming it again with a rising intonation, she reconfirming it in a tone that made her feel uncomfortably like a teacher with a student. They got to the end without incident, Ed never wavering in his focus, his laser like application of the ruler's metal edge. He was sweating; he paused to wipe his forehead while she did her quick math, but didn't look up from the page.

The last name, Arash Zahedani, also happened to be attached to the highest grade, ninety-seven, a happy coincidence that might send Ed to bed in a better mood. It was getting on four o'clock; she had to be up in a few hours. She knew she wouldn't be able to sleep; she was far too awake now to drift off again. Still, she could lie there and rest her muscles. Tomorrow was an important day at work. The Joint Commission was examining North Central Bronx Hospital, bringing with it the usual headaches. Her people were well prepared, but she would have to dig deep to perform well on little sleep. She was already exhausted from the previous week of late nights getting ready for their arrival. She'd had ten nurses call in sick Friday, and she was going to have to fire some of them, because they'd known better than to do that at the start of the weekend. Since she'd been understaffed, she'd had to struggle to handle a room full of gang members who'd burst in after visiting hours, demanding access to the ICU to see one of their own who'd been shot in the stomach. They pushed past the security guard and through the double doors in front and were advancing on the room. It could have been two dozen of them. She ran to block their way. "You're not allowed in there," she said. "You can come back tomorrow." One of them asked, "Aren't you afraid of us, white lady?" She didn't have the energy to be. Security backup arrived, two more guards, all three of them black. If the gang members didn't stand down soon, the guards might draw their guns, and who knew what would happen then? She was the only white person in the room. The guards told the gang members to leave. There was a young girl among their number; she must have been the injured man's girlfriend. She held a baby in her arms. She gave Eileen a pleading look. "I will let a few of you in, one at a time," Eileen said, "and we will all be civil to each other. And then you can come back tomorrow. And I promise you he will be in good hands, and we'll let it rest at that." The guards relented. They had the gang members line up against the wall. She could see the leader of the gang calming everyone down. He gave her a look that said, *Lady, you are all right.* It had stuck with her, that look. It had meant something to be recognized, even by this thug. She wanted that young man to give her that look in front of her husband the next time Ed was half-crazed about some absurd infraction. There was more to life than Ed's petty grievances.

She wanted to end on a high note, but a spirit of excess caution had crept into her own thinking. "Let's go through the numbers again," she said, and from his look she got the feeling he hadn't planned for it to be any other way.

"We'll switch," she said. "I'll read down the column. You call out the grades."

They proceeded through the tests, Ed dispatching his task with a new alacrity. Four tests from the bottom, La Shonda Washington, she asked Ed to repeat the grade he'd just read out.

"Eighty-six," he said.

But the number he'd entered for Ms. Washington was sixty-seven, which also happened to be the score received by Melvin Torres, the student above her in the grade book.

"One second." She rose to look at the test in his hands. The glow of the sun was filtering into the air outside. It felt more like the remnant light at dusk than the herald of dawn.

"What? What is it?"

"I just wanted to check something."

"I told you," he said. "I told you. Eighty-six."

"That's what I thought you said, honey." Her throat constricted. "I wanted to double-check."

"Is there a problem? A mistake?"

"I just need to change one thing," she said. "Give me a second."

She reached for the pencil and he slammed his hand down on it. "What is it?" He was seething. "What is it?"

"The number for the student directly above La Shonda Washington has been repeated," she said matter-of-factly. "That's all. I'm going to erase it and write in the correct number."

"Ah, Jesus!" He threw his hands up. "Jesus Christ! It's all wrong! It's all wrong!"

"Just hold on while I make this one change."

"Forget it," he said. "What's the use?"

"It was an honest mistake," she said. "You wrote the number above it. It's late."

"Yes, yes," he said dismissively. "That's it. Now let me finish this. I'll be in when I'm done."

He took the book away and closed it, then held his head and rubbed his eyes.

"We have three more to go," she said.

"It's *fine*," he said firmly. "We're finished."

She should have made the switch without saying anything. She should have come out and done it after he'd fallen asleep. Now she had to convince him to leave off his vigil.

"If we're done," she said, "then come to bed."

"I'll be in in a while."

"Come now."

"I said I'll be in. I'll be in."

"You need some sleep."

He slammed his fist on the table. "I'll be in when I'm in! What the hell else do I need to say to you? Will you leave me alone, God damn it?"

She snatched the book out of his hands. "Don't say a word to me," she said slowly, giving him an icy stare. "Not one word."

She opened to the page with the grades and looked at the last three numbers. Whitaker, seventy-three. Williams, fifty-eight. Zahedani, ninety-seven. She checked the tests and slammed the book shut.

"That's it," she said. "They're all correct. I'm going to bed. You can come, or you can stay here. I don't care either way."

She felt her hands making fists as she walked down the hall to the bedroom. She'd already wasted too much time on him. She imagined he'd spend the whole night out there, going over the numbers endlessly.

She lay in bed, counting sheep for the first time since she was a child. She bit the pillow in frustration. Then she heard him walking down the hall. She rolled over and he climbed in bed alongside her. She moved as close to the edge as she could. Even an accidental touch might enflame her so much that she'd have to go to the couch. There was no point in trying to sleep; she would lie there until it was time to get up and shower.

She felt the slight shaking of the bed but didn't register the sound as what it was until the shaking grew more forceful. Ed was doing a good job of keeping it in, but the springs of the bed gave him away. The sound of gasps followed. She had trouble identifying it at first because she had formed an image in her mind of Ed as a man who didn't cry. It wasn't macho posturing; he simply didn't shed tears, not even at his father's funeral.

She turned slowly in the bed. She was tentative with her body; there was no telling how he'd react if she touched him. It wasn't impossible that he'd get violent, like an animal in a cage. They were in a new territory, with new rules.

She shifted closer to him. When he didn't stir, she reached out to touch his shoulder, expecting him to slap her hand away; he let it rest there. She gave the shoulder a consoling rub; he sobbed a little harder. She pressed her whole body against his and he folded into its curve. She brought her other arm up against him so that she was hugging him fully. She found herself holding him to her as though he were a child. She'd always resisted cradling him in such a manner, fearing it would diminish her attraction to him, but attraction was the last thing on her mind at the moment. He sobbed as she held him, and she soothed him by making shushing sounds, long and slow and quiet, until he turned and sobbed into her nightgown.

She knew what it was about, even if he didn't. It was about getting old. She felt it too, but somehow she knew it was different for men. They got spooked when they lost their hair, when their backs gave out. Women were better prepared to deal with death and old age, especially mothers, who, having delivered children, saw how tenuous the line was between life and death. And as a nurse she had seen so many people die, people to whom she'd grown attached. Ed had taught anatomy and physiology. He'd been in the museum of death, not on its front lines. It was irrational for him to react this much to a bit of misentered data, but what was rational about a midlife crisis? Weren't they always a little absurd?

They were beginning the next phase of their lives together. She was not afraid of it. *Let it come*, she thought. *He'll be in good hands.*

Within minutes he was sound asleep, the crying having exhausted him. She lay awake until the alarm clock went off. He slept through her getting dressed. She made a neat stack of the papers on the table.

The Joint Commission sent eight people to do the inspection. She and the other administrators went into a conference room to make their presentations. She was glad she'd taken some extra time doing her hair and makeup that morning, and that she'd worn her gray skirt suit, which clung enough to give her some sex appeal while still looking professional, because the team was mostly male.

She was exhausted, but she felt confident about her staff's preparedness. She'd been readying the nurses for a year, training them in how to answer questions. They were up to date on all the standards: pharmacy, equipment, staff knowledge, patient care. It was the patient interviews that troubled her. Usually the patients were generous in their comments. Still, one disgruntled patient was all it took to get the commission sniffing around. "How is the service?" "Terrible." "How is your room?" "The place is filthy." "Are you getting the medicines you need in a timely fashion?" "I can never get anyone around here to answer my call."

She gave a rundown of the state of affairs in nursing and took a seat. She struggled to stay awake through the other administrators' presentations. Then they loosed the team.

She wasn't allowed to follow them around. It made her feel like a criminal. Accreditation was at stake; there were standards to uphold. Still, they were so damned humorless about it. They stalked the place like stormtroopers. They went through labs, making sure everything was cleaned and stored properly. They looked at every chart in the place. They pored over paperwork like district attorneys looking for a break in a prosecution. They grilled staff members. No one knew exactly how long they'd be there once they showed up. It could be three days; it could be the whole week.

Her staff could have withstood a press conference after all the paces she'd run them through. Still, things don't always go as planned. One inspector found an expired IV solution while interviewing a patient. That got the others digging. They found an expired medicine in one of the carts. The expirations killed you. You could have nurses trained to say all the right things, but if they found one bottle a couple of weeks past its prime in a lineup of fifty good ones, it negated weeks of coaching. A crash cart wasn't in the locked cabinet it was supposed to be in. They didn't tell her where it was, of course, only that it wasn't where it was supposed to be. That one hurt. She prided herself on running a tip-top ER. No one in her hospital was ever going to expire after cardiac arrest because the cart didn't have the proper medications on it. If the cart wasn't where it was supposed to be, though, it didn't matter what was on it.

Before they left for the day, they gave her a list of citations. Too many and the accreditation could be compromised. They gave her a chance to follow up the next day. It was a simple matter of a few fixes—switching out the old medicine, changing the IV, putting the cart back where it belonged—but it also served to tell her that she was on notice. She'd get through it; North Central Bronx would retain its accreditation. Nothing about it promised to be easy, though. They seemed like the kind of crew that wouldn't give them a pass on anything. It was going to be a long week. In the meantime, life continued at the hospital. People didn't stop getting sick. People didn't stop having heart attacks. One kid came in having blown off his hand with a firecracker.

She dozed off at a red light on the way home. When she pulled into the driveway she saw the sheet still over the pile in the back. In the tumult of the day she'd forgotten about it. She walked over to it and lifted a corner. It was all there, untouched. She didn't have the energy to spare Ed's ego. She whipped the sheet off. If it was a bonfire he was after, he'd have to find another way to exorcise his demons. She gathered up the pieces of lumber and put them in the garbage can; they stuck out jagged and tall. She dragged the can to the curb for pickup the next day. Ed would flip out when he saw it; in fact, that was the point. Fatigue was hardening her toward him. His vulnerability last night, and her tenderness—it felt as if it had happened a year ago. She hardly remembered it at all; it could have been a dream. It was all so stupid; how could she have indulged him in it?

She marched inside and found him hunched over the stack of lab reports they hadn't gotten to the night before. She felt she'd fallen into a film loop.

"I took your wood to the curb," she said. "I'd appreciate it if you could keep the backyard from looking like a junk heap."

"Okay," he said without looking up.

"That's it? Just 'okay'? No rage? No telling me not to mess with your stuff?"

He kept working as though he hadn't heard her. She could smell a musky odor coming off him. He hadn't showered. He had changed his clothes, thank God, but he hadn't washed before he left for work. Ed hated not to shower. He felt a layer of grime sitting on him all day when he didn't.

"What were you trying to make, anyway?"

"I don't know what you're talking about," he said, swiveling in his chair. He gave her a look that said he was only trying to get an honest bit of work done. He was one of those aggrieved husbands who had to deal with the not-always-sensible ravings of wives who meant well but made things so difficult sometimes.

"I'm talking about the pile out back," she said pointedly. "Your little Stonehenge."

"I really have to focus," he said. "Whatever I did, I'm sorry."

"You don't remember the sheet you put over the pile of wood in the backyard?"

"Yes," he said. "Yes." She could see that he remembered it, possibly for the first time since he'd done it; he was that absorbed.

"Okay, fine," she said. "Just tell me something, and I'll let you work all night. What were you making?"

"What?"

She knew this gambit; he was pretending he hadn't heard her, stalling for time.

"What were you making?'"

"Oh, you know."

"I don't. That's why I'm asking."

"I was making something. I told you what I was doing. You know this."

"When I left on Saturday you told me you had some projects in mind. Home improvement projects."

"Yes! Yes. I was making something for the house."

His answers sounded like those given over the phone by kidnapped people being watched for signs of betrayal.

"What exactly?"

"Well, it was a surprise."

"I don't need any more surprises." She looked at him for a few moments. "How did it go today?"

"Fine."

"No problems?"

"No."

"No students complaining?"

"No."

She hesitated for a moment, then came out with it.

"Do you want some help with that other stack tonight?"

"Yes," he said in an instant.

She had no energy to cook, so they ordered pizza. At the end of the meal she took a long, hot shower. Afterward, she wanted to rest for an hour before she helped Ed with the lab reports. She didn't feel like drowsing in the musty air of the bedroom, so she availed herself of the couch. It was one of those times she wished they had a television in the living room. It had been a principled stance of theirs—of Ed's, mostly, though she went along with it. At the beginning of their marriage, Ed didn't hate television, precisely; he just didn't like what it was doing to American life. It wasn't always convenient to be without a set in their living room, but there were benefits. Actual conversations took place when people came over, unlike at Ed's sister Fiona's house, where the all-seeing eye made any exchange a series of distracted monologues. And when the three of them crawled into the big bed on Sundays to watch *Fawlty Towers*, it was an event. Recently, though, Ed had grown more severe about it, insisting she shut it off when she tried to watch Johnny Carson at night. It was part of a general trend in his thinking. He was becoming more reflexive, more reactionary. She was becoming the opposite. When they moved to the new house, she would get a big television for the den.

She went to the bedroom and wheeled the little television out to the living room. She wanted to shut her brain off. She didn't care if the noise bothered him. He couldn't be doing anything of consequence, and it was only a matter of time before she'd be sitting with him at the kitchen table, running through the grades.

She woke to Ed pounding on the television set.

"Keep that off," he said. "I'm trying to work."

She was too sleepy to take umbrage at what he was saying. She waited curiously for the next thing.

"Take it inside. Take it away."

"I happen to live here too," she said, her blood rising.

"Get it out of here! I can't concentrate."

She stood and fixed the pillows behind her. "We don't talk to each other like that in this household. I didn't let my father talk to me like that, and I'm not about to let you do so. You've been a complete jerk for I don't know how long. I've had it. I can't take another day of it. Either you stop this behavior right now, or I swear, Ed, I'm leaving. I won't make a big production of it. I'll just take our son and go. Do you have any idea how tired I am? How long my day was? Because I stayed up to help you. You want to do everything yourself, fine. Do it. It's easier for me to have nothing to do with you."

He dropped into the armchair and sat looking at her. It almost unnerved her how intent his look was. Against her will, she felt herself warming to him. There was something in his gaze that could make her embers catch fire, even when they were buried under layers of ash.

"I'm sorry," he said.

"You said that yesterday."

"I'm under so much stress at work."

"I am too," she said.

"I know."

"Since when are you under this kind of stress? I thought one of the perks of your job was how low-stress it was."

"Lately it's not."

"Your head's not in it," she said. "I think your mind's not right. But you won't talk to me. You won't let me in."

"I'm dealing with a new generation," he said. "I need to be perfect."

"You're having a midlife crisis," she said. "I don't mean to diminish it, but that's what it is."

"I just need to get through the next couple of weeks," he said. "Then I'll be fine. I need the summer to recuperate. I put a few things off, and now I'm dealing with them. I've tried to shield you from all this. I'm tired. I'm making mistakes. I haven't been sleeping well. I just need to recharge my batteries." He took off his glasses and rubbed his eyes.

"I know the feeling," she said as she yawned. "When do you need to return those lab reports?"

"Tomorrow is the last day of classes."

"Go get them and we'll check them together. Then we can both get some sleep."

She put on water for tea. She felt as if she was moving through a thick soup. She stood by the stove, watching the kettle boil. She fixed her tea and with languid movements joined Ed at the table. She wanted to insist on a little ceremony. She was going to sip her tea, not gulp it. But she needed Ed to calm down first. His knees were jackhammering up and down in that way that sometimes overcame him.

"Let me drink this before we start."

"Fine, fine."

She tried to let the warm liquid have a tonic effect, but she had put too much milk in it, and it wasn't a good cup. It was foolish to make tea in order to stay awake; all her years of drinking it before bed had turned it into a soporific.

"Let's get started," she said.

He focused on the open grade book with the unwavering attention of a runner about to start a race. She thought back to the chaos at the end of the previous night's efforts, the way a spirit of collaboration had devolved into a shouting match. If only there were a way to avoid the altercation that would ensue if—when—Ed made a mistake. She could feel it as a certainty for some reason, perhaps because of the barely contained mania in that pumping leg. He was in a place mentally where she couldn't follow, where an entry error was a harbinger of doom. She thought of the bum rap women got: as hormonal as she'd been after delivering Connell, she'd never been certifiably nuts.

An idea occurred to her and she saw right away that it was the correct one, the only one. It should have occurred to her last night, but she was on Ed's terms then, and tonight he was on hers. Still, she hesitated. Any deviation from the pattern, however short-lived that pattern happened to be, promised to unleash in Ed a disproportionate fury. She had a vision of his overturning the table like a card cheat before a shootout.

She cleared her throat. "I have an idea," she said tentatively, and he didn't respond. He was tossing aside, one by one, the gestures of nicety that accounted for much of conversation. "It can save us some time. Of course, if you want to do it another way, it's up to you."

He nodded to indicate he was listening—an improvement. She sipped her tea.

"I can just enter them directly into the book," she said. "You can check it over when I'm done."

"Yes," he said, lightning-quickly. At first she thought he hadn't heard her. Then he looked up and said it again. She felt her body relax. She hadn't realized it, but she had been bracing for a shock—a blow, even.

"Good," she said as she took the gradebook from him, but she didn't mean it. He was so quick to relinquish control of the project, it was as if he had been hoping all along that she would take it over.

She filled in the grades. It took no time at all. It almost made her laugh. She had let herself be convinced that this was a task that required the gravest concentration. In fact it would have been difficult to make a mistake once the first few were in place. They were already alphabetized. She shuddered to imagine how much time Ed had spent checking the alphabetization.

"Done," she said, closing the book. She hoped he wouldn't insist on checking it himself.

"Thank you," he said, to her surprise.

"Let's go to bed."

They made love; it was a frenetic affair. Ed seemed to take his stress out on her body, but she enjoyed it anyway. They hadn't made love with vigor like that in a while. There was something less than terrifying about his anger; it was that of a man in chains. He finished with a grunt; she climaxed along with him. As they lay in silence afterward, their bodies coated in sweat, Ed looking at her intently, she felt an invisible barrier between them had been breached. It would be easier now. She would be able to tell him about the house.

26

On Saturday she drove up to Bronxville to meet Gloria. No bids had been placed yet, and she wasn't interested in seeing any other houses. Still, she drove up. The clutter on Gloria's desk infused her with a feeling of unease.

"What do you say we walk and talk." Gloria gestured outside. "Take a look at the town."

Outside, Gloria extended the pack; Eileen demurred.

"You don't mind if I do, right?"

"Of course not."

"Good. 'Cause I have to anyway!"

Gloria laughed a raspy laugh and began to cough. She lit the cigarette and took a long drag.

"Talk to hubby yet? What's his name?"

She didn't know when it had happened precisely, but Gloria had dropped all pretense of formality with her. A hint of coarseness idled in her voice. At first their familiarity had been bracing. Now that Eileen was a step closer to living there, though, she felt conflicted about it. It meant a small diminution of her ideal. She thought of all the people Gloria probably knew in town. A real estate agent could wield a lot of power if she wanted to. She could control the narrative. She knew people's secrets no less than a psychiatrist or priest did.

"Ed. Ed's his name."

"Have you gotten the thumbs-up from him yet?"

"We haven't discussed it. He's been busy."

Gloria took a drag. Eileen could feel her gaze on her.

"You're afraid if you bring it up, you'll hear a no, and then there'll be no negotiating from there. I get it. I've been there—believe me."

Eileen bristled. It was far more complicated, and even if she had time to explain the subtleties of it in a way that did them justice, she wasn't sure Gloria was the kind of person who could appreciate such subtleties. She wondered how she had managed to let her guard down with this crude woman.

"I'm going to talk to him about it soon," Eileen said, "and I'm confident we'll be in a position to make an offer."

"You have a bit of time," Gloria said philosophically. "But I wouldn't wait forever. This house is under market. You can't afford to get into a bidding war."

She had been thinking of the house as protected by the invisible bubble of her interest in it, and she felt a seed of panic take root. They did a loop around the block, Gloria waving to owners and salespeople, a few of whom came out to chat. Eileen felt edgy and ill-equipped to win anyone over. It was safer when they were in the car; it was safer to walk around alone.

She didn't admit to herself where she was really heading until she had passed the on-ramp to the Bronx River Parkway. She kept driving until she came to the street with the two stone pillars at either side that Gloria had turned onto when she'd taken her there. She felt her way up a couple of turns until she saw the house. She didn't have a plan. She just knew she had to be near it, to confirm her feeling about it.

She parked in front, figuring the driveway was too conspicuous. She sat in the car for a while, looking at the stone wall that girdled the front yard, working up the courage to walk the grounds. She knew what she intended to do was technically trespassing, even though whoever was selling the house wouldn't have minded if it helped to firm up her resolve to buy it. She walked up the driveway to the back stairs. No table and chairs sat on the patio, but she saw them in her mind. Someone was being paid to care for the plants and shrubbery. She saw where she could add a few flowers. In a house like this she would be inspired to learn to keep them alive. A

path of stone stairs led up the hill in the back. She followed it to a flat area
halfway up that had been left untended. She could put another table there.
It could be the aerie from which she looked down on her domain.

The property ran all the way up to a wall that abutted the yard of an
Italian-style villa at the top of the hill. It dwarfed this house in grandeur
and size, but there was no shame in being outstripped by a house that
majestic.

After a little while she saw a worker turning over soil in the backyard
of the house next door. He hadn't seen her, but all he had to do was look
up. She hid behind a tree and watched till he disappeared inside. Then she
scampered down the steps. The bush cover on the patio gave her courage
to try the screen door to the den. It slid open, as did the glass door behind
it, and in an instant she was in the house.

She didn't turn any lights on. Sounds echoed in the big empty spaces.
She hesitated going deeper into the house, but a rustling of the leaves outside sent her scurrying into the living room.

She headed upstairs. The place smelled different than it had; she
picked up a faint hint of mildew, perhaps wafting up from the basement.
It might only have been the close air trapped in the house. She went to the
bedroom where Connell had lain on the floor. The room felt imposingly
empty with no one else there, and she couldn't stay in it long. She went to
the guest bathroom and ran both taps. She looked at herself in the mirror,
then looked away, afraid that something would appear behind her. In the
quiet of the house every sound was magnified.

She went to the master bedroom and sat leaning against the wall,
by the windows. The longer she sat, the more nervous she grew, but she
couldn't bring herself to get up. She was waiting for external circumstances
to dictate her next move. She felt like a mountain climber who had reached
a longed-for summit and couldn't bear to return to normal life.

She didn't know how long she'd been sitting when she heard the voices.
She shot to her feet and looked for a place to hide. She gave no thought to
walking downstairs and forthrightly greeting them. She didn't know who
they might be: the owner, other prospective buyers, a neighbor, the police.
She thought to hide behind the shower curtain in the master bath, but

there was no curtain, and even if there were one, how would it look if they pulled it back and found her there? They'd call the cops for certain. She thought of the attic stairs hidden in a ceiling panel in one of the closets, but she didn't know if she could pull them down quietly enough, and where was she going to hide up there?

She stood by the doorway to the bedroom. Lights were being flicked on downstairs. She heard enough to tell it was a couple looking at the house and a real estate agent who wasn't Gloria. She decided to stay in the bathroom until she had heard them start up the stairs. If she heard them go left at the top, she would slip out and head down. If they stopped her, she would burble something and keep moving. They weren't likely to follow her or keep interrogating her. And if they turned right and headed into the master bedroom suite, she would say she had stayed behind after looking at the house.

She listened to this foreign agent enumerating the house's virtues. Hearing them presented to another couple curdled the joy she took in their particulars. They were taking forever down there. Anxiety and impatience combined to produce an unexpected boldness in her. She flushed the toilet for a bit of theater, then thrust herself out on the landing and headed down the stairs.

"Oh!" the agent said. "I didn't know anyone was here."

"Pardon me. I stayed behind to use the bathroom."

"Not at all."

"Don't let me interrupt you," she said as the couple appeared from the kitchen. "It's a great house."

"It is," the husband said.

"Well, we know the toilet works!" she said, and felt instantly foolish. The agent looked as uncomfortable hearing it as Eileen felt saying it.

"Yes—ha!" the agent said, a little belatedly.

"Do you mind if I leave through the front door? Could you lock it after me? I'd like to get a look at the front porch."

"Not at all!" The agent looked relieved. "Please!"

Outside, Eileen's frenzy subsided. She caught her breath leaning against the railing, feeling its smooth but bumpy paint. She smelled the mown grass and the lavender scent of the lilacs in the tree, and she listened to the birds, the shuffling leaves in the branches. The manicured bushes shook mildly in the wind. No police or ambulance sirens battered her ears, nor any thunder from souped-up cars. A little girl rode by on a bicycle and offered her raised hand in a wave. Eileen waved back, completing the illusion of ownership. And then it hit her, the peace she had sought in going up there, the ineffable something she'd been chasing. Then she heard the agent and the couple enter the foyer and felt the peace slip away. Their voices were muffled through the door, but she knew they were speculating about the house, weighing it, considering it. In her mind it already belonged to her. She would do whatever she had to do.

27

Connell wasn't sure why he'd told his mother he wanted to move. Maybe it was because he'd seen how much she wanted him to want to. The truth was, he didn't want to go anywhere. It felt like leaving right now would be like quitting, like saying, *I really am the pussy you think I am*. And he was heading to a new school. He'd make friends there, but if he moved, he'd lose the ones he had now; he was pretty sure of that. Farshid, Hector, and Elbert had stuck with him through all the teasing he'd endured. Farshid was going to Brooklyn Tech, Hector to St. Francis Prep, Elbert to Molloy.

When they moved, he was going to leave part of himself behind. Even the ex-friends who gave him so much trouble were part of his life. Maybe they'd all look back on it and laugh when they were adults, drinking wine around each other's kitchen tables, throwing their heads back and remembering how they were as kids. You had to stay in the same town to get that kind of rich history with people. You had to have ties that ran pretty deep.

He wasn't going to have a home anymore, not in the same way. His mother didn't seem to mind that idea. But his mother had stayed in Woodside until she was in her twenties. Her best friends were people she'd known since first grade. He saw the way they enjoyed each other's company. She said it wasn't like that anymore, that people moved around, that there weren't neighborhoods anymore like there used to be, but he knew it could be like that. All you had to do was not go anywhere.

He was playing *Mike Tyson's Punch Out!!* at Farshid's. He tried twice to get past Piston Honda, but his heart wasn't in it. He handed the controls to

Farshid and watched him work his way through Soda Popinski and Bald Bull. Connell couldn't even get to the place Farshid started from. Farshid's fingers on the buttons looked like the beating of a hummingbird's wings.

Kids pretty much left Farshid alone. He'd come to St. Joan's in sixth grade, by which point everybody had settled into cliques. He was kind of a free agent.

"My mother's going to move us," Connell said.

"Yeah?" Farshid sounded like he'd heard him but not heard him. He was moving the controller around in the air as he slapped furiously at the buttons,

"She wants to get us out of here."

"Where to?"

"Westchester."

"Where's that?"

"The suburbs."

"That's cool." He cursed and threw the controller, though it landed softly on the rug, and he retracted it by the cord and restarted the game.

"I don't want to go."

"Why not?"

"I have my friends here," he said.

"You'd get a backyard. Maybe a pool."

"Yeah."

"I'd do it."

"What about your friends?"

"What about 'em?"

"You wouldn't care about leaving?"

"No offense," he said, "but yeah—no."

"I'd miss you and Hector. Even Elbert."

"You're not gonna see us anyway, even if you stay. You're gonna be in the big city with all your nerd friends. You're gonna jerk each other off in the locker room."

"Maybe you have me confused with yourself," Connell said.

"I'm going to have girls do that for me, thank you very much."

"Everything's going to change all at once."

Farshid finished the level and paused the game. "You just need to re-invent yourself. That's what my mother said to me, 'Reinvent yourself.' In Farsi, though: '*Khodeto az no dorostkon.*' I didn't want to come here, man. There was some political shit with my father. We had to leave fast. Talk about everything changing."

"You couldn't go to Brooklyn Tech if you moved."

"I don't give a shit where I go to high school, man! Here, there, I don't care. I care about what's after that. College! Living on my own." He slapped his hands together. "Beautiful girls in my dorm room! Hah!"

Connell knew why the other kids didn't tease Farshid. He wasn't vulnerable to them; he already had a plan.

"This is home," Connell said.

"Home?" Farshid said. "What does that even mean? I'm going to work on Wall Street. I'm going to have a hot wife like Alyssa Milano that I bang a lot in my big bed. I'm going to have a big house and a big pool. That's home."

Connell felt like a child; all he cared about was getting to hold a girl's hand someday, and Farshid was already thinking of what he would do with his wife.

"Sounds good," Connell said.

"Reinvent yourself!" Farshid said, handing him the joystick. "You can start by not sucking so bad at *Punch Out!!*"

"I have to invent myself before I can reinvent myself," Connell said.

"Aw, don't say that," Farshid said. "You're already somebody. You're the biggest nerd I ever met in my entire life."

28

I started in math class. Gustavo Cruz was tapping him on the back. Connell had been resisting all year, but Gustavo hadn't given up. It was the time of year when every point counted for some kids. Usually Connell just framed his test more tightly with his arms, leaned over it more to obscure it with his body. He didn't care if it made him look like a hopeless nerd; he wanted the teachers to know he had nothing to do with cheating.

Gustavo was slapping him on the neck now. Connell couldn't turn around to tell him to stop without risking looking like a conspirator.

He thought about what he must look like to the others—a stiff kid incapable of acting normal, a former fat kid still awkward in his body, a nerd with no style or balls who would never, ever kiss a girl. He'd been insulted and made fun of a thousand times, and he'd hung from the basketball hoop, desperate to shift his hand down to cover his privates but too afraid to fall, but he hadn't suffered the truest humiliation, because his parents always told him he was worth more than other kids could see. He wasn't sure he believed that anymore.

He sat up straighter, leaned to the side, and gave Gustavo full view of his paper—the top part, at least. It was a multiple-choice test with a couple of show-your-work problems at the bottom. The multiple-choice alone was enough to get Gustavo to pass. Connell was nervous. He would have been even more nervous if Miss Montero ever even looked his way during tests, but he'd put up such staunch resistance that it must have seemed to her as if the fight on that front had been permanently won.

In the lunchroom Gustavo exulted.

"Man, that was the *shit*. Cuh-*nell!*"

"Shh . . ." Connell tried to play it cool, but he felt exposed. "Keep it quiet."

"I get you, man."

A couple of days later, when they had a surprise quiz, Connell waited until he'd finished and then leaned to the side a little. This time Miss Montero snapped, "Eyes on your own paper!" but Gustavo had probably had enough time.

"Cuh-*nell!*" Gustavo said again, and Connell thought, *Con*-null. *Con*-null.

That afternoon, instead of hustling home, he found himself sitting on the rectory steps with them. Some cosmic sleight of hand had deposited him in their midst. He hoped none of them would notice he didn't belong.

They went to Shane's apartment to make prank calls. They called Gianni's and had a pie delivered to the address in the phone book for one of their teachers. They called Antigone Psillos, a good-hearted, untouchably homely girl who had been given the unimaginative nickname of An-*pig*-o-nee. Pete asked her out, and when she cautiously agreed, he said, "Psych!" and hung up the phone.

"What's that Chinese kid you hang out with?"

"Who?"

"Your friend," Shane said. "Elbert. Elbert Lim."

"He's not my friend."

"Whatever. What's his number?"

"I don't know," Connell said.

"Here," Shane said, passing him the phone. "You dial it. Order some Chinese food."

The guys were sniggling and slapping their knees. They were in Shane's living room. His mother worked late, and his father wasn't even in the country. He was a Marine who'd been in the Gulf War. He was supposed to have come back in March, when the war ended, but he'd been sent to Bangladesh to do relief work after a cyclone. There was a picture of him in his uniform on the wall right above the phone.

"I don't know the number," Connell said.

"Bullshit," Pete said. "You talk to that kid every day."

"Hang on," Shane said. "I had to call him once for homework."

Shane got his address book and dialed the number. He made excited faces as it rang.

"Hello?" he said into the phone. "Is this Chow-Chow Kitchen? I want to order some fried rice and spare ribs."

The other guys were hooting. Connell tried to smile. Shane had his hand over the receiver. *His father,* he mouthed.

"No, I said I want to order spare ribs. For delivery."

Shane slipped into laughter and hung up.

"Call back!" Pete said. He handed Connell the phone. "You call."

Connell pretended to look at the paper and picked up the receiver. He dialed slowly, made a mistake on purpose and started again. Then he made a genuine mistake, from nerves. Shane grabbed the sheet and dialed. Connell was still holding the receiver. It rang a few times and someone picked up. It wasn't Elbert's father. It was Elbert himself now.

"Hello?" the voice said.

Connell was too nervous to speak.

"Hello? Who is this? Can you stop calling, please?"

Elbert hung up.

"He slammed the phone down," Connell said, hoping that would be enough.

"Call back!"

"Don't you want to call someone else?"

"Call back!"

Connell took the sheet and dialed the number. The phone rang for a while. He was relieved to have been spared. Then the line clicked on. It was Elbert again.

"You assholes need to leave us alone now. Isn't your break over at McDonald's? Oh wait, I forgot. Even McDonald's wouldn't hire you. I bet they'd hire your mama, though. By the hour. I hear she comes pretty cheap."

He'd always appreciated Elbert's adult air, his razor-sharp intelligence. Now it made him feel ashamed. They were looking at him intently, his new, old friends.

"Say something," Shane urged.

"I want to order spare ribs and fried rice," Connell said in a fake voice deeper than his own.

"That's really funny," Elbert said. "Original. I've never heard that before. Not even once."

Connell didn't know what to say. He felt an idiot grin spread across his face. He could feel himself getting dumber. He saw the other faces looking back at him with—could it be?—appreciation. All he could think to do was order more food.

"And some egg rolls," he said in a fake Chinese accent that made his friends laugh even louder. "And wonton soup." It made him feel sick to do it—his father would have lost his mind if he knew—but it also felt good to be one of the guys.

"Shane Dunn? Is that you? Pete McCauley?"

He was praying Elbert wouldn't say his name.

"We're not even Chinese," Elbert said. "Not that you idiots would know the difference. We're Korean. I don't even like Chinese food. Why don't you ask for some kimchi? Maybe my mother would make some for your ignorant asses. I could come over and throw it in your face."

Elbert was like that: pugnacious. Usually it was awesome; now it just scared Connell. Elbert's mother's kimchi was delicious. The first time Connell had had it, he'd felt like his mouth was on fire; he'd never had anything so spicy at home.

"Come on, Connell!" Pete shouted. "Say something."

A hush fell over the guys at this transgression of protocol. They feigned shock and started cracking up.

"Connell? Is that you?"

Connell hung up before he could answer. He knew Elbert wasn't going to talk to him anymore, so when they told him to call Farshid, he just took the phone and dialed.

"Give me that," Shane said. "I want to talk to this sand nigger myself."

Standing beneath his father's stern portrait, Shane shouted a stream of insults into the phone. He didn't bother trying to disguise his voice.

• • •

When Donny went to the bathroom, Connell stood by the hall door and listened for the sound of a flush or footsteps. He grabbed handfuls of coins from the big bowl on the breakfront, filling his pockets. He had an allowance, but he took the money anyway. It made his stomach ache to do it.

He bought food, comics, baseball cards. At a store on Roosevelt Avenue, he watched some guys buy nunchuks and throwing stars. Then he bought a curved-bladed knife that snapped with a violent click into its protective handle. He brought the knife to school and unzipped his backpack to show his new friends.

"Put that shit away," Shane said. "How can you be a nerd and so stupid at the same time?"

He didn't have a game at Elmjack, so he went to the park. All his new friends played hockey. He didn't have any hockey gear, so he played catch with one of the older guys for a while and then sat and waited.

Afterward they walked up to Northern to Dance Dynamics to watch through the blinds while the girls danced. All the girls he'd ever had crushes on were in that class, and every guy there but him was dating one of them. The class took a break for a few minutes and some girls came outside. He was the only guy not in hockey gear. He tried to hold his glove behind his back. "Baseball's gay," he'd heard Shane say, and even though he'd seen how awful Shane was in the field whenever he played softball with the older guys, he still felt like a kid carrying that glove, while the others wore protective padding and towered over him on skates and rollerblades. The girls only glanced at him quizzically, as though waiting for one of the guys to explain why they'd let Connell follow them there.

They headed to the Optimo store to steal. It was coming on evening; he knew he was supposed to have gone shopping for his mother before dinner. He should have left a while ago, but he wanted to preserve his legitimacy by doing everything they did.

The plan was for each of them to take something while the rest distracted Andy the Korean guy behind the front counter and his mother back by the storeroom. They fanned out around the store. Connell stood up front, by the baseball card display case. It wasn't hard for him to pretend to be interested, because he went in there a lot for comic books and cards. He kept Andy busy by asking a lot of questions, but he didn't steal anything. He was sure he'd be congratulated anyway for helping the cause, but when they got down the block and showed each other their loot—candy, soda, a thermos—and his hands were empty, they called him a pussy.

They went to Pete's house a few blocks away. Pete got some liquor bottles out of his parents' closet and passed them around. Connell wouldn't take a sip.

"You are such a nerd," Pete said. "I can't believe what a nerd you are. What is he doing hanging out with us again?"

Pete looked to Gustavo, who shrugged his shoulders. "My man Connell is helping me out," Gustavo said, and then he shot Connell a look that said, *You have to help yourself out.*

They went back out to meet the girls after their dance class. He could imagine what it would feel like to be able to relax, to talk to them as if he had a right to. Once, in seventh grade, he'd called up Christin Taddei at Farshid's urging and asked her out. The call had ended in humiliation. Now Christin was standing right there. She said something he didn't understand. He felt like he could barely hear anything, the way the excited blood was coursing through his system.

"You reek," Christin said again.

"What?"

"You need to use deodorant. Or cologne. Or take a shower."

The other girls tittered. "I will," he said. In his embarrassment he could feel his toes curling.

"Damn, yo!" Shane said. "My girl just dissed you *hard.*"

Shane peeled off with Christin, Pete headed home, and Connell walked down Northern with Gustavo and Kevin. They neared the Optimo store.

"You should have taken something," Gustavo said. "Everybody else did."

Dusk was coming on. The store would be closing soon. Andy had his back to the window. He was in college; Connell had seen him wearing an NYU sweatshirt. Connell bought cards from him every day practically, and comics once a month at least. Andy put together a regular bag of comics for him. Sometimes he threw him a free baseball card pack, just for being such a good customer. He liked to watch Connell open packs and find rookie cards.

Gustavo was saying something, but Connell had stopped listening. He walked into the street to get a little distance, turned, and threw the ball he'd been carrying as hard as he could. The big pane shattered with a terrific crash. Sheets of glass fell like icicles.

Gustavo shouted "Holy shit!" and he and Kevin ran down the Boulevard. Connell ran across it into traffic and kept running until he stood in front of his house, alone, his chest pounding. The front door was unlocked. He stood in the vestibule looking out to see if anyone had followed him. He wanted to switch skins with someone else, switch bodies.

His father was on the couch, wearing his headphones, and his mother was in the kitchen cooking what smelled like broccoli and ziti, which was what she whipped up when there was nothing left in the fridge. He said he was home and didn't answer when she asked where he'd been. He headed to his room. He heard a cop siren outside and started biting his nails. He went into the bathroom and stripped naked and smelled his armpits.

She was right; he did smell. Maybe he was getting ready to stop being such a damned baby about everything. He got in the shower and turned the knob for hot water all the way, with only a little cold to balance it out. The water scalded his skin and he started turning red. Steam billowed out into the room, filling it up.

He couldn't stop thinking of that window breaking. He could see it happening over and over, the glass caving in, the one big piece dangling and falling off with a crash. They would find the baseball. They would have it dusted for fingerprints. They wouldn't need fingerprints, because he went in there every day carrying his glove and a baseball. Once, he'd even left his glove there and called in, and they'd held the store open late for him to come get it. He could see Andy shaking his head in wonderment at what the hell had come over this crazy kid. He'd always enjoyed Andy's sarcasm whenever somebody said something less than intelligent or acted like an ass. Andy was in college but he had to spend all his time entertaining these little kids. Connell could see him banging his fist on the counter. He could see him locking the door and consoling his mother, and then the two of them sweeping up the shards. He pictured him emptying the window display of cards, picking pieces of glass out of boxes of packs, pulling the gate down with a muttered curse. They deserved better than what he'd given them.

He scrubbed himself with punishing quickness, but he could not calm down. He kept thinking of Christin Taddei telling him he reeked. Christin used to date Gustavo before she dated Shane, and some people said she and Gustavo had had sex. She hiked her skirt higher than the other girls did, and her blouse was always a little tight. He had an erection. He grabbed it in that steamy cloud, and after a few quick strokes he brought himself off and watched the viscous stuff disappear down the drain. He rubbed at his hand, trying to get the gluey residue off. He felt even worse now, even more scared. He was guilty, guilty. He would have to get caught. It was only a matter of time. He wanted to get out, get away. High school couldn't come fast enough, but it would not be sufficient. He wanted to get far away. He never wanted to see Andy or Andy's mother again. They would carry around the truth about him wherever they went.

He heard a knock at the bathroom door. "Dinner," was all his mother said, but he felt like he'd been called up before a judge.

29

The night before he posted his final grades, Ed didn't even grunt when she asked what he wanted for dinner, or lift his head; he just put his hand up in an imperious dismissal.

She retreated and pounded her frustration into some hamburger meat. She chopped the carrots with savage thwacks, relishing the sound of the knife crashing into the cutting board.

After dinner, as she was cleaning up, he brought all his papers into the kitchen.

"Sit with me until I'm ready for you to enter the numbers," he said.

"I'll be reading in the living room," she said. "Come get me when you're ready."

"No," he said. "I want you here. I want you ready. I'll give you the signal."

He was acting like the head of an ER team waiting for an ambulance to arrive. It was absurd that she had to be on such high alert. She didn't raise a fuss, though. She made tea and got her book and sat at the table with him.

"No," he said, looking up. "No."

"What?"

"No reading," he said. "I need you ready."

"You can't be serious," she said, and returned to the book.

"No!" He grabbed the book out of her hands.

The testy ER doctors who took their nerves out on the nurses sometimes apologized later; with the ones who didn't, you learned not to take it personally. But these men were saving lives. Whose life was Ed trying to save?

"Honey," she said. "Is it really hurting anything if I just read here next to you while you work? What's the harm in it?"

He slammed his pen down on the stack of papers. "We have a system!" he shouted. "We have a system that works! We need to follow it! Just follow the system!"

She had already figured out that they had a "system," one of his doing whatever he wanted as she looked on his work silently, benignly, unblinkingly.

"Okay." She closed her book and looked at him. His hair was graying at the temples, but otherwise it retained its deep-black hue. His lashes were still long enough to be the envy of any woman, and his crystal-blue eyes softened the sharp impression his nose and strong jaw made. It still took her by surprise how handsome he was.

She sat and waited, sipped her tea slowly. It seemed that tea drinking was something he could tolerate as in-system. She reached for a pile he'd finished with, thinking to get a head start on it. He stopped her hand and told her to wait. She stood up, just to stand, and walked over to the sink. He told her to sit down. She could feel herself messing with him. She peppered him with questions at short intervals. He ignored them and kept his head down. Eventually he looked up at her, breathing through his teeth, his eyes flashing with hate.

"Be quiet," he growled. "Sit there and be quiet and wait till I'm done."

She wanted to say something acid, to humiliate him the way he'd humiliated her. The only thing that stopped her was the vague sensation that this was not the man she'd married, that some metempsychotic transfer had occurred. She sat in the chair with one hand on the table and one embracing the mug.

When he was done he slapped the pen down and took a deep breath, rubbing his eyes. He sat back in the chair pointedly, with as much presence as if he were studying her for the first time. She was surprised by his suddenly intense look and blushed. She wanted to touch him, to dispel her nerves. She took the pile of essays and began entering the grades in the book. She made short work of it. When she was done, he produced another sheet, with numbers on it and blanks next to them.

"Now this," he said.

"What is it?"

"The final grade sheet."

"What do I do?"

"You find the student number next to the names on this other sheet."

He had everything ready for her. Considering how organized he was about all the papers, how much he seemed to have the situation in hand, it was a wonder he was asking her to do this at all.

When she was done she closed the book with a thump. Ed clapped his hands together and raised them above his head exultantly. The gesture embarrassed her—seeing him celebrate so quotidian an accomplishment. She looked for signs of irony, but there were none.

They had another bout of lovemaking. He went at her purposefully, giving her deep kisses and holding her down by the wrists. It reminded her of the way he had made love to her during their brief attempts to conceive a second child: both of their bodies moving as one; the thrust of his hips compact, rhythmic, and deliberate. The only thing that kept it from feeling perfect was her nagging worry that Connell would hear the headboard knocking against the wall.

In the middle of the night—a groggy check of the clock revealed it to be four in the morning—Ed was shaking her awake. It took some effort to figure out what he was saying, but eventually she understood that he wanted her to follow him to the kitchen.

The sheet from earlier was laid out before her, along with another that appeared identical. She looked at him, confused. Her eyes were adjusting to the kitchen light, but she could see that the grades she'd written next to the numbers had been crossed out, with new grades written in their place.

"I need you to make these changes."

"I don't understand."

"I made some changes. I need you to transfer them to this clean sheet. I have to tape it to the wall outside my classroom."

"Why are you making changes? We were done."

She wanted to put her head down on the table. She felt that if she did, he would be standing there in the same position waiting when she woke up.

"Changes!" he barked. "I made some changes! I need you to transfer them."

She couldn't make sense of it. She would simply have to submit to the logic of this inquisition. The pattern in the grades became obvious quickly: Ed had taken every grade and kicked it up a full letter, irrespective of pluses and minuses. A C– became a B; a C+ became a B; a B became an A. Ed had long held the line against rising grades. He gave out As sparingly; getting an A from Ed still meant something.

"What's this about?"

"There were other things I had to factor in. Participation. Et cetera."

"You were very generous," she said sardonically.

"There's nothing wrong with being generous."

"Not at all." She smiled. "But you were *very* generous."

"I reconsidered a few grades. It's not your concern."

"Fine," she said. "I'm tired. I don't know why I said anything." She filled in the grades next to the corresponding numbers in the new sheet and put the pen down. "There. I'm going back to sleep."

In the morning she found him on the couch. On his desk the grade sheet had been revised upward again. Now there were only two categories, A and B. Below it was another blank grade sheet. She saw that it was her duty to transcribe these trumped-up scores to the final grade sheet. Or could there be another one in store, with all As?

Standing there, she remembered how, in the years after her father retired, when she was still living at home, she would slip cash in his pants pocket for him to find when he was out at the bar, to spare him the embarrassment of not having money to buy other people's drinks. If she did this, it would be to spare Ed embarrassment.

He was curled on the couch, which was too small for his frame. It was hard to be worried about him when he was sleeping. He looked like a child, like a larger version of Connell. His hands were folded up near his face, as though he had been arrested in the act of praying. It seemed that all men were the same in the few vulnerable instants after they'd been awakened, as though they'd been called back from some universal state into the particulars of their lives. For a moment she stepped out of time and all of existence made sense; then the moment passed, and Ed returned to being her husband.

30

She sat on the stoop, listening with a new equanimity to the sounds of the neighborhood. She heard the rumble of a plane in the distance and watched it course across the sky. As a car rushed past toward Northern Boulevard, she could hear music faintly thumping within it. The laugh track of a sitcom echoed in the little valley between the two houses. It was easier to tolerate the flaws of a place when the promise of release from it loomed. Whoever bought the house would know what they were getting and willingly embrace it. If she wasn't quite going to feel nostalgic for the neighborhood, she could at least imagine that once she'd signed the papers relinquishing the deed to the house, she'd feel the rage slip from her, and she'd be able to return to survey it with detachment. She could always come back to get her hair cut; no one tamed her cowlicks the way Curt did, and his price was reasonable. And she could imagine coming back to Arturo's, though the truth was, Arturo's was a good neighborhood place, the kind that made it bearable to live there, but it wasn't anything more than that. There would be other places, better places.

Connell did a dance to avoid the back-swinging car door, pinching a plastic-sheathed comic book carefully between uplifted fingers as if holding aloft a key piece of evidence. In his other hand was a shopping bag.

"Big day at the comic book store," she said dubiously to Ed.

"He did well this year. He's a good kid."

"Looks like he did well today too, big spender."

"It's an investment," Ed said. "He knows his stuff. He didn't get junk."

She went to Connell's room. He was slotting his new comics into his long boxes with the quiet gravity of a special-collections librarian.

"Did you take advantage of him?"

"No! Why?"

"He's happy to be done with the school year. You must have seen that."

"It wasn't my idea. He just came home and said, 'We're going up the block to the comics store.' I told him I didn't want to go. He kept insisting. I kept telling him I don't go to that store anymore. I don't like those people in there."

"Why?" she asked. "What did they do to you?"

"Nothing," he said. "They're just not nice. Anyway, I don't go there anymore. He said, 'Then let's go to that store near where your orthodontist's used to be.' He drove us all the way out to Bayside. I didn't want to get all this stuff. I mean, I wanted to, but I felt bad. He just kept saying, 'Get what you want.'"

"How much did he spend?"

"A bunch."

She moved closer to him. "How *much*?"

"Two hundred. Over two hundred."

"*How much* over two hundred?"

"Two forty-eight," he said. "And seventy-eight cents."

She couldn't believe the number. She would have thought it impossible to spend that much on comic books unless you brought a wheelbarrow into the store.

"You took advantage."

"I did not," he said, indignant. He was slipping cardboard backings into the comics' plastic sleeves and ferreting them into the archival boxes he kept his collection in. If it really was an investment, she couldn't accuse him of not tending to it. "He kept saying, 'I want you to feel like you can have anything you want.' He was telling me to fill up my basket. I didn't get any really expensive ones."

Eileen shuddered, as if a cold breeze had blown through the room. She sensed a sadness at the heart of Ed's largesse. The boy seemed to have sensed it too; it had tainted his happiness at his haul. She felt a powerful sympathy for her husband, like one of those synchronized pains experienced by people miles apart, even though he was in the other room.

With a dignified informality, the ancient maitre d' directed them to a table. Arturo's hadn't changed since it opened years ago: white aprons over black outfits; napkins draped over forearms; tinted, marble-patterned wall-length mirrors; mild music; steaming sliced loaves; a reliably robust house red. There were neighborhood Italian restaurants like it all over the city—strong in the specials, respectable otherwise—but she'd always felt this place represented a bit of refinement. Sandro, Arturo's son, ran it with a seemly reserve. Still, she was looking forward to putting it behind her for places of real distinction.

Ed smiled and looked benignly at his menu, as if written in its pages were the answers to diverting but trivial questions.

"Are you happy the year is over?" she asked.

"Very happy," he said.

She fidgeted with some sugar packets. "So, Ed," she said, after what seemed like an interminable pause. She tried out a smile. "We saw a nice house. One we liked a lot."

"You found a house?"

He was looking at her with a strangely blank expression.

"Well, we didn't find a house, exactly," she said. "We did see one. It may not be perfect. There's no saying we can even afford it."

"You want to move? We can move."

"What?"

She felt a little light-headed. She put both hands on the table to steady herself. His capitulation was so instantaneous that she had to think it was because the boy was there and they were in a public place; once home, he would give full vent to his displeasure. Another thought gave her greater pause, though: that she actually believed him. It was as if he'd never truly been opposed to the idea in the first place.

Ed turned to Connell. "This is what you want?"

She took a deep breath. Her stomach was in such a knot that she felt she might throw up.

"Very much," the boy said, with a strange gravity. "I'm ready to leave."

"You are?" Ed asked.

"Right away."

"Why?"

"Well," he said, "I've been thinking it over a lot." She wouldn't have guessed he'd thought about it once since the day they'd seen the house. "And what I've come up with is that I'm starting high school in the fall, and that's a fresh start for me, and I think we should all get a fresh start."

The boy had come to her aid. She had no idea where he was getting this poise. Perhaps her dream of having a politician in the family might come true after all. Ed looked to her. She shrugged her shoulders.

"Plus," Connell added, "the house we found is great. The driveway is wide enough for almost a half-court game."

She had no need to sell it to Ed when Connell was doing so much of the work for her.

"You want to move?" Ed asked again, as he shoved more bread into his mouth.

Connell nodded.

"Why not?" Ed said. "Let's move."

"We don't have to rush into anything," she said, disturbed by the quickness of his about-face.

"You found a house, you say?"

"Yes, but—"

"We can move."

"Really?" Connell asked.

"Yes."

"Well," she said, "I'm glad to see you're open to the idea. We'll discuss it more later."

"It's a fine idea." His grin was so wide as he buttered a slice of bread that Connell broke into a goofy one of his own.

"Someone's in a good mood," she said, but Ed didn't hear her. "I said, *someone's* in a good mood." The pair of them chomped lustily. Ed signaled for another bowl of bread. When the waiter brought it, Connell ordered another Coke. "Save some room for dinner," she said, unsure which of them she was addressing. She had ripped a sugar packet open without realizing it; its contents deposited into her lap. She rubbed the crystals until they formed a grainy film on her fingers, but she refused to get up to wash her hands.

"All right," she said. "Connell wants to move. You want to move. I want to move. Does that mean we're all in agreement?"

Ed nodded as he slathered butter on a new piece.

"You don't mind if I go ahead and get some plans in motion. You're on board."

"Sure," he said.

She felt herself growing angry. "Just back up a second," she said. "Do you not remember saying you didn't want to move? Do you not remember saying it wasn't the right time?"

"I know we talked about it," he said.

"And do you or do you not remember telling me in no uncertain terms that you didn't want to—you *couldn't*—move?"

He was nodding, but once again it wasn't clear he was actually listening.

"All of a sudden it makes perfect sense to you?"

Her voice had been rising without her permission. People at nearby tables picked up their heads.

"I'm sorry," he said. "I'm sorry." He wasn't just trying to quiet her down; there was a note of real contrition.

"Hey, Dad!" Connell said. "It's okay. This is a good thing!" The boy had moved over to put an arm around his father.

"I'm sorry," he said. "I just wanted to have some of this bread."

His apologies were making her uncomfortable. "Just tell me one thing," she said. "What changed your mind? What's so different today?"

"I just feel good today. I'm so happy to be done! I don't have to go in there for weeks—months!"

He was almost giddy. Maybe this thing wasn't depression. Maybe it was manic depression.

Now that the year was over, now that he could look forward to three uninterrupted months, he'd sign off on anything she wanted. It wasn't that he hadn't wanted to move; it was that he hadn't been able to deal with anything extraneous at all. He'd had to spend so much energy managing his depression, his midlife crisis, his students, his research, that formerly ordinary tasks like doing his grades had become insuperable burdens. The strain had caused him to short-circuit. He had lost his mind over a few calculations, some entry of data into a book, some transposition of that data onto a sheet to tape to the wall. He had falsified the record for it, lost sleep over it, screamed at her because of it, cried in her arms about it. All he'd wanted was to be alone to lick his wounds, and his job never let him be alone. As long as he lay on the couch with his eyes closed, shutting out his thoughts with music, the demon couldn't get to him.

Ed and Connell scarfed their meals. Eileen stared into her plate to avoid conversation and took her time eating. After the plates were cleared, Sandro approached grandly, the waiter behind him bearing a dessert platter.

"With my compliments," he said. "I'd like you to choose one each."

Sandro had chosen this of all moments to allow his circumspection to falter. "You don't have to do that," she said.

"We're celebrating tonight," he said. "Believe it or not, we've been here thirty years. You're one of our oldest customers."

He must have seen her stiffen.

"I don't mean oldest," he said. "Longest-standing."

"We don't need *three*."

Sandro turned to Ed. "You see?" he said, a hint of pique in his voice. "This is why she still has such a nice figure."

Ed smiled warmly, registering no tension, though Connell squirmed in his seat. Sandro left.

"Here's to the end of the year," Ed said, raising his glass and taking the little bit of wine left in it down in a gulp.

"Here's to finding a house," she said. Ed held out his empty glass. Connell raised his water and the three of them clinked.

"Here's to high school," Connell said. They clinked again.

Ed looked at her. "Good luck," he said.

"With what?"

"Finding the right house."

"I told you I found the right one."

He turned to Connell. "Good luck in high school."

"Thanks, Dad."

"Good luck to all of us,"

31

His mother yelled for him to come outside. When he did, he saw her leaning on a shovel in the garden box, where she'd spent a lot of time lately. Anytime he left for a game on the weekend, she was hunched over a plant, flashing a spade in her gloved hand, or spreading enriched soil from a bottomless bag.

"I want you to bury this for me." She handed him a statue that looked like the ones on the breakfront in Lena's apartment. It depicted a man in a red gown holding a baby, probably Jesus, dressed in pink. She pointed to a space between rose bushes. "Put the hole here," she said.

"How far down?"

"Start digging. I'll tell you when to stop."

"Why are you burying this?"

"St. Joseph is supposed to help people sell houses," she said. "You have to bury him upside down, facing the street."

"Do you believe that?"

"It can't hurt," she said.

He felt the shovel strike something hard. He cleared some dirt away and saw a large rock. He trenched around it and pulled at it. It came up slowly, like a recalcitrant root. He took off his shirt, hung it on the railing, and kept digging. He was enjoying his new physique. He had grown about four or five inches that year. He watched his muscles tighten and release as he worked.

"This is the second one I got," his mother said as he dug. "The first one cost four dollars. It didn't feel right. It was white plastic. Just Joseph;

no Jesus. I brought it in to the girl at the religious store. I told her, 'I need a good one, not this chintzy one.' She showed me this. She said it wasn't intended for burial."

"How much was it?"

"Forty bucks."

It seemed like a lot of money to bury in the ground. When he had cleared the space of backsliding dirt, he dropped the statue in headfirst, covered it up, and stomped the mound to make it flat again.

"What if it doesn't work?" he asked.

"It'll work," his mother said.

32

She gave the listing to Cindy Coakley's sister Jen, who was with Century 21 in East Meadow. It might have been easier to go with someone local, but she wasn't about to leave any money in the neighborhood that she didn't have to.

The next thing she had to do was tell the Orlandos. She went up the back staircase to the second-floor landing and listened without knocking. She could hear them all in there—Gary and Lena too, from the third floor—watching *Wheel of Fortune* and laughing. Donny was good-naturedly yelling at the set, calling out answers and cursing the contestant.

Selling meant throwing them out on the street, or at least putting more burden on Donny, who wrote the checks for both apartments. Brenda didn't make much money at Pathmark; Gary's odd jobs never lasted; and Lena was past the point of being able to work.

She went back downstairs. The next day, after steeling herself, she headed up again. She heard some murmurs of conversation and knocked. Brenda opened the door onto the dining room, where Donny and Sharon were sitting at the table.

"This looks like a bad time."

"Not at all!" Donny gestured to an empty seat. "You want to join us? We have plenty."

She felt herself drift into the apartment. Brenda disappeared into the kitchen.

"Did you eat?" Donny asked.

"I don't want to trouble you."

"Sit down," Donny said. "I'll get you a plate."

The truth was, she was hungry. Ed and Connell were going to stop at a diner on the way home from Connell's game; she'd been planning to heat up leftovers. A big pasta bowl sat in the middle of the table with huge, gorgeous meatballs under a blanket of deep-red tomato sauce.

Sharon regarded Eileen with elfin eyes over a glass of soda. Brenda came in with steaming garlic bread wrapped in tin foil.

"Are you joining us?" Brenda asked.

Donny grabbed a big forkful of spaghetti and ladled out a few meatballs and poured a little lake of sauce around them. Before Eileen could answer, he handed her the plate.

"I guess I am," she said.

Sharon's plate was taken and the girl smiled silently across the table at Eileen. She had beautiful straight hair and striking features. She was nine years old, shy and gentle, the compensation for all the dead ends and suffering in the family, and remarkably unspoiled, though they all doted on her. Her radiance was like a recessive gene come to life after generations of hibernation in the bloodline.

Brenda said grace, a habit Eileen had abandoned at her own table after trying it out for a while after Connell was born. Her conscience rumbled as Brenda spoke the familiar words and added a makeshift prayer.

"This looks amazing," Eileen said nervously after everyone had crossed themselves.

"Thank you very much," Donny said, winking at her broadly. "I try."

"That's rich," Brenda said. "You can't even boil an egg."

Donny caught Eileen's gaze and gestured theatrically with his eyebrows as he spoke to his sister. "What do I need to boil an egg for," he said, "when I have you to do it?"

"Keep it up," Brenda said. "You'll find poison in your coffee one morning."

Donny smilingly bit his outstretched tongue and shivered in triumph at having provoked her. Sharon giggled through the whole exchange.

"Did you want to talk about something, Eileen?" Brenda asked. "I was trying to get everything on the table; I forgot why you came."

"Would you let the poor woman eat? Look, she has a mouthful of food, and you're asking her questions."

Eileen held a finger up while she chewed. Donny looked at her with placid interest. He had a kind, broad face with exaggeratedly fleshy features, like those of a prizefighter. He had a boxer's broad back and meaty hands. He could have become a depressive like his brother or a gambler like his father but he had sought to make a life for himself instead. He used to run with a tough crowd, the kind that in retrospect was almost wholesome in comparison to the drug gangs that roved the neighborhood now. She stopped seeing them around the house after Donny's best friend Greg from up the block wrapped his motorcycle around a streetlamp. Donny got a job as a sanitation worker through his father. He still worked on cars, but now only on his days off and more as a hobby than as a source of income. The Palumbos let him park whatever he was working on in the back of their driveway.

"What I really want to know," Eileen said, "is how you make this sauce. Mine never tastes this good."

"The key is to use fresh sausage. Spicy or sweet, whatever you like. Good stuff, nothing cheap. You have to burn it in the saucepan."

"On purpose?"

"When you have a nice charred coat, you put the tomatoes in. The acid eats the burnt part off the pan. It gets in the gravy. I'll show you sometime."

"Don't listen to her," Donny said. "Our mother's is better."

"For once this idiot is right," she said. "No one's is better than my mother's. I'm okay with that. I have time to perfect it."

"She's gotta perfect it," Donny said. "She needs something to bait the hook."

"That's enough out of you." Brenda smacked him on the head. It was impossible not to get caught up in the high spirits around the table. It was no wonder Connell didn't come right down when she came home from work, why she had to go up and fetch him.

"I've been hearing your car make some noises I don't like," Donny said as he pulled on his chin. "You know what I'm talking about?"

"I'm not sure."

"Let me take a look at it. Maybe I can catch something before it turns into a problem."

"You don't have to do that," she said. "I can take it to the shop."

"They're gonna charge you an arm and a leg. I'll do it for nothing, and I'll do a better job. I can keep that thing running forever."

"Thank you," she said guiltily. In her nervousness she had put her finger through one of the lace stitchings on the old tablecloth and broken it. This was going to be even harder than she'd thought. How could she tell him that the first chance she got she was going to buy a much nicer car? She placed her napkin in her lap and pushed herself back from the table.

"You okay?"

"I ate a bit quickly," she said.

"Brenda's cooking will do that," Donny said. "You want to get through it as fast as possible."

Sharon chuckled.

Eileen wanted to abandon the plan, go downstairs, and come back when she'd be more collected, but there were signs to put up, and she was going to need access to all the apartments.

"Who wants dessert and coffee?" Brenda said after the clinking of forks on plates had died down.

"I don't want to put you out any more."

"Nonsense. Have a seat inside. I'll make a pot."

Donny led her to the living room. She sat on the yellow floral couch, which had a pattern she'd always found garish and worn areas by the skirt and armrests. She'd considered it a telling detail that they'd bought a big new television and kept this sofa. Now, as she sank into it, she was taken by its softness. The room, which she'd always thought of as a model of how not to decorate, radiated the warmth of shared usage. In the corner sat a small, beaten piano that looked like it might have survived the ransacking of an old saloon. At times she could hear someone practicing up here, and she'd never realized until that moment that it gave her pleasure.

Donny sat on the opposite couch. Sharon came and sat next to Eileen. The television was on, muted; Donny glanced at it out of the corner of his eye.

"Are those yours?" she asked, pointing to the framed artworks on the wall. Sharon nodded.

"I don't know where she got it," Donny said. "Nobody in this family has any kind of talent like that. You should see how she does in school. Tell Mrs. Leary how you did on your last report card."

The girl demurred.

"Go ahead. Tell her."

"Straight As," she said in a quick burst.

"I didn't even graduate high school," Donny said. "Gotta be proud of this kid." He had a faraway look in his eye. "I try to help her at the table, but she don't need it. My little daughter is the same way. She's like a whip. Not even two years old and she can count to ten. She don't get it from me, that's for sure. I tell Sharon to watch you and Mr. Leary. You folks are on another plane. I tell her to be like you. I never knew what an education really meant. I tell her to look at me and just do the opposite."

"Don't say that," Eileen said. "I bet she's proud to have you as an uncle." As she spoke, she realized to her surprise that she believed what she was saying. "And you're going to be a great father to that girl."

He smiled wearily, accepting the verdict without objection. Brenda came in with a plate of Duplex cookies, followed by mugs of coffee. Eileen searched about for a coaster.

"Don't worry about it," Brenda said. "This table's older than me. It does the job."

Circular embossments emblazoned the table's surface like trophies from all-night conversations. They were suddenly so appealing that Eileen wondered for a moment why she'd always been concerned to preserve a pristine surface on her own table, which looked almost as new as the day she bought it, no history engraved on its face.

"I have to tell you something," she began, as Brenda settled into the couch next to Donny. "It's not easy to say."

Brenda, who seemed to have a radar for danger, shifted in her seat.

"Ed and I have decided to move. We're going to have to sell the house."

Donny's eyebrows rose. Brenda took a sip of coffee with two hands.

"That's great, Eileen," Donny said. "Where are you moving?"

"To Westchester," she said. "Bronxville."

"That's up by Yonkers, right? It's beautiful up there."

It unnerved her a little to hear Donny place it so quickly, though she wouldn't have been surprised to learn he knew every major road within a hundred-mile radius.

Brenda took out a cigarette and flapped the arm of her robe out to sit more comfortably, a gesture that made Eileen unaccountably uneasy. It was then that the smell of smoke, which ineluctably pervaded the apartment, came to her all at once. It was in everything; Connell came downstairs smelling of it. She hated to think of him sitting in it, or of Sharon sleeping in a cloud of the settling vapors. It also angered her that it might be a detracting factor in the minds of potential buyers.

"When is this happening?" Brenda leaked a small stream of smoke as she spoke. Her cigarette dangled at the end of her lip, just as Eileen's mother's had so often. She felt her heart hardening toward Brenda, and by extension Donny and Sharon. Brenda was making it easier on her without meaning to.

"Soon. I'm not sure."

"How soon?"

"I found a house. We're ready to make an offer."

"What happens to us?"

"I don't really know. The buyer can choose to let you stay. He can ask you to go. It's up to him."

"There's a *buyer*?"

"I'm just thinking out loud."

"I don't care if they raise the rent," Brenda said. "I'll make it work. I just don't want to move."

"You've been very kind to us." Donny stretched an arm out as if to hold his sister at bay. "We appreciate it."

They sat in silence, Brenda taking deep drags.

"It's going to be strange not having you around here," Donny said.

"It's going to be strange not *being* around here," Brenda said.

"What do you need us to do?" Donny asked. "How can we help?"

He was broad-shouldered and game, and the warm roundness of his face admitted no despair.

"I'm going to need to show the apartment, and the one upstairs. There'll be an open house. A few of them. I'll let you know when."

"Okay," he said.

"You can't be here during them. The Realtor asks that. The same is true for your mother and Gary."

"Got it."

"She might want to bring some things in. Candles, comforters, et cetera." She paused and then added, "She's doing the same thing in my apartment."

"Not a problem," he said.

"When is all this happening again?" Brenda asked, jabbing her cigarette out forcefully.

"Soon. We could start next week." Brenda called Sharon over. As the girl took a seat between her mother and uncle on the couch, the moral balance of the room seemed to shift. "I'm sorry it's so sudden. We just decided. I came to you as soon as I could."

"Don't get me wrong," Brenda said. "I'm happy for you. I don't blame you. I'd get out of here if I could."

Eileen looked down at her interlaced fingers.

"How much time do we have after you sell?"

"It depends," she said. "Thirty days. Sixty. Ninety. I don't know."

"Don't we have some kind of rights as tenants?"

"I'm not sure, since we've never worried about a lease. I can ask the Realtor."

"That's bullshit," Brenda said. "Put us on a lease. Buy us some time."

Donny stood up. "It's hot in here," he said. "Anyone else want a beer?" He left the room.

Eileen cleared her throat. "That might make it harder to sell the house. Especially because your rent is substantially below market."

"Then increase the rent. I don't care. Double it. Whatever it takes."

"Let's not worry about that right now," Eileen said. "Maybe I'll have a buyer who would prefer to have the house fully rented. I'll see what I can do when I know more."

"Maybe we'll buy it ourselves," Donny said as he returned with a glass of ice water. She saw that he had meant for the beer comment to lighten the mood. "It'd be nice to have a room for my daughter when she comes over." He checked his sister's face to see what she thought of the idea. Brenda's expression hardened, as if to say, *Who's got that kind of money?* Donny sighed. "Don't worry about us," he said. "I'm sure you have a lot on your mind. I'll see what we can come up with on our end. Whatever we can do to help, you let us know."

She thought about Lena. She knew Lena should hear the news from her, but she didn't know if she had it in her to go upstairs and go through it again. Lena was upright in everything she did; decency and morality were her default positions. She was one of those heroic old women who sat in church all day taking on the burden of saving the sinners around them.

"There is one more thing," she said.

"What is it?" said Donny. "Just ask."

"Will you tell your mother for me?"

A week later Jen had an open house. The thought of all those people gawking at her furniture, her possessions, her bathroom annoyed Eileen, but then she thought, *Let them come. Let them see the oasis we made.* Jen came an hour early to put duvets on the beds upstairs—where they'd all cleared out, as requested, despite Eileen's visions of them haunting the stoop, hangdog or angry looks on their faces—and decorative items on the tables and breakfront. She'd warmed pots of potpourri on the stovetop. It already felt like someone else's home.

She wondered who would show up. This was the time to leave the neighborhood, not discover it—but perhaps some intrepid breed of young person might fancy themselves enterprising and patient enough to secure an outpost in the neighborhood of tomorrow. It wasn't her responsibility to tell them that this neighborhood's best days were in the past.

Eileen left to get her hair done. When she returned, half an hour after the open house should have ended, she saw a tall Indian man on her stoop, talking with Jen. She stopped in front of the Palumbos' house and watched him for signs of interest. He was gesturing around and nodding at whatever Jen was saying. A woman who must have been his wife was standing on the sidewalk, along with their son and daughter, both of whom leaned against her. Eileen resisted the urge to introduce herself and feel them out. When they left, Jen told her she thought they might bid on the house. The man had said he would need it empty to make room for his extended family—brothers and sisters, nieces and nephews, grandparents. *So that's how they live*, Eileen thought.

A couple of days later, the Indian man offered the full asking price—$365,000, which Jen had originally thought a little high. Eileen called Gloria to find out whether the Bronxville house had sold. Then she called Donny to let him know there was an offer.

"How much?"

She told him. Donny whistled into the phone and there was a long pause. Did he know how much less she'd bought it from his father for?

"That's a lot," he said. "That's great, good for you."

"Thank you," she said.

He paused again. "How long do we have?"

She explained that it would be soon, a week or two at the most. She wanted to sell as soon as possible.

"Can you wait a little longer?" he asked. "I might have some options, but I could use more time."

She didn't know whom Donny was going to ask for the money, or what kind of trouble he would be exposing himself to in order to get it, but that was his concern.

"I'll see what I can do," she said, and as she hung up she understood that there was nothing she was willing to do. She had to get out while she could.

She called Gloria and told her to make an offer on the Bronxville house.

The next day—she forgave herself in advance for the lie—she told Donny there had been a competing bidder and the first bidder had gone above asking, but it was his final offer, and he needed an answer immediately.

He was no closer to having a down payment, he said.

"I'm sorry," she said. "I'm going to have to take it."

Eileen had bid below asking for the house in Bronxville, but they hadn't had another bid, so they took it without parrying.

The Indian buyer insisted on a thirty-day closing, but Eileen was able to extend it to sixty when she pled the case of her tenants. That was the most she could do for them.

Donny still fixed her car.

33

Connell woke up to his father screaming at him and wagging his finger in his face.

"*Christ!* Do you know what you've done? *Do* you?"

Connell's mind raced, but he could recall no hanging offenses.

"You left the jelly out all night!" his father said. "You left the cover off!" Connell stammered an apology, but his father waved him off. "How could you *do* such a thing?" He stamped his feet, one after the other, as though smashing grapes. Connell had never seen him make such a childish gesture, and it disconcerted him more than the yelling had.

Ten minutes later his father was back in his room, sitting on the bed. "I don't know what came over me," he said.

All that summer, he was on an energy crusade. He said they didn't need to shower every day, that every other day was sufficient. If you walked away from a stereo for a second, he hit the power button. If you ran the hot water too long for dishes, he reached across you and pressed the handle down. If you turned on the air conditioner in the car, he told you to open the window instead. When he turned off the air conditioning in the house, Connell's mother threatened to leave and turned it right back on. That got through to him; nothing else did. He let the air conditioner run, but unplugged the coffeemaker, the toaster, the stereo, the TV, the Apple IIe.

One night, while they were sitting at the kitchen table, his father howled in frustration after breaking the point off a pencil by pressing too hard. "This goddamned thing's no good," he said as he snapped it in half. "It's no good at all."

His mother took them on scenic drives in the area they were moving to, but when they parked and got out, his father just stood by the car with his arms crossed. They went peach-picking once, in Yorktown, and his father stuck his hands in his pockets and leaned against the enormous wheel of an idle tractor while his mother filled a basket with the most shapely peaches she could find. When they walked back to the barn to pay, his father reached into the basket in his mother's hands and began tossing peaches to the ground. "We don't need all these!" he said.

"What the hell is *wrong* with you?" He'd gotten about half of them out before she fended him off. She was looking around to see who had noticed the outburst. "Have you gone crazy?"

"We don't need this many!" he said, squashing them underfoot as he followed Connell's mother. "We can't eat this many!"

"I was just going to make some pies," she said to Connell, as though appealing to his fairness. The only thing he felt safe doing was shrugging.

"Not for me!" his father said. "I could go the rest of my life without another bite of your pie."

Then his mother herself turned the basket over, dumping out the remaining peaches. She dropped the basket and they walked to the car in silence. They drove home all the way like that, half an hour at least. Connell put his earphones in, but he didn't turn his Walkman on. He waited and waited to hear the silence end, but it never did, and a queasy feeling grew in his gut. The only thing he heard was a little quiet sniffling from his mother in the passenger seat when they were almost home. He hit play on his Walkman after that.

34

I t was the end of August when they moved, as hot a day as she could remember, the kind of heat that made a person happy to escape the city. She had packed boxes for weeks, and the walls were lighter in color where the pictures had hung and the furniture had stood, as if a slow-exposure photograph had been taken of their lives. The ghostly outlines of their things, together with the austere emptiness of the space and the dirt and dust gathered in the corners and wedged under the molding, increased her eagerness to get out of there. The movers came and loaded up the truck.

"Do you want to do a last walk-through with me?" she asked Ed, who was sitting on the stoop with Connell.

"I've made my peace with it," he said.

She resented the private ceremony Ed's statement implied. She'd pictured them opening a nice bottle of wine when they started filling boxes, or a celebratory bottle of champagne on their last night, but they'd had neither.

"You don't want to take a final look at it?"

He didn't respond. Connell looked as if he preferred to sit there too. Rather than squeeze past them, she went around to the side door and up the back stairs to the second-floor landing. Peeking in, she was overcome by the emptiness of the place. A spasm of anxiety rooted her to the spot; she couldn't enter the apartment. She'd half expected to see Donny and Brenda and Sharon there, but the previous week, Donny had moved them to a three-bedroom apartment—Brenda and Sharon in one bedroom, he and Gary in another, Lena in the third—in a monolithic structure around the corner that possessed none of the charm of the garden co-ops, with a cramped, concrete common area instead of generous grass. She called "hello" in the echoing dining room and stepped inside. She stood where she'd sat and told the Orlandos of her plans— which was where she and Ed had eaten when it was just the two of them, and for the first few years after Connell was born—until she got spooked and left.

She hurried down the stairs to her own apartment. She could see it that way now, as an apartment. The whole time she'd been there, she'd preferred to think she lived in a house with floors she didn't use.

When Angelo Orlando sold her the house in 1982, he'd done so in distress. Just shy of a decade later, his heirs had had an opportunity to buy back their childhood home, and they'd failed to secure it. The story of their line in the house had come to an end. They were adrift in temporary shelters: someone else's apartment, someone else's building. The great churning never stopped. Spackle was placed in the holes where nails had held family portraits, paint covered the dirt marks of shoes left by the door, a coat of varnish leveled the worn hallways, and it was ready for a new family.

The family who'd bought her house was making a stand against obscurity. It would be their nail holes puncturing a fresh coat of paint, their cooking smells sinking into the upholstery, their shouts of laughter, pain, and joy bouncing off the plaster walls. They would use all three of the house's floors. In enough time they would forget the structure had ever belonged to anyone else. It was a thought that worked both ways: it would be as if she'd never lived anywhere but Bronxville.

At the closing, she'd met the Thomases. She was surprised to learn that the husband's first name was also Thomas—though the middle name listed on the contract was something closer to what she'd expected, a tangled thicket of consonants and vowels. When she couldn't stifle her surprise at such an odd name as Thomas Thomas, the husband, who was exceptionally tall and wore tinted glasses, explained to her that he wasn't even the only Thomas Thomas in his hometown, that the name was extremely popular there, due to the fact that St. Thomas had gone there in the middle of the first century to spread the faith among the Jewish diaspora. She dismissed this idea as ridiculous; St. Thomas might have visited India, but there was no way he or any other apostle had reached there before Western Europe or Ireland. Thomas Thomas seemed like an intelligent enough man, but his dates had to be incorrect.

The fact that Indians had bought her home and were going to fill it with their entire extended family, floor to ceiling, was another reminder that Jackson Heights was a big cauldron and that it was spitting her out in a bubble pushed up by heat. Supposedly it was the most ethnically diverse square mile in the world. Someone more poetically inclined might find inspiration in the polyphony of voices, but she just wanted to be surrounded by people who looked like her family.

The only thing left to do was walk through her own apartment for anything left behind. In the guest bedroom she spotted a solitary die on the floor and went to pick it up but pulled her hand away right before she touched it.

In the kitchen pantry she found a broom leaning against the wall like a forlorn suitor at a dance. Ed and Connell were waiting outside, but she couldn't resist the urge to sweep up the dust bunnies and bits of debris on the floor. She remembered sweeping the kitchen floor in Woodside as a girl, methodically, covering every inch of that fleur-de-lis-patterned linoleum in an invisible geometric march. Back then, she'd dreamed of a house like the one she was now leaving. Somewhere along the way, she'd adopted a higher standard. Her new house was large and full of light and made an imposing picture from the street, with a sloped driveway, slatted shutters, and stone pillars to mark the front walk. It was everything she wanted, and she tried not to wonder if the new house would one day feel as old and heavy as the one she was leaving.

She stared at the pile in the center of the floor. There was no dustpan, not even a scrap of cardboard to sweep it onto. It would be dispersed by the footsteps of movers, or the Thomas family themselves. It wasn't her responsibility anymore. This was another woman's kitchen now. There'd be a victory in leaving it there and heading outside, in allowing something niggling to go unattended to, but she'd been cleaning messes all her life.

She'd heard Ed tell Connell once that skin cells constituted the majority of dust. If that was true, then there were microscopic bits of her in that pile. She got down on her hands and knees, carefully because she was wearing stockings, and scooped the dirt with one hand into the cupped other. She dumped it in the sink. When she saw a little raised ridge of residue where her pinky finger had passed along the floor, she wet her hands to mop up the last remnants of her life in the house.

She went outside. Ed and Connell were already in Ed's Caprice. She had driven the Corsica up the previous night after work and parked it in the driveway. The house had been dark, and she'd started for the train in a hurry, not wanting to linger too long there alone.

Ed didn't look angry at having to wait. He looked simply blank. Blank was fine by her right then; she could map something onto a blank. There was a roiling complexity to Connell's expression, though, an untidiness that she wanted nothing to do with at the moment. She took a seat in the back. With their Caprice in the lead and the moving truck behind them, the caravan of their belongings set out for the Triborough Bridge.

It was a clear day, and as they headed toward Northern, the sun cast a warm eye on the block's houses. Connell waved to an old man who didn't look familiar to her. The neighborhood itself hardly looked familiar anymore; it was as if she were slowly stirring from a dream. The faces she saw through the window looked benign in the heat. Pairs and trios, even solitary amblers, were carried along by an unseen buoyancy. She was no longer afraid of these people; she'd cleared that infection from her bloodstream. The previous day, when she'd realized she'd never again have to attend one of Father Choudhary's Masses or walk on the Boulevard, she'd laughed in relief.

She spotted a clerk stacking cans in a bodega and leaned back against the headrest to stare at the ceiling foam. When she looked out again, they were a couple of blocks from the turnoff for the BQE. She knew the trip to Bronxville by heart; she could see one highway turn to another, then another, until they reached the surface streets and the house where they'd begin their second act as a family. There was still this short stretch left of her present life to go through, though. She felt no stirrings of nostalgia as

she took in the Boulevard for what might be the last time. She shut her eyes
to put it behind her the sooner. There was a blessed nothingness behind
her eyelids; the darkness there could have been the peace of death. She'd
spent her whole life working toward this moment, and she was exhausted.
She felt she could sleep for years without waking.

The sounds of the streets, muffled by the air conditioning, grew less
and less distinct, and the next thing she knew the car was pulling into the
driveway. Her first thought as she took in the house through the window
was that it didn't look the way she'd remembered it. It was smaller somehow, more ordinary. She thought to tell her husband to pull back out, that
this was not their house, that they'd find their real house if they kept looking. Then she saw the truck with their belongings coming around the bend.

She stepped out and stretched her long limbs to shake off the drowsi-
ness. Ed and Connell were standing looking aimless. She remembered that
she had the only set of keys in her pocketbook.

The driveway, which had baked in the heat of a dry summer, was
scored with cracks that would only expand as the weather got colder. The
forecast called for clear skies for a couple of days. If Ed and the boy got
started first thing in the morning, there would be time for a new layer of
blacktop to dry. In a little while she would send Ed to the hardware store
for push brooms and buckets of asphalt.

She let the three of them in. They drifted to different corners of the
kitchen and stood looking at each other in silence, frozen by the unknown
future awaiting them in other rooms. She opened a cabinet door held on by
only the top hinge, and it swung like a pendulum in her hand. She had seen
the chipped paint, the peeling paper, the old cabinets, the ugly lacquer,
the Formica countertops missing edges and chunks, but somehow she had
forgotten just how bad it all was. It struck her now that this kitchen was
worse than the one she had left behind. She was beginning to understand
how much work everything was going to be and how much it would cost.

She considered saying something to christen the house, but she didn't
want to think about how inept her words would sound. Instead she just
sent them out to unload the car. There would be time later to savor the reality of their altered lives, to appreciate having arrived where they'd arrived.

She opened the front doors and stepped out onto the porch, leaning cautiously into the rickety railing. She watched the couch sway slightly as it rose up the lawn, the heavy hickory dresser behind it undulating as the movers took their halting steps. For a moment the furniture seemed borne on invisible waves, like flotsam from a sunken vessel, and she imagined she'd been hauled up from the wreck of her old life to stand on the deck of a ship bound for an unfamiliar shore.

She stepped inside and made way for the wide arcing path the couch took through the expansive foyer. She examined the bricks. The finger-thick lacquer on them would have to go immediately. She felt she was coming out of a stupor.

The movers held the couch up in the living room and looked to her for instructions, but the simple question of where it should go baffled her utterly. She told them to put it down while she thought it over. She directed the men with the dresser upstairs. She wanted the next phase of her life to remain forever potential and the rest of her things to stay in the truck. When the movers were finished, they would drive off, leaving her and her family behind in the empty spaces she'd fought so hard to procure.

She told them to place the couch flush against the wall, under the windows. She didn't get the jolt of pleasure she'd expected from making her first decision in the house, because aside from the fact that nothing would have a home for a while, certainly not the kind of permanent home that could put her restless mind at ease, she also had a nagging feeling that it was only the first of many more decisions to come, that she was the ship's captain now.

The men with the couch were heading back to the truck, but she asked them to wait a second. They stood on the steps looking up at her. They were all, herself included, waiting for the next thing she would say. She tried to freeze the moment in her mind. She knew it would be one she'd want to come back to later. The future stretched out before her like a billowing fog, nothing about it distinct. All she had was her vision for the house and their lives in it. The house itself, as it was, was not what she wanted. It could be what she wanted, but it would take time and money, and she was afraid that both would soon run out. The reality of how their lives would be lived was waiting at the bottom of that hill, in the dark of that truck. These men, on the other hand, were clearly in focus. They pulled at their damp T-shirts, leaned on the railing. She would have to say something; there would have to be something to say. If only she had another minute, she could come up with the perfect thing. She could see them growing impatient. All they wanted to do was move her things from one location to another. They had no idea that everything they placed in a definite spot brought her one step closer to disappointment.

Part IV

Level, Solid, Square and True

1991–1995

35

Connell passed through a long, dark tunnel and emerged into an enclosed courtyard, where he joined a buzzing mob of boys waiting, as per mailed instructions, for someone to usher them in. There were no adults present, so they were exposed to each other without buffering—boys used to being at the top of their class, each now merely one of many. One head towered over the others, and Connell heard speculation about the big guy's basketball prowess, the city championships he might lead the team to by dunking on helpless opponents. It was thrilling to think of the havoc he'd wreak on their collective behalf, the revenge he'd enact for the years of slights and indignities they'd suffered as grammar school nerds. His size was a metaphor for the greatness promised to them. He would reveal the past to have been a prefatory period, a chrysalis of awkwardness.

In a sudden access of courage, Connell drifted across the courtyard toward the tall boy, who up close had a childlike face. When Connell introduced himself, a startlingly deep, though gentle, voice emanated from the boy, whose name was Rod Henni. He learned that Rod also rode in from Westchester, from a town called Dobbs Ferry. They were ushered into the auditorium, where they listened to speeches, filled out forms, and collected books, before heading to the cafeteria to continue buzzing through an excited lunch. At the end of the day, Connell and Rod took the 6 down to Grand Central together, steeped in the newness of everything they'd heard. They agreed to meet in the morning by the clock.

The next day, as Connell approached the clock, Rod waved to him and leaned his crane-like form down to pick up his backpack. Connell felt the nervous stirrings of new friendship, which offered the potential for mutual understanding but also for disappointment. He didn't want to start out on the wrong foot and be unable to recover.

"What's up, man," Connell said, looking away to affect casualness as they slapped five. He tried to drain his voice of any character whatsoever.

"I'm so excited to be heading to school!" Rod said. "I never thought I'd say that!"

As Rod looked to him for confirmation, Connell realized that this boy was not going to be his salvation. Rod's eyes were bright, his body hunched in an awkward question mark. Connell wanted him to stand up straight.

When they gathered in the gym that day for a free hour of play, Rod confirmed Connell's suspicions. He couldn't catch a pass or dribble. He certainly couldn't dunk. He could barely hold the ball and jump in the air at the same time. The only damage he could do on the basketball court was to himself.

That first week of school, Connell couldn't shake Rod, who came to the cross-country meeting with him. It was an open call; there weren't any tryouts. If you came to practice regularly, you were a member of the team.

Cross-country wasn't a cool sport. Waking early on weekend mornings to run for miles, running every day after school, and enduring the ribbing of "real" athletes kept people away. Connell prided himself on being a "real" athlete, a ballplayer, but no one would know it until spring came around. He joined the cross-country team to strengthen his legs for baseball, to increase his velocity and stamina. He learned to care about the sport and his performance at it, though, and to feel frustrated by his limitations. He had long, lean muscles and was trim and fit, and he was good enough to know what it felt like to hang with the really good runners for long stretches. As they pulled away, he could feel in his body what it would take to stay with them, to be great.

In practice, Rod was deadly serious, a grinder, Coach Amedure's example for everyone else. Coach always talked about how he was going to make a hurdler out of Rod come winter. It was obvious that Rod lacked the coordination necessary to leap over a single hurdle, let alone a series of them.

Rod's times in practice never fluctuated, no matter how hard he worked. He was always a minute behind the slow pack. He excoriated himself for his slowness. The source of this ruthless self-criticism became clear early in the season, when Rod's father came to a meet. As Rod crossed the finish line, Mr. Henni screamed at him in full view of everyone else. Connell and his teammates gathered around Rod, patting him on the back, but that week at practice they took up the charge themselves, sensing Rod's weakness. They made fun of Rod's gait, his heavy breathing, his profuse sweating, even his shorts. Connell didn't refrain from joining in. He knew it was wrong, and Rod knew it too. When he laughed at Rod's expense, Rod searched him silently with his eyes. A modicum of natural ability was all that separated Connell from Rod; that and maybe the fact that Mr. Henni was sort of insane. It wasn't easy to have a father like that, but Rod didn't help his cause by walking around with an innocent, vulnerable look on his face. That was the kind of look that made people nervous, made them want to do something to make it go away.

When Connell got home from practice, his father was on his hands and knees in the kitchen, scratching at the brick floor with a metal brush to strip away the dingy varnish. He was making his way from the kitchen to the den and into the foyer, one brick at a time. Connell changed into an old pair of jeans and joined him. Hunched and silent, they worked side by side. As Connell pushed his weight into the metal bristles, he felt the ache of the five-mile run descend into his muscles.

"At this rate, we'll be done in the year two thousand," he said.

"Keep working."

"The fumes are killing me." All the windows were open and there were fans set up on the kitchen counters, but it was a hot day in September, and the solvent-smelling air barely moved. "I have a headache." Connell sat up and rubbed at his hands, inspecting them for raw patches.

"You don't want to help, don't help."

"I'm helping."

"Then do it without commentary."

They dug at the crannies in the bricks. The solvent ate at the varnish, but he had to work hard at each brick. He thought there must be a machine to do this, but his father was determined to do it this way, his way. He refused to rest, as if he was trying to make some kind of point.

Connell scrubbed another half brick clean of varnish. "I have a Latin quiz tomorrow," he said.

His father waved him away without looking up. "Do your homework," he said.

"I can help," Connell said guiltily.

"Do your goddamned homework."

That weekend, his father took him to Van Cortlandt Park for a cross-country track meet. The sunny morning, the expanse of sky, and the brisk winds all filled Connell with a feeling of possibility dampened only by his dread of what would come once the gun went off: a mile-and-a-half run through hell; acid respiration and an agony of fatigue. A little distance away on the meadow, locals chased after a soccer ball, indifferent to the impending torture.

Parents and siblings stood around in a groggy pack. On the edge of the group, Rod was bent over double, palming the ground with his long planks of hands, as diffident a presence as a six-and-a-half-foot-tall boy could be. One of Connell's teammates, Stefan, who kept everyone on edge with sarcasm, snickered in Connell's direction at the spectacle of Rod's ungainly lankiness curled up in an awkward, striving stretch. The only one of Connell's teammates who didn't laugh was Todd Coughlin, whose natural dominance on the course allowed him to be generous.

Connell's father took pictures of the team as they stretched. Lately, his father had taken pictures of everything. In protest, Connell looked away from the camera, tunneling into his stretches, concentrating on the useful burn in his hamstrings and the territorial defensiveness he felt at the fact that another team had started stretching nearby. They were hopping and flapping their thigh muscles out with an aristocratic ease.

After the gun there was some rough jockeying for position—elbows, furtive shoves—as the mob converged on a point in the middle distance. The pack winnowed quickly into a grim line; a natural order emerged. A long, flat expanse led to grueling back hills, where, except for human trail markers stationed at bridges and overpasses, he was on his own, taunted by the leisurely scrawled graffiti on the rocks, dodging horse manure, and trying not to twist his ankle in the jagged ruts in the path. The hills culminated in a precipitous downhill, which he took at a breakneck clip to avoid giving away too much ground. At the bottom, near cars whizzing by on the Henry Hudson Parkway, came a quick turn and a shock of open space, a quarter-mile straightaway flanked by spectators and hollering coaches, where he wearily approximated his best sprint to the finish, his heart and lungs in pure revolt.

He saw the distant mob at the finish line as though through the wrong end of a telescope and wanted to step to the side and vomit. A large pack of runners passed him, calling on some mysterious reserve. He could hardly keep his head up.

He heard his father's voice before he saw him. "Come on, Connell," his father shouted gently through cupped hands. "Come on, son."

He took deep breaths and flung his legs out before him as though they didn't fit and he wanted to return them to their rightful owner. He gained on the pack a bit. A wall of cheers rose up as the finish line neared. He wanted to come through with the others. There wasn't much time left to catch them. It wasn't the first pack; those guys were resting already, turning over spray-painted gold in their hands. What it was was a little cluster of competitors. There may or may not have been medals left to fight for. They always gave out so many: thirty, fifty, God knew how many. The top quarter, the top third. Gold ones, silver ones. Then bronze. Then nothing. Coach Amedure got annoyed if anyone asked how many would be handed out that day. "Why do you care?" he'd say. "Why do you want to feed off the bottom?"

He caught up to the cluster, barely. They were funneled into the rope cordon. Plenty of medals remained. Hunching over, trying to catch his breath, he watched the officials hand them out. Each subsequent medal cheapened his own a little. When the medals ran out, runners came in to less fanfare. Individual voices could be heard in the din. The crowd at the finish line began to thin.

The laggards came trickling in. Among them was Rod, upright and stiff, like a totem pole come to life. Rod's reedy father screamed at him in frustration and the other voices around hushed at once. The harangue continued after Rod had crossed the finish line. People looked away, embarrassed for the boy, and Coach Amedure tapped his pen at his clipboard in impotent censure.

"What's that boy's name?" Connell's father asked.

"Who, him?" Connell said. "Rod."

"Stay here."

Connell nervously watched his father go over to where Rod and his father were standing.

"It's Rod, right?"

Rod nodded.

"What do you want?" Mr. Henni asked sharply. "I'm talking to my son."

"I was wondering, Rod," Connell's father said, ignoring him, "if you wouldn't mind posing for a picture with me."

Rod looked surprised but answered "Not at all!" while Mr. Henni was stunned into silence. Connell's father handed the camera to Stefan, who looked around in embarrassment before getting ready to take the picture. Connell couldn't believe what was happening, how much awkwardness could attach itself to a single moment. He rushed over and took the camera from Stefan and framed the shot as fast as he could. His father and Rod were smiling; you'd never know what had been going on moments before. Connell pressed the button once; then he went to Coach Amedure to find out what place he had finished in. The coach looked away in disdain as he showed Connell the clipboard.

A kid from Connell's grade, Declan Coyne, rode the train down from Bronxville with him. He started taking Connell around with him on the weekends.

"You look like a guido," Declan said. "You need to look like a prep."

"Okay."

"That mock turtleneck, for one. You need to wear a different shirt. Something with an actual collar. Rugby shirts are fine. Polo shirts. Buttondowns."

Declan had grown up in town and had gone to St. Joseph's. He knew all the Fordham Prep and Bronxville High kids in the area, and he fit in with them easily. They didn't care that he was a distinguished piano player; what they cared about was that he'd been the goalie on the Empire State Games soccer team during eighth grade. They probably also noticed the MG Declan's father parked in the driveway on sunny days.

"That spiky haircut—no way," Declan said. "All that hair gel. Let your hair grow. Part it on the side."

Declan's unruly curls peeked out from under his cap, which said U.S. Open. Even Connell's Mets cap didn't make the grade; it was the height of naïveté to wear a baseball cap that represented an actual baseball team.

"And those pants. You look like you're jumping out of a plane. Do you see anyone else around here wearing Z Cavaricci or Bugle Boy? You don't want all these pockets and loops. You could be a construction worker in that outfit. Just buy jeans, regular jeans, not those acid-washed atrocities."

Connell's mother had bought him the jeans Declan hated. Connell couldn't help noticing how Declan's mother seemed to get every detail right: pressing his school pants neatly; wrapping his sandwiches tightly in wax paper so that they resembled Christmas presents; lining up, along-side a bright bag of mini carrots that practically screamed good health, two perfectly round, homemade chocolate-chip oatmeal cookies. She even folded his napkins into neat triangles. And it wasn't just when Declan was at school that no seams were visible: Connell couldn't believe how neat and perfect-looking everything at Declan's house was. His own house had never looked like the Coyne house. Then again, his mother had always had a full-time job.

"And don't tight-roll the bottoms either. That's totally guido."

He imagined he looked to Declan like a member of an indigenous tribe that had just come into contact with civilization.

"Throw out those Reebok Pumps. Get some deck shoes. Bass is fine. And nobody wears tighty-whities. Boxer shorts. *Only* boxer shorts."

"Boxer shorts."

"No exceptions. I can't be emphatic enough about this."

"I'll get them."

"And get some soccer shoes. Adidas Sambas."

"I don't play soccer."

"That's because you don't know what's good for you," he said. "Everybody plays soccer. Get some soccer shoes."

"Won't I look like I'm trying too hard?"

"Would you rather look like you're not trying at all?"

The park ran alongside the Bronx River. Its western border was the Bronx River Parkway. Palmer Road lay to the south, Pondfield Road to the north. Trees lined its major path, and broad stretches of grass made up its main terrain. At night kids gathered in it to drink.

There wasn't much crime in town. The police were always driving up onto the lawn from the Parkway to take the kids by surprise, sending an under-aged exodus toward Palmer Road. He'd seen them leaving the park in a hurry and wondered how he would ever hang out with these kids.

Declan led him to a large group gathered a little ways from the path. Most of the guys, Declan said, went to Fordham Prep; a couple went to Iona; a few went to Bronxville High. The girls went to Ursuline, Holy Child, or Bronxville. There were older guys too: college students, dropouts, guys who had never gone to college and were working jobs.

One guy held a flashlight up to his own face as Declan introduced Connell, so that his features jumped out spookily. He had a fleshy face situated atop a pink-and-white-striped Oxford shirt. His eyes looked bloodshot. Declan said he was a senior at Fordham.

"Here," the guy said. "Have a beer."

He pulled a bottle out of a six-pack sleeve and handed it to Connell, who felt he couldn't refuse. He tried to twist off the top.

"Let me get that for you." The guy popped the cap off with an opener on his key chain. Declan waved over a guy who looked about Connell's age.

"Brewster, Connell," Declan said.

"So you go to school with this kid?" Brewster pointed to Declan.

"Yeah," Connell said, "but I'll probably fail out. I'll probably wind up at Fordham. I don't want to work all the time."

These kids didn't need to know that Connell was pulling good grades. He didn't want to start out in this town having everyone think he was just a nerd.

"You want another one?" the older guy asked, taking the bottle from Connell's hands. Connell had drained it into the ground when no one was watching. With Declan looking at him with a slightly buzzed warmth, Connell felt the need to actually drink this one. He took a sip; it tasted bitter.

"You see that girl over there?" Declan was talking louder now. "The blonde? Her name's Rebecca. She'll suck your dick. You ever have your dick sucked?"

Connell hadn't ever even kissed a girl. "Nah," he said. "Not yet."

"She'll fool around with anyone."

He couldn't understand why a girl that pretty would fool around with just anyone.

"Did you ever fool around with her?" Connell asked.

Declan's face spread in a slow smile. "It was great," he said. "Feels awesome." He finished off his beer. "Why don't you go and talk to her?"

Declan pushed him in her direction. She was standing near the older guy who'd given him his first beer, and he chugged the bottle in his hand and went over and asked for another.

"My man," the guy said approvingly. "Plenty to go around."

He felt a burp coming up through his chest and let it out as the guy opened his beer for him. Rebecca had a cherubic face and a sweet smile. It was hard to imagine her being easy. Somebody made a joke and she laughed in a giggly way that made a wave of warmth pass over Connell's body. Declan came over and introduced him to a couple of nearly identically dressed guys, and Connell returned their desultory handshakes. He could feel the alcohol settling in. He felt a strange boldness steal into him.

"Is it always this dead around here?" he asked, and felt Rebecca look interestedly at him.

"Pretty much," one guy said.

"If I ever brought my boys from the city up here," he said, "these cops would shit their pants."

"Hard guy," one guy said derisively; Connell saw him look at another guy and smirk.

"I used to be in a gang," Connell said. He saw Declan shake his head. "I wonder what these cops would do if anything real ever happened here."

The guy made a remark Connell didn't hear, and the other guys started laughing. He wanted to say something witty, but nothing came to him. Rebecca walked off toward the trees by the river. Declan shifted his body, so he had his back to Connell as he talked to his friends. Connell couldn't hear them. When the others walked off, Declan stood there with him.

"Please tell me that was ironic," Declan said. "Please tell me you're not that corny."

Connell just drank his beer. When he was done, he went back to the flashlight guy for another.

People around him began to scatter before he realized what was going on. He was at the outskirts of the group closest to the cop car, and there was time to run and join the pack of kids leaving the park, but for some reason he just stood there. He was drunk, that was certain. He'd never been drunk before. The next thing he knew, an officer was removing the beer from his hand. "That's evidence now," the officer said. Another officer told him to stand against the car with his hands behind his back.

He'd played with handcuffs as a kid, but these were more substantial. They dug into his wrist bones. He felt himself being urged down into the car, and he sat back with a wince, the metal digging into his skin. The officers climbed in and they drove off. Through the grating he studied the impressive backs of their heads and felt strangely calm. The revolving lights illuminated the muddy grass outside. He knew he should probably be more upset, but something about this felt inevitable somehow. His parents were going to kill him.

They drove to the station house. One of the officers led him to a little room. "I'll bring you a glass of water," he said. "Have a seat."

Connell sat in the desk chair the officer pointed to, his head pounding. Above him, a framed print depicted a seafaring mission. The officer walked in with a glass, and Connell drained it.

"What I'm interested in hearing is where you got the alcohol. Did you purchase it yourself?"

Connell shook his head.

"I'm going to need verbal responses from you."

"I don't know who gave it to me," he said. "It was an older kid."

The other officer stood. "This is going to be in the paper, you understand," he said. "Your school is going to hear about this. Your parents are
on their way here."

"They are?"

"What was the kid's name?"

"I just moved here, Officer," he said. "I don't know anybody's name."

"Do you remember anything about him?" the other officer asked.

"He was an older kid. A nice guy. He had on a collared shirt."

"This kid is wasting our time."

"You're going to go to juvenile court," the first officer said. "We take
this kind of thing seriously around here. You should know that right now.
This isn't wherever you came from."

"Jackson Heights."

"Wherever the hell."

A little while later, his parents arrived. When his mother walked in, she
smacked his face. His father looked more concerned than furious.

He was grounded from everything but cross-country practice. At the
juvenile court in Eastchester, the DA offered a plea deal: thirty hours of
community service. Connell had to stand before the judge. "If I ever see
you in my courtroom again," the judge said, "you'd better have a toothbrush with you."

On the way out, his mother added her own threat. "If you ever dis-
grace me like that in this town again," she said, "don't come home. And
don't even think of taking another drink until you turn twenty-one. You're
not even close to man enough to handle it."

"Sorry, Mom."

"Not even close to man enough," she said again.

36

Because Ed's floor project had taken over most of the kitchen except for a narrow path between the refrigerator, sink, and stove, they ate their meals in the dining room. She was going to have to give up the dining room when Ed turned his attention to the rotted-out floor beneath it, but in the meantime she was determined to enjoy it. She had pinned up a bed sheet to separate it from the living room, which was packed not only with its own furniture but also with the pieces destined for the den and the foyer when Ed was done with the bricks. The dining room was her sanctuary. She had brought it to such a fastidious level of completion that it looked like a little theater in which a nightly drama was staged. The china leaned against the back of the cabinet, the polished candlesticks stood sentinel on the breakfront, the crystals sparkled in the chandelier after a chemical bath, and the white field of the lace tablecloth suggested a pristine altar.

Ed took a seat, rivulets of sweat still running from his head. He dropped his drenched forearms on the table and wiped his brow with the napkin she'd folded neatly.

When the kitchen floor was finished, the new cabinets and counter-tops could be installed.

"I don't know why you don't let me bring a contractor in for the floors," she said. "We have money for help."

"I'm doing a fine job," he said.

"I don't want to live like this. We didn't buy this house to live out of boxes. I want a real kitchen."

They had some money to work with. After they'd paid the depreciation recapture tax (she regretted the low rents she'd charged the Orlandos all those years; the house had hardly generated "income" to speak of) and put 50 percent down on the new house, they'd pulled over forty thousand dollars out of the Jackson Heights house to make improvements with.

"You'll have your precious kitchen," Ed said. "The floor will be done soon enough."

"We're already two weeks from November, Ed. We could bring guys in and have this done in a day. They probably have machines that could do this in a couple of hours."

He grabbed her by the wrist, leaned into her.

"One guy touches that floor—one *single* guy that's not myself or Connell—and I've had it. Do you understand?"

She wrested herself free. "Have it your way," she said bitterly, rubbing at her wrist. "But don't expect any help from that boy. You're going to be the hero on this, be the hero. He's not helping you. He has too much work at school."

"I don't need his help."

She could almost taste the disgust she felt. A curd of sarcasm gathered in her mouth.

"*Good*," she said. "This is just beautiful. This is everything I dreamed it would be."

37

At the gas station, when his father went inside to pay, Connell's mother whipped around to him in the backseat.

"I just want you to know," she said, "how much this means to your father. I would have preferred to stay in a nice bed-and-breakfast by the mountains and look at the foliage. But your father wanted to do this for you. You remember that, and be grateful. Do you hear me?"

"Fine," he said.

"And I have a bone to pick with you. What did you say to upset him before we left this morning? He said it was between the two of you, but I could tell he was bothered by it."

"Nothing," Connell said.

"I'm sure it wasn't nothing."

"He's right. It *is* between us."

"Don't get testy with me," his mother said. "You live under our roof. Don't you forget that."

He didn't want to tell his mother what he'd said. It would confirm that he was just the sort of brat she'd been implying he was. He didn't know why he'd said it; it had just come out. He and his father had been standing near the sink together. Connell was rinsing his dish before he put it in the dishwasher, and his father reached across him for a hand towel, and as he did so, Connell said, "You have bad breath." His father looked at him quizzically, and Connell said it again, a little differently this time: "Your breath stinks." His father put his hand up to his mouth to blow some air into his nose, and then he looked at him with a look that could have been hurt, confused, or grateful, Connell couldn't tell which. "Thanks," his father said, again inconclusively, and he left the room and headed to the bathroom. He didn't come out for almost an hour. Connell heard him brushing his teeth endlessly in there, the tap running while he brushed, and then silence, and then the tap running again.

His mother's mood brightened when they got to Cooperstown, which was full of nice little stores. They parked and walked to the Hall of Fame, a red brick structure that looked like a university building or a large post office. Outside, at his father's request, his mother took a picture of the two of them in front of one of the rounded doors. Then she left to go shopping. They arranged to meet back in front in two hours.

Inside, Connell and his father walked past the parade of plaques. His father pointed out players he'd loved in his day—Jackie Robinson, Duke Snider, Roy Campanella, Pee Wee Reese. He complained that Gil Hodges, his favorite player, hadn't been elected along with the others. He stopped at the plaques of players he'd admired for their personal characteristics who hadn't been Dodgers: Lou Gehrig, Stan Musial, Roberto Clemente. It was cool to read the plaques and see how the writers of these brief biographies condensed players' careers into a handful of statistics and a few pithy lines, but Connell would have liked it more when he was about twelve. He couldn't get enough of this stuff then.

After a little while it felt like they'd seen a lot, and Connell was thinking about lunch and wondering whether his mother might have had a point about the foliage, which, boring as it was, at least wouldn't have required him to spare his father's feelings by pretending to be as interested in this stuff as his father wanted him to be. They were passing through a big room with glass cases on all sides and people crossing in every direction when his father stopped short.

"The next time we come here," his father said, "they'll be inducting you."

Connell waited for an ironic chuckle, but it didn't come. "Sure, Dad," he said, rolling his eyes. "Okay."

He was good enough to make his high school team, but he wasn't going to get scouted; his father knew that as well as he did.

"I want you to listen to me," his father said. "I'm going to talk to you seriously for a minute."

A cute girl was standing with her parents and her little brother, looking at some old mitts in a case.

"Here?" Connell asked. "Does it have to be here?"

"I've noticed something in you that worries me," his father said. "Maybe because it reminds me of me at your age. I made life harder for myself than it needed to be. I see you hardening yourself. That isn't you. I see you closing your mind. You are open and beautiful."

"All right, Dad," he said, putting his hands up to stop him.

"Do you understand what I mean by that?"

"I don't know," he said. "I mean, I'm okay, Dad. I'm good. You don't have to worry."

"You *are* okay," his father said. "You're more than okay. You're wonderful. I know that, believe me. But there's something in you that is closing up."

"Dad," he said, "is this about me saying you had bad breath?"

His father laughed. "Listen. I'm going to ask you to do something you might find a little strange. Will you do it for me?"

"What is it?"

"You'll have to trust me."

"Is it going to be embarrassing?"

"Nobody but us will know about it."

"All right." Connell slapped his hands on his thighs in defeat. "Okay. Sure."

"Life is going to give you things to be angry at. I don't want you to be consumed by that anger or forget how much you're capable of. So we're going to do a little exercise right now."

"Are you okay? I mean, is everything all right?"

"I'm fine," his father said. "Are you ready?"

"Sure." Now Connell was genuinely curious.

"What I want you to do now is to feel in your bones that the next time we are here, they will be inducting you."

This was too much. "What does that even *mean*?" Connell asked as the cute girl passed him, meeting his gaze.

"Shh," his father said. "Close your eyes."

Connell closed them.

"I am telling you that we will be back here when they are inducting you. I want you to feel the reality of that for a moment."

"Okay," he said, relenting a bit. There was something sort of exciting in the way his father had said it. He sounded so sure. Connell wanted to believe his father could see the future or something.

"Feel it. Let yourself. You pitched for the Mets your whole career. You heard your name over the loudspeaker thousands of times. You heard the cheers. You heard the boos. You played on grass. You played on Astroturf. You killed your shoulder, you blew out your elbow, you mangled your knuckles, but it was worth it. You set aside seats at every home game. Your kids were in those seats. Your wife was. Now you're looking at a plaque with your face on it. You're thinking the portrait makes you look like someone else, but it's you—those are your numbers, under your name."

The way his father said it was like he'd been talking about more than baseball, more than the Hall of Fame. He meant it to mean whatever Connell wanted it to mean; he meant it to mean he believed in him.

And then, somehow, Connell did feel it: what it was like to have brought joy to people and done something extraordinary. He never let himself imagine outcomes like that. He didn't want to open his eyes.

"I want you to really feel it," his father said. "And I want you to remember that feeling, because it is as real as any experience you will have in your life. Will you remember?"

Connell nodded with his eyes closed.

"You have to use your imagination," his father said.

Connell could feel his mind opening like a flower in bloom. If he wasn't afraid to consider the impossible— that he would be a Major League ballplayer people would talk about for years—then in imagining it, he would not need to live it; he could have it, along with whatever else he wanted.

"Okay," Connell said. He could hear people passing by. He didn't peek, but he could see them going past, what they were wearing, the looks on their faces.

"Do you feel powerful?"

"Yes," he said, and he did; he had stepped outside time.

"Are you angry right now?"

"No."

"Are you afraid?"

"No."

"Do you know that I love you?"

"Yes," he said.

"Open your eyes," his father said, but Connell waited a bit, because something told him they would never be back where they were. "Let's go find your mother."

38

The kitchen cabinets were installed on a Friday. When Eileen came home from work after a week that had threatened never to end, and saw their pristine white surfaces, she stood leaning against the island she'd always coveted, looking around in frank amazement. Then she began opening doors and running her hand for pleasure over the sanded interiors. She couldn't wait to head to the Food Emporium. Ever since she'd emptied out the cabinets in preparation for their dismantling, she'd anticipated with great relish this restorative trip.

The next morning, she waited for the countertop man to arrive with his enormous slabs. She had settled on Corian, because granite was too expensive and she'd be damned if she'd live with Formica again. Then at the last minute she'd called and changed the order to granite.

She had thought she might like to watch them put the slabs down on the cabinets, but as the fabricator and his assistants hauled them up the back steps she realized she preferred that magical feeling of seeing the job complete, which she'd gotten as a child whenever she'd come home from school and seen the lines her mother had put in the carpet by vacuuming.

She snaked her way up and down the aisles of the supermarket, filling her cart with anything she could think she'd ever need. She hadn't even gotten through dry goods before the cart was so full that she had to check out, bring the bags to the car and start over. After this second round of shopping, not only was the trunk full, but also the back seat, the passenger seat, and the floor areas. She couldn't see in any direction except straight ahead and in the driver's side mirror. She felt the engine laboring to get her home.

She pulled into the driveway and honked for Connell to come down and carry the bags. She went upstairs and gaped at the glossy countertops. She walked their length, running her hands over their cool surfaces, amazed at how they kept going and going.

Connell came up with the first bags and laid them on the island. "What gives?" he asked.

"What?"

"You planning for a disaster?"

"I bought some things," she said defensively.

She started putting them away. Connell made an endless circuit from the garage to the kitchen. When he had nearly finished, and bags were arranged in a ring around the island, Ed walked into the kitchen and flew into a frenzy. He started grabbing items from the refrigerator and throwing them into the trash can.

"We eat too much!" he yelled. "This is too much food!"

"Would you please control yourself?"

"We need a new regime around here," he said. "We're getting fat. There are going to be changes. One meal a day! No more than one!"

"This should last us about a decade, then," Connell said.

"Get rid of it!" Ed shouted as he left the room. "All of it!"

Eileen followed him out. "You can throw it all out if you want," she called up the stairs, to his retreating back. "That's fine by me." She was trying to stay calm, not to sink to his level. "All it means is I'll have to spend more to replace it. I want every inch in that pantry filled." He disappeared into the bedroom. "I don't care if you starve to death, the rest of us in this house are going to eat." He didn't answer. "Like kings!" she shouted. "We'll eat like kings!"

39

In recent weeks, Ed had taken a hammer to places of rot in the drywall all through the basement, so that it looked like a target in a shooting range. In the minefield of the living room, he'd made a bigger mess, ripping up floorboards almost indiscriminately. The drainpipes were clogged. The garage door had stopped working. They'd suffered another flood in the basement after a heavy storm. And now that the cabinets and countertops were in, Ed refused to hire a single contractor to help.

He sat beside her at the wheel, seething in the mismatched outfit he'd passive-aggressively donned after she'd barked at him for half an hour to change out of his dirty undershirt and get a move on. They were going to the McGuires'. Ed was beset by distraction as he drove, drifting between lanes and slamming on the brakes to stop just short of stalled traffic.

"Would you pay attention? You're all over the road."

"I know how to drive," he said. "I've been driving for"—he paused—"since I was sixteen."

They'd left late and hit a bad jam, and by the time they arrived they were quite late indeed. Ed sat in the car after he'd shut it off. She stood outside the car, waving him out. Then she opened her door again.

"Are you coming?"

The light in the foyer went on; one of the McGuires would soon be at the door. She climbed back in the car. Maybe she had to try another approach. She drained the impatience from her voice. "What's wrong?"

"Just give me a minute," he said. "I can't think straight with you talking."

"Honey," she said as gently as she could, "we don't really *have* a minute."

"Who's going to be there again?"

"Just us. Us and Frank and Ruth."

"That's good," he said. "We see too many people."

They hadn't seen anyone since they'd moved, but this wasn't the time to argue. "You're right," she said. "I'll scale back. We'll just focus on the house for now."

"Thank God."

"Now, can we get inside?" She handed him the bottle of wine. Ruth opened the door and gave them both kisses. Ed's hand was shaking as he handed the bottle over; she saw Ruth notice it.

Dinner was ready and they took their seats right away as Ruth shuttled dishes in. Eileen tried to help her, but Ruth told her to sit. Frank opened the bottle to let it breathe. She felt herself begin to relax.

"How's the money pit?" Frank asked. "You find where they buried the bodies yet?"

This was where Ed would say something snappy and the two of them would be off.

"It's fine," Ed said flatly. "Coming along."

"Ed's been busy trying to get rid of the rot from the flood."

"Funny enough, I've been taking a continuing ed course in the history of water," Frank said. "Irrigation, water transport. We haven't gotten to floods yet. I'll let you know when we do. Maybe I can give you some tips."

Ed didn't say anything.

"It must be nice to get back in the classroom and learn something new," Eileen said.

"We're not getting any younger," Frank said. "We have to keep the brain going. Am I right?"

Again, Ed didn't speak. Ruth came in just in time with the platter of roast beef.

"Please," she said, gesturing to Ed. "Help yourself."

Eileen felt an instinct to serve him, but he was sitting between her and the platter. Ed stabbed at a piece with the serving fork. The tines didn't get a good purchase on the meat, which fell back to the platter with a juicy splash that sluiced grease onto the tablecloth. He went in again, stabbing with too much force, but managed to get one piece onto his plate, and then another. The third dropped into his lap. Ruth and Frank shot each other looks. Ed picked it up and put it on his plate. He didn't try to wipe the marinade from his pants. The three little strips huddled on his plate. He handed her the fork, though protocol called for him to serve her or pass her the platter. She had to stand up to reach the meat. When she was done filling her plate, she put two more pieces on his. She looked up and realized that both of her hosts were watching this transaction intently.

"You want me to serve you?" she asked Frank.

"That's fine, I'll do it myself."

"This all looks beautiful," she said, handing over the utensils. She stayed on her feet. "Let me have your plate," she said to Ruth. She felt like a chess player thinking several moves ahead. "I'll serve the potatoes." She spooned some out for Ruth; then she put some on her own plate, and then, as though it were a matter of course, on Ed's. She did the same with the vegetables.

Ed looked skeptically at his plate. After having trouble gathering food onto his fork, he started pushing it on with his finger. He transported a few bites successfully to his mouth before one dropped on his shirt.

This was a good time for Frank to make a joke about Ed being drunk. It was impossible for Ed to take offense at anything Frank said. They ribbed each other all the time, and nothing was sacred; they fell into hysterics while she and Ruth wondered what was wrong with them. Tonight, though, Frank just sat there, looking at Ed until he saw that Eileen saw him looking and looked away.

They got through the meal with some effort. "You sit with them," Ruth said, as Eileen tried to follow her into the kitchen to help clean up. "Sit in the living room and have a drink. Make sure they don't get into any trouble."

Eileen brought them drinks. There was less awkwardness in the living room. Frank helped by talking at length about the class he was taking. She was never more grateful for his long-windedness. Ed interjected here and there, and the exchange resembled an actual conversation. Ruth came in and they sat holding their glasses in the comfort that follows dining with old friends, the engine of one topic running down as the engine of another revved up.

"So how's Connell?" Frank asked.

"His grades are good, but he's struggling in biology, if you can believe it."

"I was a horrible student in high school," Frank said. "If it had mattered then the way it does now, I wouldn't have had a prayer."

"Me too," Ed said.

"It's a different world," Ruth agreed.

"He's in his second year already," Ed said. "He's got to settle down soon."

Eileen flinched.

"I thought he was a freshman," Ruth said. This was the danger of having friends like Ruth and Frank who paid attention when you talked about your kid.

"Yes, freshman," Ed said. "That's what I said."

"He likes English," Eileen said quickly.

"That's great," Frank said. "I love literature. I'm going to take a Shakespeare course next semester."

"Ed's disappointed," she said. "He wants him to love science. He wants him to go to medical school."

"Speak for yourself," Ed said. "I want him to follow his bliss."

"Maybe he'll come around," Frank said. "Listen, we were thinking of having him up for a weekend. Do you think he'd like that? Or would it be more of a drag for him?"

"He'd love it," Eileen said.

"Maybe while he's here you can talk some sense into him," Ed said. "He's having a hard time with biology, if you can believe that. He's not applying himself, is all."

"I don't know how much help I'll be," Frank said. "I failed bio the first time I took it."

"That sounds like Connell, I'm afraid. His biology grades aren't the greatest. He's focused on literature."

"Is there an echo in here?" Frank asked, laughing. "I might have to cut you off."

"Please do." Eileen tried to sound authentically relieved. "For all our sakes."

"Or maybe what he needs is not less but more." Frank stood up and took her glass, then Ed's, which was still full. He looked at it for a moment.

"Let me freshen this for you," he said.

The business of getting drinks occupied a few minutes, and Ruth re-filled the cheese and cracker plates.

"So tell Connell to think about what weekend he wants to come up," Frank said.

"You're having Connell over?" Ed asked.

"If he wants."

"Do me a favor and talk to him about giving more of his time to sci-ence," Ed said.

"Before I forget," Ruth said abruptly, "I have to tell you the funniest story." She embarked on a narrative about having had her car towed the last time she went into the city. It wasn't funny at all, and it wound up being far shorter than Eileen had hoped, but she felt her eyes well up in gratitude.

Soon it was pumpkin bundt cake and coffee. The rituals of meals had never been more of a comfort. Ed ate his cake without trouble and they sat in the pleasant ease of digestion. She could see the distance to departure beginning to narrow. They might very well escape without further incident.

Ruth gathered the coats, and they said their good-byes in the hallway.

"Remember," Frank said. "Ask Connell when would be good for him to come up."

"I will," Eileen said.

"Maybe you can talk some sense into him," Ed said. "He's slacking in science."

Frank's eyes widened. He broke into an awkward grin that looked more like a grimace. "Don't let this guy drive," he said.

Although she had had more to drink than Ed, she got behind the wheel. She felt exhausted, and more than once she had to blink away sleep. Ed snored the whole trip, like a child, oblivious of the danger he was in every time she let her mind wander.

40

The floors in the living room and dining room were still a mess. Not only hadn't he begun to lay down wood, he hadn't even bought any, and it was now the second week of December. He had put the floor job on hold to focus on the basement. It drove her crazy to have the most important rooms in the house be off-limits. She had given up on the dream of entertaining the first Christmas in the new house (when the Coakleys agreed to host, she was afraid she might have lost dibs on Christmas Eve to Cindy forever), but she wanted to be able to finally sit in her living room. He was kidding himself if he thought he was going to be able to handle it alone.

The noises of destruction and toil emanating from below made it sound as if he was overseeing a torture chamber. She never approached him when he was down there, and when he came up covered in plaster dust and dried concrete, he sat and ate in remorseless silence. When he was asleep she went down to check on his labor. The space was coming together somehow. A do-it-yourself home improvement book sat perpetually splayed on the floor, its dog-ears attesting to the concentration that had gone into making things flush and square.

She found a disposable razor on the coffee table in the den, sitting in a streak of shaving cream. She told herself that Ed had come downstairs to answer the phone while shaving and gotten distracted. When she picked the razor up, though, and saw that the book under it was his beloved fifth-edition copy of *The Origin of Species*, she let out a shriek. No one but Ed ever touched that precious volume, and it never left his study. The fact that it was on the coffee table at all was amazing enough, but for its front cover to be stained by a filmy dollop of Barbasol was simply unfathomable. Her first thought, her only thought, was to leave the razor alone so he could see he had ruined the book himself.

She'd written him notes lately—gentle reminders she would leave on his nightstand before bed, like a secretary laying out the next day's agenda for the executive she was secretly sleeping with. *We're going out with the Cudahys tonight*, or *Don't forget parent-teacher conferences at 6:00.* There had been something pleasant about writing the notes; whatever tension still hung in the air after a given evening's misunderstandings evaporated like a cup of water on a hot afternoon.

One note struck her as odd when she read it over. It grew more opaque the longer she looked at it, like one of those unfathomable koans. She couldn't escape the sensation that she'd written the note to tell herself something as much as to get a message to Ed. *Christmas is six days away, Edmund*, the note said. *Please don't forget to get Connell a new baseball glove. I've asked you three times now. I'd take care of it, but I don't know the first thing about them. It seems like the kind of thing a father should pick out. That is still you, right, a father?*

How had they gotten to the point where she could write him a note like this? She thought of the hours he spent grading papers every night, how he never came to bed before eleven anymore, how just recently she'd spent a night helping him tabulate the grades for a lab report, as she'd done during the crisis at the end of the last academic year. She thought again, as she couldn't help doing lately, of that inscrutable pile of wood with the sheet over it in the backyard in Jackson Heights. She recalled the scene with a strangely heightened clarity, as if it were an installation in a museum dedicated to preserving the unimportant details of her old life. She panned around it in her mind, studying it from every angle, attempting to understand why this nettlesome image hadn't receded into the ether of the past.

The dawning came all at once, though it felt as if it had been heading her way for a while, like a train she'd heard whistle from miles off that was now flying past and kicking up a terrible wind.

Still, she couldn't pronounce the sentence in her head, *Ed has . . .* , because it was impossible that he had it. He had a demanding job that kept him stimulated. Until recently, he had read constantly, done the crossword puzzle almost every day, exercised four times a week. He was still the fittest man in their circle.

Maybe it was a tumor. Maybe it was a glandular problem, a dietary deficiency, a failing organ.

Whatever it was, she would get him checked out.

It wasn't going to be easy to bring it up. He was going to tell her she didn't know what she was talking about, that if something was wrong with his brain he'd be the first to know, being a *brain expert*, she could hear him saying. And part of her wanted him to dismiss her fears with an imperious wave and tell her she was behaving hysterically. But she couldn't allow him to overpower her on this topic. She needed to find out if something was wrong with him.

She waited for an opening. She wanted him to forget something or say something demonstrably strange, but he just went to work and came home and started in on the basement like an indentured servant paying off his debt. He made runs to the hardware store and returned with Sheetrock, cinder blocks, and bags of cement that he hauled piece by piece from the car. She worried his body would give out on him.

When she called Ed's doctor and suggested worry about Ed's health, he told her she was crazy, that Ed was as healthy as a horse. "I just saw him, what is it, six months ago," he said. "He's got the lungs of a swimmer. Not a whisper when I put the stethoscope to him. Only thing is his blood pressure's a little high. Let him put his feet up on the weekend. Give him a glass of iced tea and put the game on for him. And his cholesterol could be lower. Maybe no cheeseburgers for a while. No more shrimp."

It sounded like an indictment of her, somehow. "We don't eat any shellfish," she said. "I'm allergic." She tried to rein in her annoyance. "Did he seem *fuzzy* to you at all?"

"Fuzzy?"

"In the head. Slower on the uptake."

"Maybe you're expecting too much of him. Men aren't perfect creatures. We get miles on the engine. We need repairs. The warranty runs out. Ed's got a good engine. He's got a lot of road left ahead of him."

She watched him and waited for the mishap, the big slipup. He continued to make incremental progress, continued to refuse outside help, but every day, as he beat himself harder and harder to finish the work, as she watched patiently, intently, she could feel the ground shifting in her favor, Ed's resilience weakening. As much as she needed to bring the work on the house to completion, as much as she couldn't wait to have a team of workers laying down boards in her living room and dining room, and as much as she was glad to see the ground ceded to her, she found herself rooting for Ed and feeling sorry for this man who spent every night hammering away. She saw him on his haunches, head in a manual, hammer poised, his back a rounded stone, and she willed him to brilliance, though she knew she was willing the impossible.

She watched Ed grow more weary at each dinner, look more disheveled, push away his plate after a few bites.

One night he didn't come when she called him to eat and she sent Connell to get him.

"He says he's not coming," the boy said when he returned.

"Tell him I said to get in here."

"Maybe you should go in, Mom."

"What is it?"

"He's just sitting there."

She went into the dining room and saw Ed surrounded by planks of wood. He had half a plank in his hands. Nails were sticking out of it, and its end was a comb of shards. She could see the other half nailed into the floor. He must have tried to rip it up in his hands.

"Get up, Ed."

"I'll be in when I'm done," he said. He was hunched over, breathing hard. He looked like he'd been whipped. He lifted himself up onto one knee in a vaguely supplicating manner, and the sight of him there put her uncomfortably in mind of the Stations of the Cross. She wasn't going to give him the chance to make some kind of poetical self-sacrifice, if that was what he was after. The only person who'd feel sorry for him if he did that would be himself. He'd had all the chances in the world to bring some-one in. They had enough money for at least the floors and the kitchen. He was too damned stubborn.

"You're done."

"I have to finish this section."

"You're done," she said. "Come and eat."

But he didn't follow. After she and Connell had finished, she brought a plate of cold sausage and beans in to him. She could barely stand to look at him as she left it on the floor by his feet. He hadn't moved in half an hour. He was in the same place in the middle of the room, a perfect vantage point from which to survey the mess he'd insisted on making.

She made the phone calls and settled on a general contractor who could finish the kitchen, do the floors, put in high-hats, and plaster and paint all the walls on the first floor.

The night before the workers were scheduled to start, she told Ed they were coming, and he didn't put up any kind of fight. She wondered whether she should have forced his hand sooner, but they gave out no manual when you got married, no emergency kit with a flashlight for when the power went out. You had to feel your way around in the dark for the box of matches.

41

The work began a couple of weeks after the new year, 1992. The bustle in and out of her kitchen was exciting. She offered them drinks and set out platters of cold cuts on the island, rolls, tubs of potato salad, bags of potato chips.

She brought home a couple of six-packs for them one day. Ed took one and threw it to the floor. One of the cans landed with a thud and shot a stream of beer all over the cabinets. A floor installer who had been using the bathroom stopped in the kitchen on the way back to the living room.

"Everything all right?" he asked.

"Mind your fucking business," Ed said.

She hadn't heard Ed utter that word in years. Maybe she'd never heard him say it.

"You okay?" the worker asked her, ignoring Ed.

"Get the fuck out of here," Ed said.

"Whatever you say," the worker said. "Whatever you say." He backed out of the room, his hands up in bemused resignation.

Eileen followed him in, carrying the unexploded beers on the plastic yoke. "My husband has been under a lot of stress," she said. "I'm sorry he spoke to you like that."

"No worries," the worker said. "We come across all kinds of people in this line of work."

"He's not the kind of man he seemed like back there."

He gave his head a sage tilt. "Some guys just don't like other guys in their house, doing work they think they should be doing."

She felt a need to protect Ed. "It's just that he's losing his job," she said, surprising herself with the lie. "Layoffs."

"I'm sorry to hear that."

"It's going to be fine. We're going to be fine."

He and the other worker looked at her as if they were waiting to see if she'd make another revelation.

"Please drink these," she said, holding up the beers.

"You don't have to tell us twice," he said. "But we have to wait until we're done for the day."

It reminded her of her father, to hear him responsibly defer having a drink. They returned to laying in the boards, and she went to the break-front to find the red velvet-lined box that held the set of crystal glasses with "Schaefer" etched into them that her father had received upon his retirement. She took them out and ran a cloth over them.

At the end of the day, when she laid the six-pack on the dining room table, she set out the glasses too, on a Schaefer bar tray she'd saved for years.

"Please use these," she said.

"Oh, we don't need glasses, ma'am," he said politely.

"It would make me happy if you'd use them. They were my father's. I'd like to see them filled with beer for once."

The roof could wait for a couple of years. The rot in the basement would have to remain for now. The tile floors she'd pictured down there were a project for another time. So was renovating the half bath between the kitchen and den. So was moving the laundry room to the first floor from the basement. There was old wallpaper on the second floor that couldn't come down, and there were walls that needed to be painted. She had pictured fresh paint and white tiles wherever she looked. She had flipped through design magazines for elaborate ideas, but in the end, white had seemed appropriate, the cleanest option, the only one she could deal with right now. She would have to wait for everything to be white. She would have to deal with gray and yellow and brown and a sickly mauve. She thought that a lot of her house looked like a waiting room. The path from kitchen to dining room to living room, though—the path that company would travel—this path was ready to go. She could keep them from going upstairs or downstairs. And as soon as she had a spare few thousand dollars, she was going to put a better half bath in for them and spruce up the den.

There was, on the other hand, the question of the furniture. She simply wouldn't be able to live with the things she'd brought from the old house, not if she couldn't fix this one up the way she wanted. Her furniture squatted shabbily and hardly filled the room. The scratched dining room table, the worn armrests on the chairs, the boxy end tables, the permanently depressed couch cushions: they were like placeholders for the real pieces to come. She saw now that she would need to replace nearly all of it. She would put it all on credit cards. Upstairs, she would create a sitting area, buy the desk she'd always lacked, and outfit each guest room with a stereo, an armchair, and a beautiful reading lamp. As soon as she got these bills paid off, she would replace Connell's childhood furniture.

She knew she lacked the aesthetic sense necessary to give the house the ambiance it deserved. She would bring in an interior decorator. There would have to be new art everywhere, and the little touches that put one in mind of real discernment. She could pay for that with credit cards too. Ed would veto these expenses if given the chance, but he was past the point of possessing veto power. He was simply going to have to place his fate in her hands. They would pay it off. Ed would get another grant. Their salaries would rise. Once everything was in place, they would live frugally, sensibly, like Boston Brahmins. They would even find a way to build their savings back up. There was always a little more money to be had every year.

42

f nothing's wrong with him," Eileen told her own doctor, when she went in about a shortness of breath she'd been experiencing, "I'm going to divorce him. I can't take it anymore."

Dr. Aitken told her to bring her husband in. She sold it to Ed as his annual checkup, that she'd like him to try her doctor, and when he didn't object in spite of having gone in for a checkup less than six months before, she knew she was doing the right thing. They sat in the discordant placidity of the waiting area before she led him into the examining room and went back out. She'd blustered about divorce, but now she saw that she would put up with anything in exchange for hearing that her husband had simply become an asshole.

After spending half an hour with Ed, Dr. Aitken came out to meet her.

"Don't divorce him yet," he said, handing her a referral to a neurology team he trusted.

She braced for the fit she expected Ed to throw once they got to Montefiore, but he sat docilely again on the papered, padded table, waiting for the doctor to arrive. His big, fleshy back looked like raw dough.

First came blood tests and a physical exam. Dr. Khalifa, the lead doctor, wanted to eliminate anything that might cause memory loss, so he checked Ed's thyroid levels, as thyroid problems had run in his family. They gave him a CT scan.

His thyroid was fine. The CT scan showed no sign of a tumor.

She took him back for diagnostic exams. Dr. Khalifa sat Ed at a table and took a seat opposite him. She sat in the extra chair and felt nervous for

Ed, as though she were about to watch his debut in a theatrical production that had limped toward opening night.

Dr. Khalifa told Ed to count backwards from one hundred. Ed got to ninety-seven before pausing. "Eighty-six," he said, then ran off a few other numbers in accurate succession, until he jumped another decile, at which point Dr. Khalifa stopped him.

The obstreperousness she'd anticipated was starting to seem like a fantasy. Ed looked vulnerable and small. He was smiling, trying to ingratiate himself with his examiner, perhaps in unconscious pursuit of mercy in the diagnosis.

Dr. Khalifa told him to draw three concentric circles, and Ed put a good one down on the page, then drew another that was ovoid and attached to the first like a chain link. The third, a shaky line meeting finally in something more like a quadrangle than a circle, sat apart from the first two.

"Great, that's great," Dr. Khalifa said dully when Ed was done. The doctor was a picture of imperviousness. She watched his eyes: he betrayed no sign of surprise, gave away no clues as to whether this was a normal result or not, the product of mere aging or something more sinister. She didn't know whether she herself would have been able to draw the concentric circles. Certainly it would be difficult under this kind of scrutiny. She had a sensation that she was watching a child take a test, and she felt a sympathy with Ed that made her question her decision to expose him to this. What right did she have to subject him in the quiddities of his middle age to a man who would be looking for any sign of deviation from a norm that was probably arbitrary in the first place? She wanted to whisk him back home and let him go at things in his own way. A category existed to describe men like him, a time-tested, venerated one at that: absentminded professor.

"I'm not an artist," Ed said, laughing. "You should see my drawings of the digestive system."

The doctor chuckled.

"This could be something abstract," Ed said.

Dr. Khalifa looked at it and shook his head. She didn't like his attitude. He was too glib, too detached. His hair was too perfect, his teeth gleamed too white. She had long wished Ed had pursued medical school, but now she felt she'd been too hard on him in her mind. She knew doctors like this at work; they thought they walked on water. The work Ed did might not have been as lucrative or flashy, but it laid the groundwork for guys like this to come to their conclusions. If Ed said nothing was wrong, then most likely nothing was wrong. She had insulted him by bringing him before this cipher who didn't deserve to carry his briefcase, let alone pass judgment on him.

"We're almost done with this part," Dr. Khalifa said. "One more question and then I'm going to have you do some physical things."

"Okay."

"Tell me something. Do you know who the current president is?"

If he wanted to insult him, this was a perfect way to do it. She almost wanted Ed to answer sarcastically or deliberately incorrectly, but she didn't want the doctor to have the satisfaction of writing it down on that little pad of his.

Ed sat with it; maybe he was coming up with a witty riposte.

"I know it's a Republican," he said. "I know that."

"Can you tell me his name?"

Ed pulled on his chin. "Reagan?" he asked. "Is it Reagan? I can see his face. It's not Reagan, is it? This is embarrassing."

"You know this, Ed," she said. The doctor gave her a look; she wanted to smack his face.

"I can see him," Ed said. "I just can't recall the name."

Dr. Khalifa wrote something down. She wanted to call the answer out. The whole thing was so stupid. She couldn't believe he was letting him dangle there like this. Ed looked ruined, as if he had failed a test not merely of memory but of character.

"Give it a second," Dr. Khalifa said. "Sometimes it's hard to think of a given thing when you have to. Think of something else. It might come to you."

"White elephants," Ed said.

"Something like that."

Ed rubbed the top of his head, as if to massage the answer from his scalp. He let out a deep sigh. "I can't remember," he said. "Who is it?"

"Bush," the doctor said. "George Bush."

"Yes! That's it! I knew it. God, I knew it! I could see his face. Of course! His running mate. It's easy to confuse them."

The doctor said nothing, just continued to write on his pad.

She thought of the time she'd had to memorize the presidents and their dates of service. She remembered Sister Alberta calling them up one by one to the front of the room to answer one question each, Sister asking her which president followed Teddy Roosevelt. So many *W* names surrounded Roosevelt— to this day she could remember them: William McKinley, William Howard Taft, Woodrow Wilson, Warren G. Harding. Though she had memorized them conscientiously, at that moment they ran together in her mind. She was terrified of being called stupid in front of the class. Her heart began to race; then her mind went blank, so she could picture only the hazy outlines of names. "*Now, Miss Tumulty,*" Sister said, and when Eileen said, "William Wilson," laughter exploded in the room.

"You're right," she said. "It is easy to confuse them."

Ed looked guiltily at her, as if she were on Dr. Khalifa's side and not his. She shifted her chair closer to him. The doctor seemed to write endlessly.

"Just one more thing I have to get down here," he said, holding up a finger as he wrote. "Perfect. Now I'd like you to change into shorts. I'm going to have you do some exercises for me."

They went into the next room and she helped him change. It felt like she was getting him ready for gym class. She wondered what humiliations awaited him. Dr. Khalifa came in and had him touch his toes from a standing position and rise from a seated one. He had him jog in place. He took notes throughout. Ed looked to her between exercises. She tried to give encouragement. When Dr. Khalifa told him to touch his finger to the tip of his nose, Ed had a hard time doing it.

"I'm not drunk," he said. "I promise. Although I might get drunk after this."

43

They were waiting for his father to pull the car up after Mass. It had snowed, and his mother didn't want to walk in it. Another light dusting was coming down, and his mother held an umbrella over both their heads while they waited.

"You're going nowhere with baseball. You know that."

The comment might have stung more if Connell hadn't known it was more about debate than baseball. His mother had been on him lately to join the debate team.

"I like baseball," he said.

"Liking it is one thing. Spending your time doing it is another. You don't have to like everything you do. Besides, you'd like debate. You're naturally competitive. You get that from my side."

"Why do you want me to do debate so badly?"

"I want you to make the most of your advantages. I want to see you use your talents wisely."

"You want me to be a senator," he said.

"I want you to be happy."

"President of the United States."

"Don't try to make me out to be some fire-breathing dragon. So I want to push you a little. So what?"

He stood in silence, thinking about it. So what, indeed? The shoveled driveway across the street was getting recoated in a sheen of snow. It might be nice to own a house like that someday, to be able to hire someone to shovel. But he had no interest in joining the debate team. Those guys were always on the verge of cutting your throat.

"What does Dad say?"

"Your father and I both want what's best for you."

"What does he *say*?"

"What does your father say?" She laughed. "'Leave the kid be,' he says. 'Let the kid do what he wants. Let him have some happiness. Let him have some innocence while he still has time.'" She was getting worked up. Some people walking past on the way to their car jerked up their heads. "'All that matters is that the kid experience joy.' If you must know, that's what he says. And you know what I say?" There was a fierce expression on his mother's face. "I say give the kid a chance to make a real mark. Those debate kids are the ones who get the best grades in the school. Get him among them, is what I say. Those are the kids who go to Ivy League colleges. Let him get into a topflight school with them, become a lawyer, a politician. Those are the kids who take home awards and scholarships. What's wrong with his being one of them? What's wrong with his making a nice living? Being comfortable?"

"It's just debate, Mom."

"They're the best. You should be the best with them. Otherwise you're wasting your time."

"I like baseball," he said.

"You're not going to be a professional player."

"Probably not."

"Definitely not."

"Fine. Definitely not."

"Look," she said, "there's your father. Don't tell him we talked about this. He just wants you to play baseball and not think about anything complicated right now. Or maybe not ever. He wants you to be like a horse in the fields or something. Unfettered." She said it with a sharp little laugh. "I don't think that's real life, though. Maybe I want to tame you. Make you useful. I guess that's just who I am. But I know one thing. You listen to me, you're never going to want for anything in this life—not with your ability. I could guide you to the good life. If I'd been born a man, I'd be there myself."

44

They went to several more appointments. Dr. Khalifa repeated some tests and added new ones. Six weeks after the first appointment—it happened to be St. Patrick's Day—they went in for the results.

She was more nervous than she'd been since her wedding day. Ed seemed past nerves. He radiated an odd calm, like a man about to receive a lethal injection.

They waited in the room for the doctor to come in. She held Ed's hand, but he patted hers as if she were the one getting the news.

Dr. Khalifa entered with a folder, giving off a vaguely metallic smell, and Ed bristled. The doctor walked quickly, without sufficient gravity. She thought, *A turnip conveys more emotion than this guy.*

"Well, I have good news and bad news," Dr. Khalifa said. "The good news is, physically you're healthy as a horse. A great specimen."

She felt a jolt of excitement, then one of fear. "What about the bad news?"

He turned to her. "The bad news is your husband likely has Alzheimer's."

She gasped; Ed's hand in hers seized into a fist.

"I take no pleasure in saying this, but from now on, it might be best to think of every day as the best day of the rest of your life. If I were you, I'd try to make the most of every day while you can."

Ed squeezed her hand so hard she winced.

"I don't understand," she said.

"If he didn't have Alzheimer's, he'd probably live to ninety-five. Heart, lungs, kidneys, circulation—all tip-top. But he's got it."

"Are you sure?" she asked.

"There's little doubt," the doctor said, with all the detached finality of one of those enormous computers in old movies that spat out answers on punch cards.

"I knew it," Ed said grimly. She realized in an instant that he probably had known it, that he might have known it for years.

"How can this be? He's barely fifty-one."

"It's early, but it happens," Dr. Khalifa said. "I'm sorry." He did look sorry, but not for her particularly, rather for himself for having to be the bearer of bad news, "I wish there were something more I could say." She looked to Ed to explain it to her better than the doctor had. "I'll leave you two alone." The doctor slapped Ed's folder on his thigh as he rose. "I'm sure you have a lot to talk about. I'll come back in ten minutes to answer any questions and talk about our game plan."

When he was gone, they sat mulling over the news. It was a paradox of sorts: nothing made sense unless it were true, and yet it made no sense whatever for it to be true. It was so obvious now that he had Alzheimer's. The news felt old already, somehow.

"What are we going to do?"

"We are going to get a second opinion," she said.

"We don't need a second opinion. He's the second opinion."

"He could be wrong," she said.

"He's not," Ed said, with an authority that made her heart pound in her chest. She felt such love for him that she had to look away.

They sat in silence. Ed's grip on her hand hadn't loosened since they'd heard the news, but now she could feel his fingers beginning to uncurl.

"What the hell," he said. "What the hell." It struck her that it sounded like both a lament and a promise—a promise to make the best of things. "What are we going to do?" he asked again.

"We are going to carry this with dignity and grace," she said. "That's what." One point of his collar was upturned, and she flipped it down and pushed the button through the buttonhole for him.

They drove to Nathan's on Central Avenue. Ed had grown up taking the train out to Coney Island, and she wanted to give him a little comfort. This landlocked outpost on an undistinguished stretch of local road was a pale copy of the faded original on Surf Avenue, but its young patrons seemed to project an aura of possibility onto it. A troupe of heavily cologned, spiky-haired Albanians in collared shirts and high-top sneakers preceded her in line, flirting with the counter girls. They hooted and clapped and spoke with great anticipation of the big night ahead. Through the window she saw a tricked-out Camaro dart into a spot in the lot, tailed by a Trans-Am.

She led Ed to the open expanse of the seating area. With a steady hand, he brought the hot dog up to his mouth and bit into the tower of sauerkraut, onions, relish, mustard, and ketchup that sat atop it. A squirt shot out and landed on his shirt. He wiped it off without a word. It used to kill him when even a fleck of ketchup fell onto one of his dress shirts, but it was as if he now saw through the ordinary frustrations of living.

They pulled into the garage. In the basement, she had him take off his shirt, then his undershirt. She sent him upstairs and went in to the laundry room. Passing the shelves along the stairway wall, she realized that someone had stolen his power tools.

Whenever the workers had been there and he'd been home, Ed had stayed in the study—working or sulking, she'd stopped caring which. They must have seen him as an easy target. In Jackson Heights, whenever they'd had workmen in the house, he'd watched over his tools with a diligence she'd always considered paranoid.

There had been two different crews in her house, the floor and kitchen guys and the painting crew, and it was impossible to ascertain exactly who had done it. It was the lowest form of knavery to steal a man's tools, especially—the thought ruined her—when he couldn't use them anymore.

She didn't tell him they were missing. Instead, she left work early the next day and bought all new ones. She threw away the packaging and nestled them into place on the utility shelves. With their unscuffed surfaces and sharp corners, they possessed a newness that seemed unlikely to escape his notice, and yet his noticing now seemed equally unlikely. For the first time in their marriage, she found herself longing to be caught in one of her gentle schemes.

· · ·

Ed was adamant about not telling the boy. They weren't going to tell anyone at Ed's work either. They wanted to stretch it out to the thirty-year pension. Including the job he'd held at the Parks Department while in college, Ed had been working for the City of New York in one form or another for twenty-eight and a half years. If they could get him to thirty, they'd have twelve hundred more dollars coming in every month than if he retired now. She was going to have to squeeze as much out of the system as she could, because someday the cost of caring for Ed was going to rise dramatically.

In the days after the diagnosis, Ed grew quiet and still. Overnight, the black-Irish touch of olive coloring in his face retreated, replaced by a gaunt, dusty pallor. His odor changed; she could almost smell the fear coming out of his pores. He had already been showering less frequently; now he stopped showering entirely, and he only brushed his teeth when she forced him to stand there next to her doing it. They both went to work as if nothing had changed. She wondered if the funereal air had settled in for good.

One night, in bed, he asked her if he was dying.

"Not yet, you're not," she said. "You still have plenty of life left in you."

"I'm scared," he said. "I *am* dying."

"We all are, in a sense."

"I have a clock on me."

"We all have a clock on us."

"Not Connell," he said. "Not yet."

She wanted to say, *Connell too*, because it was the truth, but she saw how upset Ed looked.

"No," she said. "Not yet."

"I don't want him to get this," he said. "I want him to live in peace."

She couldn't help herself. "He may not get this and still not live in peace. There are no guarantees."

"He's not going to get it. Tell me that."

"He's not going to get it."

Her answer reassured him enough to allow him to fall asleep. She lay awake for a long time thinking of the clock ticking toward its terminal moment.

Maybe Connell *would* get it. Maybe *she* would.

One never knew.

Now *that* was the truth.

Even the hospital wasn't safe enough for some of the Alzheimer's patients she'd seen over the years. Getting lost in the hallways or wandering naked out of their rooms was just the beginning. One man fell down the stairs and broke his back. Intake could be tragic. They came in with gashes, burns; once, a severed finger. She wanted to delay the onset of real symptoms as long as she could. The answer for that was drugs. There weren't any approved drugs on the market, but there were drugs in clinical trial that might be helpful. She needed to get him into a research study. He would be helping the industry he had balked at working for, and he wouldn't get a dime for it. She had once imagined getting a luxury car, foreign trips, and antique furniture out of the pharmaceutical industry; now all she wanted was a less-rapid diminishment of Ed's besieged brainpower. She had to hope some clear-eyed pragmatist not immune to earthly rewards had expertly carried out the investigations Ed had refused to take up himself.

She called around to people she knew. She found an open study at the Nathan Kline Institute for Psychiatric Research, in Orangeburg, forty minutes away across the Tappan Zee Bridge. The study was to evaluate the long-term safety, tolerability, and efficacy of SDZ ENA 713 in treating outpatients with probable Alzheimer's disease, and it guaranteed Ed a supply of the drug as long as he wanted it, until it was either commercially viable or abandoned in the United States.

After the initial evaluation she was given a stack of official forms, one of which was a "Capacity Assessment for Participation in a Research Study." It indicated that the examining doctor had determined that Ed lacked the capacity to understand the purpose, risks, and benefits of the research and make an independent decision about participation. She knew it was a pro forma thing, that they needed her to sign with his power of attorney, which she had secured, but it rankled her, because Ed so clearly understood what they were telling him, probably understood it better than they did themselves.

Her heart ached when she signed the "Assessment of Capacity to Choose a Surrogate Decision Maker" form, because during the evaluation, the doctor had asked Ed who she was. "My wife," Ed had said, as if there were nothing plainer.

"Do you want your wife to have the power to make decisions on your behalf?" the doctor asked with exaggerated deliberateness, as if to convey the gravity of what Ed was signing over.

Ed laughed and asked the doctor if he was married. The doctor nodded.

"Then it won't surprise you to hear that my wife has been calling the shots as long as we've been married," Ed said, and the doctor chuckled in husbandly sympathy before checking the box beside "This patient has the capacity at this time." It amazed her how winning Ed had been able to be even at a moment like this.

She signed with a certain stoicism a form consenting to participate on his behalf, but it was the "Record of Choice of a Surrogate Decision Maker" form that nearly made her lose her composure, because it was the only one Ed had to sign himself, and he started his signature an inch above where he should have and angled it down and through the line in a way that made it look as if he was falling down as he did it.

45

Eileen keenly missed Curt, her hairstylist, and not just because he knew how to handle her cowlicks. She missed Curt's entertaining conversation, the way he indulged her interest in politics and made her keep a toe dipped in the ocean of popular culture, the tide of which receded from her as soon as she stopped seeing him. Every time she checked out at the Food Emporium, it seemed, she recognized fewer of the faces on the covers of celebrity magazines.

She wasn't about to go back to Jackson Heights for Curt, though, so she couldn't avoid the hairstylist in Bronxville, even though it intimidated her to go in there. The salon was fancier than Curt's place, with a miniature Japanese pond and leather seats in the waiting area. She was afraid to get into political conversations there, as she never knew who felt what, or who was listening, and she wouldn't read any of the offerings on the coffee table—*People, Us, Premiere, Entertainment Weekly*—because she didn't want to give anyone a reason to look down their noses at her, even though everyone else flipped through them with guilt-free relish. She couldn't escape the feeling that there was a different set of rules for her that she'd never had properly explained.

The Bronxville salon was practically a full spa, offering nail care, massages, facial treatments. As stylists, they were skilled technicians, giving her what she asked for and leaving her a little cold. Her hair would look great for a couple of days, with a chilly perfection to it, the cut preserved so unchangingly that it looked as if she'd been fitted for a wig. Then, one morning a few days in, it would refuse to fall in line with the brush, and she would have to wait long enough until she could justify going in.

Curt gave her what she didn't know she wanted. His cuts were understated; sometimes she wondered whether he cut much at all or just stood there talking and making snipping motions with the scissors. He always swept the shorn locks away before he took the smock off her, so she never got to examine the evidence. Weeks after an appointment, though, people were still asking her if she'd just had her hair done.

One day in the last week of March, when she was waiting to have her hair cut, she heard the woman before her—who despite being a little older than her was wearing stiletto heels and had alternating streaks of chocolate, caramel, and butterscotch dye in her hair—tell the hairstylist about the miracle they'd performed cleaning her mink at Bronxville Furrier after she'd leaned against some wet paint. Eileen saw the fur hanging on the hook. It looked shiny and full, as if it had just gotten a cut, shampoo, and blowout itself. The way the woman discussed her fur, it was as though she were actually discussing something else, speaking in a secret code that Eileen could decipher only if she had the corresponding key. She'd had the thought before that a fur might just be the thing to make her feel she belonged in this town.

A week later, when she walked past Bronxville Furrier and saw that they were having a spring sale, she went in and purchased a mink. It was so plush and full and enveloped her so thoroughly that she felt as though she had shrunk down to her teenaged size just by putting it on. In some quarters, it wasn't so fashionable anymore to own a fur coat, what with all the work PETA activists had done to stigmatize the wearers of them, but fur seemed to still have a foothold in Bronxville. She had the two important things—money to buy it with, or at least a still-viable line of credit, and someone to go out with in it. Who knew how long either would last?

"What about our rainy day savings?" Ed asked when he saw it.

"If it rains any harder than this," she said, "not even Noah's Ark would save us."

The weather was too warm for her new coat, but the Saturday after she'd bought it was chilly, and she decided that this might be the last chance she'd have to put it on for half a year. She made a reservation for seven o'clock at Le Bistro on Pondfield, the fancy place across from the post office that she'd been wanting to go to for months. She and Ed parked a few blocks up, where Kraft met Pondfield, because she wanted to take a little stroll through town and be seen. As soon as she started walking, though, she felt overdressed. No one else was in fur, and the truth was that she hadn't seen many women her age in fur since she'd moved.

By the time they reached the restaurant, she'd worked up such a sweat that she took it off before she went in. She'd had a vision of the maitre d' taking it from her shoulders slowly, one arm at a time. It was heavy enough in her arms to feel like a sleeping child. She handed it over, hoping no one would see the transfer. She would have to try again next winter.

For as long as she could remember, she'd wanted to wear a mink coat. Women in minks always looked as if they had no problems in the world. She'd spent her own good money on it—the credit card payment, in the end, came from her own money. She'd pay it off as soon as the bills settled down. She was almost proud to think of how much the total had come to, even after the off-season discount had been factored in.

46

Connell's uncle Phil was in from Toronto. After dinner, Connell's father began telling a story everyone had heard before about the summer he'd spent in college doing service work in Peru. The punch line involved the drastic height differential between himself and the priest in charge.

"There I am, all six feet of me," he said, "and—"

"You're not six feet," Connell interrupted. "You always say you're six feet. You're like five eleven."

"I'm six feet tall," his father said with dignity.

"You *wish* you were six feet." Connell had just measured himself, and he knew he was five ten and that his father wasn't much taller. He went over and squared up against his father back-to-back. Then he made him take his shoes off. He took off his own Doc Martens.

"Son, I'm six feet."

"Maybe you were once," he said. "Maybe you're shrinking."

"I'm not old enough to shrink."

"Maybe you are," he said. "Maybe you're losing it early, Dad. It would explain a lot."

His father gave him a quick, deadly stare. "*Enough*," he said, and turned away. "Do you need a drink?" he said to Uncle Phil.

"I'll come with you," Uncle Phil said.

Connell followed them into the kitchen. "If you're six feet," he said, "then prove it."

"Let it go, son," his uncle said.

"Here," Connell said. "The door's right here. We'll mark you off against it. Like we did for me in the old house."

His father looked annoyed, but he stood against the door. Connell made him take his shoes off again.

"Five foot ten and three-quarters," he pronounced as he made a deep score in the side of the door with the pencil.

Connell was emptying the dishwasher. He pulled up the handle of a knife whose blade had been broken off near the base. It was nothing but a stump.

"This has seen its last day," he said, holding it up to the light. "I'm getting rid of it."

He threw it out; his father walked over and quietly fished it from the garbage.

"That knife is guaranteed for a lifetime," his mother said with matter-of-fact triumph. "That's a high-quality knife."

"I can tell," Connell said archly.

His father rubbed the handle between his fingers like a worry stone.

"I've been meaning to call that company for a while now," his mother said.

Connell was incredulous. "Can we just get rid of it? You're not going to call the company. What could you possibly do with that knife, Dad? Seriously." He strained for a tone he would take with a father he could spar with, a tone he knew would hurt him.

"You'd be surprised," his father said. "I use this knife to stir my sauces."

"I am too going to call that company," his mother said. "They'll honor their guarantee."

"We have plenty of other knives. Why do we need this one?"

"Your father bought that knife when we got married. He spent a lot of money on it at the time. Is that enough of an answer for you?"

She looked on the verge of tears. He knew he shouldn't have anything more to say.

"Doesn't mean you have to keep it forever," he said.

47

Eileen had helped Ed with his classwork here and there throughout the year, but as the end of the spring semester approached, she found herself grading more and more of his lab reports and tests. He looked over her shoulder, explaining things. They each took a stack and went through them, and she checked his work at the end.

For a year, he'd been gathering evidence toward a paper based on his government grant research, which he was going to present at a conference. After the diagnosis, he redoubled his efforts, staying late at the lab many nights. She knew she should have been proud of him for continuing to follow the faint trail of a fleeing ambition, and she *was* proud, sometimes, but she knew it would come to nothing—no new grants or appointments, no extra prestige, not even a completed paper—and she wished he were home with her instead. The nights were lonely, and it was a small compensation to imagine him sharing that loneliness with her from afar. She pictured him in his poorly lit lab, digging at his scalp as he scrutinized data skunked by faulty observations.

Ed took the study drugs twice a day. She wasn't willing to risk his missing a dose, so she watched him swallow one every morning and every evening. After thirteen weeks, she brought him in for his first evaluation.

"I feel like one of my rats," he told her as they sat in the attached orange chairs in the waiting room. She gave him a quizzical look. "In the lab," he said.

"It's not the same."

"It is," he said. "It's okay, though. I can be the rat after all these years."

"Stop that, Edmund."

"Maybe it will help someone," he said.

"Maybe it will help *you*."

"I'm not the point of this. This is a trial. Other people are the point of this."

"That's not true," she said.

"It's fine. It's science. I'm here for science."

She was silent for a while.

"I'm the rat," he said, more definitely now.

"Fine," she said. "You're the rat."

"They all died eventually," he said. "I never liked finding them stiff. It never got easier."

She imagined the stench from the cages, the dead eyes, the reduced bodies looking like cat toys. "It must have been unpleasant," she said.

"It was sad. It was a thankless job they had."

They weighed him and took his vital signs, drew his blood and collected his urine, gave him an electrocardiogram and performed memory tests. They monitored his ability to do certain tasks. They had him play with blocks. They had him cut meat. They had him write things. Writing was the hardest thing to get him to do. He hated his own handwriting. It was more proof than he was willing to look at.

At the end, they handed her enough drugs to last Ed the thirteen weeks until his next scheduled visit. There was a jolt of promise in the bag of medications. She wondered for a moment whether, if she gave him the whole bag at once, he would be his old self for a few days, an afternoon, a couple of hours. It would be worth it, even if the rest of the time he was a mess. She knew it didn't work like that, though. His real self wasn't hiding in there waiting to be sprung for a day of freedom. This was his real self now.

48

I t was a Tuesday in early July. They were lying in bed with the windows open. She tried reading a novel but felt jittery and distracted until she gave up and retrieved one of her Alzheimer's books from the pile she kept hidden under the bed. Ed was supposed to be reading, but he had his hands folded across his chest and was looking at the ceiling.

Four months had passed since the diagnosis. She had gotten swept up in the strange logic of that moment—*Don't tell a soul*—but it was clear that Ed couldn't be counted on to know when enough was enough.

She couldn't just tell people herself, because she knew Ed wouldn't forgive her for betraying his trust.

She closed her book and propped herself on her elbow to face him. "How about if we have a dinner? Invite our closest friends over. We can tell them all at once."

"I'd prefer if we didn't."

"It would be easier than telling everyone individually."

"Who says we have to tell them individually?"

"A nice dinner party," she said. "It would make it feel like a team effort to tackle this thing. I'll see if I can get it together for Saturday."

He gritted his teeth. "You sound determined."

"We'll have to tell Connell."

"*That's* where I draw the line," he said, almost growling. "I'm not telling him yet. I don't want him to see me that way, reduced like that. I still want to be his father."

"You'll always be his father," she said, but instead of soothing him she only disturbed herself with thoughts of what that "always" implied—the time when the disease would have tangled his synapses and hobbled him, when he would no longer be all there.

"In any event," Ed said, "I want to wait."

Connell was often playing baseball or in the city or at a friend's house. When he was home, he stayed in his room. If she was extremely careful, she could keep it from him a little longer.

"Fine," she said. "We'll hold it back a bit. But you'd better prepare for it. We can't keep it from him forever."

"*I* could."

"Honey, no offense—you couldn't."

"If I'm not alive," Ed said darkly, "then he doesn't have to see me like that. He can remember me as I was."

"That's nice. That's just lovely. You get that goddamned thought out of your head this instant. You're not going *anywhere*."

"If it could just stay like this," he said, his tone changing, "I could live with it." He pulled the sheet up under his chin.

"Maybe the drugs will start working," she said. "Or if these drugs don't work, there'll be others that work better. The science will catch up to this disease. And we're going to do everything we can in the meantime. We're going to be very busy. You're going to stay alert. You're going to read a lot." She looked at his book on the nightstand, which he hadn't picked up in days. "We'll do the crossword together, we'll go to plays and operas. We'll go on trips. We'll keep this thing at bay." She took his hand; it felt stiff, a little cold. She put her other hand on his chest to feel his heart beat.

She didn't know how much of what she'd said she believed, but it felt good to say it. She went back to her book. The chapter she was reading discussed how the disruption of context might accelerate the patient's decline. Familiar settings and people, it suggested, could have a prophylactic effect on memory loss.

She thought of how strenuously Ed had fought leaving Jackson Heights. Had she exposed him to harm in moving him to Bronxville? A guilty feeling took root in her thoughts and blossomed into panic.

"We can't afford to wait to tell Connell," she said. "What if he finds out for himself? What if he overhears me on the phone?"

"Don't talk on the phone."

"We have to tell him tomorrow," she said.

"Give it another week."

"Fine," she said. "This Saturday is the dinner. The one after that, we tell Connell."

"He has a game that day."

"You have his schedule memorized?"

"He plays every Saturday."

"After his game, then. Trust me. It's the best thing."

"Okay," he said. "I trust you."

She was strangely disappointed to hear him give in so easily. She understood that this new relationship of theirs signaled the beginning of the end of the old one. He would have to become something like a child to her.

The afternoon of the dinner, as she was running around getting the last things ready, Ed came in and told her to call it off.

"It's not true," he said. "It's a lie we'd be telling them."

"Honey," she said.

"It's a lie."

It was too late; the Cudahys, possibly the McGuires, were already on their way. Dishes were simmering on the stove.

"These are our friends."

"It's a lie."

"Would it be easier for you if I told them myself?"

"Do what you want," he said, waving his hand at her in a way that called to mind an angry old man.

"They'll be here in a little while. Tell me what to do."

"This is your affair," he said. He ran the tap and put a glass under it. Water filled the glass and spilled up over the sides. He held it under for a while. It looked as if he was making a little fountain out of it.

"I think we should do it the way we discussed."

"No!" he said sharply. "They don't need to know anything. It's all a lie."

"Do you think they can't tell anything?" she found herself shouting. "You think they can't figure it out? You think they don't have eyes and ears?" She paused. "And brains?" She regretted it as soon as she'd said it.

"They won't see anything," he said, seething. "There's nothing to see." He left the room.

She found him stewing on the front stairs and took a seat beside him. "We have to tell them sometime." She reached to touch him, but he flinched away. The neighbors across the street were pruning their flowers. She hadn't met them yet. She had wanted to wait to introduce herself until she felt herself to be operating from a position of strength, but that time hadn't come, and she felt too self-conscious to go over there now that they had looked at each other so many times across hedgerows without waving.

"There's nothing to tell."

"Would you rather nobody knew?"

He didn't answer.

"Because if you want to do this alone, just us and Connell, I can't. Maybe I'm not as strong as you. I thought I was, but I need all the support I can get. Now more than ever."

He turned and looked at her.

"I won't say anything tonight," she said. "We can do this when you're ready. On one condition."

He was blinking intently.

"Until then, don't make me feel like I'm alone with this. Connell needs to know. Let's deal with the reality of this. Other people, fine. But I need to know we in this house are going to deal in reality."

"Fine," he said.

"You have Alzheimer's."

"Don't say that."

"This is what I'm talking about," she said. "We need to stick together on this."

"Fine," he said. "Good."

"I know you know," she said. "But I need to hear it from you."

"I do know."

"Say it, then."

"Say what?"

"Say that you have Alzheimer's."

"You're crazy," he said. "I'm not saying any such thing"

She almost didn't care if he didn't join them. She could tell them he was sick, and if he chose to wander in, she could joke about a miraculous recovery. Maybe they'd think it strange; maybe they wouldn't. Maybe they'd notice things; maybe they'd have blinders on. She couldn't worry about managing impressions anymore. She almost couldn't care anymore whether they wandered upstairs and saw the state of disrepair her house was in, outside the carefully curated area for hosting guests.

Frank and Ruth, Cindy and Jack, Tom and Marie, Evan and Kelly: they arrived all at once, as if they'd rented a bus for the occasion. She tried to distract them with drinks and a flurry of hanging coats and shuttling dishes. She was trying to think of an alibi for Ed when he appeared in the door to a round of salutations.

She directed everyone to the dining room. She had decided to say that the occasion for their gathering was no occasion, that they simply wanted to see close friends and didn't want to wait until Christmas to do so. It wasn't a lie, exactly; she was very happy to have them there. For months now, she'd had to make excuses for not seeing them.

She used the proximity of Frank's birthday as an excuse to stick him at the head, Ed's regular seat. She sat Ed next to her. If Frank figured it out, she could count on him not to say anything. When the chatter was at its loudest, she filled Ed's plate.

She was angry at Ed for putting off the telling of their friends. She didn't care if he spilled food on himself or knocked his drink into his lap. He was on his own. She tried to absorb herself in conversations, but for the first time she derived little relief from the gathering of all these people. She ate distractedly enough to move even Jack to ask between courses if anything were the matter.

Deep into the main course, Ed tapped on his wineglass. She squeezed his knee instinctively. He struggled to his feet.

"There's something I want to tell you," he said as the voices lowered. She stood as well, to be beside him. "I wanted to have all of you here," he said. "My good friends. It's good to see you."

He paused for long enough that it seemed he had stopped. She rubbed his back encouragingly. No one knew how to react. It was sort of funny, what he'd said; it was anticlimactic. She almost expected Frank or Jack to say, "Good to see you too. Now have a seat so we can eat." They couldn't, though, because Ed looked so deadly serious.

"I wanted to tell you that we've had some news," he said. "It isn't good news."

Nobody moved; nobody said a word.

"We've had some tests done. And talked to some good doctors."

It amazed her to hear him talk about Dr. Khalifa with such equanimity. Something deep in him was surfacing, some essential fiber in his character. Then he stopped again. His leg was shaking. He was steadying himself on the table. It struck her that he had tried his best. He had tried to spare her from having to tell them, but she would have to do it regardless. She put her hand on his shoulder to urge him into his seat.

"It looks like I have Alzheimer's disease," he said.

A second of stunned silence, then a round of gasps, hands held to mouths, looks of concern. Frank pounded the table and peppered Ed for details. Jack questioned the diagnosis. Evan and Kelly moved their seats closer together and pledged their support while holding hands. Cindy cried. Marie sat morose. Ruth made attempts at jokes. Tom drank whole glasses of wine in long quaffs and kept pulling his napkin through the circle formed by his thumb and forefinger. Nobody touched their food. She wasn't sure she'd be able to serve dessert. She asked everyone if they'd like to move into the other room to sit with the news. They came up and hugged Ed one by one. He seemed more physically confident, quicker on the uptake, as if he had lanced a malignancy that had been draining his essence. She shuddered to imagine how much of his mental energy had gone into keeping everyone in the dark. In its own way, it had been a feat of fortitude.

Jack came up to her in the kitchen, chewing around his words as though they were a shell he was trying not to swallow.

"How could you do that? How could you embarrass that man like that?"

She had to hold her hand down to keep it from smacking his face. "This was Ed's choice," she said firmly.

"No man would choose that." He turned and headed to the other room with the stiff uprightness of a former military man.

She had to remind herself that men took news like this differently than women did. She'd seen that for years working in hospitals. The bigger they were, the more uneasy they acted around revelations of disaster.

"It's a matter of plaque deposits," Ed was saying when she returned to the living room. Talking about the diagnosis had empowered him; he sounded professorial.

"Plaque deposits," Frank repeated, a stunned vacancy in his voice. "I take care of plaque deposits."

"Synapses get rerouted," Ed said. "Brain mass decreases. Functionality suffers."

Whatever had happened to his short-term memory, Ed's long-term memory was, at least for now, an impregnable fortress. The clinical detachment with which he discussed what was happening neurophysiologically might have made you forget he was talking about himself. He seemed to welcome the chance to talk in this abstracted way. The faces of the people around him registered an appreciation of his aplomb, and a somber awareness settled into all of them of how terrible it was that such a fertile mind had been subject to this perverse accident of biology.

"Early-onset is the most virulent kind," she said to Marie in the kitchen. "It dismantles motor functions and speech as it erases the memory." She paused. "It's the true Alzheimer's," she said, with something like pride at the thought that if her husband were to be destroyed by a degenerative neurological disorder, it would be the undiluted article, the aristocrat of brain diseases.

Everyone stayed later than usual. No one seemed to know when it would be okay to leave. Maybe they didn't want to face the road yet, their dark thoughts, the reduced company of their spouses. Eventually Ed got cranky. "Is this thing ever going to end?" he asked, and went up to bed in a huff without pausing to say good night. Ruth raised her eyebrows, and Eileen raised hers back, and then Ruth started herding people toward the door.

After the other guests had said their good-byes and were making their way down the back steps, Ruth and Frank were all that remained. Frank filled a thermos with coffee for the trip back.

"I knew something was wrong," he said.

"It must have been obvious."

"I don't know how to process all this. It's like it isn't real."

"I feel the same way."

"It scares me," he said. "I think about it myself sometimes. When I lose my keys, when I forget where I parked my car."

Frank did look scared. The pallor on his cheeks gave him a vaguely cadaverous look.

"You can talk to him, you know. He's still your friend. He's still here."

"I don't know how to talk to him about this."

"Just open your mouth and see what comes out."

Frank shuffled out the door with his thermos held like a lantern, and Ruth gave her a long hug, and then Eileen was alone in the kitchen. Dishes and glasses were scattered everywhere, and food had to be covered in plastic or scraped into the garbage. She had never before been relieved to see her house left in such a mess. She wouldn't have to turn the lights off and head upstairs for an hour at least.

The following Saturday, they ate in the languid silence that followed games in which Connell pitched. His exhaustion passed to the two of them through some invisible membrane.

"How did you do?" she asked.

The gleaming newness of the kitchen hadn't yet faded; it still felt like someone else's room.

"Fine," Connell said.

"*Fine*," Ed said, amused. "He did more than fine. He struck out—what?" He looked to Connell.

"Thirteen."

"And not one batter made solid contact," Ed said.

"I also walked eight guys."

"His control is an issue, there's no denying it. He was pitching out of jams the whole game. He threw a ton of pitches."

As if on cue, Connell rubbed his shoulder.

"But the sky's the limit. A lefty with this kind of velocity? If he keeps working at it, he's going to be a force."

She waited for Ed to transition into the discussion of the disease. She caught his eye; he shook his head to say the plan was off. She tried to indicate displeasure, but he looked down at his soup to avoid her gaze.

"Ed," she said, coughing. He looked up.

Connell's eyes were heavy with fatigue. Ed stood up and put his hand on Connell's head for a second and tousled his locks affectionately. He walked over to the sink and gazed out the window.

"What's up? You guys fighting again?"

"No," Ed said, still looking out the window. "Just listen to your mother."

"You're getting older now," she said. "You're getting to the point where you can hear adult things." Connell sat up straighter in his seat. "The things adults talk about. What your father and I talk about."

"Please don't tell me this is about the birds and the bees. I'm way too old for that."

She couldn't hold back a thin, sad smile. She felt a lump in her throat. "We've got some bad news," she said.

The boy's jocular expression faded. "What is it?"

"It has to do with your father's health," she said after a bit.

Ed turned around and walked back toward the table. He sat. "What your mother is trying to say is that I have been diagnosed with Alzheimer's disease."

"Do you know what that is?" she asked.

"Yeah." He looked back and forth between them. "It's where you forget things."

"Yes."

"Isn't that what old people get?"

"Sometimes," she said. "Most of the time. But sometimes it happens to younger people."

"Are you going to be okay?"

"There's not a lot of medicine out there," he said. "I'm on some exper-imental drugs. We'll see. But it's going to get worse."

"Are you scared?"

This was the first time she'd seen anyone ask Ed how it affected him personally. It had always been questions about the illness. She hadn't even asked him herself.

Ed straightened up. His eyes got a crinkly, philosophical look in them. "Sometimes I am, sure," he said. "That's part of it, no question about it." He looked at the sugar bowl, the top of which he'd been clacking like a cymbal. "I like my life. I *love* my life. I don't want to lose it."

"Aren't you too young for this?"

"If you're asking me, yes," he said. "If you're asking the disease, no."

"How quickly will it get worse?"

"Honey," she said to him, "don't pepper your father with questions."

Ed put up a hand to quiet her.

"It could be quick," he said. "It could be years. Every case is different."

Connell seemed to chew on what he'd heard for a little while.

"Is there going to be a time when you don't know who I am?" he asked.

Ed's face took on a fierce expression, as though the question had an-gered him. She thought to intervene, but then he rose from his seat and leaned down to put his arms around the boy.

"I will always know who you are," Ed said, kissing the top of his head. "I promise you that. Even if you think I don't know, even if I seem not to. I will always know who you are. You're my son. Don't you ever forget that."

"You neither," he said, rising to hug his father.

She started clearing the dishes.

"Mom," Connell said. He held out his gangly arm to her.

She walked over and stood near them. Connell seemed to urge her to join them in some sort of embrace. She had wanted him to hear, and now that he'd heard, she wanted him to come to terms with it and carry on stoically, but he was a different kind of creature from her. She and Ed had worked to give him an easier life than they'd had. Sometimes she won-dered if she'd erred in not making him tougher.

The idea of a group hug embarrassed her and she couldn't comply. There was going to be more darkness than hugs could begin to dispel. She thought of this embrace he was offering as the come-on of a huckster selling a spurious remedy. She gave him three quick, sharp pats on the back, as if to punctuate some unstated conclusion, and headed upstairs.

49

After they'd finally told Connell, she could talk openly with her girlfriends about Ed's condition. She called them every night—Ruth, Cindy, Marie, Kelly, Kathy, her aunt Margie—going through the lineup, dialing a new number the instant she'd hung up with the first. She didn't want to be interrupted once she'd started, so she waited to make the calls until after dinner, when Ed was in his study grading lab reports and writing out lectures. Her friends invariably ended whatever calls they were on when she rang through. She didn't always know what she was going to talk about when she picked up the phone, but the conversations followed their own rhythms, and they always had to do with Ed. She didn't even try to talk about other things. She thought if she talked it out enough, she could make it more familiar, less overwhelming, less frightening.

Whenever she called the McGuires and Frank answered, he handed it right to Ruth. Once, about a month after the dinner at which they'd told Ruth and Frank and the others about Ed, Frank annoyed her with the way he rushed off, and she asked Ruth to hand the phone back to him.

"Where the hell did you go?" she asked. "Why haven't you called? Why hasn't he seen you? Why haven't you taken him out for a beer? Why haven't any of you goddamned guys taken him out? He's in that study night after night."

"I'm having a hard time dealing with it."

"He knows that. Just call him and say hello."

"I will," Frank said.

Frank didn't call, though, and a week later she got Ruth to put him on. She pretended Frank had called and handed the phone to Ed. She was afraid Ed would notice that the phone hadn't rung, but he just took the phone and started talking to Frank like a teenager, his excitement palpable. She listened to Ed's end of the conversation, which lasted an hour. Nothing about the disease came up. That was one difference between men and women. Men got along fine without revealing anything. She almost admired them for it. The downside was that they retreated to their islands.

When she took the phone back from Ed, she made Frank promise to call Ed again soon, but Frank didn't call, and the next time they went to the McGuires', Frank hardly spoke at dinner, and they left right after dessert.

Eileen had been telling Ruth about the anxiety dreams she was having about all her teeth falling out and her skin peeling off her body, when Ruth surprised her by suggesting she see a psychologist. She was amazed to hear Ruth speak of the positive experience she'd had in therapy. She didn't even know Ruth had ever *been* in therapy. It was nearly impossible to imagine. It wasn't that Ruth was a stone; she was in fact tirelessly empathetic when listening to the troubles and pains of others, and she always made time for her friends. It was just that she herself never gave anything away. You wouldn't catch her crying if you tied her up and strangled her cats before her eyes one at a time. For years, Eileen had taken at face value Ruth's assertion that, having more or less raised her younger siblings, she'd decided she was done bringing children up. Then, late one night when the men were asleep, Ruth admitted she'd been terrified to wreck a kid's life with drink the way her mother had done. Ever since, when Eileen saw Ruth looking at Connell with affection, she knew there was more in Ruth's heart than she'd admit to anyone, including Frank.

Eileen had dismissed therapy as an indulgence for those with too much time and money and too few friends. Besides, Catholics didn't go to shrinks; that was what the confessional booth was for. What were you supposed to do, though, when you hadn't been to confession since your early twenties? She pictured herself enumerating her sins for an hour and a half, being handed an inexhaustible list of prayers to recite, and leaving with no more clarity than she'd had going in.

Ruth's therapist was named Dr. Jeremy Brill, and his office was near

Ruth's, a block from the Flatiron Building. He greeted Eileen at the door and directed her to an armchair. Eileen looked around for the couch she'd been expecting, but there was only a mahogany desk, two armchairs, and a trio of reassuring diplomas—Harvard, Cornell, Yale—on the wall above a little bookcase. The room was dark except for a floor lamp and the little light that came through the slatted blinds.

Dr. Brill sat in an armchair and asked her to speak. She found it easier to begin than she had expected. She was talking about her mother and father, her youth in Woodside, her life in Jackson Heights, her career, even Mr. Kehoe, and after she'd been speaking for a while, she felt the first sprigs of unburdening bloom in her chest. After she'd subsided into silence, it gratified her to hear Dr. Brill—he insisted that she call him Jeremy, but that wasn't going to happen, even though he was at least ten years younger than her—say that Ed must possess superior intelligence to preserve outward normalcy for as long as he had.

"A less intelligent man might have given himself up long ago," Dr. Brill said. "Who knows how long he's been keeping this hidden?"

He prodded her to speak about the way Ed's illness made her feel, and though she'd vaguely decided beforehand to parry such questions, she began to speak with a pointedness and clarity that surprised her, until, many minutes later—it amazed her how silent Dr. Brill remained, how he seemed to draw the words out of her as though hypnotizing her with his eyes, which narrowed and widened to some hidden rhythm—she felt the engine of her thoughts wind down, midsentence. He told her their time for that session was up.

The next time, she didn't feel comfortable talking. After an initial greeting, Dr. Brill didn't say anything either. A long silence settled into the Oriental rug. It put her in mind of the silent treatment Ed sometimes gave her, or the standoffs Connell would enact as a little boy, when he stubbornly refused to speak.

"What's your biggest fear?" Dr. Brill asked after a while.

"I'm not quite sure," she said. "Probably being alone."

Another silence.

"And why is that?"

"Who wants to be alone?"

"Some people might."

"I don't," she said.

"Do you feel that your husband is leaving you alone?"

"Sometimes I do, I suppose. Yes. I guess I do."

"I understand," he said. "This is a disease where you never win. It doesn't just take down the sufferer. It takes down the spouse, the children, the friends. It can feel tremendously isolating."

It was feast or famine with him; either he didn't say a word or else he said more than she wanted to hear.

She understood that she wasn't going to win, that she couldn't beat Ed's illness, and yet she wasn't about to sit there and let someone tell her she was going to lose. She decided right then that she was never coming back. That made it easier to speak, and she spent the next half hour holding forth on all sorts of things she had no idea she was thinking about. In the end she felt relieved for having had a chance to get them out. It was almost a shame to have to cut this experiment short, because she was beginning to see value in it, though only in small doses, and for someone very different from herself.

She could see the day coming when Ed would have to stop working, and she wanted to be smart. She went to the Alzheimer's Association to find out what kind of resources might be available. The social worker told her to wait until she was impoverished and they'd be able to help her get assistance.

"*Impoverished?*"

"Medicaid only kicks in once you've spent down to the threshold. You can keep your salary, up to a certain dollar amount. Not your husband's. That goes straight to Medicaid. You'll have to liquidate investments. You can put your money into home improvements, even update your wardrobe. Buy medicines in advance, staples for the house. Set aside burial expense money for both of you. Necessary things. Not jewelry. Definitely not jewelry. Except for your wedding ring and your engagement ring, and his wedding ring. You can keep those. If you spend the money down quickly, the government can come in and ask where it went, and you might not get Medicaid. You can keep the house no matter what. And the car. The upside is, when you're nearly broke, there will be assistance available."

"You're telling me that short of—going *broke*, as you put it—there's nothing I can do to defray the cost of a nurse—or a home, if it comes to that?"

"At this point, no."

"Everything in my savings account goes?"

"Yes."

"All the stocks?"

"Indeed."

"The retirement accounts?"

"Them too."

"Let me tell you something," she said gruffly, feeling pride rise in her like a fever. "I worked hard my entire life."

"I'm sorry."

The costs would be enormous; their savings would dwindle quickly. The cost of at-home nursing care (she refused to consider a nursing home until she absolutely had to) would be the equivalent of taking out a second mortgage, which would be expensive enough on two incomes, but when Ed's pension kicked in at about 40 percent of his salary, it would be virtually impossible for her to pay it without dipping into their retirement money, which would shrink quickly.

"I should have done the cabinets in cherry," she said.

"Come again?"

"I was too prudent. I should have had the bricks ripped up and marble tiles put down. I should have bought three mink coats instead of one on sale. I should have gone to Europe every year. I should have spent my money like a drunken sailor in my twenties and thirties when everyone around me was doing it. This all would have been a lot easier to swallow if I were poor."

She went to see Bruce Epstein, a tax lawyer and the husband of her friend Sunny from work.

She sat across from Bruce in his Upper West Side office. Law books lined the shelves, as well as classic works of literature. "The best thing you can do is divorce him," he said, offering her a bowl of chocolates. "Strictly financially speaking, of course. Separate your finances. Put everything in your name. Take all the money."

Eileen fiddled with a loose string on the hem of her suit jacket.

"I know you don't want to hear it," Bruce continued, "but that's the best thing you can do. If you divorce him, he gets Medicaid right away. It might be better to be unsentimental about it. You don't have to actually divorce him in your heart. You can take care of him. Just get a different place."

"What would I tell my son?"

"Your son doesn't have to know until later."

"What do I tell Ed?"

"Tell him you're trying to be smart. Tell him you're doing this for all of you. Nothing will fundamentally change, except that you'll get assistance from the state."

"I'm supposed to divorce my husband because he has Alzheimer's?"

"I know it sounds bad," he said, "but you wanted to know. From a financial perspective, divorce is the best thing. I'd be remiss if I didn't apprise you of your options."

"How exactly would this happen? How would I divorce him and get all the money?"

"You've got a minor child, so that helps. Make up something about infidelity. There are a lot of ways to get this done. You'll get the house, so that's taken care of."

"I don't think I could do it."

"I'm not surprised," he said warmly. "But I think you should give it serious consideration. My concern here—so that you avoid regret later— is that you make a deliberate decision and not let your emotions get the best of you. Or if you're going to make an emotional decision, do that in a rational way. Decide that you want to weigh the emotions as greater in value than the financial particulars. If you were able to overcome some of the mental obstacles to proceeding in the way I've advised you, it would be the most sensible alternative. But then pure rationality isn't always the compass we're guided by. I can tell you this much: I would want Sunny to do this if she were in your situation. It would help both you and your husband. And remember: in the eyes of God you are married forever."

What he was advocating was the exertion of radical control over one's own life, even if it meant flouting cherished ideals. She had long prized the notion that she would have made a good lawyer if given the opportunity, but she realized now, as she listened to Bruce's dispassionate appeal to the facts, that she lacked the ability to see things in the unstintingly logical way he did. She didn't think she could divorce Ed just to preserve their stake. She'd rather spend the money down. She was going to have to work forever anyway.

50

Connell was in his girlfriend Regina's basement. He wanted to lay her down on the soft carpet and get on top of her, but the best he could do was squeeze close to her on the couch, which sat flush against the paneled wall. He picked at one of the grooves between panels, preparing to make his move and drape an arm over her. He'd done it twice already that day, but it still made him nervous. The first time, after they'd made out for a while, the door at the top of the stairs opened and her mother shouted down, "Everything okay?" They sat at opposite ends of the couch after that, until he worked his way back over to her, inch by inch. Just when he got there, her mother—as if she had a special sense— called him upstairs to reach a serving platter from the top of the cabinet. Regina had said her mother only let them stay down there alone because she'd heard boys from his school were nice boys.

Regina's family was Lebanese. Her father was so intimidating that Connell could barely speak to him. Connell didn't like to be alone with Regina when her father was home; it wasn't worth the anxiety.

He couldn't remember the name of the movie they were watching. He couldn't concentrate on anything but the way her hair brushed against him when she flipped it, or the way she pushed against him slightly with every intake of breath. She had kissed him dutifully for a few minutes, and now she was insisting on watching this movie, with an annoyed air that suggested she was trying to seem disciplined and mature and beyond petty lust, but really he could tell that she was just as nervous as he was.

He put his arm around her and let his hand settle on the knobby ball of her shoulder. He let it move a little lower, so that it rested on her collarbone. She was wearing a polo shirt, munching from a bowl of popcorn in her lap. He moved his hand to the triangle of skin her collar exposed and let it rest there. It was good that he had long arms, because the position was awkward. After a few seconds she shifted closer to him, leaning into his flannel shirt, but he knew it was only to move his hand away.

He had never put his hand up her shirt. He'd felt her over her shirt, but she'd always stopped him after a few seconds. One time he'd put his hand on her thigh and she'd picked it up and moved it away.

He'd told her about his father once because he hadn't had anything else to say. As soon as he saw the sympathetic look that came over her, he knew he would have that topic to return to when he needed it. It might be useful for more than filling silences.

She was watching the movie so intently that he wouldn't have been surprised if she had to give her mother a report on it afterward. All he could think of was how much like spring she smelled and whether she could tell he had an erection.

"Hey," he said.

"Hey yourself." She glanced at him and then looked back at the movie.

"I'm feeling sad."

"What's up?"

"I don't know," he said. "Nothing."

She turned to him fully now. "What is it?"

"Nothing," he said. "Let's watch the movie."

"You tell me right now." She had a deadly earnest look on her face, and he couldn't tell if she was joking or not. He felt bad when he realized she was serious. Her father's bar, and his ghostly presence at it, looked on in silent disapproval.

He put his finger to his lips in a shushing gesture, which inflamed her.

"Either you tell me or I'm not kissing you anymore tonight," she said.

"Don't make fun of me," he said. "I just don't know how to talk about it."

She put the popcorn bowl on the coffee table and sat on her legs, drawing her feet up under her. "Now you really have to tell me. What? *What?*"

"I was just thinking of my father. It makes me sad to think of him."

Her features arranged themselves into a look of concern.

"Tell me," she said. Her hand was on his knee.

"Just that he's not going to be here. He's going away. He's going to for-get me."

She started shaking her head. She looked like she was about forty years old. "He won't forget you," she said in a way that was both dismissive and reassuring. It was like she could see what was actually going to happen.

"He will. Everyone's going to go away eventually."

"Not me. I'll be here."

"You'll go away too."

"I will *not*," she said.

She went to hug him. He kissed her neck and moved up to her lips. The movie kept playing in the background, but now she wasn't watching it either. She was kissing him long and with a different level of feeling. His erection now pressed painfully against his pants. He was running his hands all over her body. He put his hand under the bottom of her shirt and moved it up quickly when she didn't shove it away. He ran his hand over her bra and slipped his hand under it. He felt his breath coming short. He moved his other hand up under her shirt, so he had one of her breasts in each of his hands. It felt like he had made it to the other side of some great divide. He started kissing her neck and ears, and eventually he had lifted her shirt up and was kissing her breasts. He would not try to do more than this. There would be other opportunities. He would keep something in reserve. His fa-ther had helped him. It was a powerful thing that he would have to use spar-ingly, what was happening with his father; he didn't want to get addicted to it. But there was nothing wrong with letting some good come from it.

The room seemed to get darker. He sucked at her nipple like he was trying to draw something out of it, which he knew was all wrong. She winced a few times at the pressure of his teeth.

The door upstairs came open, and she rushed to pull her shirt down, which was just as well, because his kisses on her breasts had turned into something he was practicing doing, and he had begun to feel guilty about losing his innocence. There was no going back for it now.

51

Virginia was in the phone book, as she'd said she'd be so many years before. Or rather her husband was: Callow, Leland. Eileen had been meaning to reach out to Virginia since the day she'd closed on the house. She'd gone for the phone several times, but the idea of fumbling through the initial conversation gave her an anxious pit in her stomach and she always hung up before dialing. She didn't want to degrade herself any more than she'd have to. She decided to show up instead.

She chose a Saturday. If they weren't home, she'd leave a note and try again the next day. She put on a nice blouse and skirt and did her hair. Virginia's address was in the town proper, up the hill, on one of those winding streets with houses set far back from the street on enormous lots.

When she was a block away, Eileen felt so jittery that she had to pull over and calm herself down. This was the encounter she'd been anticipating for years, though she hadn't realized as much until she was on its threshold. The visit Virginia had made to the dressing room planted a seed in her mind that had broken through the surface and survived long winters. She wanted Virginia to see the tree in its full flowering. Would Virginia recognize it for what it was? She hoped it would seem to Virginia like the most natural thing in the world for Eileen to be standing there, a neighbor of sorts, even if she lived across town, dropping in unannounced, an old friend, a surprise visitor.

There were so many trees on the front lawns. They seemed older than the nation itself. It was early October; the leaves had started to turn, and the sight of the street in the lightly misty air made her stop and pull over for a minute before she could continue.

She pulled up in front of Virginia's house. There was a car in the driveway. She put her own car in park and turned off the engine, and the old vehicle settled heavily. She regretted not stopping at Topps for a box of cookies, or at Tryforos for some flowers, but on the other hand it would have been strange to come bearing a gift after thirty years. She imagined handing over the rattling box of cookies and Virginia receiving it with a skeptical look, as though it were a store of keepsakes from an intentionally forgotten past.

She stood in the street, gazing at the house. It was almost perfectly beautiful. There was nothing about it she would change, nothing she could imagine anyone—even those tasteless people who ruined old houses by updating them—would ever dream of changing. The landscaping alone looked expensive enough to break a bank account. The house wore its affluence easily, though. There was a quiet about it, broken only by the low hum of a distant weed whacker. She imagined an old man roving the grounds in a pair of gloves, dragging a heavy garbage bag and filling it with weeds.

She couldn't convince herself to approach the front door. The thought of sitting over tea with Virginia had gotten her through some lonely afternoons after everything had been unpacked. She had been waiting for the moment when her house looked polished enough to show it off, when everything had settled down long enough to allow her to operate from a position of strength, but that moment hadn't come. She had kept alive the idea of a steadfast friend capable of great enthusiasm on her behalf, even after years of silence. She knew that seeing Virginia again might rob her of a consolation that had been more important than she wanted to admit.

She started up the stone path that transected the lawn. She had only taken a few steps in when a dog came running up, barking and freezing her in place. It looked harmless enough, a little Jack Russell terrier, but it barked so insistently and with such a strange, alert intelligence that she began to hear a message beyond a simple warning to stay away. The dog marked a half-moon around her, then left off its clamoring and stood with nose up and eyes narrowed, assessing her in a manner that unnerved her. She tried to hide her fear—not of the dog but of what the dog was thinking, what it saw and understood—because she thought it absurd to feel apprehension before such a diminutive creature. No one emerged from the house to call the dog off. The compact thing had an almost impossible solidity to it; its thick coat seemed to stand at permanent attention.

When the figure of a woman appeared from behind a hedgerow at the side of the house, Eileen felt her heart stop in a fear that made her forget about the dog. She thought to turn and walk away, but after she didn't immediately take the first retreating step, she knew she couldn't do so without seeming to scurry guiltily. The woman—it had to be Virginia— walked briskly to retrieve the animal, which hustled with a chastened dutifulness to meet her halfway and circle back by her side. Watching the woman approach from the middle distance, Eileen had trouble recognizing her as the gamine girl she'd last seen trying on bridesmaids' dresses. She was nicely attired, in a pair of brown slacks and a mustard-colored blouse whose sheen glinted in the sunlight.

"Can I help you?" Virginia asked from a few feet away. Her hair had gone an ashen shade of gray that somehow looked sun-bleached and healthy. She wore it pulled back in a neat, attractive bun. She'd grown thinner with age, so that she appeared almost military in her bearing. She looked inquisitively at Eileen, and Eileen thought for a moment that Virginia had recognized her, until she realized Virginia was probably simply wondering what this woman was doing on the perimeter of her lawn.

"I hope so," Eileen said. "I seem to have gotten a little lost. The road took a few turns, and I got off it somehow. I have to get back to the highway."

"Where are you looking to get?"

"I'm sorry?"

"Where are you looking to go?"

"I was visiting a friend, you see. I just need to get home."

"Where's home?"

"The city," she said, afraid Virginia would hear the nervous lump in her throat. "Queens. I believe I need the Bronx River Parkway to the Hutchinson Parkway."

"Queens? What part?"

Her heart pounded. "Douglaston," she said, the dryness in her mouth choking off the end of the word.

Virginia gave her very specific instructions, down to the approximate number of feet after the light till she'd encounter the turnoff to the Bronx River. She radiated none of the scattered, frazzled energy Eileen remembered, and Eileen felt a sudden crushing loneliness at the thought that she hardly knew Virginia at all.

She listened to Virginia describing the familiar route. She had bought herself time to catch her breath. She would never come back now, never be able to reveal herself to her or sit in her living room without a great deal of uncomfortable explaining. She searched Virginia's face for clues to the story she'd never get to hear—whether she'd had kids, whether her husband was still around, whether she'd had a happy life.

"Thank you," Eileen said when Virginia was finished.

"It's my pleasure."

"You have a beautiful house," she said. "A very beautiful house. I really can't help admiring it."

52

After they left his grandmother's apartment, they drove through the neighborhood, up Smith, along the Gowanus Expressway, and looped around to come down Court. When they hit Lorraine, they turned right and crept along.

He knew all the street names by now. This was the third weekend in a row his father had taken him to his old neighborhood to show him around. His father was trying to squeeze it in before he forgot what everything was.

They reached the Red Hook Pool. "This is where we swam when I was a boy," his father said. "It's hard to believe it's been so long. Everybody was naked and nobody realized it. It was great. We spent the whole day here and at the end we were like prunes. It's still being used today, you know."

Connell nodded politely; he was missing a Halloween party for this.

"Not today," his father said. "I know *that*. It's too cold today. Today in general."

His father stopped the car. There was an honest, open look on his face. Ugly thoughts flashed through Connell's mind.

Do you know, really? What do you know anymore? You never really were like a normal father in the first place, were you? You were always more of a dork than the others. You and your obsessively catalogued cassette and VCR tapes, your long-sleeved shirts in the summer, your never wearing shorts, your old movies, your corny jokes. You and your lab coats and sharpened pencils. You and your insistence on perfect grammar and enunciation. You and your spazzy sneakers, your sweat-stained baseball caps, your ear hairs. You and your never exceeding the speed limit by more than a couple of miles an hour. You and your beakers, your clipboards, your briefcase. You and your boring stories of the old neighborhood. I could break your heart right now if I wanted to, you big dork, you nerd, you spaz, you geek, you herb, you Poindexter.

Then his father faced the road again and they turned onto Columbia. They came to a derelict building with a long, faded sign that spelled KOHN-STAMM in capital letters. "This is what's left of the factory I worked at," his father said. Graffiti dotted its surface, and weather had worn off much of the paint, so that the ghostly outline of the words MANUFACTURING CHEMISTS could just barely be distinguished below the name. "There used to be so much manufacturing in this city. Now those jobs are gone. Factory work was a—how do I say it? It was an incubator for the middle class."

His father was having one of those extended moments of lucidity in which he could hold forth about some topic and it wouldn't seem like anything had happened to his mind. Connell always got a little charge of hope from them, a sense that some part of his father might be able to make it back from the other side of the creaky rope bridge.

"I wouldn't have gotten where I did if it weren't for a manufacturing job. We don't make anything in this country anymore."

"We make missiles," Connell said. "Movies. Hamburgers."

His father seemed not to have heard him. "I worked here at your age," he said. Then he looked at him searchingly. "No, a little older than you. In my early twenties. I keep thinking you're older than you are. You look so much like my brother Phil."

Connell turned the radio on, found WDRE. The beginning notes of "Smells Like Teen Spirit" were playing and he turned it up. He didn't even care if his father told him to turn it down, because in his mind he wasn't really there. Maybe he wasn't really there in his father's mind either.

need you to help me prepare for the tournament tomorrow."

"Okay."

"The resolution has to do with whether euthanasia is morally justified. I have to develop both a pro and a con argument. Do you know how this works?"

"I think so."

"I'm going to come at you with pro. I want you to be con. Then we can switch it up. I'll make my first affirmative. Then you do a cross-examination. We'll go from there. I'll talk you through it. Okay? Ready? My first contention is that euthanasia is justified because every human being has the supreme right of self-determination. We uphold an individual's right to determine where he lives, where he works. If we consider *those* rights to be sacred, then there is no more fundamental right a person can hold than when *he chooses* to die. Patients should have the right to maintain control over their own situations. By allowing people to make their own decisions, we preserve free choice and human dignity. Dad, you're supposed to be taking notes."

"I'm listening."

"You're supposed to take notes, so you can come at my contention and try to take it down. Here. Write down what I say. You're supposed to be scribbling fast. Come up with a counterargument. Try to find chinks in the armor of my argument. Challenge its underlying assumptions. You can argue that many people desirous of euthanasia who survive apparently terminal illnesses would wind up grateful they hadn't been euthanized. Hit me hard, Dad. I need to practice evading without seeming to. It needs to

look artless and artful at the same time. I need to stay calm and confident.
Try to goad me into saying something stupid and mean. Last week I was a
jerk, and even though I totally destroyed my opponent, the judge gave me
a twenty-four–twenty-three, which messed up my seeding in the octofi-
nals. Girls can be as aggressive as they want, which totally sucks. That Stuy
girl couldn't have been nastier, and she got a thirty–twenty-three. Then
again, if I were a better debater, I could be really nice and get points for
being so damned sweet. So that means practice, practice. I'm coming at
you, Dad. Anyway, you can say, 'It's unfeasible. It's impossible to put it into
practice equitably.' "

"It's unfeasible. It's impossible to . . . what was that?"

"Never mind. Listen, conversations about efficacy are banned. So
I say, 'My opponent is making a policy argument that has no place in
Lincoln-Douglas debate.' *Boo-yah!*"

"What? What happened?"

"I need to come up with some better hypotheticals. Something from
Plato, Jefferson. Those fluency whores at Stuy aren't going to eat my lunch
over a goddamned metaphor."

"What?"

"Nothing. Stuy is running Locke on aff. I want to be neg. I'm practically *begging* for neg. Let them play their strong hand. I'm taking that
girl down this week. I can taste it. My second contention: the 'social contract' argument. The individual sacrifices certain rights and liberties to live
under the protection of society. If an individual sacrifices the right to harm
other people in exchange for the protections of living in society, euthanasia
is justified because it is an act that has no harmful effects on others."

"I don't believe in euthanasia, son."

"This is why you should affirm the resolution that euthanasia is morally just."

"It's *not* just, son. It's not just or right at all."

"Dad! I'm talking to the judges. I can't look at you. Eye contact with
the judges is crucial. You need to rebut me. Make a 'slippery slope' argument. If we allow euthanasia, it creates a slippery slope where suicide
is justifiable. There would be rampant eugenics. Coerced euthanasia. It

would have a disproportionate racial and economic impact. People might be pressured to euthanize others for positive gain or else to avoid an economic hardship."

"Nobody is pressuring anyone to commit euthanasia. Not in this country."

"Say that it's not within the rights of the medical field to help patients die. Say that it's their responsibility to help them improve or at least continue life, no matter its quality. Because if you say that, then I can argue that many terminally ill patients suffer a great deal of pain and no longer wish to have their lives artificially prolonged."

"You lost me."

"My third contention is that at times of extreme pain for the patient, euthanasia is the most humane alternative."

"People get through pain."

"Argue that new and improved pain-relieving medicines are being discovered all the time. That the timeline for such decisions must be extended to reflect the speed of technological change."

"All I know is I don't believe in euthanasia."

"My opponent never responded to my third argument, so you should carry that through and affirm the resolution."

"What argument? Son, can we stop this? Can we just talk?"

"You want to know what's the best neg example you could have, Dad? *You* are. With your Alzheimer's. Think about it. If we euthanized people at will, maybe you would have been taken out already. For the good of the herd."

"Or maybe you would, son."

"That Stuy girl is going to wish I *had* gotten taken out when I run into her in the finals this week."

54

Early in the spring semester, Ed's chair, Stan Kovey, called her at work to let her know that they'd had several complaints from Ed's students, including, though he assured her it wasn't credible, an anonymous death threat.

"A *death threat*?"

"Not death," Stan said mildly. "I shouldn't have said death. Just injury."

"Well, isn't that a relief."

"I'm not calling so much about the threat," Stan said. "We've dealt with them before from disgruntled students. Some of these kids have learned not to trust institutions, due process, and the redress of injustices. What we need to discuss—"

"They were going to *beat* him *up*, Stan."

"More likely they were going to hire someone to do it," he said, an odd reasonableness in his voice.

"A hitman!"

"More like a thug," he said. "Ed would have gotten a warning first."

"The goddamned ingrates," she said. "The filthy, degenerate sons of bitches. He gave the best years of his life to these animals. They don't deserve him."

"They'll be disciplined," Stan assured her.

"They should be expelled," she said, and she wanted to continue, to say, *They should be tarred and feathered. They should be run through with swords. They should be brought before a firing squad.*

"They probably will be," Stan said. "Listen. This isn't about the threats, this is about Ed." He paused. "And his work."

Her heart was racing. It was the call she'd been fearing for a long time, and they still needed a year and a half to get to his thirty-year mark.

"Why are you calling *me*?" she said, thinking it safest to mask her anxiety as incredulity. "Wouldn't it be better to talk to him directly?"

"I've wanted to talk to Ed for a while, but he's stopped talking to anybody. He pops into the department office to check his mailbox and leaves immediately. He shuffles through the halls with his head down. I left a note in his box, but he's ignored it. I tried to stop him in the office to ask him to sit down, and he just brushed past me. I wanted to talk to him as a friend before I have to talk to him as his department chair. So I thought to call you."

"I appreciate that," she said, though she burned with resentment at the thought of this thoroughly average man, whom she'd hosted for dinner several times in Jackson Heights when he was a junior faculty member, claiming to speak as Ed's chair, when the only reason he held the position in the first place was that Ed had refused it.

"It seems," Stan said, "from what we've been able to reconstruct, that Ed was assigning the wrong grades to students. I saw the papers. Something was definitely going on. His fall grades were a mess."

She didn't know how the semester grades could have been a mess, because she'd supervised their tabulation. Maybe Ed had lost the sheet with the grades and had made a new one up at the last minute.

"I'm calling you," Stan said, "because, well, did you know anything about problems he was having? Did Ed say anything?"

She felt cornered. "No," she said. "I had no idea."

"I need to know, Eileen. We've been colleagues, Ed and I, for over ten years. You know that Ed's like family to me. What's going on with him?"

He might have thought himself a friend, but he was calling as the department chair. "He's had some headaches lately," she said instinctively. "Migraines. He's going in for a brain scan next week. They want to check for a tumor."

"A tumor? Jesus, Eileen. I'm so sorry."

"Thank you," she said. "We're hoping for the best."

After she hung up the phone, she called Jasper Tate. Jasper was Ed's protégé and partner on the grant research. His four-year-old daughter was Ed's goddaughter. She told Jasper about her conversation with Stan but left out the part about the brain tumor.

"You must be shaken up," he said.

"Can I trust you with something, Jasper? I mean, can I trust you not to speak to anyone about something?"

"Of course."

"Ed loves you like a son," she said.

"I feel the same way about him."

She left a long pause on the line. "He's got Alzheimer's."

"My God."

"We don't want anyone in the department to know."

"Okay."

"We want to keep him going a little longer. He wants to keep teaching."

"Of course."

"I lied to Stan."

"What about?"

"I told him Ed's being tested for a brain tumor."

Jasper chuckled warmly. She felt the compression in her chest lift.

"I don't mean to laugh," he said, trying to pull the gravity back into his voice. "It's just—Stan. He's so . . . *Stan.*"

"No," she said. "I needed that. This whole thing has been so unreal, so crazy."

"I can cover for him," Jasper said. "I'll help him prepare for class. I'll grade his things. His students can come to me for help."

She knew what Ed would say to Jasper's offer: *I can't do that to you, Tutey. You have important work to do.* She felt at times as if she was on a long trek and had lost her compass many miles back. She knew she should probably not involve this lovely man in the dissembling.

"Maybe you can help for a little while," she said.

"Yes. Great."

"Do me one favor," she said.

"Anything."

"Play dumb. Don't tell Ed we spoke. Just help him. He won't notice the difference. With the grading, yes, you may have to say something. Let him feel like he's doing you a favor. Maybe you want to compare the quality of work in different sections, I don't know. I don't need to explain Ed to you. So far as he knows, this conversation never happened."

A week later, she called Stan and told him they had ruled out a tumor but had no lead yet about what else might be causing Ed's sluggishness. She said she would get back to him as soon as she had a better sense of what was going on.

The next morning, she grabbed Ed as he was headed to work. "You leave there as soon as you're done teaching," she said. "You understand?"

He nodded.

"Don't get into conversations with anyone. Not your students, no one. Only Jasper Tate."

He nodded again.

"If you do find yourself in a conversation," she said, "under no circumstances are you to tell anyone that you've been diagnosed with Alzheimer's."

"What's Alzheimer's?" he asked, and she felt her spirit breaking, until she looked at him and saw the outline of an impish grin forming on his face.

"Don't you start with me," she said, but she was thinking, *Lord, don't let this part of his personality die just yet. If you need ideas for other parts to take away first, I can make a list.*

55

E d was already asleep when the phone rang. She'd been dreading the call for a month.

"Things have gotten worse," Stan said. "He's got to come out of the classroom. For his sake, for the students."

She put a pot of water on to try to calm herself down. The wind howled and rattled against the kitchen window.

"If you think that's best," she said. "What's the administrative protocol? Do you have some rubber room you'll put him in?"

"I was thinking he'd retire."

"He has no interest in retiring," she said. "He has fifteen years before he even thinks about retiring."

"He can't do the job anymore, Eileen."

"He has rights as a tenured professor. He's supposed to be given time to take corrective action, isn't he?"

"It would be good for the department if he retired."

She felt herself begin to shake, more in fear than in anger. She couldn't help wishing she could turn to Ed for advice; he was always clear-sighted at times like these. She knew it would be hell for him if she forced him to keep going to work. He would be in an adversarial relationship with his department; they would be looking for signs of incompetence.

"I don't give a damn about the department," she said. "He's given enough to the department. I'm interested in my husband." Her mind was working feverishly. Every passing second would erode her bargaining position. She tried to think like Ed. Ed would have worked out some algorithm in his deep subconscious to produce the right answer. He would have seen it from the beginning. "He could probably sit there for two years," she said. "That's how long the review process would take, especially for someone with as exemplary a record as Ed."

"Nobody wants to hurt Ed here," he said.

Then it came to her, as if Ed had whispered it in her ear: a palatable option for both sides that would forestall a protracted fight. His preoccupation with getting to work every day no matter what shape he was in, which she'd always found frustrating and even a little insane, would benefit her in the end. It would get him to thirty years.

"I'm not asking for a review process," she said. "He has over a year of sick days coming to him. Let him finish this year and then give him the sick days."

Stan called back the next day to say that Ed's colleagues had volunteered to fill in his classes for the remainder of the semester. The school would keep him on the payroll through the summer. The sick days wouldn't start counting down until the fall.

"I wanted to do that much for him," Stan said. "He won't have to teach. He won't have to come in at all."

"You say that like it's a good thing," she said. "Like you don't know how much he loves his job."

"Everyone knows how much he loves teaching."

She wanted to believe that, in his heart of hearts, he had never really loved teaching. That would bring them closer, somehow. She wanted to believe he'd pretended to love it, pretended to be patient in reviewing material endlessly with imbeciles, in order to get his students to respond positively and ultimately make a distasteful job easier on him. The truth, she knew, was that none of it had been a sacrifice. He'd been happier with his career than anyone she knew. It was she who had made sacrifices for his happiness.

"None of those kids will ever know how much he gave up," she told Stan.

· · ·

On February 13, 1993, Ed went to work for the last time. A week later, she went in with him to sign some HR paperwork and learned that she'd miscalculated. She'd been correct about the amount of unused sick time coming to him, but she hadn't understood that it wouldn't count toward his pension. By then it was too late to reverse course. She tried to call Stan about it, to feel him out about procuring Ed some kind of time credit, but she got nowhere. She signed off by telling him he was a jerk and slamming down the phone.

Ed would finish in June with twenty-nine years of service to the city instead of thirty, which meant he was due a lower percentage of his salary. And since he'd be retiring before the minimum retirement age, he'd see that number drop even farther. The fourteen hundred dollars a month or so he'd receive from Social Security disability would make up part of the difference, but they were going to have to adjust to new means.

Ed hadn't had a raise in four years, due to a budget freeze. There was rumored to be a raise coming in the next year or two that would have bumped him up to where he should have been all along. He'd never see the raise he'd already earned. He hadn't been holding on for just one raise, though. He'd been about to enter the period in his career in which he would make *real* money. He'd have taught until he was seventy or older, his salary rising every year.

He was also losing his grant from the government, which budgeted thirty thousand dollars a year for his efforts and was up for renewal for four more. The loss of the grant was the keenest blow for her. It was the surplus, the comfort fund, the dream of luxury, the symbol of his status.

As long as Ed was on the payroll, she'd be covered by his health insurance, but once the sick-day checks stopped coming and he started receiving his pension, that would cease.

When he'd chosen a benefits plan, a few years after they'd gotten married, he'd chosen the plan that would deliver them—and her, in his absence—the most after-tax money per month. The trade-off had been that this particular plan didn't confer health coverage on her in the event of his retirement or death. They'd made that decision with conviction, anticipating that she'd get health insurance in retirement through some job or other. They hadn't known then that something would keep her moving every few years: the promise of more responsibility; a better salary; a higher-up who took exception to a strong-willed woman; her inability to keep her mouth shut when she found something ethically questionable.

In order to retain health benefits, she was going to have to keep a full-time job, any full-time job. Thinking longer term, she was going to have to survive at NCB, or at another city hospital, for ten years if she wanted to qualify for the basic New York City pension and have health insurance in retirement. That wasn't going to be the easiest task at her age and pay scale.

She wished she and Ed had foreseen the health-coverage issues that would arise later, but who could predict the future to that degree? They'd thought he was staring at decades of work ahead. They'd bet on the bigger payout and lost. The cost to her was going to be that she would have to hold on to her job at a time when Ed needed her there most, to care for him.

If she lost her job before she'd been at it ten years, and had to buy insurance, there wouldn't be enough money to go around, because not only would she no longer have her salary, but now there would be insurance bills in addition to the mortgage payments, utility bills, food costs, Connell's tuition coming up in a couple of years (Ed had made her promise early after his diagnosis that she wouldn't let his illness stop Connell from going to the college he wanted to go to), and whatever nursing costs she'd eventually have to pay for Ed while she was at work (six hundred bucks a week at the going rate), not to mention the cost of putting him in a nursing home (four grand a month and going up), the idea of which she wasn't willing to entertain but which she knew was a possibility. And that was *if* she could buy anything like an affordable plan. The reality was that because of an episode of cellulitis that had caused one of her calves to balloon up to nearly twice its size a few months back, she might not be able to buy private insurance without spending every available dime on it—if she was insurable at all. And if she got sick without benefits, she'd be looking at losing everything. She'd worked her whole life and diligently socked away, from the age of fifteen on, 10 percent of every paycheck she'd ever gotten, and still her family's fortunes could be ruined overnight because the

American health care system—which she'd devoted her entire professional career to navigating humanely on behalf of patients in her care, and which was organized in such a way as to put maximum pressure on people who had the least energy to handle anything difficult—had rolled its stubborn boulder into her path.

56

For years, Connell had heard his father talk up how much he looked forward to teaching him to drive, but when he turned sixteen and got his learner's permit, he had to cajole his father into letting him behind the wheel. They drove through a whipping March wind to the parking lot in front of Macy's in the Cross County Shopping Center. His father got out, went around to Connell's side, and waved him to slide over.

His father sat calmly as Connell practiced accelerating, braking, turning, parking in a spot, and backing up. Once Connell worked up the nerve to venture from the lot onto the streets, though, his father looked terrified. As they approached the first intersection, he hit an imaginary brake. "Slow down!" he shouted.

"But it's green!" Connell shouted back, though he applied the brake anyway.

At the next light, Connell signaled, slowed, and turned left.

"Watch the building!" his father said, his leg pumping the floor.

He accelerated, and his father jumped back; he touched the brake, and his father gasped; he passed a car, and his father clutched the handle in the ceiling.

The next time they went out, his father screamed at him practically from the moment they pulled out of the garage until the moment they pulled back in. He then sat there miserably, apologizing, saying he couldn't help himself.

They went out a couple more times. The results were the same, and eventually Connell stopped asking to drive. He decided to wait until his junior year, when he could take driver's ed through school.

One night, at ten o'clock, his father appeared in the doorway of Connell's bedroom wearing his Members Only jacket.

"Come with me," he said.

"Where?"

"Just come with me."

His mother was drinking tea in the kitchen. His father headed past her to the basement.

"Where is he going?"

"I don't know," Connell said, and walked past her too.

His mother called down after them. His father didn't answer, so Connell didn't either. He followed him to the garage, climbed into the passenger seat. As they were backing out, his mother appeared in the doorway of the garage. His father didn't lower the window, and Connell just shrugged. She followed the car out into the driveway, a look of mild concern on her face. She had a teacup in one hand and her robe clutched in the other to ward off the chill of the spring night.

His father backed slowly down the driveway and his mother turned and headed back to the house. The driveway was curved and bordered on both sides by hedgerows anchored in stone walls that ended in stone columns. It was difficult to negotiate forward, never mind backward, and his father had scraped the car so many times that his mother had given up fixing it. His father took it slowly and made it onto the street without touching the hedge, the stone walls, or the pillars.

They didn't head down the hill toward town, but went the other way, taking back roads until they came to the entrance to the Cross County Parkway. They continued past it, turning under the overpass and taking the ramp up into the shopping center. The stores were all closed. His father pulled into a spot far from the entrance to Macy's and turned off the engine.

"You're going to drive."

They both got out and passed in front of the car. The lot was mostly dark, the lighted store signs combining with ambient light from the high-way and the low glow of the light poles to provide a mist of illumination. A few cars were scattered about, but otherwise the lot was empty. He had never driven under cover of night before. He knew the lot from his fledgling efforts behind the wheel, but there had never been so much open space, so little against which to establish a sense of perspective, and it was with a slight rush of breath that he turned the ignition over and put the car into gear.

"I want you to drive out of the lot, make a left and then a right at the light."

He drove up Midland Avenue, which ran parallel to the parkway.

"Go through the first light. After the following light, you're going to make a left to get on the Cross County East."

"I'm not allowed on the parkway."

"Do as I tell you," his father said calmly. There were no spastic jerks or fake pumps of the brake. Lately his father drifted in and out of being his old self, like a wraith passing through dimensions.

The light before the entrance to the parkway turned red as he approached it, and Connell checked to see that his belt was securely buckled. When the light turned green and he inched forward and made the left to merge, he felt like the car was running away from him.

"I want you to build up speed as you merge. We're going to head to the Hutch."

"The Hutch? What if I get pulled over?"

"Hutch north," his father said. "Get in the left lane. Don't be nervous. Just relax. There aren't many cars now. If you relax, you'll be a fine driver. Just get up to about fifty, fifty-five."

Connell pressed the accelerator. The speed was exhilarating, and he pressed it deeper, watching the needle climb to fifty, then sixty. He eased off. His father had his eyes closed.

"We have to get you used to real-world conditions," his father said. "Stay left. We're going to merge onto the Hutch north. I want you to look for signs for Mamaroneck Avenue, twenty-three north."

It felt like all the highways in the country could be reached from this one, that he could go anywhere from here. He wanted to drive through the night.

"It's coming up," his father said. "Twenty-three north. When you exit, you'll be on a ramp. As long as there's nobody behind you, when you get to the light at the end, I want you to slam on the brakes. Anything can happen at any moment, and you need to stay alert."

57

Before she could leave for work she had to get herself and Ed showered and dressed, fix breakfast, and cobble together a lunch and dinner for him.

She highlighted the start button on the microwave in pink magic marker. To the front of the microwave she taped an index card with an arrow pointing to "start" and a note that read "Press here." The last thing she did before she left was put the plate in the microwave for his lunch and then set the cook time. She waited until the last minute, because she was hounded by the thought of those dishes sitting out for hours and spoiling.

She spent all morning worrying about him screwing it up. He needed perfect accuracy to pull it off. If he hit any button other than start, he ended up gnawing on frozen manicotti or choking down cold beef stew. She came home to the time unchanged on the microwave, half the meal on the floor, a broken plate under the table, the *Times* intact in its sleeve. He had stopped reading.

The microwave routine could work only once a day. She left a plated, covered sandwich in the refrigerator for his dinner. He ate dinner early, before she got home, due to the sundowning. It would have been easier to prepare him two sandwiches, but there was something disgraceful in the idea of his eating more than one cold meal in her absence. Connell always came home too late to heat anything up for him.

She couldn't count on him to attend to a churning in the gut or notice the time on the cable box, so she called to remind him to eat and talked him through the steps.

In the morning she set the television to a channel that showed de-

pendable series in syndication in mini-marathons. It was easier to pick a
halfway-decent channel and make him stick to it than let him range off the
reservation. When he wasn't looking, she slipped the television remote and
the one for the cable box into the end-table drawer.

He made chaos out of everything he touched, but she continued to let
him handle the bills; it was a part of his masculine identity. Some bills he
paid twice, others he threw out without opening them. The phone company called to say they had five hundred dollars of her money and she
shouldn't send any more for a while. When the next bill came, she squir-
reled it away, but the following month he beat her to the mail and wrote
a check for the outstanding amount of their credit. They were almost a
thousand dollars in the clear.

She couldn't leave lists everywhere explaining how to do everything in
excruciating detail, because it wasn't clear how well he read anymore, and
anyway, where did helpfulness end and absurdity begin? Was she going to
lay out how to wipe his ass, how to aim his penis at the bowl? The easier
thing was to clean the piss off the floor when she got home from work.

When they walked into town together, he avoided the bank with phobic
deliberateness. He wouldn't even go in with her when she went to withdraw
money from the ATM. Maybe it was because he often heard her talking nervously about money, how it was a besieged resource in their household. She
knew it was hard for him to feel so out of control. He didn't realize that she
would have loved to continue ceding responsibility to him, that she would
have wanted nothing more in the world, but that had become impossible.

She decided to cancel the newspaper delivery and asked him to pick
it up from the newsstand in town. It gave him some dignity to have a task
to accomplish. He also picked up a quart of milk. She didn't always need
the milk, but routine made life easier; things got burned into his long-
term memory. Most of the time the milk made it into the refrigerator.
Sometimes it spoiled on the countertop. Connell ate cereal at all hours—it
seemed to be the only thing keeping him alive at times—so she seldom
had to dump it.

Ed also came home with a box of doughnuts every day. She didn't
know why he'd alighted on this fixation. She threw a lot away, but she also

ate her share. She'd been eating more lately in general. Stress was driving her to it. She'd gone up a couple of dress sizes in less than a year. Ed ate half a dozen doughnuts a day, but all he seemed to do was get skinnier.

When the summer came, they walked into town together on the weekends. She couldn't believe how many people he knew along the way. She learned that he liked to camp out on the bench up the block from the Food Emporium. It satisfied her to have been right in the end about the move. He would not have been able to live as freely in Jackson Heights.

She slipped money into his wallet when he was sleeping, as she'd done with her father after he'd retired, to keep him flush for his nighttime bar crawls. Most of the storekeepers knew him, which helped when he was at the register. He handed his wallet over and they fished out the right bills and put the change back in. She hoped they were patient with him. The guys at Gillard's were kind enough to simply keep a tally. Once a week, she stopped on the way home from work to settle his debts.

He liked going to Topps Bakery for coffee and a bun because they had a table and a chair. Diana, the proprietor, brought it over to him personally. "If you never paid," she told Eileen, "he'd still get it."

Once, he came home from the Food Emporium looking distraught.

"I don't think they gave me the right money," he said.

She checked his wallet. The amount there didn't match the change on the receipt.

"Did you stop anywhere else?"

He shook his head vehemently. The theft must have been obvious if he'd noticed it. Still, she didn't know if she could trust his perceptions. She could never be sure anymore if what he was saying conformed to reality.

"Let's go back," he said.

She considered the scene that might result, the whole store craning their necks, the mortifying attention, the lack of proof. Her voice would get shrill; she would need to find another place to shop.

"It's not worth it," she said. "We'll leave it alone. Don't worry, that kid will have bad luck after stealing from you."

Then she imagined the kid's sniveling, triumphal expression, and she worked herself up into such a pique that she put Ed in the car and drove him back to the store. Ed peered into the plate-glass window, hands and nose pressed like a child.

"That's him," he said, pointing.

She stood staring in at the kid. He was black, and he wore his shirt untucked in the back. He moved gracefully, economically, his quick hands passing items across the scanner from the logjam at the end of the conveyor belt. He looked like someone used to moving faster than others, escaping undetected. He had probably had Ed in his aisle a few times. Maybe Ed had handed him his wallet and asked him to take the money out. Maybe this was the time the kid had taken advantage. Her blood pumped hard; there was a metallic taste in her mouth.

"Sit on that bench," she said to Ed.

She went inside. The crisp, air-conditioned air in the store clashed with the muggy thickness of the August evening outside, and the shiver that overtook her inflamed her anger even further. She thought of going directly up to the kid's aisle, but she didn't want to appear hysterical; better to get the drop on him. She walked as casually as she could to the dairy aisle, where she picked up some eggs. When she got to the kid's register, the man in front of her was paying. She plucked a pack of gum off the rack and set it on top of the eggs. She held up a crisp twenty.

"I want all the change," she said as quietly as she could while still conveying the extent of her displeasure. "*All* of it. And I will have your job if you ever do that to my husband again. And if you think you can come into this town from wherever the hell you come from and steal from people, you're mistaken. I will have the police on you."

The kid gave the wad of gum in his mouth a few slow, aggressive chews as he slid the bills into his hand, gathered the coins, and snapped the receipt off the roll.

"I don't know what you're talking about," he said, handing them over and looking past her to the next customer, whose things he started to scan. She made a show of counting the change in front of the kid. She caught a glimpse of the customer behind her and resented the look he was giving her, which suggested it was she who was in the wrong.

She didn't move, though. She felt like she was just getting started.

"I hope you live long enough to feel the shame you made him feel," she said. "I hope you are a haunted, lonely old man someday. I hope you are sitting in a nursing home somewhere wondering where everyone is."

He told her he went to church between Masses, when the doors were left open, and sat in the back. "It's quiet," he said. "Calm."

She thought about all the tangled noise in his brain. What did it sound like in there? She imagined it to be like the static on a radio tuned between stations.

"What do you think about?" she asked.

"You," he said. "Connell. I don't want things to be hard for you when I'm gone, and I don't want him to get this. I'd do anything to avoid that."

The thought of Ed alone in that big church oppressed her.

"If I write a prayer for you, will you use it?"

"Sure," he said.

He might have been telling the truth.

"Dear God," she wrote, "I will offer this up to you without complaint, but please protect all I know and love." She copied it out neatly onto an index card that she folded and put in his wallet.

She never heard Ed ask, "Why me?" but she couldn't help asking it for him. Why Ed? Why now? Why so young? There was the obvious answer— it was random, senseless, genetic, environmental—but she didn't like that one. She also knew she couldn't sign on to any system that said it had all happened for a reason. So she took a third path, the pragmatic one. It hadn't happened for a reason, but they would find something to glean from it anyway. There didn't have to be a divine plan for there to be meaning in life. *People's lives will be better because of his illness*, she told herself. *They'll appreciate life more. He'll remind them that their lives are better than they think.* It was as good a story as any, and it had the virtue of often seeming plausible, though never when she lay awake at night, when the public life faded away, and other people vanished, and she was left staring at the back of her hand and thinking, *All of this is an illusion, even the consolations.* She was taken back to her bed when she was a child, when she would lie awake listening to her parents in the living room rehearsing their fixed roles after her father had returned from the bar, and she thought, *No time has passed since then. I'm there right now.* She remembered examining her hand then as well, and the only thing to differentiate this moment from any of a hundred in the past—the only thing that reassured her that the loop of her life wasn't about to start over again—was the crenellated landscape of wrinkles around her knuckles, which she ran her fingers over, feeling their washboard knobbiness.

58

They were staying home on New Year's Eve for the first time in the twenty-eight years since they'd met. Last year all they'd done was drive to the McGuires' to watch the Times Square telecast, but at least they'd left the house. This year she couldn't face all the work involved in getting him out. She knew she'd spend the whole night minding him and wouldn't have any fun.

New Year's, being the anniversary of the night they met, meant extra to them. When they lived in Jackson Heights, they'd go to balls, Ed in a tux, she in a shimmering gown with pearls. She'd rush around in her slip, blow-drying her hair and applying makeup, and come up short when she saw Ed wrapped in a towel, staring into the mirror as he shaved. They'd leave Connell with Brenda Orlando and come back very late. She'd be contentedly exhausted the next morning as she got the three of them out to Mass.

She sat at the kitchen table in her housecoat and slippers, her hair pulled back in a plastic clip. Connell sat across from her, reading the sports pages.

"What are you doing for New Year's?"

"Going to a party with Cecilia."

"Where is it?"

"Somewhere in White Plains. I don't know."

"How were you planning to get there?"

"I thought I'd take Dad's car."

"Have you asked him yet?"

"I didn't think I had to. I thought you were staying home."

Something in his tone irked her. "We were," she said. "But I've changed my mind. I think I'd like us to go out as a family."

"I have plans."

"The three of us are going to go to dinner. You can go out after that."

"I'm supposed to eat with Cecilia and her parents before the party."

"You'll simply call her and tell her you'll see her later."

"Whatever. Fine."

Connell left the room in a huff. She called to Ed in the den and told him to go shower. She went up and laid out a sports coat, dress shirt, tie, and neatly pressed pair of pants for him. She put on an evening gown and zipped the plastic sheath off her mink.

It was snowing out. The Caprice was in the driveway, blocking her car in the garage. Ed headed for the driver's side door. She pulled on his arm.

"You have your car key?" she asked Connell.

"Yes."

"You drive. Your father and I are tired."

There was no way she was letting Ed drive in this weather. Even when it was perfect out, lately he gave her a heart attack any time he was behind the wheel. Backing out of the driveway once, he'd hit the stone wall, torn off the side-view mirror, and dragged an ugly streak down the length of the car. Outside church, he'd have run over an old lady in the crosswalk if Eileen hadn't shouted and thrown her arm across his chest. She'd been trying to think of a way to take his car away from him without turning him against her. She didn't want to be the one to tell him that that part of his life was over. She couldn't just take away his keys or sell the car, but she couldn't just let him crash it either. Someone could end up dead. *Ed* could end up dead. She would have to figure something out soon.

Connell hopped in. Ed got in the shotgun seat, she in the back. She watched him fumble with the belt buckle until Connell reached over and snapped it in.

Connell turned to her. "Where are we going?"

"Surprise us. Take us to the city. Someplace you like to go."

"You wouldn't like the places I go," he said. "Diners. Pizzeria Uno. I went to the Hard Rock Café once. Ed Debevic's. You'd hate that place."

"Just drive. I'll tell you where."

The snow was heavier than she'd expected. The roads had iced over. Connell drove carefully, gripping the wheel with both hands. At one point he slid a couple of car lengths and stopped just before he hit a hedge-row-lined stone wall.

"We'd better not risk it," he said. "We can go out in the neighborhood. The Tap. Town Tavern."

"Keep driving," she said. "You'll be fine."

"Tumbledown Dick's."

"We're going downtown," she said firmly.

"Buckle up, please," he said.

She saw him glancing in the rearview mirror. "You just worry about the road," she said. When he looked away, she fastened the buckle.

He crawled for another block before he lost control of the Caprice again. They slid a good distance and bounced, hard, off a BMW parked in the street.

The seat belt was squeezing her ribs; she got it unbuckled. Adrenaline made her feel as if she'd touched an electric outlet. "Everyone all right?" Ed looked shocked, but he wasn't hurt. Connell was fine. So was she.

When she got out, she saw the other car's rear end had been demolished, along with most of the front of the Caprice.

"Shit, shit, shit," Connell said.

"Watch that low-class language," she snarled, and then she softened her tone. "Oh, hell. 'Shit' is right."

She picked her way carefully around the car, holding on as she walked from passenger-side door to the front fender, which was smashed into the wheel well. The frame on the chassis had buckled where it met the door. Ed sat shivering in the car, his hand fishing for the door handle.

"I knew I shouldn't have driven," Connell said.

"It's not going to open, Ed!" she yelled, and shook her head at him. She turned to Connell. "Do you think it's drivable?"

"It looks pretty bad," he said. The right front wheel was bent sideways as if kneeling toward the snowy ground. Connell scratched his ear. "I don't know how the wheel got so bent. I wasn't going fast."

"I'd say it's done, wouldn't you? A car this old?"

"Probably."

"Go up there, tell them what happened. Ask them to call the police." She pointed toward a house, atop a mound and recessed from the street, that looked like a mansion.

She slid into the driver's seat and reached across Ed—who was slapping at the top of his head with the grim determination of a mortifier of the flesh—into the glove compartment. She pulled out the envelope they'd used for years. It said "Insurance and Registration" in Ed's old handwriting. It was hard to imagine the man who now communicated in thunderous block letters writing in this fluent script.

She watched Connell disappear with the paperwork up the sloping stairs and started the car. The light from the one working headlamp diffused into the snow and reflected off the mangled BMW. She blasted the heat. When Ed reached to turn it off—it had to be unconscious, the force of habit, because no one, not even him, could be *that* absurd—she smacked his hand away and turned it up again.

She and the boy stood in the snow waiting for the tow truck to arrive. Ed was in the car.

"What a disaster," Connell said. "This is going to be expensive."

She'd fought endlessly with Ed over keeping collision on the Caprice. Time and again she'd said it was a waste of money on a ten-year-old car, but Ed had insisted.

"Maybe not as expensive as it looks. Anyway, that's what insurance is for."

"I'm sorry, Mom."

"Nobody got hurt," she said. "Nobody died. Cars can be replaced." *Or not*, she thought. She felt a hint of a smile cross her lips but stifled it. "Well," she said under her breath. "That's one way to get rid of a car."

"What'd you say?"

"I said, 'That's one way to ring in the New Year.'"

"Happy New Year," he said glumly.

"Happy New Year."

• • •

The AAA guy offered to drop them off at home before taking the car in. She sat on Ed's lap in the seat, Connell between them and the driver.

When they pulled into the driveway, Connell asked the driver if he'd mind giving him a lift to the train.

She was flabbergasted. "You're not still planning on going out?" He must have known that once inside, he wouldn't be able to leave. The driver and Connell both looked to her for approval. "Go," she said, annoyed, waving him off.

She climbed off Ed and helped him out of the truck. The snow was now a few inches thick. She held his hand as he navigated the fluffy terrain. She punched in the code for the garage door and watched the truck pull out.

Upstairs, she took off her string of pearls and changed out of her evening gown into a sweat suit. She got him ready for bed, in case he wanted to go up early.

She pulled a half gallon of ice cream out of the freezer and took two spoons from the drawer, though the second spoon was a fig leaf for her own guilt. Ed would have two spoonfuls, tops.

They sat through the lip-synched entertainment, waiting for the countdown. Ed fell asleep with his head back and his mouth open, hours before the New Year. She didn't wake him.

As midnight approached, she thought of the night they'd met, the way he'd leaned in to kiss her when the hour struck. She'd been waiting for him to do it all night. They'd been in the middle of the dance floor, surrounded by hundreds of couples. When he kissed her, she experienced a sensation she'd heard described a thousand times but always dismissed as malarkey: that everyone around had disappeared, and it was just the two of them. And now it really was just the two of them, and everyone had more or less disappeared. The ball made its languorous drop; "1994" lighted up onscreen. She tried to remember what it had felt like to kiss him that first time. All she could remember was that he had begun simply, almost politely, and then he had taken her face in his two hands and kissed her with a sudden intensity, as if he had been waiting to do so for longer than the few hours he had known her. She knew right away that she would marry him.

So many years had passed since that night that it was almost a different man she was looking at now. Hairs poked up over the neckband of his undershirt. His chest rose and fell weakly, as if he were not really breathing. She leaned over him, touched her lips to his. His eyes were closed now, as hers had been that night. She was afraid he'd startle awake and scream, or throw her off him, but he just started to kiss her in his sleep.

The Caprice was declared a total loss. She took the insurance payout and added it to their checking account.

Maybe, she thought, she should use the money for a new car for herself. She was tired of buying American cars. Maybe she'd buy herself a sporty two-door BMW like the one Connell had crashed into, or one of those E-Class Mercedes that looked perfectly enameled and invincible. She wouldn't have to cringe at the paint peeling from the roof, the felt bagging around the center light in the ceiling, the rusty creak and thunderclap of the door closing. She could get a car she wouldn't be ashamed to park in the church lot.

The boy could be expensive, but there were times he returned something on the investment.

59

People came from all over for the funeral for Ed's mother. It was the first time Eileen had seen Fiona leave Staten Island since the surprise party for Ed. Phil and Linda flew in from Toronto. Having Phil around seemed to add to Ed's grief, not diminish it. It was as if Ed had finally realized that all the years they'd spent in different countries couldn't be gotten back. The night before the funeral they'd sat at the kitchen table together for hours, Phil talking and Ed listening. Every time she went in there, Ed was crying big, unrestrained tears.

Cora had been a force in the parish, St. Mary's Star of the Sea in Carroll Gardens, and so the church was packed with a lot of people Eileen had never met. Ed didn't seem any more at home than she felt in his childhood church. His face was so red during the services that she kept reminding him to breathe. Cora had been ill for a while, and she'd had a good, long life, but it looked as if it had never occurred to Ed that his mother would actually die.

Eileen had always thought of Ed's conscientious presence at his mother's apartment, his willingness to go and change a bulb for her or pick her up groceries, as the fealty of a dutiful son, but the way he was responding to her death suggested a depth of feeling for her that Eileen hadn't imagined. It might have had something to do with his condition. He was a step closer to death than an average person.

Afterward, as everyone hurried to their cars—it was a frigid day in February—her aunt Margie asked Ed for directions to the cemetery.

"Well," he said, standing in front of the church, "where are you parked?"

"Around the corner."

"Okay," he said. "Okay." He was kneading his hands together as if they might release an answer. "You need to take the highway."

"Which one?"

"The highway around here. God, what's the name of it?"

"You mean the BQE?"

"Yes! That's it."

"Where can I pick it up?"

They were a block away from the building Ed had grown up in. He might have driven a few thousand times to the BQE from where they were standing.

"It's not far," he said. "It's only a few blocks."

She cut Ed off and gave Margie the directions. She waited until Margie was out of earshot.

"You don't know where the BQE is?"

"Of course I do," he said. "It's right around here."

She looked at Connell huddling by the car waiting to go, then back at Ed, and she was overcome by the difference in age between father and son. Ed looked more like a contemporary of his mother's than a husband to her. His shoulders hunched forward and his face was scored with new wrinkles, as if the trauma of his mother's dying had aged him. She knew she would have to play nursemaid to him eventually, but she wanted to hold that off as long as possible.

That night, although they were in mourning, and although Phil and Linda were in the guest bedroom, Eileen got on top of Ed, leaning close to him as she moved back and forth. Afterward, she lay wondering how long he'd be able to perform in bed. The thought of the loss of consort kept her awake most of the night, and it was only toward morning that she realized it wasn't the idea of physical loneliness that had been bothering her but an incipient awareness that she herself was going to die someday.

She kept a log of the first times he failed to do things. It was like a diary of a child's development in reverse. Certain failures correctly augured great changes in his mental powers. Others were false alarms, momentary hiccups.

02/19/94: Couldn't find the BQE after Cora's funeral. Losing his sense of direction.

At Karen Coakley's wedding, she turned her back on Ed to get a plate of hors d'oeuvres. When she next spotted him, he had joined a group arranged along the far wall for a picture with the official photographer. It was the groom's family, and she didn't recognize any of them, and yet Ed was smiling gamely among their number, as if he'd watched them all grow up. He was ruining the photo by his presence. When the photographer was finished, she whisked him away with a quick, pitiless jerk, hoping no one had noticed him, though there was nothing she could do about Karen and her husband seeing him there when they examined the matte prints.

A provocative beauty emerged from the group, looking flustered. "I got felt up," Eileen heard her say indignantly. "This man put his hand on my ass."

"Who?" the boyfriend asked. "Point him out."

The girl motioned in Ed's direction. The boyfriend, packed like a sausage into his suit, started punching his palm in a manner both absurdly unoriginal and genuinely frightening. Eileen shifted instinctively in front of Ed, holding up her hand to halt their advance like a crossing guard protecting a child.

"It's not what you think," she said as calmly as she could. "It's not what you think at all."

04/16/94: Grab-ass at Karen's wedding. Be there when he meets people. Stay by his side at parties. That time he held onto Susan's breast when saying good-bye? No accident.

They were invited to a party in Chelsea at the home of the chief of staff. They parked several blocks away and walked, soaking up the energy of a Manhattan evening. Ed had on a beautiful suit, she an expensive dress she'd bought a year ago and hadn't had occasion to put on. She was enjoying wearing it. It fit a little snugly, with all the stress she'd been under lately, but it still framed her shape nicely.

She didn't notice until she was a few paces ahead of him that Ed had fallen back like a recalcitrant dog on a walk.

"What is it?" She went back and tried to pull him along. "What's going on?"

"You go without me."

"This is absurd," she said. "We're a block away."

"I've never met these people."

"So what? They're nice people."

He shook his head.

"You're *going*, Ed. I RSVP'd. I can't mess around here. This guy, the chief of staff, he didn't bring me in. He's younger. I need to make a good showing tonight. I need you to rise to the occasion. Okay? I need to make it to ten years."

"They'll never know the real me," he said.

It hadn't occurred to her that Ed might think this way, but then they hadn't spent much time around people who didn't know him before.

"Half of you is better than ninety percent of people with a whole brain," she said, and was surprised to find she believed it. "Even now, you're funnier and smarter than most of those people in that room will be. Don't forget who you are. Stick by me and they won't notice a thing."

He was at her elbow all night and no one was the wiser. The good thing about parties was that no conversation had to go that deep. If Ed didn't answer a question right away, it fell back to the questioner. He only seemed more interesting the more time he took to answer. She held the plate and gave him only one-bite morsels. The dim lighting, the noise, and the crowd all helped. In his suit, Ed cut a dashing figure. He gave her an advantage with the chief, who talked with him for a long time about the research he'd done.

When they reached the street on departure, Ed was shaking so much that he could have been having a seizure. She saw that he must have exerted superhuman will to keep it together for her.

For several days, he seemed drained, and not long after, his conversation began to suffer.

05/20/94: Slurred speech after Chelsea shindig.

A few months after Frank had his stroke, they met Ruth and Frank at the Metropolitan Museum. Frank was in a wheelchair.

They'd only been there a few minutes when Ruth insisted she needed a break from her husband. Eileen understood; Ruth had Frank to herself round-the-clock now. They told Ed and Frank to wait at a bench and slipped away to a costume exhibit. Even though she was thoroughly utilitarian in her attire—a powder-blue cardigan was an extravagance for her—Ruth performed delighted astonishment at the beauty of the elaborate dresses. Eileen's gaze lingered on the cascading folds of finger-thick fabric, which seemed almost big enough for a person to hide away in.

When they returned to the bench, their husbands were gone. Eileen felt panicked, but a hunch led her to the main gallery, where she saw Ed standing, hands on the wheelchair handles, in front of his favorite painting, David's *Death of Socrates*. Between him and Frank they barely had a whole working body.

She and Ruth walked up silently behind them.

"This one in the middle is Socrates," Ed was saying. Eileen and Ruth looked at each other. "And this man with his hand on his knee. I forget his name." She wanted to say "Crito," as she'd heard him say before, but she kept quiet. "And the man at the end. I forget his name too." *Plato*, she thought. "You know the story?" Frank was nodding along. "They're making him take the cup." Frank's head was nodding like a piston. "They're afraid of the influence he's had on people." She was amazed at how much of this he remembered. Ed wheeled Frank closer to the painting, and she felt the guard's eyes on them.

"Look at his finger pointing up," Ed said. "He's saying, 'I know there's more after this.' The cup is filled with . . . with . . ." Ed grappled for the word. Frank started to say it but couldn't get it out. He stammered a couple of syllables.

"Hemlock," Ruth said tersely, but not without emotion, as she took the handles of Frank's wheelchair and began the march out of the room.

6/11/94: Went to Met. Ed forgot Crito, Plato, hemlock.

He was haunting her in the kitchen. She could tell he wanted to feel useful. She told him to chop a turnip. She had her back to him cooking and heard a lot of noise. When she turned he had lodged half the turnip on the knife and was banging both of them, turnip and knife together, on the cutting board. Connell, who had been sitting at the table looking through philosophy books for quotes for the upcoming debate season, leaped up and seized the knife.

"Give me that!" he said. "Jesus! What the hell are you doing?"

She pulled Connell into the dining room. "I will smack your face," she said, "if I ever see you talk to your father like that again. I don't care how old you are."

Ed sulked in front of the television until he went up to bed —at three thirty in the afternoon.

08/03/94: Bedtime today broke the 4:00 barrier.

60

His father stood bowlegged before the coffee machine, looking at once like a baby with a load in his pants and an old gunslinger who had walked through the desert and been struck by lightning. He was wearing a tie but it was backwards, the thin part in front of the thick part.

He shook the filter out what seemed like a hundred times, smoothed it against the swing-hinged filter holder, righting and rerighting with animal vigor what was already in place. Connell watched uneasily. His father worked as though everything depended on this, looking the way he used to look when sanding edges or sawing boards. He'd crumpled the filter, so it didn't fit properly. Connell took a new one out of the box and put it in. He took the tie off him and retied it on himself while his father laughed meekly and looked at the floor.

When his mother came home, Connell went down to the car to help with the groceries, his father following closely behind. He could see his mother evaluating the bags she handed to his father. She made sure he only had cans, lunchmeats, and boxes, nothing that would roll too far away or break.

His mother pulled out a box of Ritz and opened it before the bags were even unpacked.

Connell tore open a bag of potato chips. "I can't stop eating lately," he said to his mother. Both their mouths were full.

"Don't catch my disease," his mother said. "I eat to fill the void."

It occurred to Connell that the void was the house itself. It was too big, too empty; he could imagine eating himself into obesity in it.

• • •

He needed to go far away for college. The farther he went, the harder it would be to come back. The cost of plane tickets would be too high to make flying home a regular possibility.

He went through the list of colleges he and his mother had come up with together: Harvard, Yale, Princeton, Columbia, Penn, Williams, Amherst, Johns Hopkins, and Georgetown, along with a couple of local safeties, Drew and Fordham. Every school on the list was less than five hours away. He decided he wouldn't apply to any of them except the safeties. He made a new list: Chicago, Northwestern, Notre Dame, Stanford, Rice. Nothing small or that she hadn't heard of or whose virtues he'd have to explain. Nothing, in short, that she wouldn't pay for. He was going to force her hand. She'd never let him go to either of the safeties if he got into one of the better, farther-flung schools, even if the safety gave him scholarship money, which there was a chance they would: he had the grades, the SAT scores, and he had finished third in the state in Lincoln-Douglas debate. She would rather pay full freight and put a Notre Dame sticker on the car. She had explained how she was going to pay for his schooling: something about borrowing against the equity they had in the house and taking out private loans. All he knew was she'd told him she was going to make it so that he wouldn't have to worry about paying the loans back. And if it didn't work out, he would put the Drew sticker on the car himself—because what right did she have to be disappointed in him for going to Drew, when she'd only gone to St. John's?

He felt like he could see the whole world, clearly, all at once. He was going to leave everything behind. He was about to be born again, but this time complete with all the defenses he would ever need. He would invent the world as he went along. He would pass through a thousand years in the blink of an eye.

61

Connell ran to catch the last train out of Grand Central, the one-thirty, but it was pulling out as he arrived at the platform. He sighed and kicked the big metal newspaper recycling bin. He had already seen that when you lived in the suburbs and you missed the last train, you entered a netherworld, a night town. It was going to be a long time until the five-thirty train.

He decided not to call to say he'd missed the train, even though his mother had told him to call no matter how late if he wasn't coming home, because he felt too guilty to hear her voice. He had left that morning and hadn't checked in all day. There wasn't room in his mother's overtaxed mind for her to enforce curfews and restrictions. She just counted on him not to get into trouble. He kept up his end of the deal, but he knew she wished he were around more. She had grown accustomed to his coming home late, but she hadn't stopped feeling hurt by it. When he came in at half past two, after walking a silent path from the station, he sometimes heard her call to him quietly as he passed his parents' room at the top of the stairs. Lately, though, she had learned to sleep through the night. Tonight he was going to take his chances that he'd get in before she awoke in the morning. It was easier to avoid conflict of any sort.

He walked across Forty-Second to the B, to head down to West Fourth. A girl he'd briefly dated had told him about a place on West Tenth called Smalls, where she'd stayed literally all night once. They let underaged kids stay as long as they didn't try to order alcohol. It was a jazz club. He didn't know anything about jazz, but it was better than sitting in a diner and having to fight to stay at a table.

He handed over the cover charge. The place wasn't full. He sat at an empty table near the stage, under the lights, and ordered a Coke. The set was a mellow trumpet backed by drums, a piano, and a sax.

Faces in the crowd smiled warmly at him. The waitress didn't seem to mind that he wasn't running up a bigger tab. When the trumpeter finished blowing a solo, the audience drizzled him with applause—a comforting pitter-patter, like a summer shower glancing off an air conditioner.

The crowd could have been anyone. He decided they were important people, decision makers. He imagined they were pleased to see a young person in their midst—that they endowed him in their minds with maturity and grace. He tried to look as keen as he could, though he didn't understand the music. He performed the arousal of a true aficionado, twisting his face in agonized appreciation of a long-held note.

As the set wound down, the crowd dwindled. The performers seemed to relax. They nodded to people seated near him, spoke to a few. They took more time between numbers. He sensed that a different jazz was being cooked up, one that needed to marinate longer.

As four o'clock approached, people spread out on banquettes behind him. The players on the stage changed. His Coke glass kept getting refilled. The night felt full of possibility. Time was on his side; he could be anything he wanted.

His family, asleep at home, seemed a world away. He was ready to commit himself to the strivers, the lovers of life—these would be his new guides.

At five, the waitress began bringing out some trays of food. She left them on a long table by the front entrance. He watched a couple of people head over to them.

"Is this for us?" he asked the waitress.

"It's for whoever."

He'd never seen anything like it. First they let him stay all night. Now they were feeding him breakfast. It wasn't anything special, but it was so strange and unexpected that it felt like a feast to him.

He piled his plate with rolls and butter, spooned out some eggs, and filled his cup with orange juice, looking forward to the little ritual of ceding his place in line, the brief exchange of shared enthusiasm, but the guy behind him just grabbed a roll and sat back down, and no one else followed. Connell hovered awkwardly, pretending to contemplate the spread, until he got self-conscious and walked back to his seat with his head down and ate a lonely meal.

When he walked in at seven, his mother was asleep at the kitchen table. Tins were piled up on the island; powdered sugar dotted the floor. He and his mother were supposed to have made Christmas cookies together that night. It was a little tradition they had. He'd gone out with his friends in the afternoon and never come home, so he'd forgotten all about it.

He counted the tins; she'd made as many as always. He lifted the wax paper in one and saw some cookies missing sprinkles, some misshapen ones.

She was hunched over the table, her head in her folded arms, looking as if her back would ache in the morning.

He shook her lightly. "Ma," he said. "Go upstairs. Go to bed."

It took a moment to rouse her. She rose slowly and began to head for the stairs. She stopped in the doorway, turned.

"I will never wait up for you again," she said calmly, and his heart stopped for a moment. "I will never worry when you don't call. I will never again worry about you. I promise. You are free."

Connell drifted into his parents' bathroom, the smell of Swedish meatballs giving way to lavender soap. It was Christmas Eve. The radio in the bedroom was tuned to the same Christmas station as the radio downstairs, as though his mother couldn't be away from "Rockin' Around the Christmas Tree" for long enough to change her clothes.

His father had applied the shaving cream in a grotesquely liberal dose. He picked up a blue plastic razor, one of those bulk-pack, single-blade jobs he insisted on using and with which even a dexterous man could injure himself. Connell watched him raise the torture implement to his face and begin to make groping stabs at his jaw. He had to leave before the carnage began.

He went downstairs. His mother was checking on the turkey in the oven.

"Your father has informed me that he doesn't like Christmas, that he never has, that I go overboard, that things are out of control." She doused the bird with a baster and the juice that escaped from the tray sizzled on the bottom of the oven in loud hisses. "Do things seem out of control to you?"

All around were trays of prepared foods, folded napkins, polished silver, washed crystal, proliferating decorations, cookies she'd baked alone, scores of gifts she'd bought and wrapped herself.

"Not on your end," he said.

"I try to preserve niceties like Christmas because it's going to be hard no matter what I do or don't do. The mind needs to be tricked sometimes."

He had no idea how she withstood the deluge of inanity that flowed from his father. Connell couldn't even be in the same room with him. He brutalized her, and when you confronted him on it he denied it like a scheming boy. He wanted her ready to attend him at a moment's notice, yet he showed no sign of gratitude.

When his father came downstairs, bloody bits of tissue clung to his face like a swarm of exploded mosquitoes.

"You should use another razor," Connell said. "The ones you use are cutting up your face."

"There's nothing wrong with my razor," his father said.

"You should try the Mach Three."

"Mine are perfectly fine," his father said through gritted teeth, kneading his hands angrily.

"Or maybe an electric razor."

"Why is everybody picking on me?"

"No one's picking on you," Connell's mother said. "He's trying to help you."

"I don't need any help. I do fine by myself."

"You use too much cream," Connell said.

"Goddamned ingrate!"

"Edmund!"

His mother followed Connell into his bedroom. "You should just love your father," she said.

"I do," Connell said. "I know."

"These fights you're having now—they won't mean anything in twenty years."

Connell cut her off. "And whatever I have to put up with is less than anything you had to put up with, I know."

His mother seemed to be considering what he'd said. He couldn't remember the last time she waited before reacting to him. It made him feel worse than when she just blew up.

"You need to think long and hard about what kind of person you want to be. That's all I'll say. Did you get your father anything for Christmas?"

Connell looked away.

"Here," she said, and went to her pocketbook. She handed him a pair of twenties.

"What's this for?"

"Go to the mall," she said. "Get him an electric razor if you care about his face so much."

On Christmas morning, after he'd given him the razor, Connell heard his father shaving with it. His father came down holding a Bic in his hands.

"This time, as it happens," his father said, "I didn't cut myself."

"Good," Connell said. "How do you like the electric razor?"

"I didn't use it."

"I heard it going."

"You heard nothing of the sort," his father said indignantly.

"I *heard* it."

"You don't know what you're talking about." He jabbed the Bic in Connell's direction. "This is what I used."

"No way. I heard it."

His mother sighed, then abruptly snapped, "Would you leave your father alone?"

"Fine, fine." Connell got ice from the freezer. "No, you know what? That's bullshit."

"Watch it!" his mother said.

"I *heard* it. Why won't he admit it? Why won't you admit it, Dad? It's stupid."

"I used the Bic."

"You didn't!"

"I used it like this." His father put the razor up to his face and started digging at his dry cheeks. He winced, kept going. "Like this."

"Stop!" Connell's mother screamed. "Stop, stop!"

Connell went to take it from his hand. A dewdrop of blood clung to his father's chin. His father shifted and lunged the razor at him. Connell reared his head back.

"Ed!" his mother screamed.

"Okay!" Connell said. "You used the Bic!" He tried to wrest it from his father, but his father dropped it and grabbed him by the wrist, twisting it.

"I did use it."

Connell was in pain. "Will you use the other one for me, Dad? Because it's Christmas. I got it for you for Christmas."

"Sure." His father released his grip. "What other one?"

"The razor I got you."

"I used it already," his father said, smiling. "Works like a charm."

Connell eyed the razor on the floor. It looked like a piece of bloody evidence. His wrist throbbed. He thought of picking the razor up and holding it at his father himself.

"I'm glad you like it," he said quietly.

"It's a great gift," his father said, rubbing his chin and looking curiously at the blood on his palm. "A great gift. You're a good kid."

Connell saw his mother's face twist up as she turned to the dishwasher. She seemed to be fighting back tears.

"Now can we please have a nice Christmas, please?" she asked. "Can we all forget everything and have a nice Christmas?"

62

In the middle of a Valentine's Day commercial, his father stood and went out without his jacket. He was halfway down the driveway when Connell caught up to him.

"Where are you going?"

"It's Val, it's Valen, Valtine's. I'm going to get a Valen-en-tine's card for Mom."

"We can go when Mom gets home with the car. It's freezing."

His father turned and headed down the street. Connell called after him, then ran inside, grabbed their coats, and caught up with him. His father was shivering as he walked with purpose. Connell could barely stop him long enough to get the coat on him.

"I'll go with you," he said. "Slow down."

They walked into town, buffeted by wind. Connell took his father's elbow and led him into the stationery store and to the aisle of Valentine's Day cards. His father picked up card after card and made a pile of them in his hands.

"Wait, Dad." Connell laid a hand on his shoulder to calm him down.

"I need it," he said, panting.

"Let me help you." Connell wrenched the pile of cards from his father's hands. He led him to the cards for wives. "Everything from here to here," he said, drawing an imaginary rectangle with his finger.

His father quickly made another pile. Connell tugged them from his hands.

"Do you want me to pick out a good one for you?"

"Yes!" his father shouted joyfully.

Connell found one embossed "To My Beloved Wife" in cursive above a bouquet of flowers. Inside was one of those generic sentiments that made him wonder how people ever brought themselves to purchase these things. It looked the part of the cards his parents had exchanged in the past, though, and he didn't want to get too particular. He handed it over.

"That's very nice," his father said quietly. "Very nice."

As long as he was there, he figured he might as well pick one out for Kaitlin. He found one that, oddly enough, more or less captured how he felt about her, and he knew he was going to have to undercut the sincerity of the message with a little humor, to make it less awkward, so he bought a joke one too.

63

She liked the Starbucks by the train station. She'd heard some grumbling when it opened; Häagen-Dazs had been the lone exception to the town's embargo on chain stores. But she saw no reason not to patronize it. She liked the Italianate style of the building, the tiled roof, the real wood. The patio and its tables reminded her of one of the piazzas she'd seen on her trip to Italy with Ed. Sometimes she took her coffee out there and watched the professionals heading to the train and the purebred dogs pulling their owners forward, though usually she sat indoors.

She went on Saturdays, to get away from Ed for half an hour. She didn't gravitate there for any caffeinated talk. She went because it was acceptable to sit alone among strangers and because order prevailed: the line moved quickly, pastries were stacked neatly behind glass displays, the pleasant smells of frothed milk and espresso grounds suffused the air, the music never hurt her ears, and the overheard conversations never devolved into table-slapping self-indulgence. She liked that it lacked the ambience of smaller cafés, with their intimate conspiracies. There wasn't that feeling that she was missing out. People were islands even when they sat together. She liked that no matter how often she went in, the staff never seemed to recognize her. She wanted not so much to be alone as to be left alone. They let her stay as long as she wanted.

She sat inside, reading the *Times* she had brought from home. When she let her glance drift from its splayed pages to the neighboring table, she saw that the woman seated there had begun to cry. The woman was younger, perhaps in her midthirties; she was not unattractive, with her hair pulled back in a neat ponytail and a close-fitting business suit. She was sitting with her hands tucked under her knees, and her whole torso was heaving with sobs. Eileen tried to read but couldn't stop looking over in embarrassed amazement. The sobs got louder. The people seated at nearby tables shot each other looks. One man raised his eyebrows at Eileen, as if to say, *Can you believe it?* It felt as if the calm waters of her reflecting pool had been disturbed by the entrance of a wild animal.

She thought about getting up to leave but sat, transfixed. She had all of five more minutes before she had to get home to Ed. She wondered what this woman expected anyone to do. Was Eileen supposed to say, "Whatever it is, it's going to be fine"? Was she, a total stranger, supposed to press her to her chest and say, "There you go, that's it, just let it out"? Maybe that was the right thing to do, the only thing. But how did she know it was going to be fine? Could she make those assurances?

She decided to bury her head in her newspaper again. Out of the corner of her eye she saw the woman stand up and leave, heading toward Pondfield. She had an impulse to go after her, but she didn't want anybody to think she knew her. She waited a minute and then walked out slowly, throwing out her half-full cup.

Outside in the fresh air, she felt her resolution wavering. She headed toward her car in the train parking lot and got as far as the first row of cars before she turned around and started running toward Pondfield. She couldn't remember the last time she'd run like this. She didn't know if the woman would still be visible anywhere, but she had to at least look for her. As she ran she saw herself reflected in the shop windows and thought she looked ungainly and ridiculous flinging her tired body after so foolish a person, especially when she had no idea what she was going to say if she managed to track her down.

She got to the corner of Park and Pondfield and looked in all directions. She spotted the woman up past the drugstore, walking in the direction of the train station. She knew what she would say. She would stop next to her and ask if she could help in any way. She would say, "You're not alone in feeling like this."

She hurried toward her, feeling her heart pound. When she got within a few car lengths of the woman, who was past Cravens by this point, she slowed down so as not to seem hysterical when she started talking. She was only a couple of feet behind her now. She took a deep breath.

As she passed the woman, she picked up her pace and followed the curve of the block back around toward her car. She walked all the way there without turning around. When she got to the car, she had second thoughts and decided to drive around the block and see if she could find her. She could pull into a parking space and get out and walk up to the woman and just stand there in silence if she had to, if she couldn't bring herself to speak. She could just stand near her and that might help a little. She saw the woman not far from where she'd passed her. She hesitated for a second and then kept driving. In her shame and embarrassment she found herself driving the back way home instead of her usual route. Whatever it was, the woman was going to have to work it out herself. That was just the way life was sometimes: you had to handle your own grief. There wasn't any sense pretending otherwise.

64

Connell was leaving for college soon. His mother told him to take his father out for the day. Batting cages and driving ranges, their go-to spots for years, were out, and there wasn't a game at Shea. He brought him to the Metropolitan Museum of Art, because he couldn't think of anything else to do with him.

The lobby was aswarm with refugees from the rain. "It looks like a waiting room for a train station," his father said, and the remark's aptness took Connell by surprise. He was taken back to another time, years before, when the two of them stood at the top of the Met's steps, about to go in. "This is what makes our country great," his father had said as he rubbed two quarters together. "This is more than enough to get us in." He had handed Connell the coins. "Bygone philanthropists, men of vision and character, gave something back to the people. To see all this priceless art, you pay what you feel you can." His father had paid the suggested rate anyway.

Connell led him up the endless flight from the lobby. They stood in front of a painting called "The Gulf Stream" that depicted a lone man on the deck of a small, broken-masted boat in a little plateau between substantial waves on the open sea, sharks circling. The man leaned back against an elbow, looking like a champion of calm, or else like a man resigned to his circumstances.

"Homer," his father said.

"You know him?"

"He's one of my favorites. When I was a kid, I picked up a book on him in the library on Union Street. I didn't know who he was. I just liked the picture on the cover. I kept that book for months."

"I didn't know that." Connell was taken aback at the thought that his father remembered aesthetic preferences. He thought with a pang of the many afternoons they'd spent on different floors of the house. He wanted, one day, to be a person who went out of his way to find out what made other people happy.

"This looks like dire straits," his father said. "I wonder what he did when he was in dire straits."

"Who?" Connell asked. "Homer? Or the guy in the boat?"

His father only nodded. "Thank God all these artists did what they did," he said, "or we'd have nothing."

Connell laughed. "Maybe not nothing," he said.

The rain was coming down in sheets when they left. His father's hands were shaking. Connell put a hand in his armpit and guided him down the wet stairs, rain whipping at them from all directions.

At the bottom, his father stopped short, and Connell was annoyed. He wanted to get out from under the stinging droplets. In the thick gray of the avenue he could hardly see his father's face behind the rain slicker's hood and his wet glasses.

"You all right?" he asked, and then he saw the bright flash of a toothy smile.

"It's so beautiful," his father said.

"What is?"

"This," he said, gesturing around. "Everything."

He went looking for some tape in his father's study and found him sitting there staring up at his diplomas. Some books on the ends of shelves had fallen over, and Connell stood them up. A fine layer of dust covered everything.

A couple of hours later, he brought the tape back and found his father in the same position. At first he thought his father must have fallen asleep, but then he saw that he was awake and staring at the wall. Connell asked him what he was thinking about.

"It must have taken a lot of work to get these," his father said.

• • •

Basically I tried to love all my characters with a full heart without turning a blind eye to their flaws, prejudices, or failings. The more I let go the reins of how they would be perceived or judged, the more human they became and, I hope, the more lovable, despite their sometimes unsettling idiosyncrasies and predilections.

What do you hope readers will take away from Eileen's story?

I hope readers will find solace in reading about another person going through what Eileen goes through and coming out the other side. I hope the book inspires people to feel hope in the face of despair and believe it's possible to preserve dignity amid experiences that profoundly reduce one's power and dignity. I hope it leads them to conclude that we're always capable of learning something, even the most intransigent among us and even late in life; that, while people might never really change, they can evolve into more loving versions of the selves they already are. I hope it might make some readers who live lives outside the margins of what the media considers "important" feel recognized and perhaps less alone. And I hope it inspires people to value the time they have, and their relationships, and maybe give the people who matter to them a hug.

Are you working on anything now? Can you tell us about it?

I'm writing a novel about a different kind of family from the one in my first book. It, too, is rooted in the lives of its characters. I don't intend to spend ten years writing it, that's for sure. But who knows? We can control only so much in life.

momentum. It was only when I switched back to handwriting that I began to make a real dent in the story.

I had an idea of how it would end, and I progressed toward that ending, though the textures of the idea changed in the course of my writing the scenes leading up to it. Part of the pleasure of writing a novel is watching your initial conceptions evolve as the characters guide you in different directions than you'd imagined going in.

Charles Bock calls *We Are Not Ourselves* "a true epic in the best sense of the word." Were there great American epics that inspired you while you were writing? What were they?

Invisible Man. The Great Gatsby isn't epic in size, but it's epic in scope, and the dream Gatsby pursues is the quest of an epic hero. *Moby Dick. Light in August. Blood Meridian. The Adventures of Huckleberry Finn. The Adventures of Augie March. The Grapes of Wrath. An American Tragedy. Ironweed. Lolita.* John Berryman's *The Dream Songs.* William Carlos Williams' *Paterson. Mrs. Bridge* and *Mr. Bridge* together form an epic of ordinary lives. *Charming Billy.* The Rabbit Angstrom books. The first two of Richard Ford's Frank Bascombe books, *The Sportswriter* and *Independence Day*, had a big influence on me. *The Moviegoer. To Kill a Mockingbird. Beloved.*

Each of Ed's friends and family members reacts differently to his illness, and you present each of their reactions with great empathy. How were you able to do so?

I tried to take cues from the characters themselves in presenting a range of possible reactions that might capture the manifold ways people handle bad news. Within scenes I saw that each character would respond in his or her own way, according to the logic of how I drew them, and I tried to let them have autonomy to an extent. I think presenting them empathetically was made easier because I wasn't writing a book that was trying to skewer anyone. I was trying to capture some of the truth of the lived experience of a people in a particular place and time—a tribe, a dominant culture, a subculture, whatever you choose to call it—as best as I understood them.

It's apparent that Ed loves teaching and that, until his illness manifests itself, he's widely respected by both his students and colleagues. How did your own experiences in the classroom inform Ed's character?

Teaching at a Jesuit school, where an ethic of service is inculcated not just in the students but in the faculty and staff, gave me insight into how a teacher like Ed, who is so dedicated to his students, might think. Ed derives genuine spiritual sustenance from his work, and I'm not sure I could have understood that if I hadn't been a teacher myself. Teaching is a job in which something critical—the molding of the minds of others—is always at stake in the routine performance of the task. In its purest form teaching is a vocation, and as is true with the performance of any vocation, you get back from it more than you put into it, even when you put *a lot* into it and even when it's not always "fun." It's a privilege to teach. It's a privilege to spend all day helping people with their writing and their thought processes. And it's a privilege to discuss books with developing minds. Early in my career, when we were digging into "Ozymandias," I remember thinking, *What an extraordinary thing this is, to be standing here talking about this poem with these young people at one in the afternoon.* I never forgot that feeling, even when exhaustion made the profession a challenge. Certainly, grading papers late into the night, and experiencing the foggy mind that results from sleep deprivation, enabled me to write my way into the section where Ed is having a hard time getting his lab reports graded.

When *We Are Not Ourselves* was first acquired for publication, you told *Page Six*, "I'm humbled. . . . Working on it for more than a decade, I faced a lot of self-doubt and threw out hundreds of pages." Clearly, your writing process involved a lot of self-editing. Can you tell us more about it? Did you know how the novel would end when you began writing?

There was an enormous amount of self-editing, particularly in the final two years of composition. Self-editing, in fact, was part of what made the book take longer than I would have liked. When I began the book, I was writing by hand, but I switched to the computer about halfway through and found that I was editing everything as I wrote it and not getting enough forward novel. This was more than a diversion for me. I see baseball as being woven inextricably into American social history. For years, baseball was a point of entry into American culture for immigrants who found they could share a language with established Americans in the joys and tribulations of fandom. And it was a primer for many males in the performance of the rituals of masculinity, beginning with stickball or Little League or playing catch with Dad, and continuing, the idea went, into one's relationship with one's own child. Baseball fandom became a signifier of one's willingness to assume certain ratified, prescribed male roles. And affections for teams were tribal, and epic in scope. If a girl's father was a Yankees fan, then she was a Yankees fan. That bone-deep identification is fertile territory for fiction, because it activates the most basic impulse of storytelling. *This is who I am—a Yankees fan.*

The kind of research I found most compelling (aside from the fun of figuring out which styles of watches, cars, and clothing were popular at different junctures) was the sort not readily available in documentary texts, the sort James Joyce wrote back to Dublin about when he was composing from abroad. What's the name of that store on the corner? How far is it from such and such a church to such and such a house? The facts on the ground. The Internet is an extraordinary resource for this kind of thing. Google Earth is a miracle for fiction writers. But nothing is as fruitful as naked-eye observing. So I went to sites and looked around. I got a feel for places whenever I could.

Aside from my research into New York, I researched nursing practices, the state of medical insurance practices and Medicaid and Medicare law in the last couple of decades, the history of the development of Alzheimer's drugs, intake procedures for nursing homes, and the effects of Alzheimer's on the bodies of sufferers, including the rates of deterioration and so forth. But I never wanted to write a case study. I sought to write a novel first, and a novel that had to do with Alzheimer's, second.

Probably the most productive research I did was simply interviewing friends and family members. Eyewitness accounts might lack the rigor of historical sources, but they preserve an unusual amount of the rich human texture of the past.

In general, the novel came fully to life when I allowed my characters to be characters and abandoned any attempt to mimetically reproduce the fathomless humanity of any individual person.

Beyond my mother in specific, I was also trying to evoke the spirit of some of the women I'd admired when I was growing up: strong, career-minded women at the forefront of the next wave of feminism, making historic inroads into a male-dominated professional hierarchy.

Eileen's story manages to be both highly personal and universal. *Publishers Weekly* **praises it in a starred review, saying Eileen's "life, observed over a span of six decades, comes close to a definitive portrait of American social dynamics in the twentieth century." Did you do any research about American social history while you were writing** We Are Not Ourselves**?**

Writing about New York is almost by definition writing about American social history, because New York is freighted with so much significance in the American imagination and perhaps the human imagination in general. The city bears the weight of nearly limitless thematic importance as a symbol of capitalism, immigrant opportunity, decadence, urban decay and renewal, race and class relations, and inequities in the distribution of resources. I wanted to render New York as accurately as I could on the page, so I ended up doing a good deal of research into the city's history, the history of Queens in particular. I researched immigration patterns, to see which neighborhoods different ethnic groups settled in, because I wanted to place my characters correctly on the map. I researched the manufacturing sector in New York, to see what was sold and where, because manufacturing jobs—paints and pigments, watches, the garment and meatpacking districts, the millinery industry—were the incubator of the middle class in the area, and the loss of those jobs was the loss of that incubator. One thinks immediately of Detroit when one thinks of the collapse of manufacturing, but the boost given Ed by the manufacturing sector was once fairly typical in New York, and its loss has had an impact on social mobility.

I consulted box scores, recaps, and newspaper articles to learn as much as I could about the specific New York Mets games that appear in the trusted person has read it and provided feedback that has allowed you to see its flaws clearly and attend to them faithfully, and you know it's ready, *really* know it's ready, it will find a home. Despite the doomsday scenarios we hear about the death of reading in general, there will still be people looking to publish good books whenever you're done with yours. Having a day job helps take the pressure off your earning a living as a writer while you're working on your book. Take as long as you need. Go alone down the stormy peninsula of your thoughts and trust that when you return there will be someone at the other end of your travels and you won't regret the journey, however discouraging or frightening it might be at any given moment.

Write by hand, if you can. It's the easiest way to eliminate distractions, and it provides tremendous forward momentum, because it's harder to stop and edit when you're writing by hand, and it's especially difficult to get caught up in trying to perfect every sentence as you write it. Writing a first draft on a computer often yields the spectral experience of watching your sentences disappear off the screen shortly after you write them because they're seldom just right the first time, and if you give yourself any chance to get rid of them, you will do so. It's harder to delete bad sentences when you handwrite; you really have to cross them out a lot, and a vestige of them remains behind despite your best efforts. And that's good. Because when you go back and look later, with a kinder eye than you possess in the white heat of composition, at the first sparks the unconscious mind threw off, you often find something in them worth preserving.

Chad Harbach calls your protagonist Eileen Leary "a real addition to our literature," praising her as a "mother, wife, daughter, lover, nurse, caretaker, whiskey drinker, upwardly mobile dreamer, retrenched protector of values." She's so vividly rendered that she feels familiar. How did you come up with her character? Is she based on anyone in your life? If so, can you tell us a little about them?

Eileen was rooted originally in my mother, who is a more dynamic and complex person than I could ever have hoped to capture on the page. Eventually I found creative freedom in letting Eileen be who she wanted to be.

A Conversation with Matthew Thomas

Congratulations on publishing your debut, *We Are Not Ourselves*. What has the experience of having your book published been like? Did you find anything surprising? If so, what?

I'm thrilled to have my book published and grateful that it found a home at Simon & Schuster, with the extraordinary Marysue Rucci as its editor.

What has surprised me is just how many people play a vital role in getting a book into the hands of readers. Once its writer is done with it, a book owes it eventual existence on shelves to a remarkable team effort by untold talented people—editors, copyeditors, jacket designers, production editors, sales reps, book reps, publicists, even publishers themselves—who make crucial, often unsung contributions.

You've said it took you more than a decade to write *We Are Not Ourselves*. What made you keep writing? Do you have any advice for aspiring writers?

I kept going because I didn't want to regret not finishing it. I'd invested a great deal of time, energy, and spirit in it and passed up many other opportunities while working on it. I think of that famous line of Macbeth's: "I am in blood/Stepp'd in so far that, should I wade no more,/Returning were as tedious as go o'er." I would say "I had to finish it," but I'm uncomfortable invoking the idea of a ferocious creative mandate that needed to be fulfilled, because I think that's too highfalutin a notion to describe an activity, novel writing, that's more often like long-haul trucking than some ineffable mystical experience. It's closest to the truth to say that not finishing it would have dealt my psyche a blow whose imagined pain was worse than the considerable frustration of facing my limitations every day.

To aspiring writers, I would say: Don't give up. It's never too late. You're never too old. The success of others is proof of the possibility of your own success. There's enough opportunity to go around. When you've taken your book as far as you can take it on your own, and at least one

Enhance Your Book Club

1. Baseball is important in the Leary household. Ed and Connell relate to each other through the sport. When Eileen goes to a game with Ed and Connell, she realizes that "she did some of her best thinking at ball games, or while Ed was listening to them on the radio" (p. 172). Watch a baseball game with your book club. Discuss why Eileen might find watching games calming. Did the experience have the same effect on you?

2. When Eileen is a young girl, her father takes her to visit friends in Jackson Heights and she feels an amazing sense of peace because "The people who lived in this building had figured out something important about life, and she'd stumbled upon their secret. There were places, she now saw, that contained more happiness than ordinary places did" (pp. 15–16). What is it about the building that feels exceptionally special to Eileen? Are there any places like that in your life? What makes them so important to you? Share your thoughts with your book club.

3. When Matthew Thomas sold *We Are Not Ourselves* for publication, it was major industry news. Read more about it at: http://www.the wire.com/entertainment/2013/04/high-school-english-teacher-who -sold-his-debut-novel-1-million/64342/ and at: http://www.media bistro.com/galleycat/high-school-teacher-lands-deal-for-debut-novel _b68806.

4. Go on a virtual walking tour of Queens, New York, by following this link: http://www.thirteen.org/queens/ to learn more about the neighborhoods where Eileen grows up and where she raises Connell. Eileen knows "it was possible to see the changes as part of what made the city great . . . but only if you weren't the one being displaced" (p. 128). Talk about how Eileen reacts to the changes in Jackson Heights with your book club. Were you surprised? Explain your answer.

11. When Connell tells his friend Farshid that he and his family will be moving and expresses reticence about it, Farshid tells him, "You just need to reinvent yourself" (p. 240). Do you agree with Connell that "I have to invent myself before I can reinvent myself"? (p. 240). Why does Connell tell his mother that he wants to move even though he's ambivalent about the prospect? What does moving into a new house mean to each member of the Leary family?

12. When it comes to dating, Eileen would "rather be alone than end up with a man who was afraid" (p. 51). What traits is Eileen looking for in a partner? How does Ed measure up to Eileen's ideal partner? Were you surprised that she ends up marrying him? Eileen sees them as "co-conspirators in a mission of normalcy" (p. 124). What does she mean? Describe their relationship. How does it evolve?

13. After Ed gets sick, Connell avoids going back home. Why is he so afraid of going home? Connell tells Eileen that caring for Ed is "too hard for me. It's too much" and that "I'm not you. . . . That's the problem right there" (p. 466). How does Eileen react? Is she justified? Compare and contrast the way that both Eileen and Connell deal with their sick parents. In what ways, if any, are they alike?

14. After Ed's diagnosis, Eileen takes "a third path, the pragmatic one. It hadn't happened for a reason, but they would find something to glean from it anyway" (p. 382). What does Eileen's reaction tell us about her character? Describe your first impression of Eileen. Did you like her initially? Did your impression of Eileen change as you read on? In what ways and why?

15. Eileen's mother tells her, "Don't ever love anyone. All you'll do is break your own heart" (p. 12). Why does she offer this advice to Eileen? In what ways has Eileen's mother's heart been broken? Do any of the other characters in We Are Not Ourselves suffer heartbreaks? What has caused those instances of suffering?

6. After Ed has lost his temper and "flipped out" on Connell, Eileen tells him that "it had better not [happen again]. I don't give a damn what your father did to you. That boy's not him" (p. 186). Why do you think Ed is so reticent to talk about his relationship with his own father? Does Ed's relationship with his father inform his parenting style with Connell? If so, in what ways?

7. On moving day, when Eileen arrives at her new house, "Her first thought as she took in the house through the window was that it didn't look the way she'd remembered it" (p. 278). Contrast Eileen's memory of her new house with the reality of what it looks like. What accounts for the change in the way that Eileen views the house? Why is she so baffled when her movers ask her where they should place her belongings within it?

8. Connell attends one of Ed's classes in order to complete a school assignment. Describe Connell's experience in the classroom. Although Connell is unnerved by his time in Ed's classroom, he keeps his word to Ed and decides not to tell his mother how strange it had been. Why do you think Connell chooses to keep this information to himself? Do you agree with his decision to do so? When Ed apologizes to Connell, Connell tells him, "It's all right . . . I already know what kind of teacher you are. You teach me every day" (p. 162). How does Ed teach his son?

9. Who is Bethany? Do you think her friendship with Eileen is healthy? Why or why not? Why does Eileen agree to accompany Bethany to the faith healer? Compare and contrast Eileen's experiences with Vywamus with her experience going to a therapist. Why does Eileen think that going to the faith healer is "better than therapy" (p. 444). Do you think going to the faith healer has helped Eileen? How?

10. Ed is reluctant to attend a party with Eileen at the home of one of her colleagues and tells her, "They'll never know the real me" (p. 393). What does he mean? Were you surprised by Ed's diagnosis? Were there any instances of foreshadowing in the novel that led you to anticipate what Ed's illness was? What were they? Who do you think is "the real" Ed?

Topics & Questions for Discussion

1. Thomas begins his novel with two epigraphs, one from Stanley Kunitz and one from *King Lear*. Did the epigraphs inform your reading of the novel? How did they relate to each of the members of the Leary family? Why do you think Thomas chose to use the phrase *We Are Not Ourselves*, taken from the *King Lear* epigraph, as the title of his novel?

2. When Eileen is growing up, she's aware that "men were always quieting down around her father" (pp. 3–4), whom "everybody called . . . Big Mike" (p. 6). Describe Big Mike. Why does he command so much respect from the outside world? Does this influence Eileen's behavior? In what ways? How does Big Mike's legend compare with the reality of what he is like when he is at home with Eileen and her mother?

3. Even after Eileen buys the apartment building from the Orlando family, she's obsessed with the idea of owning her own house. Why is this so important for Eileen?

4. When Eileen enters nursing school "she knew that even if nursing wasn't the field she'd have chosen, she'd been training for it without meaning to from an early age" (p. 38). Describe Eileen's childhood. How have Eileen's experiences with her mother helped prepare her for the job? Occasionally Eileen feels the instructors are "treating her with something like professional courtesy" (p. 38), and it makes her think of the way men in the neighborhood treat her father. Why? And why does this make her uneasy?

5. When Ed turns down an offer to be the chairman of his department, he tells Eileen, "It's all about having the right ambition" (p. 85). What does Ed think the "right" ambition is? Why is Eileen so upset that he has turned down the job? How do his ideas about ambition conflict with Eileen's?

Introduction

Epic in scope, heroic in character, and masterful in prose, *We Are Not Ourselves* is a multigenerational portrait of the Irish American Leary family.

Born in 1941, Eileen Tumulty is raised by her immigrant parents in Woodside, Queens, in an apartment where the mood swings between heartbreak and hilarity, depending on whether guests are over and how much alcohol has been consumed.

When Eileen meets Ed Leary, a scientist whose bearing is nothing like those of the men she grew up with, she thinks she's found the perfect partner to deliver her to the cosmopolitan world she longs to inhabit. They marry, and Eileen quickly discovers Ed doesn't aspire to the same, ever bigger stake in the American Dream. Although she encourages him to want more, as the years pass it becomes clear that his growing reluctance is part of a deeper psychological shift. An inescapable darkness enters their lives, and Eileen and Ed and their son, Connell, try desperately to hold together a semblance of the reality they have known and to preserve, against long odds, an idea they have cherished of the future.

Through the Leary family, novelist Matthew Thomas charts the story of the American Century. At once expansive and exquisitely detailed, *We Are Not Ourselves* is a riveting and affecting work of art—one that reminds us that life is more than a tally of victories and defeats, that we live to love and be loved, and that we should tell one another so before the moment slips away.

About This Guide

This reading group guide for *We Are Not Ourselves* includes an introduction, discussion questions, ideas for enhancing your book club, and a Q&A with author Matthew Thomas. The suggested questions are intended to help your reading group find new and interesting angles and topics for your discussion. We hope that these ideas will enrich your conversation and increase your enjoyment of the book.

Simon & Schuster
Reading Group Guide

We Are Not
Ourselves

Matthew Thomas

About the Author

Matthew Thomas grew up in New York City. A graduate of the University of Chicago, he has an MA from the Writing Seminars at Johns Hopkins University and an MFA from the University of California, Irvine. His *New York Times*–bestselling novel *We Are Not Ourselves* has been shortlisted for the Flaherty-Dunnan First Novel Prize from the Center for Fiction, longlisted for the Guardian First Book Award, nominated for the Folio Prize, and named a Notable Book of the year by the *New York Times*. He lives with his wife and twin children in New Jersey.

Connell's mother was at work when it was time for him to head to the train to go to the airport to leave for Chicago for the first time. He wished she'd taken the day off. He slung an army duffel bag over each shoulder and got his backpack on and started walking. His father was walking into town to go to church, so they walked together.

When they crossed the overpass that stretched across the Sprain Brook Parkway, Connell saw cars streaming by in both directions and thought of how much a map of roads and highways, when it included all the little ones like this, looked like a map of rivers, or an illustration of the circulatory system. He stopped and watched for a while. He was having another of those inchoate ideas that he couldn't entirely articulate to himself. He knew that these cloudy notions would come into sharper focus when he was away at college, where he would divest himself of the stultifying habits of personality and the false conclusions of biography and shine the light of pure reason on experience.

When they reached the bridge over the Bronx River a block from the train, his father was the one to stop. He leaned over the stone wall. At first Connell thought his father's mind was just wandering, but then he wondered whether his father might not be imitating him from a few minutes earlier, so he put one of the bags down and tugged on his father's sleeve as cars sped past. "Dad!" he said, more exasperated than he had intended. His father shook his head and pointed down at the water. "What is it? What's up?" Then Connell saw a frog on a rock, lazing in the sun. Maybe this was the frog's habitual spot. Maybe his father had seen it before and remembered to look for it. He seemed pleased that Connell had been there to see it too. He clapped, and it jumped into the river and left a ripple on the water.

He was half a block away when he saw the 12:23 train pull into the station. If he ran, he could make it. His father looked stooped and pale from the heat and uneasy on his legs. Connell could take the next train, at 12:55, or even the one after it; he had plenty of time to make his flight.

He led him under the tracks to Slave to the Grind, the coffee shop he had haunted all summer.

"Two brain freezers," he said when they got to the counter. After he'd

said it, he felt like a fool. If his father noticed, he didn't seem to care. Connell bought a corn muffin for them to split. He led him to a table in the back, where they drank and ate slowly.

"I'm sorry to be going so far."

"Have fun," his father said. "Study what you want."

"I'll miss you."

"Forget that. Live your life."

Outside, heat radiated off cars, and the sun pounded through a severely clear sky. The town thrummed with end-of-summer energy. He had another twenty minutes until the 1:23.

"You okay getting back by yourself?"

His father nodded. They walked to the station.

"You didn't make it to church."

"That was just as good," he said, pointing toward the coffee shop.

He watched his father walk off to get the newspaper; then he took a seat in the shade on the cool concrete bench and pulled a book out of his backpack. Thoughts of his father walking home alone to the empty house kept distracting him, so that he had read only a single page when the horn announced the approaching train, but in his flurried efforts to put his book away and get his baggage settled before the train arrived, he was able to forget about his father entirely.

65

One morning in October, she went to turn the television on for him and found that there was no picture. The repairman couldn't come in right away, and she had to go to work. She left Ed on the couch, knowing he'd have nothing to do but sit and think. She couldn't imagine how he'd pass his day without television to distract him from his thoughts.

She hardly got anything done. She must have called him half a dozen times. Every time she called, he hurried off, saying very little, as if he had to get back to something.

When she came home, she found him sitting in exactly the spot she'd left him in on the couch. She wondered if it were possible that he'd sat there for nine hours straight. She checked the microwave and the refrigerator. At least he'd risen to eat. Evidence of urine on the floor of the powder room gave her spirits a strange lift. She was glad she'd called and made him get up.

Another day passed in the same way, and then the repairman finally came on the morning of the third day, before she went to work.

It turned out that all he had to do was reprogram something on the television and the cable box. She gave him a forty-dollar tip on top of the fee his company charged.

"If I ever need you again, please put me at the top of the list." She tried to affect a breezy manner to hide the desperation she felt. "We simply can't get on without television in this house."

66

Connell stayed up all night trying to finish *Crime and Punishment* in time for class. In the predawn hours, as he battled fatigue and a fractured consciousness that felt, appropriately given the book in question, something like "brain fever," the story took on a diabolical urgency, and his experience of it became more personal. It felt as if it could have been the story of the mental collapse of any college-aged kid under pressure, or at least any kid far from home, huddled under a Siberian chill.

At nine o'clock he put his head down to rest his eyes for five minutes. The next thing he knew, the clock said ten fifty and he was scrambling not to be late for his eleven o'clock class. He was once again grateful he'd put in for a single room, because the dorm with the most singles, while being a Brutalist eyesore, also happened to be close to campus.

He threw some clothes on and dashed down the stairs, jumping five or six steps at a time and coming down hard on the landings. He ran through the courtyard of the structure which was designed by a prison architect and seemed to be made entirely of concrete—and marveled, as he did every day, at how violently it clashed with the neo-Gothic elegance of so much of the campus. He had missed breakfast again. With two classes back-to-back, he would miss lunch as well. He had wasted so many meals in his plan that he could hardly tell the difference anymore between hunger pangs and pangs of guilt. He ate often at the Medici, the Florian, or Salonica, because the theater people he hung around with went to those places before and after practice. They staked out a table and sat at it in shifts all night.

He ran past Rockefeller Chapel and onto the quad. The sprint across

the length of the campus to Cobb took his breath away, and by the time
he arrived he was panting hard. There was a time when this run would
have been nothing to him, but when he decided to pursue the life of the
mind, he stopped taking care of his body. He considered it a noble choice,
except when he examined the evidence that he was falling apart. His muscle mass had melted away considerably. He was long and lanky and now
almost certainly too thin. Instead of gaining the traditional fifteen pounds,
he had probably lost twenty. He figured he looked like he was taking drugs,
though in fact he was scared to try any. It would have been enough that
his father had been a drug researcher, but on top of that, in his father's
Alzheimer's he had an up-close example of the effects of haywire brain
chemistry. He didn't want to do anything to damage his brain. Of course,
he understood that sleep deprivation was as ruinous as many drugs. The
strongest drug he ever took was caffeine. He drank coffee throughout the
day, enough to make him faintly jittery most of the time. He had a thick
eraser of fifties-style hair, and his glasses were big, plastic, and chunky and
looked like a stage prop. Once October bled into November, the weather
provided the model for the persona so many around him cultivated: brisk,
astringent, clarifying, with intermittent flashes of manic warmth.

He paused in front of Cobb to catch his breath and gaze at the indefatigable smokers, who stood in the mouth of the big stone C-Bench in
any weather, puffing at Galoises and Lucky Strikes, anything unfiltered, to
hurry the heat into their lungs. In the winter, with puffs of condensation
escaping lips, everyone on campus looked like a smoker.

In class, he took a seat at the round table, and then he was snapped awake
to see the class all looking at him. The professor had called on him to
speculate about what motive Raskolnikov might have had for the killing,
beyond his stated philosophical one. Connell replied that he wondered
whether Raskolnikov might not have been struggling through some kind
of Oedipal problem. His father was dead; there was tremendous pressure
on Raskolnikov to succeed, to provide a life for his sister and mother. He
had his landlady at his back, a surrogate mother figure. Maybe the pawnbroker was herself a surrogate for those unresolved feelings.

The professor, a Russian American with a Mephistophelian goatee, had an amused smile on his face. This had happened before—slumbers of Connell's punctuated by sudden outbursts of insight. Connell figured either that the professor possessed that elusive quality, the so-called Russian soul, or else that he had been similarly sleep-deprived at one point in his career himself. Something had allowed him to understand Connell's bizarrely derelict behavior as an expression of authentic scholarship. Certainly it would have been harder on Connell if he didn't do the reading. But to fall asleep like that in class, in brazen view of the instructor, and spring awake to provide a take that the other students seemed to chew thoughtfully on, even if they wore looks of scorn or pity: this seemed to strike the professor as being a natural mode for the study of Dostoyevsky.

Connell couldn't help it. He never got enough sleep. He would drift off standing up, sometimes midconversation. If he leaned against a wall too long he would lose his legs and nearly topple over. There was so much to read, and the conversations he found himself in often lasted deep into the night. He watched the night owls go to sleep and pressed on.

Class let out and he went outside for the few minutes between classes to stand in front of the building. He spotted that professor he always saw with his son, a redheaded boy about four or five years old. He watched them walk across campus hand in hand, the professor gesturing around at something, the two of them stopping to watch a squirrel slip down the sloped lid of a garbage can and land in a crash of plastic containers.

He wished he had his own father with him. They could share an apartment off campus. His father could wander the grounds all day and they could meet for dinner. His father could trail him to classes. He would love the state-of-the-art labs, the brilliant students, the sense of higher purpose. His father had never gotten to hang out on a campus like this, though he'd always maintained that all campuses, in spirit, were essentially the same, that the differences between classes of institutions were more in degree than in kind.

After his second class, Connell want back to the dorm and did a little work. Then he went to dinner and rehearsal. He had gotten the part of Orlando in *As You Like It*, because his experience as a debater had lent him a

certain rhetorical polish. The problem was, he didn't know how to be anybody but himself, and he wasn't sure what that self was yet, so he studied other people for traits to grab and fashion a personality out of. He liked to think this was what all college kids did, but when he ran into one of those hale, relaxed young men whose character, in the Heraclitean sense, seemed carved out at birth for him, he felt foolish and guilty. It helped that the character he was playing in *As You Like It* was a little naïve, because he could be breathless and overwhelmed up there and it would just about make sense.

They had spent a week choreographing the fight scenes, which were the only parts of the play he had any mastery of. He hadn't exercised in months—was it a full year now?—but he still had a wiry energy, and he executed the flips with an ease that made him embarrassed about the rest of his performance. His father would have enjoyed watching him practice the fight scenes. He loved swashbuckling movies about adventures on the high seas, and World War II flicks with buddies fighting side by side and striding into danger.

The cast went to the Medici afterward. He found himself in the middle of a spirited conversation about the nature of free will. Several people packed into the booth, jamming him against the wall. The girls, Jenna included—Jenna whom he'd made out with a few times and who was on the verge of agreeing to make it exclusive—doted on a stage crew member whose carpentry skills lent him a virtuous concreteness in the abstracted arena of campus life.

Hopped up on an endless series of coffee refills, Connell was eating a plate of baked ravioli and idly playing with one of the sugar packets in the little tray when he was overtaken by an insight into the nature of time and space that made his mind fairly crackle. All at once, he could see the whole chain of hands through which this packet had passed on its journey to him. He could see the sugar cane growing, being gathered, being refined. He could see its manufacture. He was about to enact its consumption. He could see the future too: the packet heading to the landfill, decaying in the earth, disintegrating. In one moment, the packet in his hands didn't exist yet, and in another he was holding it, and in another its remnants were

sitting in the trash bag waiting for pickup. He knew he wouldn't be able to explain it to anyone if he tried. The other actors were now carrying on some kind of debate about Williams, O'Neill, and Miller, and Connell was there and not there. He thought, *Domino Sugar. Dad made the sugar that went into packets like this. He is holding one of these now, in the past.* He could see his father looking into the future and seeing the blurred outlines of a life, a wife, a child. His father would be dead and in the ground. Connell would be too. The sugar would keep getting made.

He wanted to call his father and tell him his fevered thoughts, but he knew that even under the best of circumstances it wouldn't have made sense to anyone, and it surely wasn't going to make sense to his father now in the state he was in. Still, he wanted badly to share this insight, and he could feel it slipping away. There wasn't even time to turn to the guy next to him and try to get it across, so he just formed a mental picture of his father as a much younger man, standing in a white smock, holding a clipboard, as he squeezed the sugar packet and sent the thought to that young man in his image, wherever he was in space or time. He ripped the packet open, poured it in, and watched it dissolve.

The director of his play had seen his polish and misunderstood. She hadn't realized that polish was all he had. He could stand before people and make stentorian declamations, but the only reason he could project a convincing air of youthful ignorance was that he was stuck inside himself, and he knew he was—it was the one thing he could say with real conviction that he knew about himself—and he wasn't playing a part.

The next morning, he woke up late again and bounded down the stairs, but this time he came down too hard on the landing and felt something snap. He hobbled to class and then to the hospital, and that night, when he showed up at rehearsal on crutches, with a broken foot, it was as if the director had been waiting for this to happen all along. There was no understudy, of course, so Connell had to play the part himself. They had to rechoreograph the fight scenes, which he and his counterpart had brought to such a high level of polish that someone suggested that when he recovered they should put on an avant-garde show that would consist exclusively of

them playing out their grapplings over and over. They turned them into arm-wrestling scenes instead.

Connell felt safer, somehow, up on crutches. He had to practice walking around onstage in them, and the new physical demands of the part took the urgent edge off his desperation to remember his lines, which allowed him finally to get off book right before the show went up. It was pure chance that he'd broken his foot, but it was lovely to imagine that it wasn't merely chance, that there was a higher order working in life, that the mystical flashes of insight born of staring at a packet of sugar in a noisy restaurant might actually connect to a truth of the universe. It was lovely to consider the possibility that he'd been somewhere else with his father, in another neighborhood of time and space, just because he'd been able to conceive of it while watching some crystals dissolve into a coffee cup.

He had to remember to give the old man a call.

After the eleven o'clock Mass, they took a walk through the neighborhood, then went to the Food Emporium. They were having the Coakleys over for dinner, and she needed to pick up a few things. As they passed through the first electronic door heading out of the store, Ed came to a halt in the vestibule and started yelling "No! No!"

"Not now," she said. "We have to get home."

"Not with her!" he yelled. "Police!"

She yanked his hand. He grabbed on to the sliding door to pull back. Somehow he managed to hold on to the bags.

"We have to go," she said. "Please!"

"Not with you! Police! Police!"

She pulled harder. He stumbled two steps and threw himself to the ground. The cantaloupe he was carrying spilled out of its bag and rolled into the street. She couldn't budge him. At first people gave her curious looks as they passed, but then a few stopped to gawk, and then a crowd gathered as Ed continued to call for the police. She offered them sheepish smiles as they thronged around her. Workers from the store came out. Someone must have called 911, because the next thing she knew two officers were parting the crowd.

"Police!" Ed shouted frantically when he saw them.

"The police are *here*," she said desperately. "Shut *up*."

The flash of anger didn't help her cause. She told them she was his wife, but Ed's continued shouting made them question her. A neatly dressed woman in a shearling coat whom Eileen had never seen before came forward from the crowd and said she knew who she was. "I see her around,"

the woman said quietly, as if to downplay the connection. "In church. She takes care of him. It's not abuse."

Eileen was relieved, but she felt a profound gravity come over her at the thought of what a spectacle she'd become. The police were mollified by this character witness; one of the officers told the crowd to disperse, while the other asked what was wrong with Ed and whether she had anyone to call for assistance. In her confusion she could think of no one, not a neighbor, not a single friend.

"You don't have anyone to call?"

"I don't know anyone around here," she found herself saying, to her own amazement. The officers looked heavily at each other, as if they had been conscripted into helping her move a roomful of books. They hooked arms under Ed and led him to the car.

When they got home, she called the Coakleys to cancel. He was raving about how he wasn't going to eat anything from her, he wasn't going to eat a single thing she gave him. Eventually she convinced him to go upstairs to the bedroom, and he fell asleep.

"Wasn't it wonderful?" he asked a few hours later when she woke him to give him his medicine. "We had such a nice day."

"What are you talking about?"

"Didn't we have a wonderful day?"

After dinner, Ed went right back to bed. She returned to the kitchen and opened the wine she'd bought for the Coakleys' visit. She'd consulted the salesman to make sure it was a bottle to satisfy an exacting taste. For the last few years, Jack Coakley had been educating himself about wine. He was becoming—he'd taught her the word—an *oenophile*. The salesman had handed her a Bordeaux whose label she didn't recognize and said it had big mouthfeel, with strong but creamy tannins, a blend of fruity aromas, and a smoky finish. She'd nodded and tried not to seem lost. It had been more money than she'd planned on spending, and she'd thought about getting a cheaper bottle she was familiar with, but the way he'd looked at her, seeming to evaluate her, had made her carry it up to the counter.

When she was nearly done with the bottle, she called Cindy.

"I almost went to jail," she said. "And he's saying, 'Didn't we have a

wonderful time?'" She drained the last glass. "This is the best bottle of wine I've ever tasted."

She hung up and began eating her way through the food in the refrigerator—the hors d'oeuvres she'd bought for dinner, leftovers, the cake she'd made that morning.

She felt the tremors of an incipient headache. The headaches were the reason she stayed away from alcohol. She could see the appeal of it, though: the obliteration of the day's concerns, the loosing of the reins of control, the preoccupation with something as simple as the next drink, the forgetting. The forgetting could be wonderful.

Eileen knew facing the crowds and the cold might not be a good idea—Ed was more sensitive to cold than he'd ever been, and the excess stimulation might put him in a frenzy—but she couldn't help herself. Though they'd gone every year they lived in Jackson Heights, she hadn't been to see the Christmas windows on Fifth Avenue since she'd moved to Bronxville. She was loath to miss them again.

She parked in a garage close to the strip of stores. She expected him to gripe his way through the wall of humanity, but he didn't pull against her as she led him by the hand.

They started at Lord & Taylor. "Jingle Bells" poured down from the hidden speakers above, and in the first window, figures revolved and bobbed mechanically in a mute and tireless tableau of Christmas morning. A boy moved up and down with his arms spread wide as though in a Cossack dance as he beheld the miracle of his new bike; a girl swung her new baby doll back and forth as if it were a model airplane; and their father forever pulled a stocking from the mantle above the fireplace. Ed jabbed her shoulder.

"Isn't it the greatest thing you've ever seen?" he asked in a surge of enthusiasm more unlikely than any she'd seen from him over the course of their marriage. "Look!" he said. "Look!"

It was the same at the next window, and all the windows from Fortunoff to Macy's. His childish wonder never abated, and his expression was blank with anticipation as she led him to the next garland-wrapped queue.

Later, in bed, she was disappointed not to be able to recall any of the scenes. Instead, all she could see was Ed's huge smile and his glasses reflecting the lights of the displays.

Connell called the next day to let her know he wasn't coming home for Christmas. He had decided to spend the holiday at the house of his new girlfriend. He'd had the same excuse at Thanksgiving.

"Who is this girl? Thanksgiving and now Christmas? Sounds like someone we need to meet."

"You will," he said, to her dismay.

"Well," she said. "Your father will certainly be disappointed."

She decided to cancel the little Christmas Eve party she'd planned. Ed wouldn't know the difference; they could eat frozen dinners and watch television. She'd have followed through if her cousin Pat hadn't called shortly after she'd gotten off the phone with Connell and said he and Tess and the girls were going to be able to make it after all. Pat was as close to a brother as she had. He used to come over to her parents' apartment every year, starting in her late teens, to put up the Christmas tree with her father. He reminded her so terribly of her father. When he heard how upset she was that Connell wasn't coming home, Pat said they'd come on Saturday the twenty-third and stay through the long weekend.

"The girls will help you get ready," he said. "They'll cook, they'll clean, they'll do whatever I tell them to."

She knew she should have been touched, but it wasn't as she would have planned it, and she wanted something, anything, to go exactly as she'd planned it.

Ed was there to greet Pat and Tess and the girls when they arrived, but a few minutes later, when it was time to eat the big lunch she'd prepared, he had disappeared upstairs. She found him sitting on the divan at the foot of the bed, looking confused.

"Are you planning to join us?"

"That lady downstairs," he said. "I know I should know her. Who is she?"

"You mean Tess?"

"That's her name?"

"Tess," she said. "Yes."

"Okay," he said, rising. As they got to the door and were about to head downstairs, he stopped her. "Don't tell her I don't know her."

"But you do know her."

"Don't tell."

"I won't," she said. "Believe me."

"Good."

"Do you remember her name?"

"Don't test me."

"It's not a test," she said. "I'm trying to help."

He stood there thinking. "What is it?" he asked after a bit.

"Tess."

"I said don't test me."

"No," she said, laughing. "Not *test*. *Tess*. Tess is her name."

He repeated the name a few times. "And how do I know her again?"

"She's Pat's wife."

He looked annoyed. "Pat, your *cousin* Pat?"

"Yes," she said, unable to keep from laughing.

"Well," he said, "why didn't you say so?"

"You know who Pat is?"

"Your cousin Pat," he said, as if she were being obtuse. "Of course I do."

"Of course you do," she said, chuckling. She straightened his glasses on his face and led him downstairs.

In the morning, Ed went for the paper. She was relieved to get him out of the house for a while. She had a lot to do for the party, and her nieces were there to help her. It was unseasonably warm, so she imagined he might take a seat on the bench by the Food Emporium.

Elyse helped her chop potatoes and Cecily polished the silverware. She showed the two of them how to make quiche. The Christmas music gave her movements an upbeat, cheery punctuation, and as she directed the girls she remembered the joyous way Ed, in the days before he switched over to headphones, would stand in the living room conducting along to the symphony recording with an invisible baton. She enjoyed watching him work himself into a frenzy. She loved how he laughed at his own ridiculousness.

She was happy enough that she could almost forget that Connell hadn't

come home. Watching Elyse and Cecily work in their purposeful way, she wondered what it would have been like to have a daughter instead of a son. Daughters didn't leave the way sons did. Her friends' daughters never seemed to move more than a few miles away from their mothers.

Ed had been gone an hour and a half. With his slow gait it wasn't unreasonable to think he was still in transit, and anyway she was enjoying herself. A little while later, though, Tess asked, "Where's Ed?" and Eileen began to worry: not that anything bad had happened to him, but that he'd gotten lost. She had allowed herself to get complacent.

"Topps," she said. "The local bakery. They spoil him there. I'd better go and save the counter girl from him. He'll haunt that place all day if they let him."

She drove slowly down Palmer, stopping at storefronts to peer inside, feeling like a criminal casing them out. She did a circle of the town. He wasn't on any of the benches. It had grown colder since he'd left; the wind had picked up. She regretted giving in to vanity, both his and hers, in not getting him a MedicAlert bracelet. He was wandering the streets with nothing to explain his situation.

She drove down Kimball Avenue to double through the back streets where he might have gotten turned around. When she got to Midland, she saw a man approaching a car at the stoplight under the Cross County overpass, waving his hands, and it took her a second to realize that he was her husband. She threw the hazards on and walked toward him, and when he saw her he started clapping his hands. She pulled him back by the sleeve. A blue Mercedes honked and slowed as it passed. At first she thought it was her neighbor from up the block, but she was relieved to see a gray-haired man she didn't recognize. Still, had he recognized her? Would he recount the scene over dinner?

She was too angry to speak. She tried to imagine the melee Ed had caused since he'd gotten to the intersection. How long had it been? She was lucky the police hadn't gotten to him yet.

She buckled him into the passenger seat and returned to the driver's seat before saying anything. "What were you doing so far from the house?" she asked finally.

"You found me," he said. "Don't make a big deal of it. Let's go."

"Did you get lost? Were you disoriented?"

Ed looked at his feet. She noticed that the soles were separating from the leather of his shoes. He needed a new pair, or at least a resoling. She had been leaving details like this unattended to. Her secret thought, the shameful thought she'd been harboring more frequently lately, was that Ed wouldn't notice anyway.

"I was trying to get to the mall."

"What in the hell!" she shouted. "Tell me the truth. Did you get lost trying to get home?"

"No." He shook his head.

"I need to know, Ed."

"I wanted to get you something."

"We *decided* about this. Remember? You and I aren't exchanging presents this year. It's just easier that way."

"Not for Christmas," he said.

"For what, then?"

"Our anniversary." He stretched out his hands and poked at his ring. "New Year's Eve," he said.

"We got married on January twenty-second, Edmund."

"But we met on New Year's Eve."

She was quiet. She pictured Tess's concerned look when they got home. The look would say, in the most well-meaning way possible, *Why did you let him go out in the first place?* Ed sat heavily in the passenger seat. "We need to get back," she said. "Everyone is worried sick."

When they were nearly home, she looked over and saw him holding his wallet.

"I didn't have any money anyway," he said.

She hadn't put any in his wallet in a while. She'd also taken the cards, to prevent someone from taking advantage of him.

She turned the car around and drove back to the mall, parked in front of Macy's. She fished her own wallet out of her purse. A hundred-dollar bill flashed up at her, along with a couple of singles.

You stirred up emotions in a man when you gave him cash. She'd

practiced defusing that ticking bomb during her father's retirement years, when she still lived at home. When Ed handed her his wallet, she folded the hundred in briskly, economically, as though she were giving a flu shot.

They went inside. She told him she'd wait in the purse section and watched him amble off. He stopped to talk to a salesgirl, who pointed him toward the escalator. As he began to rise, clutching the thick rubber rail with both hands and looking over the side as though it were the edge of a ship, she decided to follow him from a distance. She trailed him into the women's section. She had a vision of him throwing dress after dress over his shoulder in a frenzied spree, but he walked the aisles deliberately, like a big cat stalking its prey, looking at dresses without touching them. He moved from rack to rack, evidently making quick decisions, and stopped in front of a row of dresses along the far wall. He appraised them as she pretended to look at clothes across the aisle. A salesgirl came over and he waved her off. As if he had read Eileen's mind about the dowdy-looking dresses in front of him, he headed to an adjacent rack and, after a sweep of those offerings with his eyes, held up a dress. She could see it shimmering in the light. The pattern was tasteful, the cut elegant. He waved the salesgirl over again with a frantic hand, holding the dress in front of him as though it were a banner in a parade.

She watched a strange exchange between Ed and the salesgirl. A look of patient confusion crossed the girl's face as he passed her his wallet. She held it dubiously as he jabbed at a pocket behind where his credit cards would have been. Frustrated, he took the wallet back, removed a slip of paper, and handed it to her.

The girl nodded and returned with an identical-looking dress. He must have written Eileen's size on the slip of paper. She couldn't imagine the effort he'd expended in memorializing this detail. Still, there was little chance the number was correct. She needed a ten now.

As Ed approached the cash register, she realized that the dress must have cost well over a hundred dollars. She rushed over. She knew Ed would be furious, but she couldn't worry about that now. She tapped him on the shoulder. He sprang forward, startled, and let out a little cry. When he saw it was her, he yelled her name a few times in manic excitement, the trapped heat of emasculation radiating off him.

"Funny meeting you here," she said.

"You like this?" he asked. The girl, who had arranged her features into a beatific grin, handed it over for inspection.

"It's beautiful," she said. She glanced at the dress size: eight. He was closer than she thought.

"I like you in blue," he said. The simplicity of the declaration put an ache in her chest. He directed no animosity at her for having rescued him in the transaction. He seemed to feel only a naked desire to please. He was being stripped of pride, of ego, ruined, destroyed. He was also being softened.

"We'll use this." She handed her credit card to the salesgirl before Ed could reach for his wallet, which was sitting on the counter. The girl passed her the index card Ed had written on. It said, "Eileen's size," with a big "6" crossed out and an "8" written in its place. When Ed turned away, she took a pen and crossed out the "8" and wrote "10" next to it in as close a hand to his as she could manage. She would come back and exchange it for a ten. She slid the paper back in his wallet and put the hundred into her own. There was no reason for him to be walking around with a bill that large.

The McGuires and Coakleys couldn't make it that year. They had excuses— the Coakleys had been talking about heading out to Arizona to see Cindy's brother for years, and Frank's niece in Maine had just had a baby—but she couldn't help being annoyed at their not trying harder to be in town. They'd been so strange around Ed lately, the women tentative, the men garrulous and impersonal, that she imagined they were relieved to have a reason to get away. It seemed to her that she had graduated from the ranks of ordinary wives into a rare stratum inhabited by widows whose husbands were still alive.

At one in the morning, she and Tess sweated to get the mess cleaned up. Just when it looked as if she might escape the evening without a major disturbance, Ed woke and wandered out of the bedroom. He paced back and forth in the upstairs hallway, screaming and flailing his arms violently. She couldn't silence him. One by one the houseguests gave up the pretense of sleep and emerged from their rooms—Pat, Tess, the girls, her aunt

Margie, who had also decided to stay. Pat tried to intercede, puffed up by macho gravitas, but she held him off and allowed Tess to help her corral Ed.

The morning saw no enthusiastic ripping open of presents; the girls handed them around with a perfunctory languor. As Connell had grown older, she'd worked hard to keep alive the Christmas morning ritual, and she tried to pump some life into the girls, but their exhaustion won out. They put in a lackluster effort at breakfast as well, nursing cups of coffee and leaving heaps of food untouched. She thought, *Connell was right not to come home.*

As she scraped scrambled eggs into the trash, she resolved to have one more real Christmas, with all the trappings and ceremonies of the occasion. Next year, the big green star would make its way to the top of the tree. She hadn't felt safe when she'd been on the top step of the ladder, leaning over the branches, and she certainly wasn't about to ask Ed to get up there and do it, and by the time Pat arrived she'd moved on to other tasks for him to do and had forgotten all about it. When she'd sat at dinner, though, all she'd been able to focus on, other than her anxiety about Ed's embarrassing her, was the treetop sticking up like a tumor, even though it was out of sight in the den. It was in plain view in her mind's eye. She hadn't realized how important that star was in rounding out the scene she so carefully constructed. When the lamps were off, it winked with a hazy, emerald loveliness that seemed to pull you toward it. Next year, she would need Connell there to put it up for her. After that, he wouldn't have to come home for another holiday if he didn't want to. She was going to wring enough perfection out of next Christmas to last her the rest of her years on earth.

Part V

Desire Is Full of Endless Distances

1996

69

When Paula Coogan, who had hired Eileen at North Central Bronx, moved to another hospital, Eileen was surprised and dismayed to learn that Paula's replacement was Adelaide Henry, whom Eileen had supervised at Einstein many years before. Adelaide promptly put Eileen on nights, claiming she needed someone of Eileen's stature watching over that shift, but Eileen guessed she was trying to get her to leave, maybe out of insecurity, maybe out of revenge. She remembered being tough on Adelaide, but only because she'd noted her potential and hadn't wanted to see her waste it, especially as executives making promotion decisions were going to be more exacting with Adelaide because she was black.

If Adelaide wanted to get rid of her by putting her on nights, though, she would fail. Eileen would've held on in the midst of a flaming apocalypse to last the two more years she needed to get health benefits. And it was actually a blessing to be put on nights, because with the sundowning, Ed was going to bed early, and he mostly stayed in bed, and the dark of night had begun to frighten him, so that even if he got out of bed he would never leave the house. Short of his filling the place with gas from the stovetop burners, there was very little she had to worry about if he went unsupervised at night, so she would climb into bed with him in the late afternoon and awake at ten to report for duty at eleven. It was working out better than she could have hoped for: she didn't have to pay anyone to be there; she could take care of him when she came home in the morning and still get adequate sleep.

Maybe she spoke to the wrong person about being comfortable with

the night shift, or maybe she didn't affect a sufficiently beleaguered air, because within a month she was switched back to days. She had made it work with Ed home alone for a good while, but the idea that he would get lost worried her, and he was now a known quantity at the police station. She wanted to keep him home with her as long as she could.

She asked around at the hospital to see if anyone knew a good in-home nurse who worked off the books. She found a girl to stay with him, a robust Jamaican who wore her hair in a tower, radiated ease, and seemed perfect for the job until she made Eileen late for work one morning when she showed up late herself, claiming bus trouble. The girl's commute involved two connections and a longish walk, so Eileen didn't dismiss the excuse immediately; besides, she wasn't in a position to act rashly, not without a backup in place. She gave the girl a warning; it happened again; she gave her another warning, one more than she would have given any of the nurses on her staff. The third time, she fired her, but by then she already had her replacement on call.

The second girl got to work on time, but Eileen came home early once and found Ed in the armchair in the living room, where he never sat, picking at his hands like a chimpanzee while the girl stretched out on the couch in the den watching a soap opera and talking on the cordless phone. Eileen told her that part of her job was to sit with Ed and make him feel like a human being. She came home early again the following week and ran into the girl on the phone again, this time on the patio. She paid her for the full week, even though four days remained in it, and told her not to come back.

It would have been easier if she'd been able to stay home and watch Ed herself. Even thirty years into her career—twenty-five in management—she was still better than all of these kids. When she was coming up through the ranks, the care of the patient had been the paramount concern. Now they had other things on their minds.

She had a bad feeling about the third one during the trial hour, when she saw how difficult it was for her to calm Ed's flailing long enough to feed him, and how she could barely lift him from the toilet, but it was hard to find great help when she couldn't pay a tremendous amount, so she

hired her anyway. Then she got a call at work saying Ed had fallen and she couldn't pick him up.

A nurse was supposed to be capable of outsized feats of strength, like a lifeguard or an ant. The girl had looked hale enough, but there lurked in certain people a softness you couldn't see.

She'd gone through three nurses in four months. She didn't have the patience to try another. Instead of replacing the third girl, she gave Ed strict instructions not to answer the door for anyone he didn't know. She told him not to leave the house. She prayed he'd listen, at least until she could figure something out.

She gave in and got the MedicAlert bracelet. If people wanted to look at him as an invalid, she didn't have the energy to stop them anymore.

Somehow Eileen's old friend Bethany had heard what was happening with Ed, tracked down her new number, and called to offer her support.

Bethany had been a fellow nurse at her first go-round at Einstein. Shortly after Eileen met her, Bethany married a corporate executive and quit working, but for a few years they'd stayed in touch, aided by the fact that Bethany's daughter Teresa was Connell's age. Every summer, Eileen, Ed, and Connell went out to Bethany's beach house in Quogue for a handful of days. In the mideighties, though, when Walt took a position at Pepsi, they moved to Purchase, sold the summer house, and dropped off the map.

Bethany told Eileen she was living nearby, in Pelham, and that she and Walt had gotten divorced. Teresa had dropped out of high school in her junior year and moved to Los Angeles with her boyfriend, an actor.

"Walt is heartbroken," she said. "I tell her I only want her happiness. I've been trying to convince her to let me come out and visit. Maybe I'll just show up."

Bethany called every day that week to check in. Eileen welcomed the attention, as many of her friends had receded. She had always gotten along with Bethany, who had a frank, Jamaican sense of humor and could take the stuffing out of anyone. Eileen needed a little more frankness in her life. The friends who had stayed close tiptoed around conversations about Ed.

She invited Bethany over for tea. Bethany told her she'd become a spiritual guru in the years since her divorce. "I guess I began before the divorce," she said, laughing. "It might have had something to do with our *getting* divorced. Walt wasn't exactly clamoring for me to get enlightened."

She took out a photo of Walt, a gesture Eileen found strange. She couldn't understand why Bethany was still carrying it around. Walt looked like he hadn't aged a bit, as though the Jamaican food Bethany had fed him kept him young. Bethany also showed her a photo of Teresa, taken before she'd left. She was just a kid; she still wore braces.

She'd gotten involved with faith healing, she said. Her healer channeled a spirit named Vywamus. "You should come with me sometime. You might like it."

"I'm not interested in any voodoo religion," Eileen said.

"It's not voodoo," Bethany said. "And it's not religion." She laughed. "I'll let you off easy this time. But I'm very persistent when I want to be." She laughed again. "I'll pursue you to the ends of the earth."

Eileen laughed too, though she couldn't help feeling a little unnerved. She poured another cup of tea to cut the tension.

Bethany made friendship easy by always driving over to see her. One Tuesday evening, just as Eileen was about to fix a quick dinner, Bethany appeared at the back door and told her she wanted to take her somewhere.

"I have Ed," Eileen said. "I can't leave."

"He'll be fine. Come."

She called up to Ed, who was in bed with the television on, and then followed Bethany down the back steps.

"Where are we going?"

"It's a surprise."

She was happy to get out, and touched by the thoughtfulness of a friend who knew she needed a break. She imagined a packed restaurant, a coffeehouse buzzing with conversation.

Bethany looked happy. She wore a poppy-colored blouse and light rouge on her brown cheeks to match, as well as lipstick. She put her hand on the back of Eileen's headrest and backed out of the driveway.

"Where is it, though?" Eileen said, as mildly as she could. "Now you have me curious."

"I want you to keep an open mind," Bethany said.

As they pulled onto Midland Avenue, it occurred to Eileen that Beth-

any was not taking her for a gourmet meal or on a shopping spree. They were driving to her cult. "Oh no," Eileen said. "No, no."

Bethany grinned. "I know," she said, and let out a hearty laugh. "But it's not like that. It's going to be relaxing and fun. You'll like these women, I just know it."

"I told you I'm not interested in that," Eileen said, but Bethany kept driving, and they passed through towns, and soon they were parking the car in Pelham.

"There's nothing to be afraid of." Bethany put her hand on Eileen's. "You don't know what you think about it yet."

She took a long look at Bethany's narrow face and close-set brown eyes, her skin that hadn't aged in the ten years since they'd lost touch. She felt sorry for her for needing all this hocus-pocus. She decided she would go in, just this once, as a favor to her friend and an exercise in openness, like sitting through the character breakfast at Disney World when Connell was four, because it was the right thing to do.

Inside, a circle of women rose to greet her. She sat and joined them, and a woman walked in from another room, evidently the psychic chan-neler. She was small, no taller than five two, and her hair had a sort of de-liberate unkempt quality, as if in demonstration of her ascetic bona fides. She sat without ceremony and looked serenely around at the group until her eyes fell on Eileen. She held Eileen's gaze awhile, smiling in a way that forced Eileen to smile back uncomfortably.

The woman called them to order with a breathing exercise. Eileen took part in it, stifling her laughter.

"I'd like to welcome Eileen Leary to our midst tonight," the woman said. "Bethany has brought her to us. Thank you, Bethany. Eileen has been going through some difficulty with her husband. We're here to help her."

Eileen felt herself blushing. She hadn't expected the group's attention to be directed at her so soon or so completely. "Please don't worry about me," she said. "I'm just here to watch."

"Eileen's husband has Alzheimer's disease," the woman said as if Eileen hadn't spoken, and clucks and knowing looks passed through the room. "But as we have seen so often, not everything is as it seems. We are going

to discover today what is happening in her husband's soul. Bethany tells me his name is Edmund? Edmund Leary?"

Eileen had an impulse to shield Ed's name from them, as if by incanting it they might affix to it one of those exotic, long-distance curses that could cause a man to drop dead in the street.

"That's correct," she said.

"My name is Rachelle. In a minute I am going to call on Vywamus to visit us. He will talk to you about your husband. I will be channeling him. It may appear that I am talking, but I will only be a conduit. There is nothing to be afraid of. We will link hands, so you will only have to squeeze the hand of the person to either side of you for reassurance. My spirit will not be in the room during this time. I will not be able to answer any questions once Vywamus has entered my body. You must direct any questions to Vywamus. But it is advisable to simply let him speak. You may notice a slight change in my voice. That's a result of Vywamus using my body as his vessel."

Rachelle started to breath rhythmically and to move her hands in circles. She made guttural chanting sounds, random syllables, like a flautist playing scales to warm up. Then she began speaking. Her voice became almost comically low in pitch.

"I am Vywamus," she said. "I am here to speak to you, Eileen Leary. I am here to tell you that your husband is one of the most repressed souls in the universe. For many lives, he has been fighting a battle with his spirit. He has been an Atlantean for centuries."

Eileen knew that Bethany had never really gelled with Ed. Bethany had had a bit of this New Age streak even when they used to spend time together, and Ed had had little patience for it. She wondered how much Bethany had told this lady.

"This time through," Rachelle said in a painful-sounding husky baritone, "he is fighting for his soul. The battle in his body mirrors the battle in his soul. It is not this disease that is making him obsessed with control. It is the other way around. His obsession with control has culminated in this disease. He needs to learn to open up in this life to save his soul from the battle it has been fighting for centuries."

She had to hand it to her: once Rachelle started channeling Vywamus, she didn't break character. Still, Eileen was having a hard time taking it seriously. She had to bite her cheeks to keep from making editorial grunts. It was all meant for someone else, someone weaker of will or less educated. Whatever kind of cult this Rachelle was running, she was mistaken if she thought she had a potential convert in the room. Eileen may have been through some difficult times, but that didn't mean her brain had gone soft.

71

There had been times she'd wanted to kill Ed; now that he was declining so quickly, she just wanted him home until Christmas. It shocked her that her goals had dwindled to one, but that was all she could focus on, even now, eight months away from the holiday. Once Ed left, she knew, he was never coming back.

There used to be so many goals. They'd made a list at one point. Learn some Gaelic together. Visit the wineries in Napa Valley. She couldn't remember what else was on the list. They hadn't accomplished any of them.

They hadn't finished the house. Much of the first floor looked new and appealing, but a good deal of the second floor was dilapidated and run-down.

She hadn't gone back for a doctorate. She hadn't learned to play better tennis. They'd never take another trip to Europe. They might never take another trip anywhere.

They didn't need to go anywhere anymore, though. If she could get him to Christmas, she would take without complaint whatever was coming. A proper send-off was all she asked, surrounded by the regular crowd on Christmas Eve, the kitchen—the beating heart of the house—full to bursting. By midnight, no one would have left. Smiling Ed in his suit on the couch would be incident-free. Then Mass in the morning; then a short drive to someone else's house, some coffee cake and a modest second round of gifts. Then let it come down. She didn't need the whole day. Let him have a fit at four o'clock. Let him be raving and dangerous and inconsolable. She'd drive him over to the home herself. She'd always hated Christmas night anyway. It was the loneliest night of the year.

Eileen agreed to let Bethany take her back to her faith-healing, channeling psychic, whatever-she-called-herself friend Rachelle. She decided to experience it as a cultural phenomenon, like the be-ins and happenings she'd missed out on while she was in graduate school. She didn't have to keep up a wall of suspicion if she went in knowing these people were doing something entirely weird and that she was going to study them anthropologically.

She joined the others in the circle and waited for "Vywamus" to come out. The woman, Rachelle, walked in barefoot, on the balls of her feet like a cat, gathered her robe under her and sat, Indian-style. Eileen couldn't have gotten into that position if she'd been drugged and stretched into it by a team of men.

Rachelle/Vywamus started speaking to another member of the circle, the focus of the beginning of the session. When Eileen thought about the actual message Vywamus was delivering, and not the spooky way it was being delivered, she grew almost intrigued at how familiar and unthreatening the ideas in it were. The whole thing was a charade, but there was something quaint about the idea of conveying sturdy old wisdom through the medium of performance art. She imagined many of these suburban wives might be impressed enough by a brush with the avant-garde to actually hear a message they'd have dismissed if delivered by a priest, rabbi, or shrink.

After a while Rachelle/Vywamus turned her/his attention to Eileen. Rachelle had homed in on something essential about Ed right away. Eileen wouldn't have put it the way Vywamus had, and Rachelle might have had help from Bethany, but she also appeared to be a master psychologist.

Under the absurd pretense of this character, she was saying something borderline sensible.

At the end of the session, after Vywamus addressed a few of the other women and Rachelle made a big display of being physically drained, everyone stood in a circle talking and eating snacks. Rachelle returned in a different outfit, having shed the robe she was wearing, and mingled.

When Bethany drove her home, she said that she had covered Eileen for the first couple of visits, but next time there would be a one-hundred-dollar fee, and if she wanted to do private sessions it would cost one fifty.

For days, Eileen fretted over how to tell Bethany she wasn't going back to Rachelle, but on Tuesday morning, as she dressed for work, she realized she was actually looking forward to Bethany's visit that night. Bethany was the only one of her old friends who had gotten more involved in her life, rather than less, with the news of Ed's condition. Eileen dug through her closet and found a pair of slacks she could still squeeze into, and a loose jacket that would hide the bulge forming at her waist. She hadn't been indoctrinated into Bethany's cult, and she wouldn't ever be, but as she ironed her clothes and thought about which lipstick would work best with her green jacket, she knew she needed to be out in the world.

Ed was already in bed when Bethany rang the bell at twenty to seven. Eileen applied a last spritz of hairspray, shut the powder room light and yelled "Entrez!" toward the kitchen door. Bethany came dressed smartly again, in a turquoise blouse and white jacket. As they got into the car, she pulled down the visor and dabbed lipstick on her top lip and rubbed her lips together to smear it in. Bethany handed her a tissue to blot.

It was satisfying to be in the company of strong women, most of them semiretired professionals. Maybe she was exactly the sort of woman in a vulnerable state of mind that Rachelle sought to target, but these women didn't seem that way. If they were, she didn't care. She wasn't planning to get to know them. She trusted herself not to be bamboozled by Rachelle's charisma. There was a spiritual vacuum she needed to fill. She'd never imagined she'd find herself in the living room of a cult leader, or sitting unperturbed as she listened to the rates for future sessions.

She wondered what the others were getting out of it. The world, as Vywamus presented it, didn't seem to matter very much; our real existence was taking place somewhere else as we lived out a shadow existence. She didn't need to be signing on to a whole new program in her fifties. She was going for the hour it got her out of the house.

At the end of the session, she didn't even feel awkward writing the check. Bethany took it with a smile and presented it to Rachelle. Eileen knew she was being played, but she was content to let it happen. It was good to have someone thinking of her, and she liked that Vywamus did so much of the talking. It was better than therapy. Eileen couldn't stand the silence in Dr. Brill's office, the fact that she was expected to open her mouth and let all the words she'd apparently kept stopped up come pouring out.

73

If you'd told her at her wedding that one day, years on, she'd be picking her husband up at the police station on a balmy evening in late May, she would have laughed and said, "You don't know Ed," but she'd gotten a page, and then she was nestling into a spot between a pair of squad cars in the quiet lot at dusk. She shut the engine off and sat considering the possibility that fate had finally caught up to her.

She headed toward the sign-in desk and saw Ed sitting in the waiting area with an officer, his shirt untucked, his hair a mess. He wore no anguish on his face, only an aspect of resignation. In his rigid posture he looked surprisingly regal, like a statue of an ancient Egyptian king.

She introduced herself. The officer's name was Sergeant Garger.

"I'm so sorry about this," she said.

Seeing her, Ed emitted a low moan that suggested he'd been caught with a prostitute or committed some other unspeakable indiscretion.

"Officer Cerullo will sit with your husband," Sergeant Garger said. "I'd like you to come to my desk to sign some papers."

She wanted to get out of there as quickly as possible. She didn't want them to conclude that the situation was completely out of hand, because there was no telling what they might do then. She could endure any embarrassment, as long as they didn't take him away.

"Your husband was wandering back and forth in traffic in front of the church," Officer Garger said quietly. "He was stopping cars, waving his arms. Cars were backed up all the way to the train station. When we approached him, he was wild. "

"I'm sorry."

"If the responding officer hadn't seen the bracelet on his wrist, we would have booked him for disturbing the peace and resisting arrest. We ascertained that he was trying to find his way home." He took out a breath mint, asked her if she wanted one. "It's Alzheimer's? Is that correct?"

"Yes," she said.

"He seems young to me."

"Fifty-four."

"I understand this is not the first incident," the officer said. She nodded silently. "He comes into town?"

"He doesn't," she said. "This is an exception."

"What nobody wants is for this to turn into a legal situation. If your husband is deemed a threat to himself or others, or if the home situation creates an impediment to his safety—"

"I'm a nurse. I know the law."

"Do you let him out alone?"

"We usually have a nurse, but I had to let her go. I haven't found a replacement yet. I got him that bracelet in case something happened. I have to go to work; I can't stay with him."

"Have you considered a nursing home?"

"Not as long as I can help it."

"Are there any family members who can help?"

"No," she said.

"Nobody?"

She thought of Connell at school. She had hoped he'd grow up when he went off to college, but he couldn't even remember to call home on his father's birthday without a reminder.

"Well, there is my son. But he's away at school. He's in a play this summer. I can't ask him to come home."

"You know what I think, Mrs. Leary? If you don't mind my saying?"

"What?"

"You sure can."

In bed that night, she thought about the way Officer Garger had looked at her. She'd gotten that look lately from men—repairmen, deliverymen—

who came to the house and saw what kind of shape Ed was in. She had a few more wrinkles now, and a hint of crow's feet, and the other day she thought she'd seen the makings of a jowl. Still, she knew she remained beautiful and that a distressed situation like the one she was in with Ed might bring out the chivalry in even unenlightened men. Lately she had told them the story as soon as she opened the door. She considered it her duty to explain that Ed was incapacitated. He had come to pride himself on his hard-won home improvement skills and would have hated for the professional craftsmen he respected to write him off as another eunuch of a househusband.

They looked at her with pity, some with more than pity. They didn't like to look at Ed or raise their voices around him. It made conversations more conspiratorial than they might otherwise have been.

She couldn't avoid admitting to herself that she'd given Officer Garger a look of her own. She knew it hadn't communicated much but a vague dissatisfaction, but guilt still crept through her. When Ed's hand explored her shoulder, she rolled over and went to sleep.

74

I t was the day of their first practice as a cast. He and Jenna had arranged to meet beforehand at the Medici. He walked past the place and circled the block, then steeled himself enough to go in. He found her in a booth in the back.

"Sorry I'm late," he said.

At the first read-through, Jenna had been a revelation as Puck, sexy and feral. Connell had read his own lines in a workmanlike fashion that was accidentally appropriate for the role of Francis Flute, the bellows mender given Thisbe to portray in the mechanicals' play-within-the-play. He liked to think he would have made a good Oberon to her Puck, but the director knew better. Oberon went to an upperclassman whose magnetism attracted the available attention of much of the cast, Jenna included. When the director announced that Thisbe would be wearing a pink prom dress, the loudest laugh in the room came from Oberon.

"It's okay." She leaned down to reach into her backpack, her long red hair shifting forward to block his view of her. "Here, let me give you this. We should get going."

"Hang on a second," he said, beginning to panic. "Let me sit down." He creaked in the joints as he bent into the seat. When he squared up across from her, he felt the nervous energy he had been carrying around in his chest settle with a queasy finality into his gut. She was not going to reconsider. If it had been a moment of betrayal that had driven her away, some passionate carelessness in the predawn hours, perhaps he could have pulled her back to him. She had a peculiar tolerance, even a fondness, for

the self-absorption of dynamic young men. There had been no regrettable evening though; likely he had been too ready to offer his devotion. The little sedimentary deposits of his need had piled at her feet until they blocked her view of him.

"I think we have time for coffee," he said, "and to talk a bit."

"Let's have some, then." She signaled to the waiter, frowning in that lovely way she did when she was taking care of tasks. It was something in the way she gave in without a fight: their relationship had already receded into the past for her. "What do you want to talk about?"

"I just want to talk." He couldn't say the undiluted truth, which was that he needed her not to leave him. They sat in silence. He dug his knife into the candle wax poured in one of the many grooves furrowed into the table by generations of undergraduates. He couldn't look at her.

"How's your father? Are you going home?"

He drummed his fingers on the table. "I don't have to, if it would make a difference for me to stay."

"You should go," she said. "You need to be there."

"I miss you so much," he said, finally cracking. "I don't know what I'm going to do without you."

"You're running from something. You need to look at that."

"I'm sorry," he said.

Her lips pulled into a little knot. "For what?"

"For not planning anything for your birthday," he said. "For any mistakes I made."

She laughed. "The only thing you did wrong was ask me to marry you. The only thing I did wrong was not say no right away." She looked at her watch and pulled out a sealed envelope. "Can I give this to you now?"

The ring made an airy bulge in the center. He felt his chest tightening.

"We're too young for this," she said. "We're *nineteen*! I should never have taken that thing. I was in shock, I guess."

In his silence he was laboring to deepen the groove, but the dull knife had no effect.

"Let's not be so serious all the time! Let's have fun."

"We could make it work," he said.

"Let's get the check. We're late." She patted his hand, looked for the waiter. "We've had some great conversations here."

He sat, quietly despairing.

"This wasn't one of them, Mr. Cat-Got-Your-Tongue. Mr. Eeyore. And any other animals I haven't mentioned."

He couldn't help smiling. "Could you try, for one second, not to be so damned adorable?"

"I'm not adorable," she said. "You just see me that way. That's the whole problem. I'm fucked up inside, just like you."

They arrived as the rest of the cast was stretching. It was going to be a physically challenging production, so Dale, the director and a theater professor, wanted them limber. Since it would be performed under the stars, outside the Reynolds Club, they would be practicing outdoors to get used to projecting their voices.

As Connell stretched, he rehearsed what he would say to Dale. He hardly knew the man, beyond taking one of his classes, but he'd already come to see him as something of a father figure, and he dreaded disappointing him. He went to office hours and listened to Dale hold forth about plays. He hadn't read or seen most of the works Dale brought up, but he tried to nod along at all the right moments, and when he left Dale's office, he marched straight to the Reg to check them out. He scrambled to read them before he saw Dale next, but he was always a discussion behind.

"This is where we'll be for the next two months," Dale said as he called them together. "There's no intimacy out here. It's vast, echoless. The acoustics are awful." He gestured to the heavens. "The open air swallows all but the loudest sounds. There will be no microphones. You will have to fill this space with your voices."

Connell watched over Jenna's shoulder as Dale spoke. She was alarmingly buoyant. He saw her exchange a few looks with Oberon.

"Now," Dale said, "I want you to spread out." Connell tried to stay by Jenna. "Form two rows. Everyone has a partner on the opposite row."

When the shifting of bodies finished, Connell saw that Jenna was his partner. "Get up real close," Dale said. "Closer. Put your face right near your partner's face."

Connell wasn't an actor; he knew that by now. He was never sure where to look when he was onstage. He had tried out for this play to let some more Shakespeare run through his head and carve out some shared space with Jenna, who now was staring right into him. He didn't know what to do with his arms, which swayed awkwardly by his side.

"We're going to do a little exercise. I want both rows to take one step back. Okay. Do you notice a difference? Look into your partner's eyes. Are they looking into yours?"

They were. She was laughing with what seemed like genuine mirth at the irony of their pairing.

"Now," Dale said, "I'm going to ask you to do something a little unusual. I want you to tell your partner you love them. Don't be shy. Tell them you love them now."

"I love you," Connell said, separated from her by a few feet. She said it too, her brows raised, a big smile on her face, as though she were trying to get him to laugh along with her. It occurred to him that she had never said those precise words to him before.

"Now take another step back," Dale said, "a big one. You have to try harder to see each other. Maybe not much, but a little. What happens when you get farther away? What do you have to do to compensate? Out here, you'll be trying to reach people a long way off. Now, tell your partner you love them again."

Connell said it a little louder than before. Jenna seemed to mean every bit of it. There was no denying her talent.

"Now take another step back. Forget about the distance. Say it as if they're right next to you, only louder."

"I love you," he said weakly across the expanse. He didn't know how to use his diaphragm, and his breath ran out too soon.

"Now two steps. This time shout it! This is love that gives a damn."

He did as asked, coughing as he did. She was a figure in a row of people.

"Two more steps. Again!"

This time he didn't say anything, only listened. He couldn't make out any individual voices, only a collective one making an urgent appeal.

"One last step! Give it your best shout!"

Jenna was a blur on the other side. His throat hurt. He threw his arms back and shouted as loud as he could.

His mother had called and asked him to come home and he had said he had a responsibility to the director and the cast to be in the play. He could hear from her silence that she was shocked to hear him talk of responsibility in refusing to come home and help, and the truth was that he had shocked himself by saying it.

He hadn't realized how scared he was to see his father until his mother's call. He hadn't intended never to return; he just had no immediate plans to do so. Jenna had been the best excuse possible, but now she didn't seem like much of an excuse anymore. He could say he was staying in Chicago to work on things with her—*my future wife*, he could hear himself rationalizing later, *or at least that was how I thought at the time*—but he saw the truth of their relationship too clearly to allow himself to pretend later that he hadn't.

Had he tried to grow up quickly to cover up feeling like a child? Had he asked her to marry him because he needed a grand unifying theory to explain his absence? The thing was, he himself had been scared of marrying her. He didn't want it, really, any more than she did. He was more relieved than brokenhearted, but now he had to think about everything he wasn't doing. He had run out of excuses not to go home.

He quit the play, crammed his pair of army duffels full of dirty clothes, and got on a plane. His mother said she couldn't pick him up, so he took the bus and train and walked from the station.

He squeezed through the back door with the bags and was struck by the punishing volume of the television coming from the den. He remembered his mother saying tests had revealed that his father had lost some hearing. He headed toward the den but found his father in the vestibule, balanced precariously on a stepladder, looking through the little windows set into the front

doors. Connell muted the television and went back and called to him, but his father only mumbled something, so Connell walked over and touched his shoulder. "Dad!" he said, more forcefully. "I'm *home*." The news seemed to leave no impression at all, though he'd been away for almost a year.

"He's out there." His father gave Connell a serious, confidential look.

"Who?"

"The man," he said darkly. "That man. He always comes."

"Where is he?"

Connell raised himself on his toes and looked out. No one was there except the gardener, who had finished pruning the hedges and moved to the house next door.

"Do you mean him?" he said, pointing. "You mean Sal?"

"No, no, no." His father's eyes flashed; his hand twitched; his hushed tone and terrified stare implied that anything was possible. Connell wanted to believe in his father's continued ability to perceive danger accurately. Had he arrived just in time?

Connell turned again to the window; then he backed away, feeling foolish.

"Come down off there," he said, holding his father's elbow, but his father stood frozen. "It's just a step. Just put your leg forward." His father offered a tentative foot, then retracted it and tried the other. "Lean on me," Connell said, and his father did. Once on firm ground, he clapped a couple of times before he seemed to register his son's presence and looked embarrassed. He went to the window again. He was animated now, his finger jabbing at it.

"He's there! He's there!"

Connell darted over. His father was right: the man *was* there, and he was famously unstoppable. He might deliver death and destruction; he might deliver circulars for the Food Emporium.

"Dad!" he said. "Don't you know that's the mailman?"

The mailman disappeared behind the hedge. "I don't trust him," his father said, and then headed for the kitchen with a surprising quickness in his step. He lifted one of the blinds in the window above the sink so high that his whole face would have been visible from the other side.

When his father moved aside, Connell saw that the blinds were bent in several places. His mother must have reconciled herself to living with them rather than replacing them over and over. This one change amounted to a revolution in her thinking.

His father opened the door and then the screen, which swung back hard and crashed into him as he headed outside. When he returned, he was pressing a bundle of mail against his chest with both arms. Some pieces fell to the floor and he released the remainder onto the island like a cascading pile of apples.

"What are you doing?" Connell asked, flabbergasted.

"I get the mail."

"Just like that."

"I get it every day."

"But a minute ago you were saying you didn't trust him. You were totally spooked."

"He comes every day," his father said. "I don't know who he is."

"He's the *mailman*," Connell said desperately.

"I don't trust him."

"Dad," he said, "he's the *mailman*."

"I don't trust him."

"But you know he's delivering the mail?"

"Yes," he said reasonably. "He comes every day."

"So why are you suspicious of him?"

"I don't know who he is," he said. "I get the mail every day. That's my job. I have other jobs."

He shuffled into the den and sat down. Connell followed him and un-muted the television. The volume shot out like a cannon report. Connell retreated to the kitchen and picked up the fallen letters, wondering when the last time was that his father had opened a piece of mail and whether he'd ever open one again. He made himself a peanut butter and jelly sandwich. The den was drenched in noisy static, and he went in and found his father watching the electronic snow of a lost signal as though it were a program. His father didn't stir in that crashing noise. He clutched the remote like an amulet. Connell tried to take it from him, but his father had

an iron grip on it. Connell went to the television, lowered the volume, and changed the channel until the picture came up.

"This thing," his father said disgustedly. "It doesn't work." His mouth hung open, and a little drool leaked out. Connell used his father's own shirtsleeve to wipe it up. His father gave him a knowing look. Connell wondered how much awareness still lurked in him. A faint whining hum emanated from him.

"It's good to see you," Connell said, throwing an arm around him.

His father kept looking at the television but patted his own knee. "Good," he said. "Good."

They watched *Columbo*. Peter Falk's Beckettian detective wore his trademark trench coat and screwed up his face in his world-weary, gently bemused way—experience and innocence mingling in him. Connell thought, *Thank God for* Columbo. *Thank God for* Law & Order *reruns*. He didn't know how he would ever fill the time with his father without television.

When the commercials came on, he had no idea what to say. His mother would ride in on a barge of stories about family friends or simply accounts of her day. Connell felt disrespectful delivering reports from the front lines of experience. He felt a little better talking about things his father knew already or that they had experienced together, but it felt awkward to introduce them into conversation. Still, he could feel it coming, the need to revert to the familiar.

"I have to say I like Paul O'Neill," Connell pronounced academically. His father continued to look at the television. "I'm not one of those Mets fans who hate a guy like that just to hate him. He's the heart of that team, a blue-collar worker." The silence on his father's end of the exchange was growing desperate. "Yankees or not, it was exciting to have a New York team in the playoffs again." This last remark seemed to have gotten his father's attention, because his face brightened into a smile, as though it were news to him; and then Connell realized that it *was* news to him, even though he'd watched all the playoff games the previous October and Connell had called after every one.

"Yeah!" he said. "Good!"

Connell felt stupid for trying to tread carefully around the old man. It was time to face facts: his father's short-term memory was shot. He probably didn't remember anything longer than a few minutes. As soon as Connell left the room, his father wouldn't even know he had come home in the first place. He wouldn't have wanted his son to sit around with him on a Friday night; it would have embarrassed him, and Connell didn't want him to be embarrassed, so he went upstairs to get ready, because there were people he hadn't seen in a long time.

He still had his first bottle of cologne, which he had made last a few years by dabbing it sparingly, once behind each ear, once on either side of the neck. He had sweated it out on dance floors and left its trace in heated grapplings on couches. When he'd departed for college, he'd left it behind on the counter in his bathroom, a little offering at the altar of adolescence.

He found the bottle in his parents' bathroom, down to the dregs. A vague horror crept into him, turning to fury. His father must have scooped the bottle up in his wanderings through the house. He could see him struggling to open it, sloshing its contents around, watching it pour through his fingers into the sink. He imagined him clapping it to his neck and chest in big cupped palms and uncoordinated splashes, trying to steal some of the future that stretched out before his son. How much could he even *smell* anymore? And what use did he have for cologne anyway? That part of his life was over.

Connell marched downstairs with the bottle. "Did you do this?" he asked, thrusting it under his nose. "Did you take this? There was more than half a bottle in here."

"I don't know," his father said, looking scared. "I don't know."

This time he didn't soften it for him.

"I get it," he said. "*You don't know.* Well, you used it. I know it's just a bottle of cologne. But it was special to me."

His father's eyes widened; his forehead wrinkled; his mouth turned down. He sat back in the couch. "I'm sorry," he said. "I don't know. I don't know. I'm sorry."

Part of Connell wanted to say it was no big deal, but he couldn't somehow.

"Look," he said. "Just be careful with my stuff. Okay? Whatever I left in my room. Maybe you could leave that stuff alone."

"I'm sorry," he said.

He felt his resolve wavering. He had to resist comforting him. His father ran roughshod over everything, and everybody was supposed to go around picking up the pieces. You couldn't get mad at him; you were supposed to feel sorry for him all the time. Well, forget that. Connell was the son, not the father. It wasn't his job yet to pick up the pieces.

He went to a friend's place in the city. They hit a few bars, closed the last one down. He took the first train home in the morning, the five-thirty.

He awoke to his mother shaking him.

"Your father has his routines now," she said. "You're disrupting him. He needs this couch for the TV. Go up to your bed." The room was dark, but a sliver of light filtered through the sliding door. He smelled coffee and the eggy sweetness of batter on a grill. "Just go upstairs." A frown flashed across her face. "You didn't have to come home."

"What are you talking about? I'm getting up."

"I need to know what I can expect from you while you're here."

"I'm here," he said. "What do you need?"

"Can you stay with your father? I don't want to leave him alone today."

"Yeah," he said.

She stood there for a second looking him over.

"Can I count on you?"

"Of course," he said.

"Just stick around the house, make sure he eats, make sure he doesn't get hurt. Sit with him awhile. Don't sleep too late."

"Okay," he said.

"He's excited to have you home." She made it sound hopeful, but a sad note crept into her voice. "You're all he asks about. 'Where's Connell? Where's Connell?'"

His mother had dressed his father in a long-sleeved shirt and slacks. He looked as if he was about to go to work. One detail remained, though: his shirttail hung out. She undid his belt, then hiked his pants up high and rezipped them.

Connell passed through the kitchen. The pancake batter bowl was empty. She hadn't made enough for him. He threw his thumb over his shoulder. "It's all yours," he said, not as gently as he could have.

His mother stopped him on the stairs.

"Are you going to be here?" she asked. "Tell me now. I'll try to figure something else out. I can't afford to have you acting irresponsibly."

"Mom, relax," he said. "I'll take care of him. Go to work."

At the top of the stairs he heard his mother tell his father she was putting on the television, and his father gurgle in response, and then he heard the volume rising, step by step. "If you need anything," his mother shouted over the television, "Connell is upstairs." If his father responded, he couldn't hear it. "I love you," his mother said. There was a pause. "Can you say it back, honey?" He didn't know if his father hadn't responded or if he simply hadn't heard him over the loud volume, but after a while he heard the garage door opening.

He thought it important to let his father drink his own soda. His father grabbed the glass by the brim and pulled it toward him too quickly. The glass dropped to the bricks and shattered. Connell picked up the biggest chunks of glass by hand and got the dustpan and broom to sweep the slick shards into the garbage. He toweled the pool from the floor. So it had come to this: you couldn't give him anything to drink by himself. He had to be in a bib, practically. You had to hold it up to his mouth. You had to give it to him in a plastic cup, maybe even a sippy cup. And he just sat there defenseless as you reached into his lap with a sponge to soak up the spillage. He didn't even try to brush you away and say he would do it himself. He just sighed and offered himself up. And the fragile, helpless look on his face, the way he didn't even try to argue that everyone made mistakes, made him seem like a whipped dog, complete with sad, soulful eyes and a desire to please.

"Don't move an inch," Connell said. "Not one inch." But he didn't know why he'd said it. He had cleaned up every bit of the glass.

His father was picking at his belt, trying to get it open. He was pumping the waistband up and down like he was trying to fan out a fire. Then Connell smelled it. He went to unbuckle the pants, but his father wouldn't let him.

"No," he screamed. "No! No!"

"Dad!" he said. "Calm down. We have to get you clean."

His father was whimpering as he kept his hand on his backside, trying to hold the stuff in place. In the struggle, some crap soaked through his pants. Connell maneuvered him upstairs somehow and into the shower, still in his clothes, but when he tried unbuckling the belt, his father started yelling and keening again. He undid the button of his father's pants, then stopped. This wasn't the time to rush stupidly in. He would get the shoes off first; everything else would follow from that.

"Can you sit down? If you sit down this will go a lot easier."

"Go away!" his father shouted. "Go away!"

Connell moved behind him and pulled his father down onto him, breaking his fall with his body. His father crashed an elbow into his chest and flailed around like a man on fire. He would have punched Connell in the face if he could have turned around.

Connell held him in a tight grip. "It's okay," he said, over and over. He had to slow everything down.

He climbed out from under him, cradling his head. He tugged off his father's shoes, unzipped his pants, and started pulling them off. His father grabbed at them and kicked at him, but Connell got them past his butt and off his feet. Crap clung to his father's legs and fell to the tub in clumps. Connell heard it splat and realized he could never be a nurse like his mother. His father was breathing hard and staring at him with an eerie intensity, as if to keep his gaze from drifting to his nakedness.

Connell dropped the pants in a heap on the floor. He didn't have the heart to tackle the underwear yet, so he went after the button-down shirt. His father was slicked with crap all over and hard to grip, but Connell got the shirt off; only the socks and soiled briefs remained.

"Will you stop, Dad? Will you stop for a minute?"

"Go away!" his father shouted. "No more!"

"You are going to have to listen to me," he said sharply.

"Leave me alone! Leave!"

As he took his father's underwear off, Connell looked away, partly so as not to mortify his father and partly because he hadn't seen his father's penis since he was a little kid in the shower with him. The smell in the hot shower overpowered him, and he gagged. Some of the crap fell out of his father's underwear, which Connell cupped like a diaper and dropped into the little trash bin with the grocery store bag in it. His father lay there naked. Connell would have to pick him up and wash him, but he would have to get the tub clean too, or they would both track it around the house. His own clothes were going to get sopping wet, so he quickly undressed. He left his underwear on. He needed all his strength to lift his father up. His father wasn't resisting anymore, but he was dead weight. Once Connell got him standing, he closed the curtain and turned the water on. The crap stuck to the bathtub began to wash toward the drain. He grabbed a towel from the rack and started wiping the crap from his father's legs and butt. It seemed that no amount of wiping could get him clean. His father's head hung down and his shoulders slumped. His chest heaved in deep, mournful sighs. When the towel was too filthy to continue, Connell rolled it up and dumped it on the floor. He grabbed the bar of soap and another towel and made it into a giant washcloth with which he washed his father's genitals and gave his legs and backside a good scrubbing. He had never touched his father so much in his life. He soaped up his hands and washed his father's feet and his own. He washed his own arms and legs and scrubbed at his hands, then turned the water off. "We're almost done," he said, opening the curtain, taking his father's hand, and helping him out into the steam-filled room. He ran to the closet and grabbed more towels. His first thought was to wrap one around his waist and remove his sopping underwear beneath it, but something told him it would be a great indignity for his father to be naked while his son was clothed, so he took his underwear off and stood exposed. He toweled his father down and they stood naked together. He wrapped a towel around each of them. He

found his father's cologne in the medicine cabinet, made a little well of it in his hand, and clapped it to his father's neck. The smell rushed up at him, and he was reminded of when his father showed him how to shave. "Go with the grain," his father had said into the mirror. "To avoid bumps. Take it easy. Take your time. Don't go over the same spot twice if you can avoid it." Afterward, he'd leaned down to let Connell pull at his cheeks and feel the cool, smooth skin of his face.

Connell put some underwear on his father, and a T-shirt, and led him to the bed and tucked him in.

When his father was asleep, Connell left the house to go buy a box of adult diapers. He didn't know why his mother hadn't thought of this sooner. It would save everyone a lot of trouble and be a simple fix. He couldn't think of a single reason not to use them.

"He wants to leave you his desk when he's gone," his mother said at breakfast the next morning, before she left for work. His father was upstairs. "The rest you'll have to wait for me to die to get."

"Jesus."

"You want to be a kid forever? You have to hear this stuff eventually."

Connell knew that getting that desk had been one of the few happy experiences his father had shared with his own father as an adult. It was of no use to his father anymore, though. Now it was where his mother did the bills. She could use the little desk in Connell's room for that; he could switch them out.

The desk was five feet wide and three deep and made of solid wood. It wasn't an heirloom, exactly. The wood was scratched and nicked from the banging by the chair. A set of drawers on either side formed the base on which the desktop rested.

Taped index cards ran along the front and side edges. One card listed the day, month, and year of all three of their birthdays. One had a little family tree branching out from his grandparents to his aunts, uncles, and cousins. Off EILEEN TUMULTY LEARY (WIFE) and ED LEARY (SELF) was CONNELL LEARY (SONN). One card read SOCIAL SECURRURITURY #, as though his father had picked out a syllable at random to keep the thread going. Inside the

desk was a card with a pump pin affixed to it and the caption, PIN FOR
BLOING UP OF BACKET BALLS.

While his father watched television in the den, Connell lugged the
heavy thing up the stairs piece by piece to his room. When he was done
reassembling it, he felt energized by a sense of possibility. He would fill in
the drawers and get down to whatever important work lay ahead, which
would reveal itself to him if he sat there long enough.

His own desk was so light that he could carry it downstairs without
removing the drawers. He shoved it into place where his father's desk had
been. It looked miniature beneath his father's diplomas. He taped the index
cards to the desk's surface.

All that remained was to bring his father's chair up and carry his own
down in compensation. His father's chair didn't just swivel and wheel; it
pivoted back, to allow for those periodic bouts of idleness deep thinkers
required for their important ideas.

The chair, which was heavier than it looked, was anchored in a metal
base. Once upstairs, it lent his room an appealing seriousness. He sat in it
and picked at the remaining tape on the desktop. He leaned back, to let his
mind wander wherever his thoughts would go.

He must have fallen asleep, because he awoke to his father shouting.
He went downstairs and found him in the study.

"My desk," his father said plaintively.

Connell pulled at his shirt's hem. "Mom said you wanted to leave it to me."

"Yes," he said. Tears were streaming down his face. "For you." He
pointed at Connell, jabbing him in the sternum. "You."

"I brought it upstairs."

"When I'm dead," he said. "When I'm dead."

The weight of a lifetime of kindnesses done him fell on Connell at once.

That night, when his mother told him to take it back downstairs, he
felt almost relieved.

For a moment, he hoped that his father might forget it ever happened,
but then he realized that the condition didn't work like that. He forgot
things you wanted him to remember. He remembered things you wanted
him to forget.

The next day, he sat at his little desk again and tried to write Jenna a letter, but nothing came. He covered both sides of a sheet of paper with his signature, trying out different styles.

The weather was nice. He decided to try to take his father outside for a catch.

He found the gloves in a tote bag on which his father had written the family name multiple times in permanent marker during the period when he'd gone around labeling everything. The longer Connell looked at those insistent capital letters, the more they sounded like the cry of a drowning man.

His father had bought them both new gloves the year they'd moved in. Connell felt ashamed at how pristine his father's looked, scuff-free and auburn-lustrous. They'd spent almost no time playing catch since. Connell's glove was more worn, its leather cracked in places. When he'd quit baseball to do debate, the shift from body to mind had felt final. He hadn't even considered taking his glove when he'd left for college.

He put a tennis ball in his glove's pocket and led his father outside. When they got to the bottom of the stairs, he held his father's glove out to him.

"Let's play catch."

His father could hardly hold the glove on his hand, so Connell decided to ditch the gloves. He stood him with his back to the wall and walked a few paces away, then bounced the ball to him, trying to get it as close to his hands as he could. When he didn't catch it, Connell fetched it and placed it in his hands. His father couldn't throw, but he could bounce it to him in a rudimentary way. He could tell his father was throwing because he would hold it for a while and then it would leave his hand.

He felt like he was losing his mind, or at least his intelligence, sitting there watching that much television with his father. He started spending most of his time in his room, reading novels, trying to drown out the noise of the television downstairs, and writing and rewriting a tortured letter to Jenna that got longer and longer the more he realized he'd never send it. He understood he was writing it for himself now, to try to figure out what had gone wrong with him, why he'd asked her to marry him in the first place. She was right: he *was* nineteen. He was embarrassed to think of how he'd

behaved for most of the last semester—like a child and an old man all at once.

He heard his father cry out and dashed down and found him lying facedown in the kitchen. The runner was bunched up on the floor; he had evidently tripped on it. Connell rolled him over, saw that his mouth was bloody and that he'd broken one of his front teeth. Connell sat him up and soaked a dish towel and put it in his mouth. He saw the piece of tooth lying on the floor and laid it on the island. The quantity of blood on the bricks made Connell worry that his father might have bitten part of his tongue off, but when he forced his mouth open he saw that he had only cut his gums and split his lip. Blood pooled under his tongue. Connell leaned him over the sink and got him to spit, then sat him at the table. A broken plate rested facedown on the floor. He must have thrown it as he'd fallen. Connell gathered its halves and the plastic-wrapped sandwich into a saggy bundle that he deposited in the trash.

The runners formed little rolling hillocks. He had even slipped on them himself a couple of times. He remembered now—how had he forgotten it?—that his mother had asked him to buy double-sided tape to secure them to the floor.

He watched his father's Adam's apple rise and fall as his father swallowed blood. He gave him ice in a wet towel to suck on. After a while, he brought him up, got him changed, and returned him downstairs. He mopped the floor of the blood and put the piece of tooth in the little pocket of his jeans, because he couldn't bring himself to throw it out and was too ashamed to leave it on the counter. Then he sat with his father on the couch and waited for his mother to come home and see what had become of both of them.

He heard the garage door. His mother came up the stairs carrying some bags of groceries. She handed them to him and slung her pocketbook onto the island. She told him to put them away.

"Leave that chicken out," she said. "I'm going to make it."

She called in "Hello" to his father and filled a glass with water. Connell emptied the bags purposefully, trying not to look at her. When there was

nothing left to find a spot for, he turned to see her taking down a second glass of water with deliberate sips, as though it were medicine. She was looking at him over the glass.

"I might send you to the store for garlic," she said. "I forgot to get garlic."

"Okay."

"I've got to turn that down. I can't hear myself think. Edmund!" she called again. "I'm home."

She put her glass in the sink. There was a strange buoyancy in her step.

"Mom, wait."

"What?"

"Something happened earlier. Dad got hurt."

She started in his father's direction. "What is it?" she asked with surprising panic in her voice. "What's happened?"

She took the remote and lowered the volume on the television.

"What's happened?" she asked again, sounding more alarmed than Connell had heard her sound, perhaps ever. "Are you going to tell me, or what?"

His father sat there like a statue, looking past her at the screen's flashing, unaccompanied images.

"He fell down. I was out of the room. He landed hard on the bricks."

"Let me look at you, Edmund. What did he hurt?"

"He fell on his face. Cut his chin. Broke his tooth."

"Let me see your mouth, Edmund."

His father sat stone-faced.

"Open up!" she said, sounding shrilly desperate. She turned to Connell. "How bad is it?"

"There was a lot of blood."

"Open up!" she said. She sat on the couch and put her hand to his father's mouth. She pried his lips open. He had his teeth squeezed shut, but Connell could see the space where his tooth had been. His mother didn't turn and yell at him. She smoothed out his father's hair and kissed his cheek.

"Oh, Edmund," she said mutedly. "What are we going to do with you?"

"Nothing," his father said finally. "Nothing. Leave me alone."

He hadn't taken his eyes off the television, but now he took one glance at Connell. There was embarrassment in the glance, but also something like a flash of defiance.

Connell waved his mother into the kitchen. She didn't follow him right away. He stood away from the doorway while he waited for her, because he didn't want his father to see him. He was ashamed.

The volume went back up, and a few moments later his mother came in.

"What is it?"

"I don't think I can do this," Connell said, his hands against the edge of the countertop.

"Do what?"

"This thing with Dad. I don't know."

"What *happened*?"

He looked down. "He fell. That's all."

"Well, you just have to keep a better eye on him."

"That's what I'm saying. I don't think I can do it. I thought I could do it. But I can't. It's too hard for me. It's too much."

"I did it when I was ten years old."

"But I'm not you," he said. "That's the problem right there."

"Well, that's just terrific," she said. She motioned for him to move and took a cutting board out of the cabinet below.

"It's driving me crazy," he said.

"What do you think it's doing to me?"

"You go to work."

"I never go anywhere," she said. "All day long, I'm right here in my mind."

"I'm sorry. I don't want to disappoint you."

She sliced through the thin layer of plastic on the chicken. "Don't worry about disappointing me. Worry about leaving me in the lurch. I need help, goddammit!"

"I can get a job. Bring some money in. You can pay someone with it."

"Keep your money," she said. "You're going to need it for therapy later."

"That's cold."

"I thought it would be good for him, for *you*"—she pointed with the knife—"if you were around. If it's not, it's not."

"I wish I could do it," he said.

"You can," she said. "You just don't know it." She had started to cut the chicken, but she set the knife down. "Here," she said. "You do this. You think you can handle it? Or you want me to find someone else to do this too?"

He felt the blood drain from his face. His mother seemed to notice. "Thin slices, across the breast," she said a little more softly. She went to the refrigerator and brought back some broccoli. "Cut this when you're done with that. Small pieces. My feet ache." Then she went into the living room. He cut the chicken and rinsed the broccoli, but before cutting the latter he went to the doorway and leaned into the dining room to look at her. She had her legs up on the couch. She was holding one of the sheer curtains aside with one hand and rubbing at her foot with the other. She was looking out at the street and didn't notice him there. He had an impulse to tell her he would rub her feet for her. When he was a kid, she would ask him to rub them, and he would grumble his way through it, because she worked all day and her feet were clammy and smelly. Her feet had only gotten more forbidding over the years, the soles tougher, the cracks deeper, but he wanted to rub them and not complain. He couldn't find a way to tell her what he was thinking, so he just looked at her for a while. It seemed she was watching for something. He couldn't remember the last time he'd seen her sitting there. When they first moved in, she sat there all the time.

He went back to the broccoli and cut it with heavy chops, because he remembered her saying she found the sound a knife made on a cutting board satisfying. When he was done he hacked at the bare board for a while, rhythmically so that it would sound like the real thing. He went into the living room. She had stopped rubbing her feet. She wasn't looking out the window anymore but was sitting on the couch. She gave him a weary glance as he approached.

"What is it?"

"Can I help?"

"You chopped the broccoli?" He nodded. She let out a faint sigh. "I'll be in to cook. Just leave everything there."

"Can I help with your feet?"

"My *feet*?"

"Do you want me to rub them?"

She had a wry expression on, as if she was weighing making a dry remark. Then she seemed to consider it further. "You're offering to rub them," she said dubiously.

He thought of the gap in his father's mouth, the pool of blood under his father's tongue.

It had been years since he'd touched his mother's feet. He had half expected he'd never touch them again.

"Yes," he said.

She raised her brows. "That would be nice," she said.

He settled into the couch and took one foot in his lap as he used to. He was almost queasy with embarrassment at his proximity to her. He pressed a tentative hand against the ball of her foot. It was all there, the familiar moistness, the tufts of knuckle hair, the burst blisters, the gunky nails.

"Is your father all right?" she asked.

"He's fine. Just watching TV."

She seemed to relax, let her head fall against the pillow. He gave himself over to the task, using both hands to apply the proper pressure. Somehow he'd always been good at this. He'd had a certain amount of practice. His father would be busy in the study and his mother would put down the paper and ask if he'd rub her feet. There was something sweetly cajoling in the way she told him that she never sat down at work; it was the only time she ever behaved that way around him. Now, even more than before, he saw the evidence of what she'd been talking about. There was a history of her career in the bulging veins, the cramped muscles, the corns and bunions, the calluses and cracks. She wore neat shoes, but they covered a sprawling account of an overtaxed life, and there was no hiding the truth when she took them off.

He went after the pain, tried to free it up. She gave a muted cry of relief. He would be a disappointment to her later, when she remembered how he had failed her, but for now she was probably only thinking that she didn't want him to stop. He had more strength in his hands than he

used to. He used to ask to quit and she would wheedle another minute out of him and he would say he was tired and she would give in, but now he wouldn't tire so easily. He would let her be the one to tell him when she'd had enough. The television roared in the other room. He brought her other foot up so that he could move between the two feet. He thought of the tooth in his pocket. There was a chance this would be the last time in her life that she'd have her feet rubbed, because circumstances might not conspire again to bring them together like this. There was a limit to his ability to reach out to her. It was easier with girlfriends. He was always offering to rub their feet. He threw all his affection at them and hoped that some of it would stick, maybe even come back to him, though if it didn't he gave it anyway, he gave it more, even, because everyone had something that needed to come out.

She wasn't going to be able to rely on her son, but she didn't want to just bring another nurse in. The time had come to approach the problem differently. The fact was, she was handcuffed to Ed. Everything she did when she wasn't at work, she had to do with him. What she needed was someone who would be there more of the time and in a more unstructured way, who could free her up to have a bit of a life; someone who could effortlessly pick up Ed when he fell. Maybe this person could even help around the house in a handyman capacity. Maybe what she'd needed in the house from the beginning had been a man.

If she was going to bring someone in full-time, she had to find the money to pay for it. She decided to take advantage of the fact that mortgage rates had gone down significantly since she and Ed had bought the house. She refinanced to bring her rate down from 10.3 percent to just over 8 percent, which gave her a little more to work with every month.

She put out feelers at work and posted flyers, but she didn't get any promising leads. Then one of her nurses, Nadya Karpov, said her older brother Sergei was reliable and strong—too strong, Nadya said, to be driving a cab nights. He didn't have nursing experience and he was in his fifties, but she thought he'd be good at it, as he was patient and calm. He didn't have a car and he lived in Brighton Beach, but he was willing to make the long trip on the A train and the Metro-North. Eileen knew the nine hundred dollars a week she was offering would be a significant raise. The amount was just shy of what Ed's pension and Social Security payments added up to, after taxes. Nadya said Sergei would probably jump at

the chance to spend part of the week in Westchester and get away from her sister-in-law. "She's Russian," Nadya said simply, with raised brows, and Eileen nodded back, as if she knew something about the terror of Russian wives.

"We're having company today," she said to Ed shortly before Sergei was scheduled to arrive with Nadya for an interview. "A friend from work and her brother. Sergei's his name. I think you're going to like him. He's excited to meet you. He doesn't have many friends in the area. They're from Russia. So I'll need you to show him a good time." After she'd said this, Ed sat at the kitchen table and wouldn't move. She wanted him in the den, out of the way, to give Sergei a few minutes to walk around and get acquainted with the place. She could bring him in to meet Ed after he'd seen how nice everything was, what kind of people she and Ed were. But Ed wouldn't budge. She could already envision the scene—Sergei in the house less than a minute, Ed wringing his hands and wailing, decision flashing across Sergei's face: this is too much, too weird, too uncomfortable, he'll find something else, it's nice to meet you and your husband. Then he would say a polite good-bye, would leave her with Ed again, with Connell drifting through like a ghost until he flew back to school.

She tried to entice Ed into the den with a plate of cheese and crackers, but he just muttered at the kitchen table. She waved to him, patted the pillow at her side. Something must have told him she was plotting a betrayal.

She turned the television off and joined him in the kitchen. She put some potpourri on, as if she was trying to sell the house, and in a way she was. She understood that Russians were big readers. Maybe Sergei would get a kick out of all Ed's books. Maybe they'd stoke a fire in him to work on his English, make his way through the rows.

She poured a glass of wine and tried to read the paper but kept staring at the same sentence over and over. When the doorbell rang, she leapt from her seat and rushed to adjust Ed's collar, which was pointed up. Through the glass she saw Nadya smiling broadly, her brother hulking behind her. Sergei doffed his cap as he crossed the threshold, seeming to fill the room. He shook her hand, then walked over and did the same with Ed's. A bald patch rested on top and gray nibbled at the sides of his head, but otherwise

Sergei was the picture of virility: a ruddy glow, hair sprouting out of his collared shirt, a quiet formality about him, even in his jeans and leather jacket. He was shorter than Ed but bigger in the trunk.

"What a beautiful house!" Nadya gushed. "What a beautiful neighborhood! Isn't it beautiful, Sergei?"

He nodded. Eileen invited them to sit and took their coats into the den. When she returned, Nadya was seated beside Ed, Sergei across from him. Nadya was looking at Ed with sensitive eyes, though Eileen had told her to play it like a regular visit. The relief was how calmly Sergei was carrying it. He too wore a compassionate expression, but he was sitting back, giving Ed space. His bearing said he understood something of what Ed was going through. His hands reminded her of her father's. She could picture those hands grabbing barrels of beer from a truck, securing a big metal hook to their rings, and dropping them into cellars. She could see Sergei jamming metal rods into barrels to tap them without getting his head knocked off by the pressure they released.

She left Ed with Nadya and gave Sergei a tour of the house. In the spare bedroom she heard the floorboards creak under him, and for a moment she was sure he would break through, that the house couldn't bear his weight.

Ed woke up raving at three in the morning. She tried to rub his head, but he batted her hand away and seethed through his teeth. Then she felt the wetness of the sheets. He might have drained his entire bladder into the bed. She was careful about making him pee right before sleep, but maybe she'd forgotten. It wasn't the first time. It had gotten to the point where she could sleep, and felt comfortable letting him sleep, in a little wetness of the sheets. This was a full-on soaking, though.

For a few days, she'd experimented with putting adult diapers on him before they went to bed. He complained about the way they cinched his waist and the loud crackling noise whenever he moved, but the real problem, she understood, was the humiliation he felt wearing them. One night he took them off and peed the bed anyway. She gave up trying to get him to wear them after that.

Moaning, flushed with agitation, Ed left the bed and began to roam mindlessly, bent on something inscrutable. She alternated between securing a corner of the fresh sheet and shooing him away from the stairs so he didn't spill down them. When she was done, she tugged the T-shirt off him, but he wouldn't let her change his underwear. She was too tired to argue, so she let him crawl sopping into the clean sheets. She didn't sleep the rest of the night; her hand kept drifting over to his underwear to feel if it had dried.

She cleaned the house top to bottom in preparation for Sergei's arrival. She felt nervous taking a strange man into her home. It was a Sunday, the start of his work week. She'd never liked Sunday evenings, which filled her with a creeping dread that went back to grammar school.

In the days leading up to Sergei's arrival, she mentioned him often, casually, hoping through these hints to make his presence in their lives seem natural in Ed's mind. She felt the way she imagined Ed must have felt when he used to condition his lab rats with tiny, nonfatal doses of pure cocaine. "Sergei is going to help us around the house," she said. "Sergei is going to take care of a few things for us." "Sergei will be here on Sunday." "Sergei might stay the week."

That morning, after they stopped in at Mass for a few minutes, she walked Ed around town for two hours. He behaved better when he was tired. Still, when she answered the bell and led Sergei in, Ed said, "No, no!" again and again, until he wasn't speaking anymore but yelling in a high-pitched wail that sounded like a baby's cry.

"This man is here to help us," she said. "Can I tell you something?" His face was turning purple. "This man is not here for you. Do you understand? He's here so I don't have to worry about you when I'm not here. He's here for me."

He began to quiet down, and the violent color drained from his face, and he looked as if he could breathe again.

She woke in the middle of the night to find Ed half on top of her trying to make something happen. She wasn't sure if he knew what he was doing, or

if he was even awake at all. She laid him down, calmed his pounding heart, and got on top. It was awkward and a little heartbreaking, but the blood still raced through her veins, and it was more attention than some of her friends had gotten in years.

Sergei stayed until she got home from work on Friday. She might have been able to give him less than nine hundred a week, but she wanted to convey the gravity of the job in the pay, and she was taking this man from his home, his wife, even if Nadya said he was happy to get away.

Sergei's main job was to cook Ed's meals and keep him company. Friday evenings were awkward; the transactional nature of the relationship couldn't be avoided. She counted out a pile of fifties and handed them over in a folded stack, avoiding Sergei's eyes. Some Fridays he finished watching a program with Ed before departing. Others, he was waiting by the door when she arrived. Even when he seemed content to chat, he didn't speak much, owing to his poor command of English. In that respect, he and Ed made a good pair. She imagined them grunting at each other like cavemen when she wasn't there. It wasn't the worst thought in the world. She may have had to act disgusted if it happened around her, but that didn't mean she couldn't take private delight in the idea of it.

His mother wondered what he was still doing there, why he hadn't gone back to school. The truth was, he was okay thinking of himself as a screwup, but he wasn't comfortable thinking of himself as a sociopath. To just leave like that, to turn his back utterly— this would be too much for him to take. He wanted to think he was a better person than that, so he stuck around. He told his mother that he would be there to help when he could but that he didn't want to be primarily responsible for his father, and she told him not to bother. Eventually he just said he was sticking around because he didn't want to go back to Chicago for the summer.

One morning over breakfast he told his mother that he was going to go in to see his old teacher, Mr. Corso.

"That's nice," she said in the flat tone she'd assumed for talking to him now that he'd made his decision.

"I thought I could get some direction from him. Maybe he could help me figure a few things out."

"That's not something you go to your teacher for," she said, abandoning her flat affect. "That's something you bring to your father. He's still your father."

"I don't know what I'd say to him. I don't know how I'd explain any of it."

"What are you planning to say to your teacher, then?"

"Mr. Corso knows how to figure things out fast."

"There's no one who figures things out faster than your father."

"Come on, Mom. Dad's not himself."

"Your father is still the person to go to with this. I don't care how great Mr. Corso is. Is he King Solomon? Is he Marcus Aurelius? If not, then you talk to your father. He's still here."

They sat in Mr. Corso's trophy-stuffed office, surrounded by photos of past teams and Mr. Corso standing with students who'd made good—a prominent attorney, a major Hollywood executive. He wasn't sure what he was there for—support, direction, or just to be near the man for a while. Connell remembered seeing ex-students in Mr. Corso's office when he was a student. It wasn't hard to understand why they returned even decades later. Mr. Corso was the kind of man who knew how to cook a perfect steak at his summer house in Breezy Point and explain why Dostoyevsky beat Tolstoy on points after ten rounds. If all of life was a competition for Mr. Corso, somehow he seemed to draft everyone around him for his team.

"I still can't believe you quit playing ball," Mr. Corso said, leaning back into the red leather of his chair with his hands locked behind his head. "An arm like yours. And to join the army that talks you to death."

Mr. Corso hadn't stopped needling him since his sophomore year, when, just before baseball season started, Connell decided to switch to debate. Mr. Corso liked to argue over ideas almost as much as Mr. Kotowski, Connell's debate coach, did, but after school he assisted the varsity baseball coach, strategizing on the bench as he crunched sunflower seeds. He had a friendly rivalry with Mr. Kotowski, who had stamped generations of students with his trademark brand of razor-edged hyperarticulateness, and who, Mr. Corso liked to grumble, mined his freshman speech class for prospects. Between them, they seemed to divide the world.

"I declared an English major," Connell said. "I wanted to thank you. You had a lot to do with that."

Mr. Corso laughed and rocked in his chair, the springs creaking beneath his weight. "Don't come crying to me in twenty years when you look at your bank statement."

He shifted forward, knitting his hands together at the front end of his desk. Connell could see the pink dots of his peeling tan. His eyes were keen and probing, soft brows hovering above them. His craggy, pockmarked

face gave him extra gravity and toughness. Connell spent his sophomore year afraid of Mr. Corso, after he quit baseball, but when it was time to pick his senior elective he chose Mr. Corso's modernist literature class. After a semester of *Ulysses*, *Absalom, Absalom*, and *The Sound and the Fury*, what Connell remembered best were those bits of fatherly wisdom Mr. Corso slipped into his lessons. One time he explained the impact supply and demand had on pricing by asking them to imagine approaching a hot dog vendor with a lone dog floating in his cart as rain began to fall. "What do you think he'd take for it?" Connell remembered him asking. "You think the price of things is chiseled into tablets handed down from a cloud?"

"Where are you working this summer?"

"I came home to help with my father," Connell said nervously, "but I don't think I'm up to playing nursemaid. You know?"

Mr. Corso looked at him in silence for a few moments. "What makes you think it's okay to drop the ball like this?"

"My mother's bringing someone in," Connell said nervously. "It's the best thing for everyone."

"Your family is good people," Mr. Corso said with a slight growl in his voice. "You don't have a clue yet what that means in life, do you?"

Connell looked away. Another silence followed.

"Those guys you debated with. Do they have summer jobs?"

"More like paid internships," Connell said. "At blue-chip companies."

"Do you want to work?"

Connell guessed that was why he was sitting across from Mr. Corso, though it wasn't clear until now that that had been his purpose. "Yeah," he said, nodding. "I need a job."

"Can you do *real* work?"

Mr. Corso drummed his fingers on his desk. The tips were fat, and the nails were neatly trimmed. Another silence followed, in which Connell felt the hair on his arms and bare legs rise in the air-conditioned office.

"Sure."

"The super of a nearby building on Park called to offer summer relief jobs to our graduating seniors. Doorman, porter."

He fingered through a pile on his desk and pulled out a piece of paper as if he'd known where it had been all along.

"Does this guy have a son?" Connell asked.

Mr. Corso chuckled. "Poor kid's only ten. They're starting the application process early these days."

Connell tried to hide his embarrassment at being offered this job. "You want me to go break the news to him that you can't buy your way in here?"

"Better keep that under wraps," Mr. Corso said, folding the paper into thirds and handing it to Connell in an official manner. "If you do a good job, we should be able to make this a regular tradition for—what—five more summers at least? Maybe beyond if the kid gets in here. We'll call it the Connell Leary Memorial Fellowship in honor of your deceased athletic career."

Connell was stationed in the basement, beside one of four service elevators, where he waited for the buzzer to ring and the indicator to light up and tell him his fortune. Gate shut, he shot up to the proper floor, to shuttle nannies to the laundry room and shareholders to the little fiefdoms of their storage cages.

There were some Albanian guys down there with him—college-aged but not in college, or a little older. Connell saw in the snappy way they spoke to Mr. Marku that they had ambitions to make it up to the lobby. Some of them were rough-looking; others, the more recent immigrants, didn't speak English all that well. He knew he'd have had a better shot at promotion than any of them, if only he trimmed his unruly hair and shaved his scraggly goatee, but he didn't care. He was just passing through, and he was pretty sure Mr. Marku had taken one look at him and known he'd felt that way.

He was summoned by a gorgeous au pair. While she moved her employers' sheets to the dryer, he fantasized about going in and seducing her, then stopping the elevator between floors and having sex in it. After he'd returned her upstairs, he stood on the landing imagining the bedrooms on the other side of the door. He went down to the basement and sat in the chair thinking about her, until he rose and headed to the stall in the locker room. Sadik interrupted him, banging on the door, and he didn't finish.

He put the garbage can in the elevator and went to the top floor to do a run, dumping the contents of their cans into his own. Ancient Mrs. Braverman on the twelfth floor opened her door and handed him a Coke from a mini fridge filled with them. She seemed to remain alive for the

sole purpose of bestowing little gifts on the porters. The strange tenement squalor of her digs disconcerted him, the old abandoned furniture, the peeling wallpaper. There was none of the splendor he saw in other apartments, the slabs of stone stretched across kitchen islands as big as docks on a lake. She had kids but they never visited. Money was not a guarantor of dignity.

His presence surprised Mr. Caldecott in 10B when the latter opened his door to toss his garbage bag into the big can. Mr. Caldecott hurried out of there. Connell felt like a Peeping Tom a flashlight had settled on. The feeling wasn't unfounded: even the proudest of porters from time to time did what Connell had done the previous day, when, once he'd taken it to the basement, he'd gone through the garbage and paper recycling, in search less of salvageable goods than of documentary evidence of the power the shareholders wielded—bank statements, work memos, eye-popping receipts, all the marvelous details of their lives.

In the afternoon, the building settled into a postlunch siesta and he leaned against the painted brick wall next to the service elevator to read *Invisible Man*. Instead of a brilliant campaign against Monopolated Light & Power, he was stuck with severe stretches of hallway intermittently punctuated by feeble fluorescence. The elevator car contained the only source of incandescent light, a single exposed bulb. For a few minutes he placed the chair directly in the car, but he lost his nerve the first time he heard footfalls down the hall.

Officially, he wasn't supposed to be reading at all. The activity was tolerated as long as it wasn't comfortable. And so he stood for hours on the threshold of the elevator and stashed the book when he heard someone approach. Whenever Mr. Marku passed—he was in a generous mood that day, announcing his presence with a stagy, whistled tune—Connell trained his gaze on the light-up panel like a laboratory monkey waiting for an experimenter's stimulus. One time, though, Connell didn't lose the book quickly enough. Mr. Marku didn't give orders or ask questions. He just announced what Connell would do, as though he possessed powers of psychic intuition. "You'll go outside and sweep the perimeter," he said. "Then you'll go to the store and get me a Marlboro Lights hard pack and a six

pack of Heineken." (The first time Mr. Marku told him to buy beer, Connell said he wasn't old enough, and Mr. Marku replied—accurately, it turned out—"When they see you in that outfit, nobody asks questions.") "When you're back you'll start on those fire stairs." No one ever used the fire stairs, but Connell had mopped them three times already that week. There were four sets to mop, sixteen flights each. They never gathered any dust.

78

It was an unusually warm night. The musk of the flowers she'd planted rose up as she walked from the car. Sergei was standing at the back of the house, smoking under a clear, star-filled sky. She greeted him awkwardly, unsure of whether to invite him in, as he could come in on his own when he was finished. It almost seemed he had been waiting for her.

She went upstairs. A while later, his quick, hacking cough announced his presence inside. It was strange to hear a man in the house when her husband was in the bed next to her. Since Sergei arrived, she'd been able to sleep through the night. She wasn't even bothered by Ed's nocturnal ravings anymore; she just stayed in bed with a foothold in sleep and let him walk around the room.

She heard Sergei climb the stairs. She lay in bed awake listening to the quiet voices and laugh track from his television, and his own occasional muffled laughter.

It was a mystery what happened in Sergei's room after he closed the door. She'd gone in when he wasn't around and found little more than was present when she'd first turned the room over to him. There was the television, the radio, the armchair, and the side table. There was a small stack of Russian volumes in English translation, a Russian-to-English dictionary, a bottle of aftershave, and the suitcase he lived out of. And there was the bed, of course.

From deep within her, she felt a tremor of unwelcome desire rumble up. She lay there trying to ignore it, but it seized her attention so thoroughly that she felt a buzzing in her fingertips, the room became stiflingly hot, and the sheets lost their softness and scratched at her skin. Even though she

knew she shouldn't, even though it felt like a betrayal, even though Ed was sleeping next to her, she began to touch herself, something she hadn't done in years, and she didn't stop until she had brought herself off with a little involuntary cry that sounded vaguely mournful to her ears, after which she lay taking quick, dry breaths and feeling a tingling lack of satisfaction. An attempt at a second round produced no results.

Connell hadn't heard Mr. Marku coming, and when he looked up from the book and saw him standing there, he let out a strangled yelp.

"Come to my office," Mr. Marku said. Connell rose to follow him. "First, tie up those newspapers."

When Connell entered, Mr. Marku was staring at the wall-length aquarium.

"You read a lot," he said.

Connell nodded nervously.

"You've heard of Camus's *The Fall.*"

He suspected a trap. Mr. Marku always dropped his bombs at the end of a shift, when you had little time to react. Connell was in Mr. Marku's doghouse for coming in late on a seven-to-three shift on a Saturday. He had thought that Mr. Marku never slept, that he had cameras trained on every entrance and exit, until he figured out that Sadik had ratted on him. The guys built up capital however they could.

"Yes," he said, "but I haven't read it."

Mr. Marku was proud of the year he'd spent at Iona College before family responsibilities forced him to drop out. More than once he'd mentioned that he'd planned to be an English major.

"It's a parable of hell," Mr. Marku said. "The devil is this bartender." He just waved his hand. "It's too much to get into." He knocked a smoke out of his pack and lighted it in the windowless office. "You'll come in Wednesday at six forty-five in the morning." He handed him a bundle of folded clothes. "You'll wear this doorman uniform. You'll shave."

80

As Bethany backed out of the driveway, Eileen saw Connell coming up the hill. Most nights he came home after midnight, and sometimes, when he didn't have to work the next morning, when the sun was rising. Eileen rolled down her window.

"There's chicken in the fridge." She expected him to wave and keep walking, but he stopped.

"Where are you going?"

She turned to Bethany, who took her hand and gave it a squeeze.

"Out for a while," she said. "There are potatoes too. Just put one in the microwave."

When she came home, Sergei was waiting in the kitchen, sipping from a cup of what looked like coffee, but it could have contained vodka for all she knew.

"Hard work today," he said.

"Is everything okay?"

"In Russia, even, I don't work this hard."

"What's up? What happened?"

"Is no good to talk about it."

"Is Ed okay?"

"He is asleep."

"That's good," she said.

"I don't mind to work hard," he said. "But he is very hard work."

He said it with a whistle that indicated a certain professional appreciation. She nodded in solidarity.

"He wipe shit on walls in bathroom," he said. "I clean it up. Between tiles. Is all gone."

"Thank you," she said. "I'm sorry."

"You mind if I . . . ?" He had taken out his pack and already had a cigarette in his mouth. He was flicking the lighter absently.

"Let's go outside," she said.

They stood on the patio and he lit the cigarette. She didn't know what to say, so she said nothing. He pulled on his cigarette and looked at her. Behind it his eyes smoldered. He was stocky and his hair was thick where it wasn't sparse. He stood in the middle of the patio but seemed to take up much of its space.

"You want?" he asked, extending the pack.

"No, thanks, I don't smoke."

"Try," he said. "One time. Is very relaxing."

She had never had a cigarette. Aside from the pure brain-dead imbecility of subjecting yourself willingly to an avoidable carcinogen, she had always found them vile, noxious, smelly things—except for a brief period in high school when she loved a boy who smoked and she was intoxicated by the aroma mixed with his cologne and sweat, and the taste of it in his mouth and the rush she got when she kissed him just after he'd had one. But the memory of watching her mother smoke had permanently soured her on them. Her stomach turned whenever she saw a full ashtray; she imagined being made to eat it, butt by butt, and gagging on the ashes.

"Fine," she said, and she took a cigarette from him. Life, she thought, was like that sometimes; for years, things were a certain way, and then in an instant, almost without conscious thought, they weren't that way any longer, as if all the hidden pressure on their having been the way they'd been had found release through a necessary valve. She reached her hand out for the lighter, but he just took his own cigarette out of his mouth, lit hers from the flaming tip of his own, and handed it to her.

"You have to light it right," he said.

She took a few breaths without disturbance. Sergei told her to take a deeper puff, and she did so, looking at him for confirmation. He was smiling an amused smile. Her lungs filled with heat and she fell into a loud cough.

"Don't laugh at me," she said.

"This always happens," he said.

"Usually to teenagers," she said. "Not to fifty-four-year-old women."

"It happened to me," he said smoothly. "You are not fifty-four."

"I am."

"You may have fifty-four years"—he was gesturing in an inscrutable way that she assumed would have conveyed more to a Russian native—"but you are not fifty-four."

She blushed. "I think I'm done with this," she said, dropping it and stepping on it. It was nearly the whole cigarette, and her embarrassment made her kick it behind her toward the house.

"You work very hard," Sergei said, continuing to smoke. "My wife has no job for thirty years."

"Thank you," she said, absurdly. Talking to Sergei made her uneasy. At first she thought it was the language barrier, but now she was beginning to think it was something else, a tension rooted in the strangeness of having a man living in her house.

"I didn't want to have job past sixty," he said, finishing his cigarette and stepping on the butt. They went back inside. Sergei sat at the table glancing at the newspaper while she put dishes away.

She didn't hear him on the stairs, and her back was to him when he entered, but there was no mistaking that Ed had joined them, because her stomach seized in nervous anxiety. She heard the clicking sound he made when he was trying to get words out, like the distress call of a bird.

Sergei put down the paper and gave him a long-suffering look.

"Why don't you sit and I'll make you some tea," she said.

"My," Ed stammered, and the clicking became more desperate.

"Ed, honey. Please."

Sergei held up a hand to silence her. He gestured for Ed to take his seat as he rose and passed out of the room. She heard his heavy footfalls on the stairs and unconsciously poured the water out of the kettle she'd been heating instead of filling the cup she'd set out. The steam rose from the sink. When she'd caught herself, there wasn't enough left for a full cup.

"Look what you made me do," she said.

Ed calmed down once Sergei had left the room. He sat where Sergei had been and shook his head, continuing to click, but in a softer way, like a cooing bird. "No," he stammered, quietly.

"It's okay," Eileen stood behind him and rubbed his back. "It's okay."

"Mine," he said.

81

The summer uniform had short sleeves and no jacket, but the pants were a thick wool-poly blend, and he wasn't allowed to take off his hat. There was no air-conditioning in the atrium, so they opened all the doors to the enclosed quadrangle and hoped for a breeze.

The one benefit to the heat was that it kept many of the residents away from the city. He ushered their mounds of bags and cartloads of hanging clothes into Range Rovers and Jeeps, and they handed him ten bucks and headed for the Hamptons or Long Beach Island. Even Mr. Marku went out of town for the weekend. He came into the lobby with his golf clubs and polo shirts on Friday afternoons and said to get his car, his sweat fresh with aftershave. Connell loved when Mr. Marku was away, because it was safe to read in the open.

The shareholders who remained in town weren't much trouble. There was the shipping magnate of Olympian means who spread the last scant lengths of hair across his glossy pate. He hustled through the lobby with his head down, polite and preoccupied, as though he were sorry for trespassing. Then there were the younger sharks who hadn't yet acquired a house in the Hamptons. They talked sports with Connell, checked out women with him, and as long as he didn't act as though they were equals, they didn't pull rank. They hailed their own cabs, told him to stay in his chair when he rose at the sound of their approach, but if he took for granted that they would, they cracked him into action with a chilly look, all camaraderie forgotten.

Mr. Shanahan in 12C was probably the most successful shareholder in the building. He wasn't the richest—that was the shipping magnate—but he was the one who held the most power. He was in charge of an investment bank. He had the sort of reassuringly large cranium common to movie stars, and perfect teeth, and very little body fat, and he treated the doormen more like regular people than probably anyone else in the building. It wasn't a shock to learn that he'd been a doorman once himself, in college.

Mr. Shanahan spent a lot of time with his son Chase, who was home from boarding school for the summer. Mr. Shanahan got dropped off in a town car and met Chase for lunch. Sometimes he came home early and reappeared in the lobby a little while later with the boy, both of them in jogging outfits. They stretched in the courtyard before they went out for a run in Central Park, and they did push-ups there afterward. They weren't technically supposed to be in the courtyard doing that, but everyone looked the other way because Mr. Shanahan was such a good guy and never got to see his kid during the year.

Sometimes Mr. Shanahan and Chase sat on the bench in the lobby while one or the other tied his shoes on the way out or caught his breath on the way back in. They teased each other in a good-natured, prep school sort of way, and Mr. Shanahan took evident pride in the boy, who, at a couple of inches over six feet, was almost as tall as Mr. Shanahan himself, even though he was only fifteen. Whenever they left the lobby in the beginnings of a jog, Connell felt a jolt of yearning.

All in all, Connell liked being upstairs. In the early afternoons, though, when the sun washed the lobby in clarifying light, and the thick, humid air muffled the car horns, he was set upon by remorse. Not only had he abandoned his father to a stranger, he had cost his mother unnecessarily by doing so. She was paying Sergei twice what he was earning at the building, and to do a job that Connell should have done free of charge. There had to be a way of looking at it that wasn't so dark. There had to be an explanation for his selfishness. Maybe something was going on that was too big for him to see. Mr. Grossman, his junior year English teacher, had lectured one day about how the Oedipal complex worked in *Hamlet*. Hamlet didn't under-

stand all the forces that conspired in his own mind, the conflicting desires and obligations. Losing a father early, being given all that responsibility, Mr. Grossman said, had made it hard for Hamlet to act. Maybe something like that was working in Connell's mind too, something big, something hidden. He was afraid he would never see it clearly.

She scheduled a solo session. Bethany picked her up and brought her to that too.

To assert ownership of the transaction, Eileen tried to present Rachelle the check when she walked in, but Rachelle cannily brushed it away and told her they could handle that later. Rachelle had her sit in the middle of the living room. It struck Eileen that no sign of Rachelle appeared in the pictures on the walls, that it could have been a house lent for the meetings by one of her acolytes.

They got quickly to work. Bethany sat close to her and held her hand as they listened to Vywamus speak. Eileen could almost physically *feel* the web of rhetoric being spun around her, but she relaxed in Bethany's grip regardless.

"The true story of your husband is more complex than it appears," Vywamus said effortfully, trailing into a long cough, as if Rachelle hadn't gotten into character yet. Eileen liked to think she was above superstition, but she could feel herself hoping that Vywamus wouldn't pronounce anything bad. "You only know him in this life, but your son and he have been struggling for many lives. This time around, your son has the intellect and the emotions. Your husband has only the intellect. He is fighting for his soul."

"Really?" Eileen said doubtfully. The assessment of Ed was off base, and Eileen wanted to challenge it on principle. Anyone who knew Ed knew he felt things deeply, but how was she supposed to go about reasoning with Vywamus?

"But he is doing good things for himself," Vywamus said. "He is putting others before himself."

She thought of how Ed prayed for Connell and herself and not his own salvation. Maybe there was something to what Vywamus was saying. Or maybe Rachelle knew that letting Eileen leave with bad feelings might hurt her business.

"Your son left because he was angry at his father."

"Funny," she said. "I thought he left to go to college."

She tried a smile, but Vywamus would have none of it. "He has been battling your husband for thousands of years."

The whole act was so absurd, so transparent, but Eileen decided to shut off the critical voice in her head. She chose to let her mind be soaked in Rachelle's narcotic wash of words. Eileen knew that she was the one actually spinning the web. For a couple of hundred dollars a week, she was being given the gift she needed more than any other: to be taken out of her life.

"It seems like that sometimes," she said.

"You are guarded," Vywamus said. "This is because of certain childhood experiences. We both know what these are, and I need not utter them now. You must open a window in your heart. There is a need for fresh air in your soul. You need to reach out to those you care about and give them a loving embrace. Remember that touch plays a crucial role in how we communicate love."

"Okay." She had the feeling of listening to a deathbed monologue. She felt strangely poised to carry out whatever Vywamus called for.

"You have a good child. And a good husband. This battle of his has nothing to do with how he feels about you. In this life, you have helped his soul."

"Thank you," she said. "Thank you very much."

On a slow afternoon in early August, Mr. Marku snapped his fingers as he passed and motioned for Connell to follow him downstairs. They entered the office, and Connell sat on the worn leather couch as Mr. Marku yelled at a contractor on the phone. He watched clown fish and angelfish chase each other through the coral in the saltwater aquarium and had one of those crystallizing insights into the order of things that always seemed less profound a few hours later. The guy wanted weekend access so his workers could finish sooner, and Mr. Marku wouldn't give it up. The doormen and porters took it for granted that Mr. Marku let his palm get greased for things like this, but as Connell listened to Mr. Marku standing this man down, he considered the radical idea that sometimes there wasn't a cynical story to uncover, that Mr. Marku was probably just a man of principle.

He thought of his mother and the phone conversations he'd been eavesdropping on. He felt guilty listening in, but he couldn't help it, because when he was around, his mother was so squirrelly about not talking to whoever this lady was, this friend of Bethany's. His guilt turned to anger that his mother was getting taken for a ride.

Because Mr. Marku knew everybody, he probably knew the kind of people who could strike some fear in the heart of this lady, make her leave his mother alone. A couple of men would show up at her door, and they wouldn't have to say much.

Mr. Marku hung up and leaned back in his chair. He lit a cigarette and gave Connell a long look that betrayed no malice, which made it more intimidating. He never prefaced anything with pleasantries; it was always speeches.

"You don't shave, I give you a razor and tell you to shave," he said. "You take long lunches, I say he's a growing boy. You talk too much to the shareholders, I say I'm glad he speaks such good English. But when you don't wear the hat; when you don't wear the hat, and you're standing in front of me . . ."

"Are you letting me go?"

"Not yet, I'm not," Mr. Marku said. "I told your teacher I'd keep an eye on you, whip you into shape. You're coming back down here to work."

She added a weekly phone call to the Tuesday night groups and the Thursday night solo session. The rate was cheaper for the telephone session, one twenty-five an hour.

One day Connell sat at the table giving her dirty looks while she was talking to Rachelle. She tried to shoo him away, because she felt too self-conscious with him there, but he wouldn't leave, and she told Rachelle she'd call back.

"What's going on?" he asked when she hung up.

"What?"

"What's up with Bethany?"

"Nothing, why?"

"I saw a show about this the other day. They'll take you for everything you have. People end up homeless."

"Look at this kitchen," she said. "Look at that countertop. Does it look to you like I'm going to be homeless?"

The next time Bethany came to pick her up to go to Rachelle's, a strange mood hung in the air. Connell came into the kitchen, followed by Sergei, and then the two of them went down to the basement. When she called down to say she was leaving, she got no reply. As Bethany backed out of the driveway, Eileen saw the garage door rising and Connell pulling out with Sergei in the passenger seat. It was something she hadn't seen before, the two of them in the car together, and she spent the whole trip wondering where they could have been going. She usually enjoyed these rides to Rachelle's, singing along with Bethany to pop radio, but she was

distracted by the thought of Ed in that house alone, even if he was already asleep when she left.

The bell rang as she was settling into the floor. When Bethany opened the door, Eileen saw Connell and Sergei there. Connell started to enter. "Excuse me, young man," Bethany said as she tried to stop his advance, but Sergei moved her aside with an effortless sweep of the arm and followed him in.

"What are you doing here?" Eileen asked.

"I wanted to see where you went."

"You followed me?"

"I don't know what's going on," he said, "but I don't like it."

She was oddly comforted to see him there. She felt, for a moment, as if she wasn't on her own.

"Where's your father?"

"He's home. In bed."

"You need to get back there," she said.

"*You* need to get back there," he answered. There was an unexpected authority in his voice; he seemed to have matured by ten years in an instant. She found herself on the point of heading for the door.

Rachelle walked into the room with a natural, confident air and placed a hand on her shoulder. "This must be your son," she said. "I'm so glad to meet you." Her voice was full of disarming warmth. "I've been hoping for this chance."

She put her hand out. Connell took it automatically.

"You're every bit as spirited as I understood you to be."

"Thanks, I guess." He turned from Rachelle. "Come on, Mom. We have to go."

"And who is your friend?" Rachelle asked.

"This is my husband's caretaker, Sergei," Eileen said.

Sergei stood there with his arms crossed, impassive. Connell must have prepared him for his role; the thought of it touched her.

"Come *on*, Mom," Connell said.

"Now, I understand you're feeling a lot of different things," Rachelle

said to him. "Anger. Confusion. A loss of control. And I know your heart is in the right place. I probably know more about what you're going through than you think. You might like to talk to me yourself sometime."

"Nope," he said. "You can keep your snake oil."

"Watch your mouth," Bethany said, stepping toward him. Sergei shifted in front of Connell, and he and Bethany looked like a big dog and a little one squaring off. The tension in the room was thick.

"Why don't we all take a deep breath," Rachelle said. "Please, sit down."

"I'm not sitting," Connell said. "I came to get my mother out of here."

"Is that why you brought your friend?"

Connell nodded.

"The body is one thing," Rachelle said. "The body can be held captive. The mind is something else entirely. The mind seeks its natural state, which is freedom. You can't imprison a mind forever. If your mother seeks freedom, she'll be back. There's nothing you or I or anyone else can do to fetter that desire. You can try to put her in chains, but her mind can break them. What we do here is train minds to break chains."

Connell looked as if he was waiting for her to come to his aid, but she was frozen, partly out of curiosity about how he'd handle this challenge with a year of college under his belt.

"I don't know what to say about all that," he said. "I'm sure you're a nice person. I just came to get my mother."

"You don't get to tell your mother how to live her life," Bethany snapped. "If she's discovered something you can't understand, it's not your place to stand in its way."

Eileen bristled. "Take it easy, Bethany."

Rachelle put her hand up in a pacific gesture. "You're a bright young man," she said calmly. "Are you willing to consider that there might be a reality beyond the comprehension of your senses? That all might not be as it seems?"

"Mom!" he said, exasperated.

"Why don't you ask her what she wants?" Bethany strode over to stand behind her. Eileen felt Bethany's fingertips on her back urging her into the loveseat, and she sat, surprising herself. "She's had a lifetime of males

telling her how to behave, and she's not about to start taking orders from her own son."

Connell fell back against the wall, looking spent. Sergei remained standing with his arms folded across his chest. She knew it must have seemed to Connell that she was under Rachelle's spell. She wished Connell could see the granite vein of skepticism that ran through her, which Rachelle could never mine clean, no matter how long she chipped away.

"I want you to know something," Rachelle said to him. "Your mother is in good hands here."

"Can we get out of here, Mom?"

"I'm fine," Eileen said. "I don't want you to think anything weird is going on."

"How much money have you given them?"

"He's only concerned about his inheritance," Bethany said. "Typical."

"That's not fair to the boy," Eileen said.

Rachelle took a step toward Connell. "I'm saddened to hear you speak in such simplistic terms about the relationship your mother has formed to the truth of the universe. I may draw a modest fee for facilitating her enlightenment, but it's only to cover basic administrative costs, nothing more."

"You're preying on her in a time of weakness. You should be ashamed."

"Mind your manners," Bethany warned.

"Leave my mother alone."

"You're nothing but a punk," Bethany said.

"And you're a crazy cult lady." He pointed at Bethany and Rachelle. "You and you."

Eileen knew she should step in, but she couldn't make her mouth form any words.

"I've tolerated you here out of deference to your mother," Rachelle said. "You're no longer welcome. Please leave now."

Bethany stepped forward; Sergei did as well.

"Mom," Connell said, simply, plaintively.

"You've offended me," Rachelle said. "I've asked you to leave. If you don't, I'll have no choice but to call the police."

"I'm not leaving without my mother."

"I'm quite sure that's not your decision to make," Rachelle said. "Why don't you go peacefully and let us get back to trying to do some good for your mother, instead of causing her needless anxiety."

Connell didn't move.

"*Now,*" Rachelle said.

"Mom!"

"It's okay," Eileen said.

"You heard your mother." Bethany stepped toward Connell. "Now go. If Rachelle doesn't call the police, I will."

Sergei was pleading with her through the dark pools of his eyes. She sensed a controlled fury in him; she could imagine it erupting if anyone so much as grazed Connell with a finger.

"You're just going to stay here with these people? That's it?"

She wanted to say, *I'll be home later,* but the words still wouldn't come.

"You're ignorant," Bethany said. "You're an ignorant kid and you don't know what you're talking about. I feel sorry for you."

"Don't talk to my son like that," Eileen heard herself say, and the room grew still and quiet. She rose. "He's not ignorant. He means well. And I'm sorry if he offended you. I'm sure he's sorry too. Yes?"

"Sure," Connell said, evidently trying to seize the momentum. "Sorry."

"I'm going to go home." Before she knew it, she was paces from the door. "I'm tired. I want to thank you for everything."

"You don't have to let guilt rule over you like this," Rachelle said. "You're on the verge of a major breakthrough."

"You've helped me," she said. "You've made a great difference."

"You still have a long way to go," Rachelle said. "Don't fool yourself."

"I'm sure I do."

"I'll call you later."

"I don't think so."

"Don't let him influence you," Bethany said. "He's no better than your husband."

Eileen got very still. "You don't know the first thing about him." She dug into her pocketbook for the check and extended it toward Rachelle.

"Don't be silly." Rachelle tried to reach for her wrist. Eileen shook her off and left the check on the table. "You're always welcome here. Take some time to think it over."

She must have stood there too long, because Connell was calling her over. She walked toward the door. Bethany moved to head her off, but Sergei slid in front of Bethany like a gravestone rolling into place, blocking her with his massive body as Eileen continued out to the street.

"It's going to be okay," Bethany called after her, but Eileen didn't turn around. Connell raced ahead while Sergei led her down the stairs and up the stretch of the block to where the car waited. He opened the door for her in the back. Connell took the streets with the grim purposefulness of a getaway driver.

In the silence that prevailed in the car, she wondered how her son had plotted this thing, how many people knew, how he had explained it to Sergei.

They pulled into the garage and went upstairs. Sergei headed to his room. She and Connell stood in the kitchen, eyeing each other warily.

"You didn't have to do that," she said.

"Yes, I did."

"I wish I could explain this to you. I know it sounds like I'm making excuses. But I was never in any kind of danger. I was in control the whole time."

He just looked at his feet. She wondered when exactly he had gotten so big. She was having one of those moments she hadn't had in years, where he seemed to grow before her eyes. It occurred to her that he might have seen her as being as out of control as his father was. Maybe he thought both of them were losing their minds.

"Anyway, I want to thank you for caring. I was fine, but still."

"No problem," he said.

"I mean it. You're a good kid."

"Come on. You're my mother."

She wanted him to hug her, but he just stood there dubious of the way she was looking at him.

"Come here." She put her arms around him. She felt his breathing

against her chest and was reminded of holding him when he was a baby, his laundered pajamas soft and fresh as he was, the whole of him fitting in her two hands, his little behind on her palm. He'd looked at her then as the source and giver of love. She hadn't had to hide anything from him, and she hadn't needed anything from him but his presence. And it was that way again now, for at least this day, this moment. His presence at Rachelle's had meant everything, and his presence now in her arms meant everything too.

When they were done hugging, he looked at her strangely.

"What?"

"Maybe those crazy ladies helped you after all."

"What do you mean?"

"That was the first time you ever did that."

"Did what?"

"Hugged me first."

She shook her head. "That's not possible," she said.

"In my memory, anyway."

She shook it again. "There's more that's happened than what's in your memory."

When she got to the top of the stairs she ran into Sergei leaving the bathroom. He gave her a diffident wave, as though they were schoolchildren passing in the hallway during the change of classes. She stood in the antechamber to the bedroom for a while, hearing Ed's labored breathing under the sheet.

She walked to the bed and found him lying awake in a spooky silence, looking right at her.

"Where?" he asked, sounding as if he were half dreaming. "Where were?"

"With Bethany."

"Who?"

"Someone I used to work with. It's not important."

Ed had always had quick and accurate instincts about people. She crawled in and lay beside him. He drifted off. She lay awake listening to the unified murmur of televisions, her own, Sergei's, and the one in the den. She pictured Sergei awake, keeping a solitary vigil like herself.

85

Ed had lost faith in the physical properties of things. On the way up the stairs that night, he stopped on every step. She had to follow closely behind him and tap a leg to indicate which one was next, then lift it for him. He was frantic when his foot was in the air. They proceeded at a glacial pace, and then he stopped and simply wouldn't budge, despite how hard she pushed his leg, which still had considerable strength in it, the atrophy notwithstanding. She couldn't get him to let go of the banister. This was one of those moments—they had been coming more frequently lately—when she wished Sergei didn't go home on the weekends.

By the time they reached the top, they were both exhausted. She steered him into the bathroom, where she undressed him with great difficulty. Getting one leg over the high lip of the bathtub was no mean feat; getting the other over seemed an impossibility. He straddled the bathtub wall like a rodeo performer athwart two prancing horses. She upset his balance enough to get his other leg in, but then her troubles started. Laying him down was out of the question: she would never get him up again. Showering him, though, presented the risk of his slipping and cracking his head open. A visit to the hospital for something so severe almost certainly meant he would be taken from her care. While the tub was dry, her anxiety was contained; when the water came on, she began fretting in earnest. Whatever purchase he had on the tacky mat was tenuous, and there was nothing for him to grab on to but her body if he started falling. She turned the shower on and cleaned him, but when the time came to emerge, his anxiety spiked. He simply wouldn't step over the lip of the tub. She tried

coaxing him, forcing his leg up, making feints at him, but nothing budged him. His legs shook from standing so long in that fixed intensity of opposition, and his body quivered under a dew of cold droplets. She decided to turn the water back on to warm him up. He stood wordless in that superfluous rinse until she shut it off. They could not go on like this. She thought to get the cordless phone and call for help, but she didn't want to leave him alone for even the several seconds it would take her to retrieve it, and besides, she didn't know whom to call, and she didn't want an ambulance to come for fear of his never returning. She could shout for help, but no one would hear.

She attempted a few more times to tap and lift his leg, exhorting him to cooperate and be a man about this. She tried luring him into a sense of ease and then going after his leg when he wasn't expecting it, but he stiffened as soon as she wrapped her arms around his calf. She wished she'd bought the goddamned shower chair. He was in a kind of agony of fatigue now. He didn't want to resist her, but he couldn't help himself. He wanted to sit and he couldn't sit; he wanted to leave and he couldn't leave. He somehow had the strength to stand, though she knew he couldn't do it forever; he would eventually fall like a felled tree. She sat on the tile floor and looked at him in his nakedness.

"Please, God, tell me what to do," she said aloud.

Something in her aspect of defeat might have triggered some atavistic impulse to protect his mate from suffering, because he motioned to step out of the tub. She leapt up to offer a steadying hand. He lifted the leg with a vigorous thrust, as if it had come unstuck from mud after a struggle. She walked him into the bedroom and saw that it had been two hours since they'd started up the stairs. It felt like an augury: his brain was freezing up. Their time left together in the house seemed precariously little.

She dressed him with deliberateness and care. He sat on the bed in the bright white of his underwear and T-shirt and she felt tenderness for him and a yearning that she almost couldn't bear. She laid him beneath the sheet and tucked it up under his arms. She curled up to him, clinging to his side, trying to memorize the feeling of his corporal presence in the bed with her. She did not sleep. She lay listening to his breathing, watching

his chest rise and fall, staring at his face in the moonlight coming through the window. Sometime in the middle of the night she felt his erection and pulled his underwear off. He did not startle awake but rather came to gently and with tender murmurings and she climbed atop him and took him inside her. She looked into his eyes as she used to when they were first married and he did not look away. Despite his incapacity in almost every area of his physical life, he was still able to climax, and she was startled into a giggling joy at the wide-eyed surprise that overtook him as he did so. She lay in his arms for a while afterward, and in the drift of her thoughts she was brought around to her parents. This unlikely coupling with Ed tonight was proof that what was visible to others was only a sliver of the spectrum of a couple's intimate life. A hunger for contact could overcome intractable impediments. She began to reconceive of her parents' lives, to imagine that a shadow passion overtook them when they might least have expected it to.

She had to get some distance if she wanted any hope of falling asleep, but she wanted to be close to him, so for the first time in years she attempted to sleep facing him. She didn't think she would actually drift off, but the next thing she knew the room was flooded in light.

That morning, a Saturday, she wanted to pay a visit to Cindy, who'd had her gall bladder out, but she didn't want to bring Ed. She left him with Connell and drove to Nassau University Medical Center.

When she walked in that night, she found all the lights out except for a cabinet lamp in the kitchen, and Ed lying on the cold bricks of the vestibule. She cursed herself as much as she did Connell, because she'd had a strange intimation of disaster when she'd left. She knew she couldn't trust him, and she'd left Ed with him anyway. She called his name and got no answer.

She couldn't lift Ed, couldn't even get him to sit up. It was as if rigor mortis had set in while he was still alive. She rushed to the cordless phone and saw a note that said that Connell had gone to the city to meet some friends. Rage coursed through her. She brought the phone back with her to Ed and set it down. She didn't want to call anyone until she absolutely had to. She tried to get under him and wedge him up under her thighs, but she

couldn't get a purchase on him. She tried to roll him onto the rug, but he was raving, and she gave up and tried to soothe him, to no avail. He was making his clicking noise. His body was seizing up. He had never felt heavier. She wondered whether she could manage the situation until Connell got home, but most likely he would take the last train out of Grand Central.

The ambulance arrived in minutes. Two guys strapped him to a gurney and she rode with them to Lawrence, where he was admitted. The trip in the ambulance must have revived him, because he walked in with assistance, but in the ER he went wild, screaming, flailing his arms and striking one of the orderlies. They used restraints to tie him down.

"Why?" he kept asking. "Why? Why?"

He looked less healthy than he had even a few days before. It amazed her how quickly catabolic processes could take over a body once they'd begun. She hadn't noticed how skinny he'd gotten, how bad his teeth were, how much he needed a haircut.

She stayed as late as she was allowed. At home she couldn't bring herself to go up to the bedroom, so she just sat at the kitchen table. She hadn't consciously intended to wait up for Connell, but after a while she realized that was what she was doing. She tried to watch television in the den, but she couldn't concentrate on any of the shows. The only thing that made any sense to her was to sit in the silence of the kitchen. She chewed her rage, grinding her teeth.

He walked in at two fifteen. She sat silently looking at him.

"What are you doing up?" he said, throwing a canvas bag down on the island.

"I asked you to stay with your father. Why did you leave him alone?"

"It was only for a little while."

"What made you think it was okay to leave him alone?"

She had shouted. She saw the boy flinch, his eyes widen with fear. He picked the bag off the counter and put it across his chest as if he might make a run for it.

"He was asleep in bed when I left. He wasn't going anywhere, and you were coming home in an hour."

"Well," she said. "He went somewhere."

• • •

She went upstairs to put her head down for a moment. The next thing she knew, the room was bright and Sergei's throaty greeting was booming up at her from the bottom of the staircase. It was one o'clock in the afternoon. She couldn't remember the last time she'd slept so late. She remembered that Ed was in the hospital.

She went to the banister and looked down the landing. "I should have called you," she said. "With everything that was going on, I forgot. I didn't need you to come."

He stood in the vestibule holding his hat against his chest. "You not go to church today?"

Lately he had taken to coming earlier on Sundays, to be there when they returned from twelve o'clock Mass.

"Something's happened with Ed," she said. "He had some kind of collapse. He's in the hospital."

"I stay here with you," he said.

"I'm leaving soon."

"I stay anyway."

"That won't be necessary."

"I stay with you," he said again, this time more decisively.

Connell wasn't in his room. She called downstairs to him, but he didn't answer there either. She dressed without showering, not because of the late hour but because with Ed's absence it felt like Sergei was a guest in the house, and even though Sergei had passed many hours there sitting and doing nothing, she had a strange feeling of having to attend to him.

When she got downstairs she found him sitting at the kitchen table in a state of contained agitation. She could see his deep breathing, the tautness in his fists, one of which still clutched his hat. He asked what had happened. When she told him, his hand on the hat squeezed tighter.

"I stay here," he said.

The nurse was trying to get him to eat when Eileen walked in, but Ed was resisting mightily. He flung his arms around as she approached with the fork, and then shut his lips tight. When she managed to get the food in, he

calmed down and chewed it thoughtfully for a few seconds, then reconsidered and spat it out on the tray.

"He did this with breakfast too."

"I'll take over," Eileen said. She spoke sharply to him, told him to cooperate or else—what? What could she hold over his head?

"If you don't eat," she said, "you're not going to be allowed to come home."

He raised his eyebrows dramatically and took the rest of the meal with little protest. The doctor came around and they discussed how he'd been admitted for altered physical status, an acute sudden change in his condition. The goal would be to rehab him. They agreed on benchmarks: if he could stand on his own and walk to the bathroom, they would release him. Judging from his condition, that seemed sufficiently far off to give her time to adjust to her new circumstances. She needed Ed to do poorly enough for long enough to allow her to figure out what came next.

The next day, she stayed late with Ed. She was famished when she left, and on the drive home, as she contemplated the empty shelves of the fridge, she realized she'd have to order something, though she barely had the energy to make the phone call, let alone figure out what she wanted. She'd never again be able to turn to Ed and say, "What should we eat?" She didn't want to heat up anything in the freezer. The thought of those frozen carcasses disgusted her. It felt like they were food from a lifetime ago, and indeed they were: they were from her life with Ed.

When she walked into the kitchen and saw a smock draped over the island and a pot on the stove, she was so relieved that she almost exclaimed her joy.

Sergei rose from the couch and insisted that she sit. He warmed up the pot and brought a glass of water. He ladled out a healthy portion and presented her with it, then stood watching to see her reaction. It was delicious, a beef stew of some sort.

"Give me the receipt," she said. "I'll reimburse you."

He did his habitual hand waving. It would always be like this with him: he was stubborn as a molar. He had cleaned up the evidence of his

preparation, so that only the stewpot was left on a clean stove. The sink was empty, the dish drainer clean. Maybe he'd made it for himself; maybe he'd tired of eating cold-cut sandwiches. She had the sensation that this was probably how Ed experienced his meals now: they appeared before him as if by magic.

She grew uncomfortable at the sight of Sergei gazing down on her. "Please sit," she said, and he did. He drummed his fingers on the tabletop until his hand latched onto a mail-order catalogue, which he rolled up and used to gently beat the time against the table's edge as he watched her eat.

In the morning, she woke early to take Connell to the airport. When she was stuck in traffic, she looked at his sleeping form in the passenger seat. Everyone said he looked like Ed, but she didn't see it.

He woke up right before they reached the terminal. The need to remove the bags from the trunk promised to make the good-bye mercifully brief. She got out of the car and stood there with him in that scant minute of grace allowed to a person unloading.

"If you need me to come back—" he said, looking past her through the doors.

"Not before Thanksgiving. I can't afford it."

"I'm sorry I won't be here to help."

"I have Sergei," she said. "I'll be fine."

He nodded slowly. He seemed on the verge of speaking, and then he dropped his eyes and looked away before meeting her gaze again, warmly.

"You're going to miss your plane," she said.

He hugged her and picked up his bags. "Call me back if you need to," he said. She could tell he intended an air of gravity, but the way he squinted at the sunlight reminded her of when he was a small boy on her lap reaching for the curtains behind her head. How could the years have brought both of them here?

"Go," she said, and he turned and went through the sliding doors. She watched him disappear around a corner. A cop pulled up beside the car and told her to move along. She watched the planes out the window and in the rearview mirror until she couldn't see them anymore.

She hadn't been at work long when she received a call from the hospital saying they were going to discharge Ed. The woman said they'd be sending him home around two o'clock.

"That's unacceptable," Eileen said. "I'm not home to receive him. This is too sudden."

"It says here you have help with you at home."

"Yes."

"Then he will be delivered to your home aide. He's not eligible to stay any longer. He's stable, his blood pressure is down, he can eat. We have to send him home."

"Is he standing?"

"He can stand with assistance."

"Tell me, was he standing on his own when he went in there?"

"I wasn't here when he was admitted."

"I'll tell you, then. He was. He walked in from the ambulance. So he is not stable, if you ask me."

"I am telling you that he is ready to be dismissed."

"We agreed that he had to be able to walk. He has to be able to go up and down stairs."

"He can walk with assistance."

"I'm going to appeal. I do not agree with the discharge. Medicare gives me two days, no?"

"That's correct."

"Keep him there, then."

She slammed the phone down. Once he was back within her walls, she would have to keep him there until the end. It would be almost impossible, emotionally, for her to deliver him personally to a nursing home, without some event like this interceding to take the guilt away from her. And then she would just be waiting, possibly even hoping in some dark part of her unconscious mind, for something bad to happen to him. She didn't want to live like that. And the hardest truth was that—no matter how good a nurse she thought she was; no matter that she'd proved, during staffing crises, or strikes, or untimely bouts of mass absence, that she could do the work of three nurses; no matter that she wanted to believe she could give

him better care than anyone else could—she wasn't sure anymore that a nursing home wouldn't be better for him. This might have been the time for her to summon up the courage to take Ed back into her home, but she couldn't do it. She had run up against her limit. If this was her only chance to get him out of her hands—and she saw that it was—then she had to take it and live with the guilt later, maybe for the rest of her life.

She spent the morning calling nursing homes in the area. She couldn't afford to wait until the end of the day, because the offices would be closed. It wasn't easy to do; Adelaide seemed to watch her every move.

When she didn't have any luck on the phone, she left work early with a knot in her gut and drove up to Maple Grove Nursing Home in Port Chester, half an hour north of her house. They had a place for Ed, and they'd accept her application, but they told her that they wanted three years' payment up front. It was obvious to her that they didn't want Ed to go into the Medicaid pool, which paid less than private citizens, bargaining for lower rates. Three years up front, factoring in planned increases every six months, was over $225,000. She would drain her cash reserves to zero and still not even be a tenth of the way there. She'd have to cash out the retirement accounts, because they'd already taken out a home equity loan to pay for Connell's tuition. Even then, she couldn't get it done in time.

She hadn't spent an entire career in health care not to pick up any allies along the way. Her friend Emily, whom she'd hired at St. John's Episcopal, had an in with the state attorney general's office. Emily had a representative from the office call Maple Grove and get them to drop the demand for up-front payment. Eileen would pay the fee for the first month, $5,800, while the Medicare paperwork got sorted out. Medicare would cover the first twenty days at 100 percent and the next eighty days at 80 percent after a copay. Then she was on her own.

She called Lawrence Hospital and had them fax in the application for her.

"They're going to transport him tomorrow," she told Sergei. "Maybe you can stay awhile in case I need help with anything. He may be coming back, for all I know."

Sergei nodded as if to say he hadn't imagined it going any other way.

"I'll pay you, of course," she said, but she had no idea where she was going to get the money. She would have to figure out these details later. Right now what was important was getting through a difficult time.

In silence they ate the dinner he had prepared. Something in his face, maybe the roundness of it, took the edge off her anxiety. He seemed to prefer mute expressions to speech, two in particular: a half glower that reminded her of her father's, and a wide-eyed, almost innocent smile.

After they finished eating she dismissed him as he started to clean the dishes. He protested and would only leave the room when she insisted that she needed to use the kitchen phone to spread the news about Ed. She called as many people as she could, until it got to be too late, even accounting for time zones. She left the bunker of the kitchen to face the rest of the first floor, turned off all the lights, and walked up the stairs to the lonely bedroom to pack a bag for Ed.

It was a preposterous exercise. She couldn't reduce his wardrobe to a few essentials at a moment when everything seemed essential. There was also the problem that what was essential to Ed wasn't always essential to her. Some of his favorite shirts should have become cleaning rags long ago. She took out the bag they used for short trips and started filling it with three or four of everything; then she brought down a bigger bag from the attic. She would have time later to figure out exactly what he needed, but she wanted him to have enough in case of mishaps the first few days. Then she saw his peacoat. It was missing buttons and threadbare at the elbows, wrists, and collar. He looked like a homeless man in it, but he'd insisted, perversely, on holding on to it, as if he'd never left the cold-water flat he'd grown up in. His stubbornness drove her crazy. And yet his lack of interest in material things had allowed them to save a good deal of money relative to their incomes. She held the peacoat in her hands until she almost broke down, then put it back on a hanger and took a newer coat from the closet.

She walked through the day in the haze of her lack of sleep, feeling her boss's eyes on her, as if Adelaide could sense her mind was somewhere else. They moved Ed at noon, but she couldn't call. She wanted to pull Adelaide aside and assure her that she had no aims on her job, but how could she do

so without seeming insubordinate? She felt lucky to have a job, but she saw no way to communicate that without smelling of desperation. Once Adelaide sensed weakness, she would surely seize on it. Eileen didn't blame her entirely. Mayor Giuliani's office, in its push for health care efficiency, had HHC working middle management to the bone. Ruthlessness was more or less demanded of Adelaide if she wanted to keep her job. Eileen had been on the other side of these managerial squeezes, at St. John's Episcopal. It had bothered her at first to think that her days of carrying the heavy burdens of upper management were behind her, but now she didn't care at all.

It was time now to be smart—smart and strong. She wondered whether she'd ever have a chance to be foolish and weak. She feared it would be when everyone else was foolish and weak again too, only this time around there wouldn't be anything romantic about their foolishness; they'd be old and doddering and needy. At least she wouldn't be alone in it, the way Ed was. Ed was surrounded by people, but there was no one in that building like him at all. He was younger; he'd given up more of life. But there had rarely been anyone anywhere like Ed, even when all had been well. He was smarter than most, more sensitive. In that regard he was more prepared for the loneliness of senescence than she was. He'd been a stranger in the world for most of his life.

After work she drove up to the home. She made her way to the circular reception desk from which the hallways radiated. Below the counter ran a ring of binders with red labels on their spines bearing the letters DNR, for Do Not Resuscitate. She had indicated in her application that she wanted this designation for Ed, but still that stark, resigned lineup took her by surprise. An odd few didn't say DNR, and it filled her with shame to see them, because it meant those families hadn't given up hope, or they were willing to stick it out until the end, the very end, the end of science and technology.

She was directed to a television room. Wheelchairs were arranged around the perimeter. The room was full of women older than her husband, some by decades, whose gazes seemed directed less at the program than at the light the set cast. There were a few men, frail and reduced; she didn't spot Ed at first, but then there he was, hidden behind a man who distended and released his cheeks as though blowing on a tuba. Ed looked as if he'd been caught in a traffic jam. He was moaning quietly. When she stood before him, his moan turned into a wail, and he pumped his arms up and down. She wheeled aside the tuba player, who looked at her skeptically as he puffed out, with an audible pop, the air he'd been holding in. She asked at the desk to be directed to a common room, thinking not to disturb Ed's roommate.

Ed wailed and thrashed, trying to twist in his seat to get a look at her. When he made to rise, the seat belt stopped him, and if he tried to rise farther, the barest push on his shoulder made him fall back in the chair. After making a couple of turns at the end of corridors, she arrived at the

common room, which was blessedly empty. She closed the door behind her and wheeled him to a wicker chair, where she sat facing him. He continued to wail. She tried to soothe him with a hand on his shoulder and he slapped it away. She tried to touch his face and he motioned to bite her. He was seething through his teeth. She insisted on smoothing his hair. He looked wild, unkempt. Already they had dressed him in an outfit that looked shabby and unmatched. She would have to speak to them about that. The easiest way to get them to give him good care was to let them know that she would be around, that they couldn't slip. It was the same with the nurses she supervised.

For a few moments he suffered her attempts to pat his hair down, but then he put his hand to his scalp as though deliberately to mess up the work she had done.

"I know you don't want to be here," she said.

"No." He shook his head. "No, no, no, no. No."

"I'm here. I'm going to be here. I'm going to be here every day."

There was a confused sadness in his expression, a struggle to convey what he was feeling.

"I couldn't take good enough care of you at home," she said, swallowing hard. "I couldn't keep you safe."

He fell quiet. She was finding it hard to keep herself together. She was determined to get through this without breaking down.

"No," he said.

"Okay," she said. "This is just for now. It's temporary. When you stabilize, we'll get you out of here."

He snorted at the word "temporary," as if a bit of the old humor were back. Then he slipped back into the wailing, only now it was weirdly dislocated from the conversation and seemed almost meditative. He stared into the distance. She shook him to make him stop, and finally, mercifully, he was quiet.

"I can't be here during the day," she said. "But I'm going to come after work, every day. Do you understand me? I'll be here all the time. You're going to get sick of seeing me."

His eyebrows shot up. "No, no, no!" he said.

"Don't worry about me," she said. "I'm going to be fine. I'll have help." She reached to pat down his hair again, and he batted her away with a shocking directness and force.

"No!" he shouted, less in plea than command. He was pointing a finger at her. "No! No!"

"No what, Ed?" She had a creeping feeling he understood something. She hadn't said she was keeping Sergei on, but she sensed that it was the topic between them now.

"What is it?" He grew quiet again, brooding, his bottom lip pushed out, his chin tucked, his eyes searching hers.

"No." His voice was meek, but the note it struck was final.

"No what? You don't want me to have help?"

"No."

"All right," she said. "I'll get by. I'll manage."

"No," he said again.

A vestige of evening light lingered in the air as she headed back. She decided to take a detour through town. She took Valley off Pondfield and drove up the hill, into the warren of expensive homes. The road curved quickly and with little give; she had to pull over once to let a car pass. Lush trees shouted their vigorous greens, balancing the calm of the Tudor revival homes, every one of which seemed perfectly placed and spaced.

She stopped in front of Virginia's home. She wondered whether Virginia had ever seen her there, whether she'd noticed how often the same car stopped outside her house or across the street for a little while and then drove off.

She drove down the hill and took Garden, stopping next to the empty tennis courts. When they lived in Jackson Heights, she'd bought Ed private lessons with a pro at the tennis center in Flushing. She never forgot her admiration at the way he held his own with Tom Cudahy the first time she saw him play, or that he'd so thoroughly assimilated the little coaching he'd gotten that he'd turned himself into a decent player. Tennis seemed like the perfect sport for him to take up, or at least the perfect one if he arranged his life the way she wished he would. The exercise would satisfy him, tiring

him out as effectively as the long jogs he liked to go on. The courts were
state-of-the-art, and the pros who taught there were trying to get on the
US Open circuit or just coming off. It was the kind of place where Ed
would meet people, make the right contacts, and form an ambitious plan
he might not otherwise conceive of. It lacked that deliberate grandeur of
a country club that she knew he would balk at. Still, he objected to the extravagance and didn't attend a single session. Connell wouldn't go either.
The two-hundred-dollar credit never got used.

She circled through town and doubled back on Pondfield past the
restaurants with outdoor tables that would be pulled in in a few weeks.
She'd imagined dining at those tables with Ed, a drink in hand as towns-
people stopped to greet them by name, but now she would have to sit at
them alone, or with friends from elsewhere, or not at all, because she didn't
know anyone in town.

She parked and walked past the post office, Le Bistro, the stationery
store and Topps Bakery, Lange's Delicatessen, the Alps, Tryforos on the
other side of the street, past Botticelli Bridal Boutique, which had in its
window a beautiful dress beaded from bodice to train, and arrived at
the northbound platform of the train station, where she took a seat on a
bench, looking at Lawrence Hospital in the middle distance, the place that
had originally brought her to this town. The temperature was pleasant, the
summer humidity ceding to the dry air of autumn. People began to amass
on the opposite platform in anticipation of a city-bound train. She felt an
impulse to get on that train and see where the night took her, but Sergei
was at home, and she had to go home too.

A train approached on her side. She watched its light grow from a
speck around the bend into a bright flash as it roared into the station. The
platform rumbled under her feet, and after a few pregnant moments the
train slid its doors open and allowed the emergence of people. The passengers weren't in a hurry, but neither did they dawdle; they ducked into the
tunnel or fanned out into the streets with determined efficiency to meet
spouses in waiting cars or begin the walk home. The platform emptied
quickly, leaving her alone again, and after another minute the train on the
opposite side came in, and that platform emptied too.

She would never be picked up by Ed nor pick him up. There would be no one waiting for her in the rainy dark, taillights guiding her to him, no respite in the front seat as someone else manned the wheel. She would have to take a cab if she ever wanted not to walk from the station. The fleet of cabs waited for trains, their drivers' expressions stony. They never pulled into your driveway but only continued up the street with their other fares, leaving you standing outside an empty house, listening to the muffled sounds of trucks on the distant highway and the drowsy hush of oncoming night.

She went back to the car and drove a long way home, drifting once through town and taking back roads. She pulled into the garage and shut the car off and sat in it long enough for the light in the door track to go off, so she was swallowed in darkness. She listened to the rhythms of the house, its quiet heartbeat. The water heater hummed in the basement, and from a couple of flights away she could make out the faint whisper of Sergei's radio.

She went up to the second floor and stood outside his door. He was listening to classical music. There was something about men needing to listen to classical music alone, as though the emotions it stirred in them embarrassed them too much. She waited until she heard a pause in the movement and knocked. When he came to the door, the racing stripes of his track pants and the blazing whiteness of his sneakers looked slightly comical under the solid square of his polo shirt.

"I wanted to let you know I was home," she said. "Thank you for staying."

He waved her politeness off.

"Do you want some tea?"

"Yes," he said.

"It's not from a samovar, but it's Irish, so it should be strong enough."

"Any tea," he said.

She put the tea on and set out what was left of a cake she'd made earlier in the week, a treat for Connell before he left for school. When the kettle whistled, he came down the stairs. She tucked into the preparation of the tea to escape the silence of being in a room with him. The language barrier robbed her of her instincts. She didn't want to talk down to him, but she found herself talking slowly and loudly when she did talk. After a while,

there was nothing left to prepare, and she brought the teapot over and served him and sat with him.

"You like classical music?" she asked desperately. He arched his brows and then merely nodded, deflating the little hope that she might spark an exchange with this question. She had the feeling he wasn't much of a talker in any language. "My husband and I go—*went*—to Carnegie Hall, for the symphony. We had a subscription."

She was just at the point of asking him, idiotically, if he knew Carnegie Hall, when he cleared his throat with an authoritative growl and said that his daughter had played there. She was glad she had put the mug to her lips, because she was able to hide her astonishment.

"Student at Juilliard," he said.

It occurred to her that she had never really spoken to him about his family. She knew he had two kids and that the older one, his son, whose name she could not remember, worked on the West Coast; she wondered now if it were for one of the software developers in Silicon Valley. She had pictured him as a security guard.

"Carnegie Hall," she said. "That's quite an accomplishment."

"She plays violin."

"It seems like the hardest instrument to play," she said. "Then again, they all seem hard to me."

"Is, and is not," he said sagely. She was curious to hear more, but she didn't want to ask. She wondered about the life he led when he left her house on Friday evenings. She pictured his daughter coming home for weekends, the three of them sitting around a table at some massive hall in Brighton Beach, drinking flavored vodka and listening to music. She considered the reality that the time he spent at home was his real life and the time he spent at her house was only a job.

"I appreciate your staying," she said. "I want to say that again. I can't say for how long it will be, exactly. I'm just not sure Ed is going to stay at that home. I'm going to pay you your regular wage, of course, for the trouble of being here."

He gave her another wave of the hand, to dispense with so pedestrian a topic. She might have been offended if she didn't find it so reassuring. He

settled back into his seat and seemed to appraise her. The warmth that settled into his features would have made more sense had he been drinking
vodka rather than tea, and for a moment she wondered if he hadn't been
taking swigs from a flask or a bottle upstairs.

"I need job," he said, chuckling. "I stay even if you don't pay me. I don't
mind getting away from my wife. You know?"

She took a quick sip of her tea.

"She is not like you," he said. "She not work hard. She not work at all.
Russian woman, not American. I was driving cab. I should be retired."

"Life would be easier without money to worry about."

"Life is easy when you have good wife who don't need to be taken care
of. Who take care of you."

She cut another slice of cake, which she began eating nervously.

"But," he said, "when I bring home money, she is happy."

"I have some jobs for you while you're here," she said. "Home improvements. There are things my husband didn't get to do that we had talked
about doing. Are you handy?"

"I was engineer in Russia," he said proudly. "I once built violin from
scratch for hobby. I can do your jobs."

"You won't need to do anything quite that complicated," she said, trying to hide her amazement. She said the first thing that came to mind: "You
can just help me get this place in shape to sell it." As she said it, she realized
that she was never going to sell the house, that deep down she suspected
she would die in it.

"Is beautiful house," he said. "Sell for a lot of money."

"You'd be surprised. The market around here isn't great right now.
They put in some low-income housing not far from here. People turn up
their noses."

"You get a lot for this house," he said dismissively.

"We took out a home equity loan to pay for Connell's education." She
hesitated, "You know what that is?"

"Home equity, yes," he said, looking annoyed. She was once again
mortified, but it was such an odd negotiation, trying to figure out what he
understood. She was getting the feeling that he understood more than she

suspected. She poured them both another cup of tea, even though she'd had too much already. She could feel a buzzing pressure in her temples.

"So I still have a lot to pay on it," she said. "If I move into a smaller place, I'd probably break even." She didn't know why she was telling him all this.

"You'll be fine," he said. "You have good brain."

She could feel a slight shift in the mood, a softening of his edges, if not of hers.

"I don't know when Ed might be allowed to return, if his condition stabilizes." She was riffing now. "I'd like you to be here if something happens to change his status. For a little while, at least. Please tell your wife that I appreciate her patience as I adjust to this new reality. I'm sure she's wondering why you're still here if Ed is no longer in the house."

"My wife, she does not know that your husband is in nursing home."

"She doesn't?"

"*Nyet*. No." He was laughing. "What difference it makes? As long as I bring home money."

Eileen was silent.

"How long you want wait for your husband to come home?" Sergei asked.

Eileen felt herself redden and began piling up the dishes.

"Only as long as necessary," she said. "Only until I know he's not coming back."

She switched into a recitation of the things she wanted him to do the next day while she was at work—clean out the garage, dig the leaves out of the drain gutters, change the burnt-out floodlights on the side of the house. She wondered if he could tell she was making them up on the fly. It wasn't a long list, but it would last a few days at least. She went upstairs and got ready for bed. A couple of her girlfriends called and she stayed on the phone until after ten. She didn't mention Sergei.

She lay in bed after the calls wondering what she would find when she went to the nursing home the next day. She feared spending the night there might cause Ed to lose whatever grip he had on his old life. She couldn't shake the thought of him staring at her in that reduced state with a crystal-

linc, hateful gaze, as though she had betrayed him by putting him there, as though every day she left him there would be another betrayal.

When Sergei came up she heard him settle in. She listened to the shifts and squeaks he made in the bed, until she heard the muted whistle of a snore. In the glow and muffled insistence of late-night television she drifted off, though the loud commercials hectored her to intermittent wakefulness, and then the sun recalled her to life.

She encountered the social director on the way to the main desk. The woman had a big tropical bird on her arm that she tried to present to Eileen.

"This is Calypsa," the woman said, extending her arm. "Say hello, Calypsa."

"Hello, Calypso," Eileen said, with forced brightness.

"Calyp*sa*. With an *a*. Say hello, Calypsa." The woman's name tag read Kacey, but she hadn't introduced herself, even though she was the social director. The bird just sat on her wrist, giving Eileen an eerie stare.

"I'm Eileen."

"She'll go up your arm if you hold it there for a minute." Eileen could think of nothing else to reduce the awkwardness of the moment, so she stuck her hand out reluctantly. "Straight," the woman said sharply. "Put your arm out straight. She'll walk right up."

Eileen straightened her arm. After a few moments the bird hopped decisively onto her wrist. Eileen had to restrain herself from crying out as the bird made its way to the soft skin inside her elbow, where it stopped and dug its claws in.

"It pinches a bit," the woman said.

"It certainly does."

"You'll get used to it."

"I suppose so," Eileen said tersely.

"I take her around to the patients. She loves to crawl on them."

Eileen was incredulous. "*Crawl* on them?"

"All over."

It was hard to see how this was going to be something Ed would enjoy. The bird was making its way up her arm to the shoulder, where it settled

in with a certain finality, as though it had planted a flag. Eileen was able to relax slightly, though it was kneading her shoulder through the fabric.

"It—*she*—doesn't hurt them?"

"She wouldn't hurt anyone," the woman said with a hint of indignation. "They can scream at her and flail around and she just acts like a lady." The bird pecked at Eileen's collar and seemed about to engage her ear when the woman whisked her away, clucking, ostensibly at the bird, but Eileen felt it directed at herself.

Ed wasn't in the dense crowd in the television room.

"Where is my husband?" she asked the attending nurse at the main desk.

"Who are we talking about, ma'am?"

"Edmund Leary," she said. "He was admitted yesterday."

"He could be sleeping. He had an eventful day." The girl raised her brows.

"What happened?"

"Sometimes there's an adjustment period."

"What *happened*?"

"He had to be restrained. He didn't want to be changed. He's a little younger than our average patient. He's got more pop in him."

She felt a twinge of pride beneath her concern. She ached to see him. She walked down the hall and found him staring at the ceiling, the radio at his bedside playing at a low murmur. After a couple of seconds she realized it was tuned to a rap station. She shut it off angrily and headed back to the desk.

"There was a rap station playing on my husband's radio."

The girl gave her a blank look. Her straightened hair—whether it was her own or not—was piled on her head in a colorful tower that looked like a piece of glazed ceramic. She should have known better than to think this girl would understand.

"There should *never* be a rap station on his radio."

"I'm sorry about that, Mrs. . . ."

"Leary. *Eileen Leary*. My husband is *Ed* Leary, and I will be here every day. And I do not want rap music on his radio."

"I'm sorry—"

"I'm a nurse. I understand they may put the radio on when they're changing the sheets, doing up the room. Under no circumstances should the radio in his room be set to a rap station." She could feel herself sweating. "I'm trying to make myself perfectly clear."

"Would you like to speak to my supervisor?"

"I will call tomorrow," Eileen said. "Thank you."

"This won't be a problem," the girl said, "I assure you."

"I know it won't," Eileen said, and she went back to Ed. She could hear in her head all the things that nurse was thinking about her. She'd heard this narrative in her head for as long as she had been supervising nurses, and she was fine with it.

Somewhere deep down, she knew that if Ed were his former self enough to take in the rap music with all his faculties, he might very well be curious enough to give it an honest listen. There had been times when she had suffered Ed's open-mindedness like a thousand little cuts, but it was tolerable because he gave in to moments of tribal loyalty himself sometimes, and even displayed occasional ill-temper about the things that got her blood going—like that night she'd never forget, when a couple of Hispanic kids, who had been leaning against the streetlamp in front of the house for an hour, cursing up a storm, drew Ed out to the stoop. He dressed them down and told them to take that kind of low-class language elsewhere, because this wasn't that kind of house, and she stood in the vestibule and watched over his shoulder as they skulked away. Now, though, that he could hardly discern the differences between things, there was no appeal she could make to a reasonable, mutual, even generational abstention from the noise around them. The silent radio reproached her. She put on a Nat King Cole CD for him.

At the end of her visit, she had a hard time navigating her way out through the identical hallways that seemed to loop back on each other. She asked for the "front entrance" because that was what she'd heard it called, even though it was at the back of the building, and even though facing the street was an entrance she imagined should have been called the "front entrance." That entrance was the "back entrance," and if she went out that

door, she would have had to walk all the way around the facility to the "front entrance" to get to her car.

The place seemed designed to make you crazy. Maybe the idea was to make you want to stay away. Judging from the sparse population of visitors in the television room, most people obliged them.

She wasn't visiting. What she was doing was seeing her husband after work. It was simply a part of her day. She was showing them that Ed might be there with them instead of home where he belonged, but nothing else had changed.

They could put his room in the middle of a maze and she would find her way to it every night.

She was going to be the woman who wouldn't go away, in the marriage that wouldn't die. Her idea of her husband wasn't going to be diminished when orderlies looked at him as if he was just another old fool. They had no clue what kind of man had fallen into their lap, but she wasn't going to explain it to them, because they didn't deserve to hear it. She was content to let them think he was a gibberer, an invalid, an idiot, because she knew better. She would always know better than them.

She had him pour a layer of blacktop in the driveway. She had him paint everything that could be painted, and then she had him move outside to paint the cedar boards, the fences, the window moldings, the heavy metal gate to the stairs, even the bricks. He removed the old wallpaper and installed new paper with fresh patterns. She had him rip out the attic insulation and replace it, haul junk from the basement and attic to the dump, and dredge the drainage gutter in front of the house. He ripped out the horrible toilet in the first-floor half bath and installed a bright new one, along with a new vanity. He didn't need assistance for most jobs; for the biggest ones, she paid the gardener to help him off-hours. He used his own tools, leaving alone the ones she'd bought for Ed. He patched the waterlogged wall in the garage. He reinforced the retaining wall at the end of the driveway, where the property shot up into a slope, because it had begun to lean slightly and she had been told it would eventually give way if left untended. He erected a temporary wooden buttress to keep the wall from pitching forward, dug out the backfill down to the footing, filled in the resultant gap with concrete blocks and fabric to keep the silt out, and then repacked the dirt. For a platform top over the two layers of wall, he built a wooden frame into which he poured concrete that he smoothed out so faultlessly that it reminded her of fondant atop a fancy cake.

Her friends marveled at his work. In their marveling she could hear a hint of prurience, but if they weren't going to make their surmises explicit, then she was content to let them harbor them silently. Maybe they thought he was taking Ed's place. Maybe they thought that she was in some fundamental way *out of control*. Maybe they thought it was sad that she needed a

bridge between her old life and her new one. Maybe they thought she was sleeping with him. *Let them think whatever they want*, she told herself. *Let them speculate and conjecture and cluck their tongues and drown in pity or disapproval or whatever else.*

She was proud of the caliber of improvements to her property. Neighbors who had never said two words to her began to ask who had done her work. She made vague demurrals about his being a friend, and when she relayed these inquiries to Sergei, he radiated a pride she hadn't expected. She would have preferred him to stand aloof from appraisals of the quality of his labor, because if he remained eternally elsewhere in his mind, somewhere more rarefied and abstract, then she didn't have to think of him as reduced to his circumstances. When she saw how delighted he seemed by the compliments, though, she decided to stop worrying that she was condescending to him when she assigned him tasks, which made her more comfortable keeping him in the house, which was what she had been trying to feel for a while. She didn't know what she would do with herself once he was gone.

As October gave way to November and the stream of bigger jobs slowed to a trickle, the house began to take on the patina she'd envisioned when she'd signed the papers aligning her fate with its own. She understood that it would have to remain incomplete: she wasn't going to launch into finishing the attic or basement. The electrical would never get upgraded or the oil tank dug up or the piping replaced or the asbestos hauled away. She wouldn't be able to keep paying Sergei the nearly four thousand dollars a month she'd been paying him. The Medicare-paid hundred days were coming to an end soon, whereupon she would start paying six thousand a month to the nursing home, which would come right out of the retirement accounts and what was left of the home equity line of credit.

She wanted to talk to him about leaving, but it was easier each week just to spend down her income and dip a little into her savings and promise herself that she'd bring it up before the next payday. *As long as I bring home money, she is happy*, she remembered Sergei saying.

One day Sergei asked if he could stay at the house on weekends as well. The request dismayed her; she had been sure this would be the day

she would say something to him about finishing his stint there; in fact, she had just been about to bring it up. Then he told her that he had left his wife a couple of weeks before and had been staying on his sister's couch on weekend nights.

She was stunned. "I can't afford to keep paying you full-time."

"You don't have to pay me," he said. "I pay you to stay here."

"Pay *me*?"

"I do handyman work," he said. "I work for your neighbors."

This radical-sounding proposal had about it the seductive reasonability of the most outlandish schemes. She affected a dubious air, but she knew its adoption was inevitable.

"I like this neighborhood," he said, to fill the gap her thoughts had opened up.

"You're not paying me," she said. "You can continue to do jobs around this house while you get your feet under you." She felt her heels come together involuntarily. "That will be compensation enough for use of the room. Eventually you'll have to find your own place, of course."

She made a sign for him with her home number on it, though she didn't include her name. She photocopied it and put it up on the tackboards at Slave to the Grind and Lawrence Hospital. She placed an ad in the *Pennysaver* circular. She knocked on the doors of the neighbors who had asked about him.

Calls started coming in. She dropped him off at Smith Cairns on her way to work and he bought a used Taurus. Most mornings he left before she was awake. Usually he put a pot of coffee on for her. He never drank coffee himself.

She stopped feeling guilty about having kept him away from home in the run-up to his separation. Leaving his wife had been his business; it had nothing to do with Eileen, and from what she understood it had been a long time coming. If some time apart every week had been enough to drive a wedge between them, then maybe a separation had been in order.

He left more than enough money every Friday to cover his portion of the food. He hardly used any electricity.

It would have been too intimate for them to eat meals together. They would have had a lot of time to fill across a table. When she cooked, she ate first and left it for him on the stove; when he did, he left it in the fridge. She would knock and tell him through the closed door that there was something for him downstairs. He would leave a note for her in his pidgin English: "Am make dinner tonight. Don't you do it."

He took his clothes into the bathroom with him when he showered, and he dressed before he emerged. Once—he must not have known she had come home—she watched from the base of the stairs as he took a few thunderous steps into his bedroom, around his waist a dull white towel that might have been taken from a gym. Its ends met in a strained cinch at his hip, his abdomen pushing against it but not hanging over, as if his excess flesh were made of sounder stuff than her own. Remnant steam trailed him into the hall. The ruddiness of his face and chest suggested a lobster that had survived a boiling, while the whiteness of the rest of him ran almost alabaster.

He did his own laundry and often hers as well, though he never mixed their clothing in the same load. She didn't have to ask for this hermetic separation; he had arrived at it independently.

They watched television in their own rooms. The set in the den was almost never used, except sometimes in the late hours, when, assured that he was tucked into his quarters for the night, she padded downstairs and turned it on, keeping the volume low and the lights off. She heard the stairs creak with his weight and muted the volume, but it was a phantom creak. The tenebrous dark in the kitchen fluttered for a moment, as if he had entered that space, but he never did.

She took the *Times* with her to work, not because she needed it during her shift but to be able to leave it for him in its entirety later and avoid awkward negotiations about sections. She dropped it on the island when she came home, and he was discreet enough to collect it when she was out of the room and put it in the recycling bin when he was done. Most days he left the *Post* for her in turn, which was a guilty pleasure she hadn't indulged in since the days in Jackson Heights when she used to retrieve Connell from whichever Orlando apartment he was at. She'd forgotten how much she'd

enjoyed sitting at the Orlandos' dining room table, flipping idly through the *Post's* pages and chatting while Connell made his entreaties to stay.

The prospect of Thanksgiving had been haunting her for a while. She would have to justify Sergei's continued presence in the house to Connell. Somehow she had managed to keep it from him. It helped that he didn't call much. She had also told Sergei not to answer the phone, though she knew she needn't have bothered. Finally, she called Connell and told him not to come home and to apply the credit to another flight. Money was tight, she told him, and he'd be home in a few weeks anyway. He protested, though halfheartedly enough to allow her to feel a little better about what she was doing. She could tell he felt guilty, but his guilt wasn't just about not being there; it was also about not feeling more guilty about not being there.

Several well-meaning friends invited her over for the meal, but she told all of them that she was going out to her cousin Pat's. She went up for breakfast that morning with Ed and then made Thanksgiving dinner for herself and Sergei, the full orchestration, with all the sides and a bird large enough to yield leftovers for weeks.

It was the first American Thanksgiving meal Sergei had ever eaten. She watched him assemble on his plate a heaping mound of the offerings. After he had devoured it, he filled his plate again. When he reached for a third helping of marshmallow-topped sweet potatoes, she felt a warm pride settle into her, like a sip of mulled wine. He ate a whole can of cranberry sauce himself.

One night in early December, after a few frustrating hours at Maple Grove, during which Ed refused to eat and emitted a persistent, plaintive whine, and an enervating day at work before that, while she was washing the pan from a meatloaf whose crusted end she had polished off without so much as sitting down, she heard Sergei walk into the room behind her. She looked up into the window and saw his reflection standing in the doorway. After a few moments she couldn't pretend she didn't know he was there; his steps had been too heavy, and now there was an electric charge in the air. She put

down the scrubber and took a fortifying breath, then turned to face him. He was perfectly silent, looking at her with a strange intensity. He began to walk toward her. She had rubber gloves on her hands and raised them instinctively. He came around the island and stood before her. She could feel her own breath coming fast. He inched closer to her. The tentativeness she detected in him alarmed her; it was as if he feared for both their fates, as if he couldn't help whatever he was about to do. She reproached herself for sheltering this stranger in her house. He could do anything he wanted to her and she would be powerless to stop him.

One of his hands went to her waist; she felt she was watching from outside her body as she didn't move it away. His other hand joined in.

"What are you doing?"

"It's okay," he said.

He pulled her to him. Her arms went up in halfhearted protection and the cold, wet rubber sent a tingling across her skin. She felt bloated and squishy against him. She'd put on sixty pounds in the years since Ed's diagnosis, nearly a pound for each her husband had lost, as if she'd been eating to maintain their equilibrium. Sergei's face, as he moved in to kiss her, was smooth enough that she wondered whether he had shaved right before he came down. His drugstore aftershave, liberally applied, did not repel her up close as she had imagined it would. She felt a pounding through his chest. His hands moving over her left ghostly sense impressions everywhere they'd been. She found herself ascending the stairs with him.

Afterward, in her room, she locked the door and moved the armchair in front of it. She knew it was ridiculous, but she felt the need to protect herself, to hide. She climbed into bed and wept for a while, and then somehow she slept, the body doing what it had to do. She woke in the middle of the night to the unsettling light of the lamp and heard the low hum of Sergei's television. Somehow she knew that he wasn't awake.

In the morning she showered and dressed before she moved the armchair. When she ventured out of the room, she saw Sergei's door wide open. She walked over to it and looked inside; none of his things were there. She ven-

tured downstairs and was startled to find him sitting at the table sipping a cup of coffee, the suitcase next to him.

"Forgive me," he said.

"For what?"

"I understand you want I should leave."

"Don't be ridiculous," she said. "You have a job to get to. You can begin to look for a place. In the meantime, this is where you live. There's nothing more to say, as far as I'm concerned."

88

Connell had hatched his plan over Thanksgiving, when he learned that his mother was going to have her Christmas party on Christmas night instead. Cindy Coakley was planning to host Christmas Eve again, as she had the previous year and probably would indefinitely now that the old order had been toppled. It wasn't ideal, his mother said, as there wasn't as much to look forward to, and people couldn't stay out as late, but it was important to her to have a party in the house this particular year, with the usual cast of people. She understood that it would be redundant, the same people going to both, and she understood that they would go if she insisted, and she was going to insist. She said she wanted it to be as nice as any Christmas they'd ever had. He knew it was going to break her heart not to have his father in attendance, so he was going to make sure his father was there after all.

They went together on Christmas morning to see him. The nursing home was decorated for the holidays. Small clusters of visitors amassed at every sitting area, and many of the rooms were packed, with an air of festivity. The nurses and orderlies were less formal with his mother than with the adult children and grandkids who flew in from far-flung places, but they were also more circumspect. It must not have been convenient for them that she came every day, particularly as she was a career nurse who wasn't afraid to assert herself.

They found his father asleep in his bed, his mouth hanging open. They didn't wake him but sat in chairs on either side of the bed waiting for him to come to on his own. Connell got the creepy feeling that they were look-

ing at his corpse. Just as he was about to reach out and shake his father awake, his mother did it herself. His father opened his eyes without startling and began babbling hushed syllables. He lifted his hand slowly to scratch his nose, as if moving through an invisible viscous substance.

Connell's mother had tried to prepare him for how much his father had deteriorated since summer. When they transferred his father to the wheelchair, his father couldn't push himself up off the bed without help.

After his father was in the chair, Connell watched his knee for some vestige of the gesture that had bound them over the years. It had begun when he was young, when his father would throw his arms around him and declare, "What a good boy I have here." Early on in the illness, whenever Connell hugged him, his father squeezed back and said simply, "Good boy." When his father began to lose his strength, the squeezes turned to pats; when he lost his coordination, the pats became pounding slaps. "Just rub," Connell said once, as they clutched. "Rub. Now just keep your hands still for a second, like this." Then his father started to slur his words, so that all he could say clearly was "Good, good, good," and then eventually that "good" gave way to an inarticulate sound— but Connell knew what it meant, even if no one else could have interpreted it. Then Connell would lean down to initiate a hug, and his father would reach up from the couch, until eventually his father didn't reach up anymore but just patted his own knee. The final stage came when Connell noticed that his father patted his knee whenever Connell was even in the room. Now, though, in the wheelchair, he didn't move at all.

Connell wheeled him to the big picture window that looked out on the lawn. Remnant clusters of white from a recent snowfall dotted the landscape. It was too cold to take him out on the veranda. His mother had not mentioned the possibility of taking him home for Christmas, and seeing his condition, he knew why. He was undaunted, though. He would lift his father up into the car and carry him up the stairs and give his mother a little of her life back for a day.

They had brought a couple of presents, which they opened for him. The muted quality to the exchange, the way it was over in less than two minutes, made it feel as if they had come empty-handed. His mother had

had them dress his father for the occasion, in the gray knit sweater he liked to wear on Christmas, with the band of snowflakes around the middle, and a collared shirt and dress slacks, but it looked like the outfit of a much larger man had been put on him by accident. Connell hadn't had the buffer of incremental change to reduce the shock of seeing him swimming in it.

His mother was uncharacteristically quiet, and Connell chattered until the engine of his monologue ran down and they gazed out at the leaves getting whipped up in the wind and sent swirling around the grounds.

Kacey, the social director, came by with the tropical bird on her arm. "Look, Mr. Leary," she said. "Calypsa wants to wish you and your family a Merry Christmas and a Happy Holiday!" The parrot wore a miniature Santa suit with a black belt, and a red felt hat with a pom-pom on top. It did a little shimmying dance. Connell couldn't help bursting into laughter. *Maybe that's the point of dressing it up that way*, he thought. *Maybe there's a method in her madness.* His mother barely raised her eyes to acknowledge either woman or parrot, and after holding the bird for a bit, Connell decided he had to get her out of there before her mood darkened any further. "Let's go," he said. "There's a lot left to do." He wheeled his father back to his room. When they reached the car, he told his mother he had to run to the bathroom, and he went back in and told the desk attendant of his plan to return that evening and pick his father up. She checked to see if he was on the sign-out list.

"It's not a problem," she said, as she closed his father's binder. "I have to remind you that he is your responsibility once you've signed him out."

"I got it," Connell said as casually as possible, failing to hide the tremor in his voice.

He would have to wait for the right moment to leave. His mother would be leaning on him for help. She had outdone herself this year: new strings of lights, new boxes of ornaments, a second crèche, a new star for the tree, expensive-looking wreaths.

A different level of intensity attended this year's preparations. While Sergei did a last-minute grocery run, Connell hauled the last boxes down from the attic. He added a final platoon to the small army of Santa Clauses,

wooden soldiers, and snowmen that already occupied the first floor. Artificial holly hung from every wall, bedecked by bows, with wreaths affixed to every door. The tree was heavy with ornaments, strings of lights, and tinsel clumped thick as cooked spinach. Rivulets of lights ran along the fireplace and the baseboard molding, around the doorframes, up the banister. Plugged-in candles sat on end tables and the breakfront, and illuminated manger scenes fought for space with ceramic Christmas trees. Everything seemed to have a light in it or on it or behind it. Somehow, despite the overwhelming number of individual pieces, the house still felt underdecorated once everything was plugged in and turned on, as if the dark spaces were more apparent than the lit ones.

The amount of food in the kitchen suggested a team of cooks and not a single determined individual. Plates, pots, and pans took up every countertop and the island. The dining room table, at full extension with all its leaves in, was covered in white lace atop red linen. A smaller table pushed against it spilled into the living room. Drummer-boy napkin holders topped the place settings. Even on that sprawling surface, there wasn't much room to set a drink down.

The guests started arriving, and Connell carried their coats down to the rack in the basement. They amassed in the kitchen, mugs of eggnog in their hands, glasses of wine, cheese cubes, butter cookies, chocolate truffles, nuts from bowls, Swedish meatballs on toothpick spears, crackers plucked from dwindling rows, boughs of grapes snapped off a larger bunch, chips dunked in chunky dips, bread wedges spread with baked brie, gourmet pigs in handmade blankets, slices of cured imported meat—the orchestral tune-up for the symphony to follow. There would be leftovers for a week.

He watched his mother slide through the kitchen to kid Tom about saving room for dinner, as she cleared plates of toothpicks and crumbs and swept back into conversation with Marie. She was her best self at parties. She had a gift for putting people at ease. She always said she'd have made a first-rate diplomat or politician, but Connell knew she'd have been content with his becoming one in her place.

Incandescence and bodies combined to heat the den quickly. He

opened the patio door, but it brought a violent chill into the room, and he had to close it again. The living room's wing chairs, folding chairs, and couch were packed with people balancing plates of appetizers on their knees. By the bar in the atrium, Jack Coakley and a man from up the block had planted themselves, guests weaving between them to refresh their drinks. The door to the front porch was cracked for air. Connell opened it fully and saw the team of wooden reindeer Jack had made one year in his garage workshop, and the lights that fringed the fence and lined the walkway and festooned the shrubs.

He went outside, closing the door behind him, and unplugged a strand of lights, throwing the right side of the house into darkness. He went back inside and told his mother that a light string was broken and that he was going to the store for a replacement. He knew that she wouldn't be able to tolerate such a prominent blemish on the evening's perfection. He got in the car and headed for the nursing home, pausing in front of the house to look at the dark patch he had created there. He could see her point in worrying over details like this, because it filled him with a vague foreboding to look at it. He found a Christmas radio station and set off into the rapidly darkening evening.

He parked in the lot and waited to be buzzed in. As the vestibule gave way to the hall, a red canvas band spanned the width of the hallway at waist height, secured at either end by Velcro. It looked like an oversized winner's tape, but in fact it was an effective deterrent against escape. Connell removed one end, passed through and felt a creeping sadness as he matched the furry strip in his hand up to its rougher twin.

He found his father in the Crow's Nest, a small room overlooking the front lawn where the noisier residents took their meals in sequestration so as not to disturb the others, and where they spent the better part of their afternoons. A dozen or so other residents were there. With the meal over and the orderlies somewhere else, wheelchairs abutted each other like bumper cars. His father was moaning a low moan. He registered a small change of expression when he saw Connell standing there, but he hardly seemed to stir out of his hazy state. It was past his bedtime; they had left him there for Connell. The television on the wall was set to the evening news.

Connell wheeled him out. When they reached the canvas band, he stopped.

"I'm going to punch in the code," he said. "I can tell you what it is, if you don't tell anyone I told you."

He waited to see if his father's eyes would light up to indicate that he'd been longing for this key to liberty, but his father didn't seem to notice what he'd said. The low, keening hum persisted. He punched in the code and replaced the strip and wheeled him out. He had a feeling of springing his father from jail. After they had been outside for a few moments, his father stopped moaning.

"That's what you wanted?" Connell bent down to ask. "To go outside?"

His father's silence seemed to confirm it.

"If only I'd known! It's a little too cold to stay out long. Besides, we're going someplace I think you're going to be happy to see."

He got to the car and opened the door and got both arms under his father's armpits to get him standing. He got him seated in the car and secured the belt and put the folded wheelchair in the trunk.

It was the first time his father had been off the grounds in months, and Connell wondered how it felt to him to be driven down the long driveway. The trees were bereft of leaves, and strong winds whipped the denuded branches, which in the reflected glow of the headlights looked like guards reaching their elongated arms out to stop his father's escape. They made their way down the road, his father slumped against the window, silent, his hands in his lap, his neck at an uncomfortable angle.

"Sit up straight, Dad," Connell said, but his father didn't move. He reached over and pulled him upright and turned the radio on. He wanted him to look out the window and see the lights strung on fences in front yards, the candles in the windows, the lawn ornaments, and, in a larger sense, the world outside the confines of the nursing home, the fact of its being Christmas, the fact that such a thing as Christmas existed at all, but it was as if his father hadn't noticed he'd left the Crow's Nest. It didn't matter; when they got home, he would see the house done up for Christmas and be recalled to the seasonal cheer. He would be brought back to his life. It would make Dad happy, but the bigger consequence would be his moth

er's joy at having everyone together for one last Christmas at home. She'd mentioned it so many times before his father had gone into the nursing home, and it must have been bitter for her to watch that possibility die. For his father, nothing hung on this trip, but that was because he didn't know where he was going. Once there, he would understand that Connell had spared him a lonely drifting off in a room whose sole concession to the holiday was a drugstore-purchased Santa Claus sign taped to the door. For the night to pass without any observance, for his father to slip into an ignorant slumber, was too much for Connell to take.

Traffic was light, and they arrived quickly enough that he might almost have been gone that long had he set out in search of a string of lights. The block had filled up with cars and he had to park a little distance away from the house. He had been intending just to walk his father in and guide him to a seat on the couch, but instead he retrieved the wheelchair and wheeled him. As he neared the driveway he saw Ruth McGuire hitting the button on her keychain to lock her car. She must have left Frank at home. Her eyes widened as he approached. She met them at the foot of the driveway.

"What's this?"

"Merry Christmas," Connell said, leaning in for a hug, though Ruth was strangely stiff.

"Hi there," she said to his father, bending down to kiss him. She stood back up. "What's the deal?"

"I thought the whole family should be together for the holidays."

Ruth put down the bags of gifts she was carrying. "Your mother doesn't know about this?"

"It's a surprise."

"No." She shook her head. "Not a good idea. She doesn't know he's coming at all?"

"It's all me," he said.

"Oh, God." She seemed to be thinking quickly. She picked up the bags again, made a quick circle, and put them back down. "What to do. What to do?"

"It's fine," he said. "It's good. We're going to have a nice night. She wanted this."

"Your mother is under a lot of strain right now," Ruth said. "She's not having an easy time of it, and the holidays make everything harder. Believe me, I know." She gestured toward the passenger seat her husband would have occupied. "I left Frank home with the nurse because it's just too hard to make it work with nights like this, and I didn't want to upset your mother. She just wants to get through the night and move on."

"She's in a good mood. She's going to be happy to see him."

Ruth walked a little distance away and motioned him away from the wheelchair. He locked it in place and headed over to her.

"Believe me," Ruth said, "she's doing whatever she has to do to get through it. She's doing the best she can. Why don't you take him back to the home?"

"I brought him all this way," he said. "I don't want to upset him."

She gave him a hard look. "You will *not* be upsetting him. He won't know the difference. Why don't you take him back? We don't have to mention anything to your mother."

"She'll be angry at me for disappearing for that long."

Ruth threw up her hands in exasperation. "*Let* her be. Don't make it harder for her than it has to be."

"But it's Christmas. She's going to be happy to be spending it with him."

"At least go in and tell her what you're thinking. I'll stay with your father. Tell her your plan and give her a chance to decide. Don't spring this on her."

Ruth went to the wheelchair, put her hand on his father's shoulder, and patted it.

"I want her to see him in the kitchen," Connell said. "I want to see the look on her face. I want to see his face."

He took the handles of the wheelchair and released the wheel lock.

"Would you listen to me? I've known your mother for decades."

"She's my *mother*."

"Connell." She glared at him.

"I can't take him back now."

"You *can*."

"It's cold out here," he said. "I want to bring him in."

"At least give me a chance to go explain this to her."

"It'll be fine," he said, but she had already picked up her bags and was heading up the driveway ahead of him. He wheeled his father between the cars to the house. He pulled his father to his feet and they started up the stairs. There was no handrail, so he had to push against the wall with a stiff arm while the other wrapped around his father's waist as he dragged him up a step at a time. An anxious expectancy rose in his chest. Again his father was emitting that low moan. They advanced slowly toward what felt like a climactic moment, though he hoped it would be more of a prelude to a memorable night and a conclusion on his mother's part that the holiday had turned out perfect. He felt suddenly queasy. He tugged the screen door open, hoping to catch it with an elbow, but it swung back with a bang as he secured his grip on his father. Then the door behind it opened and Jack Coakley smiled warmly until Jack saw Connell's father and his expression changed and he held the screen door open and made way for Connell to bring him in, which he did just as Ruth came in from the vestibule with his mother, the two of them moving in a brisk conference punctuated by restive hands, neither looking up as they walked swiftly, and then his mother raised her eyes and saw the two of them there and stopped, and everyone gathered in the kitchen was turned toward him with either confusion or gravity on their faces, and it was only then that he realized that he had made a costly error in judgment. His mother didn't rush over as he'd expected her to but stood there with her mouth moving silently for what was surely only a moment but felt like a lifetime and would surely last that long in the slow-exposure image his mind was capturing of it. Sergei shifted on his buttocks in his habitual seat, and glasses of punch dangled from fingers as if arrested in their journey upward, and then a quick, throaty sob emerged from his mother as she said, "Oh, *Ed*," once with a falling cadence and put her hand to her mouth. He turned to consider his father for the first time since he'd arrived at the home to pick him up, his hurrying having prevented it, though he was starting to feel now that he wouldn't have seen him even if he'd paused to look. A thick rope of drool hung from his father's mouth, indecorously refusing to break off and fall to the floor. Connell wiped it off and stood there in an agony of regret as the gathered

crowd, led by his mother, converged on his father to pull him back toward
the fireplace in the den with purposeful seriousness. The party was over
before it had begun. Sergei rose and left the kitchen as if compelled by the
heat of wordless gazes. Connell would have to wait for another day, perhaps another life, to feel redeemed. He had never felt so far from his father,
who disappeared behind a wall of backs as his mother approached him to
deliver the rebuke he knew he deserved.

"Help me with the coats," she said with a quiet urgency that had no
time for rancor. She had spent a lifetime adjusting hopes downward and
knew what order to handle things in. "Get some drinks going. We have to
make the best of this."

When he was done, he went out to the front porch and picked up the string
he had disconnected from the others and plugged it in. The lights came on
at once, completing the outline around the railed fence that his mother
had drawn for passing cars and those making the turn into the driveway.
It made a neat picture, and he stood taking it in, trying to derive a simple
pleasure from the lights, trying to forget that they and the hundreds more
inside had not prevented the encroaching of a fathomless darkness. His
father was gone, gone.

She had worried that the party would last late into the night, everyone frozen by Ed's presence, unsure when they could leave, *if* they could leave, but then one by one they started to go. Before everyone had departed—because she knew it would be impossibly painful for her to get him out of there once they had—she announced that she was going to take Ed back to the home, and she had Jack and Connell get him down the stairs, said some quick good-byes and asked Ruth to handle everyone's coats. Connell wanted to drive Ed himself, or go with her, but she insisted on doing it alone.

When she got to the home, she parked by the front door, even though she wasn't supposed to stop there. She left the wheelchair in the trunk, helped Ed out of the seat in a bear hug and shuffled him over, as if she was dancing with a passed-out man and trying to keep him up. Everything inside was dark except for a single light in the entry to the foyer. She rang the bell and held Ed up with both arms, regretting that she hadn't just left him in the car while she waited, or stopped to get the wheelchair out of the trunk, but she hadn't been thinking clearly. She rang again. He was shivering, and she rang again and she thought of bringing him back to the car, wondering whether they were going to come at all, but then an attendant came to the door and Eileen asked for a wheelchair. She'd return the other one another time. She wheeled him in, got him into bed, kissed him good night, and left before she could feel what was starting to well up in her, which she whisked away by shaking her head quickly from side to side and throwing her hands out like she was trying to dry them off.

She hadn't been able to bring herself to let Ed stay in the house that

night, because it would have broken her heart to have him there one more time only to have him have to leave again, and there was also the matter of Sergei. She hadn't been intimate with him since that night she'd gone into his room and let what was happening happen, the first spark catching the kindling and sending flames up quickly, and she had almost gotten to the point where she'd convinced herself it hadn't occurred. Lately, though, they had fallen into a habit. He would come into her bed after she'd turned in and hold her for a while. At some point in the night he would get up and go to his own bed, but there had been mornings she'd woken up and found him there, and once she'd even woken up in his arms. She couldn't have had Ed sleep in the bed, because it didn't feel like her bed with him anymore. It wasn't hers with Sergei, either, and it felt less and less like her bed, period. She could hardly sleep in it. She had been thinking of getting a new bed for years, and now she saw that she would have to do so right away—tomorrow, even. Now that Ed had been back in the house, it couldn't continue the way it had been.

She was glad Connell had slept in late. Sergei was waiting for her in the kitchen when she came down. He made it easier on her by stopping her quickly into her speech and making a gesture that showed he understood. She got the feeling she might not have had to say anything to him at all, that he would have figured it out on his own. He always made things easier on her. He had gone up to his room the night before as soon as Ed came in, and he hadn't come back down, and Ed's presence had caused such a distraction that she was sure no one had drawn any conclusions from Sergei's departure, and she had been grateful because leaving the room had been the perfect thing for him to do and she hadn't had to ask.

He gathered his things quickly; there wasn't much to gather. She asked where he would go and he said he would stay with his daughter until he figured out what was next. Something told her he would end up back with his wife, that he had been going to end up back with her from the beginning, that this had been something he had been doing for himself as well as for Eileen, that it was a life-giving escape for him too.

He stood in the door and she felt a rush of something like panic and asked if he wanted to go into town and get some breakfast with her. When

he said he did, she spirited them out quickly, as it felt somehow that the reality of what had been happening between them would become more permanent in her own mind if her son came down and saw them leaving for town together.

She got in Sergei's car, which she'd never been in before. It touched her to see how neat and clean it was, not a scrap of paper or food wrapper anywhere. There was an air-freshener smell in the car, and the smell of broken-in leather, and the smell—she wouldn't have guessed she'd recognize it—of Sergei himself.

She had thought of Pete's, or the other diner in town whose name she could never remember, but as he drove she realized it would be uncomfortable to sit with him and have a full-on meal and have to wait for a check and manage all the time, the silences, and have to look at each other that long, because she realized she felt more for him than she'd ever admitted to herself, and she knew he did too, or else he wouldn't have put up with being intimate with her just the one time.

She had him pull into a spot on Palmer outside the bagel shop, and they went in. It surprised her to realize that it was the first time they had ever been in public together. She asked him what he wanted and he told her to get what she thought he would like. She remembered seeing him eat an egg and cheese sandwich once, so she ordered him one with American cheese, which he loved, a fact that had always surprised her somehow, on a plain bagel, because that was the safest choice, and a black coffee. She got the same for herself, except for the cheese, cheddar in her case, and she was so nervous paying that she had to hand over another dollar to have enough, and she felt a little of what she imagined Ed had felt when paying, and she also felt a pang of sadness or guilt, she wasn't sure which, run through her like an electric shock. She glanced over while paying and saw Sergei looking at her, taking her in frankly and unapologetically, maybe because he was free to do so now, and she was sure the woman behind the counter would be able to see the whole story of their relationship—she had to call it that, if she was being honest—from that one look.

She brought the food over and sat at the little café table with him, in a plastic chair, and they talked about the safest of things: the weather, how

the coffee was. He asked her to get him another napkin, because they kept them behind the counter and it would have required some negotiation on his part to get one, and she felt a surge of connection to him that made all the nights of his holding her settle in, like a dog going to sleep with a sigh by a fireplace, and she wanted to reach out and touch his face, but she knew that she would never be with him, that something about the circumstances of how they'd come together made that impossible, that their lives were too different, too incommensurable, and that while they'd had this thing that she saw meant more to her than she'd understood while it was happening, it too, now, was gone.

When the sandwiches were eaten she ordered a muffin for them to share, and they picked at it with a tender deliberateness that gave the sadness she'd been feeling room to breathe. After every crumb was gone, and there was no reason for them to be sitting there anymore, they sat and looked at each other for a little while. She didn't care now what the woman behind the counter thought, because she was going to take this moment for herself and not let it slip away. She could tell he was feeling the same thing she was, though she wasn't prepared to give it a name. They sat there and let that nameless feeling pass over them like a wind in an electric storm. Then she got up and he followed her out. She walked him to the car and he offered to drive her home, but she said she would walk, and the moment for him to get in his car was upon them, and people were coming at them from both directions, and she was nervous to be seen there with him, because she knew everyone would know, that it would take only one look at her for them to know. She put her arms around him quickly before she could stop herself and sank into his arms as he pressed her to him one final time. She wanted not to forget any of it: the fresh smell of his shirt mixed with cologne, smoke, and sweat; his jacket rough against her face and the strange innocence of its red and black checks; the strength of him squeezing her; the sound of his breathing. She felt rise up in her the years of Ed's illness and the months since he'd been gone. She felt it in her chest but she didn't let it out, because she didn't think she deserved to do so. She would have to carry it around in her a little longer at least. He gave her small kisses on the neck and said something to her in Russian that she

didn't understand, and then he took her face in his hands by the ears and gave her a few smacking kisses on the forehead and walked around to the driver's side door. He took one more long look at her before he dipped his big body down into the car, which shook with his entry into it. She listened to it starting up and watched it pull out and waited for him to come around the circle and head back the other way toward the Bronx River, and after he was out of sight she went back into the store to buy some bagels for Connell. She would eat again with him when he was up. It would give her less to explain, and it would make it less real, what she'd been feeling sitting there, and it would make it more real, in a way, it would make it more hers, something that didn't have to exist for anyone else, something she'd done for herself, for once, and there was no need to apologize for it. She looked the woman in the eye and handed over her money and left to start the walk home. The second half was all uphill. She knew she'd barely be breathing by the time she arrived.

Part VI

The Real
Estate of
Edmund Leary

1997–2000

S he had a hard time leaving him at night. It was better not to say good-bye. She'd tell him she was going to run an errand or to take a nap—trying to imply, in the way she said it, that she'd be returning. "I just need to run to the store," she'd say, and then mechanically make her way through the corridors and out the back door, the whole time telling herself she could turn around and go back.

Once, when she said, "I'm going to get something to eat," he seemed to laugh sardonically, and she looked at him, trying to find a deliberate message in his expression, some chastening meant for her, but she saw only that familiar blankness as he stared at something she couldn't see. This disease was making her paranoid too.

She went every day. She never accepted the invitations for weekends in the country or at the beach. Her friends said she was being too hard on herself. She thought she was being too easy. *I could bring him home*, she wanted to say. *I could take care of him.* They told her she needed to have some semblance of a life, that it was too much. And she thought, *It's not enough. I'm a nurse, for God's sake, that's what I do*, but all she said was, "I'm fine. I'm fine. I'm fine."

His wallet was still on the mule chest. She rubbed her fingers on the worn, smooth leather, took out the driver's license and looked at it, read the prayer they'd written together. Inside was everything she'd allowed him to carry in his final ambulatory years, and everything he'd been carrying on his last day as a full-dressed member of civilization: seven dollars cash; an index card listing his name, address, and phone number and her work phone

number, written in her own hand; his Alzheimer's Association Safe Return card ("If I appear lost or confused, please help me by calling . . ."); his Mobil and Amoco gas cards; his AAA card ("Membership year 27"); two different Board of Elections voter registration confirmations; his Waldbaum's Valued Shopper Card with Check Cashing Privileges; his PriceCostco card under Jack R. Coakley Consulting; his AARP card; his ID from BCC; an index card with the number for the car phone; his Sears card ("Valued Customer Since 1973"); his Blue Cross/Blue Shield card; his GHI card; his PSC-CUNY card indicating he was a member in good standing of the AFT Local ?334 (AFL-CIO); his New York Academy of Sciences membership card; a picture of her from June of 1968, when she had been thin; a picture of Connell in his baseball uniform from his freshman year of high school; a picture of Connell from preschool; a picture of Connell graduating from St. Joan of Arc; and the edited index card with her size written on it. She opened the card. She was going to cross the "10" out and write "12" in its place, and then throw it in the garbage, but when she saw that the "10" was in her own handwriting, the tears came all at once.

His roommate was named Reinhold Huggins. Mr. Huggins had been a celebrated piano teacher. Now he pushed a walker around and refused to wear an undershirt under his hospital robe, his naked back bisected by the tight string, his steps tiny and shuffling, his posture slightly hunched. He was surprisingly alert. He didn't say anything unprompted, except to ask for water, but if she asked how he was doing he would say, "Rather well, thank you, and yourself?" always quietly and gently, so that she had to lean in to hear him, and without the rising intonation that would have made the statement a question. Despite his manner of speaking, he was fearsome-looking, with a hoary, streaked beard and an unsmiling visage. The one time she had tried to direct him to the piano in the lounge, he gripped her shoulders with his long, bony fingers and squeezed hard. She didn't do it again. Often when he spoke or sat in his chair, he raised his forefinger and beat it back and forth like a metronome. Other than that, he wasn't a bad roommate; there were worse in the building.

Mrs. Klein and Mrs. Sonnabend liked to sit in the lounge and talk

by the picture window. Eileen was surprised at how present they were. Watching from a distance, she became convinced, by their facial expressions, laughs, hand gestures, and the way they interrupted one another to make an excited point, that they were gushing over their grandkids. After she'd seen them there enough times, she grew fascinated enough to get up close to listen in. Mrs. Klein said, "My daughter, my daughter, she's going to come, my daughter, with a hundred dollars," and Mrs. Sonnabend responded, over and over, with something that sounded like "Gesundheit."

On December 2, 1997, she made it to her ten-year pension. Before she left for work, she called Connell in Berlin, but he wasn't home, and she was almost relieved not to get him. She wasn't sure he'd have appreciated the full significance of the news, and she didn't want to feel silly or diminished about it, so she left a message for him to call her and figured she'd hear from him in a week or so, when it would be just another curiosity to report. On this day, the actual day of the event, she felt too raw to mention anything about it and risk not hearing back from him. It meant more to her than she would ever have guessed it would. She hadn't always been sure she'd get to this day, and it wasn't even about health insurance anymore so much as having something to strive for, something that allowed her life to hang together.

She went to the home after work with a half bottle of champagne. A drum circle had been organized in the community room; Kacey the social director was standing in the center, her own drum suspended from a strap around her neck. Eileen stopped in the doorway to watch. Kacey was slapping at her drum, which was fancier than the others, and looking at the patients with a manic grin, trying to get them to imitate her. The gathering was mostly women, though a few men were scattered throughout. Eileen was glad Ed's physical infirmity kept him out of activities like this. She watched long enough to hear the haphazard drumming peter out. Kacey slapped each hand down once in quick succession, generating a popping sound like that of a plastic cup hitting a hardwood floor. "Now you!" Kacey said, earnestly, casting about with imploring eyes. An old woman sighed and said, "Oh, come *on*," and Eileen wanted to hug her in gratitude.

She found him in his room. The popping cork startled him; his eyes widened, though he didn't move. She had to pour the champagne slowly into his mouth to keep him from dribbling it all out, but once he could feel the bubbles on his tongue he lapped it up. She could have sworn she detected a smile on his lips when she told him her news.

For years she had imagined she might be moved to retire the day she'd secured the pension, but as she sat there finishing off the little bottle, she realized that even if her financial situation had worked out better, and even if the cost of the nursing home didn't go up every six months, to almost seven thousand a month now, she wouldn't be giving a passing thought to quitting. If she retired she would have nothing to do but spend all day at the home, and she still had some life left to give. One of the inescapable facts of her existence was that she was good at her job. She had spent her life thinking of all the other things she might have been—a lawyer, she'd often concluded, or a politician, which was probably the best career for any child of Big Mike Tumulty's, even if that child didn't happen to be male— but now it struck her that she was doing what she did best. Her profession had been becoming hers the whole time she'd been looking away from it. The point wasn't always to do what you want. The point was to do what you did and to do it well. She had worked hard for years, and if she had nothing to show for it but her house and her son's education, there was still the fact of its having happened, which no one could erase from the record of human lives, even if no one was keeping one.

91

The morning after Thanksgiving of 1998, Connell went up to the home alone. After his visit, he got halfway down the hall before he headed back to his father's room and stood in the doorway looking in; then he left again. When he was about to turn the key in the car, he went back in again, but this time he entered the room. He sat in the chair next to his father's bed and took his father's hand as though he'd just arrived.

At noon, they went to lunch. The lunchroom was noisy with women calling for help or screaming incoherently, which pierced the fog in which his father was generally lost and caused him to tremble and start in his wheelchair. Connell attributed this to his father's chivalrous nature. The men's screams didn't have the same effect.

After lunch, in his father's room, Connell quickly came to the end of everything he could think to say. He told him about how the Mets barely missed the wild card after collapsing in the final week of the season, losing five straight, and about how the Yankees won the World Series again after winning the most games in regular season history. He told him how his last year of college was going. There was no way to tell whether his father understood anything. When his mother was there it was easier. She spoke as if he might answer her at any moment. She would tell him something that had gone wrong at the house and say, "You always told us not to do that," or "You knew that already, didn't you?" But he couldn't bring himself to speak rhetorically to his father. He couldn't suspend his disbelief that his father would answer, and he felt like he was disrespecting him if he phrased his sentences as questions. He sat with him in silence instead or put music on.

The room was quiet, peaceful. A small piano on Mr. Huggins's side was the resting place for a flowerpot and a pair of framed pictures. He had never seen Mr. Huggins sit down at it, but then Mr. Huggins was almost never in the room. He walked the halls endlessly, pushing his walker as though trying to wear himself out.

"You know Mr. Huggins is German? I know I've told you about Berlin, but let me tell you about it again. Berlin is great. The art, the culture, the literature. The whole city is a construction site. They're making everything new. They're also trying not to make *anything* new, in the sense that they're unwilling to paper over anything in the past without tremendous deliberation. They're trying to deal with the legacy of the past in a thoughtful way. It's not perfect, and they know they'll never live down the atrocities of the Nazi era, but they're trying to be the world's historian, or at least the world's agonized conscience. They look relentlessly inward. They guard ruthlessly against historical revisionism or sentimentality about the old ways of life or anything that smacks of even the slightest hint of the kind of thinking that led them down the road to hell. Sure, there are some neo-Nazis there, just as there are racists and xenophobes anywhere, but as a culture, at least the intellectual culture, they are tremendously deliberate about quashing that sort of thing before it gains a foothold. You can't accuse the Germans, or at least Berliners, or at least intellectuals in Berlin, or at least the intellectuals at the Freie Universität that I came to know—you see? I learned from them to qualify my statements down to the point of the granite and the unassailable—of trying to pretend the Nazis never happened. They even guard against the idea of getting angry at having to be so thoughtful and conscience-stricken all the time. There's a kind of unwavering discipline about their watchfulness about conscience fatigue. Consciousness fatigue. Conscientiousness—no; they wouldn't say conscientiousness; that suggests something of 'good manners.' They're almost brutal to themselves in their unwillingness to feel good about the fact that they remember to feel bad about the evils committed in the past, before they were born. They admit their lack of discipline and prosecute it even when it's not there. We could learn a thing or two from them about how to address the legacy of slavery, or the treatment of Native Americans, or the Japanese internment

camps, or Jim Crow, or the Tuskegee syphilis experiment, or any number of atrocious episodes that leave a stain on the soul of America."

They sat in silence again until he put on some Mozart from the boxed set he had bought his father as an early Christmas present. He had decided not to fly back for Christmas that year, though he hadn't told his mother yet. He figured it would force her to accept the invitation to the Coakleys' instead of spending another depressing Christmas Eve at Maple Grove, as she had the previous year, when he'd been in Germany. If he came home she'd want the three of them to spend it together, and he didn't want to do that to her, so he was going to force her hand, make her let someone—Cindy, whoever—take care of her for a change.

His father began to clap and cheer in the middle of a movement, and Connell clapped along, which reminded him of sitting next to his father in Carnegie Hall as a kid, when he would watch for his father's hands to come together with authority to know when he himself should clap.

At the end of one movement—a check of the liner notes revealed the symphony to be Mozart's fortieth—his father smiled deliriously and then started sobbing deeply enough that it was impossible to hear the music. Connell couldn't tell if it was the symphony making him react so strongly or else something bubbling up from his unconscious mind. He began to get unaccountably angry. Rather than let that feeling come to the fore and allow the visit to turn ugly, he wheeled his father out to the television room and left, this time for good.

For weeks, she had seen the end coming. His color was ashen, his breath sulfuric. His gaze was vacant, without any bouts of clarity. His head was stuck in a permanent loll, as if the muscles in his neck had stopped working. The clonic twitches almost flung him out of his seat.

A month before he died, he did something that she turned over in her mind later whenever she wondered how much he was aware of in his last days. He often exhibited what looked like glimmers of awareness, but she knew they were more likely her own projections. It was less painful to believe he couldn't remember all he'd lost, but another part of her—she knew it was selfish—wanted him to know who she was.

A few days before Valentine's Day, she was wheeling him down the hall to his room. The home was decorated with pink streamers and heart-shaped cardboard cutouts, as though it were not a facilitator of human expirations but a middle school full of yearning adolescents. She had to walk close to the wall to avoid someone being wheeled in the other direction, and in that instant, Ed had reached out to one of the hearts on the wall and plucked it off. *Reached* was too strong a word; likely it brushed against him and his hand closed around it reflexively. He clutched it the whole way down the hall and into the room. It was only when she wheeled him into place and sat beside him that he dropped it and it fell on the floor between them. His hand twitched after it; he could almost have been pointing. She picked it up. She was on the verge of asking if it was for her when she realized she didn't want to hear the lack of an answer, so she just placed it on the nightstand.

Glue pooled in the corners of his mouth and a pasty spackle of plaque sat on his teeth, which could no longer be cleaned effectively and which had darkened so considerably that they had gone past yellow to a necrotic shade of blue.

She wet a paper towel and wiped his face. "Happy Valentine's Day," she said, and when she kissed him on the mouth for the first time in longer than she liked to remember, she was surprised at how sweet he tasted.

Something in his mother's message compelled him to return her call right away and not merely resolve to do so before the weekend was over. She would never have delivered bad news on an answering machine, but there must have been a hint, a subtle quaver, and a hint was all he needed. For years, he had been tuned to the peculiar frequency of disaster. It was irrational, he knew; his father's disease augured no sudden change in fortune, only a long decline; nevertheless, whenever the phone rang in his sleep, he awoke with a start and sprang to his feet.

"Your father is sick," she said when he reached her.

He looked around at his apartment. Papers were strewn everywhere; a thick layer of dust had settled on every surface. Neither he nor his roommate had done any cleaning in weeks. It was their last stretch in college, and each of them was responsible for wringing as much as he could out of the dwindling days. He considered the smells: the faint ammonia reek of dirty clothes, the mildew musk that drifted out from dishes in the murky sink, which only got washed when his roommate's girlfriend complained.

"He's not going to make it through the night," his mother said, with none of the bluster that entered her voice when she knew she was right. She sounded vulnerable. It might have been the first time he'd ever heard her sound that way.

"Are you sure?" he asked, but it was an idle question; she'd watched hundreds of people die.

"He has pneumonia," she said calmly. "That's bad for someone in his situation."

"Why didn't you call sooner?"

"I was waiting to see if he'd make it through. I didn't want to pull you away unnecessarily. Anyway, I'm calling now."

"How is he?" It was a dumb question, but he hoped, even half expected, that his mother's answer would be different this time—modulated, hedging.

"Everything's quiet," she said. "I'm by the bed. I'm trying to make him comfortable."

He could see the nursing home shrouded in darkness, the hallway dark but for the sliver of light shining out under his father's door. He could see his mother's hand on his father's chest, the labored breathing, the terror in his father's eyes.

"We'll have to hope he lasts until you get here," she said. "Call JetBlue. Put it on the American Express."

He didn't have a credit card of his own. His mother had given him the Amex the day he left for college. It listed his name in full caps, CONNELL J. LEARY, and above it, Member Since 67. "In case of emergencies," she'd said as she handed it over before she headed to work that morning. The very last thing she'd said, as always, was "Be careful."

It was with a sense of ceremony that he packed for his trip. The nervous excitement that attended any travel filled his chest, but he was preparing for a greater journey. They said that a father's death was a defining moment in a man's life, perhaps *the* defining one. He was about to be ushered into an immense and silent club of men who shared the knowledge of one of life's singular passages. He was humbled by the possibility of waking up a different person, one with the stamp of legitimacy on him. Every shirt he folded into the bag, every pair of socks he picked out from the rest, he envisioned outfitting the better self that was, perhaps, being born into the world. A solemn suit, sensible slacks, his best shoes: the destiny for which he had been preparing was coming into focus. There were matters to attend to: taking out the trash, washing the dishes in the sink. He dispatched them with an intensity he had never been able to summon before. They were the precursor to the larger duties he was about to perform, as son to his mother and ambassador for his family—in short, as the man of the

house. Every move he made had the imprimatur of purposefulness. There was no time for sentiment, only for the handling of tasks that a man ought to do well and uncomplainingly.

He stood in the doorway for a moment, looking out, for perhaps the last time with eyes of an adolescent, at the view of the street from his place. He breathed deeply the evening air, the smell of trees and car exhaust. His apartment seemed suddenly quaint; he felt a tremendous affection for the life he had been leading. He would leave it all behind. He would begin anew. Nothing could stop him; nothing could hurt him; he could walk on coals and get to the cool other side.

Before he left, he called again. "How is he?" he asked, because he couldn't ask the obvious: *Is he alive?*

"He's in pain," she said, "but he's still here," Her voice broke. "I told him you were coming. He squeezed my finger."

At Midway, he checked in, passed through the detectors, and took a seat at the gate. There wouldn't be much of a wait; he had arrived shortly before departure. He settled in and tried to read a book, but he was seized by panic at the thought of his father dying. He had been living without his father for some time already, but he still made pilgrimages to him, for the advice he listened for in his father's heartbeats, ear pressed to his chest; for the reassurance in his constancy; for the comfort he felt when he nuzzled him close and registered the soft, unconscious rhythm of his breath on his neck. He was still the standard-bearer; he was still his father.

They started boarding the plane. The back rows, his group, boarded first. He felt like a horse stomping at the gate, ready to dash off the plane when it landed. He hadn't checked any bags; his uncle Pat would be waiting for him at the airport.

He was the first to his row. He put his book into the seat pocket, lowered the tray table, and drummed his fingers. Stragglers filed in slowly. Soon he would have to get up for the person in the window seat, or watch the one in the aisle stuff his things into the overhead bin. He wished he hadn't rushed aboard. He didn't need to use the bathroom, but he replaced the table and rose anyway.

He pressed close to the mirror, leaned his forehead against it. His

breath collected on it. He would stay there as long as he needed to. He was looking for something, some confirmation, though of what he wasn't sure.

Then he saw it. It was all there: his father's aspect of perpetual surprise; his father's widow's peak, which seemed to climb his scalp in flight; his father's nose, which flared out slightly at the nostrils; his father' s jaw, which gave ballast to the rest; the cavity in his father's chin; the black hair; the slightly overlarge ears.

He bared his teeth. They were, against all odds, perfectly straight. As a kid he had avoided the nighttime headgear designed to supplement the corrective pull of his braces. He had faked the log that documented his wear time. At the panic-stricken last minute before heading to the orthodontist, overwhelmed by the enormity of so much squandered time, he had switched pens and varied the numbers, composing fictions that attested to his discipline and endurance. His father drove him to the orthodontist once a month for two full years; every time, Connell waited to hear the guilty verdict; every time, he was spared. His father never called him on it either; he was happy enough to take him for a ride, happy enough to shell out bucks he didn't have for the sake of his son's smile. The world of adults seemed to budget for the carelessness of children.

His teeth were not his father's. His father had a bridge that he washed under the faucet and click-clacked for Connell when he asked him to. He had a cracked front tooth that he lost half of when he fell to the brick floor in the kitchen while Connell brooded in his room.

"You are flying home," he said to the mirror, hoping to ground himself in the reality of what was happening. "Your father is dying. He is your best friend. You will never be the same again."

It didn't work. By the time he got back to his seat, he had forgotten what he had felt in the bathroom. An attractive woman around his age or a few years older had taken the window seat. In the aisle sat an older businessman who couldn't be bothered to flirt with her. Connell squeezed past him, insisting that he needn't get up, and the man didn't flinch.

As they waited for takeoff, Connell looked at the tiny television on the seat back, which showed a map with their location, the plane icon as big

as a state. It looked as if it could cover the distance in a quick sprint, but it just sat there.

"I've heard that's good." He gestured to the book in the girl's hands.

"Oh, it is," she said. "It's beautifully written. I've liked everything I've read by her."

"What brings you to New York?"

She seemed startled by the sudden shift, but he hadn't read the book or any of the author's others. "I'm going to see a friend," she said. "My college roommate. She moved there to work for a fashion house."

"My name's Connell." He jammed his elbow awkwardly against the seat as he tried to extend his hand.

"Karla," she said. "Nice to meet you."

He thought he heard the businessman sigh.

"Have you ever been to New York?"

"I haven't. I'm excited."

"How long will you stay?"

"A week."

"What do you have planned?"

"Not much," she said. "I don't even have a guidebook yet. All I know is I'm staying with my friend. I'm so busy, I haven't had time to sit down and plan anything."

"Make sure you ride the Staten Island Ferry. It's the best view of the city, and it costs only fifty cents."

The businessman coughed. "It's free now," he said.

"Sorry?"

"It *was* fifty cents. It's free now."

He resumed making notes on his stack of papers, but not before giving a look that said he knew what Connell was up to, that Connell had been away too long, that he was a fraud, that he was going to lead this girl astray.

"That sounds great, either way," Karla said. "I love boats. And bargains."

Connell and Karla looked at each other for a second. Her smile was charming, open. Then she resumed her reading and he took his book out of the seat pocket. After a while she asked whether New York was home,

and he said it used to be, and she asked why he was going there and he told her his father might be dying after a long illness and she said she was very sorry. The revelation seemed to sink them deeper into silence, and part of him wished he had made something up. The plane took off with a rumble. He noticed she made the sign of the cross and pressed her hands together, kissing her fingertips lightly.

Near the end of the flight he asked if she liked Indian food.

"You know?" she said. "I don't think I've ever had it."

"There are these two adjacent Indian restaurants," he said, "at the top of this stoop on Second Avenue, off Third Street. They're identical: the same décor, the same hanging lights. Strings of plastic chili peppers. They've been warring for years. A host stands outside each door, trying to usher you in like it's Shangri-La on the other side of that door. You make your choice: right or left. Then you're part of that tribe. They remember you. God forbid you go the other way the next time."

"Which way do you go?"

"Right," he said.

"Then how do you know they're identical?"

"I never thought about that," he said. "I guess I've been too scared to find out. You don't know how intimidating those guys are."

She laughed; he could feel interest stirring in her. For most of the flight, he had waited for that moment when the dynamic between them would change, when she would cease being a stranger. Maybe this was his chance.

"Maybe we should go while you're in town," he said. "We can go left, if you want. I'm willing to risk it."

"I'm not one to tamper with loyalties," she said, and she shifted in her seat. He feared he had spoken too soon. It could get uncomfortable; they still had a little ride ahead of them.

"You're right," he said. "Better safe than sorry."

"Are you sure you have time? I mean—your father."

"I can make time," he said.

"You don't have to worry about me," she said. "I'll have enough to keep me busy. You've got things to take care of."

"It'll be fine," he said. "I'll be able to slip away. Besides, he's probably going to be fine. This has happened before."

"Well," she said, "only if it's not a disturbance."

"I'll give you a call to set something up."

They exchanged numbers. There was a hint of bafflement on her face. She seemed shocked by him, the way one is shocked and refreshed by diving into unexpectedly cold water. The way she searched his look for an extended moment, as if to ask whether he were sure he wanted to entertain her with so much else going on that was far more important, cemented his belief that he had impressed her as a man delightfully open to suggestion, with an imagination large enough to find time, even in the depths of despair, for the important things in life, those accidents without which our existence was little more than a schedule of dry routines.

They landed and filed off the plane. She had to retrieve her things from the overhead bin, and a few passengers shot between Connell and her. He waited at the mouth of the corridor, averting his gaze from the other passengers, embarrassed at the thought they could see what he was up to. It felt important to walk with her to baggage claim. She was about to greet the rest of the city; he would become merely the first in a line of men she encountered in her travels. Whatever primacy he held was about to yield to the manifestly transient quality of their acquaintanceship. He could easily be forgotten. These last few hundred meters would make a difference in ensuring that that didn't happen.

As they snaked their way through the terminal, he made some dry observations about New York that got her laughing. He was riding a wave of euphoria. His bag felt like nothing on his shoulders. She seemed to be taking quick steps to keep up with his longer stride. He was filled with a sense of possibility: this might be the prelude to something they could continue in the city they had just left. It was the first day of his trip; there was no way of knowing what was to come. And there was this woman striding along beside him, bursting with expectation. To an onlooker he could have been her boyfriend, visiting the city for the first time himself.

They were almost running when they hit the corridor that opened onto the baggage claim area. He was turning to look at her the whole time.

As they headed down he remembered why he was there and looked for his uncle Pat through the frosty glass. He couldn't yet distinguish any faces.

The revolving doors loomed at the bottom of the downward slope, and anxiety began to creep into him. He found himself slowing his pace and flattening his smile. He was looking less at Karla and more toward the revolving doors beyond which waited his uncle Pat. And then he was really slowing down, enough that Karla asked what was wrong. He could make out the faint image of his uncle and his mother through the glass. The fact that his mother was there could only mean one thing. He was drifting slowly away from Karla and not answering. He didn't want his mother to see him talking to her, to see him as the frivolous fool he suddenly knew he was. Soon Karla had stopped addressing him and walked on, and he walked several paces behind her, knowing what he had seen through the glass but not admitting it fully to himself until he got right up to it and could not avoid any longer the sight of tears streaming down his mother's face. That was when he knew that his father had died while he had forgotten him entirely.

He pushed his way through the revolving door. His mother was fanning her face with her hand as she tried to tell him what he already knew. His uncle stood by, saying nothing.

"I'm so sorry," she said.

He had missed his father by two hours. His mother had gotten permission to keep his father there long enough for Connell to say good-bye.

His uncle Pat drove to the home like a Formula One racer, leaning into the turns. While his mother sat on the divan by the entrance, Uncle Pat walked him down the hallway to his father's room and left him alone. His father's eyes were open. Connell stared into their beautiful blueness awhile, though they stared at something else, and he smoothed his hair down as he always did when it stuck up. He kissed his forehead and cheeks. He was cold. He talked to him, though he knew he wasn't there anymore. His mouth was open. He looked at his cracked tooth. He wouldn't need teeth anymore. He wouldn't need anything.

His mother came to get him after a while. "That's probably enough," she said.

He gave his father another kiss, and on the way out he stopped in the doorway and turned and looked back. He was about to return to his father when he saw the stern, imploring look his uncle was giving him. The expression on his mother's face said it was painful for her to be in the room with his father, that she'd been holding out for Connell to come home but the time had come to say good-bye. It must have been difficult for her to look at his father the way she'd looked at the corpses of so many patients over the years. It must have seemed like there was no difference between him and the rest of the numberless dead. He closed the door with a quiet click and they all walked out to the car.

94

I t was pneumonia that killed him. As the brain had deteriorated, the body parts had stopped working. His lungs filled with mucus. He drowned in it.

After he died on March 7, 1999, she decided that if there was such a thing as a next life, she wanted to return under another sort of banner entirely— something ebullient like "Holiday" or "Sunshine." This time through, though, she was Eileen Leary; she'd never remarry. This was life: you went down with the ship. Who was to say that wasn't a love story?

She slept on his side. She didn't like his side particularly, but she couldn't bring herself to sleep on her old one. Whenever she did, she lay there thinking of all the nights she'd slept facing away from him, and she wanted one of them back—a single one would be enough—so she could turn her body toward his.

She knew he would have wanted his remains to contribute to the body of knowledge. The neurologists who'd diagnosed him weren't going to order an autopsy, though; they were convinced that it had been Alzheimer's and had long ago closed their investigations. The team that had conducted the drug study wasn't going to order it either.

She could have paid to have him autopsied anyway. She would have had to do a little paperwork to have the body moved from one county to another. The whole procedure would have cost eight thousand dollars, or about how much she'd been paying per month at the end to keep him at

Maple Grove. It struck her as unseemly to attach any dollar amount to the privilege of peering into the riddle of a mind as fine as Ed's. They should have been clamoring to do it for the honor alone.

In the end, she couldn't bring herself to have it done. She couldn't stand to think of someone cutting her husband's head open. His teeth were broken, his gums had grown red and swollen, he had straggly hair, his once-proud muscles had atrophied to saggy sleeves, he had cuts and scabs everywhere, his skin had turned hoary from lack of exposure. She couldn't imagine destroying his body any further. And the thought of his being dissected like that, when he had so often been the dissector himself, filled her with a palpable revulsion. He went intact into the earth, all the questions answered that would ever be answered, all the unasked ones forever unasked. Science had reached the end of its utility. All that remained was the body, and she wanted to give it tenderness.

After all that trouble she'd gone to to put a leather band on the LeCoultre watch, Ed had never worn it. It had sat in its box for thirty-two years.

She took it out of the case. Under the velvet platform in the bottom of the box the gold band lay like the desiccated skin of a snake. She went to a jeweler and had it put back on. The restored watch was worth a good deal of money, due to its pristine condition, its collectible nature, and the high price of gold, but that was immaterial now, as she buried him wearing it.

The new tools she'd bought after the workers stole his old ones had never been used. A few weeks after his death, she paid someone to haul them away, along with the contents of his office: crates of records, VHS tapes, his science textbooks. The books were outdated. No one listened to records anymore. The tapes were fuzzy recordings Ed had made on the black-and-white set, old movies and documentaries about cathedrals and bridges. Connell had no interest in any of it. It had all run out of currency.

In the surfeit of time that widowhood allowed, she had a recurring vision of her husband in the early days of the disease, after he'd retired. He was still handsome. His hair was thinner, but it had not lost its striking

blackness, and his blue eyes coruscated in the light, though the whites had yellowed. He was smaller than he used to be; his clothes fit loosely on him. It was early afternoon, but the room was dark, save for the glow of the television and some sunlight filtering through the drapes on the patio door. When the trees shifted in the wind, the room pulsed with greater light. The lamp on the end table could have offered more lasting illumination, but in the flurry of activity that accompanied her departure she had forgotten to turn it on. He could not summon the fine motor skills to turn it on himself. He had been sitting there since eight in the morning, watching the channel that she had decided offered the best chance at diverting him for the length of her workday. He had, by then, seen every episode of the detective show he was watching, though his failing memory offered an ability to see familiar things afresh. He lost the plotline somewhere in the middle of the episode. What caught fire in his mind were the rudiments of narrative: a ringing retort, anguish on a face, a happy reunion. He could still feel. He could still cry. He did cry, without knowing he was doing so. He felt the tears drying on his face afterward, and it was as though he had awoken from an unhappy dream. He could no longer read. By the time he reached the end of a sentence, he had forgotten where it began. He could decipher headlines in the newspaper; from them he cobbled together a sense of what was happening in the world. He was left with television, and when she was around, listening to music or her reading to him. He was hungry. He tried to go to the kitchen. He had a hard time rising from the couch. It took a couple of attempts, but he eventually succeeded. When he returned he couldn't find the remote control. He didn't want to watch this channel anymore. He couldn't follow the story. He knew there was something about a murder, some kind of investigation. Those detectives who were always there were working on the case. There had been some kind of theft. Something was missing.

There was a skull in a box in the closet. It was a specimen of Ed's; he'd taught anatomy with it. He'd called it "George," but she refused to call it anything but "the skull." He'd taken it out every now and then to show it to Connell and his friends, a grisly spectacle she'd always insisted on cutting short. The

boys poked their fingers through the eye sockets, dug their nails into the grooves in the pearly skullcap, probed the crenellations in the ivory teeth and clacked the hinged jaw in dummy conversation. One year—Connell must have been eight or nine—she threw a Halloween party for all the kids on the block. "George will be making an appearance tonight," Ed said to Connell at the breakfast table that morning, and when the party was in full swing, all the kids assembled in the basement, Ed donned a black robe, charred the bottom of a pan, and spread the black char all over his face. He shut out the lights in the basement as he descended the stairs, and when he reached the center of the circle in which they'd been arranged in anticipation of some kind of surprise, he spoke in a deep voice and held the floating skull up to the flashlight. The kids shivered and screamed in delighted terror—including Connell, who knew it was coming.

Ed said once that when he died he wanted his skull to be used in anatomy classes. He had been delighted by the story of a classically trained stage actor who willed his skull to the company he'd been in, to play the part of Yorick in Hamlet, thereby assuring his immortality.

She took the box down from the closet and set it on her desk. She had never opened it. She lifted one of the cardboard flaps, then another, then the last two, slowly. She shuddered to see the top of that cranium, but she lifted it out of the box and set it facing her on the desk. Despite her years of nursing, her encounters with death, the anatomy classes she'd taken, she'd never been able to shake a basic awe in the face of relics of the body. She sat staring at that empty gaze. The whole time she knew Ed, there had been a skull behind his features. The man whose skull this had been, whose flesh had hidden this bone, had had his own ties of family and friendship. It struck her that she was much closer to the end than the beginning.

She thought of donating it to the science department at Saunders High School, then decided against it. There would simply have to be an orphan skull lying around after she was gone. Connell would find a home for it or take responsibility for throwing it out. He would be the arbiter of its fate, as he would decide what to do with her body, as she had decided what to do with her husband's, as someone would decide what to do with his.

• • •

The more she thought about Ed's turning down NYU all those years back, the more she began to entertain other, more mysterious possibilities: that he may have had reasons other than vocation for evading ambition's prod; that he may have needed BCC more than they needed him; that he may have been afraid of changing his routine or exposing himself to closer scrutiny; that he may have known more than he let on; that he may have known it earlier than she'd ever thought possible.

The study had lasted three years. She'd kept him on the medicine another two, until it was too hard to get him to swallow the pills. It wasn't entirely to spite her that he resisted: he had an instinctual fear of choking.

The drug didn't have a name, just a string of letters and numbers—SDZ ENA 713. Later it acquired a name, Exelon, and could be prescribed. A lot of things were different later. Later they put patches on people so they didn't have to take pills. That would have prevented a lot of trouble.

She asked herself, when she was feeling low, whether it was the medicine that had caused him to go so rigid that he couldn't be picked up when he collapsed at the end. Rigidity was one of the side effects. Would she have been able to keep him home longer if she'd taken him off the drugs? Would he have avoided dying in a strange bed?

Sometimes she lay in bed thinking that somewhere they might be making drugs that would have changed everything. She knew she would find that bittersweet, though Ed would be thrilled. Advances in science were the things that made him happiest in life. Advances in science, and Connell. And herself, she had to admit. That was usually when she broke down.

Many nights, she worked herself into a panic trying to imagine what would have become of him in his last years if she'd divorced him as she'd briefly considered doing before an explanation emerged for his sudden cruelty. Try as she did, she couldn't picture where he would have lived or who would have taken care of him. As time passed she came to believe that she had been fated to be there for him at the end, that being there for him was what everything in her life—her care of her mother, her career in nurs-

ing—had prepared her for, that it was, in a sense, her life's great work. In this way she was able to sleep soundly again.

This was his final gift to her: to silence her regrets about the paths she hadn't taken.

She kept going to the nursing home. She'd grown attached to seeing the other patients. She brought them cookies and sat in the television room with them, watching the evening news or reruns until it was time to go home. Some nights, she read to Mrs. Benziger from a magazine, but mostly she made herself useful by changing the channel when they grew restless with whatever program was on.

One night, as she was leaving, Mr. Huggins came toward her down the hall, pushing his walker. The overhead lights had been shut off for the night, and the only illumination came from a dim table lamp, which, reflecting off his stark white hospital robe, made him look like the herald of some malevolent spirit.

"Hello, Mr. Huggins," she said as she neared him. He had stopped moving forward and was standing with both hands on the walker. He lifted a hand and pointed at her in apparent remonstration. He was saying something but too quietly for her to hear, so she leaned in closer.

"No more," she heard him say, gently as a baby. "No more."

She studied his face to see if he meant what she thought he meant. She couldn't hear him without putting her ear almost directly up to his mouth, but she could read his lips. He was saying, "No more," over and over, and he was shaking his head.

It occurred to her that she could elect to take this as a sign if she wanted to. No one was hanging on her decision; it was only her left with her life. Mr. Huggins was right; she couldn't keep coming here forever. She had needed someone to give her permission to stop.

She kissed his hairy cheek. "Thank you," she said. "Good night. Goodbye." She passed through the barrier and out the door, where she stopped to turn and look. The last image she had of the place was Mr. Huggins's gray-white back, like a glimpse of a surfacing whale, as he stepped in front of the lamp in his slow turn into the room that he had shared with Ed and

that now was his alone. She wondered if he missed Ed too. She hoped he didn't even remember him.

Everyone told her to sell the house, find someplace smaller, cheaper, sock away the difference. But she didn't need the money. The life insurance payout allowed her to pay back the home equity loan she'd taken out to cover Connell's tuition and the nursing home bills. It even let her put the new roof on that she needed. She had little in savings, but she had the house, and she had Ed's pension and her salary as long as she worked. There was no more nursing home to pay. She wasn't paying Sergei anymore. Connell was almost done with school.

Besides, where would she go if she sold? Back to Jackson Heights? Nothing was left for her there. When she bought the house, she had planned to die in it. Her plan hadn't changed.

Cindy Coakley said, imploringly, "The ghost of your former life is here."

Not my former life, Eileen thought. *My former* future *life. That's the ghost that's here. The ghost of the life I almost had. As long as I don't leave this place, that former future doesn't have to die.*

And then she thought, *We move around too much in this country.*

Heading into his final quarter of school, which began three weeks after his father died, Connell had only one course left to take in his major. He also needed to finish one science requirement, and he was taking a theater elective, the plays of Tennessee Williams. He had planned to write a thesis on Bellow's influence on Amis, but he couldn't get his act together to do so, and he'd stopped caring about graduating with special honors in the department. General honors in the college would do.

Shortly after the start of the quarter, he started dating a girl named Danielle and going to the Tiki or Jimmy's with her and their friends. He played pool and foosball and Addams Family pinball and had long conversations deep into the night fueled by caffeine, and he had a lot of sex with Danielle. There were people crashing on his couch nearly every night, friends of his or of his roommates, and it felt like a single endless party. He started skipping classes. He still made it to the Blue Gargoyle tutoring center three times a week to meet Delores, the fifth-grader he'd been helping with her reading since September. He started staying in Danielle's apartment while Danielle was at class. He would be there waiting when she got back, and because she always seemed happy to see him, he didn't let himself wonder whether he was wasting his time. He worked on his role in Williams's one-act, *Talk to Me Like the Rain and Let Me Listen*, a lonely play about a man who comes home to his quietly suffering girlfriend and narrates to her the story of his night spent wandering the streets, which felt quite a bit like his life, except for the part about coming home to his girlfriend, as it was always she who came home to him. His other classes

fell to the side. There was a paper he didn't do in the medieval literature class, and then there was a project he didn't do in the science class, and then the halfway mark came and went and he knew he was going to fail, but he couldn't stop himself from failing, and he couldn't drop any classes because he was only taking three. He knew he was in a whirlpool, and he could feel himself going under, but he couldn't grab anything firm. His mother wasn't going to be able to come out for the graduation, because she'd gotten a recent promotion and couldn't take time off, so he didn't have to do a lot of explaining about why he wasn't walking with the others, and it wouldn't be the worst thing to let her think he had graduated. Danielle was still in her third year. She told him she'd had fun with him and left for a summer in Florence to study Renaissance art. He sold what he could, shipped his books, and got on an Amtrak train in honor of his father, because they had talked of riding the rails across America together. The Lake Shore Limited left at night, passing through Indiana, Ohio, and Pennsylvania before it entered upstate New York. When the sun came up, he saw small cities, former hubs, gorgeous Hudson views. He read a little, didn't sleep, didn't talk to anyone. Mostly he looked out the window and thought of his father, who would have found it fascinating, the history of manufacturing in America written on abandoned factories, rusty buildings, heaps of scrap. Somewhere after Poughkeepsie he started crying, and he cried on and off for an hour and half until they pulled into Penn Station. He hadn't taken this trip intending to mourn his father, but it occurred to him that that was what he was finally doing, that when he'd boarded in Chicago he'd undertaken a twenty-hour vigil of silence for him. It took seeing the haunted glory of upstate New York, and being unable to talk to him about it, for him to understand what it meant that his father was gone.

When he entered the lobby of the building on Park Avenue, he beheld a scrawny kid in an ill-fitting doorman's uniform looking as if he was playacting in his father's clothes, and another in a porter's outfit giving a sopping mop a desultory pass over the tiles. "Where did you go to high school?" he asked the kid at the control panel, and he cringed to see that familiar mix of deference and condescension in the kid's eyes that said that

this was a pit stop for him. The kid confirmed his suspicion: there had been a steady stream of graduates since his own stint.

He asked for Mr. Marku. The kid spoke into the intercom in a muted voice that strained after maturity, and a few minutes later Mr. Marku emerged from his apartment and hugged Connell with a warmth that caught him off guard. They went into his office. The fish in the tank were smaller now, but there were more of them, and they were more colorful.

"You're feeling well," Mr. Marku said, lighting a cigarette. "You're looking well. You finally shaved." He rubbed his hand on his own chin, his eyes betraying his delight. "You came to pay me a visit."

"And to see about something," Connell said. "About work."

Mr. Marku gave him a long look. "You're finished college."

Connell clicked a pen on his thigh. "Yes."

"You want to come back here."

"I do," he said. "I'm sorry about how things ended."

Mr. Marku waved his hand as if swatting away a fly. "Summer work."

"I was thinking beyond that," Connell said.

"You have other options. A smart kid like you."

"I'll do a good job," Connell said. "I'll do a better job than before."

Mr. Marku stopped blinking, his lightly appraising gaze shifting into a harder stare.

"These guys have wives, families, bills. It's a steady paycheck for them, a respectable job. Maybe not for you."

"No more books," Connell said. "I won't read, I'll wear the hat. I'll shave every day. I know the ropes."

Mr. Marku shook his head. Maybe he was remembering Connell's flaws—the tardiness, the way he nosed his way into people's business in the building, how he sat down at every opportunity.

"I'm not a kid anymore," Connell said. "I get it now. I'll never be late, I'll keep my mouth shut and my nose down. I won't ever sit down."

Mr. Marku laughed. "Even I sit down." He shook his head again, but this time it seemed as if he was trying to work it out. "I don't have anything full-time."

"Anything," Connell assured him.

"You want to look somewhere else with your college degree," he said. "This doesn't make any sense."

"I like it here," Connell said. "I don't want to go to an office, sit at a desk all day, push paper."

A long silence followed, punctuated by a sudden frenzy of activity in the fish tank.

"You'll show up tomorrow at eleven forty-five," Mr. Marku said finally.

"Thank you, sir."

"Summer work," he said, and Connell nodded. "That's all I have. Then you have to move along."

Connell covered for the doormen when they rotated out on vacation, or else worked by the service entrance gate, where he logged the entrances and exits of the crews and ran the A elevator line. He'd earned more money three years before, but since then the union had struck, and a concession had been made toward a hierarchy of seniority. The summer relief rate was now only eighty percent of the fully vested rate. He would have to wait a year to make what the other guys made, but he was fine with it; maybe they'd look at him as less of an upstart that way.

He kept his face shaved and his hair cut short and wore the hat. The high school kids deferred to his seniority, regarding him with wary politeness. They saw him, he suspected, as a man who'd fallen through a sinkhole in his life.

At the beginning of August, a beloved doorman and tribal elder known variously as Scottish John, the Scotsman, and Scottie, though never simply John, retired to a little salute of cake and coffee after thirty years on the seven-to-three shift, leaving a vacuum of leadership. Mr. Marku called Connell into his office.

"Tell me how long you plan to stay here."

"How long can I? I thought my time ran out in September."

Mr. Marku luxuriated in a pause. "You've come back to make things right."

Connell felt an uneasy gratitude hearing this declaration and looked at Mr. Marku in silence.

"You'll show up tomorrow morning at six forty-five," Mr. Marku said.

"Scottie's shift?"

Mr. Marku nodded. Connell nodded back, feeling as if he'd graduated into adulthood. Seven-to-three was the only shift that presented a modicum of complexity, with shareholders leaving for work and school, nannies and contractors reporting for duty, packages arriving, and mailmen dumping teeming bags of mail to be sorted into little cubbyholes in a big rolling sorter.

After a little while, he saw a subtle shift in the way the full-timers related to him, as if he were separating himself from the gently self-absorbed youths around him, whom he covered for whenever he could, masking their incompetence at practical matters and wringing what assistance he could out of them the way any doorman would. When they went to college in September, he felt he'd become one of the regular guys. The only difference between him and the other doormen was that during breaks he read books instead of the newspaper, and he didn't bullshit in the locker room during lunch but took walks around the neighborhood, peered into the Guggenheim Museum, or sat at restaurants with a book open before him.

He became a reliable fixture in the lobby. He knew all the shareholders' names and apartment numbers. He knew the names of their kids who came home from college on the weekends. He knew their nannies' names, the names of their masseuses who arrived with portable tables, the names of the lovers they never discussed. He kept their secrets and knew the front desk as a mole knows its burrow. As soon as a familiar figure appeared in front of the building, he had his finger on the button to hold open the appropriate elevator door. When someone unfamiliar approached, he had the intercom receiver in his hand, ready to put it to his ear and hit the proper buzzer.

He could tell his presence made a few shareholders uncomfortable. It would have been easier for them if he spoke halting English or hadn't gone to college or hadn't gone to a *good* college or looked a little Balkan or Mexican. To avoid fanning the low flame of their unease, he talked as little as possible about himself. The summer kids were one thing; they caused a temporary ripple in the waters of class identity and were tolerated, even

indulged. By collecting a decent check and moving along to good schools, sometimes even schools the shareholders' children didn't get into, they confirmed the rightness of the shareholders' way of life and the durability of their meritocratic ideals.

His mother pressed him about graduate school or another line of work. How could he explain that he'd never finished college, after all the money she'd spent on his education? He heard her talking as though through a body of water, the sounds muffled by some mysterious viscosity in his spirit. He felt his mind working slowly, his imagination straining. He felt himself becoming thicker all over.

The one purely bright spot in his failed last year of college had been the time he'd spent tutoring Delores. He started giving time to Mr. Marku's kid Peter, who was in eighth grade now and hadn't gotten anything lower than a ninety since third grade. Connell drilled him on vocabulary words and sat him in the little room off the lobby and made him practice taking standardized tests.

Over Thanksgiving break, the college freshmen dropped in like conquering heroes and asked to see Mr. Marku, who came out and gave them big hugs that made Connell unaccountably jealous. They deferred to Connell like a cool older brother, but he didn't feel cool, and their condescension stung.

He shared an apartment in Greenpoint with a guy he'd met through Todd Coughlin, his old cross-country teammate, whom he'd run into at a concert at the Bowery Ballroom and who lived across the hall. In the evenings, he went to galleries, parties, shows. He dated a girl named Violet, an actress who worked as a bartender. She never questioned his choice of a job, only assumed it was a temporary solution while he figured out the creative direction of his life.

He wrote a check to his mother to pay down some of the college loan principal. She ripped it up in front of him. "Don't do this on my account," she said. "I took this tuition on. Don't think you can pay your loans back and not have to feel guilty about staying at that job."

He couldn't figure out why he hadn't gone back to school in the fall. Partly it felt as if returning would be a lie; as if it would be making a prom-

ise to himself, or to his mother, that he couldn't keep. Then there was the matter of telling his mother he hadn't graduated in the first place. It wasn't that he didn't care to do anything ambitious with his life; he just wasn't sure what that ambitious thing was yet.

After a few months had passed, the cup of guilt he'd been carrying around—for having gone away when his father needed him, for letting him go into a home—simply dried up, and he was left holding the empty vessel of his routine. He'd stopped feeling he was living someone else's life, but he hadn't started feeling he was living his own.

He never checked his bank balance, just kept depositing the checks. There was always enough to pay the bills. He didn't want to consider the long-term implications of his financial decisions, because the idea of so many years strung together—twenty years, thirty years, forty years—filled him with terror.

In early January, when Peter Marku was admitted to Regis, Connell felt a surge of joy. He wanted Peter to grab the world by the throat, and he took pride in having helped him.

He was invited to a celebratory dinner at the Markus' apartment. He found it remarkable how quickly he forgot that it was his boss's quarters. It could have been any Park Avenue apartment. A couple of times the intercom rang, and Mr. Marku rose to answer it. Tony brought a large envelope to the door. Otherwise, it was as if Connell were a valued tutor who had been invited into their home as a reward for his role in securing their son's advancement. They ate ravioli, shared a couple of bottles of wine, and polished off a delicious cake that Mrs. Marku said was traditionally Albanian.

As they sipped their coffee, Connell looked at Peter's proud face. The boy's gratitude was palpable, but it wouldn't have mattered if it wasn't, because Connell knew the difference he'd made. That was when it struck him, all at once, that he would very much like to be a teacher. The thing to shoot for, of course, was a college professorship. Even if he managed to get into a decent doctoral program, though—he would have to get his BA first—he wasn't sure he could survive it. He had enjoyed writing papers in college, but he didn't have the zest for the professional side of academia—the specialization, the obsessive focus on publication. The most he could hope to

do would be to teach high school. That wouldn't do, though: every generation was supposed to do better than the previous one; every man was expected to surpass the achievements of his father. If he were to become a high school teacher, he would have to accept that he'd never be as successful as his father had been. His mother wanted big things from him, and instead he was manning the door at a building. But at least at the moment he inhabited something that must have looked to the outside world like a chrysalis. If he did this thing he was now imagining doing with his life—which he could now see he might enjoy quite a lot, this helping people through the thorny thicket of adolescence—he would not only remain a disappointment, he would be a bigger disappointment than ever.

He was now a favorite son among the doormen. He had helped deliver the super's kid to the doorstep of respectability. There would be privileges attached to his new status, something subtly easier about his experience on the job. And something like a home was available in the building—in the lobby, in the locker room in the basement, in this, the super's apartment. He could come over for more of these dinners. He could live through Peter for at least four years, guiding his decisions, giving him the benefit of his perspective, sending him off to a good college on a scholarship. And when Peter came home from college, and later when he came up to visit from his loft apartment downtown, when he pulled up in front of the building in the company town car, dropping in for dinner with the folks, Connell would open the car door without resentment, because by then he would be old enough not to feel resentment anymore. All he had to do was bide his time. Everything would get simpler once enough years had passed. He wouldn't need to go anywhere; he could stay in the lobby and the years would come to him.

If you had to pick a perch from which to watch the world go by, Connell thought, the lobby wouldn't be the worst—especially on quiet summer evenings when you had all the doors open and you got a nice breeze going and dusk was overtaking the city, the setting sun reflecting off the windows on the other side of Park.

When Mr. Marku proffered the coffeepot, Connell held his hand over his mug. Mr. Marku looked determined as he asked if Connell were sure

he didn't want another cup. Mrs. Marku cut another piece of cake, and a queasy feeling of betrayal set in as Connell watched it cover his plate. He knew it was only cake, but it took on a strange, almost numinous power. It felt as if he would be giving up on an idea he had of how his life would go if he ate it. He would be declaring a new oath of allegiance. They were buying his future off for so little: a home-cooked dessert, the promise of further intimacy, a hint of family, an elder brother status of sorts. He had no energy to fight them, not when he had nothing better to argue for. His hand was drawn to his fork and he pressed down into the cake, watching a chunk separate from the rest. He took his hand away from the mug and let it be filled. Peter looked on quietly, taking everything in, an observer more than a person observed. Connell was surprised to suddenly see, with a piercing keenness of perception, that this was no longer his own experience. He was in the middle of an experience Peter was having. He hadn't seen the usurper coming.

When Eileen was a teenager, she had dreamed of going to Death Valley and sleeping under the night sky and its canopy of stars. As a fifty-eight-year-old woman, she compromised and stayed at the Furnace Creek Inn, a luxury resort.

She went in February, during the cool season, because she'd never been able to stand the heat and didn't want to bake her pale skin in the sun. Despite this precaution, after the first day, when she took a walk out into the immense emptiness of the desert and felt spooked, she found herself indoors most of the time. She stayed on the resort's grounds, splitting time between the dining rooms, the fireplace lounges, and a deck chair by the heated pool.

One night she went with a group into the national park. She stood on the Racetrack Playa, which was cracked and dry enough to resemble the skin of a lizard. She didn't need a guide, or even a rudimentary understanding of astronomy, to know what she was seeing when she looked up, because it was simply and unmistakably the Milky Way. The guide pointed out sailing stones: wandering rocks, he said, pushed along their lonely way by means that had never been explained to anyone's satisfaction. One of the tourists held forth about how the movement of these rocks might be due to the effects of wind or ice. His grip on the science was shaky, Eileen could tell, his knowledge anecdotal and obviously derived from popular magazines, a pale shade of Ed's earned erudition. Ed wouldn't have spoken unless he knew what he was talking about. She would have enjoyed watching him soak it all up, the flickers of a theory in his gaze. She could have taken a lesson from his patience with this nattering tourist. He would have liked the way these stones left a long trail, never coming to rest, defying explanation.

On the first anniversary of his father's death, Connell took the train to Bronxville to go to the Gate of Heaven Cemetery. His mother picked him up at the station and drove to Tryforos & Pernice.

"Get something nice," she said.

He was overwhelmed by the choices and selected a premade, mixed-bouquet arrangement. When he returned to the car, his mother was annoyed.

"They didn't have any roses?"

"I don't know," he said. "I just got what looked nice."

"Those are mums and daisies. You should have gotten roses."

"You didn't say anything about roses." His mother looked genuinely upset. "I can go back and get roses."

"No, those are fine," she said. "Your father wouldn't know the difference anyway. He probably would have picked the same ones you did."

Gusting winds rolled across the burial yard. His mother cleared her throat.

"Dear God," she said, "watch over the soul of my dear husband Ed." She looked at Connell. "Let him know that we miss him and love him." She looked at Connell again. "I've never been much good at prayer. If there's a heaven, your father is there. That's one thing I know. Ed," she said, turning back to the grave, "there's not an hour goes by that I don't have you on my mind. Maybe you know that already. Maybe you can listen in on my thoughts. If so, that's a nice thing. That means I probably don't need to speak at all. But I can't stop talking now that I've started. Sometimes it feels like

you never left. I go to tell you things and you aren't there. I fold the paper down to tell you about an article and you aren't sitting across from me. Connell misses you. I'd catch you up on everything that's happened in the last year, but if you can hear me, then you know it all already. If not, I'd just be talking to myself. I love you dearly. I guess we'll say the Our Father now."

She started to say the Lord's Prayer and Connell joined in. It had the soft familiarity of a bedtime routine. The words came easily to him; he wondered if they were stored so deep that they'd be among the last things he remembered when he died.

When his mother finished, she patted the ground in search of pebbles to leave on the gravestone. It was a Jewish custom she had picked up like a magpie building a nest of grief. The capillaries in her cheeks were red, but the cold seemed to have no other effect on her. She was tough, but as they stood in that astringent wind, Connell thought of her living in the house alone, so many empty rooms, all of them still and quiet. After he left the house later, after tea and cake, she would remain behind in it. He had been glad when she told him she was thinking of selling it, but in the end she hadn't put it on the market; something held her back.

His mother put two pebbles on the gravestone and stepped back, buffeted by wind. "Your father picked this spot out," she said. "We looked at the brochures right after we moved. This was before we knew anything about his illness. It sounds morbid, but it wasn't. He wanted to see the plot of land, so we came out here and looked at it. This area wasn't filled in yet, but they had it all planned out. Your father wanted to be on this hill. He would have loved a day like this, chilly and misty, the sky full of rain clouds. I don't know if you remember, but he loved cemeteries. Any trip we took, we had to stop at a cemetery. He liked to read the inscriptions on the gravestones. Maybe I should have come up with something better."

He considered the carved words: "Beloved husband and father." It was boilerplate, but novelty wasn't called for on a headstone, and it was a fitting summation of his father's life, even if it fit a lot of men's lives. Beneath that spare etching was a space where the inscription for his mother would go. She was standing with him now, and the day would come when she no longer would be, when he would arrange for the lowering of her into the

earth. He wanted to put his arms around her and shield her from what was to come, and he felt a kind of panic bloom in his chest. The most he could do to try to chase it away was drape an arm across her shoulders.

"This was the only real estate your father ever really cared about," she said, as if in answer to a private thought. It was a paltry plot, but the view was beautiful. If you added the adjacent space that Ruth and Frank Mc-Guire had bought, it started to look like a little neighborhood. They'd been trailblazers when they'd secured the plots, but in the intervening years the march of mortality had swept past the area and filled it up, and another vanguard was forming a little way up the road. There wasn't room there for Connell, which was just as well. He would make his own decision about a final resting place, or perhaps someone he didn't know yet would make it for him.

Real estate. He couldn't help hearing another meaning in the phrase. What was his father's real estate? There was the investment portfolio, and the house and the things in it; there was the contribution to science; there were the altered lives of the students he'd taught, and the impacts those students had had, and would have, on others. And then there was him. *He* was his father's real estate. At the moment he was an underwater asset.

He picked up a pebble and added it to the little pile atop the gravestone. They headed toward the car.

"Your father got a kick out of the fact that Babe Ruth was buried here."

Connell remembered reading about ballplayers driving to Ruth's grave to soak up some luck, but he hadn't realized this was the cemetery in question.

"Where's the grave?"

"Not far."

"Did Dad ever see it?"

"He stood in front of it for a long while." She chuckled. "Silent. Sort of solemn. The way you two get about baseball."

They drove until they reached a tall marker set back from the road, with a plinth that said RUTH in big block lettering under a large central stone that depicted Jesus gesturing to a little boy. One smaller stone bore a quote from Cardinal Spellman: "May the divine spirit that animated Babe Ruth to win the crucial game of life inspire the youth of America"; another

listed the years of Ruth's birth and death, as well as those of his wife, Claire. There were baseballs stacked in a little offering, a solitary bat, baseball cards taped to the stone.

He thought of his father down the road, ignored except by family members. Death may have been the great leveler, but there were still hierarchies in cemeteries.

He went up and rubbed his palm on the gravestone. He wasn't above asking for a little luck. He might even have knelt if his mother hadn't been there. It felt for a moment as if he were back in church as a little boy, as if he'd placed a quarter in the box and lit a votive candle and now the time had come to say a prayer. Saying a prayer, making a wish, having a thought—were they all the same? Was anyone listening? Was there anything other than a void in the universe? *Help me*, he thought. *Help*. But the Babe just stood impassive in his frieze, a gray block, silent as the stone it was quarried from.

When they got to the house, his mother put on a pot of tea. Connell went into the study to use the computer. The study still smelled like his father, or at least like things he associated with his father—old books, pencil shavings, the heated metal of the desk lamp. His mother came in and picked up something from the desk.

"I was going through these file cabinets," she said, "and I found this." She handed him an envelope with his name on it. "Your father wanted me to give it to you a while ago, but with everything that was going on, I must have mislaid it."

He tried not to let her see the anger that was coursing through his system like a poison. "What does it say?" he said, calmly as he could.

"Well," she said, "I didn't exactly steam it open. I remember he wanted to get some thoughts down for you. He wanted me to wait until he wasn't compos mentis to give it to you. But obviously he didn't want me to wait this long."

Connell held the letter warily. "Thanks," he said.

"Maybe you want to be alone for this," his mother said, and left the room.

Instead of opening the letter, which sat like an unread verdict, he went to the filing cabinet and looked through the drawers. One was full of mementoes from his youth—report cards, honors certificates, birthday and Father's Day cards he'd written his father, art he'd made in the early school years, a once-essential stuffed rabbit he'd forgotten about. As the years passed, his father had saved increasingly more things, no doubt as mnemonic devices, until he had stopped saving anything.

In another drawer he found shoeboxes full of those four-by-six photo albums that used to come free with a developed roll. The albums didn't have dates, but one contained shots from a cross-country meet of his, so it must have been taken during his freshman year. They were mostly shots of Connell, though there wasn't a single photo that depicted him looking at the camera. It was as though his father had been waiting for him to turn and look at him. A terrific loneliness came over Connell as he imagined his father looking through the camera and calling for his gaze silently with his own. He was relieved to see a few landscape portraits of the meadow at Van Cortlandt Park, but when he came to a photo of his father standing with his arm around his old teammate, a sensitive kid who left the school after an unhappy freshman year—he had to jog his brain to remember the kid's name was Rod--he felt jealous. Rod dwarfed his father; he appeared to be leaning down to be in the shot with him. Their faces were close together, and they had such smiles on. It looked as if Rod was his father's own child.

He was terrified to read the letter; he saw that clearly. He went to the bookshelves. All that remained of his father's library were two shelves of reference books and some hardcover volumes of philosophy and literature that his mother hadn't parted with. Another shelf held his father's intellectual output—a shrine of published papers, notes, and notebooks. Connell remembered how much time his father spent in the lab just before he retired. He saw now that his father must have known he'd have to give up his lab soon. Was it possible to imagine him chasing an understanding of, even a cure for, the disease he was afflicted by? Whatever he'd been working on had come to naught, but maybe it would have had an impact on the larger world. If so, then these notebooks could hold the key to reclaiming

him from the forgotten dead men on that hill. He wanted people to visit his father someday, paying posthumous respects.

Connell found a notebook from this later period, but there was no cache of revelatory notes, no raw materials from which he might fashion a second act for his father in death. There were only scribblings in a wavering hand and endless, unlabeled columns of numbers.

He sat back down and held the envelope before him. His fear of the verdict had waned as he read his father's notebooks. He flashed with a juvenile hope that it contained something he urgently needed to hear, and now he hesitated to open it out of fear of disappointment. He wanted to preserve the seal of possibility on it; to reserve the option to project whatever he wanted onto it; to use his imagination to drag himself out of the hole he found himself in.

98

My dear son,

I wanted to take some time to tell you a few things that I think you should hear and that you can only hear from me, because a while ago I got some bad news, and to the extent that your knowing the things I will tell you here can answer questions you may have someday, I want you to know them. I don't mean to insist on their importance by telling you them; I want my presence in your life when I'm gone to be a hand on the shoulder, not one around the throat; but if these things are important to you, then they are important to me to precisely that extent. I hope you can read my handwriting, let alone follow the train of my thoughts, which I fear may be hazier than I understand it to be at any given moment. I want to write this before the opportunity slips away.

I want you to remember me, but only if you want to remember me. I tried to be the kind of father that a son could recall with a full and open heart and not out of a sense of duty. The way you know me as your father is the way I most purely am. The understanding between us goes beyond words, and it is there that I live most fully, there and in the mental space I inhabit with your mother. It may be important to future generations to know the biographical facts of my life, to place some leaves on a bough of the family tree, but that is an abstract notion; you are the reason I am writing, you whom I feel in my blood and bones. I don't want to leave you with questions. I want you to carry me around to the extent that it makes you happy to do so and gives you strength. I want you to forget me if you need to. I want you to suck the marrow out of life.

I am going to slow down. I am going to take a deep breath.

If you want to remember me, remember all the things we did together. The times we ran through words for your spelling bees, hours and hours of words. You used to sound like a monk chanting. We started before dinner, picked it up afterward, went until your bedtime. Remember the driving range, emptying buckets of balls. Remember the fishing trips, the canoe trips. The catches we had, the games we went to. Remember the radios we built together, the remote-controlled car. Remember the trips to the comic book store, the trip to Italy, the trip to Disney World. Remember us going through your homework together. All the times we went to the batting cages. When I taught you the names of birds and plants and animals. When we went bird-watching. The symphonies we went to. The plays. The Mobil games at the Garden. The time we watched the pole vault record get broken. The long-jump record. The mile-time record. The Knicks games. The wrestling matches. George "The Animal" Steele. King Kong Bundy. Andre the Giant. Hulk Hogan. The way I rubbed your back until you fell asleep. The Mets games we listened to on the radio together. The times we read together at night. The ground balls I hit you. The fly balls. The times I drove you all over the five boroughs and beyond to your friends' houses, or picked you up from the train when you called. The trips to the museums. The trips to the barbershop. Getting our hair cut side by side. The way we went to get you your new baseball gear every year. The jogs we went on. The push-ups we did together. All the times we went out in the cold to throw the football around. The way we got you over your fear of the rope swing at the Coakleys' summer house. The way we got you to jump off the train trestle. Making Easter eggs. The way you loved to watch the tablets dissolve and the cloud of dye suffuse the water. All the times we shoveled snow.

What matters most right now is that you hear how much I want you to live your life and enjoy it. I don't want you to be held back by what's happened to me.

I want you to know that I loved my work and did some good with it, and I believe that is worth more than any amount of money. I have not given you a lifetime of riches, but I have faith I have given you a father you can be proud of.

You will not have me there to speak to about the major events of your

life, the ups and downs. But when the hardest times come, I want you to think of this:

Picture yourself in one of your cross-country races. It's a hard pace this day. Everyone's outrunning you. You're tired, you didn't sleep enough, you're hungry, your head is down, you're preparing for defeat. You want much from life, and life will give you much, but there are things it won't give you, and victory today is one of them. This will be one defeat; more will follow. Victories will follow too. You are not in this life to count up victories and defeats. You are in it to love and be loved. You are loved with your head down. You will be loved whether you finish or not.

But I want to tell you: this is worth summoning some courage for. It doesn't matter that you win; it matters that you run with pride, that you finish strong. Years will pass in an instant, I will be gone. Will you remember me on the sidelines, cheering for you? I will not always be here, but I leave you with a piece of my heart. You have had the lion's share as long as you have lived.

When I am gone, I want you to hear my voice in your head. Hear it when you most need to, when you feel most hopeless, when you feel most alone. When life seems too cruel, and there seems too little love in it. When you feel you have failed. When you don't know what the point is. When you cannot go on. I want you to draw strength from me then. I want you to remember how much I cherished you, how I lived for you. When the world seems full of giants who dwarf you, when it feels like a struggle just to keep your head up, I want you to remember there is more to live for than mere achievement. It is worth something to be a good man. It cannot be worth nothing to do the right thing.

The world is closing in on me. I have begun a race of my own. There will be no laurels waiting at the finish line, no winner declared. My reward will be to leave this life behind.

I want you never to forget my voice.

My beloved boy, you mean the world to me.

99

His mother was reading the newspaper over a cup of tea. There was a plate of cookies in front of her. She had set him up with a cup and saucer.

"Well?" she asked. "What did it say?"

He stood in the doorway. "I didn't finish."

"Why didn't you finish? You look like you've seen a ghost. Here, sit down."

He made his way to the chair. He had the letter in his hand. He placed it on the table next to his saucer.

"Why didn't you finish reading it?"

"I read it," he said.

"You just told me you didn't finish it."

"I finished it, Mom." He could feel his lip quivering. "Give me a second to think."

"Fine. Tell me when you're ready."

He took a cookie in order to do something. They were the jelly-topped ones she liked, butter cookies. He took a bite but didn't chew it. He let the little chunk dissolve on his tongue.

"I said I didn't finish," he said. "I didn't mean the letter. I meant something else."

"Didn't finish what? What the hell are you talking about? You're not making sense."

"College," he said. "I didn't finish college."

"Of course you did," she said quickly, taking a cookie.

"I didn't."

"What are you telling me?"

"I didn't finish college. I was a couple of classes short, and I just came home."

She gave him a long, hard look and chewed slowly.

"You're telling the truth now?"

"Why would I lie about this?"

"*You* tell *me*. You've been lying all along, apparently." She took another cookie and ate it quickly. He did the same, to distract himself from the anxiety he was feeling.

"I didn't lie. I just didn't tell the truth."

"You're telling me you don't have a diploma?"

"I don't," he said.

She sighed, put her face in her hands. "Is that why you're working at that goddamned building?" Her voice was muffled a little from talking through her hands.

"Yes," he said. "Maybe. I don't know anymore."

"It is," she said, practically shouting. "That's exactly why you are." Her face had brightened, not with joy but with the glow of an insight. "That's *exactly* why. That's not the kind of kid I raised. I knew it. I knew something was fishy. I should have seen this myself. I don't know how I missed it."

She had a faraway look in her eye, as if she was figuring out the solution to several problems at once. Her expression opened up in a way he hadn't seen in a while. The stress of the last years with his father had taken some of the fullness from her face and left lines in its place.

"I'm sorry," he said. "I know you're angry."

"Oh, you're damned right about that," she said. "I'm furious. Make no mistake. You had no right to do what you did. I don't care if it's your life. There were other lives involved here. Not just mine or your father's. My father's, my mother's. Your father's mother's. A lot of people worked hard to put you in the position you were in. There was a lot of money involved."

"I'll pay it back."

"What you will do," she said sharply, "is quit that godforsaken job immediately and go back to that school and take the classes you need to take to graduate. I don't care if I have to drive you to Chicago myself. I don't

care if I have to sit there and watch you do your work like I had to watch you when you were a child. I don't give a good goddamn what kind of reasons you thought you had for doing this. Let me tell you what those reasons were. They were bullshit, is what they were. You will get that degree, and you will make a real life for yourself. And I will be goddamned if you think anything will happen other than that." She clapped her hands. "I can't believe I didn't see this. I knew this wasn't you. I *knew* it."

"What wasn't me?"

"This ridiculous life you're leading."

"What if it is?"

"It's not," she said. "I carried you in my womb. I know a thing or two about you."

"What's wrong with the life I'm leading?"

"Don't you get superior on me," she said. "My mother pushed a mop around for thirty years. Understand? She cleaned up the vomit of snot-nosed kids. There's nothing wrong with hard work. What's wrong with it is that it isn't your life. It never was. It belongs to someone else. You've been borrowing it. You're simply not allowed to do that anymore, is all."

"You can't make me go back to school," he said.

"I can, and I will, and I don't care if you're too thick to see I say that out of love. You can thank me when I'm dead and you're not getting up to open the door for some goddamned punk. I will be damned if I let that happen to my son. I'm still your mother."

100

When Eileen heard that someone at work was selling a pair of tickets to the Mets game, she remembered the time, the spring before they moved, when Ed told her he'd bought tickets of his own at work. Back then she'd thought of it as a subterfuge, but now she liked to think of it as a troubled man's authentic attempt to give his family a carefree afternoon, even if he couldn't share in it fully with them. She had been hard on him in those days, before she understood what was happening. There was room to be easy on him now.

She bought the tickets and went alone, the empty seat for Ed. It was the first day of October 2000. The leaves had begun to turn. It was warm and a little cloudy—*A good day for baseball*, she could hear Ed saying. It was the last game of the season. She had been told that not much was at stake. The Mets would be in the playoffs no matter what happened. She arrived late and found the stadium packed. They were playing the Montreal Expos, whom she remembered as being not very good, but it hardly seemed to matter who the opponent was. A palpable energy hung in the air, the kind Ed would have loved, especially if he'd had Connell with him.

She placed her pocketbook and coat in the empty seat and settled in. A hot dog vendor made his breathless way up the aisle, stopping a few rows below her. She watched him cradle an open bun, deftly spear a floating dog, sift through the bulging apron pocket for change. She was hungry, but she felt too raw for his sweaty humanity, the workaday intimacy of the moment of transfer.

She had been trying to clear her mind of the interfering noise of everyday life, including the loud silences when she was alone in the house,

and this was a good place to do so. She kept her seat when the others stood. She didn't clap along to the rhythmic thumping coming from the giant speakers, and she didn't shout "Charge!" when everyone else did, but she allowed herself to siphon off some of their excess spirit.

The Mets held a narrow lead until the seventh inning, when the Expos tied it up. The score remained tied heading into the bottom of the ninth; after the third Met out, she slammed her hand down on her knee and looked at her bitten nails and realized that it mattered a great deal to her that they win this game, even if it didn't matter to the team. It would have pleased Ed to see it head into extra innings: the decision of fate forestalled awhile, both teams working on borrowed time. The outcome's importance rose with every out, as if all would be right in the world if the Mets prevailed.

She understood what had made these games so compelling to her husband: every day could bring the breaking of a new record, but the larger world would persist undisturbed. There was always news, even if little of it was newsworthy. Every pitch was different, every swing, and yet they all were variations on a familiar theme. The lines on the field, the fences around it, the neat geometry suggested that these, for a discrete but somehow infinite period, were the limits of the world.

The tenth inning gave way to the eleventh. A pair of base hits and a sacrifice bunt—she could never forget that term, because the sacrifice bunt, when executed perfectly, was nearly Ed's favorite play, surpassed in his esteem only by the hit-and-run and the triple—put runners on second and third with one out, and they walked the next batter, but the Met pitcher got the last two men out without incident, and she allowed herself a deep breath. After two quick outs in the bottom of the eleventh, the next batter hit a single, and the one after him followed with a thrilling line drive to center, but the center fielder threw to the shortstop, who threw to the catcher, who tagged the runner at home for the third out. The Met pitcher struck out three straight batters in the top of the twelfth—*struck out the side*, she could hear Ed saying while pumping his fist—and the Expo pitcher retired them in order in the bottom half of the inning. No one reached base in the top of the thirteenth, and she heard someone behind

her say that this was the longest game the Mets had played that year, and she thought, *Of course it is*, and that her heart would not be able to take it.

When the first batter up in the bottom of the thirteenth walked, she could hear Ed saying, *It's the leadoff walks that kill you*, and then the next batter was the pitcher, and she knew pitchers couldn't hit and the team usually pinch-hit for them in situations like this or had them bunt, but somehow he was swinging away, and somehow he got on base safely with a little ground ball that didn't leave the infield, and she found herself standing and shouting "Go! Go! Go!" as her voice was swallowed in the mounting chorus of thousands of others. The next batter squared up for a bunt—she remembered Ed calling it that, squaring up, facing your fate head-on—and when he laid it down, the third baseman came rushing in for it and made a bad throw and the runner on second came all the way around to score. She squeezed her hands into fists and felt her throat constrict as the cheering cascaded around her.

It mattered so little that they'd won, and yet nothing mattered more. A fugitive joy stole through her as the players cleared the field. She sat in her seat and watched the fans leave, the emptying stadium growing quiet. Shades of runners lingered on the base paths. When the groundskeepers began sweeping dirt into piles and smoothing them out, she made her way to the car.

101

She rang the buzzer for the apartment number she had listed in her address book. A shy and small-framed woman answered the door, speaking Spanish. Eileen could see a crib in the living room behind her and a shirt spread out over an ironing board. She asked about the Orlandos, but the woman didn't seem to know what she was talking about. Eileen excused herself and went back downstairs. The Orlandos' name wasn't anywhere on the lobby registry.

She went around the corner to the Palumbos' house. Mr. Palumbo came to the door. In the eight years since she'd last seen him, he had aged considerably; he must have been pushing eighty by now.

"It's me, Mr. Palumbo," she said. "Eileen Leary. How are you doing?"

She couldn't tell whether he didn't recognize her or didn't want to let on that he did. She'd never talked much to him, but he'd been her next-door neighbor for years, and she wanted that to count for something. When he extended his left hand, palm down, she took it gratefully in her own. The knuckles were like ball bearings, but the skin was smooth. He squeezed her hand tighter and started patting it with his other one. His hands felt like little furnaces.

He said his wife had died. Eileen offered condolences but couldn't bring herself to tell him about Ed. He said his son had moved out of the apartment upstairs. "It's hard to be a landlord at my age. My daughter wants me to sell the house and move out with her family in Hackettstown. I think about it, but what am I supposed to do out there, in the middle of nowhere? Watch the grass grow? The kid on the third floor, nice Colombian kid, he takes care of the handyman work. I go up there and play poker." He laughed. "He takes all my money."

She asked after the Orlandos. Mr. Palumbo started to speak about Donny and then disappeared inside for a long time. When he came back, he handed her a business card for an auto body shop in Garden City. He explained that Donny had opened it a few years back and now he had a few locations, with car washes.

"Very successful," he said. "He got remarried too. Nice lady. He has two girls with her."

She felt a joyful smile spread across her face. Beleaguered Donny of the inauspicious circumstances had made a miracle happen. Ed would have been so proud.

"Wonderful," she said.

"I went out to see them. Beautiful neighborhood. Gary lives in a carriage house on the property. Brenda keeps the books for the shops. You should see Sharon. What a beauty. She could be a movie star."

"My goodness," she said. "And Lena?"

"She passed right after my wife."

Mr. Palumbo crossed himself, so Eileen did too. When Mr. Palumbo asked about her family, she spoke vaguely, sparingly. She felt like a fool not admitting Ed was gone, but she couldn't help herself. She needed this man to believe Ed was still alive.

They said their good-byes. As Eileen turned to leave the stoop, she heard the sound of something falling inside the apartment, and she had an eerie sensation that Mr. Palumbo had keeled over, dead. She knocked on his door again in a panic that surprised her. When Mr. Palumbo answered the door, she said the first thing that came to mind, which was that she wanted to wish him a happy Thanksgiving in case she didn't see him before then. He looked a little bemused and thanked her for the wishes and she was left alone again. A sudden thunder overtook her heart and the tinny taste of fear stole into her mouth. She sat on his stoop to calm herself. She decided that she was afraid of getting left behind—but that was impossible; she had left before that could happen. Happy as she was for Donny, it unnerved her to learn that he hadn't been living in the neighborhood all this time. She'd never imagined he would get his act together enough to make the radical moves he'd made. She had derived a certain comfort from

thinking of him as living out the trajectory of his known life, keeping her past in place by staying put for her, even if he didn't know he was doing it. It was much more frightening to think of the world in a state of permanent flux.

She hadn't built a dynasty. She wasn't even sure there would be a continuation of the line. Her son had gone back to Chicago to school, but she couldn't help worrying about him, and in a more elemental way than she'd ever worried before. She'd begun to worry less about what sort of foundation he was laying for her future grandchildren—God willing, he would meet a nice girl and settle down and have kids—and more about his own future.

She wanted to rejoice with Donny, but she didn't know how to begin to reach out to him after all this time and silence. She fingered the business card and then put it in her wallet. She thought, *I hope you have a wonderful life. I hope you have a lovely big backyard. I hope you flip steaks and watch your daughters run around and think*, I could die in peace.

She rose and walked over to stand in front of her old house. The new owners had let the garden grow up over the garden box and had restained the doors, and new drapes hung in the window in a style she didn't prefer, but it was unmistakably her house. She'd stood so many times where she now stood, appraising it, and a surge of affection shamed the memory of her desperation to escape it. She stepped onto the stoop.

The lights had come on in the streetlamps, but the evening hadn't yet submitted to night. She wanted to be transported back to a time when this had been her life. The birds in the trees made their entreaties, cars flew down the street, and the smooth paint of the banister brought the skin of her palm to life. She closed her eyes and listened to the familiar sounds of a disappearing plane and a distant horn and breathed in that strangely appealing mix of car exhaust and leaves. She could have been arriving back after a long day at Lawrence, or following Ed and Connell up the stoop after Sunday dinner at Arturo's. She could go inside and find Ed on the couch wearing the headphones. She would say to him, *Listen as long as you want. Listen to all your records. I'll be right here when you're done. I'll wait years if I have to.* She would take his hand in her hands and kiss the back

of it with enough tenderness to show him it wasn't a gambit. *Let's just stay right here*, she would say. *Let's stay here forever.*

She didn't know these people, but she was beginning to feel she couldn't return home without seeing the house. She'd spent a lifetime running, and she was tired. There had to be some way to fit the past into the present, even if she'd turned her back on it.

She took the knocker in her hand and gave the door three quick, emphatic taps. A young man answered. It was hard to reconcile him with the boy—he must have been seven or eight then—she'd seen standing out front when his parents were leaving the open house. He was tall and broad, and his hair was neatly brushed. He had the bright, white smile of an elected official.

"Can I help you?"

It unsettled her to be greeted as a stranger at her own house. She had to squelch the pride that threatened to ruin this venture before it had even begun.

"My name is Eileen Leary," she said. "I used to live here."

She felt like one of those furtive talkers who went from door to door proselytizing for obscure faiths and doomed causes. She wouldn't have been surprised or blamed him if he'd closed the door before she finished her halting appeal. But he invited her inside.

"I don't want to be a bother," she said as she crossed the threshold.

"Not at all," he said. "Would you mind taking off your shoes?"

It was a custom she'd long thought of putting into practice in her own home, but she'd never found a way to introduce it. The vestibule tiles were cold on her stockinged feet, but the plush carpet sank pleasantly under her as she entered the living room. They kept a television where her armchair used to be. The set looked so inviting that she wondered why she and Ed had deprived this space of one for so long. She watched the father, Mr. Thomas as she remembered it, slap his elegant hands on his knees and stretch his long body as he rose from the couch.

The boy began to introduce her, but his father cut him off. "I know who you are," he said affectionately. "Welcome back! Does it look the same to you? My wife is making dinner. Anabel! Come in here."

The décor was so different that she had trouble gauging the depth and width of the room; it seemed that the space itself, which had given her so much trouble in her decorating efforts, being always a foot too wide or too narrow, had compliantly shifted its dimensions to fit the needs of the new owners, finding its natural harmony in the process, as if it had been waiting for them to arrive. When she looked into the dining room, though, and saw the old wall-sized mirror, she was seized by a pang so strong it made her stomach lurch. There was a greater profusion of things both big and small, the kind that would have nettled her in her own home but that here suggested a fruitful multiplication.

"I like what you've done with the place," she said, and felt instantly foolish. It had been almost eight years. They hadn't "done" anything with it; they'd simply made it their own, or what they'd done with it had been done so long ago that it was absurd to speak of it.

They stood around in one of those benignly awkward circles that obtained whenever men were responsible for making introductions. She saw the boy sneak a look at the television and felt her heart bloom with an instant affection, because it was what her son would have done in the same situation.

Casting about for something to say, she noticed, on an end table, a trophy capped with a winged figure arching her arms in triumph. "What's this?" she asked brightly, picking it up. It was heavier than she expected, not like the flimsy trophies for dance recitals or participation in Little Leagues.

"He won it in debate," the father said. She remembered that his first name was Thomas too. "The state championship. We're very proud of him."

"Don't let him fool you into thinking I was the champion," the boy said. "I came in second."

"This year he will be," the father said.

She saw that the boy was uncomfortable with the attention, and she put the trophy down. She remembered they were Catholic. "Did you go to St. Joan of Arc?" she asked.

"I did," the boy said. "From third grade on."

"So did my son." She guessed the boy was attending the same high school as Connell, which was a powerhouse in debate, but she didn't want

to embarrass him by asking, in case he hadn't gotten in. "You have a sister, I remember. Is she here?"

"She's at Yale," Mr. Thomas said proudly. "We don't see her often. Only holidays—and every other weekend, when she needs to do the laundry." He chuckled at the absurdity of her coming all that way to wash her clothes, but Eileen also heard delight in the fact that his daughter, while being a high achiever on her way to a rewarding professional life, was still, in the end, his daughter.

Just as a heavy feeling was about to settle into Eileen at how long it had been since her son had washed his clothes in her machine at home, which she now ran only about once a week, Mrs. Thomas emerged from the kitchen and let out a surprised cry at seeing a stranger there. She must have been so absorbed in her cooking that she hadn't heard the knock at the door. Eileen knew that feeling well—the exigencies of household duties, the making of a meal for a pair of mouths that showed their appreciation by the way they wolfed it down. It had always moved her to watch her husband and son eat.

"Hello," the woman said, turning to her husband for an explanation.

"Anabel, this is Mrs. Leary."

"Mrs. Leary?"

Of course it was the husband, and not the wife, who recognized her, because her perpetual industry allowed him a clear head, and she barely had a brain left at the end of a day of housework. Eileen felt herself straighten up in respectful solidarity.

"Mrs. Leary, from whom we bought the house," he added.

Her hand went to her mouth to stifle the sound of her shock. "Oh! Welcome! What brings you here?"

"I was in the neighborhood."

"Forgive me, I'm a mess." She gestured to the apron tied around her waist, a prominent, fresh stain on its front. "Vijay, please take Mrs. Leary's jacket." So *that* was the boy's name. It had taken the wife's entrance for this crucial detail to emerge. Thomas Thomas could have been Ed standing there in a somehow still-charming dereliction of protocol. The boy came over and helped the jacket off Eileen's shoulders one at a time. "May I

show you around?" the woman asked. "I'm sure you're curious to see the house."

Eileen *was* curious. She was so refreshed to behold how accurate the woman—*Anabel*—had been in her perception, how sensitive to nuance, that she almost didn't answer right away.

"I would love to see it," she said. "My name is Eileen."

Their shake was firm, appreciative—collegial. Anabel led her to the kitchen, which smelled like cardamom and curry. They had turned it into a galley kitchen. There was much more counter space now. They had granite slabs, not unlike the ones in her house. There was even a space to eat, with bar stools pushed under it, but she could tell they ate their meals in the dining room. The renovations were tastefully done, the sort she would have approved of had she and Ed committed the money to making them—had she not known in the back of her mind that she was thinking of some other house every time she looked at her own. Anabel gave her a quick tour. They had redone the bathroom: new tiles, a new clawfoot tub, a beautiful pedestal sink. They had converted one of the closets in the master bedroom into a little bathroom. She'd always wished for an extra bathroom on that floor, so she wouldn't have to walk down to the basement when someone else was using it. New baseboard molding lined the house. Everywhere were elements obviously Indian—silk tapestries, carved wood figurines, an enameled brass vase—but there were also crosses on the walls, and a picture of the pope in the master bedroom. It took her a moment to register that this had once been her bedroom with Ed. Nothing in it looked the same. The bed seemed to radiate the life and energy of years of a couple sleeping side by side in it.

"How are your husband and son?"

She didn't have it in her at that moment to deflect the question in an obfuscating ramble. "My husband died last March," she said.

"Oh! I'm so sorry! Mrs. Leary!"

"Thank you," she said. "And please call me Eileen."

"It must be strange to be back here."

"It's nice, actually."

"Please stay for dinner. We're just about to eat."

She knew what to say when politeness was extended in the due course of decency: *I have to get going* or *I really can't stay*, whatever made it easier for everyone to save face and return to their regular lives. But she didn't want to say any of that right now. She was so very tired. She wanted to stay there with these people in the attractive home they'd made of what she'd left behind. Something about these environs struck her as oppressively and irreducibly different, and yet she could imagine never leaving them. She didn't look forward to returning to her empty house, with the wind screaming, the branches shushing against the siding, and the fear of someone creeping in through the window troubling her sleep. So much life filled this home that there was no way to feel dread in it, but then she'd seen that there was no way to feel dread in anyone's home but one's own. Something was sacred in being a guest.

She was led to the dining room table and directed to sit. Thomas and Vijay shut the television off and made their way to the table with murmuring contentedness in their voices.

"Do you like Indian food?" Thomas asked, breaking the spell as Anabel slipped into the kitchen. Eileen froze in terror. She'd sat already, had begun to arrange her napkin in her lap, so there was no way out. The last thing she wanted was to act discourteously to these people, but the truth was that she hated Indian food, hated the very sight of it—its little lakes of earth-toned sauces, its hillocks of meat in blasted landscapes of mud. She had smelled the spices but thought of them as an inevitable detail—a tribal marker, not part of the daily routine. She had somehow failed to consider that the Thomases actually made Indian food at home. Wasn't the way forward to assimilate? She didn't know how to read these people who blended in but didn't, who were like her but weren't, whose kids got where her own kid got, or even beyond, but started somewhere else entirely.

How could she say she hated their food? She would have to explain everything—how she'd come to feel about the neighborhood, about her life, about the world as she'd wanted it to be: simple, predictable, familiar. It wasn't about their food. It was the smell, the spices, the strangely proliferating condiments, the mystery of its preparation. It was the fact that she'd had no choice about it. So many Indians were there all of a sudden

and so many of her friends were gone. At some point all the restaurants in the neighborhood had become Indian restaurants. Then the last of her friends had left, and the Indian restaurants had remained and seemed to multiply. She couldn't stand the sight of the stuff, and now she was about to be served it.

"I don't know," she said. "I've never had it."

And that, finally, was the truth. For all her revulsion, for all the times she'd insisted she couldn't take a single bite without gagging, she'd never actually tasted it. It had been easier to say she had, because there had been less to explain. It had been easier to say, "I don't like it," instead of, "I'm too angry to try it." But you couldn't lie to yourself forever.

Her throat was constricted and dry. She took a long drink of water, almost the entire glass.

"You're in for a treat," Thomas said upon the entrance of his wife bearing platters. He listed names of dishes; Eileen was too keyed up to register them. He spooned out a plate for her as Vijay passed her a bowl filled with bread that resembled thin, soft mattresses. After she had her plate, the others filled theirs in turn, and the scent wafting up at her was not as offensive as she'd imagined it would be; there was a sweet pungency to it. The mound on her plate was the color of Mars. There was no turning back.

Thomas said the name of the dish again, and she speared some on her fork. As she bit into it, she registered that it was chicken, and also that there was tomato in the sauce, and cream of some sort, as well as some indeterminate spices. There was something complex and contradictory about it, a mildness and a stoutness that competed for primacy, and on top of these a pleasing fullness in the mouth, the medley of textures bolstered by stray grains of rice. She was aware of how she had no competing memory with which to dull the vibrancy of this experience. If to taste forgotten foods was to reanimate the past, then a different kind of reminder, a reminder of future possibility, waited in unfamiliar flavors. She was making a new memory. She was eating Indian food. She'd never thought she'd live to see the day.

"It's good," she said, trying to be measured, until she couldn't hold back. "It's really very good." She placed her fork on her plate, straightened

up in surprise, and saw them looking at her warmly. It was only then that she registered that they were sitting in the same arrangement she and Ed and Connell had sat in in that room—the father nestled into the table's head, his back to the window, the boy with his back to the mirror, the wife across from him, ready to shuttle dishes. Eileen was in the seat that had often gone empty at her own table. She'd looked at it in the middle of meals and thought how nice it would be to have someone drop in unannounced and bring the world to her. She'd never imagined the scene from the visitor's vantage point, how complete a picture of life it might have presented, how much it might have looked as if everything that mattered in the world was there already.

"I didn't know what I was missing," she said, and because there was no way to say what she was thinking without telling her whole story, she picked up her fork, took another bite, and hoped they'd see something more than mere politeness in the smile that was spreading across her face.

Epilogue

2011

The day had been a muggy slog, everything moving at half speed. He had the windows open and the fans on, but the air just sat in the room, menacing them. The looming final exam made him rush through the lesson, lecturing more than he liked to. Ordinarily, once the weather turned this warm, sophomores would do anything to avoid the indignity of actual learning, but the extreme heat had sunk them into a state that resembled attentive silence. It was also the class period before lunch. They didn't draw chalk-dust penises on loose-leaf paper and slap them on each other's backs, or put on goofy accents when asked to read, or read unbearably slowly on purpose, or read the last word of every sentence in unison. He used to love these muggy days at the beginning, but now that he was a veteran, now that he commanded respect and attention, they were the days he enjoyed least, because he could feel the limits of his craft. There was always room for improvement. He felt almost pleased when Carmine Priore threw his book in the air and told him to end the charade and let them out early: at least it was a sign of life.

Toward the end of class, he realized he'd forgotten what they were discussing, what point he was about to make, even what book they were talking about. He turned to the blackboard for help, but found no clue there, save for a single word, "Empathy," scrawled and underlined, apparently by him. He looked to one of the desks in front. *The Metamorphosis*. He began to panic. His first thought was Alzheimer's, and terror moved through him. He was only thirty-four.

He took a deep, deliberate breath. He simply had to relax. He knew *The Metamorphosis*. He knew these kids too: there was Nick Indelicato and Tommy Daulton; there was Marvin Neri; there was Brendan King; there, asleep—he slapped his hand on the desk and the boy jerked up violently— was Carmine Priore.

As for him, he was Connell Leary, Con-Man to his friends, Mr. Leary to his students. He would be Mr. Leary to them when they were forty and had kids of their own.

He tried to shake it off, but the waterlogged, blank feeling persisted in his head. Terror welled up in him. It was no dream. His room, an ordinary classroom that he shared with a colleague in the history department, was appointed with maps of the ancient and modern world, a poster of Shakespeare, another of Thomas Jefferson, a framed reproduction of David's *Death of Socrates*. The faces of the boys flashed with delight as the electric silence deepened. They looked at each other and began to murmur.

"Quiet!" he shouted. "Quiet this instant!" He heard his own voice and thought he sounded not like himself but like one of those teachers in the movies, impossibly stuffy. He needed to act quickly if he wanted to maintain authority. "I will wait here all day until you gentlemen are ready to learn," he said, walking over to his father's desk. "And you can wait with me." He paused, long and fruitlessly. "We're going to do something important. We're going to take control of our educations. You gentlemen are going to own this material. You're going to teach it to me as if I don't know it. One of you is going to come up here and be the teacher." They emitted a collective theatrical groan. "Or else we can have a surprise quiz," he said, to louder protests. He settled on Justin Nix in the back row—Justin of the kind, broad face and the nearly perfect indifference to the grammatical conventions of standard written English. Justin pointed to his chest and mimed looking behind him for another student as the kids laughed.

"Okay, Mr. Leary," Justin said, rising and high-stepping toward the front of the room. "Here I come. I'm going to be Mr. Leary, guys."

He handed Justin a piece of chalk. "Go to work," he said. "What do we know? What do we need to know?"

He fell into his chair, overwhelmed by the hothouse smell of teenage boys baking in the heat. He heard Justin at half volume, as though from the bottom of a pool. Justin wasn't teaching *The Metamorphosis*. He was doing an impression of the way Mr. Leary stood at the board, the way he rubbed the top of his head and pushed his glasses up. Justin had his gestures down cold. A minute into this pantomime, Connell felt the air come back into

his lungs. The kids were watching for his reaction. "You've really helped," he said, trying to sound calm, sarcastic. He didn't want them to know he meant it. "I think we've all benefited enormously from this little display. Give him a hand."

They burst into exaggerated applause, ironic hoots, and arm pumps—a release of pent-up energy. He brought another kid up, and a third; they said some things about the book. Then he rose from his chair, willing himself to feel refreshed and in possession of all his powers.

"What I want you to consider," he began, "is that as soon as the door is opened and Gregor's parents see the enormous bug for the first time, they immediately know it's their son. Did this strike any of you as strange? Why didn't they rush to check for Gregor in the closet? Why didn't they go to the window to make sure he didn't break his leg jumping out? Why do they instantly assume their son has been transformed into a—what is he again, Trevor?"

"A cockroach," Trevor said.

"We've gone over this. What Kafka called him in the original German can be translated as something more like *vermin*. We also know that toward the end of the story Kafka has the cleaning lady describe him as a certain kind of insect. Justin, since you've done such a good job already?"

"A dung beetle," Justin said.

"Great! A dung beetle. Which eats, as we've discussed, feces."

They groaned in unison. He felt himself in something like a fugue state. He knew he'd be able to finish what he'd started. He'd stood before a class and guided it through a text often enough to do it now without falling apart, without even an apparent hitch in his delivery. Inside, though, he was boiling with fear.

"Just for that extra bit of humiliation for Gregor. Anyway, how do we explain his parents' instantly knowing that that dung beetle is their son? Maybe it's not a stretch for them to see their son as a vermin. Maybe they've been seeing him as less than human all along. He's been serving their needs, propping them up. Maybe his spirit, as they see it, has finally found the body it deserves."

The bell rang. He reminded them to do the reading and gathered his

things. He kept his head down. He could sense a couple of them assembling at his desk. Danny Burbano was there, as well as Justin. Danny was always there. Danny was embarrassed to speak in front of the others, but he liked to talk about the books they read. Connell usually indulged him.

"Not today, Danny," he said as he brushed past. "Tell me tomorrow." He could sense the hurt pooling in Danny's chest. He was gruffer than he should have been, but he had to get out of there. Justin followed him out the door, hustling to keep up.

"Am I in trouble?"

"*You?* For what?"

"That impression I did."

"Nobody's in trouble," Connell said. "Everything's going to be fine."

He was down the hall and through the doors before Justin could respond. He looked up from a flight below and saw Justin watching him descend the stairs. He knew he must have looked like a man on fire.

Outside, he broke into a trot. The light at the corner was turning red and he sprinted across the avenue. He ran several blocks, all the way to the park along the Hudson's edge, where he slumped on a bench and tried to catch his breath. His shirt was soaked with sweat. He hadn't run that hard, that long, since high school. He took deep, fugitive drafts of the river air and tried to focus on the sun on his neck. A passing tugboat let out its foghorn. The sound reminded him of a bullfrog lowing, and he had a strange, familiar feeling that he couldn't place. He looked at the diaphanous vapors in the atmosphere and out at the boats passing slowly and the competing skyline across the river, and he thought of the way life arranged itself around water.

He'd had intimations of this moment before. Once, he'd stood in the predawn dark in the kitchen, unplugging his wife's phone from the charger and plugging in his own, and as he held it in his hand he realized that he could not recall the device's name. He pressed his hands against the countertop's edge and leaned his forehead into the microwave, fighting through a thick, aphasic fog, and, after at least a minute had passed, he began to feel a panic like the kind he felt when he cut off the circulation

to his arm in his sleep and woke with a start and called out, shaking and flapping it uselessly for so long that he was sure he had lost the use of it forever, until the blood came pumping back in and he recovered sensation in painful stages. All he'd been able to conjure had been the last line of a vaguely recollected poem—*blackberry, blackberry, blackberry*—and then he'd remembered the poem's title—"Meditation at Lagunitas"—and finally realized with a mixture of relief and fear that BlackBerry was the very name of the thing he was holding, that his subconscious mind had been faster at retrieving it than his conscious mind, and that this could be an augury of what was to come.

Babe Ruth hit 714 home runs in his career, Hank Aaron 755, Barry Bonds 763. Hack Wilson set the single-season RBI record with 190 in 1930, though decades later historians found a discrepancy in a box score and changed the number to 191. Lou Gehrig played in 2,130 consecutive games, Cal Ripken 2,632. Orel Hershiser pitched 59 consecutive scoreless innings in '88, eclipsing Don Drysdale's record of 58 1/3. Cy Young won 511 games, Walter Johnson 417, Christy Mathewson and Pete Alexander both 373. Barry Bonds walked 2,558 times, Rickey Henderson scored 2,295 runs, Hank Aaron drove in 2,297 men, and Pete Rose got 4,256 hits, passing Ty Cobb's 4,191—some say 4,189—in '85. Mickey Mantle finished with a .298 lifetime batting average because of some mediocre seasons at the end of his career. Ted Williams lost the MVP award in 1941 to Joe DiMaggio and his 56-game hitting streak, despite hitting .406 that year. Dwight Gooden struck out 276 men as a rookie. Ralph Kiner won 7 home run titles despite playing in only 11 seasons.

Maybe he should have committed other facts to memory. Maybe he should have learned the dates of elections and political coups d'état. Maybe he should know the presidents in chronological order and their vice presidents and the dates of their elections and deaths, or the history of Mesopotamia or metallurgy, or the basics of quantum mechanics, but he didn't know those facts, he knew baseball facts. He'd learned baseball facts originally because his father had known baseball facts and he liked having them to share with him, and then eventually they were just what rattled around in his head.

Roberto Clemente had a .317 lifetime batting average, was voted to start

17 All-Star games, and finished with exactly 3,000 hits. His plane crashed in Puerto Rico during an off-season relief mission he attempted to fly to Nicaragua in 1974 to deliver food to starving people. He was elected to the Hall of Fame immediately, the Baseball Writers' Association of America forgoing the five-year waiting period they gave themselves to consider the value of a player's contribution to the game.

He waited for the sensation of panicked blankness to come back, and after a while he started to wonder whether it had happened at all or whether he'd conjured it out of his fears. Something in the scene in the classroom had triggered it, some nagging déjà vu. He kept circling back to the moment when he turned to the board and saw the single word and didn't remember how it got there. It hovered inscrutably, an insistent message in it.

He thought of the visit he had paid to his father's own classroom before anyone knew what was really going on with him. He had watched his father come apart before his eyes.

Empathy. He hadn't always had it. It was a muscle you had to develop and then keep conditioned. Sometimes he thought his real goal wasn't to teach them to write better essays but to get them to think more about what it meant to be human.

Michelle had been trying to persuade him to reconsider his firm stance against having children, a child. He had told her from the beginning that he wasn't comfortable taking the chance he'd get the disease or that the kid would. The line was going to end with him, he had said, and she had accepted it, until she lost her mother after Christmas.

He took out his wallet and dug around in the recesses of its folds for the little piece of tooth. He held it in the sunlight, felt the smooth enamel against his fingertips. It could have been a sliver of seashell, a shard of stone or scree. He had transferred it from wallet to wallet over the years. He had to stop torturing himself with it. He wasn't helping anyone with all this regret.

He had agreed the night before to go in for genetic testing. She had gotten him to commit to having a child if he definitely didn't have the gene. It struck him now that what he had been thinking about when he drew a

blank before the class was an idea of this potential child. He could see a suggestion of this child's face, an amalgam of his wife's and his own. The truth was that even if he had the gene, he'd be willing to have a kid anyway, and not just because there was a chance he wouldn't get the disease. If he got it, he'd do whatever he needed to do to shield the kid from it as long as he could.

The truth, he saw now, was that he wanted more than anything to have a child with his wife. Her life was as sparsely populated as his was, familywise. After her mother's passing, her father had moved out to California to live with her brother, Ricky. Except for a cousin in Houston, Michelle didn't have anyone else. Michelle and his mother had circled around each other for a few years. At first he thought it had to do with Michelle's being Nicaraguan American, but lately he believed it had more to do with the fact that Michelle and his mother both had such strong personalities. They butted heads without the release of ever actually meaning to do so. Maybe it had something to do with the fact that Michelle was a lawyer, that she'd been a clerk for a Supreme Court judge and was now at a corporate law firm. She'd already lived a lot of the life his mother might have wanted to live, and she wasn't even thirty-five. His mother and Michelle had gotten close enough lately, though, that Michelle was now the one who called his mother when they had to make plans with her, and when they went over to his mother's house, Michelle and his mother sat at the kitchen table after dinner playing backgammon while he watched television in the den. He knew that if he had a kid, Michelle and his mother could pull together even more, and it wasn't hard to imagine Michelle calling his mother "Mami" soon enough, which he thought would make both of them happy.

He could honor his father by loving the kid the way his father had loved him. And if he had to be vulnerable in front of the kid, if he had to be defenseless and useless and pathetic, if he had to forget things and piss himself and get lost on the way home, then so be it. If the kid didn't handle it well—well, that was what kids did. They went out too often, they stayed out too late, they said things that cut to the quick, they forgot responsibilities, they broke your heart. Years later they thought about it all.

And what did parents do? They saw more clearly than their kids did.

They forgave their kids, even if they didn't say so. Even if they couldn't say so. They did.

He couldn't wait to get home to his wife. She would be surprised by his change of heart. She might be more surprised by how much he had to say. She was always trying to get him to talk. Well, tonight he was going to talk. She wasn't going to be able to shut him up. He was going to tell the whole story, even the parts he wasn't proud of. He would have to find a way to tell it so it made some kind of sense. He would have to tell it from the beginning. He'd have to give her enough detail to let her see it for herself. It was lucky that he had such a good memory for that kind of thing. It was all in there somewhere, he was sure of that. He would dig it out.

He rose and walked to the fence that cordoned off the edge of the island. He took one last look at the little chip of tooth and tossed it in the water. It disappeared without even the tiniest detectable splash, to settle unseen on the riverbed. Maybe in a few thousand years it would make its way out to the ocean. Maybe in another few thousand it would wash up on the shore of a wholly different world, with new species, a different atmosphere, and a tenuous place for man. For now, while he breathed and moved, while he felt and thought, there was still, between this moment and the one of his dying, the interval allotted to him, and there was so much to live for in it: the citrus snap of fresh black tea; the compression and release of a warm stack of folded towels carried to the closet between two hands; the tinny resonance of children in the distance when heard through a bedroom window; the mouth-fullness of cannoli cream; the sudden twitch of a horse's ear to chase a fly; the neon green of the outfield grass; the map of wrinkles in one's own hand; the smell and feel, even the taste of dirt; the comfort of a body squeezed against one's own.

He would hug his kid as much as he could. "Good," he'd say. "Good. Good."

Acknowledgments

For the titles of parts I, III, IV and V, I am indebted to *The Great Gatsby*, "Skunk Hour," by Robert Lowell, "Love Song: I and Thou," by Alan Dugan, and "Meditation at Lagunitas," by Robert Hass.

Many thanks to: Stephen Boykewich, Aidan Byrne, Joshua Ferris, Chad Harbach, Christopher Hood, and Tracy Tong, for careful reads and useful notes; Aaron Ackermann, Bonnie Altro, Charles Bock, John James, Matthew McGough, David Moon, Bergin O'Malley, Brad Pasanek, Amanda Rea, Chris Wiedmann, and Boris Wolfson, for friendship, encouragement, and support; all my teachers, especially Tristan Davies, Eric DiMichele, Stephen Dixon, Judith Grossman, Michelle Latiolais, Alice McDermott, Jean McGarry, John Mullin, David Powelstock, Mark Richard, Jim Shepard, Malynne Sternstein, William Veeder, Michael Vode, Robert von Hallberg, Greg Williamson, and Geoffrey Wolff; my classmates at Hopkins and Irvine; the staff and community at Paragraph, where I wrote a substantial portion of this book; my beloved colleagues at Xavier High School, especially Margaret Gonzalez, Ben Hamm, Mike LiVigni, and the entire English department; my extraordinary agent Bill Clegg, along with Chris Clemans, Raffaella De Angelis, Anna DeRoy, and Elizabeth Sheinkman at WME; my brilliant editor Marysue Rucci, publisher Jonathan Karp, and so many others at Simon & Schuster, especially Elizabeth Breeden, Andrea deWerd, Cary Goldstein, Emily Graff, Jessica Lawrence, Christopher Lin, Carolyn Reidy, Richard Rhorer, Lisa Rivlin, and Wendy Sheanin; copyeditor Peg Haller; Clare Reihill at Fourth Estate; Caroline Ast at Belfond; Mickey Quinn, for sharing his memories with me; my sister Liz Janocha and brother-in-law John; my mother and father, for a lifetime of love and stories; and my wife, Joy, for her indispensable edits and remarkable forbearance in giving me time to write while we raised twin babies in a one-bedroom apartment.